THE COTTAGE ON WINTER MOSS

By

Allie Cresswell

This book is dedicated to my granddaughter Molly.

I am sorry I could only get one unicorn in.

Chapter One

My story began about five years ago. I call it a story. As it's true, maybe I ought to call it a history. Then again, I read somewhere recently that history is never wholly, objectively true because it is seen through the eyes of people, who are not objective and sometimes not entirely truthful. Their comprehension of it has to pass through the perhaps rose-tinted filters of their understanding, and their recounting of it further skews the facts; they emphasise one thing and underplay another, according to their own recollection, yes, but also according to lots of other things: their prejudices, their politics, their guilty consciences. And then, their medium is language, which is a lithe and slippery creature, shaded with nuance.

I call it "my" story, but that isn't quite accurate either. Truer to say, this is my version of a story that also belongs to other people. It is a concoction of what they told me, what I inferred from the bones they unconsciously threw me, and the correlations I made between these things—some of which, I tell you frankly, I made up.

I'm a writer. What can I say?

So, I first met the man you might know as Ivor Kash about five years ago. His name isn't really Ivor Kash, it's Ivaan Kashyap. Don't judge him; I use a pseudonym too. That's two stories already, two adaptations Ivaan and I have spun for ourselves because we find them more palatable—certainly more marketable—than the original. And we are only in paragraph four.

His star was in the ascendancy then. A long overdue hue and cry had suddenly meant ethnically diverse actors could find roles hitherto denied them and he had been cast in a supporting role as an ex-pat Indian curate in a lavish period piece boasting a handful of headliners. He was nominated for two BAFTAs and won one of them: Rising Star. The film was just pipped at the post for best picture but won a smattering of other gongs. Not best screenplay, unfortunately for me; but still, it was a solid success with critics and at the box office and I had to be content with that.

I *was* content with it. More than content. It was based on my fourth novel. I had been writing between parttime jobs for years. I published independently, since my applications to agents and publishers—carefully crafted enquiry letters, the single page synopses that literally dripped with the blood and sweat of their production, the beautifully bound booklets containing the first fifty pages—went unacknowledged. Not so much as a "thanks, but no thanks," let alone a request for the full manuscript. Never mind. My books had been well-received by readers but sold only hundreds of copies rather than the hundreds of thousands or even millions I had hoped for.

Then, the death of my lovely dad had brought with it enough money to allow me to give up the waitressing and chambermaiding for a year and concentrate on my work. I had taken a twelve-month lease on a cottage in Yorkshire, to mourn Dad and to try to come to terms with the sudden but irrevocable estrangement his death had brought about between my brother and me. My disappointment in Daniel—my brother—was eclipsed only by the anger and resentment I felt for his controlling wife, who had bulldozed her way through Dad's last will and testament, torn up his letter of wishes and monetised every piece of his property she had been able to get her grasping hands on. Somehow, in Daniel's eyes, our estrangement was *my* fault. My sense of betrayal had been monumental, but I had poured all my angst and loss and woundedness into my writing and my fourth book—*The House of Shame*—was the result. To my astonished delight it had been snapped up by a publisher and optioned for a film. I'd insisted upon including myself in the deal as script consultant, although I'd never written a screenplay in my life and had zero experience in the movie industry. I spent a rollercoaster few months in LA doing my best to keep the souls of my characters alive, the essence of my plot intact and to make sure my Regency personae never uttered the word "gotten."

From the sun-baked streets of LA we moved to Yorkshire to begin filming the exterior sequences. It is hard to conceive of two places more opposite in geography, climate or culture. To me, it felt much more like home, but the crew shivered and complained. The cast huddled in their trailers and drank the caterers out of tea and coffee before we all moved south to the studios, where the beautiful Regency interiors had been lovingly recreated. I will admit to tears as I looked upon the opulent drawing rooms, the lavish upholstery. The grandeur and style seemed to have been plucked from the realms of my imagination and conjured, solid and three-dimensional, before me. I suppose no writer can ask for more; that the world she imagines, the characters she creates from nothing, the emotional nuance and complexity of plot she sees in the privacy—even the secrecy—of her mind's eye should become a vision shared by others—a reality, even if only yet another manufactured one.

Ivaan and I met on the studio set. I'd like to tell you what drew us together was that we both felt a teensy bit more anchored in the real world than the rest of the cast and crew, but the truth is probably that we were both absolutely swept up in the world of artifice and carried away by it. Film is, after all, the ultimate actualised expression of the make-believe world I'd been escaping to my whole life. I think I can be forgiven for letting it go just a little bit to my head. Anyway, we gravitated towards each other and embarked on a fevered affair that lasted for the duration of the production but fizzled out as soon as the rushes were in the can and the editors took over. He got a role in a space odyssey that was to be filmed in Oman. I returned to London, rented a bedsit and chewed my nails, waiting to see what impact *The House of Shame* might make.

The answer came swiftly—it was a smash hit, feeding the public's insatiable desire for extravagant costume drama, the elegance of a by-gone age and the thrill of timeless romance. Unfortunately, in the way of these things, its bright star shone all too briefly. People flocked to see it, loved it, raved about it and bought the book. My back catalogue saw a resurgence of sales. A month later it was "old news." Some other phenomenon became all the rage until that, too, slipped off the popular radar.

I earned a lot of money. A less sensible person than I might have made the mistake of buying penthouse apartments and flashy cars, but I was rational enough to perceive the fickleness of the industry. Only another successful book, and then another, would keep my name on the best-seller list and sustain that level of income. Also, I did not want to be a one-hit-wonder. I wanted to establish myself as a critical and a commercial success.

I wrote two more novels. One of them was optioned by Netflix but never made it onto the screen, the other climbed only the lowest rungs of the best-seller list. My agent began to ignore my calls.

Ivaan and I kept in touch, but his success went to his head. He lived the high life for a couple of years, hobnobbing with the great and the good of Hollywood, doing photoshoots and interviews and appearing on popular chat shows. It seemed you could hardly move without seeing his handsome face on magazine covers, his sartorial form elegantly arranged over some celebrity settee. But then he got involved in a scandal—underage girls, drugs, some sleezy nightclub—that looked like it would land him in prison. In the end it came to nothing, but his reputation was soured and after that the publicity about him was all bad. The next I heard he was back in the UK and living in a mean little flat in Hackney.

I looked him up, and … you know how it is … one thing led to another and I found I had moved in with him. I suppose I felt sorry for him, and the flame of our passion still burnt hot despite existing now in the unpretentious air of a south London suburb. He explained the scandal to me in a way that made me believe that, while he was guilty of naivety and stupidity, he was guilty of nothing else. We commiserated with one another, moaning about how capricious the industry was, how full of fair-weather friends. He was broke, applying for auditions for all kinds of bit parts, adverts and audiobook narration—jobs that two years before he would have considered way beneath him—but hardly ever getting past the door. I encouraged him to keep trying, and never reminded him of the fact that I paid the rent and for all our groceries, our meals in restaurants and our seats in theatres. He was always complaining about having no cash but I wasn't stupid enough to let him access my bank account, which was the only sour note between us.

Oh. That, and the dog.

Chapter Two

The dog appeared one morning after one of Ivaan's protracted absences. I had got used to these. He would go out "for an hour" and return three days later with a haggard look in his eye and a chin full of stubble. When I quizzed him about it, he would come out with some shaggy dog story so I should not have been surprised that, on this occasion, a shaggy dog was exactly the outcome. This tale began with a chap he had met who had told him about an audition. He'd gone along, waited around to see the director, been taken to a party that had turned out to be a casting session. He'd been asked to read for an amazing part, driven to Dorset to meet the producer, but the car had broken down and they'd got a lift with a man in a Land Rover who was on his way to the vet with his dog … you can guess the rest. Normally, at the end of Ivaan's narrative was some crock of gold, some "fantastic opportunity," some invaluable connection that was sure to come good—but somehow never did. This time the conclusion was the dog which, it seemed, was to live with us from this point and be a very good thing. My argument—that we lived in a small flat, with no green space conveniently accessible, with lifestyles not geared up to the kind of commitment a dog needs—fell on deaf ears. Ivaan told me, with a light of boyish eagerness in his eye that I could never resist, that he had always wanted a dog. Then, oddly for a man who so badly wished to own a dog, he argued that as a writer who stayed home all day, *I* was exactly the kind of person whose lifestyle made *me* a perfect dog owner. Piling on the pathos, he said this one had been on its way to be euthanised when he had met its owner and I must be heartless to be able to look it in its soulful, sad eye and tell it that it couldn't stay.

'Don't be ridiculous,' I said. 'I'm not telling him, I'm telling you. He doesn't understand a word we are saying.'

'Dogs are particularly intuitive,' he said, kneeling down and fondling the dog's—admittedly silky and rather beautiful—ears. 'They pick up on emotion. Look at his face. Look into his *eyes*, Dee. If you can do that and still want to throw him onto the street, there must be something wrong with you.'

'I wouldn't throw him onto the street,' I muttered. 'There are dogs' homes …'

'Poor old lad,' Ivaan crooned, stroking the narrow dome of the dog's head. 'Poor old lad.'

The days passed and I didn't get round to taking the dog to the dogs' home. He was a brown and white spaniel of indeterminate age—five? six?—and rather overweight. He seemed pretty content to sit on his bed while I wrote, and two tours of the nearest park, night and morning, seemed to suffice him for exercise. I began to look forward to the thump of his tail on the floor when I returned from shopping or some other errand. Sometimes while I was reading or watching television, he would put his head on my lap and look at me with eyes that both expressed and invited trust, and it was hard not to respond. He stayed. We called him Bob, an uninspiring name but one he seemed to respond to.

On the whole, having Bob was a pleasure rather than a problem, so long as I was the one to feed and exercise him. If it fell to Ivaan to take care of things, poor Bob got a raw deal. I was still invited, from time to time, to speak to book clubs, do readings at book expos and appear at literary festivals. These affairs invariably took me away overnight and sometime lasted a whole week. Before I went, I would always impress on Ivaan that he could not, while I was away, go off on one of his jaunts; that he must feed and walk Bob twice a day and not leave him alone for more than a few hours. But when I got home it would be clear that Bob's routine had been neglected. I would find his water bowl empty, no dog food in the cupboard—and more than once, a puddle or deposit on the kitchen floor told me Bob had not been taken out. Nobody was more appalled at this than Bob himself; while I cleaned up, he looked at me with embarrassed, anxious eyes, his tail tucked under his belly.

Two things happened to make me realise that the situation in the flat in Hackney, and my relationship with Ivaan, could not continue. First of these was a new family who moved into the neighbouring flat. They were the Bensons, a single dad and three teenaged daughters. Mr Benson was out all day at work. He came home with bags of groceries and I caught the whiff of things singeing as he attempted to cook dinner for his daughters. His washing machine flooded on two occasions, and on one of these the water came under his door, across the landing and soaked our hall carpet. We started having trouble with the drains, and it transpired—after a pricey visit from Dyno-Rod—that the girls had been flushing industrial quantities of make-up wipes and sanitary products down the loo. Neither of these things would have been too terrible on their own, and I felt rather sorry for Mr Benson as he tried to provide for his family under circumstances that had been foisted upon him by the untimely death of his wife. But the acrimony that existed between the girls was awful. They shrieked and argued from morning till night. At least two of them should have been in school, but they must have been habitual truants because their noise continued unabated during school hours. I could hear them through the paper-thin walls of the flat as they hurled insults and more solid things at one another, slammed doors, played various types of dreadful music *at the same time,* trying to drown each other out. Sometimes they even came physically to blows. I could hear china being smashed, furniture being pushed about, the ricochet of bodies against the walls and hitting the floor. Twice I had to go round and hammer on their door when it had seemed to me one of them was likely to be seriously harmed—and indeed, on one of these occasions I did end up calling an ambulance. It was simply impossible for me to work in the midst of this cacophony. I lost my train of thought. The bubble of my imagination was popped. I found their invective intruding into my dialogue. I tried taking my laptop to libraries and cafés. Ordinarily these venues are excellent sources of material for writers; I have never met one who is not an inveterate listener-in to other people's conversations and an avid people-watcher, but these places also held multitudinous distractions, and of course I had to leave Bob behind.

It became increasingly clear to me the flat in Hackney was untenable. It wasn't even an especially nice flat—gloomy, shabby and cramped, with a view of a carpark. The bedsit I had given up in order to move in with Ivaan had been nicer, certainly quieter. In truth—because I had been careful with my money—I could afford somewhere quite spacious in a trendy neighbourhood like Southwark or Clapham, but something prevented me from taking on that financial commitment while Ivaan remained out of work. It would alter the dynamic of our relationship, and not in a positive way. While I had paid the rent on his flat, he had felt, I think, that there was some measure of equality between us. The furniture and fixtures were all his. His name was on the tenancy agreement. If things were to go wrong between us there would be no question of *him* moving out. These things were important to him and he showed his sense of possession by complaining if I rearranged the furniture or bought something new—curtains, a coffee machine—without discussing it with him first. I might be paying the bills but it would always be *his* home. If we moved somewhere else, all that would change and I could not imagine he would feel happy about it. He, then, would be the weaker partner, the guest—patently the freeloader. It might make him angry and discontented. That he was capable of truculence, of unreasonable resentment, had already been amply demonstrated to me on a couple of occasions. One of my books had received a glowing review in *The Guardian* and he sulked for three days. A lady had approached us while we drank coffee and asked me to sign a copy of one of my books. Of the two of us, Ivaan was far more famous but she had ignored him completely. He had not liked that. No, I did not think in the face of his precipitate fall from grace that he would like to have my modest success rubbed in by a removal from *his* flat into one that would be mine.

Also, it might make him complacent. He might begin to ask himself why he should bother attending auditions, putting himself out there. It was one thing to feel sorry for a man who was doing his best to make his way, to support and encourage him, to tell him—as I had to repeatedly—that I believed he had talent and the potential to get back to the bigtime. But it was quite another to put up with someone who had stopped trying, who was prepared to rest on *my* laurels. The idea of him loafing around the flat—even if it was a much nicer one—wanting my attention, suggesting we go out for coffee or lunch when I ought to have been working, did not appeal. Under those circumstances I would have to allow him some access to funds, and that seemed like the top of a dangerously slippery slope.

Though I was fond of Ivaan, the initial passion of our affair had cooled. He was ten years younger than me and while a twenty-five-year-old stud was a decided plus in bed, when we were out of bed, I had begun to feel more like his mother than his lover. He wanted to go out every night, was no sooner doing one thing than wanted to be doing another, thought nothing of visiting half a dozen bars in an evening. To be frank, I was finding it hard to keep up; but the suggestion of a "cosy night in" would have him rolling his eyes, sighing and pacing the floor like a caged animal. Having no work himself he was impatient when I wanted to settle down and write. He could be a distraction and a drain. What's more there were times when he was mean, taking out on me the frustration and dissatisfaction he felt at his situation. Sometimes being around him was like walking on eggshells. At last, I asked myself the crucial question: could I really see a future with him? The answer was no, I couldn't.

Having come to this conclusion I began to feel restless and discontented and thought that a complete change of scene would benefit my writing. Day followed day and my word count was woeful as the Benson girls pulled each other's hair out and yelled blue murder at such volume the glasses in our cupboards chimed. I found it harder and harder to draw forth the storylines that I knew were there, glimmering like gossamer threads in a sort of inner creative crucible. It may be only other writers who will understand what I mean. Writing is hard work, a labour of daily discipline, but there is something spiritual about it too. We bring forth— from literally nothing—character, plot, the structure of a world that is so vivid readers can step into it and lose themselves. It is vivid to us too. Before the reader, only the writer's footprints mark the sand. If it is not too precocious to say so, we are like God in the beginning. From what is formless, dark and empty we bring forth … not light, always, but something that wasn't there before. That's the point I'm trying to make. It's a kind of alchemy. From *outside* of ourselves—conversations overheard in cafés, the people we have met, our understanding of human nature—and from a place *inside*—some creative ventricle—we conjure up raw, unrefined material to knit and meld and sculpt into something, if not beautiful, at least believable.

Anyway, with every day that passed I felt my ability to perform this alchemy became less potent. Something had to change. The feeling was vague, uncrystallised. I nursed it in secret while I cleaned Ivaan's flat and washed his clothes and fed and walked the dog he had landed us with, and waited for one of his "very promising prospects" to come good.

It took a second catalyst to really galvanise me. I began to notice things missing. Money from my purse, a pair of emerald earrings that had been my mother's, a designer evening bag I had treated myself to for the BAFTA ceremony and stored away—carefully wrapped in tissue in its own monogrammed box—on a top shelf of the wardrobe until I should have need of it again. The money I supposed I could have spent without realising. The earrings could have been lost—although it seemed unlikely *both* could have fallen out—but the bag was different. I *knew* I had packed it away and stowed it on the shelf Ivaan had cleared for me when I moved in. The sense of having been stolen from, taken advantage of, was sudden and infuriating. I fulminated the whole day long, waiting for Ivaan to come home from wherever he had been so I could confront him. Poor Bob got frogmarched round the park at double speed and, in my fury, I slammed down the Pyrex dish containing the casserole I was going to reheat for our supper too hard and broke it.

It turned out to be one of those nights Ivaan did not come home at all, and I was left without an object for my ire, tossing and turning in bed, feeling angry and betrayed.

He finally called me from somewhere in Wales—he said—where he had got a last-minute call to play Captain Tom Cat in a remake of *Under Milkwood* that was being produced on a shoestring budget by an independent co-operative of film-makers.

My cynicism kicked in immediately. 'In Welsh?' I asked him.

'No,' he said, 'in English. Aren't you pleased? It's the part Peter O'Toole played in the original. One of the producers is David Roberts. Don't you remember he won the award for Outstanding Debut the same year I got Rising Star?'

'Not really,' I said. 'How long will you be away? What have you done about clothes? You didn't take any with you.'

'I picked a few things up on the way to the station,' he said. 'There wasn't time to come home. I'd have missed out if I hadn't got the train there and then.'

'How long is the shoot?'

'It's weather dependent. We're in Wales, so you know what we're up against. It could be a fortnight, or more.'

'It seems a very odd time to be shooting a film in Wales,' I said. It was almost the end of September.

'Yes, it is. They were waiting for some funding, and by the time it came through the bloke who was to play my role had got another offer. So, in a way, it's worked to my advantage; although, I must say, it's wet as hell here, *so* dreary. I'm in the shabbiest B&B and the sheets are damp. But what does it matter, Dee? It's work, and so long as I'm here I'll get paid.'

'It matters because I'm going away too,' I said, surprising myself, because I hadn't absolutely decided until that moment. 'I'm not sure how long for. There's Bob ...'

'Oh?' he said. 'Are you going to that literary festival after all? I thought you'd been turned down.'

'It isn't the festival,' I extemporised, 'it's something else, a creative writing workshop that's being organised at Warwick University. There's *some* flexibility, but the deadline is ...' I did a quick calculation, '... the end of October. Will you be back by then?'

'Oh, I expect so. Warwick? An easy hop to Stratford Upon Avon from there. Perhaps I could come. It would be nice to get away for a few days together, wouldn't it?'

'There's Bob,' I said again.

'Lots of hotels allow dogs. Chrissie Bix is playing Rosie Probert and she has one with her. It goes without saying, *she* isn't staying in the B & B.' He sounded sullen and bitter and I could understand why. Two years ago, *he* would have been the one installed in the best hotel room.

'Look,' I said. 'At this point I don't know where I'll be staying or how long I'll be away. The point is, *you* wanted Bob, Ivaan, and you'll have to look after him. So, can you be back for the end of October, or not? If not, I'll have to sort something else out for him.'

'I can be back by then,' said Ivaan, but sulkily. 'I have to go. They're waiting to go to some restaurant.'

'I can't find my Loewe bag,' I said. 'Have you seen it?'

'I have to go, Dee. I'll call you tomorrow,' he said, and hung up.

A quick search on the internet told me David Roberts was indeed involved in a remake of *Under Milkwood* and that Chrissie Bix had been cast as Rosie Probert, so I did believe Ivaan's story. I was glad for him. David Roberts was a respected young producer and it seemed to me likely that if Ivaan could keep his nose clean this production might turn the tide on his fortunes. It would make it easier for me to plan my exit from the relationship; I would not be leaving him high and dry. In fact— I told myself—I had helped him through his dry patch and had nothing to feel guilty about in looking to a future that did not involve him.

Of course, my creative writing workshop at the end of October had been a fiction. I was not infrequently invited to lead sessions for various courses and so it had been easy to invent one. I had calculated how long it would take to get myself organised and how long Ivaan might reasonably need for the shoot and decided a month was about right. I disliked telling falsehoods but I just knew—with the Bensons caterwauling through the walls and the empty Loewe box sitting on the dressing table—that I had no alternative but to go away. I knew also, that to tell Ivaan as much would be to invite trouble. He could be calculating and manipulative. Who knew what obstacles he might throw up? A clean break would be better. I would go somewhere Ivaan could not follow me or even find me. Not that I was afraid of him exactly, but just because I wanted to avoid the ugly scene that would inevitably result in him realising I had not just "gone away for a while," that instead I had actually "left." There was also a part of me that wanted to punish him; he had stolen from me, after all, and there ought to be some comeback for such low behaviour.

I wanted a complete break, complete peace. I had in mind somewhere quiet, rural, where I would not be bothered by the distraction of friends asking me for coffee, shops and cinemas. I had to reconnect with the creative source that had produced *The House of Shame* and I was convinced that could not be achieved in London or anywhere near it.

As tempting as it was to plan, to look at maps, to make reservations at hotels, I didn't. I decided I would simply set off and see where I ended up—in the same way that when I start a new book I begin with a blank document, start writing and let the story develop by its own organic impetus. In fact, the more I thought about it—as I sorted through my clothes, bundling some up for a charity shop, packing others, and gathered together the few possessions I could legitimately call mine—the metaphor of a journey to and in a strange land was one that applied exactly to my writing methodology. Each day at my laptop was just that, a foray into a new territory where I would encounter strangers, become acquainted with their histories and their personal idiosyncrasies, and connect them with each other and with their surroundings, having no preconception. It did not do to impose my agenda. *They* and the landscape and the chemistry of their interactions must dictate the plot.

So, no. I would not plan, I would not book ahead. I would simply get into the car and set off.

The car was one I had inherited from my dad, an MGB he had lovingly restored over several years in the little garage attached to the family home. A car, in London, was really a liability but I had not liked to sell it and so had stored it in a lock up. Ivaan and I had used it for the odd run to Brighton, and once he had borrowed it without my permission, making me incandescent with anger when I found out, as he was not insured to drive it. While Ivaan was away, I took it to a garage and had it serviced and overhauled. It needed quite a bit of work and I was glad to have allowed myself the time to have it properly seen to. My great escape would have been a bit of a damp squib if I had broken down on the M40 and had to be towed back to Hackney.

All the while, Bob regarded me from his basket by the radiator with curious, anxious eyes. None of his belongings—his food, his water bowl, his lead—made their way into the increasing collection of holdalls that began to accumulate in the hall. I told myself it was impossible he could understand the significance of my activity but his reproachful gaze did release a worm of guilt in my innards.

I telephoned the bank to cancel the direct debits that paid the rent and utilities and told them to stop sending my statements to the flat. I extracted my passport and birth certificate, my NHS card and my paper driving licence from the file where Ivaan and I had stored our personal documentation. I phoned my agent and told her I was going away and would email her when I had found somewhere to stay. To be honest, she didn't seem particularly interested and I foresaw the day when I would be back to doing my own marketing, sourcing editors and cover designers, wrangling with the algorithms of the big on-line book shop.

Two weeks passed. Three. The clocks went back and the longer nights seemed endless. I saw friends—saying goodbye without actually speaking the words—and walked Bob through the mushy leaves that carpeted the park in the premature gloaming, thinking I would quite miss the old boy. I bought myself a new phone and took out a contract with a new provider. Ivaan had my old one on his "find my friends" app and although I thought he would be too shocked and angry to think about pursuit, I couldn't risk it. The future was going to be all about me and my writing. A clean break. A new start.

Chapter Three

The final week dragged by, and if it hadn't been for Bob, I would have up and left regardless of any deadline I had agreed with Ivaan. I had spoken to him a few times, making no mention of my departure; not broaching the topic of the missing bag, the money or the earrings; concealing my anger and disappointment in him. I did complain vociferously about the Bensons, using words like "untenable" and "unsustainable" and "impossible", giving a creditable performance of a woman on the edge of her patience, creatively compromised, a rubber band about to snap. It wasn't difficult as I *was* all of those things. I spoke firmly about the creative writing workshop I was supposedly to attend on 31st October. I flattered myself he would be upset if he knew things were over between us, and I wanted to spare him that while he was on set, but the truth was I would not have put it past him to delay his return home deliberately to prevent me from going if he suspected I was leaving for good. He knew I would not leave Bob home alone. I enquired about the shoot, about potential opportunities that might be presenting themselves, urging him to make contacts *now* that he would be able to call on later. But his reports were not hopeful. Everyone in the cast, it seemed, had work lined up. Chrissie had already gone, off to Acapulco for a role in a glamorous all-action movie. David Roberts was contracted to co-produce a big-budget police drama for Sky. Bill Todd, who was performing First Man in *Under Milkwood*, was due in Stratford Upon Avon to begin rehearsing *Lear*.

'My best hope is a possibility on a daytime soap called *The Cottage Hospital*,' he told me miserably. 'They're looking for an Asian staff nurse. My agent has put me forward. But the auditions begin next week and, so far, we haven't heard I'm to be called.'

'All the more reason for you to be *here*, though,' I said. 'You'll definitely be home on Friday, right? That's what we agreed.'

'Probably,' he said. 'It depends.'

'But you promised,' I reminded him. 'Friday is the last day of October and I have to be in Warwick then.'

'I'll try,' he said, but bullishly. 'If I can't, you'll just have to delay. Surely, twenty-four hours won't make that much difference?'

'It *will*,' I said, trying to keep the panic out of my voice. 'You must think of Bob. He can't be left on his own and I can't take him with me. You *have* to come home on Friday. I'll wait until noon but I won't wait any longer. Friday, Ivaan. It's what we agreed. I've already put my arrangements back to accommodate you.'

Our call ended and I looked around the flat. I had cleaned it thoroughly, stocked the fridge and even made meals Ivaan could reheat in the microwave while he came to terms with the fact I had gone and wouldn't be coming back. I presumed he would have the *Under Milkwood* money to tide him over, and the proceeds of the sale of my Loewe, which had been £1200 when I had bought it.

The next day, which was Thursday, I brought the car from its lock-up and parked it behind our local delicatessen by arrangement with Giulia, the shop owner, who had become a friend. I cleaned the flat again, pulling pots and plates from the cupboards and wiping at the sticky marks on the melamine. I defrosted the fridge and scrubbed at the grill pan until my fingers were raw. Bob's eyes were doleful. He sat in his basket and emitted little whimpering noises, and when it was his suppertime, he refused his kibble.

In the evening I sat on the sofa and sent a text to Ivaan. *I've looked up your train for tomorrow. The 13.08 will get you into Paddington at 16.10. Allowing an hour for you to cross London that will mean Bob's on his own for five hours. Long enough. Don't let him down.*

I didn't get a reply and, when I went to bed, I had an ominous feeling. My bags lay along the hall wall. The flat was pristine. My affairs were all in order. I gave Bob a stroke before switching out the light, but once I was in bed, I heard the bedroom door creak open and his flop and sigh as he settled himself on the rug. He had never done that before.

21

The next morning, I stripped the bed and made it up again with clean sheets. While the washer churned, I took Bob to the park and bought breakfast from Giulia, thanking her for the use of her parking space. Bob was reluctant to get into the car. The space behind the front seats was small, a ledge barely big enough for him to settle on. He didn't like the noise of the engine or the flap of the flimsy roof. I drove to the flat and parked in the car park across the road. It took me several trips to load up the car. The boot and the place behind the seats were full, as was the footwell on the passenger side. I felt anxious leaving the loaded car unattended even though it was locked; those old cars are easily broken in to and are unprotected by alarms. I had a crook lock but that was all. It was a quarter to twelve by the time I was ready—a last sweep of the drawers and cupboards done, Bob settled in his bed with a chew which he ignored, his chin on his paws, his eyes never leaving me. I watched the clock hand tick the minutes away. At noon I texted Ivaan. *Are you at the station?* There was no reply. He might be somewhere there was no signal. I waited quarter of an hour and texted again. Still nothing. Damn him. Bob had begun to tremble, an involuntary tremor that shook his entire body. A dribble of drool escaped his lips and pooled on his blanket.

'He'll be here soon,' I said, with more confidence than I felt. 'You won't be on your own long.'

I waited until twelve-thirty. Surely, I thought, Ivaan would be at the station by now. I rang his number but got only his voicemail. 'Ivaan, it's me,' I said. 'I really can't wait any longer. I hope you're on your way. Poor Bob has come over all trembly. He knows I'm going away and you're not here ... I don't know what to do. If I leave him and you don't come home ... he'll die, Ivaan. He'll die of thirst or hunger ...'

I ended the call. Next door a vicious argument sawed on between two of the Benson girls. I wondered about knocking on their door, asking them to take Bob in until Ivaan came home. But I did not think I could subject Bob to such acrimony. I dithered until ten past one, when Ivaan should have been on the train, should have been on GWR's Wi-Fi. I googled the timetable. The train was 'on time.' I called Ivaan again but still there was no answer and suddenly, in a stomach-plummeting, temper-twisting onslaught of reality I knew Ivaan wasn't on the train, wasn't coming home. I fastened Bob into his harness—probably more roughly than was necessary—and clipped his lead on. I stuffed his food, bowl and blanket into a carrier bag and hoisted his basket awkwardly under my arm. I slammed the door of the flat shut and posted my key through the letter box. When I got to the car, I had to repack it to accommodate Bob and his luggage but, fifteen minutes after my pay-and-display ticket had expired, we were on the road.

Chapter Four

Although I had deliberately planned neither a route nor a destination, at the back of my mind I had an idea that the north Norfolk coast might be the perfect spot for my sabbatical—wild, unfrequented, inspirational. But when I approached the M25 one of the gantry information boards informed me of long delays on the M11. So I turned left instead of right and considered my options as the squat little MG fought bravely for its place on the road against the snarling saloons of businessmen and the thundering wheels of juggernauts. Spray hurled itself against the shallow windscreen, the stubby wipers ineffectual against its onslaught. Bob, clipped safely into the passenger seat, rested his head on my knee as though to give moral support. As much as I had not wanted to bring him along, I must say that having him beside me was a comfort.

There was no point in going south. That coast—I had decided that coastline was required—was crowded and expensive and much too close to London. I had already, by turning westbound onto the M25, discounted Essex and Kent. Cornwall, Devon and Dorset—far to the west—were all possibilities. So was Wales but, because Ivaan was—or had been—there, I felt disinclined for it. That left me with the north, and when the slipway for the M1 came into view I pressed the indicator.

As the major arterial route connecting north and south, the M1 is never a pleasant drive, and especially not on a Friday afternoon when people are heading out of the city to their weekend retreats. But, on this occasion, I found the traffic quite manageable, and the squall that had lowered over London soon cleared to offer a pale blue sky.

The sound system in the MG isn't very sophisticated but I found BBC radio 4 in time for *The Archers,* which is my guilty pleasure, and then the afternoon play.

By three-thirty we had come to the junction with the M54, which would take me to my make-believe creative writing workshop at Warwick University, and, at the last moment, I took it. We stopped at the services and I walked Bob around the lacklustre, litter-strewn dog walking area before returning him to the car and heading to use the loo myself and to buy a cup of tea. I sat in the café. There were no messages or missed calls from Ivaan and, there and then, I wrote him off. I removed the SIM card from my old phone and activated my new one.

Perhaps there was something theatrical about deliberately obfuscating my whereabouts. What did it matter if people knew where I was? Who would even care? I had a few friends who might wonder, after a month or two, why they hadn't seen me. But writing is a preoccupying, distracting business. We writers lose ourselves in our plots and characters; quite often they are more vivid to us than corporeal company. Even when we are surrounded by people, our minds are elsewhere. My friends are used to this trait in me, an emotional and intellectual absence that supersedes my physical presence. They understand the need for seclusion. They expect *not* to see me for weeks or even months. I could have simply said to them, 'Look, I'll be off the radar for a while. Don't worry. I'll be in touch when I'm done,' and they would have accepted it. But something about this adventure called for a cloak of subterfuge, a mysterious element. I felt like Alice or Dorothy, or Lucy from the *Narnia* stories—all characters who had crossed some peculiar divide between reality and make-believe. As a child I'd always been something of a daydreamer, drawn to the world of make-believe. It may well have been my way of coping with Mum's illness and death. Fiction, primarily, is escapism, isn't it? A place where we can find a better world and be better people. I'd always thought of my writing as a foray into a strange country, but as a metaphor, not literally. Now I was making that journey and I wanted no bread-crumb trail, no skein of thread, to tempt me to turn back.

When I crossed the car park and eased myself back into the MG I felt like a different person. I had sloughed off the old—specifically Ivaan and the whole Hackney episode—and from now on would embrace whatever fate provided for me.

I drove for hours, taking—at what felt like random—the M6, discounting the North Wales option because a slow-moving lorry ahead of me indicated he was going that way. Darkness fell somewhere north of Preston but I drove on. The traffic seemed to fall away the further north I got. I passed slow lorries as they lumbered up the inclines, and was passed by faster cars, but there were times when I had the dark, unfurling ribbon of roadway to myself. The sky was clear, a dark arch of blue-black pricked by stars. To my right and left the shoulders of slumbering hills rose up, and a gibbous moon hovered above me, throwing a milky light that rendered everything in shades of pearl and pewter.

I listened to the news, more *Archers,* an arts programme and a political debate before the petrol gauge suggested a fill up was required and my bladder indicated an emptying would be timely.

I took the next exit, which brought me to a roundabout. A petrol station—unnervingly illuminated by flickering fluorescent tubing and echoing with the ghostly strains of eighties rock music—was the sole sign of civilisation. Beyond it, to left and right, I could see no glimmer of light, no sign of habitation at all. The kiosk was dimly lit but the pump worked and, while I dispensed petrol, I looked around me at the deserted, eerie—but immensely satisfactory—scene. Presently a youth shambled into view from some garage behind the kiosk where, I imagined, he had been tinkering on some decrepit engine to the accompaniment of Guns N' Roses. He wiped his hands on a rag and then pushed open the shop door for me.

'Do you have a loo I could use?' I asked him.

He nodded towards the far corner of the tiny sales area and I spotted a door, half hidden behind a stack of baskets displaying crisps that were declared—almost proudly, on a hand-written sign—to be "Out of Date."

I used the loo and selected a few bits and pieces from the shelves: a bottle of water, a bar of chocolate, a packet of nuts. There were sandwiches, also soggy-looking sausage rolls and doubtful pies, but I didn't like the look of them. I would have liked some fruit but there was none.

When I had paid, I pulled the car over to a layby and let Bob out for a snuffle along the verge before pouring half of the water into his bowl and scooping a couple of handfuls of his kibble on top of it. He looked at it askance for a few moments as if to say, 'What's this? No gravy?' but then, with a sigh, began to eat it. I ate a few squares of the chocolate and wished I had a hot drink. The air was decidedly chilly, somehow thinner than London air, but noticeably clean-smelling. Apart from the sound of an occasional car passing below on the motorway there was no noise at all. I felt strangely peaceful, free and happy, but also quite tired, and I decided I would stop at the next hotel in the hope they would accommodate Bob.

The roundabout offered only two exits apart from the ones that led back to the motorway. I toyed with the idea of getting back on and going further north, but it felt wrong. There were signposts at the other exits that had names I didn't recognise, which I saw as a thoroughly good omen. One of them—Hogget-in-the-Hole—appealed to me because it sounded like somewhere in Middle-earth and accorded with my idea of having crossed into a land of make-believe. I headed towards it.

The road was a decent enough "A" road, though twisting like a switchback in places, steeply climbing and then just as precipitously plummeting. We went through one or two places that might have been villages—clusters of literally three or four houses, all darkly curtained—but passed no pub, hotel or guest house. I saw no signs that pointed to anything that might be a town. There were no streetlights. The beams of the car raked endless hedgerows, copses, fields and paddocks.

Gradually, we seemed to leave the hilly country behind us. From time to time I could glimpse, over the neatly trimmed hedges, vast flat plains as dark and featureless as oceans. In the far distance what I took to be masts—but what kind, and for what purpose I could not guess—were gaily arrayed with red lights. It seemed to me the road was gradually wending me in their general direction. Occasionally there was a junction and I sat at it, the engine idling, while I peered down the dark throats of the lanes and tried to make out the words on the signposts. These were old, the lettering obscured by clinging tendrils of ivy or flaked away into rust. If they were legible, they meant nothing to me. They promised nothing in the way of overnight accommodation or dinner. I reached over to where my phone balanced on the dashboard. It was 11 p.m. 4G signal was nil. I drove on—further and deeper into the dark, strange landscape.

After about an hour the road became notably less good, narrower and more winding. I had not, that I knew of, turned off the road I had been following but it—like me—suddenly seemed less certain of its way. I was tired, and, perhaps, slightly panicked. I took the first turning that offered itself, but this lane took me between high hedges that leaned towards each other to form a sort of tunnel. It offered no possibility of a three-point turn. The surface of the road was loose gravel, with a ribbon of grass down its centre; decidedly worse than its predecessor, and my sense of anxious disorientation increased. The darkness outside the car was so intense and heavy it felt oppressive. I slowed to snail's pace, inching forward through the black velvet of the night. Then, abruptly, the lane came to an end at a T junction. There was a signpost but the top was missing, leaving me clueless. I threw my hands up in despair, my sense of being trapped in a maze augmented. I looked at my phone again—still no signal and, in any case, I had no navigational app.

I plumped for a left turn. This lane was tortuously winding and potholed, then, suddenly steeply descending. An owl came out of nowhere, gliding on outstretched wings that just skimmed over the hedge. It almost hit the windscreen. I braked hard, throwing Bob forward and making my luggage shift, but thankfully I hadn't been going fast because of the potholes and so we escaped unscathed. I put the car into gear and continued, but my hands trembled on the steering wheel. The car carried bravely on along an avenue of what I took to be ancient trees. I felt as lost, as disorientated and as desolate as I had felt when Dad died; having my hands on the steering wheel where his hands had so often rested deluged me with a sense of abject loneliness.

I began to feel cold. The heater of the car wasn't very efficient and the soft-top let out more heat than it kept in. The imperative to find somewhere to stay, to eat, to rest was strong, but it was clear these remote areas of the country were not like London, where there is a Brewer's Fayre and a Travel Lodge on every corner. There, twenty-four-hour coffee outlets and burger restaurants are everywhere, but that rabid consumerism had clearly made no inroads in the desolate, unpopulated region I had come to. If I had been less tired and less overcome by grief I might have been delighted; what else had I wanted, after all, than somewhere different, unspoiled, quiet and remote? But as I guided the car down the seemingly endless, aimless lanes I was forced admit to a sensation of overpowering fright and panic. I reached out my hand and caressed Bob's head, feeling extremely glad that I had him by my side.

Suddenly the lane came to an end at a junction. In front of me was a line of scrubby-looking grass and then ... nothing. Beyond the grassy fringe I could see no landscape at all. The canopy of night reached down from the heavens to the horizon. It felt like the edge of the earth sailors of old used to believe in. I turned off the engine and opened the door. I was parked on the junction, but it seemed so unlikely any other vehicle would appear *now*, when I had not seen a single one for the past two hours, that I did not worry about it. I unclipped Bob from his seatbelt and, before I could get out of the car myself, he had scrambled across me and climbed out. He planted his feet on the grey ground and gave a vigorous shake before lifting his muzzle and sniffing the air. Slowly, I got out of the car, pulling a fleece from behind the seat and putting it on.

There was an odd tang—sharp, briny, mineral—and dampness in the uncannily still air, and yet there was a sense of gigantic movement, shifting and surging, not far away. The earth's crust felt thin beneath me. A noise that was not wind, not traffic, not mechanical, rumbled across the road. Bob's tail began to wag and he padded across the road towards the line of spiky grasses. I followed him, scrambling up the verge with difficulty because the ground really did give way underneath my feet; it was dry, soft and yielding. The grasses were long, as high as my knee. The verge stretched for perhaps five yards and then fell away. Everything beyond it was shade and gloom, a vast lake of impenetrable dimness; but far, far out, the reservoir of shadow was relieved by the occasional glimmer of reflected starlight. It heaved and shifted and, at last, I identified the rumble, crash and suck that reverberated in the air and shook the ground—it was the sea.

I don't suppose Bob had ever seen the sea before. It awoke something in his sedentary soul and suddenly he was off, down whatever precipice there was beyond the dune. I saw the flash of his tail and then he was gone. My sense of desolation was sudden and overwhelming. I called his name but my voice was lost, snatched up into some strange vortex of night and eddying air. I stepped closer to the edge, but with no idea of its steepness or height, or what might lie in the pool of gloom at my feet, I did not dare follow him. I don't know how long I stood, whistling and shouting into the abyss. Once or twice, at an immense distance, I heard him bark. I could imagine him running along the tide line, snuffling in seaweed, dancing in and out of the waves that must, somewhere a long way across the beach, be curling onto the shore.

Far away to my right I thought I could see pinpoints of lights—a settlement of some kind, I speculated—hunkered down on the coast, where, surely, there would be a hotel or a B&B, *somewhere* I could lay my head. But when I blinked and looked again I could see only shades of night, layers of shadow and dim. I decided I had imagined the lights, dreamed them into being. How could there possibly be, I reasoned, any civilisation out here in this utter, desolate wilderness?

Finally, overcome by fatigue, I crossed back to the car and drove it to a sort of indentation in the dune—a layby, a passing place, a car park? I had no way of knowing and, in any case, was too tired to care. I reclined the seat as far back as it would go, pulled a travel rug over me, and closed my eyes.

At some point in the night, Bob came back. His whines roused me to half wakefulness and I opened the door to let him in. He crawled across me, damp and smelling strongly of seaweed, and settled himself on the passenger seat. He sighed once, heavily, and in a manner that communicated extreme contentment, and then went to sleep.

I woke, cold and stiff, at dawn. The windows of the car were steamed up, running with condensation. My rug was beaded with moisture. A warm fug of doggy-dampness rose off Bob as he snored. His coat was thick with some greenish brown crust that, last night, had undoubtedly been primordial slime. The seat beneath him was silvered with fine particles of sand. I reached out and stroked him fondly, glad he had found his way back to me and suddenly sure, from now on, he always would.

Chapter Five

As I climbed out of the car and stretched my back, the scene that greeted me was nothing short of spectacular. Where, the night before, there had been only an endless expanse of formless murk, now a panorama of ultraviolet luminosity arrayed itself before my eyes. In the night, the cloud had dispersed to leave a dawn sky that was the colour of mother-of-pearl. The hardly-risen sun behind me stretched my shadow to a grotesque length on the shivering grass but illuminated the soft grey beach and the benignly shimmering sea in a facsimile of the sky's colours: pearl, mercury and pale mauve. The beach was dotted here and there with tortured sculptures—black, gnarled and faintly terrifying—which became, on a closer look, ancient tree stumps, logs and branches I supposed had been washed ashore long ago, now bleached and petrified permanent features of the landscape. The coastline to the left arced to a headland beyond which I could see nothing at all. To the right it curled in a perfect bay of shingle enfolded within a fringe of flat, sage green dune. At the furthermost reaches of this—I had to squint to make it out—there was a line of what I took to be buildings. A village! At the very least a hamlet! The buildings sat low, squat, as though crouched to the ground, an intriguing gaggle of roofs and chimney pots only just emerging from the twilight, but so promising to *me*. I could make out nothing more than that they *did* exist and were not, as I had told myself the night before, a figment of my exhausted mind.

I thought of breakfast, a pot of tea, a hot shower, and could have wept for joy.

Beyond the settlement the land rose again to a bluff that reached out into what, I saw now, was a firth, separating this coast from another. Across the iridescent waters lay a far hilly country of fields and clustered copses and, in the distance, a substantial mountain. The whole promontory was wreathed in mist—hazy, ethereal. It was breath taking, scarcely real. I knew I was tired and needed food and drink, but standing there in the dawn half-light did make me feel as though I had come into some fantastical domain. On the other hand, it disappointed me to find I had not, as I had thought, reached land's end. There was more over there, and I could go further. Perhaps my journey was not done. There was only one way to find out. I got back into the car and turned the ignition.

The name of the village alone should have answered my question— Roadend. What clearer signal did I need?—except for the two hanged figures that dangled from a twisted, cobweb-swathed tree just beyond the village boundary. Both corpses were festooned in shapeless black capes. Skeletal feet drooped from the hems about four feet above the ground. Their heads lolled, half-severed by the thick hemp of the nooses, their faces mercifully covered by hanks of woolly hair. My sharply intaken breath exploded in a gale of laughter when I saw the placard one of them clutched in its bony fingers. *Hallowe'en Night at the Winter Arms, 8 till late.* Of course! Last night had been Hallowe'en.

I passed a large farm—an ugly, flat-fronted farmhouse surrounded by barns and ancillary buildings, grain silos and silage stores. A number of impressive tractors were parked in an open-fronted shelter and in the yard two meaty-looking pickup trucks and a swanky Range Rover pushed a number of less well-favoured vehicles into the weedy perimeters. A dog on a chain raised its head as I passed but there was no other sign of life about the place.

The whole village slumbered in an enchanted sleep in the chill dawn. No curl of smoke rose from any chimney. No glimmer of light shone from any tightly-curtained window. I felt embarrassed that the noise of the car would disturb the inhabitants' dreams as they recovered from the excesses of their fright-night celebrations.

It was not a pretty village and yet it had about it a certain characterful appeal, conjuring images of a frontier—an outpost on the edge of the map—beyond which there be dragons. As I drove, I counted perhaps two dozen cottages, all old and small and covered in unattractive grey stucco, strung on either side of the narrow road like molars or knuckle bones on a tribesman's amulet; there was something grisly and primitive about them. Suffice it to say they were not friendly, and I instinctively felt if I were to knock at one of the doors, I would not receive a welcome.

The next cohort of houses in the village was built differently and more sociably, I thought. They had been built at tangents, arranged around irregular-shaped cobbled yards, their roofs abutting in awkward gables and overhangs. Several were constructed of reddish stone but most had been cement-rendered and painted in pastel colours, a cheerful and pointed contrast to the dour terraces. They clustered on both sides of the road, interspersed with greens where benches offered places for rest and conversation. There was an inn—the Winter Arms—and a farmyard that, curiously, also seemed to house a shop. I saw a Post Office sign but of course, at this early hour, both pub and shop were tightly shut. A hump-backed bridge spanned a stream. Beyond that were more houses—ugly modern bungalows—until, at the very far end of the village, a small, squat church sat within a large walled graveyard. Beyond them were rough fields and unfenced pasture that seemed to melt into the long grass of the dune. The tarmac of the lane terminated at a cattle grid. The way continued but turned to loose gravel in two deep grooves either side of a grassy hump, climbing the slope towards the headland I had seen from the other end of the bay. Now I was closer I could see the ruined remains of an old building on the crest of the rise, close to where the land dropped steeply away to the sea. It looked as though it had been burned out long ago; two walls and a crumbling chimney were all that had survived. But the track was sufficiently well-worn to suggest traffic still used it; I supposed it led to a farm. There seemed no point in risking the MG's low suspension. It seemed I *had* gone as far as it was possible to go.

My phone's battery had died in the night and of course, like all modern people, I wore no watch. The church clock suggested it was seven fifteen. It was lighter now, the lavender air a warmer, pinker hue, the sun struggling higher into the sky. Up to this I had been looking at the houses and, when I could glimpse it between them, the sea. But now I looked in the other direction, eastward, and saw a landscape of enormous, rugged hills and sheer ridges; the terrain I must have driven through the previous night. The contrast was so stark between that massif and this plain that I stood and gawped at it for quite a long time, until Bob indicated, by a polite little mew, that he needed to get out of the car.

I parked and we made our way through the wicket gate into the church grounds. Bob disappeared into the undergrowth behind the wall. I tried the stout iron handle on the thick, studded church door but it would not turn. A few fluttering notices pinned to the board in the porch informed me there would be a Eucharist the following day, and a Service of Remembrance a fortnight later. I wandered around the graves. Those at the front of the ground were the oldest. Most of these stones were so ancient that any lettering they had ever borne was worn away. They teetered at angles or slumped sideways, half swallowed by the soft earth, and it was a long time since anyone had left flowers. The grass around them was long, although someone had mown a path, so I was able to amble down the rows without difficulty.

As I strolled, I began to see newer graves, of marble rather than sandstone. They spoke of elderly residents of the village who had lived good lives to ripe old ages and died peacefully in their beds. A memorial plaque on the church wall mourned the young men of the village who had been lost in the world wars and subsequent conflicts—young scions of the local family trees, lost as barely-budded flowers. Probably in anticipation of Armistice Day, a plinth beneath the memorial had been swept clean and a bench freshly painted. Somewhere, in this remote, forsaken, slumbering place, there was someone who swept and painted. This proof of human endeavour—human *existence*—cheered me. The ordinary business of everyday life was carried on here. I had not wandered into an enchantment or stepped through some mystical veil. Soon—*very* soon, I hoped—there would be breakfast and the prospect of somewhere to stay. That I *would* stay was beyond doubt, now. *This* was the place. I had arrived.

I rounded the rear wall of the church to find another early-morning visitor. It was as though my mind had conjured him into being. He stood at the farthest end of the graveyard, hard against the low wall that held back the heathlands beyond. He wore mannish, but woefully shabby clothing: a brownish woollen jumper—out at the elbows and frayed at the welt—over a shirt of indeterminate colour, baggy trousers that might once have been corduroy, sloppy green wellingtons. No coat, but he had a shapeless hat squashed down on his head. A good deal of scraggly white hair formed a fringe between his hat and his shoulders. I took him to be a tramp. His size was considerable, even though, as I later gathered from the way he walked, he was past the best years of his life and sadly decrepit. He stood with his feet firmly planted next to the freshly turned earth of the newest grave, his body looming over it in a way that seemed to me more belligerent than doleful. I hung back at the corner of the church, so as not to intrude. The mourner was muttering to himself in a manner that suggested he was less than sane, and every so often his murmurings increased in volume, as though muted speech was not sufficient to convey the forcefulness of his feelings or the scope of his delirium. Snatches of his diatribe carried on the wind. I couldn't make out any words but I got the impression the hapless resident of the grave was being given a thorough dressing-down. From time to time the man flung an arm out, shook his fist, or leaned down to speak with particular emphasis, as though into the face of a bitter adversary. His list of indictments went on and on, a catalogue of wrongs he seemed to hold against the dead man. At last, his tirade seemed to exhaust itself. He swayed, wearied by his own invective, and wiped his arm across his mouth. I thought he was done, but he leaned over one last time and spat deliberately onto the brown, turned soil. Then he turned away. He walked unsteadily, bowleggedly, and not in a straight line, taking an erratic route away from me, into the nether corner of the graveyard. I pressed myself against the wall, reluctant to encounter such an angry and sacrilegious man, even one in his full faculties, which I could hardly suppose this one to be.

When I was sure he had gone, I made my way over to the grave. It belonged to John Forrester; his name was inscribed on a temporary marker. There were flowers in abundance, and a cluster of woebegone teddy bears. The funeral must have been only one or two days previously. The sight of these tributes, and the thought of the cold corpse beneath, deluged me with a sudden wash of grief. I supposed John to have been a man of some age, a much-missed father and grandfather, to have garnered these tributes. The gob of spittle—glinting and viscous on the black earth—both revolted and angered me. I could see Mr Forrester had joined a good many of his ancestors; I counted two other Forrester graves alongside his. I bent down to decipher the names. Todd and Rose were in one, with two infants, and, beside them, Caleb and his wife Ellen.

Two figures appeared around the corner of the church. One, aged perhaps fifty, was a diminutive figure, appearing somewhat plump although, as she was swathed in a capacious Macintosh, I supposed it was unfair of me to judge her. She had a full head of wonderfully curly grey hair and bright, lively eyes. She carried an old tin bucket that contained some sprigs of greenery, a few blowsy dahlias and some purple flowers I identified as asters. Her companion was even smaller, with straight, mouse-brown hair kept off her face with a tortoiseshell slide. She wore thick-lensed glasses with luminous green frames. Although probably in her twenties she had the physical exuberance of a child, half skipping along the flagstone path. Her face was round, her eyes—behind the lenses—small and almond-shaped, her mouth wide and her utterly benign expression characteristic of Down Syndrome.

'Oh! Who's *this?*' said the older lady, seeing me amongst the graves. Her tone was enthusiastic, friendly and confident; designed, I conjectured, to encourage and buoy her companion. Her accent was plummy—wholly Home Counties—not at all what I had expected in this northern outpost.

'Hello,' said the younger woman. 'My name's Olivia.' She came and stood right in front of me and looked up into my face with no trace of awkwardness.

'Hello,' I replied. 'I'm ...' I hesitated just a fraction of a second. I could be anyone I wanted, in this newly hatched—newly *re*hatched—iteration of myself! Christened Dolores, I had ditched that in favour of Delilah for my *nom de plume*. But Dee did just as well for both. '... Dee,' I concluded. 'I'm new here.'

'Hello Dee,' said Olivia, smiling broadly. 'Why have you come to Roadend? Have you run away?'

'I suppose I have, in a way,' I began, but the other woman said, 'Olivia, dear, we mustn't pry.' She shifted her bucket to her left hand and proffered her right. 'I'm Marjorie,' she said. 'Forgive me, dear, but you look exhausted. Have you driven all night?'

'I have,' I admitted. I liked the fact that, even though I had confessed to running away, she made no enquiry as to why, or where from. I could be anyone; an escaped convict, a lunatic, one of those needy, leeching types who attach themselves and won't let go.

Just then Bob made his appearance, tongue lolling out of the side of his mouth and one ear inside out. I thought Olivia might be frightened of him but she clapped her hands and said, 'A dog! I love dogs. Is he yours?'

'Yes,' I said, reaching down and clipping Bob's lead on. It occurred to me he ought not to have been allowed to roam around the graveyard unsupervised. 'He's Bob. I'm afraid he's a bit smelly. I think he's rolled in something on the beach.'

'Patty does that,' said Olivia, matter-of-factly. 'It's a dog thing. They think it makes them smell nice.'

'Is Patty your dog?' I enquired.

But Marjorie forestalled Olivia's reply by announcing, 'You must come home with us immediately. I'll just pop these into the vestry.' She drew a bunch of large and ancient-looking keys from her coat pocket and walked away from me to where there was a small door I had not seen before, hidden behind a buttress. She wrestled with the lock for a few moments and then disappeared inside.

'We don't use the front door, except on Sundays,' Olivia told me confidentially. 'Unless it's the summertime. Then we put a sign out and visitors come and put money in the collecting box. But in the winter Mummy says the church needs a rest, and so does she.'

'Is Marjorie your mummy?' I asked.

Olivia nodded. 'She's the vicar as well, and the chairperson of the village hall committee, and she runs the book club. She's teaching me to play the ukulele.'

'How splendid,' I said. Marjorie, it seemed to me, was the perfect person for me to have met.

Olivia swept a theatrical arm across the churchyard. 'Such a lot of dead people,' she said.

'Yes,' I said, plastering a look of sober condolence on my face.

We stood for a moment in mournful silence until, with a hundred-and-eighty-degree alteration of countenance Olivia said, 'If you're coming home with us, it means I'll get two breakfasts.'

Marjorie's house—the vicarage, I suppose I must call it—turned out to be one of the soulless bungalows. Inside was neat and trim but bland. The lounge was furnished with far too many chairs of all shapes and sizes and I realised this must be the venue of prayer meetings, Bible studies and perhaps also the book club. One wall was covered in bookshelves and I longed to go and run my eye over the spines. A desk in front of the window held a Bible, a note pad and a laptop computer. The placement of the desk interested me. No one would be able to pass along the village street, visit the pub or the shop without Marjorie seeing them. It occurred to me that, from here, she might have seen an unfamiliar car pass by half an hour before. Her bucket of flowers may well have been a ruse.

Thankfully–because it was a cold and unappealing space, more like a waiting room than a lounge—I was taken beyond it into a large kitchen with its original 1970s Formica units. Patty turned out to be a border terrier. She greeted Bob affably enough before returning to her basket. It was clear to me I was not the first waif-and-stray to have been brought home and I probably would not be the last.

After discreetly directing me to a cloakroom, Marjorie sat me down at a little gate-leg table, spirited dog food from one cupboard, a box of cornflakes, a bowl and spoon from another, put the kettle on, flung tea

39

bags into three mugs and slapped bacon onto the grill in a fluidly choreographed sequence of moves that was almost beautiful to watch. Beneath the coat she was, as I had suspected, rather fat, with multiple tyres of flesh separating her capacious bosom from her wide, well-covered hips. She wore a pilled green sweater over pull-on tweed-effect trousers and, having removed her brogues, a pair of fluffy moccasin-style slippers. Olivia wore an almost identical ensemble except her sweater was pink and her slippers had rabbit ears.

In the way of most writers, I managed to steer the conversation away from myself, mining information about my hosts by making a series of enquiries. How long had they lived at Roadend? Had Marjorie known her vocation for a long time, or was it a more recent calling? Did Olivia's father work locally? Might there be a room, a house or studio—anywhere at all, really—that I could rent for a few months? Marjorie and Olivia answered all my queries. I had the feeling the information would have poured out of them even without my judicious prompts. Both were natural chatterers except on the subject of Olivia's father who was dismissed as, "off the scene." Marjorie talked in a way that was calculated to inform and guide Olivia. In between her testimony—she had been called to serve the church out of the blue, on location as a PA to a BBC producer covering a news story about a tsunami—she said things like, 'I mustn't touch the grill. It's hot,' and, 'We use both hands to hold the milk bottle, in case it slips,' and, 'We must top up Patty's water bowl. Dogs need fresh water every day.' Olivia's response to these remarks was a weary, slightly irritated, 'Yes, Mummy. I know.'

In no time, I was eating bacon and eggs, then toast and marmalade—Olivia's own homemade, she told me proudly—and drinking mug after mug of steaming tea. Olivia, as she had predicted, got a second breakfast, but Marjorie contented herself with tea as she flitted with surprising speed and grace around the kitchen, wiping surfaces and washing the grill pan. At last, she brought a mindfulness colouring book and a pencil case and set them before Olivia. Olivia rolled her eyes, but then applied herself to one of the pictures. Marjorie sank herself on to the chair opposite mine. Her flow of verbiage dried up and I found she was looking at me with kind but expectant eyes.

'Now, my dear,' she said, 'in fifteen minutes I'll be packing you off to bed, but in the meantime, you might like to tell me a little bit about what brings you here.'

I found my eyes sliding away from hers. There was no earthly reason why I shouldn't explain things to her, except I thought it might shatter my sense of having abandoned myself to the vagaries of the universe, and it might compromise my desire to throw myself, body and soul, into something new and wild and improvised. But sitting there, in Marjorie's prosaic bungalow, surrounded by her fifty-year-old kitchen, holding her Marks and Spencer's mug between my hands, it crashed upon me that, for all my dramatic departure from Hackney, my reckless drive, my sleepless night, my end point was hardly distinguishable from my beginning. I was like a time-traveller whose machine had malfunctioned.

'My boyfriend turned out to be a liar and a thief,' I said at last, trying not to sound self-pitying. 'So I left him. I have some work I need to do, so I just got in the car and drove and drove and … ended up here.'

'I see,' said Marjorie, lifting a wiry eyebrow. Perhaps she had wanted more. More drama, more peril, more anguish. Perhaps an escaped convict or a psychopath would have been more to her preference. I thought again about the books on her shelves; grisly murder-mysteries? Political thrillers? 'You know, my dear,' she said, steepling her hands, 'living in the remote countryside is not like *The Archers*. It can be hard, especially at this time of year. You don't think you might be more comfortable in a town?'

'I love *The Archers*,' I admitted. 'My personal opinion is that Shula will make a very good vicar. But I know it isn't real. I've done this before,' I went on, in a mitigation that was, effectively, that I was a repeat offender. 'I lived in Yorkshire for a year, in a little mill town. I did some good work there—probably, my best—and I want to get back into the routine I had there.'

41

I waited for her to ask me what the nature of my work was, but she didn't. She breathed in through her nose and turned her mouth down at the corners. 'Oh dear,' she said, shaking her head. 'Two very bad mistakes *already*.'

Olivia lifted her head from her picture and grinned. 'Don't tell anyone here you're from Yorkshire,' she said. 'They won't like it.'

'Oh, OK,' I replied. 'And what else?'

Olivia lowered her voice to a conspiratorial whisper, 'Mummy thinks *The Archers* is *real*,' she said, 'and she is a bit in love with Alan. She thinks Usha is the wrong woman for him.'

'Oh!' I said, giving an exaggerated wink, 'I *see*. And which Ambridge resident do you like, Olivia?'

She blushed. 'I like Jazzer. Do you know, in real life the actor who plays him is blind?'

I stifled a yawn. 'I didn't know that,' I said.

'Come on.' Marjorie pushed her chair back. 'Go and get your bag from the car while I throw some clean bedding on the spare bed. Then you can sleep.'

Chapter Six

I slept for about five hours, and once I had showered and changed my clothes, went in search of coffee. Olivia was nowhere to be seen. Bob raised his head from a rug in front of the electric fire in the front room. Its single bar glowed redly and emitted a smell of singeing dust. Marjorie left her desk to show me where the cafetière was.

We took our coffee back to the front room because, with the aid of the little fire, it was warmer than the kitchen. From the window I surveyed the scene. In the time I had been asleep the weather had changed. Low clouds now shrouded the sky. The sea had turned turgid and brown—frankly, not particularly attractive—but the waves that rolled onto the beach were dramatic, topped with cream foam. As I stood in the window alcove a smattering of drops hit the pane. Rain.

In spite of the threatening weather, the village had come to life. The people who walked along the seafront, visited the shop and stood and chatted with each other on the roadside were far from the quirky tropes I had imagined, though. They were not *characters*. Certainly, they were not *caricatures*. They were ordinary, wrapped in thick coats and scarves, carrying newspapers and shopping bags, holding the leads of their dogs. Some few everyday cars made their way along the street, as well as the occasional tractor. Children scrambled on the play equipment in a little park.

Marjorie nodded in the direction of a shaled area opposite her house. 'Visitors tend to park up there, and then walk along the dunes,' she told me. 'Even at this time of year we get quite a few at the weekend. Mrs Harrop does a roaring trade in hot drinks and she makes cakes, too, and sells those. That's where Olivia is. She goes and helps out on Saturdays. Mrs Harrop runs the local shop. I recommend you tread carefully. She has delusions of grandeur and expects a certain amount of due deference. I must warn you she is also the town crier, so far as other people's business is concerned. Don't tell her anything you don't want the entire village to know. Oh, but that's mean of me. She's a good sort, and I'm sure the shop barely breaks even out of season. But thank heavens for it. I don't know what some of our older folk would do without it. The pub doesn't open at lunchtime during the winter months. I always think that's short-sighted of Bill and Julie. They're the landlords. They'd get trade if they could be bothered. Who doesn't want a bowl of soup and a sandwich after a good walk? Or a cream tea? But,' she sighed, 'they want to retire. The place has been on the market for three years. Frankly, it's getting a bit tired. I hope someone will buy it off them. A village without a pub is worse than one without a church, in my opinion.'

'You could hold a church service in a pub,' I ventured.

'You *could*,' she cried. 'But you can't pull pints in a church. The bishop would never agree to it.'

'Did you see me drive past here this morning?' I asked on impulse. 'Is that why you came up to the church?'

Marjorie blushed. 'You must think I'm a nosey old do-gooder,' she said, 'but yes, I saw the car, and Olivia and I love a slice of intrigue with our morning cuppa so we got our coats on and hurried over.'

'Well,' I admitted, swallowing the last of my coffee, 'you've been a lifesaver. But I must think about what to do now. Having set off on this hare-brained scheme I have to think of practicalities.'

My heart sank as I spoke the words. I wanted to stay at Roadend. It was exactly the kind of place I'd pictured. Here, I was sure, I would be able to write. But where could I stay? Not here, at the vicarage, nice as Marjorie and Olivia were. I'd seen no "to let" or "vacancy" signs along the village street.

'Well, on that front, I think I have a possibility,' Marjorie said. 'Mrs Harrop has a holiday let, out beyond the church. She doesn't usually have holidaymakers in the winter months and I happen to know her Christmas booking cancelled. So, the place is available until Easter. Would that suit you?'

I could have wept. 'It sounds perfect,' I said. 'What is it like? Not that it matters. I'd take anything, more or less.'

Marjorie shook her head. 'I have no idea. I've never stepped foot inside. But how bad can it be? Families come back to it year after year for their holidays.'

Suddenly I was impatient to be off, to close the deal with Mrs Harrop and to see the house. I assumed it was a house although of course it could just as easily have been a damp old caravan or a spider-strewn bothy.

Marjorie must have sensed it. 'Come on,' she said, getting to her feet. 'Let's go and see, shall we?'

Roadend's village shop and Post Office had been fashioned from what I took to be an old dairy or other ancillary farm building that was attached to the farmhouse. Roadend Farm was situated up a sloped, cobbled access. The farmhouse itself was older than the one I had seen at the beginning of the village, stone-built, and much larger. It might have been Georgian—quite grand, with a porticoed porch and sash windows. With the demise of the edifice on the hill it must have become the most affluent house in the village. It had the highest site in the otherwise flat plain of the village and as such commanded a considerable view of the street, the beach and the other houses. All this provided suitable illustration of Mrs Harrop's sense of superiority and entitlement. Stepping through the tinkling door of the shop was indeed like stepping into an august presence.

Mrs Harrop was a tall, angular woman, with closely cropped grey hair and gimlet eyes made hawkish by the half-moon spectacles she wore perched on her beaked nose. Clearly, she had been expecting me. Although she did not deign to move from her swivel chair in the Post Office cubicle her attention swooped from whatever she had been fiddling with and fixed itself onto me, taking in at a glance my face, figure and apparel.

'And so,' she crowed, looking down on me from the height afforded by her stool, 'looking for somewhere to stay, are you?'

I decided to meet her direct manner with equal candour. 'I can see you like to get straight to the point, Mrs Harrop,' I said. 'Yes. And I believe you have somewhere that might suit.'

She sniffed. 'I might,' she said. 'I haven't decided yet.'

'Oh,' said Marjorie in a peremptory tone, 'I do beg your pardon. I understood from our telephone conversation that you were very open to the idea. Never mind. I'll take Dee down to see Mrs Ford. She has that nice little apartment above the studio.' She seized the handle of the shop door and wrenched it open, setting the bell jangling and a carousel of cards spinning.

Clearly, Mrs Harrop hadn't anticipated this gambit and her smug air of having something that somebody else wanted evaporated. Her mouth fell open. Marjorie raised a questioning eyebrow and waited for Mrs Harrop to make her move.

At that moment Olivia emerged from some nether region of the shop, carrying a plate of iced buns. In truth they were rather inexpertly iced but I was sure they would be fresh and I understood some delay was required to enable Mrs Harrop and Marjorie to face each other off across the shop.

'Oh! Hello again Olivia,' I cried, taking the two or three steps required to bring me to the counter. 'Those buns look delicious! May I buy three of them, please?'

Behind me, Marjorie approached the Post Office counter and uttered a few *sotto voce* sentences through the grille. Olivia found a paper bag and used a pair of tongs to manoeuvre three of the buns into it.

The shop was small, its shelves crammed with goods, from tinned peas to padded envelopes, firelighters, fancy goods, toiletries and tobacco. A huge, refrigerated unit took centre stage, with homecooked hams, pies and confectionery. The carousel of greetings cards stood awkwardly just inside the doorway. The floor beneath the stand shimmered with a haze of trodden-in mica—glitter, which, over the years, had dropped from the cards leaving only a gluey shadow where sparkle should have been.

Negotiations complete, Marjorie stepped back from the grille and Mrs Harrop said, to the shop at large, rather than specifically to me, 'Easter's late next year. First weekend in April. I'd need you out by then.'

'That suits me,' I said, not turning, pushing some coins across to Olivia. Then, in a casual tone, 'What are you charging?'

She named a figure that, at Hackney prices, would barely have covered three months' rent, let alone the five months that would take us to Easter.

I did swivel towards her then, my bag of buns clutched in my hand. 'That sounds fair,' I said. I struggled to keep my voice level but my amazement must have shown in my face.

'Of course, it will include all utilities,' Marjorie put in quickly, 'plus logs and coal and so on.'

Mrs Harrop frowned. 'Mrs Ford wouldn't do as much,' she muttered, but she did not disagree.

'But Mrs Ford doesn't need the peace of mind, does she?' Marjorie observed. 'She can see from her kitchen window that all's well. Having Dee at your place will mean you won't have to worry about the place, empty, all through the winter. Wasn't there a burst last year? Or a leak in the roof? I can't remember now, but by the time you found out …'

'Cost me a new landing carpet,' Mrs Harrop admitted.

'Is there broadband?' I asked. 'Or a decent phone signal?'

Mrs Harrop fixed me with a beady eye. 'If you're going to be picky …'

'Oh no,' I forestalled her. 'I just wondered.'

'There's a box with a blue light on the hallstand,' she told me.

'It's called a hub,' Olivia said. 'Jamie set it up, didn't he? But,' with a heavy sigh, 'to be truthful, none of us gets very good bandwidth.' She shook her head apologetically. 'We have no fibre.' A mischievous glimmer in her eye invited me to share her joke, the image of Roadend's populace: limp, insubstantial, and susceptible to moral dissipation.

'I'll need three months in advance,' Mrs Harrop said, getting us back to business. 'You can pay with a card. I have a machine.'

I hesitated. I hadn't even seen the place. What if it was awful? Why, exactly, had the Christmas guests cried off? But my determination to follow the flow of narrative as it unspooled in front of me made me push my reservations away. I set down the buns and reached for my purse. 'I'll need a few groceries,' I said, looking round me at the dusty tins and packets. 'A few staples, to get me started.'

'To get you started?' Mrs Harrop sniffed. 'Waitrose doesn't deliver *here,* you know.'

'I can make up a box,' said Olivia. 'Do you like chocolate?'

'I do,' I told her, 'but I was thinking more along the lines of fruit and vegetables, eggs, milk …'

'Gin,' Marjorie offered, 'if you hope for a visit from the vicar.'

I smiled. 'Gin then, and whatever the vicar likes with it.' I looked doubtfully at the shelves. 'Do you have ground coffee?' I ventured, 'and Earl Grey tea?' All I could see were some inferior brands of instant coffee.

'Certainly,' Mrs Harrop shrilled. 'We keep those in for Her Ladyship. Olivia, you'll find the things the lady wants at the back of the storeroom, on the top shelf. Make a careful list, mind. Don't let anything slip in there that won't get paid for.'

'Don't you usually offer a welcome hamper for your guests?' Marjorie said mildly. 'I would have thought the first box of supplies might be included.'

'Not if she wants premier brands,' Mrs Harrop snapped. Clearly, she felt she had given quite enough in allowing the utilities.

'I'm happy to pay,' I said, proffering my debit card, 'but not through the nose.'

'Oh,' Marjorie said, in a fulsome tone, 'Mrs Harrop cuts her margins to the quick. As I told you, the older residents would be lost without this shop. She'd be the last person to take advantage of anyone.'

The shopkeeper narrowed one eye as she slipped my card into her machine, not quite sure if she'd been insulted or praised.

'Jamie will collect your groceries and bring them out to you,' Olivia said, and I thought I discerned a blush on her smooth, round cheek.

'She won't want *him* getting his feet under the table,' Mrs Harrop countered hotly, handing me the machine for my PIN. 'Although,' addressing me, 'if you find yourself in real need, I expect he'll help you out. He'll be your neighbour. But the apple never falls far from the tree, so you can't expect *much* ...'

'He's a perfectly pleasant young man,' Marjorie said.

I tucked my card back into my purse.

'What time do you finish here, Olivia?' I asked. 'These buns won't eat themselves.'

Chapter Seven

By the time we'd had tea and eaten the buns and I had manoeuvred Bob and the boxes of groceries into the MG, it was almost three o'clock in the afternoon. The earlier showers had concentrated themselves into a steady downpour. The sky was leaden, the sea a roiling brown soup. The village inhabitants had retreated into their houses; the carpark was empty.

I waved to Marjorie and Olivia and pulled off their drive feeling thoroughly optimistic in spite of the weather. I had been directed over the cattle grid past the churchyard, up *Winter* Hill and told to look for a gate at the top of the gravel track which would lead me to my new abode, *Winter* Cottage. What could be more auspicious for a writer seeking a *winter* retreat? It was meant to be. The keys to the cottage dangled from the overdrive switch on the dash.

The MG rattled over the cattle grid and I proceeded cautiously up the track. The wipers did their best to keep the screen clear but the rain was heavy, a grey curtain, obscuring the rough heathland to the right, the dunes to the left. The burned-out ruins at the top of the hill were invisible. I concentrated on the track, hearing the brush of grasses beneath the car's low-slung chassis, fearful a protruding boulder might impale the exhaust or ruin the prop shaft. Slowly, we climbed. If the day had been clearer, I would have liked to have stopped, to have looked back down at the village from this vantage point, but there was no possibility of that. The rain pounded the roof of the car. It was like being inside a drum. Bob regarded me with anxious eyes. I kept in a low gear, quelling wild misgivings. What had I been thinking of? The MG could not possibly handle this kind of terrain on a regular basis without incurring some severe damage, and winter was coming. Things could only get worse. Unless I was prepared to walk, Roadend might be all but inaccessible to me from the cottage, wherever *that* was. Again, I had not enquired; it could be miles away.

My reverie was interrupted by the sudden glare of headlights, the scrunch of tyres on gravel and the pounding of a horn. Another car was coming down the track. There was no passing place and the banks were too high to allow any vehicle to mount, certainly not mine, not even the four-by-four, which is what I took the on-coming vehicle to be. It ground to a halt in front of me. I stopped, of course, but with a redoubling of anxiety as I doubted I'd be able to get going again. The track surface was so slippery, running with rainwater, as well as the small shower of stones the other car's tyres had dislodged. I could barely make out the other driver. His windscreen was so much higher than mine. I had a much better view of his snarling radiator grille, but something told me it was a pretty good representation of the driver: irritated, impatient, entitled. He must have thrown his car into reverse. It began to pull back up the slope, throwing more stones against my bumper. The speed and violence of his manoeuvre confirmed all my suspicions—there was one angry man. I put my car into first gear and, mercifully, felt the wheels grip as we continued up the way.

In fact, it wasn't very far, not more than twenty yards. The slope plateaued out onto a smooth, close-cropped area of short turf. The four-by-four—a Range Rover, I made out, top of the range—waited for me to pull onto the grass and then roared off down the hill, not seeing—or at least not acknowledging—my wave of thanks. Across the grassy common, to the seaward side, the stone walls of the tumbledown house reared up. They were blackened by the rain and also by fire. The one or two remaining windows stared at me blindly, fringed by weeds that had somehow become embedded between the stones and managed to grow, bedraggled and windswept, in that unpromising situation. Of course, the tragedy of its demise, its forlorn isolation, the possible romances of its history all intrigued me, but I could do no more than make a mental note to research its history. I had to get myself and Bob installed in our new home.

I looked around me. Ah! There, almost straight ahead, was the gate.

I must say it was far grander than I had anticipated. A tall, ornate, wrought iron affair with gilded finials, flanked by stone columns. The stones looked old, as old as those of the derelict house, but the orbs on top were new, large, and rather showy. A drystone wall stretched out to either side of the gate. To the right, the landward side, it skirted the common and disappeared into a scrubby copse. A handful of sheep cowered in the lee of the branches that overhung the wall. I felt sorry for them, and sorry for myself—desperate now to be indoors, sheltered, to have arrived at last. Through the gates I could see trees—not ancient ones but young, not much more than saplings—struggling to contend with the wind and weather, their semi-denuded branches whipping backwards and forwards in a frenzy. There were several tended shrubs and some modern sculptures, a gazebo from where, I imagined, the last rays of the setting sun would be visible, should it ever emerge from its shroud of cloud. A driveway curled elegantly around these features and dipped out of sight over the brow of the hill.

I drove to the gates and got out of the car. The power of the wind almost snatched the door from my hand. Outside, the sound of the rain was less but the noise of the sea was more. It growled and pounded at the beach down below like a bad-tempered beast. I could hear the grind of stone on stone as the beach shifted beneath the waves, trying to accommodate its angst. I hurried to the gates and, with difficulty, turned the handle and began to swing one of them inwards. It was stiff, almost as though anchored by some mechanical brake. I needed both hands and all my strength to get it to move at all. The rain pelted my thin coat, quickly soaking it through, and ran down my face like a river of tears. The wind tore at my hair. I managed to get one gate open and secured to a latch, although it fought me all the way. I decided it would be enough; I could squeeze the car through without needing to fight the other gate. I had begun to return to the car when a frenzied bark and a woman's equally furious shout made themselves heard through the roar of wind, water and tide. Inside the car, Bob began to bark savagely, showing an impressive array of teeth. He threw himself towards the windscreen, scrabbling at the dash with frantic paws. I think, if he had not been clipped in by his harness, he may well have come through the glass.

'What the hell do you think you're doing?' thundered the woman. She came stomping up the driveway—a tall, unusually broad figure, swathed in a capacious, hooded waxed cape. She wore expensive wellington boots, the designer kind favoured by the Royal family, and carried a walking stick, which she brandished.

I brushed hair and water out of my eyes. 'I'm the new tenant,' I said, trying to balance righteous anger with good-natured explanation. Her dog—large, brindled—bounced around me but I could see it was all noise and bluster. He had no intention of biting me. Bob continued to yell from inside the car. Of the two of them, he sounded much more fearsome. 'By arrangement with Mrs Harrop,' I added, shouting into the teeth of the weather.

The woman came to a standstill. From what I could see of it her face was large, round and mannish, and unembellished by make-up. 'That gate is automated,' she shouted. 'You need a fob. It doesn't open manually. If you've broken it, you'll pay for the repair.' I couldn't place her accent, but she wasn't British.

'Mrs Harrop didn't give me a fob,' I said.

'What do you think you were doing, forcing it like that?' she went on, ignoring my remark. 'Didn't you realise?'

'No, of course not,' I retaliated. 'Mrs Harrop said nothing about the gate, other than that I should go through it. I'm the new tenant,' I repeated, matching her spleen. 'I have the key.'

'Not to this house, you don't,' she spat out. She clicked her fingers and the dog immediately fell silent.

'I *do*,' I insisted. 'Winter Cott—'

'Oh! *This* isn't the cottage,' she interrupted, scornfully. 'This is Winter *Hall*. This is where the Lord of the Manor lives.' She waved her arms to indicate the grandiose gates, the tended shrubs, the elegantly curving drive. 'I think, if you're expecting *this,* you're going to be disappointed.' She nodded her head to indicate I should look behind me, back out onto the grassy plateau, at a gap thirty yards or so along the drystone wall, past the sheep, where an ordinary farm gate hung lopsidedly from a post.

Suddenly, I felt really foolish. Of course.

'I'm very sorry,' I said. 'I can see I have made a mistake.'

She raised an eyebrow. Her gaze was steely, unyielding. What else did she want me to say?

'It's a poor beginning,' I stammered, 'as we're to be neighbours. I've taken the cottage for five months ...'

'Pshaw,' she spat out, dismissing any possibility that, even without this misunderstanding, we could ever be remotely associated. This, I realised, must be the 'Ladyship' to whom Mrs Harrop had referred—the Lady of the Manor, the person who had her own shelf of premium brands and speciality produce in the storeroom behind the shop. It mollified my crippling shame, to think that, at least, I could equal her discernment in taste for beverages.

I began to retreat. 'Would you like me to—' I began, indicating the gate.

'Don't touch it!' she cried. She walked slowly to where I had secured the gate and unhooked it, got something out her pocket and pressed it. The gate began to swing closed. She watched it all the while, an expression of supreme haughtiness on her large, ill-favoured face.

'I'm sorry,' I said again, as the gate clanged closed.

She turned away and began to stomp off down the drive. I watched her retreat, her menacing, caped figure reminding me powerfully of something ... oh yes! The hanged witches.

Chapter Eight

Water had begun to pool on the spongey grass of the common, so it was no wonder, really, I had missed the much fainter track that led across the turf to the farm gate. The sheep scattered as I approached them, and I got the car through the gate and the gate securely closed again with no danger of any of them sneaking through.

The track—if possible worse than the previous one—snaked through the copse of trees and down behind the bluff. Few vehicles came and went this way. What kind of isolation had I let myself in for? The lessening of wind and noise was immediately apparent. It was a relief after my exposure to both, not to mention the displeasure of Her Ladyship, which had rattled me more than either.

The track exited the copse, bottomed out and travelled between waist-high banks of bracken. It was dying back now, its lower fronds turning bronze. From my low-slung seat I couldn't see much above or beyond the brakes on either side of me. The sky seemed like a murky lid, pressing down. Skeins of rain draped in billowing sails across my letterbox of vision. At last, I made out the low roofs of a terrace of dwellings. They stood with their backs to the hill, facing out across whatever expanse of pasture or heathland lay beyond the bracken. As I crept closer, I saw that each individual cottage in the row had a square of garden in front of it, with a gate, the gardens divided from each other by stone walls. I crawled along at a snail's pace to find the sign I had been promised, especially eager not to make another error.

The first cottage in the terrace looked as though it was in some process of gradual restoration. Bare stonework around the windows suggested these had been recently replaced, but the glass was dirty, with faded curtains hanging limply inside. The render was patched, awaiting painting. Its garden was filled with what looked to me like junk: building materials, tumbles of stone and bags of sand. What actual garden remained was tidy enough, gravelled, with a number of flower tubs, a birdfeeder and a wrought iron seat. Beside the cottage was a wooden structure with a few hens scratching around inside.

The next cottage—the middle one of the three—looked derelict. My heart sank. Was *this* ...? But no. A roughly carved sign hanging lopsidedly on the dilapidated gate declared this to be Winter Farm. It was a sorry It was a sorry place indeed, its grey, neglected render, its boarded-up windows and door giving it a blind, ravaged appearance. Its garden really was a junk heap: a freezer with its door hanging off, various crates, a stack of pallets, rubble, broken chairs ... and all scrambled over by brambles and some other pernicious vine. It was obvious no one lived there and I heaved a sigh of relief, thinking of the Bensons, and the boon of blessed quiet that having no neighbour would offer me. On the other hand, I couldn't help wondering about damp, vermin, rot ... the kinds of things that could easily be as much a nuisance as wayward teenagers. I looked at the middle cottage with a critical eye. It had an oddly mournful, shrouded appearance. I found I felt rather sorry for it.

The last of the cottages had a sign on its freshly painted gate: Winter Cottage. Beyond it, the track terminated in a five-barred gate that seemed to give access to a stand of willowy trees. I really had come to the end of the road. I was home.

I switched off the engine and gave the MG's steering wheel a little pat. Dad would be proud of it, I thought to myself. It had brought me safely, more or less unscathed, from one end of the country to the other, through tribulation and storm and what had seemed like an endless night. The silence was sudden and intense, like a blanket. Even the rattle of the rain on the roof seemed muted. I looked at the cottage through the passenger door window and Bob, following my gaze, gave a little sigh.

As much as my writerly instincts might have savoured a gothic hovel with shadowy corners, cobwebs, creaks and a resident ghost, my human frailty craved warmth, comfort, cleanliness and security. And here it was. Winter Cottage was the largest of the three in the row, double-fronted, with windows either side of the solid-looking front door. Cheerful curtains hung in the windows which, though timber, were of a modern type, certain to debar draughts and prohibit leaks. The cottage had been painted in a shade of pale blue. The roof was of slate and, as I craned to look up at it, a wisp of smoke could be seen coming from a squat chimney. Someone had lit a fire.

Suddenly, I couldn't wait to be inside. I scrambled out of the car and released Bob from his restraint. I grabbed the box of groceries and the keys and pushed through the gate. The garden was well-tended; a traditional cottage garden, although most of the perennials were past their best. A few nodding asters and late-flowering anemones brushed the legs of my trousers as I passed along the brick path, bejewelling them with diamonds of moisture. The key slid easily into the lock and I stepped into a narrow hallway of wide, wooden boards topped by a carpet runner. A radiator oozed heat. There was a hall table with the promised router, and a place to hang coats and store boots. Stairs mounted to one side. Beneath the stairs was a cupboard, but it was locked. I assumed it contained cleaning materials and so forth; things Mrs Harrop did not wish her guests to access.

Past the stairs the passageway continued down to what I instinctively knew would be the kitchen. I followed my instincts to find a room that stretched the full width of the house, with sage green painted kitchen units and an Aga at one end, a scrubbed kitchen table in the middle, a comfortable settee and a fireplace with log-burner at the other. Here was the source of the smoke—a heap of coals and a log glowed dully behind the glass. The floor was practically tiled. Bob's claws clicked on it as he investigated the corners and scoped out a spot in front of the fire for his bed. A rear door gave access to a small yard where a Calor gas tank, a stack of logs and a coal bunker were located. I put a tentative hand out and touched the Aga. It was warm. I thought, if the house had contained no other room than this one, I would have been well-pleased. I put the groceries on the table and went back out to the car.

I investigated other rooms as I brought my belongings inside. To the left of the hall there was a dining room, furnished in dark wood, with a gateleg table and what looked to be an ancient sideboard. A number of leaflets had been spread out on the top: tourist attractions and the like. I glanced around but then closed the door. I did not anticipate using that room at all. To the right of the hall was a small sitting room. Another fireplace, with an open fire this time, was flanked by bookshelves stocked with paperbacks presumably left behind by holiday makers. A three-piece suite and a coffee table made up the rest of the furniture. There was a television—not Smart—and a DVD player with a selection of films. Everything was clean and neat, good quality without being high-end. I could see myself, after a day of brisk walking and busy writing, relaxing in here. Upstairs were three bedrooms and a bathroom. I chose the largest bedroom to sleep in—a double, with views to the front. I could now see—beyond the bracken border—some kind of marsh or wetland. Deeply dug trenches filled with water intersected areas of scrubby terrain. More bracken, heather, spiky bog grass, sedges and reeds made an undulating carpet almost as far as the eye could see, interspersed with clumps of contorted trees, sculped by wind.

The back bedroom was a twin, rather dreary in comparison, but good enough to store my luggage. The other front bedroom was tiny, so small there had been no attempt to put even a single bed into it; a futon offered further sleeping accommodation should it be needed. But it had a desk in front of the window and I immediately knew it was where I would set up my laptop and write my new book. The views over the marsh were inspiring, the room cosy with sprigged wallpaper and a plush carpet. I could hear, above the ceiling and through those doughty roof slates, the hum and sigh of the wind as it skimmed the bluff behind me, came scouring down over the ridge-tiles and exploded out across the marsh.

I emptied the car and pulled it round to the side of the cottage where a substantial, timber-built garage looked as though it belonged to the property, but might not. I made a mental note to try the keys in the padlock later. I hoped it was part of my tenancy. The MG would not thrive if left outside in this environment. But I did not wish to presume, to be caught attempting to break into an outbuilding that might belong to someone else. Once bitten, twice shy.

I was eager to settle in, to put the kettle on, to find my slippers, to investigate the grocery boxes Mrs Harrop had supplied. But by this time it was past four o'clock and the light was fading. Bob needed a walk and so, I realised, did I. I checked the fire was safe, adding another log but closing the vent down, switched on one or two lamps and pulled my coat back on. It was too thin, soaking wet, completely inadequate for the climate, but it was all I had.

We stepped out of the cottage and I pulled the door closed behind me.

We didn't walk far. In the fading light, and tired as I was, it would have been foolhardy to stray too far from the cottage. But it had stopped raining and the wind had quietened down. We traced our steps up the track until I spied a wide wooden bridge spanning one of the drainage rills. It was wonky, slick with moss, but seemed to lead to a tamped down path that wound between the tufts of heather and bracken. It may have been an animal track for all I knew, but Bob bounded along it with his nose to the ground and his tail waving like a flag behind him. We crossed one of the quadrants, wobbled across another much-less-substantial bridge, came to a bank, and thence into one of the copses. Through the densely coppiced trees I could see something blue. My curiosity piqued, I pushed my way in. I had to force my way through. The whip-like branches smacked my back as I let them go behind me. At the centre of the copse was a sort of clearing, where a blue plastic barrel had been set up as some kind of feeder. I guessed it was for pheasants. In the middle of the cleared area was another tree—a much older tree than those around it, with gnarly silver branches and slender leaves. It was a silver birch, but a very unusual one, far more like an oak in its shape and size than the normally tall and willowy habit of silver birches. One of the lower branches had grown out horizontally, long enough, and at just the right height and thickness to make a private seat for lovers. I immediately named it the trysting tree. Its privacy—screened from the world by the surrounding willows—and the provision of a branch where two could snuggle close together, made it the ideal spot for a clandestine assignation. I stood in the clearing and looked at the tree. Stray beams of late afternoon light illuminated its bark so that it glowed with an eerie luminescence. There was something enthralling about it—its age, its shape, its potential—and I found myself mesmerised as though caught in some enchantment. Story threads seemed entwined like gossamer in its very branches, and I let my mind pursue the delicate skeins—of tragic lovers, lovelorn men and ruined women, lost children ...

The sudden clatter of a disturbed pheasant brought me back to myself. I fought my way out of the copse in time to see it lumbering into the sky, Bob in pursuit. I stopped to catch my breath and take my bearings. Everywhere, to left and right and beneath my feet, was the trickle and ripple, the ooze and suck of water. My boots—wholly inadequate for the countryside—were soaked. I breathed in and smelt the vegetation, the tang of moisture in the air, the faint brine of the sea, the acrid whiff of woodsmoke. I stood still, beneath the overhang of the trees, and let the openness press itself into me, or expand me. Somehow, it seemed to do both. The effect was both liberating and strangely unsettling. On the one hand I felt relieved—my exodus from London and my random drive up the country could have ended so badly. On the other I felt oddly vulnerable—everything here was *so* strange, so foreign. I felt alien, exposed. Even now, I speculated, someone could be watching me. I could be murdered, kidnapped ... I could disappear from the face of the earth and no one would have the least clue. I looked back towards the cottages. *Was* someone watching me, from behind the smeary windows of the first cottage? I gazed over the marsh. What malevolent presence might lurk in its undergrowth? Bob shared none of my misgivings. He dashed from one place to another, following scents, burrowing in the undergrowth, sending a second screeching pheasant flapping panic-stricken into the purpling air. Every so often he came back to me and sat at my feet, looking up at me, his mouth laughing, his tongue lolling, in a sort of delirium of happiness.

Twilight fell like a stone. I almost lost the path and missed the wooden bridge. Without Bob's unerring sense of direction, I think I *would* have missed it. I told myself I had been stupid not to bring a torch. I had left my mobile on the kitchen table, so I didn't even have that. We stumbled through the bank of ferns back onto the track and groped our way along; the lamps I had left on in the sitting room threw a pool of yellow welcome into the gloom. We passed the first cottage. A low light shone through the uncurtained window. The dark rectangle of doorway moved and a man stepped out. After my ghoulish imaginings on the marsh, he startled me and I gasped. Bob grumbled a warning.

'Sorry,' he muttered. 'Didn't mean to frighten you.'

He made his way down his path and lifted, rather than swung his gate open. 'I'm Jamie,' he said, but rather than offering me a hand to shake, he squatted down and lifted his hand to Bob's nose. Bob gave it a perfunctory sniff, and then licked it.

'Mrs Harrop mentioned you,' I said.

'But not favourably, I bet,' he said, under his breath.

'She said if I needed anything, you'd help. Was it you who lit the fire? Thank you.'

It was so dark now that I could make nothing out of his features, his demeanour or even so much as his age. I knew he had caught Olivia's fancy, so he could not be very old.

'The vicar sent me a text,' he said. 'Walter was only here yesterday afternoon turning the Aga off and battening the place down. He wouldn't have had time to come back before you got here, so I went in and turned things back on. It was no trouble.'

'Walter?'

'Mr Harrop. She has him do all the maintenance here, although I've offered often enough. He'd rather see to the farm though. He hasn't the patience for holidaymakers. I know how he feels. But he has to do as he's told.'

'Under the thumb, is he?' I asked, but then thought it was unwise to become embroiled in village factions. 'I'm not a holiday-maker,' I explained. 'I'm here to work. My tenancy is for five months.'

I sensed, rather than saw, a shrug, inferring that it was all the same to Jamie. He didn't care either way.

'I did wonder about the garage, over there,' I said into the gloom. 'Does it belong to the cottage? I don't want to leave my car out, really.'

Jamie considered. 'No,' he said at last. 'It's our garage. But, as it happens, there's not much in it that couldn't be moved. You could put your car in it if you want. It's dry enough.'

I dithered. I really did want to get the car under cover, but I didn't want to find myself fleeced for an exorbitant sum of money, or to be a nuisance. 'I wouldn't want to put you to any trouble,' I said.

Again, I sensed a shrug. 'Suit yourself,' he said. 'The offer's there.'

I was on the point of accepting when a sudden noise from inside Jamie's house, a series of bangs and crashes that might have been a tower of furniture collapsing, or someone falling downstairs, had him leaping through his gate and disappearing into the shadow of his door.

'Talk about it tomorrow,' he threw over his shoulder before the door closed with a slam.

Bob and I settled ourselves into the cottage. Mrs Harrop's box of groceries yielded up a readymade—but homemade, I am sure by her own hands—cottage pie, which I placed in the Aga, and a bottle of red wine, which I opened immediately and left on the hearth by the log burner to breathe. There were numerous other commodities which, if I was careful, would see me through the next few days while I found my bearings and googled what other, more cost-effective, less monopolistic sources of shopping there might be. If all else failed I might survive for quite a few days on all the chocolate Olivia had provided. I set up the coffee machine I had brought from the flat and placed a few framed photographs on the dresser: of Mum and Dad on a cruise; of my brother and I when we were younger, before he had married his harridan of a wife and before we had fallen out with each other.

As I ate my dinner, I made a list of herbs and spices and other condiments I doubted Mrs Harrop could supply, the brand of washing powder I preferred, the dog food Bob liked, other bits and pieces I liked to have handy. I would need a strong torch, too. Once I had stacked the slimline dishwasher with the few things I had used, I considered opening up my laptop, but the thought of the emails that would certainly be waiting for me from an angry, or possibly worried, Ivaan, stayed my hand. I'd have to faff about finding the Wi-Fi code and, at that point, I was so comfortably ensconced on the settee in the kitchen, with a second glass of wine in my hand and my toes stretched out to the fire, that I couldn't be bothered.

I woke up two hours later. The wine glass—empty—had fallen from my hand but, by some miracle, had not broken. The fire was a heap of glowing ash. Bob snored in his bed by the hearth. The silence in and around the cottage was all-encompassing. The darkness, when I peered out from between the drawn curtains, was as substantial as something solid, a screen drawn down upon the land.

As I climbed the stairs my phone bleeped. An unknown number. I opened the text. It was from Olivia, who, I now recalled, had asked for my number. *Mummy says you'd be welcome to come to church tomorrow, the service starts at 10.30. Don't worry. She knows you won't come. Have you met Jamie yet? xx*

I texted back. *Yes, but it was dark. She's right, I won't. But thank her for the invitation. xx*

The bed was soft, clean, well-aired, with sheets that smelt of fresh air. I sank into it and fell immediately asleep.

In the night, though, something woke me. I lay awake and listened for a while. Had Bob made a noise? If he needed to go outside, he would do it again. But no. From inside the cottage there was no sound at all. And yet … I concentrated my hearing. There, in the roof-void—not right above my head but somewhere not far away—a creak, as if someone had shifted their weight from one beam to another. I held my breath. My heart hammered in my chest. There was a soft, hollow thud—to my fevered imagination like a cupboard door being carefully, slowly, *secretively* closed.

Across the marsh an owl hooted and then, from the slates right above the window, there was a skitter of talons, the flap of a wing, an answering screech as the owl's mate launched itself into the night.

Chapter Nine

It might have been the disturbed night, but more likely it was simply a precipitous drop in the adrenalin levels that had seen me through the past few weeks. Whichever it was, I woke on Sunday morning beset with doubts. The shimmering mirage of my adventure in a fantasy world had dissipated. I lay in bed for a while, looking up at the strange ceiling, tuning in to the sounds of the unfamiliar house, the eerie cry of birds over the marsh. Deciding to leave Hackney, to end things with Ivaan; planning my departure, executing it; and then the journey, like casting myself adrift onto a magical sea; a night without sleep; and my surreal arrival at Roadend—all these had roller-coastered me along—and now that they were done and I had landed, rather than feeling relieved I felt critically unsure. I was a fish out of water. Could I really manage to live for five months in this sequestered corner of the country?

A quick review of my wardrobe told me most of the clothes I had brought with me would be useless. I pulled out one thing after another despairingly. Everything was too thin, too trendy, too towny. I needed a shopping centre, or at least a retailer who would deliver, assuming there was one who would venture this far out into the wilds. It annoyed me I had come so unprepared, that I would fulfil the locals' woeful expectations of a city girl come to play at country life. Had not Marjorie suggested I ought to rethink? I added to the list I had begun the previous evening some much less fanciful items than miso paste and balsamic vinegar: sturdy boots, a waterproof coat, warm underwear and plentiful sweaters.

The day was fine, the squall of the previous one having blown itself away. A thin blue sky and a watery sun illuminated the dripping marsh in shades of ochre, sage and forest green. Bob and I walked across the marsh again, following different paths, hopping over black, peaty bogs, stumbling through tufts of whispering reeds, but not losing sight of the cottages. Such as they were, they were my only secure anchor in this remote and alien environment. We saw no one, heard nothing that was not wild, natural, emanating from earth and sky. One part of me exulted in it. But another admitted to feeling vulnerable and out of place. I regretted having so peremptorily rejected Marjorie's invitation to church.

I got back and rubbed Bob down with an old towel and then made coffee, which I took out into the garden and drank perched on the stone wall. There was garden furniture, but it had been swathed in a tarpaulin and secured with bungees for the winter, and I did not like to undo it. Why? Perhaps, in my heart, I was not sure I would be staying.

I hoped to see Jamie, as much to see a human face as to accept his kind offer of the garage, but the curtains of his house were tightly closed and no coil of smoke rose from his chimney. His hens had been fed, though, and in fact I had found half a dozen eggs on my doorstep. I was curious about him, what manner of man he was, his family situation, how life had brought him to his unprepossessing cottage on the edge of the marsh. How did he live? As my only neighbour, he would be my main and perhaps my sole human contact. I wondered how he got around. I had seen no vehicle. For that matter—again, a kind of vague despair threatened to engulf me—how would *I* maintain a connection with the village? The track to it was so awkward I did not like the idea of driving the MG along it very frequently. I sighed. Perhaps, after all, I would have been better with the apartment over Mrs Ford's studio. Why hadn't I investigated that? It might have been better in every way, at the heart of the village. A studio suggested someone with an artistic bent. Might they have been a kindred spirit?

My thoughts returned to Jamie. Perhaps he was at church, I mused. Perhaps the whole village attended religiously. The Lord and Lady of the Manor no doubt had a private pew; I could not see Her Ladyship crushed in with the hoi polloi. I imagined Mrs Harrop in a tall and imposing hat, further augmenting her sense of being *above* her neighbours. Her husband—in my mind's eye a diminutive, cringing creature—would creep down the aisle in her shadow. She would have scrubbed him raw for his weekly appearance in church. I peopled the nave with the other inhabitants of Roadend of whom I knew anything at all; Olivia, neat and devout, watching as Marjorie delivered her carefully prepared homily. The publicans—what were their names?—Bill and Julie, disillusioned, disengaged, thinking only of their retirement in some Spanish ex-pat community as the prayers and gospel reading echoed past their inattentive ears. The widow of the man recently buried, Mrs John Forrester, her eyes red-rimmed, a damp handkerchief balled in her gloved hand. I added, for good measure, the two hanged witches, slumping them into a shadowy pew, propped against a pillar, their black capes dripping onto the flagstone floor, their skeletal hands clutching hymnals. Again, I was sorry I had not accepted Marjorie's invitation to the service; there would have been no hypocrisy in it. I could have made no bones about the fact that I was there simply because I was new to the area and wanted to meet more of the villagers. That, probably, was all Marjorie had had in mind.

The day, like the marsh, stretched out in front of me, and I felt small and lonely. I put my hand on Bob's head. Thank goodness I had him with me.

I went back indoors and wandered through the rooms. Everything was *nice,* but impersonal, bland, provided for holidaymakers who would stay—at most—a fortnight, and then go home to their family mementoes, their familiar comforts, their drawer of useful bits and pieces like batteries and Sellotape and sticking plaster and postage stamps. I had no home. This, as pleasant and comfortable as it was, wasn't mine and wasn't home. I had an overwhelming desire to call my dad, which of course was impossible; and then, in desperation, my brother, to hear, if not a friendly voice, then a familiar one. But that was impossible for a different reason.

I set about trying to put my own stamp on the cottage, bringing a nice, crocheted blanket down from the twin room and laying it over the back of the settee, swapping the cushions around, exchanging a drear oil painting over the fireplace for a cheerier one that had been in the hall. I put away three leering toby jugs that sat on the dresser and set out instead some nice blue and white china cups and saucers I had found in the dining room sideboard.

In the afternoon I set up my laptop in the small bedroom, carrying one of the dining chairs up to sit on while the machine booted up and my emails loaded.

My fears were realised; there *was* an email from Ivaan, but not a worried or angry one. His tone was blithe, casual, full of his own concerns.

> *Dear Dee,*
>
> *There must be something wrong with your phone. I tried calling a few times but it didn't even ring out. Has your contract ended or something? You ought to sort that out.*
>
> *So, I'm in Acapulco. I got a message from Chrissie that there was a role for me on her film if I could get here quick, so I went straight to Heathrow and got the next plane. I knew you'd understand. There wasn't time to call you straight away because I had all my travel to sort out, and by the time I was at the gate your phone had died. It isn't a big part; all I know so far is that I'm to be one of a team of henchmen working for Chrissie's love interest, but I've skimmed the script and I'm the only one with any lines. I feel I can work with what little there is and hopefully I'll convince the producer that, in the follow-up Chrissie says is definitely in the pipeline, my character has the potential to grow. I need to put on some muscle pretty quickly, but Chrissie's in a nice condo with a gym and a pool and she says I can stay here and get into shape until I'm needed on set, which won't be for a while, I don't think. I guess I'll get to meet the director on Monday, which is ... tomorrow. God! I'm exhausted. It's the middle of the night and my body clock is all over the place. The flight was 29 hours with two stops. The only seat I could get was business class, but Chrissie's pretty sure my airfare will get reimbursed, which is a good thing.*
>
> *I need to crash. I'll email you again soon.*
>
> *Love, Ivaan x*

I quelled my instinct to send off an irate response but expiated my angst by stacking up the theoretical indictments against him. If I *had* been at my fictitious writing seminar in Warwick, Bob would have been alone in the flat for thirty hours before Ivaan had sent his message. And if, as he implied, Ivaan would not actually be needed on set for some time, why could he not have returned to Hackney, even if only for the duration of my course? Why did he have to fly *immediately* to Mexico? For someone who was supposed to be in a relationship, how could he think it was OK to fly off *anywhere* without even letting his partner know? Selfish! Impulsive! Thoughtless! Plus, I had my misgivings about Chrissie Bix. She and Ivaan had become suspiciously friendly, hadn't they? Of all the out-of-work actors she knew, why had she picked him for the part? And sharing her condo with him? Perhaps they'd started a fling in Wales and were now carrying it on in Acapulco. I felt betrayed, jealous—which I knew was unreasonable, since I had already decided to end my relationship with him. Then, I thought, she was welcome to him. And I hoped she kept her designer handbags under lock and key.

I slammed the lid of the laptop and stamped off down the stairs leaving Bob bemused, but not inclined to move from the futon, where he had settled himself. While I waited for the kettle to boil, though, I admitted I had made myself unreachable by swapping phones. And hadn't I, supposedly in a relationship, taken off without letting my partner know? If Ivaan's actions were irresponsible, they were at least in character, whereas I had acted rashly, melodramatically. Neither were traits I would have called typical of myself. My conclusion was that Ivaan was as much sinned against as sinning.

I carried the tea carefully up the stairs, in a much humbler frame of mind for composing a cool, but not caustic, reply. Just at that moment a beam of sunlight pierced the bathroom window and shone into my eyes. I squinted. I would not have seen it had I not been at such an oblique angle, and had the sun not, just then, at my eye level, shown up the slightly embossed ridge of dust on the grey, flecked carpet. I frowned and continued to climb. The line joined another at each corner, and those a fourth, to make a barely discernible—but quite definite—square of grey, powdery dust on the ashy pile of the carpet. How odd. I had not made it, I was sure. And although Bob did leave footprints and doghair, it was beyond him to have left such a perfect rectangle of dander. My eye travelled up, to where a square loft access hatch was set into the ceiling. I recalled the noise in the night, that quiet thud of what I had taken to be a cupboard door closing. Could it have been the loft hatch? Had somebody been in the loft?

Were they still there?

The horror of such an idea threw me into a panic, and I think it topped off a teetering stack of doubts and anxieties that had been accumulating all day. I abandoned my tea, pulled my coat from the peg and called to Bob, and we were soon striding up the track at a fast pace.

I didn't know where I was going, only that I needed to be out of the house. I needed people, company, reassurance, someone with a ladder.

We soon gained the slope through the coppice and let ourselves through the farmgate. The open aspect, the view of the sea, the intriguing ruin of the old house plus the exercise all seemed to help me find perspective. I walked up the camber of the hilltop, giving the imposing gates a wide birth, and made my way to the shattered remains of the building. It stood perilously close to what turned out to be a precipitous edge that dropped sheer to the beach below. Sheep, grazing in the lee of the broken walls of the tower, ambled away. I was proud of Bob; though not on a lead he took no notice of the sheep. He seemed to sense I needed him close to me.

Two walls of the old structure remained, making a right angle within which the grass grew long, knitted with nettles and brambles. Some litter had got caught up in it but it was what I would describe as clean litter: empty beer bottles, crisp packets and the like. Hackney litter had been of a much more nefarious ilk: needles and other drug-taking paraphernalia, used condoms, human excrement. The rest of the site was grassed over, with only a line of squared off foundation stones showing the extent of the former construction, which was not large; I had an idea it might have been a pele[1] tower, a fortified family home with provision for the protection of livestock on its ground floor, accommodations above. It would have had an unrivalled view over the firth, towards what I fancifully thought of as "the far country" across it. With a ninety degree

---

[1] Pronounced peel

turn it also provided an uninterrupted view over the village, then the plain and the massif beyond. I presumed the landowner had wanted to watch his back, as well as the coast. The pele's elevated situation would certainly have provided an excellent vantage point, as well as an unassailable defensive position. But this had been much more than a military outpost. The neatly dressed stones and some ornate detailing around the first-floor chimney breast told me this had been a gracious—if exposed—house at one time. Time and tide, however, had done their work. At the rate the bluff was being eroded by wind and sea, it seemed to me not unlikely the whole ruin would tumble to the beach before too long.

Any old house gets a writer's juices flowing and this one was no different for me. I walked the full perimeter of the ruin, hoping to find an information plaque, but there was nothing. I could only ponder about the family who had lived here; the Winters, I assumed, since everything round about seemed to bear their name. I speculated about their allegiances during the War of the Roses, the Civil War, the Jacobite uprising. What battles, what tragedies, what romances had the old place seen? What ghosts might linger? The answers might be waiting for me behind the self-important gates, where presumably the most recent descendants of the family now lived, but probably I had scuppered any chances of mining them by my foolishness the day before. I tucked away the idea of a story based on the burned out pele tower. I didn't need a fully formed record, just a hook of some kind, a germ of an idea from which, in a manner that was sometimes linear and sometimes centrifugal, my writing gland would spin out the story.

I turned to face the sea, which lay like a whipped mercury mirror far below. It was grey-blue, sparkling and exuberant with winking lights. The tide was out but coming in, covering boulders, groynes and sandbanks, marching towards the shingle tideline. A few walkers strode along, bent against the breeze, and I could see a dog gambolling in the surf. The bluff and the ruin upon it projected into the firth, protecting the sweeping curve of the bay and the village from whatever lay on its other side. *That* I could not see. The stone wall and the formal gardens of the Lord of the Manor's demesne kept it from view.

I looked with a kind of yearning down at the village. The pub was open. I could see cars pulled up on its forecourt. I imagined Marjorie and Olivia sitting down to their Sunday lunch. An ice cream van, or perhaps a mobile coffee van, was parked on the main carpark and a small queue of people waited to be served. Children played on the playpark. I felt reassured. There was nothing here to be afraid of. Even the imposing gates behind me, and their intimidating warden, held less fear for me when considered from this wide-open, exposed perspective. I had behaved foolishly and she had been understandably angry. That was the beginning and end of the incident. And now that I had put some distance between myself and the cottage, I realised how ridiculous I had been to believe someone had been creeping about in the loft. There might be a birds' nest up there. Hadn't I heard an owl? The wind could have disturbed dust and sent it seeping round the loft hatch. I only needed to mention the matter to Mrs Harrop next time I saw her and I was sure she would send Walter round to check the roof was sound.

Out of the wind, the sun was quite warm, and I sank down on one of the square stones, pulling Bob close to my side. I decided I would not walk down to the village on the off chance of seeing Marjorie and Olivia. I must be self-sufficient. I closed my eyes and concentrated on the glow of sunlight on my face, the sound of the waves below me, the cries of gulls.

Another sound added itself to the mix. A faint beat, a pulse in the air, a dull, percussive sound that grew in intensity and volume. I opened my eyes. There, over the water, coming from the open water side of the firth, a dark speck moved below the thin, high cloud. A helicopter. I watched it approach, high, but I thought in a descending trajectory. The sound became louder, almost uncomfortable in my ears. I wondered if it was a military flight, or an air-sea rescue mission, but, as the helicopter drew near enough, I could see no identifying mark on it. Bob's ears lay flat and he licked his lips in a way I knew denoted anxiety. I stroked his head and murmured reassurances, but the helicopter came inexorably on, seemingly right towards us, and so low that I feared for the crumbling chimney of the pele tower behind me. The twin runners, the whir of the blade, the glazed dome of the cockpit, all were clearly visible to me. My hair was caught up in its maelstrom, the hood of my coat flapped. Bob cowered beside me. Was it going to land on the plateau? I considered waving, to alert the pilot to our presence, to the tower behind me. The aircraft seemed to hover right in front of us, just over the lip of the bluff. Very deliberately it hung there, not forty yards from where Bob and I shrank against the stones of the tower. The noise and the downdraft were assaulting. My whole body vibrated with the mechanical thrum. I could see the pilot—a bulky man in a red helmet, wearing mirrored sunglasses. He seemed to be regarding me with dispassionate interest as I struggled against the tumult, crouching low and shielding Bob with my arms. What the hell was he thinking? Fear turned to anger and I half stood and raised my arm in a gesture I hoped would encapsulate all my fury, but at that moment the helicopter swooped up, passed right over my head, cleared the derelict tower and the wrought iron gates and disappeared over the headland. It must have landed close by. The whine of the engine abruptly lowered in pitch and decibels and the air around us stilled, leaving Bob and I shaking amidst the old walls.

Chapter Ten

When we got back to the cottage Olivia was patiently waiting for us, perched on the garden wall, with Patty by her side.

'Mummy was here too,' she greeted me, 'but she had to go back for a baptism preparation class. I said I didn't mind waiting.'

'I'm so glad you did,' I said, meaning it, as I opened the door and ushered her inside. 'You're my first visitor.'

'Hasn't Jamie been?' She peeled off her coat, a cerise, padded anorak. In spite of the lurid colour, I found I envied her it. My coat, an unlined gaberdine, had hardly kept out the autumn chill.

'I haven't seen him at all today,' I told her, leading the way to the kitchen. The heating was off and of course last night's fire had long since gone out, but the range emitted heat. 'I'm frozen,' I admitted. 'Do you know how to light the fire? I'll make us some tea.'

Patty leapt onto the settee and did a few pirouettes before settling herself down against one of the cushions. Bob, who was not generally allowed on the furniture—his earlier incursion onto the futon notwithstanding—turned an outraged eye towards me, but then settled down in his basket. Olivia knelt on the hearth rug and opened the door of the log burner. She used a lever at one side to shift the bed of ash and then she laid four pieces of coal and two logs carefully in the grate. 'There aren't many firelighters,' she said, peering into the kindling box.

'I'll add them to my list,' I said.

She added a firelighter and several sticks to the fire and then struck a match, holding the box and the match well away from her, and striking away from her body. It wasn't until the fire was burning brightly it occurred to me there was neither log burner nor open fire in Marjorie's bungalow.

Olivia remained kneeling on the rug, her face brightly illuminated by the flames, which were reflected also in the glass of her spectacles. She stroked Bob's fur with an automatic hand. Her thoughts must have run in tandem to mine. She gave a happy sigh and said, 'I've always wanted to do that, but I've never been allowed, before. I've watched it done *loads* of times, though.'

I made the tea and we settled onto the settee together. 'How was church this morning?' I asked. 'I almost wished I had come. I felt a bit lonely, here by myself.'

'We thought you might,' Olivia said matter-of-factly. She held her mug with both hands and sipped the tea. 'That's why we came to visit. Church was alright. Mummy preached about All Hallows Day. It's when the church remembers all good Christians, but especially the dead ones. All the John Forresters were there.'

'Ah yes,' I said. 'I saw Mr Forrester's grave.' I wondered whether I should mention the angry old man but decided against it. 'Was he a good Christian?'

Olivia gave a snort of laughter. 'No! He was angry and mean. I'm friends with Lucy, his daughter ...' she paused and sipped her tea again. '*Sort* of friends,' she qualified. 'We sat next to each other on the school bus a few times, but that was a long time ago. She's married now, with a baby.' Olivia stopped again and went into a kind of reverie. I wondered if she was privately pondering the probability of *her* ever marrying and becoming a mother; or perhaps she was sad her friendship with Lucy had lapsed. Presently she rallied and said, 'I think Lucy was afraid of her dad. He had a bad temper. I saw him fighting lots of times. I don't mean just shouting, although he did a lot of that too. *Actually* fighting, with fists and feet. Once, I saw him and his brother ramming each other with their tractors. It was worse if they'd been drinking. But Mrs Harrop says that's normal, for Forresters. *She* says, "Forresters come out of the womb fighting. They'll fight anyone who crosses them, but, most of all, they fight each other."'

This idea intrigued me; another narrative possibility to be filed away and ruminated upon. A family feud, warring brothers ... 'I gather they've lived in the village a long time, the Forresters?' I probed. 'There are lots of them in the graveyard.'

'The Forresters *are* the village! Well, *they* think so. Mrs Harrop thinks differently. But it's true they used to own all the land. But then old Todd Forrester divided it up between his sons. John had a big family but he got the smallest farmhouse. It wasn't fair and he never got over it. They fell out. He did alright in the end, but he never lost his grudge.'

I recalled the prosperous-looking farm I had seen at the far end of the village. 'Is that the one you pass as you come into Roadend?'

'Yes. Low Farm. Mr and Mrs Forrester had six children and they're all involved in the farm, one way or another. They keep poultry and sell eggs. They have rare breeds of cows and sheep for holidaymakers to look at, and they sell the breeding stock for thousands!' Olivia put her cup down and began to count off John Forrester's progeny on her fingers. 'Johnny is the oldest. He's taken the rare breeds over now. Adam comes next. He has a herd of goats. They sell the goat meat to Indian restaurants all over, and on the internet. Then Harry. He looks after all the farm machinery. Ben does the accounts. Ben is ...' she stumbled in her inventory and looked suddenly shy. 'Ben has a partner who is ...'

'A man?' I put in.

She nodded, and I thought I would have to say something inclusive that, at the same time, encompassed what I assumed would be Marjorie's take on same-sex relationships. But Olivia got past her embarrassment to surge on, 'Of course, with so many of them, they didn't need the farmworkers' cottages so they converted them to holiday lets and Lucy and Anna manage those. Mrs Forrester is supposed to run the dairy. They make award-winning ice cream. But in reality, she's always too ill. We *say* she's ill. Mrs Harrop says she's just lazy and always has been. Oh!' Olivia checked herself. 'I shouldn't have said that. We mustn't say anything *about* a person that we wouldn't say to their face.'

'You didn't say it,' I reasoned. 'Mrs Harrop did.'

This seemed to satisfy Olivia. 'Yes. You're right. Well, she's supposed to run the dairy but in fact the girls do it. We buy goats' milk and cheese from them. I'm lactose intolerant. It gives me … erm …' she lifted a finger to her cheek and stroked it meditatively.

'Eczema? I wish you'd said so,' I cried. 'I used cows' milk for your tea.'

'Oh, it'll be alright. A little bit won't hurt. I eat ordinary ice cream whenever I get the chance, and it doesn't seem to do me much harm. But don't tell Mummy that.'

'I won't,' I promised, but I wanted more information about the Forresters. 'What about the other brother?' I asked.

Olivia shrugged. 'He got the best farm but, with only one son, he couldn't manage to run it. The John Forresters wouldn't lift a finger to help and it all went to pot. Eventually he sold out. The new squire owns it all now.'

'What a pity,' I said, but privately pleased by the satisfyingly distinct arcs the two brothers' narrative trajectories would make. 'The new squire. That will be the man behind the fancy gates. Does he fly a helicopter?'

Olivia nodded.

'So, he's only recently inherited, but I suppose his family has been connected with the area for centuries. Their name is Winter, isn't it?' I hoped Olivia might be able to give me some background on this other intriguing creative possibility; how and when their old manor house had been razed, family annals of derring-do, the skeletons that might be rattling in the ancestral closets behind the gates. My preliminary sketch of the squire was not a flattering one: an inbred toff, with buck teeth and a hee-haw voice, equal to his wife in *hauteur* and spleen.

'Yes and no,' said Olivia, shattering the bubble of my imagination. 'You're almost right. The Winters used to be the squires, but the last one died without a son and so that was the end. These people aren't Winters. Their name is Forster. They bought the title when they bought the land. Mummy says it's jumped-up silliness. Anyone can be a Lord of the Manor, you know, so long as you don't mind your 'manor' being a five-metre square patch of bog. Well,' she conceded, 'his is bigger than that. But no one knows why he wanted land here. He's Canadian. It's a mystery.'

As much as I am intrigued by a mystery—what writer is not?—my thoughts turned to more practical matters since it was clear my scheme for a novel based on the ruined pele tower and its unbroken succession of barons would come to nothing. 'I know Mrs Harrop said Waitrose doesn't deliver here,' I began, 'but does *any* supermarket? I need a few things I don't think Mrs Harrop will stock.'

'You'd be surprised,' Olivia offered, loyally. 'She can get most things. What do you need?'

I thought of my list. The things on it seemed appallingly pretentious. Did anyone really *need* Macadamia nuts or Ibérico ham?

I ignored the question. 'And I suppose she's quite pricey. Not that she's greedy, of course, your mum said the margins are small, but, in comparison to an ordinary supermarket …'

Olivia lowered her voice to a conspiratorial whisper. 'Occasionally, we go to town and get things from the supermarket. It's usually when we need shoes, or the dentist, or when we fancy a film, or when Mummy needs new glasses—things crop up quite often and we find it just can't be avoided. We could pick things up for you, or you could come with us.'

'Isn't it …' *A long way away* is what I was going to say. But I hesitated, for the truth was I didn't know *exactly* where I was. I still hadn't consulted a map. It pleased me to think of myself in some far, sequestered domain, a place so far off the charts it wasn't quite real. I didn't want to know there was an ordinary town a half hour's drive away. 'I expect it's quite a long way away,' I concluded, sliding my eyes away.

'We usually make a day of it,' Olivia confirmed, helpfully abetting me in my fantasy. 'And, if we get back after dark, Mrs Harrop can't see what we unload from the back of the car.'

'I see,' I nodded sagely. 'And, if I order things on-line—clothes and things—can they be delivered, this far out?'

'Oh yes. Amazon, Next, Marks & Spencer's, Santa Claus. They all deliver here.'

Again, Olivia's dry sense of humour amused me. I entered into her joke. 'By teleporter?' I suggested, 'or a mystical portal?'

'By Hermes,' she said. 'The winged messenger. Locally known as Brian.' She picked her mug up and looked hopefully into it, but it was empty. 'So,' she began with specious casualness, 'you did meet Jamie, but you haven't seen him today?'

I made more tea as I filled her in on my meeting with my neighbour, emphasising the darkness, its brevity. I could see it didn't satisfy her, but it was all I had.

Our pleasant *tête á tête* couldn't last long. Beyond the windows of the cottage, the November light was fading fast. While Olivia was putting her coat on to go home it occurred to me I ought to offer to drive her, although the prospect of negotiating the tortuous lane at dusk didn't appeal.

'Oh no, that's OK, I'll walk,' she said, when I made the suggestion. She pulled a torch out of her pocket. 'I'll be quite all right. I'm equipped, see? And I have Patty.'

'Did you walk here, Olivia? Or did Marjorie drive you?' I hadn't heard a car labouring up the hill as I had sat in the lee of the old manor house.

'We came along the boardwalk,' she said, attaching Patty's lead. 'It's one of the first things the new squire did, when he came. The marsh can be dangerous, especially after a lot of rain. But he had the boardwalk put in, to connect up the village and his estate. Having said that, Her Ladyship prefers to shop by email. She sends her orders in to Mrs Harrop that way. Haven't you seen the boardwalk?'

I shook my head. 'I've walked on the marsh a couple of times, but I didn't see a boardwalk.'

'Come on,' she said. 'I'll show you.'

I put my damp coat on and hauled Bob out his bed for the third time that day to follow her up the lane in the gloaming light. We had hardly passed the derelict cottage when Olivia stumbled into one of the potholes and had to reach out to me for support.

'Oh,' I cried, 'are you alright?' The inadvisability of allowing her to go home *alone* assailed me again.

I had resigned myself to accompanying her all the way when she said, 'Whoops! No, I'm OK. Mummy's always telling me to watch where I'm going. She expects me to fall over all the time but really, I'm nowhere near as clumsy as she thinks I am.'

The effect of the little incident was that we walked on along the lane arm-in-arm, lingering together as we passed Jamie's house when my instinct was to hurry by. It was obvious that Olivia hoped to catch a glimpse of him, but the place was still deserted; no light shone through the still-drawn curtains.

I threw her a sympathetic glance. 'No sign of anyone being home,' I observed with manufactured lightness. And yet, oddly, when we passed the chicken run, I could see the hens had all been put away and the door of their house was firmly shut.

'Maybe I'll meet him coming home,' she said. 'He's sure to come this way.'

Past the place where the wide planked bridge crossed the dyke, just before the track began to rise, where the thicket of elder and silver birch marked the bend in the track, a fingerpost I could not have seen from the car pointed off to the left. Through the bruised light that mazed the marsh in tones of violet and grey I could see the sturdy poles and connecting planks of a boardwalk leading off across the marsh.

'It's a shortcut,' Olivia said. 'It comes out at the back of the church. Halfway along there's a hide, for watching birds, but no one uses it.

I felt swamped with relief that there was a nearer way to the village than the twisted path and precipitous slope, that the gates of shame could be avoided, that if I had to encounter Her Surly Ladyship again it would not be on the crest of her own hill.

Olivia turned to me, disengaging her arm from mine but, to my surprise, replacing it with a warm hug. 'Can we be friends?' she said, looking earnestly up at me. 'I haven't got a *real* friend.'

'Neither have I,' I said. 'I'd love to be friends with you, Olivia.'

We both beamed, ridiculously pleased. Then Olivia said, 'We're going away tomorrow. Mummy's on a diocesan course. But we're back on Friday and there'll be a bonfire on the beach, you know, for Guy Fawkes. A couple of days late, but we always have it on the Friday. Will you come? You can leave Bob at our house with Patty. I don't suppose he'll like the fireworks. Oh! And if you text me the shopping you need, I'll make sure we get it for you. There's a Waitrose not far from the cathedral.'

I nodded enthusiastically. 'Oh, yes *please*. Are you *sure* you're all right walking home alone?' I asked. It really was quite dark by that time.

Olivia said, 'Mummy and I spend a *lot* of time together. Sometimes, it's nice to be on my own. And I promise I'll watch my step.'

I watched her little figure recede into the gloom of the boardwalk, Patty trotting jauntily at her heels. It must have been a trick of the light because the pink glow of her anorak seemed to disappear as if through some kind of veil. One moment she was there, the thin beam of her torch waving farewell, the next the boardwalk was empty.

I walked slowly back to the cottage. The day had all but ended, the twilight pressing down from above and also creeping in across the marsh. Sepia clouds scudded across the sky. Everything—the bracken, the trees, the oozing marsh, even the row of homely cottages—seemed leached of colour, like a panorama shot in monochrome. Only the lounge lamp I had left on threw a splash of muted light. My footsteps on the crunchy gravel sounded shockingly loud in the hush. The hens in the coop were silent, the willows at the end of the track shushed and whispered in the little wind. Perhaps Jamie had left the window open a fraction—as I went by, I thought I saw the curtain move.

I made some pasta for my supper and finished the bottle of wine I had opened the evening before. I wondered about going through to the sitting room to see if there was anything on the television but the idea of leaving the warmth of the kitchen did not appeal, so I chose a novel from the bookshelves and settled down with that. I was yawning by half past eight and at nine o'clock I stopped fighting the fatigue.

I was rinsing my wine glass at the sink when a clatter outside the back door made Bob bark. The noise of it, after the absolute silence of the evening, was startling, and sent adrenalin coursing into my veins. I dried my hands, hushing him urgently in a way that was counter-intuitive because I was glad any interloper should know I had a dog, and a brave one too. I summoned courage and turned the key in the door, opening it to throw an envelope of light onto the rough slabs that paved the yard. Bob bolted past me, launching himself into the gloomy corners. The yard wasn't much more than a roughly fenced enclosure, holding back the hill and trees that rose up behind the cottages. A gate to the left gave access to an alleyway that ran the whole length of the row. It was shut, but not locked. I shot the bolt firmly across. Apart from that, I couldn't see anything amiss. Bob toured the log store and the adjacent shed, his nose to the ground. Underneath the small window that looked into the kitchen, a galvanised metal bucket lay on its side. Had someone used it to stand on, to spy on me through the window? I had closed the curtains, but they didn't stretch quite all the way across ... I gave myself a shake and told myself not to be ridiculous. More likely an animal—a fox, perhaps, *en route* to the hen coop—had knocked it over. I picked it up and put it into the shed.

I let Bob out for a final wee at the front of the house, and while he mooched around in the long grass across the track I looked out across the marsh. The earlier wind had subsided and now only the clandestine whisperings of the willows and the shushing of the grasses on the marsh told me a vestige of it remained. There was no moon, but the sky was strewn with stars, pin-prick punctures in black velvet—a number so vast it was impossible to comprehend. Below their canopy, the marsh was a sea of shadows, the topography undulating away from me, as fathomless as the sky above. Then, somewhere in the dim, I saw a light; thin and wavering, it seemed to move across the swell of the marsh. It was sometimes clear—I could follow it for ten, fifteen, twenty seconds together—and then it disappeared, emerging at a point further to the left. I strained my eyes to make out its trajectory, to discern the darker anthracite silhouettes of the trees from the ashy gloom of the undergrowth. Who could be walking across the marsh at night, and why? It probably wasn't safe, and with those deep-cut channels of water hidden by fringes of bracken, it would be easy to misstep. But what could I do about it?

I stepped through my gate and onto the track to peer through the gloom at Jamie's house. No light shone, so there was no aid to be got there.

I gave it up, whistled Bob and went to bed. My dreams were peopled by the Forresters, the feuding brothers, who morphed—in the way of dreams—into my own brother and me.

Chapter Eleven

My second night at the cottage passed without any disturbance more bothersome than my dreams, and I woke in a much more positive frame of mind. The day, again, was bright and clear, with high scudding clouds over the marsh and a cacophony of birdsong in the willows.

As I dressed, I remembered I had not answered Ivaan's email the previous day. I woke my laptop and fired off a quick reply, not stopping to think too carefully about it before I pressed "send."

> *Dear Ivaan,*
>
> *Thank you for your message. I knew in my bones that you would not return, regardless of any suffering that might cause Bob (or me). Accordingly, I arranged to leave the flat and we are now living elsewhere. As I ceased to pay the rent and utilities beyond October, you should put measures in place to meet those commitments. Both are due on 30th November, so you have a little time.*
>
> *I genuinely wish you the best of luck with this film, and with all that follows it.*
>
> *Kind regards*
>
> *Dee*

I closed the lid and put him out of my mind.

My boots were still soaked but I pulled them on, and Bob and I set out for our morning walk. To my surprise, the door of Jamie's cottage was open, the curtains pulled back, and a few items of washing hung out to dry on a rotary drier that had appeared in his front garden. He was in the chicken run, sweeping up the soiled straw bedding, the poultry clucking and cooing at his heels. I was able to take in a few details of his appearance before he saw me because he had his back to me and, being tall, he had to stoop to fit in the coop at all, further limiting my scope of vision. I gathered he was well-made, brawny, with wide shoulders tapering to a narrow waist. His shirtsleeves were rolled up and I could see thick, muscly arms haloed, in the slanted morning light, with blond hair. He worked the broom with short, efficient strokes. His hair—fair— was wavy and would have fallen to his collar if not for the odd angle at which he was forced to hold his head. He wore blue jeans stuffed into brown boots. This was as much as I could take in before Bob bounded up to the coop and alerted him to our presence. He swung round and lifted a hand to shade his eyes from the sun. Crouched within the low-roofed chicken enclosure, his stance reminded me of Quasimodo and I wished I had a cup of water on me so I could play Esmerelda.

'Good morning, Jamie,' I said, stepping closer and trying not to laugh. 'It's me, Dee, from next door.'

He gave a little upwards gesture with his head. 'Oh. Yes. Good morning,' he replied, and returned to his sweeping.

I got only the briefest glimpse of his face. It was handsome, certainly, in a rugged and unkempt style—square, lightly stubbled jaw, broad forehead, deep-set eyes. I couldn't make out their colour and peered more closely. 'Oh!' I burst out. 'You're hurt.' His left eye was purple from brow to cheek, the lid swollen. I could see now, his bottom lip was split, crusty with a scab.

He gave an irritated shake of the head. 'It's nothing,' he muttered.

I hesitated. Either he had been in a fight, or it had been him on the marsh the previous night, and he'd had a fall. Either way, he clearly didn't want to talk about it. I found his reticence mildly hurtful, which was silly; we were hardly friends. Even so, my sense of being snubbed made its way into my voice. I took a step back. 'Thank you for the eggs,' I said. I heard the stiffness in my voice and he must have done too. 'That was very kind.'

He shrugged and carried on sweeping, although the floor of the henhouse was now clean, the dirty straw all piled into one corner. The hens scuffed about in it, as eager to redistribute it as Jamie was to collect it. It was another comical circumstance and I wished we could share a joke, but his turned back and surly air warned me he was in no mood for levity. I waited for him to make some conversational gambit. Had I settled in the cottage? Did I need anything? Wasn't it a pleasant day? Nothing. I filled the awkward silence with, 'I have been thinking about your kind offer.'

He made a noise I interpreted as a query, although it was not much more than a grunt.

'Yes,' I laboured on, 'about the garage. I'd like to put the car in it if it wouldn't inconvenience you too much. You mentioned a few things would have to be moved around. I'd be happy to help.'

He opened the door to the coop and stepped through it, straightening up his back and coming to his full height, which must have been six foot two or three. Apart from the black eye and the split lip, he was a good-looking bloke and it was no wonder to me that Olivia had fallen for him. I put his age at somewhere around thirty, but he could have been as young as twenty-five or as old as thirty-five. I had a strange sense of disconnect between his robust physicality and his emotional state; he seemed burdened, weary, careworn. He looked lonely. It was there in the set of his shoulders, in the way he let his arms hang loose at his sides. His gaze slid around, looking anywhere but at me. I wondered where he had been all yesterday, who he had fought with—if he *had* fought—and what about. Why did he live alone? Why was he even here, in this isolated place, instead of in a town or city? I wanted him to look me in the eye so I could make him some offer of understanding, of sympathy. But he only stood long enough to ease the crick from his back. Then he stooped down to fondle Bob's ears before taking hold of the handles of a dilapidated old wheelbarrow and manoeuvring it awkwardly back into the enclosure.

'No need,' he said at last, seizing a pitchfork and beginning to lift the straw into the barrow. 'It won't take me long to sort things out in there.' His eyes flicked me briefly up and down. 'No offense, but they're heavy and …'

'All the more reason why I should help,' I interrupted.

'… and dirty,' he finished. 'I'll get to it later. I'll leave the key in the padlock for you.'

'Thank you,' I said. He made that shrugging gesture again, and I was left feeling like someone who had thrown a lifeline to a man in deep water, only to have him refuse to take hold of it. I gathered our conversation was over. I called Bob and we went on our walk.

We walked out across the marsh in the direction of the light I had seen the previous night. The meandering path through the russet bracken and tall, waving fronds of loofah-coloured grasses brought me to the thicket where I had found the trysting tree. It did seem to me—although it could have been wishful thinking on my part—that the interwoven screen of twigs and branches had been bent back and broken. It felt easier to access the little glade than it had before. And, once there, it looked like the grass had been flattened. I imagined an assignation of some kind; it certainly was a private spot for lovers to meet. How romantic to risk the dangers of the marsh for a few snatched moments ... but then I recalled the wild-haired old tramp I had seen in the churchyard. The trysting tree was an ideal spot for a homeless person to doss down; well-sheltered, safe from discovery. I cast about me for the kind of detritus I imagined a homeless person might leave behind them. There was nothing.

There was no sign of Jamie when we came back. I made coffee and took it upstairs and got busy with my laptop and credit card. I placed an order with a well-known country outfitter for boots and stout shoes. I ordered two coats; a warm, padded one and another similar in design to the one the Lady of the Manor had been wearing—long, capacious, thoroughly waterproof. I added thermal underwear, roll-neck sweaters, zip-up fleeces, walking trousers, a hat, scarf and gloves to my basket. I visited an on-line pet store and bought Bob a coat with a fluorescent stripe, a collar with a flashlight, some dog shampoo, a hundred rolls of poo-bags and a bulk supply of the food he liked. I ordered a sturdy torch and some spare batteries, a DAB radio and a book about pele towers from the ubiquitous on-line store that sells everything. For a finale of utter profligacy, I added an iPad to my order. When I'd finished, I felt almost drunk with the excess of spending and the sense that I had, now, committed myself irrevocably to this remote dwelling and its lonely marsh.

I was so busy with my purchases I did not at first tune in to the odd reverberation that had communicated itself to the air. The hum of my laptop, the creak of the radiators, both might have masked the separate sound that seemed to emanate from … from where I could not exactly say. Houses are rarely absolutely silent; they have their own rhythms and sighs, their own particular vibrations. The cottage was old and there were any number of causes for the strange hum I now felt and heard. The window frame, perhaps, had a chink where a pulse of air could squeeze through. The cavity wall between the cottages might allow the ingress of some stray draught. The beams and trusses overhead could be flexing, reacting to heat or cold. This was not to mention the tree-clad slope that rose up behind the cottage or the windswept marsh in front. But the longer I sat in that little room the more keenly I was aware of it—a curious drone that rose and fell in pitch, and came and went in volume, like a radio left on in a distant room. A voice? Perhaps. But as much tremor as sound. To my fanciful mind it was the echo of a quiver of emotion.

I sat for a long while, trying to tune my senses to it, but at last I had to abandon the effort, and when I went downstairs I could hear only the rumble of the fridge and the murmur of wind in the trees.

In the afternoon the sky clouded over, taking all the brightness from the copper bracken and the swaying grasses, and turning the slowly flowing water in the ditches from amber to a dun brown. I felt sure more rain was coming, and if I wanted to get into the village today, via the boardwalk, I had better do it quickly.

On again with the boots, which were beginning to disintegrate now, their seams oozing some nasty tea-coloured moisture, their laces fraying in their eyelets. On again with the thin, damp gaberdine. We walked up the track and then took the planked causeway that went around the thicket and along the periphery of the marsh. The topography was extraordinary, with depth as well as distance, like an enormous, dense feather quilt. Mounds of bracken and marsh grasses, heather and other low-growing shrubs tessellated between the animal tracks I had followed on earlier days and the crisscross of little canals in a crazy appliqué to which there was no design, no pattern, but yet which formed a beautiful, perfectly balanced landscape. The trickle of water was constant. I could see silvery glimpses beneath my feet, between the boards. Above my head skeins of geese crossed the marsh in ragged chevrons. They squawked and chastised each other. *Don't fly so fast. Keep up at the back! Bank right, you're off course!*

The boardwalk felt solid, its sturdy poles planted deep in the ancient peat of the wetland. The surface of the boards had been covered in chicken wire to stop them from being slippery but this was peppered with a mosaic of fallen leaves like an ancient Roman pavement. Bridges crossed the waterways and these had handrails, but the sides of the main path were open. It would have been easy for Bob to leap off the boards and into the brush of the marsh, but he plodded contentedly at my heels, even when we disturbed a pheasant from beneath the track. It chattered away in a flurry of wings. He stared after it, but made no move to pursue it.

After about ten minutes a spur divided off towards the centre of the marsh, running for about a hundred yards and then terminating in a pontoon with a timber structure on it; the hide Olivia had mentioned. I could imagine it was an excellent spot to observe the wildlife but I hadn't time to explore it. Above me the sky was filling with thick, ominous-looking clouds.

At some point impossible to quite determine, the undulating marshland turned to ordinary bog. Here and there were blackish pools of water, and cows had poached up whole swathes of the ground. The path followed the line of a barbed wire fence, turned sharply right and terminated in a gate at the back of the graveyard.

The graveyard was quiet. No angry tramp today. It occurred to me he must have left by the boardwalk gate, as I had not seen him at the front of the church when I had met Marjorie and Olivia. This made it seem more likely that it had been him I saw the night before, making his way across the marsh to some sequestered little bivouac; not the trysting tree, but some other similar, sheltered spot.

The flowers on John Forrester's grave had been augmented, I presumed by the family before or after the previous day's church service. The bouquets and tributes now spilled onto the paths on either side of the grave. A solar lantern had been added. I was curious that a man who, by Olivia's account, had not been popular even with his own children, should have warranted this excess of memorials. I wandered around the other Forrester graves for a while, summoning the details I had gleaned from Olivia. Todd, I recalled, was the man Olivia had mentioned as the family patriarch. He had been laid to rest in 1993 with his wife, Rose, who had died some seventeen years before him. Also memorialised were two infants, both girls, who had passed away within two years of each other. John Forrester appeared to be the first adult of his generation to join his parents.

I thought of my own parents, buried in an environmentally friendly greenwood plot not far from their home. There was no marker to show their place other than a birdbox that my brother and I had arranged to be placed on a nearby tree. Dad and I had wandered beneath the ancient beech and horse chestnut trees every year on the anniversary of Mum's death, but I had not been back since taking him there for the last time. I had a sense that, now he had been reunited with her, he would not need me. I held him fast in my memory; that was his memorial.

I let myself out via the lychgate and put Bob on the lead.

There were no customers in Mrs Harrop's shop. At the tinkle of the bell, she emerged from the room behind the counter, wiping her hands on a tea towel. I was struck again by her raptor-like demeanour, the vulturish way her head seemed to thrust forward, the beady, watchful glint of her sharp grey eyes. It was ridiculous but I found her intimidating. I was sorry there were no other customers with whom I might form an alliance against her.

'Good afternoon,' I said gushingly, 'I'm so glad you're open. I wasn't sure of your opening hours.'

'I'm always open,' she barked, 'or I *can* be. Just come round the yard and knock on the kitchen door if you need anything.' She indicated the room behind her. 'I've just put a batch of flapjack in. The school bus will be here in an hour and the children come in for sweets and cakes before they go home. Settled in, have you?'

I assured her I had. 'I need a few bits and pieces,' I said, looking around at the crowded shelves. I had texted Olivia with most of my list of foodstuffs, saving a few everyday items to placate Mrs Harrop. 'That shepherds' pie was delicious. Do you do any others? Milk, please, butter, firelighters …' I reeled off a few things and she moved efficiently round the shop collecting them together for me.

'Made lasagne this morning,' she said. 'Want some of that? And there's a quiche. That was left over from Saturday but it'll be perfectly alright. Do you need eggs?'

I shook my head. 'Jamie gave me some, thanks.' I looked at the vegetable display; dirty carrots and potatoes, some tomatoes that weren't quite ripe, onions, and two rather lovely cauliflowers. 'I'll take a cauli, please, and two big potatoes. I'll bake them in the range.' Some devilry prompted me to add, 'And do you have some local cheese? Or ought I to go down to Mrs Forrester's dairy for that?'

She sniffed. 'I stock an excellent local cheddar,' she said. 'No need to traipse all the way down there. Anything she does, I can do, and cheaper too. Her stuff is priced for tourists. My shop is for the locals. And as for her baking … she's no hand for pastry, never did have. Mary did all the cooking, when Todd was alive.'

My writer's antenna pricked up. Mrs Harrop didn't like Mrs Forrester. Ingrained antagonism was a rich mine no self-respecting writer could afford to leave unexplored. Hadn't Marjorie told me that Mrs Harrop was a gossip? And here was my perfect opportunity to find out a bit more about the Forrester clan.

'I gather Todd was quite a character,' I murmured, pretending to examine a tub of hot chocolate.

Mrs Harrop busied herself with packing my purchases into a bag. The interaction of shopkeeper and customer went on in the ordinary way. I added things to the counter; a tin of soup of a brand I wouldn't normally buy, some lack-lustre sliced bread. She waved the scanner over them, but all the while her voice spooled out a sketch of Todd Forrester: tyrant, misogynist, reprobate, thief. It was as though we were both listening to the narrative broadcast on the radio. We were not gossiping, simply tuning in to an item of village history. When she had finished, I felt the bones of the man she had described to me like an unwieldy skeleton in my grasp. It was disorganised, its ribs misaligned, its joints dislocated. It was bald and fleshless, aching to be properly assembled and clothed with character. And with fairness—for there was no doubting Mrs Harrop's prejudice against him. No one in fact or in fiction is wholly, one hundred percent bad. Nevertheless, there was no mistaking Todd's potential as a powerful catalyst on which to build a story.

In one sense I felt rather overwhelmed, like someone who had hoped for a new mug for their birthday and received an entire tea service. Ideas for stories didn't usually come this easily; they had to be teased and prodded, brought forth with much travail. This one had landed virtually gift wrapped! I ought to have been suspicious of it but instead I felt rather blessed. I couldn't wait to get home and start.

At the last minute I remembered to tell Mrs Harrop about the strange noises I had heard in the attic, and the dust-fall that seemed to have come from the loft hatch.

'Probably a bird,' she said. Now her storytelling was done she was prosaic again, eager to get back to her flapjack. 'I'll send Walter down.'

'Jamie might ...' I began, but she curled her lip at that suggestion. 'No good sending a lad out to do a man's work,' she said. 'Walter will come. He might as well bring your shopping. This bag's quite heavy.'

Chapter Twelve

It was tempting to take Bob onto the beach. I stood on the little hump-backed bridge and watched the tumbling water cascade between its banks and out onto the grey shingle. The car park to my right was empty, the playpark tenanted only by one young mum and her toddler. Bob lifted his nose to smell the sea, the seaweed, the scents carried on the brisk wind. The water was churned, dark with silt, topped with creamy froth, the tide quite high and crashing in relentless waves onto the hissing shingle. About a hundred yards along the beach stood the village bonfire, built from driftwood and old pallets and the upper branches of a felled tree, also broken furniture and other bits of rubbish the villagers had contributed. It was quite an edifice, and I wondered about walking just that far. But the sky presaged rain. Like the sea, it was murky and brown, whipped up into cappuccino peaks. There was no glimmer of sun. It was barely four o'clock but already it felt like dusk was with us. I shivered in my inadequate coat and turned for home.

Halfway there the rain began. Spiteful needles stung my face and plastered the front of my coat with water, but this was only the canapé for the banquet that was to follow. The heavens literally opened, drenching us with a deluge of cold, merciless rain. In moments my hair was running with water, my coat was soaked, my jeans sodden and sticking to my legs, my oozing boots squelching with every step. I began to run along the boardwalk, although, in hindsight, I have no idea why. I was already as wet as possible. It was like running with a cold, high-pressure hose fixed to my head—there was no escaping it. Rain smarted my eyes and it was all I could do to keep them open. The marsh was covered as though by a thick curtain of moisture. Through my half-closed eyes I could see it billowing in arcs and folds—grey, gauzy, quite graceful, but ruthless. The hide came into view, shrouded by rain, but a place of refuge. I took the spur and ran towards it. The wind felt like a hand on my back, chivvying me forward. I wrenched open the door of the hide and fell inside. Bob bounded in behind me and the door slammed on us as if by a meteorological turnkey.

The hide was dry, but cold. The floor was bare boards, dusty. I picked myself up and wiped my hands. Bob shook himself and water sprayed from his coat onto the plank wall and onto me, but I was so wet already more could hardly matter. Only a small amount of light entered from an opening high up under the eaves. I wiped my face with the lapel of my coat but the fabric was so saturated it made no difference. A narrow bench ran along one side of the hide. The shutters over the viewing apertures rattled in the wind but kept out the rain, which I could hear pouring in sheets from the roof and splashing onto the platform. On the opposite wall I could see a few posters and information sheets I presumed would detail the local wildlife. I tried to make them out, but the light wasn't good enough. I turned from them and was about to perch on the bench when something in the corner caught my eye. Bob noticed it at the same time and took a step or two towards it to investigate, but I pulled him sharply back. Something was slumped against the wall, deep in the shadows of the gloomy space. I gasped, and shrank away, thinking immediately of the tramp. Was he dossing in the hide? In this weather, who could blame him? But he certainly wasn't a man I wished to be in close confines with. The thing in the corner remained still. Surely my entrance would have disturbed even the drunkest sleeper. I listened intently but could hear no sign of breathing. Eventually I began to think reasonably, fumbled in my pocket for my phone, located the torch and switched it on. The thing in the corner was a large rucksack, patterned in army camouflage, and another cylindrical bag I took to be a sleeping bag. I approached cautiously. Closer inspection told me the cylinder was a tent, not a sleeping bag. I had no idea a tent could pack up so small, but there it was; what did I know? They were not old but they were well-travelled, the seams of the backpack somewhat ragged, one of the straps repaired with a leather patch, a stain on the cover of the tent. A number of things were attached to the rucksack: a skillet, some walking poles and a rectangular shape I made out to be a solar panel. Ah! And yes, there at the bottom was the bedroll. None of these things were dusty; they hadn't been in the hide long. Neither were they wet, so they had been there before the heavens had opened. On balance they didn't seem to be the possessions of a down-and-out. The homeless people I had seen in London tended to have worldly goods that were bundled less professionally than this, and would rarely leave them unattended. On the other hand, it was a capacious pack and looked as though it could contain enough for a trek of some duration. Its owner could be a hiker, likely ex-army, perhaps someone doing a trek for charity. Or they could be a runaway, a fugitive. Either way, I posited the theory that having stashed their gear in the hide they, like me, had been caught out on the marsh in the downpour and would be making their way back here as quickly as they could.

I cranked open one of the shutters. The rain still fell, but the day was gone. Night was smearing itself across the marsh like black paint across a window and I could make out no feature of the landscape other than the broad ribbon of the walkway. I checked my phone. There was no signal and my battery was low. If I wanted to make it back to the cottage with the aid of the torch, I needed to leave immediately. Otherwise, I would have to spend the night in the hide, presumably in the company of the owner of the camping gear.

I shortened Bob's lead. He looked up at me. I could see his eyes shining in the dimness, trusting, but also fearful. His ears lay flat along the dome of his head. I gave him what I hoped was a reassuring smile and pushed the door of the hide open.

The rain hit us again as we exited. The wind was in our face this time as we made our way along the pontoon, back towards the main boardwalk. The assault of water on my skin was dreadful. It hit my coat and legs like a hail of shot. We forged on, reaching the turn and moving at something between a fast walk and a slow jog along the planks. I held my phone out in front of me, but its light was meagre, scarcely penetrating the wall of water or the pressing gloom of the night. The dark shoulder of the thicket emerged from the murk. Beyond it I could just make out the outline of the cottages. I tightened my grip on Bob's lead and extended my stride. Then, the heel of my boot must have caught between the planks, or perhaps it came away from the sole. Either way, I stumbled, was yanked to a standstill and then thrown into a sprawl on the boardwalk. The chicken wire sliced into my palms. My ankle wrenched and a thunderbolt of pain stabbed up my leg. I screamed. My phone shot from my hand and skittered away. Bob stopped in his tracks and turned back to where I lay. I could feel his hot breath on the back of my neck as he stood over me, confused.

The boardwalk began to shake. Heavy footsteps pounded towards us. The tramp? The hiker? The escaped convict? But it was Jamie. Water poured off him. He wore no coat. His sweater was saturated. I felt the ooze of it as he lifted me up. He carried me in his arms, scooping me up easily in a way that conjured Rhett Butler carrying Scarlet O'Hara up the stairs, or wicked Willoughby rescuing Marianne Dashwood. I could feel the rasp of his beard against my scalp. But there was no romance in *this*. My ankle jarred in agony with every step as his long strides covered the walkway.

'My phone,' I gasped out.

'Gone,' he barked back, 'or soaked. Useless anyway. What were you thinking? Couldn't you *see* what was coming?' His tone was curt, almost reprimanding.

'I thought I'd make it back,' I said. 'I didn't know … I didn't know it *could* rain like this. It's biblical.'

'It's Cumbria,' he said witheringly. And I was conscious of a surge of anger, because he had broken the spell, and plucked me from my make-believe realm to somewhere commonplace that anyone could find on any map.

I stiffened in his arms. 'I can probably walk,' I said. 'I'm not Marianne Dashwood. I don't need a Willoughby.' He made no reply, and I realised he had no idea what I was talking about.

He strode up to the cottage and pushed the door open. It was only later that this struck me, as I had locked it on my departure earlier that afternoon. He carried me down the hall and into the kitchen, where the log burner was lit, and the lamp on the dresser emitted a low but comforting glow. He set me down on the hearthrug. I stood on my good leg while he removed what was left of my boot and peeled my coat off me. Then he plucked the crocheted blanket from the back of the settee and wrapped it round me.

'Sit down, before you fall down,' he said. He kicked off his own boots before padding across to the kettle and putting it on. 'Have you got any spirits in the house?'

I thought of the provisions Olivia would be bringing back with her, from what I had thought of as *beyond the veil*, but that I now realised was probably only Carlisle. A bottle of Spanish brandy had been on my list.

'No,' I said. I had eased myself sideways down onto the settee and lifted my injured foot up onto the cushions.

'Right.'

Jamie left the kitchen and I heard him mount the stairs. A minute later he was back with a bundle of towels. He threw one at me and began to dry Bob off with the other.

'Mrs Harrop won't thank you for that,' I said sharply.

'Stuff Mrs Harrop. This dog's soaked and chilled to the bone.'

Jamie himself was as wet as possible, the water dripping from his trousers and the welt and sleeves of his jumper. His hair was plastered to his head. But he made no attempt to dry himself off, rubbing Bob down thoroughly instead. The bruising to his eye looked worse than ever. In the low halo of light from the lamp he looked more threatening than any convict or unhinged hobo my imagination had conjured in the hide. He put another couple of logs on the burner and made me a cup of hot, sweet tea before thrusting his feet back into his boots and striding out of the room. I thought he'd gone for good, angry at the trouble I'd caused him and my lack of gratitude—and part of me wondered how we'd managed to make such a poor start to things when we had hardly exchanged half a dozen sentences. I concluded it was *because* we'd had no meaningful conversation that we had failed so signally to connect with one another. I laid the blame squarely on his shoulders for this failure; he had been so uncommunicative. His opinion of me was very apparent—the naive, bumbling town girl, ill-equipped for country life, unable even to predict a rainstorm. My own estimation of him was crystalising with amazing speed—he was an ignorant country bumpkin, rude and resentful.

I looked down at my hands. They had left smears of blood on Mrs Harrop's towel. They were badly grazed and stung like mad.

Five minutes later he was back. He had changed, and wore an oilskin type coat over his dry jeans and sweatshirt. His towelled hair stood up in tufts. He must have removed his footwear at the front door; he wore socks, clean, but holey. He produced a bottle of whisky from an inner pocket of the coat and splashed a generous measure into what was left of my tea.

'For the shock,' he said.

He fumbled in another pocket and brought out a packet of painkillers. 'For the pain,' he added, unnecessarily, popping two from their blisters and handing them over. Then he saw my palms. He gave an irritated tut, marched across to the sink and began to rummage in one of the cupboards for the first aid box.

I swallowed the tablets down and let him bathe my hands with antiseptic. It stung like hell but I was damned if I was going to let him see that. I winced inwardly, and when he had finished I drained my cup. The whisky was fiery, but it was helping. I closed my eyes. He stood and regarded me for a moment, and I wondered what he was waiting for, but then it occurred to me—I opened my eyes and looked at him. 'Thank you,' I said, without much warmth.

He had not removed his oilskin and I presumed he only needed a gesture from me to release him. But he stood on. I looked around the room. I had not left the fire alight, nor the lamp on. Now I thought about it, I didn't remember seeing the car outside.

'You ... put the car away for me?' I asked.

'Yes,' he said. 'I could see the rain coming. I didn't think you'd want it left out.'

Had there been a note of sarcasm in his voice, that *he* had seen the rain coming, implying *what idiot would not?* I couldn't tell. 'No,' I agreed. 'I wouldn't. Thank you *again*.'

'And Walter was here. He's been in the loft. There's a slate shifted. We've put a bucket under it for now, but he'll come back when the rain's passed over and fix it. We put your shopping away for you.'

Their joint endeavour surprised me. I'd got the distinct impression Mrs Harrop disliked Jamie and assumed her husband would feel the same way. 'You helped Walter?'

The whisky was doing its work; I felt the soothing creep of it as it permeated my body. I hadn't eaten since breakfast and the glow of the whisky compensated for the lack of food. I felt less cold, although the wetness from my clothes was soaking into the blanket and I knew I ought to strip off.

'Of course,' said Jamie, as though it was obvious. 'I'd have looked in the loft for you, if you'd asked. I did offer …'

'I didn't remember, until I was in the shop,' I said. 'And, this morning, you weren't very … communicative.'

He looked away. 'No,' he said. 'I had things on my mind.'

I decided to accept this admission as an apology because it was clear it was the closest Jamie was going to come to one. 'Will you have a whisky?' I asked, gesturing to the glasses on the dresser.

'No thanks,' he said. 'I never touch the stuff. Does your ankle hurt?'

'Like the devil,' I admitted. 'It might be broken.'

'Can I look?'

I nodded, and suppressed a smile, thinking again of the scene in *Sense and Sensibility*. How had Willoughby couched it? *May I have permission to ascertain if the bone is broken?*

99

He crouched down and ran his hand over my ankle, pressing gently here and there and watching my face to gauge my reaction. 'Hum,' he said at last. 'Just a sprain, I think. Those painkillers will kick in soon. You should go upstairs, take off your wet things and get into bed. Have you eaten?'

I shook my head. 'But I'm not hungry,' I said. 'If you could feed Bob, before you go, that would be helpful.'

'Sure.' He cast around for Bob's bowl, and I pointed out the bag of kibble.

'He likes it with a drop of warm water,' I murmured. My mouth felt woollen, all of a sudden, and I had the overwhelming urge to fall asleep. Perhaps I did fall asleep. The next thing I remember was being lifted up and carried upstairs, my head lolling against Jamie's shoulder. He sat me on the chair in the bedroom and drew the curtains. I wondered if he would undress me, and the idea made me smile. As hale and manly as he was, there was a shy uncertainty about him that gave me the impression he was not experienced with women.

'You'll have to take it from here yourself,' he said, and closed the door softly behind him. In spite of myself, I felt a little twist of disappointment.

Chapter Thirteen

I don't know what those painkillers were, but they were strong. I slept until nearly noon the next day and although my ankle was swollen and sore, I could bear to stand on it. I showered and got dressed and hobbled downstairs.

Everything in the kitchen was tidy. The damp blanket had been draped over an airer and placed before the range, and was now dry. The towels must have been through the washing machine. These, too, were on the airer, back to pristine whiteness and nearly dry. The sofa cushions, no doubt wet where I had sat on them, had been propped up against the radiator.

I was suddenly deluged with guilt. Jamie had done all this for me, a virtual stranger. He had got himself soaked last night, putting himself to considerable inconvenience and perhaps even in some danger. He must, I realised, have been looking for me; or at least, looking *out* for me, knowing I was out of the house, knowing the storm was coming, adding up those two circumstances and predicting—quite rightly—catastrophe. I found myself standing in front of a mirror, absent-mindedly twitching my hair into better shape, as these thoughts assembled themselves and impacted my conscience.

There was no doubt he was an extremely attractive man. And kind. And he would not be the first thirty-year-old I had … but then I thought of Olivia and dismissed the ridiculous fantasy that had been forming itself.

I glanced down at Bob's basket. It was empty.

I opened the front door. It was as though the previous day's rain had never happened. A speciously innocent blue sky scudded with white clouds. Fallen leaves bounced blamelessly along the track. From somewhere came the rhythmic thud of an axe on wood.

I limped along to Jamie's house and found him splitting logs. The action was smooth, efficient— no doubt the result of many years of practice. Bob lay nearby, gnawing on a stick. He leapt to his feet when he saw me, his whole back-end wriggling in pleasure. I bent down to greet him, my joy at being reunited with him bringing a tear to my eye.

Jamie put his axe down and came forward. 'How are you feeling?' he asked.

'Fine,' I told him. 'A bit sore but, you see …' I held out my hands as though to say *Here I am*. 'Thank you,' I went on, pouring genuine appreciation into the words. I almost reached out to put my hand on his arm, maybe even to take his hand, but stifled the impulse. 'Thank you *so* much for all you did yesterday. The car, and coming to find me, and helping Walter, and … well, just everything. I'd have been in a real mess without your help.'

He shrugged and examined a callus on his palm. 'No bother,' he said, and I thought, with relief, that we had turned a new page. But then he looked me in the eye and said emphatically, 'Only, you know, you must be careful.' He threw his arm out to encompass the marsh, and his gesture implied an even wider purview. While his words conveyed concern, somehow his tone was scolding, and I felt the nascent connection between us begin to shrivel. Then he said something that really took me by surprise. 'It's much more Thomas Hardy round here than Jane Austen. More Brontë than Trollope. I know you understand me.'

'I think so,' I said, stunned. This was an aspect of his character I had not for one moment suspected. How had I labelled him? An ignorant country bumpkin. Well, he was far from that. And I did understand his inference. What he meant was that this territory I had stumbled into, via poor planning and happenstance and some romantic notion of following the story, was not a rural idyll; neither was it an enchanted country. It was hard, cruel, unforgiving. Marjorie had implied much the same thing. I gathered she and Jamie both doubted my ability to hack it. I had doubted it myself, but now I was committed and I was damned if I would give up. I was already bridling at his tacit rebuke, so instead of the honesty that his remark should have prompted in me—a frank admission that I was ill-informed and ill-prepared and out of my depths in every possible way—what surfaced was pride.

I gathered myself up. 'Thank you,' I said again, but coldly.

Jamie breathed out slowly through his nose, a resigned sigh, and closed his eyes. He could see—as could I—that whatever window of connection he had prised open last night, and whatever reciprocating flag of truce I had proffered only moments ago, we had screwed it up *again*.

'I do understand your reference ...'

'But you're surprised to hear me make it,' he snapped, reaching down for his axe.

'Only because, last night, when *I* made a literary reference, you didn't acknowledge it,' I cried. 'It wasn't an unreasonable conclusion to draw, was it?'

'I had other things on my mind last night,' he flung back.

'And yesterday morning, also,' I retorted. 'What a surprisingly cerebral person you are!'

He emitted a harsh bark of laughter. 'We may be off the beaten track,' he sneered. 'But we do have *books*. We can *read*.' He took a swipe at another log. He mustn't have set it up properly. It bounced awkwardly off the anvil he was using and flew out at a tangent, narrowly missing me.

'Steady on!' I shouted. 'There was no need for that.'

'You know it was an accident,' he shouted back.

It was a standoff. We remained, equally adamant, equally angry. Speaking for myself I was also dismayed and sorry things had got so out of hand. A quiet—a very quiet—voice told me I ought to break the impasse. It was my pride, after all, that had reopened the schism. I opened my mouth, but as I did so a series of resounding bangs emanated from inside Jamie's house. It sounded like a succession of explosions, or someone taking a frenzied sledgehammer to a metal tank. Bob jumped up from where he had been sitting and took up a defensive stance.

'Oh shit,' Jamie spat out. He dropped his axe and ran into his house, closing the door behind him with a slam.

I retreated to my cottage, made coffee and toast, collected my novel and went into the lounge. Although the sun had moved over the roof, the room was still warmed by it, and the sofa cushions were dry. I eyed the fire, but the thought of hobbling about to gather the logs and kindling required to light it was too much for me, so I contented myself with dropping down onto the couch, hoisting my legs up and pulling the crocheted blanket over me. I tuned my ears to the house next-door-but-one, but whatever catastrophe had erupted there had ceased for the time being. It was the second time some unexplained occurrence had summoned Jamie unceremoniously indoors and I wondered what nefarious business he had going on in the gloomy confines of his cottage. If he was renovating, which the stacks of stone and the scaffolding poles in his garden suggested he might be, could it destabilise the entire row?

My ankle throbbed, and I wished I could ask for more of Jamie's painkillers. I had some over-the-counter ones somewhere, upstairs probably. I added the annoyance of this to the stack of irritations I was accumulating. I was seething, but also hollow with dismay, my exasperation humming like a swarm of bees around an empty hive. How had things gone so wrong again? Jamie had been quite right to warn me about the marsh. Olivia had done the same and I had not taken *that* personally. His use of literary references must have been designed to resonate with—rather than alienate—me, calculated to make a platform we could build upon, although how he had *known* that I could not tell. He had been in the cottage last night, helping Walter. What could he have seen to give him a clue about me? I looked down at the paperback I had laid over the arm of the chair. From the shelves of Lee Childs, Danielle Steels, Stephanie Meyers and Nicholas Sparks, I had chosen a book by Kazuo Ishiguro. Perhaps that had been enough of a clue? Also, upstairs, I supposed he might have seen my precious collection of Oxford Pocket World Classics, partly unpacked in the little front bedroom. So, he was observant. Or perhaps nosey? How would an investigation of the attic have necessitated intruding beyond the landing? Whichever it was, he had used that nugget of information about me to reach out. And I had thrown it back in his face.

I sipped my coffee which, in my distraction, I had allowed to get almost cold, and ate my toast, peeling off the crusts and feeding them to Bob.

Outside I heard the putter of an engine—not a car, it sounded more like a motorbike. Was *that* how Jamie got about? Whatever it was roared away up the track. Silence descended on the place like an enveloping shroud. Rather than feeling released by Jamie's departure, I felt strangely bereft.

I must have slept. When I opened my eyes, the afternoon beyond the undrawn curtains was fading into a purple gloaming. I did not know what had woken me. Bob lay on the hearth rug but his head was up, cocked to one side, listening. The room was ashy with shadow. Something rumbled beneath us, the oddest sound, like the shudder of something shifting below. My suspicions about Jamie's renovations revived with a vengeance. What *could* he be doing, at his end of the row, that would cause my foundations to tremble? I honed my ears, and even lowered my good foot to the ground, so I could feel any vibrations in the floor that my ears could not catch. The house, the ground beneath it and the air around it all held their breath, and so did I. The stillness was absolute, and yet thick with some presence. I could feel it—a curdled texture, a miasma. I sat, frozen, and waited, but no further sound or quiver came. Then, with a volume and sharpness that had me leaping to my feet and sent a jab of pain up my shin, someone knocked on the door.

Jamie stood on the doorstep, his arms full of parcels and cardboard boxes.

'These were in the box for you,' he said. 'There are more.'

He dumped the packages into the hallway and stumped off down the path to gather the rest, leaving me panting and pale, grappling onto the doorframe for support.

'The box?' I gasped out.

'Yes, at the top of the track, by the gate, there's a box where the post gets left. They don't come down *here*.' His tone suggested I was an idiot not to have known.

'Mrs … Mrs Harrop didn't tell me,' I stammered out. 'I'm … sorry. And thank you.'

He dumped the rest of the boxes down. 'What's in them?' he enquired in a surly manner.

I swallowed down my hysteria, determined not to make myself ridiculous with stories of ghosties and ghoulies and bumps in the night, and repressed also my sense of outrage because, really, what business was it of his what I bought? 'Some proper clothes,' I said, struggling to keep my voice even. 'Boots and so on.' Something made me add, 'I didn't have the right stuff … I didn't know … I hadn't planned …' I struggled for a literary allusion that might help me out. 'At least Lucy had had the forethought to take one of the fur coats from the wardrobe before stepping into Narnia,' I said with a self-deprecating smile.

'Narnia?' he half-shouted, his indignation written large. 'Is that where you think this is?'

'No … of course not,' I faltered.

He shook his head. 'Pity you can't order common sense online,' he said, turning away.

I slammed the door before he reached the gate.

I looked with a sort of despair at the parcels stacked around the hall, all my pleasure in them utterly evaporated, and my suspicions about the noises that had woken me still unresolved. My ankle throbbed atrociously the longer I stayed upright. I limped into the kitchen and found the tin of soup I had bought from Mrs Harrop and heated it on the stove. I ate it at the kitchen table, feeling forlorn and wretched; let Bob out for five minutes; and then took myself with difficulty up the stairs, taking them one at a time, using the banister as a support. I sought painkillers and the oblivion of sleep.

The next morning I limped through my chores, walking Bob only so far as was necessary for his needs before returning to the cottage. The weather was damp and drear, the marsh veiled in misty vapour. I made my coffee and carried it upstairs, opened my laptop and began a new document.

The Trysting Tree
1906 ~ 1924

If Todd Forrester's infancy had been happy, he did not remember it. Like all babies, he had no recollection of his time at his mother's breast, of being cossetted in blankets or sung to sleep at night. That these things had occurred he took for granted because he thrived. His bodily strength was evidence of regular feeding and rest. That his mother had provided them was also a matter of unarguable fact to him. Who else could it have been? In the dimness of his childish recollection there figured no other being in the stone-flagged kitchen, which was the entirety of his domain. No being of significance, anyway.

When he learned to walk his purview widened to include the yard, where hens pecked at the dirt and a fat cat lolled on the water butt in the sunshine. There was a tumbledown barn that housed a teetering stack of straw bales and mice that streaked in blurs across the floor. Swallows nested in the eaves in the summertime, and in the autumn strings of wizened onions dangled from nails hammered into one of the beams. There were two goats. His mother would milk them, her head pressed against their bony flanks, her eyes closed but oozing tears that dripped into the bucket with the thin, blue milk.

From the yard, Todd could see more. Men—distant, indistinct, their gaze averted. They drove cows or pigs along the street, wheeled stacks of lobster pots on trolleys or shouldered billhooks and other savage-looking tools whose use he could not imagine. Across the pitted track that served as a street were the beach and the sea; a heaving, shifting, grey expanse that was terrible to behold. Todd was not permitted further than the gate so the world those men inhabited—where they came from, where they went, what they did with that brutal ironmongery—was closed to him. Beyond the gate, he gathered, the world was not a safe place to be. His mother kept it at bay. Indeed, his mother kept all the world's ills away from him. Dirt, mud, dust and mould could not on any account be tolerated. All day long she swept and mopped, scrubbed and cleaned. She beat the rug and washed the curtains and scalded her hands pounding their laundry, as though pursued by a fiend. At night she scrubbed his hands and face until they burned.

'We must be clean,' she muttered, fervently, as though it was a prayer. 'We *must*, little man, or else—Oh Todd! Todd! What filth is this? We must be clean or ...'

She watched him like the buzzard that wheeled above the farmyard and cast its shadow on the coarse cobbles, blocking out the sun and causing the hens to crouch in fear at its passing. His mother's watchfulness meant that while little in the way of mischief could be achieved, the catastrophic consequences of mischief were also mercifully averted. Todd, like the hens, had an inkling of some impending penalty that could accrue ... but to what, *for* what, he did not know. The threat of it was a shadow that hovered, an unnamed peril that lurked just beyond his understanding.

His mother was generally unhappy; he knew *that*. She cried and sighed a great deal, and wrung her hands, and fretted—but he felt *he* was the alleviation of her misery. Singing to him, telling him stories, watching him eat his food and play his games—these things gave her pleasure. He was her world, the epicentre of it. It was as it should be, as all children believe it to be—tyrants of self-importance as they are—until the truth crashes upon them and breaks the bubble of their egotism.

It was not surprising, then, that gradually it dawned upon Todd's rousing consciousness that her world encompassed more than just him and that this *other* must be a man. The shirts and trousers on the washing line were large, too large for either of them. And then there were three plates of supper—and one of them a large one—even if that overloaded plate was covered and left on the range to keep warm. Todd and his mother ate theirs in the orange light of the setting sun that made a path across the sea and pointed its fiery finger right through the polished kitchen window, illuminating the dustless shelves and the pristine upholstery and the wetly shining gloss on the fresh-mopped floor. His mother's paleness was made rosy in the glow. But then the sun would set and the shadows would rush in from the corners, and his mother's eyes would grow wide and flicker repeatedly towards the door. Then, in a rush, she would light the lamp and hurry Todd up the wooden stairs to his cot.

A deep, gravelly, long-droning voice in the night-time would come to him through his dreams, and the sound of a heavy tread on the stair.

His first positive sight of his father came when Todd was about five years old. He had been ill with some childhood ailment, his mother remaining by his truckle bed throughout the hours of the night, bathing his brow with cool water and feeding dribbles of water between his parched lips. Then one morning he had been better, his head clear, his body released from the shivers and sweats that had gripped him for the past week. He got up from his bed and used the chamber pot that rested beneath it. It was early—the air still blue with darkness—but birds twittered in the ivy outside his window and he was ravenously hungry. He descended the stair in search of his mother and some bread, but found instead a man seated at the kitchen table, a bowl of porridge before him and a pint pot of tea in his hand. The man had straw-coloured hair and bushy eyebrows and a large, unkempt beard. His eyes were the palest blue Todd had ever seen, and of an intensity that pinioned him to the spot.

Todd stopped in his tracks and stared at the apparition.

The man stared back, as still as a statue apart from his eyes, which blinked, slowly, hawk-like, in patient rhythm. Then he said, 'Hungry, are you?'

Todd opened his mouth to reply but his voice would not come. He swallowed and got out a hoarse, 'Where's Mam?'

The man flicked his eyes upwards, indicating the room above, where Todd's mother slept, and then repeated his query. 'Are you hungry?'

Todd nodded.

The man rose from the table and fetched a second bowl and mug from the shelf. He divided his breakfast equally amongst the receptacles and then took up his spoon. 'Come on then, boy,' he said.

Todd approached the table, climbed onto his chair and picked up his spoon, only to have it abruptly knocked from his hand.

'You'll thank the Lord God, I hope, before you begin.' The man's eyes were shards of ice, his whole expression suddenly fierce, although, only just before, he had seemed benevolent enough.

Todd swallowed—painfully, his throat was still sore—and felt tears well. He sat, mute, and looked at the man.

'Do as I do,' said the stranger. He folded his hands and closed his eyes. Todd did as he was told.

The man—his father—was a source of mixed blessing to Todd from that time. His father hoisted him onto the old horse and took him into the fields. This was exhilarating, but once in the field the boy was expected to work, to glean grain from the field margins, to place stones in heaps ready to repair the walls, to spread dung along the furrows. He was not permitted to play, or just to watch; and once in the field he could not return home until the day was ended although it was but a short walk to the farmhouse. Under his father's supervision Todd was permitted beyond the gate, to see the ship-breakers at work and the women gutting herrings on the shore. His mother was left behind, her face a rictus smile, the echoes of her admonitions—to be careful, to stay close, to be good and mind his father—following them down the rough street. Todd held his father's gnarly hand and listened to the staccato conversations he had with other men, understanding little but amazed at the breadth of the newly opened world beyond the farmyard.

Another world also opened at his father's advent, but this was not one that Todd liked. This was a world of judgement and sin, a world of brimstone and everlasting torture. It required an hour's walk to chapel every Sunday, across the Moss—a large expanse of wetland and peat-cuttings behind Winter Hill— and along the dunes, an hour of trudging no matter what the weather. Two hours of haranguing by the preacher, followed by an hour of fervent prayer left Todd famished, his innocent spirit assaulted and fluttering like a trapped bird to escape his body. His trembling legs were hardly able to carry him back home. Now, at night, Todd was required to stay downstairs until the nightly long-droning was done. His father read from the Bible, his voice flat and halting as he stumbled inexpertly through the words. Should the child's eyelids flutter and fall, even for a moment, the devotions would be extended by a further half an hour.

School gave Todd some respite from this regime, although he was still expected to complete his chores before and after lessons and to endure the evening observances. Rest from the drudgery of the farm came at a cost, however. At school, Todd discovered his family was looked down upon. Their farm, he was told, was the poorest and worst managed. His father, Caleb, had a reputation for being "odd." He was "an incomer," treated with suspicion just on that basis regardless of his other eccentricities, the chief of these being that he never touched alcoholic drink. He was a "methody," although the boys who affixed this label could not explain to Todd what it meant. So much was Todd prepared to accept, but when a child described his mother as "a slattern" he drew the line, bloodying the nose of the boy who said so. The furore that ensued ended with Todd being taken into the barn and beaten by his father. The impersonal way in which the punishment was administered hurt more than the blows. It seemed to Todd his father was a man without feeling himself but inhabited by a rabid spirit that would from time-to-time lash out using his unresisting frame. There was no knowing when this fury would manifest itself. It was a conundrum Todd felt unable to fathom and he did not put much effort into trying. He was careful to keep himself at arm's length from his father's unpredictable ways. If it had only been a question of himself, that might have been all right. But the child could not escape the reluctant awareness that his father was the bird of prey under whose shadow his mother cowered—and she could not escape it, as he could. As he *would,* one day.

Escape came, however, in 1916, when Todd's father was conscripted into the Yeomanry. He made a final appearance in a scratchy brown uniform and then disappeared. Todd, then aged ten, prepared himself to take upon his shoulders more of the work around the farm. As perplexing a figure as his father had been, he had been a hard-working one, yielding from the boggy acres just about sufficient crops to sustain the family. Now this would fall to Todd, and to his mother, and to such itinerant labour as could be found—and paid—from those unfit for military service. School must be attended for another two years and Todd did not think his mother sufficiently able to do more than her usual, light tasks with the hens and goats and in the house. He viewed the future with trepidation and wondered why, since *he* could see the problem so clearly, his father had not been able to do so. Other farmers were exempt from conscription. Why was Todd's father different? On the other hand, for reasons Todd chose not to articulate, the idea of the farm being restored to the halcyon days of his childhood, of his life reverting to just him and his mother, was appealing. He was determined to cope, somehow.

In the summer of 1916, Sir Hector Winter brought his family to their rather rusticated manor, the pele tower on the outskirts of the village. Winter Hall was not by any means his favourite house, but it was, now, the only roof left to him. His London house had been destroyed by German bombs and his country residence in Buckinghamshire had lately been sold in order to offset sundry debts. In truth, Sir Hector came to the north a disappointed and disgruntled man. He was the last of a line of Winters unbroken since 1624, and likely to remain so since the death of his wife—without male issue—two years before. He had a daughter, to be sure, but a daughter, however dear, could not be a baronet. Winter property and Winter blood seemed doomed and Winter wealth was also compromised to an extent that Sir Hector had been forced to retrench. He brought only a very small retinue to Winter Hall: himself and his daughter, her governess and only so many servants as could be accommodated in the lofty, draughty quarters of the ancient tower.

Sir Hector was a hale and healthy man in his middle thirties, and ought to have found usefulness in the military, but he had been injured in the Boer War to a degree that active service in the current conflict was impossible. *Inactive* service was insupportable to him. Not for him the lounging around in the corridors of power, the loafing in clubs, the trumpery of uniform and braid unstained by mud or blood. Sir Hector came north, therefore, to take up residence in the place that had been his forebears' stronghold since 1624—back to where it had all begun.

He found the tower's accommodations to be penal; nothing his servants could do seemed enough to heat the place sufficiently, or to banish the draughts and strange moanings that came off the sea and down the chimney. The countryside around about was drear, devoid alike of game and suitable society; to his chagrin, every other member of the local gentry was involved in the war effort to greater or lesser effectiveness, swinging the lead in Whitehall or mismanaging troops in France. He was bored and lonely, frustrated and depressed. He had neglected his northern property in recent years, leaving an agent to collect rents, to arbitrate in disputes and to ensure that the infrastructure was kept in good repair. Looking around the cottages and tenant farms, the water mill and the public house—all of which were owned by him—and the church, whose living was within his gift, and the schoolhouse for whose upkeep he had paid, he was dismayed at what he found. The agent had certainly been neglecting his duties. The vicar seemed rarely to visit the parish and almost never to hold services in the church. The schoolmaster was a dissipated man with little interest in the education of his pupils. Upkeep of the buildings was poor, repairs left undone. The accounts of the miller were suspect, the beer in the alehouse watered down. Sir Hector rolled up his sleeves and got to work.

He found the yeomanry to be surly and uncooperative, little inclined to make the repairs he suggested or to adopt new farming methods he assured them would yield excellent results. They resisted mechanisation, for example, even when Sir Hector offered to buy—from his own pocket—a tractor and a threshing machine that would save them hours of back-breaking labour. The miller's account books found themselves to be inexplicably fallen in the mill pond. The vicar took ill and was sent on doctor's orders to a sanatorium in Buxton. The beer at the alehouse was as weak as ever. Sir Hector despaired. He was sure it would only take one of his tenants to trust him, to follow his advice, to allow him to intervene benignly on his farm, for all the rest to drop their guard and follow suit. They could only benefit from his paternal interference, although naturally, in time, he too would reap the rewards, as better run, more profitable farms would be able to afford higher rents.

In due course the squire's activities brought him to the gate of Low Farm, the smallest and most barren of his tenancies—the Forresters' farm. It was July, and the area was enjoying a period of warm weather. School had closed for the summer and so it was Todd—who was the same age as the squire's daughter—who opened the gate and took the reins of his horse while Sir Hector inspected the barn and henhouses. The boy ran off to find his mother, his father being "away at the war." The woman who came out of the farmhouse was harried and careworn, her hair—blonde and strikingly abundant, if rather dirty—tied back in a kerchief, her eyes as blue as periwinkles, her face—beneath the sweat of washday—of the particular prettiness that appealed to Sir Hector's taste. Here, he thought, was the ideal beneficiary of his advice and governance. A lone woman, hardly able—by the look of her—to manage singlehandedly. The land looked unpromising but *she*—Sir Hector eyed her narrowly—was the type who would hearten the most down-spirited of men.

'Your husband is away, the boy says,' said Sir Hector in a kind and sympathetic voice.

The woman nodded. 'That's right, sir.'

'And how are you managing? Will you be able to get your harvest in?'

The squire looked past the sorry little farmhouse to the flat field beyond. The spring wheat was well up, but choked with weeds,

'We will do our best, sir,' said the woman.

'Your neighbours will assist, I am sure,' said Sir Hector with more confidence than he felt.

'I don't know, sir,' came the reply. 'They have their own farms to tend.' Her hands toyed restlessly with each other. Sir Hector noted that, though chapped and red, they were small and delicate.

'Have you any complaint to make about the house? The roof is sound, I take it?'

Mrs Forrester raised her eyes to the squire and stuck out her chin. 'Complaint? Oh no, sir. The roof is sound enough. We're good tenants, sir, and no one else wanted this farm. It had lain empty for five years before my husband and I took it. The land is poor enough. Not that we complain, sir. Only it gets so waterlogged in the winter. Winter wheat does no good, nor potatoes. They rot in the ground. But we pay on time, and the bailiff has no complaint to make. Oh, please, sir ...' Her chin began to wobble, and then she burst into tears.

Todd, behind her, took hold of a fold of her skirt and wrapped his hand in it, but whether to receive or to lend comfort, it was hard to tell.

'My dear madam,' the squire cut in. 'You mistake my intentions entirely. I am here to assist you, if I can, not to turn you out.' He took a step towards the poor, exercised woman and made so free as to place one hand under her chin. With the other he brought forth a large, clean handkerchief which he pressed upon her. 'Do not disquiet yourself to any degree,' he said softly. 'Let us go inside, and I will look the place over, and we will be comfortable.'

Sir Hector did not wait for permission but ducked his head to enter the kitchen. The woman followed, amazed but still hesitant. The boy disappeared. The squire took his time, peering up the chimney and pressing his hand to the walls in search of damp, allowing his tenant to compose herself. He mounted the stairs and looked up into the roof. She followed, blushing and flustered, to remove her nightdress from the pillow and stuff it out of sight. Sir Hector pretended to be oblivious to her discomfort, humming and haa-ing and occasionally stroking his abundant sideburns.

Eventually he said, 'There now. Everything seems to be in order. Have you your rent book to hand? And let us have some tea, ma'am. I'm in sore need. I am sure you are, too.'

Mrs Forrester found the rent book and flapped around the kitchen making tea for the squire, doling out tealeaves she could ill-afford and dusting off her best cup and saucer from where she normally kept it on a high shelf. At last she placed the cup before the master and withdrew to a far corner of the room, as though she were a servant and not the hostess. Sir Hector, however, urged her to join him at the table, which she did with extreme reluctance. He perused the rent book with minute interest, or at least appeared to do so, whilst casting covert glances at the lovely profile of Mrs Forrester. Of her own tea Mrs Forrester drank not a drop.

When he had finished his tea, he got to his feet and handed back the book.

'This is quite satisfactory,' he said. 'But I can see that you are going to struggle with running this farm on your own.'

'Oh no,' Mrs Forrester interposed. 'I can manage very well, and the boy …'

'The boy looks to be a capable fellow indeed. Do not be afraid, ma'am, you have nothing to fear. Your tenancy of Low Farm is quite safe. I shall encourage your neighbours to lend you their assistance, and I myself will do what I can for you. I have a limp, you will have observed,' he struck his game leg with his riding crop, 'but I have a strong back and, to tell the truth, I long to be of some use. You will be doing me a great service if you will permit me to assist you. Now then, what else? Ah! I see you have a flock of hens. I shall require eggs to be delivered to Winter Hall every week, about two dozen. Can you manage that? And I saw, in your barn, that you have a store of apples from last year. I'll buy those from you also, a dozen or so to be delivered with the eggs, more if my cook requires them. Now then,' he paused to stroke his moustache which, to be fair, was rather fine, and to give Mrs Forrester a franker appraisal, head to toe, than he had yet allowed himself. 'What else can you offer me?'

Mrs Forrester paled and then blushed and looked anywhere but at the squire's face. At last, she mumbled, 'I am a fair needlewoman, sir. I can mend shirts and so on.'

'Capital!' said the squire. 'Two afternoons a week, I shall expect to see you at the Hall. My little girl goes through petticoats and stockings at a truly prodigious rate. She is about the age of your boy. How would he like to take charge of her while you do your mending? I am sure he knows the country hereabouts and that she would not come to harm in his care. What do you say?'

What *could* she say?

The next two years passed pleasantly for Todd and his mother. The squire was as good as his word, sending aid when aid was needed, and frequently appearing himself, in shirtsleeves, to hoe and scythe and walk behind the horse guiding the plough. Decent crops were coaxed from the soil and the squire found a buyer for the willow that grew in such abundance in the wet rills of the farm, for the making of baskets, mats and chairs. The extra money provided little comforts about the house, and food was never wanting in the pantry.

What Sir Hector lacked in practical application he made up for in effort and gallantry. He was unrelentingly civil, overlooking the poorness of the fayre Mrs Forrester provided for their midday repast and the faded and much-mended state of her attire, and attributing to her—a poor and practically illiterate farmer's wife—all the delicacy of feeling and womanly sensibilities of any titled lady of his acquaintance. His chivalry confused her at first—she thought he was patronising and teasing her—but in time she came to accept him at face value, believing he genuinely wished to make himself useful amongst his tenants. She bloomed. Perhaps it was because the long shadow of her husband had passed away from her; or perhaps the notice of the squire encouraged her. Perhaps she simply emulated the other women of the village, who slowly put aside their enmity and prejudice against her and took her into their circle. She stopped attending chapel and went instead to the parish church, where Sir Hector had appointed a diligent and kind-hearted curate to minister to the Roadend flock. She was seen to smile, and even sometimes to laugh. She gained weight and countenance. Her hair, in those days, was never dirty; and her frocks, though old, were less puritanical, gradually augmented by lace trimmings and the occasional ribbon.

Todd was happy to see it. He was, in those days, generally happy about everything. He was a strong boy by this time, and no one at school would dare to say bad things about his family. The curate, whose duties included assisting the dilatory schoolmaster, praised Todd's progress in the three Rs and encouraged him to even greater academic endeavour. His world was now by no means restricted to the farmyard. Once his work was done, he was at liberty to roam all over the village—down to the beach where the herring women teased him and ruffled his white-blond hair with their fish-gut fingers and along to the breakers' yard where the skeletons of ships were hauled up like leviathans to be prised apart. He roamed the Moss and found birds' nests and frogspawn and climbed a silver birch tree that had grown to prodigious size within a little copse of willow and elder. He ventured further, along the windswept dunes and up towards where the estuary narrowed. He liked his own company, the freedom to do as he wished. He relished the conviction that he was his own master.

One aspect of his life caused him dissatisfaction, and that was the arrangement his mother had made—that twice a week after school he would take the squire's daughter beneath his wing.

It was not that Miss Winter was a demur little girl only interested in her dolls and her books. Although tedious, *that,* he felt, he could have endured. But no. She was, on the contrary, a feisty child who was restless for adventure, fearless in the face of danger and decidedly adamant that anything he—a boy, and a stupid one at that—could do, *she* could do better. If they climbed trees, she would climb a limb higher. If they leaped over the peat cuttings on the Moss, she would leap further than him. If they dared the tide, she would wait a minute longer before running before the encroaching stampede of water, often soaking her skirts and once having to wade up to her armpits. He had felt sure she would drown. She talked *incessantly*— a tirade of speculation, observation and gossip picked up from the servants filled Todd's ears with nonsense until he thought his head would burst. It was hopeless trying to creep up on the badger set or the fox den to see the cubs at play. The little girl's high-pitched voice and endless repertoire of chatter would be heard by them from a mile away. Having her in tow limited Todd's sphere of activity. He could not play with the other boys in the village when she was in his charge. He could not be certain one of them would not overstep the line; although, in a fight, he would tend to back Miss Winter—she really was quite fearless—he knew the squire would look dimly on such an outcome and his patronage of Mrs Forrester could be at risk. He could not take Miss Winter to the herring women; their language was too coarse. The ship breakers' yard was too dangerous. True, she liked animals, and would spend hours fondling puppies if he knew where there were any, or playing with kittens, so long as he was sure not to tell her they would almost certainly be drowned before many days were done. These occupations were tiresome to Todd but it was not even that, which most irked him. It was the sense that his companion was in some way laughing at him; that—though only a girl—she was superior to him and she felt it. She spoke of London and Brighton, of the circus and the zoo as though they were ordinary, as though *everyone* could and should have been there. She could read and write better than him, and was derisive when she discovered he had not read this book or that one. His knowledge of nature was piecemeal, culled from observance. Hers was authoritative, from the books in her father's library. She had a teasing, provoking manner, and a smile was never far from her lips, and Todd felt *he* was the cause of her humour, without knowing why. She made him feel generally at a disadvantage, a step behind, and he did not like it.

~

The war ended and Todd's father returned, and all the light and pleasantness disappeared from life at Low Farm.

It being November, the squire had left the pele tower and returned to London. Miss Winter had returned to her boarding school and, with a reduced household and the end of hostilities, Sir Hector felt, if he was careful with money, life in the metropolis could be sustained.

His patronage of the Forresters' farm ended. His departure left a vacuum that his agent had no instructions to fill. And also, the return of Mrs Forrester's husband made it injudicious. Caleb Forrester was resentful of the squire's meddling and would certainly have vetoed any further involvement on the part of Sir Hector had it been offered. In truth, Caleb was resentful of everything that had transpired while he had been occupied in France: the improved productivity of the farm; his wife's restored bloom; his son's growth almost to manhood; the giving up of chapel-going. The very fact that his wife and son had survived—not to say thrived—seemed to irk him, and he was quick to re-establish his adamantine control. The hour-long trudge to chapel was reinstated with immediate effect and the long-droning insisted upon with renewed urgency. The willows that had been planted along the periphery of the fields were pulled out despite the fact that they had brought in valuable additional revenue *and* helped to keep the land from being waterlogged. Ellen Forrester's new circle of acquaintance amongst the village women was broken up and the family was again viewed with suspicion and dislike by their neighbours. Ellen's comely features and thickened waistline were both soon reduced to their former thinness.

Forrester had not been physically injured in the war but that he had been psychologically damaged was beyond question. He was thin to the point of emaciation, those preternaturally pale eyes sunken into deep hollows. He had no tolerance for either heat or cold, would shiver uncontrollably before a roaring fire, but then throw off the blankets that had been draped over him and insist on having all the windows wide even when snow lay on the ground; no one else's comfort gave him any concern. He demanded food and then threw his plate on the floor. He slept ill, often shouting out in his dreams, and he frequently soaked the bed in sweat and urine. He sat in the best chair and barked out his orders. His wife scurried about, trying to please him. Todd followed his instructions, but with as defiant an air as he could muster.

It seemed to Todd that the war had in some way expanded and exaggerated the arc of his father's moods. The former neutrality of attitude, the detachment that had so confused Todd in earlier days, now seemed to be simply a vessel that contained a legion of devils, any of which could rise up at any time. Where previously he had been taciturn, now he was morose. The sudden flares of righteous anger that had assailed him before were now white-hot incendiaries, and not always righteous ones. Pious fire had given way to explosions of profanity that made Todd blush and his mother weep with distress. Caleb's temper was such it would throw him to the floor in its excess, rendering him heedless to the pain he might inflict upon himself from broken glass crushed under foot or burning brands snatched up in his hands. Whereas the old Caleb Forrester had prided himself on his abstinence, the new one indulged himself with liquor to disgusting extravagance. It was not infrequent that the long-dronings were slurred and interrupted by sudden slumber. Hangovers were common, but not on Sunday mornings. At chapel, Forrester presented himself as boldly as any pharisee, and added his amens with an audacity that defied challenge.

In one other regard was the returned Caleb not the one who had gone away. Now, he was work-shy, and it fell to Todd and his mother to do all the work on the farm. The squire having left the area, the assistance that had been forthcoming for his sake was now not to be had. All farmers were struggling with the shortage of labour created by the death and incapacitation of their workforce, and no one had time to spare for the mistress of Low Farm. Todd was thirteen by this time, and had completed his education. He was a strong boy, and very capable, but he was only a boy still and the physical rigours of farm work were often more than he could manage. If the squire had made good on his promise to provide a tractor, all might have been well, but the single—now rather elderly—horse was all the propulsion available for ploughing, hauling stones, dredging ditches, fetching and carrying. The rest was down to Todd's own strength, which was simply insufficient.

He got up before dawn to see to the livestock—a dairy cow, now, as well as the goats, the hens and a pig, plus the horse who would be expected to labour all day. After breakfast he would go out to the field to weed, to plough, to harvest, to mend walls and shore up the dike that, after rain— and without the thirsty willows—was forever threatening to swamp their acres entirely. He did whatever the season demanded. It was backbreaking work, and although his mother helped all she could, the querulous cries of her husband would often require her to return to the farmhouse. Rarely indeed could his father be persuaded from the house and urged to—literally—put his shoulder to the wheel, and so often was he inebriated that his aid, in any case, was hardly worth the effort. He would stumble in the furrows, fall into the stream, injure himself on the tools. He was as likely to pull out the wheat as the weeds, and so only when in sore need did Todd call upon Caleb at all. Todd worked alone in pouring rain, ankle-deep in mud, in bitter cold, his hands blue and his eyelashes iced. He laboured in wind and baking sun, in drizzle and drought, returning home after night had fallen to eat whatever food his mother had prepared for him—and saved from being dashed to the floor by his father—and then to fall into bed in his room beneath the eaves. But Forrester's night terrors and the sound of his mother being harangued, beaten and occasionally raped were unendurable to Todd. He intervened on her behalf and was soon banished to the barn. He made a cot for himself in the least draughty and leaky corner and slept there, with the animals, for five years.

123

The years passed and Ellen Forrester's beauty diminished to nothing; the little summertime of happiness and blossom she had enjoyed under the squire's benevolent interest seemed like a dream. Her hair lost its lustre, her skin its bloom. Her husband's ministrations cost her two teeth. They cost her also the baby he had foisted upon her, a brother or sister for Todd. Harsh weather and harsher treatment, cold, deprivation and misery made her old and she was in her grave before she had reached her forty-fifth birthday. Todd also suffered. Often was he hungry, always was he tired. Before her demise he would take upon himself the brunt of his father's temper in order to save his mother; he was rarely seen without bruises on his face or arms. After her death it was a different matter, and the two would fight—Forrester's drunkenness making him an equal match for Todd's youth. Then both of them wore the scars of their battles.

Todd stopped growing, reaching, at seventeen years of age, all the inches he would ever achieve. The Forresters were genetically a tall tribe, and his sons would inherit that characteristic, but Todd himself was ever to be a small man.

Todd himself sunk physically under the weight of his burdens; yet, within himself, he grew. What grew inside him was a towering, incandescent anger. Against his father, principally, and against the general unfairness of his lot. He absolutely determined his helplessness would be temporary, his inability to control or change his circumstances was a purely interim situation that time would change exponentially. For now, he lived in the thrall of his father, but the time would come when he—Todd himself—would rise. Then, the Forresters would not be a family to be sneered at and derided. Then, they would not be relegated to the poorest patch of land. Then, they would not live hand-to-mouth, scraping food from the barren earth with their bare hands.

The fiery ore of Todd's determination hardened into a steely core that sometimes he felt would split open his skull and tear his ribs from his spine. It sustained him through all the unhappiness of his early years and it sweetened his dreams—the foretaste of power, the enticing vision of what his life would become. It hardened him, and returned him to that state of selfishness he had known as a baby. *He* would be the centre of his world. He, and only he, would matter, and anybody else—any wife, any child, any lover—would only be as a satellite, revolving around him, serving his will and his ambition.

In 1924 Mr Forrester at last succumbed to the reaper, and Todd was alone in the world.

Chapter Fourteen

The days after my fall in the storm passed uneventfully, apart from on the page, where Todd's history spilled from my fingertips. From his tombstone I knew Todd had died in 1993, aged eighty-six, so he must have been born in 1906. This had given me a timeframe for the family saga that I envisioned; it would span about a century from that date, a pleasing scope of history. In my imagination, Todd was bitter, resentful and calculating. Mrs Harrop's extreme antipathy towards him had coloured her picture and it was no surprise therefore that it had infected mine. That Todd must have had a cold and manipulative streak I distilled from the fact of him dividing his farm, Lear-like, between his sons. This, Mrs Harrop—and Olivia also—implied, had fatally stoked the already acrimonious relationship between them. But a character's traits—like a real person's—can never emerge from a vacuum. It is the fiction writer's job to create a facsimile of reality in her work, a representation that, while false in fact, *feels* true, and adheres to the laws of real life. So, I had invented a father for Todd who came back from the first world war changed: wounded, troubled and sporadically violent. Many men, I conjectured, must have gone off to war as one person and come back another. Not all would have been brutalised by their experiences in Flanders. Some would have been broken, traumatised. Some—the already arrogant and unfeeling—might have come back as humbler, kinder, better men. But the beauty of being a writer is you can determine the history of your characters and its impact upon them, and I cast this shadow over Todd in order to shape the man he would later become.

I didn't see Jamie. Although he continued to bring the remainder of my purchases down from the box he didn't knock on the door, he simply left them on the step for me to fall over. He also found and returned my phone. He had removed the battery and sim card and put the whole collection into a Tupperware box filled with rice. I left it in the box for a day or two to dry out and then reassembled the parts, but the phone was dead. I considered resurrecting my old phone, the one I had switched off at Warwick services, but decided against it. I had my new iPad, so I could log into my account to retrieve my contacts and use other messaging apps to get in touch with them if I needed to. Of course, on my new phone, these had numbered only one—Olivia. I texted her with my news and she was comfortingly sympathetic to my plight, although obviously thrilled by Jamie's part in my rescue.

I unpacked my purchases and found places for them in the cottage, folding away my old life and storing it in the divan drawers beneath the spare room beds. I saw no more lights across the marsh, heard no more strange bumps in the night, dismissed the camping gear in the hide as just the belongings of a twitcher or a hiker passing through.

Ivaan's reply to my email was predictably angry and wounded, alternating high dudgeon with abject remorse and pitiful wheedling. I did not reply. Moving his tirade to the waste basket and marking his email address as "junk" felt like the symbolic sprinkling of earth on the grave of the past.

The weather was dry, cool, the sky veiled by high cloud. I walked Bob short distances, avoiding both the marsh and the headland. I chastised myself—why should I not walk across the marsh, or along the boardwalk, or up the track to the ruined pele tower if I wished?—but these destinations held an ambivalence in my mind. I had made a fool of myself and until my ankle was healed and my confidence restored, I did not feel able to venture there again. But more, the version of the area that I was pouring onto my page, day after day, was a shimmering mirage I wanted to hold before me. To see the pele tower in its broken-down state would break the spell of it I was weaving in my story: austere, uncomfortable, but whole and habitable. Low Farm *today,* with its modern buildings and unimaginative farmhouse, would hardly feed *my* version: tumbledown, primitive, stark.

Instead, I explored the path that led beyond the cottage, through the five-barred gate and the willow wood. The path was what I thought of as a bridleway—wide enough for a horse but not for a car. In contrast to the marsh, it was dappled and benign, a meandering path through trees that skirted the hill and would, I presumed, have come out on the beach beyond the headland if I could have walked that far. My new footwear was perfectly suited to the terrain, although one boot was from necessity only laced up halfway. In my new layers I felt warm for almost the first time in days. Bob seemed content to snuffle around in the undergrowth, the intense interest of the scents he found there making up for the lack of distance we covered. By Thursday the swelling on my ankle had gone down altogether, although the skin was bluish green in hue, and I found I could manage without painkillers, which was a good thing since I had almost run out. I ate the food I had bought at Mrs Harrop's, eking it out until my delivery via Olivia should arrive. And I worked.

As always, when I begin a new story, my head was filled with it, the characters crowding for my attention. I found my mind barely on the radio or television as I pursued the various story avenues that were opening up to my imagination like enticing paths between trees.

The family at the pele tower had insisted on being included in the Forresters' narrative although I had no way of knowing if their story arcs had ever coincided. In a way, it did not matter. My tale was flowing of its own volition and it would become its own truth. But I was pleased with the idea of a slightly lascivious squire impinging on the Forresters' lives, even if only briefly though my instinct was that the impact of the Winters on the Forresters would be far, far more.

Since Dad died and I have been able to write more or less fulltime, I have always treated it as a job, being at my desk by a set time every day and writing for a proper number of hours with infrequent breaks for refreshment and exercise. In fact, it is not unusual to find many hours have passed since I took my seat. I will look up to find the day has ended, the tea at my elbow is cold, but two thousand or so excellent words are on the page. I found I settled easily back into this routine—rising early and walking Bob, taking my coffee upstairs and not looking up until a polite grumble from him indicated it was time to stop.

The peculiar strains of sound that came to me from time to time from along the row intrigued and confused me. What *was* Jamie up to? No explanation I could conjure could account for the weird creakings that emanated to me through the wall that separated my house from the rest. The house was supposed to be unoccupied, but the low grumblings continued even when I knew Jamie to be absent. Unfortunately, our relations were such that it was impossible for me to enquire. In the end, they ceased to disturb me. They became one, in my mind, with the whistle of wind down the chimney, the rattle of slates overhead and the patter of rain on the windows. They were *not* the same. They were—in some mysterious way I could not define—sentient, human: the echoes of sighs, the rumble of some historical discontent. I wove them into the weft of my story and it adopted a mournful, plangent tone. At times I almost felt sorry for poor Todd.

By the end of that first week in November the evenings were drawing in, to the extent that if I left it until later than four to set out on our evening constitutional, I would find myself returning in the dark. But the path though the willows was safe, without the trip hazards and sheer-sided waterways of the marsh. I felt more secure—less exposed—within the shelter of the trees than I had done on the wide swathe of the wetland. The phantoms of my fevered imagination—rabid tramps, escaped lunatics, marsh sprites and the like—were kept at bay with the beam of my small but powerful torch, which I kept firmly in my hand. I did not worry too much about the dark. The moon rose early in the clear, pearly sky, even before the sun threw out its fiery finale as it sank behind the hill. I enjoyed hearing the birds as they returned to their roosts, the sigh and settle of the remaining leaves. I found that the prospect of the cottage with its warm, welcoming lights and the fire laid ready in the burner evoked feelings of comfort and contentment. My writing left me satisfied, emotionally fulfilled.

I did not feel lonely. The thoughts and feelings of my characters and their underlying psychological constitutions played in my mind as I walked, and also in the evenings as I sat and stared into the flames. Of course they were imaginary, but real to me, and less problematic than my real neighbour. On the whole I found my inclination was to avoid Jamie. There was nothing phantasmagorical about *him*. He was real, warm, flesh-and-blood; I had felt his strength when he lifted me. And he was not malevolent; indeed, he had shown me multiple evidences of his kindness. But there was, between us, some prickly antipathy I could not fathom but could not deny. I was not proud of my own behaviour towards him, but neither could I account for the peculiarly scratchy nature of his demeanour. We seemed to repel each other, like matching poles of a magnet. Our every encounter had left me feeling unnerved. I found myself listening for the putter of his motorbike coming and going and timing my own perambulations accordingly. I knew it was silly. Just because we were clearly not going to be friends did not mean we could not be perfectly affable neighbours. As much as I avoided him, I also wondered about summoning my courage and trying to make amends. I considered going round with a bottle of wine but did not know whether his dislike of spirits extended to all alcohol. It was a conundrum I felt unable to solve and decided that, on the whole, it would be better to let the dust settle before making any attempt to build bridges.

So it was that my return through the dusk to the cottages, Bob at my heels, was always a slightly cautious procedure. I would douse my torch and cover the last few yards to the five-barred gate stealthily, peering over it and down the track to see if there was either light or movement from the far end of the row before pulling the screeching spring-bolt that held the gate closed and scurrying the last few steps home. It was ridiculous. I knew it and, on one Thursday evening, I found that he shared my view. As I closed the door I heard, quite distinctly, the sound of hollow, derogatory laughter coming from the gloom of his garden.

Chapter Fifteen

On Friday I steeled myself to avoid my laptop, ignoring the importunate cries of the Forresters to be released from their state of narrative petrification, and attended instead to domestic chores like changing the bed and running the hoover around. It took me a while to find the hoover. The door to the cupboard at the bottom of the stairs—surely, its obvious location—was stubbornly locked and no key I had been provided would open it. Eventually I located a sorry looking antediluvian cylinder machine along with a mop and bucket and various other pieces of cleaning equipment in the shed in the back yard. I spent the morning quite happily clearing the grates and bringing in fresh supplies of logs and kindling. The vacuum did a reasonable job of eradicating the tumbleweeds of Bob's hair that gathered in the corners and beneath the sofa and table, but my feeling was it emitted as much dust from one end as it ingested from the other and I made a mental note to ask Mrs Harrop about an alternative. Walter had not returned to deal with the roof despite the fact that the weather had been dry all week, and this was another matter I needed to broach with my landlady.

I made a sandwich with the last of my bread and cheese and took it outside to eat, perched on the garden wall, determined to rise above my neighbour's derision. The day was gloriously bright and sunny, the trees on fire with gold, amber and ochre, the marsh a splendid textured carpet of russet, olive, honey and umber. No breath of wind disturbed the foliage. Overhead, geese chevroned across the pale blue sky. I had made no precise plans with Marjorie and Olivia. I knew they were returning from their diocesan confab that day bringing—I ardently hoped—my black-market supplies with them. I felt sure the village bonfire would go ahead—the weather was perfect—and their invitation to attend would still stand. I was looking forward to it. My quiet, uneventful week had banished my qualms, my sense of being alien. Time had given perspective to the strange vibrations that had woken me in the sitting room. I was ready to admit they had been a product of shock, pain and a fevered imagination. You might argue I had simply swapped one make-believe for another, and that living—as I had done—in the company of fabricated characters in a fantasy world did not count as authentic living. Whatever. I relished the prospect of an evening in company with flesh-and-blood companions, of meeting more of the *real* villagers, of broadening my sphere beyond the isolated and claustrophobic confines of the cottage and the marsh.

I had gone inside to hang my washed bedding over the maiden and put in a fresh load when the noise of a vehicle pulling up brought me running to the front door. Marjorie drove an ancient Land Rover, blue and battered, that emitted clouds of acrid-smelling smoke and sounded like a bag of nuts and bolts being put through a food processor. She climbed out of it with no sign of concern, however, and began to unload my bags of groceries. Olivia and Patty scrambled out of the back door and an angular young man I didn't know stepped from the passenger seat.

'Hello! Hello!' Marjorie cried, hefting my provisions over the garden wall. 'How are you my dear? All settled? How's that foot of yours? Oh! Watch that one. Bottles, I think. Hello Bob. Hello, hello, hello.' She stooped and fussed Bob. Patty barked and described wide circles round the car and its three occupants. Olivia smiled broadly and tried not to look too obviously at Jamie's house.

I waved a greeting to the newcomer. 'Hi,' I said, 'I'm Dee. Pleased to meet you.'

The man was in his mid-twenties, of middling height, with prematurely thinning, wispy blond hair. He was painfully thin, his face almost cadaverous, with prominent cheek bones over sunken cheeks. Ice-blue eyes swam in hollow sockets. He stood back as the women bustled up to greet me, just nodding in response to my wave.

Gently, Olivia took his arm and guided him forward. 'This is Patrick,' she said, coming to stand beside him. 'He's exploring his vocation. He's come to do work experience with Mummy. Patrick, this is my friend Dee.'

Patrick mumbled, 'Pleased to meet you,' before busying himself with the shopping bags.

Marjorie said, 'I don't suppose there's any chance of a cup of tea, is there?'

'Of course,' I almost cried out with relief, ushering them all inside. 'But you'll have to excuse the laundry.'

'Patrick doesn't drink tea or coffee,' Olivia whispered to me as we manhandled the groceries inside.

'He doesn't look very well,' I replied. 'Has he been ill?'

She nodded, but, of course, could give me no further detail.

It was so wonderful to have corporeal company in the cottage. I fussed about making tea, opening a carton of orange juice for Patrick, arranging biscuits on a plate and breaking off to show my guests what small alterations I had made to the arrangements in the cottage, my study and the views over the marsh from the front windows.

Spying my laptop and a notebook that was covered in scrawl—character notes, dates and a rough sketch of a farm—Patrick asked, 'What are you working on?'

'It's just at a very early stage,' I prevaricated, closing the notebook and herding them out of the room. I felt sorry to be so abrupt. Patrick had hardly uttered a word before this, but I certainly wasn't ready to talk about my work.

I pointed up at the loft hatch. 'I'm expecting Mr Harrop to come and look at the roof,' I shrilled. 'There were some funny noises up there on my first night. Probably just a bird. I have heard an owl.'

Credit to Patrick, he gave it another shot. 'What kind?'

'You'll know better than me,' I said. 'I'm afraid I'm a city girl. Do different owls have different calls?'

'Yes,' he said. 'A female tawny owl goes "ke-wick," while the male makes a wavering "hoo-hoo" sort of noise. But that's been misinterpreted into

133

'te-wit to-woo,' as though it's one bird when in fact …' he trailed off, suddenly losing confidence.

'It's actually two?' Olivia finished for him.

He nodded, tongue-tied again.

'That's fascinating,' I said. 'I had no idea. You're obviously a keen birder. You'll enjoy the hide, I should think, along the boardwalk.'

'The roof should be sound,' Marjorie observed, taking the conch from Patrick. 'It was all renewed when the cottage was renovated. That would be three or four years ago now. That was its second renovation, of course. Mr and Mrs Harrop did the place up to an extent, when they moved in, I believe, but that was years before my time.'

I made a mental note of this information. 'I worry about the house next door,' I confided, as we descended the stairs. 'An empty house attracts all kinds of interlopers …'

'I'm sure Jamie keeps on top of that kind of thing,' Olivia put in. 'Have you seen much of him?'

I hesitated. 'Not much,' I said. 'He was helpful when I fell. He was a lifesaver, in fact, but … the truth is we haven't really hit it off.'

'Oh?' Marjorie lowered herself on to the sofa. 'I find that very strange. He's such a personable young man. Then again, I suppose it can't be easy …'

'His family …' Olivia began.

I held my breath. Would they give me some clue about my moody, temperamental neighbour?

No.

'We mustn't gossip,' Marjorie declared. She gulped her tea down, draining the cup, and in my mind's eye it was as though she effectively swallowed any hope I might have of understanding Jamie. Then she said, 'Now then Dee, why don't you put your shopping away and get a few things together, and then you can come back with us in the old jalopy.'

She picked up her handbag and began to rummage about in it. 'I have your receipt here somewhere,' she muttered.

'We always have sausages and baked potatoes, on bonfire night,' Olivia said. 'We make too many, and then take them to the beach to give away. Bill and Julie don't like it. They *sell* food, but Mummy says it's a metaphor. People *eat* sausages and jacket potatoes, but they *taste* loaves and fishes.'

'That's good,' said Patrick who, in my opinion, could use all the bangers and spuds going. 'I'm not much good in the kitchen, though.'

'That's no problem,' said Marjorie. 'I've arranged for one of the church wardens to come and take you down to the beach. They'll need all the help they can get there, finishing off the fire, checking for hedgehogs and so on, and it will be nice for you to meet a few folks.'

Patrick, already pale, whitened further.

'Every one's *very* friendly,' Olivia told him. 'They'll be ever so glad of the help.'

I felt doubtful. Patrick didn't look to me as though he had the strength to hold a sparkler, let alone to move the logs and pallets I had seen stacked up on the beach. But I was not going to pass up the chance of a little girl-talk with Marjorie and Olivia back at the vicarage.

I threw my groceries in the cupboards, grabbed my new, padded jacket and laced up my boots. Bob leapt into the rear of the Land Rover without being asked and I thought I remembered a detail in Ivaan's shaggy-dog-Bob story—hadn't the car that had picked Ivaan up on the way to the audition been a Land Rover? Perhaps it was what Bob was used to.

Marjorie executed a tortuous five- or six-point turn at the end of the lane and we set off back along it, passing the cottages and the hen coop. I felt a frisson of excitement, as though I was escaping. The week I had spent at the cottage felt much longer and I resolved I would not go so long again without going to the village, having guests over or seeking out company of some kind. Marjorie had mentioned a book group, hadn't she? I could join that; and Mrs Ford's studio still intrigued me. As we entered the copse at the turn in the road something made me look back. From the angle of the track and its slight elevation I could see the gable end of Jamie's house and, foreshortened, the three chimneys that stood above the long line of the roof. It was odd, but it looked to me as though a thin, grey pencil-stroke of smoke was rising from the middle one.

As it turned out my expectation of a pleasant afternoon of confidential chat with Marjorie and Olivia was disappointed. People came and went with relentless regularity. A couple came to ask about banns. Someone else had the draft of the parish newsletter for her to proofread. A man came to report a leak in the church roof. Several brought offerings of cake to welcome them home, also jars of jam and sundry other homemade offerings. A snivelling child who had tripped on the pavement and cut her knee was brought in for first aid. The child bawled without ceasing while her wrung-out mother tried to wash the cut and eventually Marjorie took the job in hand while Olivia made the exhausted mother some tea.

As the light began to fade Patrick returned from the beach looking as pale as a ghost and clearly chilled to the bone but smiling. He said he had enjoyed helping the team on the beach. He took himself off for a shower while Olivia and I heated baked beans and Marjorie had a protracted conversation with someone in the front room. Then we were crammed around the kitchen table, the four of us plus five or six others who happened to be in the kitchen when the sausages were cooked. I'd have killed for a glass of wine but only water appeared on the table, so I had to make do. I gave Bob a portion of Patty's kibble and then Marjorie and I took the dogs for a quick walk along the village street while Olivia and Patrick stacked the dishwasher and wrapped the remaining food in silver foil.

After the hubbub of the vicarage the village was thickly quiet, curtains closed against the evening, Mrs Harrop's shop light the only bright point.

'She's still open?' I queried. It must have been almost six o'clock.

'She's always open,' Marjorie replied.

'I meant to go in,' I said. 'Apart from supplies—I need to throw her off the scent of my illegal delivery—I need to speak to her about the cottage. Will she be at the bonfire?'

Marjorie shook her head. 'No. She never goes to the bonfire. You can scribble out a list and give it to Walter. He will be on the firework team. You'd do better speaking to him about any maintenance issues, anyway. Is it the roof?'

I nodded. 'Yes, and I can't find a key to the cupboard under the stairs. There must be a better vacuum cleaner in there, the one Mrs Harrop uses for the changeovers. Plus …' I hesitated, '… there's Jamie. I think he's doing some kind of renovation at his place and sometimes … there are these peculiar noises. One afternoon I felt sure the whole foundations shook.'

'I don't think you need to mention anything like that,' Marjorie advised. 'Jamie is sound as a pound, but he isn't Mrs Harrop's favourite person. I wouldn't want to stir up waters that are already fairly muddy. He's had a difficult hand in life.'

'Has he?' I dropped my question like a pebble into still waters and waited for the ripples to come.

But Marjorie zipped her lips closed, saying only, 'It's impossible—for a newcomer—to assimilate the years of family history and village politics that go into a place like Roadend. Suffice it to say that here, if you kick one person, five or six others will limp. Do you know what I mean?'

'Of course,' I said. 'But that's just what I want to understand. I want to know all the background.'

'Do you, dear?' Marjorie said tartly. 'And why would that be?'

She had me there. 'I just take an interest in people,' I mumbled. 'And I'd hate to put my foot in it by just not knowing what "it" is.'

Marjorie breathed out through her nose. 'Hmmm. I find that if I'm honest with people for my part, they're happy to reciprocate. But these stories you're so eager to uncover? They can be painful. People don't want to scratch the scabs off them again and again.'

I felt vaguely chastised. What did Marjorie mean about honesty? Did she suspect that I hadn't been honest with her? I supposed I hadn't, in-so-far as I had obfuscated my profession. But I had been perfectly frank about my reasons for leaving Hackney. The cheating, lying boyfriend was perfectly real; and, in fairness, she hadn't *asked* about the nature of my work. If she had, I probably would have told her.

'I suppose I mustn't rush things,' I said. 'I've only been here a week and I haven't had the chance to meet many people. I'm looking forward to the bonfire very much. I suppose the whole village will show up?'

'Some people never join in with community events. The folks down at the far end of the village, for example. We won't see hide nor hair of them. They're the really ancient families in the village. Their forefathers were ship-breakers and herring fishermen. They've never really forgiven the rest of us for invading! But lots of the others will come along I should think. It's such a perfect evening for it.'

'Patrick seems a nice chap,' I said. 'Will he stay with you for long?'

'Until Christmas, initially. He is testing his vocation, but he needs to improve his health as well; his *mental* health, that is. To be honest, it's as much a convalescence as a placement.'

Marjorie sealed her lips and would say no more.

Sensing another firmly shut door on her repository of secrets, I cast about for another topic of conversation. 'I don't suppose we will see the folks from the manor house. I did encounter Her Ladyship. I'm afraid I made a mistake about which gate I was supposed to go through. She wasn't pleased.'

Marjorie threw me a wry smile. 'Oh dear, no. She wouldn't be. I'd have paid money to witness *that* encounter.'

I gave a hollow laugh. 'I'm sorry to say she had the best of it. I came away with my tail well and truly between my legs.'

'You aren't the first,' she replied.

Chapter Sixteen

By the time we had settled the dogs at the vicarage and got ourselves down to the beach the bonfire was already alight. Sparks showered into the pewter sky. The moon's light was milk-pale in comparison; it cast a wavering pathway across the still surface of the sea—far out, the tide was low—and the smooth, dun sands below the shingle line.

A group of doughty-looking chaps was in charge of the fire, pacing its perimeter with spades and rakes, teasing reluctant tinder back into the inferno. Their faces were red, glistening with sweat. One of them seemed to be in charge. At first, I thought it was Jamie; the man was head and shoulders taller than the others, with a shock of fair hair that the fire lit up in glints of auburn. But his left eye was unbruised, which Jamie's, even so many days after his fight, would surely not be. More of this man's face I couldn't see because he had his scarf tied across his mouth and nose even though what smoke there was billowed upwards in the windless air. He moved between the other men pointing out pieces of glowing cardboard that might break free, branches that needed repositioning, and occasionally he stood back to survey the whole fire and the crowd with an authoritative eye. Every so often he nodded to a big lad with a paunch that separated his t shirt from the waistband of his tracksuit bottoms, a cue that the lad should hurl more gash timber into the flames from the back of a trailer.

Children—be-wellied, wrapped up in thick scarves and topped with bobble hats—stood at a safe distance twirling sparklers. Olivia drifted in their direction, Patrick in tow carrying an insulated box we had packed with hot food. Marjorie was immediately absorbed into a crowd of middle-aged women who had set up a trestle table and were doling out soup in polystyrene cups. I was offered one but declined; I had eaten plenty already. I needed alcohol, and quickly, to steady the nerves which I was surprised to find fluttering with importunate fingers at my innards.

There were perhaps a hundred people on the beach—families and couples, groups of friends, some of whom clutched cans of lager in their gloved hands. Their thick outerwear and woolly wrappings made them look like overweight spacemen, and the rocky beach—grey and indeterminate—like the surface of a faraway planet. I felt their eyes on me as I stood uncertainly on the periphery of the proceedings, but their happy chatter did not falter and no one broke away from their friends to say hello. I plastered a smile onto my face and watched the children forming letters and drawing circles of light with their sparklers, and remembered when my brother and I had done just the same. That memory deepened still further a yawning chasm of emptiness. My eyes began to swim with tears and I looked away. On the shingle carpark I saw a well-illuminated marquee—a makeshift bar—with the glint of glasses and bottles, the hum of recorded music. I crunched off in its direction.

A woman I assumed was Julie stood behind the bar, where beer taps had been rigged up and a glass-fronted fridge had been manoeuvred into position. I heard, from behind the marquee, the percussive grumble of a generator keeping everything going. Julie had a pinched, narrow face, a knife-like nose and lips that were pursed in a permanent expression of disapproval. Whenever she was not pouring drinks or wiping down the bar—a thankless task, it was constantly a-swim with beer—she was rubbing her hands together as though she believed they might generate a spark. All in all, she gave a powerful impression of a woman who would rather be anywhere else but there, at a carpark on a cold November night. Her morose demeanour seemed not to deter customers, however, and I had to wait a while behind a phalanx of broad backs before I could catch her eye and get served. I offered her my friendliest, most winning smile and ordered a large gin and tonic, but my charm offensive fell utterly flat and I came away from the marquee without a single person having said hello.

I stood and sipped my drink alone, outside the circle of light cast around the marquee, excluded from the drinkers who pressed together against the bar. Excluded full stop, I thought morosely. In spite of Marjorie's advice earlier, I still resented the feeling of being so alien, so out of the village loop. Why were people being so unfriendly?

At the far side of the carpark, beyond the marquee, the play area was in near-darkness, but a slight movement caught my eye; the barely-perceptible twirl of the roundabout. Its wooden platform and metal handles moved with inexorable slowness. I had to stare at it to convince myself that it was moving at all—whether some trick of the feeble light made it seem as though the shadows were moving across it, or whether indeed the thing itself was in motion—each segment just penetrating the yellowish glow of the lights before melting back into the dimness. I stood almost mesmerised by it until, from the thick gloom, a figure emerged, an old man, perched awkwardly on the platform. A shock of white hair, a tatty pullover, ragged boots, the glint of a bottle. The graveyard tramp. For a second, he was visible in the slice of light, then the murk swallowed him.

A pot-bellied man with a scraping of thin hair over the dome of his head moved burgers and sausages around on the grill of a large barbecue that had been set up at the far side of the marquee. He was benign, reassuringly corporeal in comparison to the spectre on the playpark. He had no customers at all, his air of busyness a thin veil for the frustration and perhaps even despair that he must have felt. Seeking any port in my storm of sudden horror, I took a few tentative steps in his direction and he looked up hopefully at my approach.

'Burger, love?' he enquired. 'Sausage?'

I shook my head, but stiffly; my jaw was half clenched, my neck a ramrod. 'I'm sorry,' I said, 'I've already eaten.' I looked across at the park again. From this angle it was enveloped in darkness. I couldn't see anything moving within its thick veil. 'I didn't know there would be caterers,' I stammered out. His face fell, but I surged on in a voice that sounded thin and tense. 'I just thought I'd come over and introduce myself. You must be Bill, from the pub. I'm Dee. I've rented Mrs Harrop's cottage for five months.' I was standing so close to the barbecue that the smoke rising from the fatty meat made my eyes sting. When I lifted my hand to wipe them, I saw it was shaking.

If Bill noticed, he did not say anything. 'Oh, that's you, is it?' He moved three or four sausages onto a plate on a side table. They were burnt. 'I wondered if you might come in for a meal one night, but you never showed.'

'I would have done,' I assured him, too earnestly because I was desperate to ingratiate myself with the only man who stood between me and the mad old man in the play park, 'but I fell and twisted my ankle. This is the first time I've been out since I did it.'

He nodded, as though this was not news to him. 'It was quite a downpour we had, on Monday,' he admitted. 'You were lucky Jamie came across you. Are you alright, love? You're as white as a sheet. Here,' he indicated a plastic garden chair. 'Sit down for a minute.'

'Thanks,' I said, sinking down. 'I'm OK, really.' I glugged some more of my gin and tonic. Bill occupied himself with the food for a minute. Presently I said, 'You know Jamie, then?'

'I know everyone, love. Wouldn't be much of a landlord if I didn't. Jamie does odd jobs for me, and he puts in a shift or two on the bar if we're busy. Not that we are, these days. Mrs Harrop charged you a pretty price, I'll be bound, for the cottage?'

We both looked across the road, to where the light in the shop still shone. My heart rate had returned to normal; my hands had stopped shaking. 'I didn't think it was unreasonable,' I said in a voice more recognisably mine. 'I was lucky to find anywhere. I just pitched up out of the blue, you know.'

'On the run, are you?'

I couldn't tell if he was joking but took a chance on it. 'Why?' I replied. 'Has my probation officer been sniffing round?'

He laughed and wiped his forehead with his sleeve.

I looked over my shoulder to where the bonfire snapped and crackled, and where the crowds stood shoulder to shoulder. Bill had been kind and I felt sorry for him. 'It's a pity you couldn't get the barbecue a bit nearer,' I remarked. I finished my drink, the glow of alcohol finally finding its way into my bloodstream, and took a deep breath. 'If you have a tray, I don't mind carrying a few hot dogs and things along the beach, see I can find any takers,' I said.

He jumped at my idea, hastily wrapping food in napkins and putting them on a tray. I carried it to the far side of the fire, away from the free-soup-dispensing women and the little circle of children munching sausages and potatoes which surrounded Olivia and Patrick. A group comprised mainly of men and just two or three women—I identified them as the hunting-shooting-fishing set because of their Hunter wellingtons and Barbour jackets—stood well back from the fire talking amongst themselves. One or two sipped from silver hipflasks. It crashed upon me I had chosen the wrong group to approach; *they* would hardly be in the market for cheap burgers, I thought, but it was too late to retreat and I trudged on across the shingle with my tray like a Christian entering the Colosseum. One of the men—no word of a lie: he wore a deerstalker and a handlebar moustache—broke off his diatribe mid-sentence and looked in my direction. A woman who had her back to me swivelled her head. My nerves—already heightened, despite the gin and tonic I had drunk so quickly—escalated further when I glimpsed, a few yards behind the tweedy cohort, the dim outline of a sleek, black Range Rover, surely *the* black Range Rover I had forced to reverse up the track on the day of my arrival. Was *he* here amongst this huddle of hurrah-Henries? Was *she?*

More heads were turning my way. There was no possibility of retreat. I could not pretend all the food on my tray was for me, that I was simply in search of a quiet place to scoff it. I gripped the tray more tightly and continued my approach.

'Good evening,' I cried, forcing joviality into my dry mouth. 'Bill's cooking up a storm over in the carpark and asked me to see if there were any takers. Would anyone care for a bite to eat?'

To my surprise there was a gale of enthusiastic guffaws and a wholesale rummaging in pockets for money. I moved along the line of waxed jackets dispensing food, not daring to look up into any of the faces until a drawled, 'No, *thank you,* not for me,' told me I had come face to face with my nemesis. I raised my eyes to her. I had to crane my neck—she was so much taller than I was. She looked down with vinegarish disdain.

'Oh,' she said, 'it's you.' Again, I discerned—but could not identify—that twang of accent.

'Yes,' I said, fixing a smile to my face. 'Hello again. How are you?' Her face was as I recalled it from our previous awkward, rain-soaked encounter: round, unlined, not ugly but nowhere near as elegant as I suspected she would have wished. This close to her I could see the grey at the roots of her artificially blonded hair. I turned to indicate the fire, the grinning children and sociable groups illuminated by its amber glow. I said, 'Isn't this a lovely occasion? The fire certainly is splendid, isn't it?'

Then I moved on down the line of her friends, one of whom remarked in a horsey voice that was perhaps meant to be muted but which in fact carried with perfect clarity, 'Who's that, Caroline?'

'Oh,' she replied, and I could sense the dismissive wave of her hand, 'that's the fool who tried to force her way in through our gate.'

'Oh,' came back the reply, 'fancy that. Rather nice looking though, eh?'

I was desperate to look back, to identify the man I assumed must be her husband, the helicopter pilot; the chinless would-be toff who had bought himself a title just for fun. I wanted to remind him he'd already helped himself to an eyeful of me from his helicopter cockpit. But my pride wouldn't let me. My tray was empty, my pocket jingling with coins. My work was done.

I had begun to make my way back to the carpark when the tall, broad bloke who had been supervising the fire unwound the scarf from his mouth to shout, 'Have you sold out? Oh, what a pity. These chaps could use a burger, I should think.'

His face was glowing, hot with the fire. I suppose mine was glowing too. But something else was making *me* light up. I had rarely seen such a handsome face: broad brows over deep-set eyes; wide, well-defined cheek bones; a square chin shadowed by a neatly trimmed beard. Good lips revealed even teeth in a friendly smile. He strode towards me, pulling off his glove.

'Hi,' he said, holding out his hand for me to shake. 'I'm Hugh. You're new. Oh! And now I'm a poet, what do you know?' His broad shoulders shook as he laughed.

'I'm Dee,' I said in a squeak I hardly recognised as my own voice. 'I'm Mrs Harrop's tenant ...'

'Oh,' he cried, as though I had solved a problem that had long been baffling him. 'I saw the lights in the cottage were on, and I was surprised because I felt sure she had told me there were no more guests until Easter.'

So he knew the cottage. Had been past it, at night. I recalled the strange light I had seen across the marsh. Could that have been him? 'That's right,' I gushed. 'But that was my good fortune, because I found myself in need of somewhere for a few months.'

Found myself in need? What was I implying? That I had been made homeless? As if it wasn't absolutely at my own choice! Why did I feel the need to play the victim? I shook myself. 'What I mean is, I needed a place, and Mrs Harrop was able to help.'

Hugh cocked a quizzical eyebrow but said, 'Well, that's excellent. Excuse me. I must get back to the fire. But if you would be so kind as to bring a few sandwiches our way ...'

'Of course,' I said. 'Coming right up.'

I walked past him, doing my best to make my gait across the shingle—awkward, because the stones were loose, and because my ankle was still weak—into something approaching an elegant sashay. From further down the beach, the first rocket whooshed into the sky. In its light I could see the whole of the play park—swings, slide, climbing frame, roundabout. Deserted.

From then, the evening hurried by. I took a second tray of food to the men who were looking after the fire. Hugh threw a £20 note onto the empty tray.

'Shame you didn't bring us beers,' joked one of the men.

Hugh grinned but said, 'Not until the fire's burnt down, Jim. Then I'll stand you all a pint.'

Jim shrugged, but nodded. 'Fair enough.'

My efforts on the beach alerted customers to Bill's barbecue and he began to do a fairly brisk trade. The bar was busy and, with the beer, the crowd became garrulous. Marjorie managed to extract herself from the soup quorum and I bought her a large gin and tonic.

'Oh, naughty,' she said with a conspiratorial smile when she tasted it.

I'd treated myself to another, too. We clicked our plastic glasses together. 'You've been an absolute brick, Marjorie,' I said. 'Thank you.'

She waved an airy hand. 'All part of the service, dear,' she said. 'Now then, let's introduce you around.'

We made the tour of the fire, Marjorie throwing out a barrage of names I couldn't possibly remember, 'Here are Leonard and Amy, from The Dunes. I expect little Henry is around somewhere. This is Arnold, been in the village man and boy, haven't you Arnold? Lost his wife last year, poor old thing. Here are the John Forresters, out in force! Lucy, and her husband Mike. Johnny—Beth not with you this evening, Johnny? Oh, I'm sorry to hear that. Send her my love. Ben and his partner Alan … Mrs Ford! Can I introduce Dee … Oh! I don't think I know your second name, Dee! How odd! Never mind. Mrs Ford has a studio where she makes exquisite …' And so it went on, until my head was in a whirl but at least I felt I had begun to make progress.

By the time we got to the far side of the fire the tweedy brigade had disappeared and the black Range Rover with it, leaving only tyre tracks into the dunes. Only two chaps remained to supervise the fire, neither of whom was Hugh.

Later, when the fire had sunk to a mound of bright hot ashes, the children had been taken home to bed, the marquee emptied of stock and the barbecue extinguished, I sat on a log with Olivia and Patrick. The fireworks over, we had popped back to the vicarage and now the dogs sat contentedly on the shingle beside us. A little way from us a circle of young people had gathered around a man with a guitar. The strains of *Wonderwall* rose up into the night air. A few others hovered at the periphery of the fire's glow, toasting themselves in its warmth. One of them was Jamie. He wore a hat pulled down low over his head and a headtorch, unlit.

Olivia must had seen him at the same time as me. 'He will have been helping with the fireworks,' she told me. 'They set them up on the edge of the dune, well away from any livestock. Good, weren't they?'

'They were splendid,' said Patrick, but then he gave an involuntary shiver. I didn't blame him; outside the orbit of the fire, the air was decidedly chill. I wasn't sure how much longer I would stay; even my thickly padded coat was beginning to feel not thickly padded enough, and Patrick only wore an ordinary anorak.

'Do we have to make a donation for the fireworks?' I wondered.

'Oh no,' Olivia told me. 'Bill and Julie fundraise all year, for the fireworks, and for a Christmas party for the children and another for the old folks. The squire tops up the fund if there isn't enough.'

'*Does* he?' I said, surprised. He had not seemed the altruistic type to me, keeping himself and his hunt-ball cronies at a firm distance from the hoi-polloi.

I glanced across at Jamie again. He took a swig from a bottle of beer. So, I noted, not a complete teetotaller then. He kept himself slightly apart from the others—not alone, exactly, but not part of the crowd either. Every so often I caught him looking our way and eventually I raised a hand in greeting. He lifted his chin in a sharp jerk of acknowledgement and turned away.

I sighed. 'I have no idea what time it is,' I said, groping for my phone in my pocket, then remembering I didn't have one. 'But I feel sure Bob and I ought to be heading back to the cottage.' I levered myself off the log, dusting down the back of my coat.

Olivia and Patrick got up too. 'Would you like us to walk with you?' said Patrick. 'Or me, at least.' He turned to Olivia. 'Perhaps you'd rather take Patty home?'

'Oh, I don't mind,' said Olivia. 'But Jamie might be going that way. *He* could …'

'I don't need anyone to walk me home,' I declared. 'It's a perfectly still, dry night. I have my torch …' I drew it from the inside pocket of my coat in evidence, 'and Bob here is all the escort I need.' The spectre of the old man I had seen earlier did not alarm me now. So what? There was a local hobo, but he would surely be harmless. If he were not, Marjorie would not allow Olivia out alone.

'If you're sure,' said Patrick, and I saw the fatigue around his eyes. It had been a long day for him, I realised.

We began to crunch our way along the beach to the carpark, where our ways parted.

Olivia hugged me goodbye. 'Don't be a stranger,' she said.

'I won't,' I promised. 'Goodnight, Olivia. Goodnight, Patrick.'

I began to walk along the road towards the church. Away from the fire the air was cold and smelled of frost. The last lamp-post in the village, outside the church, cast diamonds onto the verge beneath it. My feet crunched on crystals. Behind me, in the carpark, I heard the familiar spurt of a motorbike engine starting up.

As I approached the gate into the churchyard the sound of Jamie's motorbike grew closer. I could hear it putter and stutter as it struggled in a low gear. I supposed that, like me, he would take the boardwalk shortcut home. I wished I had set off just a few minutes later, to allow him to get ahead of me, or that he would accelerate and overtake me. I knelt down and retied the laces of my boots as a gambit to allow him to do just that, but the engine idled some few yards behind me, hidden in a pool of shadow. I couldn't prevaricate any further. I straightened up and walked briskly towards the gate. I had my hand upon it when a shout from a little further up the track, and the hollow, metallic clang of footsteps on the cattle grid, made me peer into the gloom beyond the church wall.

'Dee,' called the voice, and Hugh strode into the halo of light cast by the lamp-post. He wore a thick, Aran pullover topped by a gilet, blue jeans and substantial boots. 'I'm so glad I caught you,' he cried. 'I wanted to buy you a drink.'

'Oh,' I said, wrong-footed. 'I was just heading home.'

'It's early,' he said, shooting out an arm, revealing a thick wrist and a large, expensive-looking watch. 'Hardly past nine-thirty. The pub will still be serving. Won't you let me buy you a nightcap?'

I hesitated. Behind me, the motorbike revved a couple of times. It sounded an odd note. An objection? A warning? Or just impatience, that I should get out of the way? I couldn't tell. But it decided me. 'Alright,' I said, turning back in the direction of the pub. 'Just one, then.'

Chapter Seventeen

The inside of the pub was more or less what I had expected—banquettes of seats around the perimeter of the room, upholstered in balding red plush, an L-shaped bar with a jar of pickled eggs at one end and Bill at the other, nursing a tumbler of whisky. The ceiling was low, beamed; the beams plastered with beer mats advertising more varieties of beer than I thought it possible to exist. Between the beams the pitted ceiling was yellowed with old nicotine, although of course smoking had been banned in pubs for years. Some dreary paintings covered the worst of the faded, discoloured wallpaper. Taxidermy—a snarling, flea-bitten fox and a dusty, dishevelled pheasant—stood in appalled, atrophied juxtaposition on the window ledge. Beneath my feet the carpet was both slick and threadbare.

The place was busy, though, with groups I had seen together on the beach now crowded around the small tables. The man I recalled as Arnold was playing dominoes with some other old-timers by the fire. The paunchy young man spilled over a barstool, the waistband of his tracksuit low enough to reveal the cleft of his bottom. His companion was the harried mother I had seen in Marjorie's kitchen. The two were clearly together but exchanged no words.

As Hugh and I entered the bar there was a kind of hush, as though everyone in the place had paused in their conversation to take a breath at just that moment. Heads turned. I saw the light of recognition in people's eyes when they took in Hugh, and the lifted, curious eyebrows when they saw I was his companion. Hugh held the door open for me and indicated a space at the bar, pulling a bar stool from further along. I unzipped my coat and slipped it off. After the frosty temperature outside, the room was stifling. Bob lay down on the stone flags that surrounded the bar.

Hugh took my elbow as I scrambled onto the stool, then hung my coat with his gilet on a hook by the door. 'What will you have?' he asked.

Bill, suddenly animated, moved from his place at the end of the bar. 'Gin and tonic, isn't it?' he queried, his hand hovering over the glasses that were ranked on a shelf behind him. 'A double, if I'm not mistaken. This will be on me.'

I nodded. 'But only a single, please. I can't afford to fall over on the boardwalk *again.*'

Bill smiled and plinked ice into a tall glass.

Hugh said, 'Did you fall over on the boardwalk?'

'Oh yes.' I shook my head at my own stupidity. 'During that downpour on Monday. My boot gave way, or got caught. I don't know. Something. But there I was flat on my face. I've been limping all week.'

'That was quite a deluge,' Hugh agreed. 'I was out in it myself.'

Bill put my drink down in front of me. 'What'll you have, Hugh?'

'A whisky,' Hugh said. 'My usual, if you have it.'

Bill reached a bottle from a high shelf and free-poured a generous measure for Hugh and one for himself.

'Cheers,' he said.

Hugh slipped his wallet from his back pocket but Bill waved it away. 'I told you,' he said, 'these are on me.'

'Thank you very much, Bill,' I said, sipping my drink. I turned to Hugh. 'When I was out in the rain, I took shelter in the hide for a few minutes. There was some camping gear in there. Was that yours?'

He nodded. 'Yes. I'd packed it up when I saw the rain coming in, but then got caught short halfway back, so I dumped it.'

'You'd been camping? For fun? Or professionally?'

'Both, really. It's my job to monitor the countryside hereabouts, and I'm a bit of a wildlife nerd. Early mornings and dusk are the best times for seeing some species, especially the deer, so I often camp on the Moss ...'

'The Moss?'

'Winter Moss. Yes. It's what the locals call the marsh. There's a certain tree—'

'I think I know it,' I said, certain he meant the trysting tree.

'... or sometimes I camp on the dunes. Have you ventured out there yet?'

I shook my head. 'There's a path from the cottage that goes through a willow wood. I think it will take me to the dunes on the far side of the headland. But I haven't made it that far yet.'

Hugh picked up his glass and swirled the amber liquid before taking a sip. 'It's beautiful,' he said contemplatively. 'There are natterjack toads— quite rare. But ... I don't know what it is, but *something* on that side feels so different. The weather, for a start. It's quite uncanny. The mist seems to come from nowhere, sometimes ...'

I felt my spine tingle. Perhaps I gave a little shudder.

Hugh turned to me. 'Does that give you the creeps?'

'No,' I said, 'but I will admit to you, when I saw that camping stuff in the shadows of the hide, I jumped half out of my skin. And, since then, I've been imagining an escaped lunatic roving round the ... moss. On my first day I saw ...' but I checked myself, remembering Marjorie's warning. '...and so I haven't set foot on it since.'

Hugh laughed. 'How funny,' he said. 'No lunatic, I'm afraid. Only me.'

'I'm reassured,' I said. 'I have an active imagination. It doesn't take much to set it off.' It was true my imagination at that moment was conjuring all kinds of foolishly romantic scenarios. Staying in the warmth of the pub and getting drunk with Hugh was one of them. Walking home with him along the moonlit boardwalk was another. Slipping my key into the lock and pulling him into the darkness of the hallway, the feeling of his arms around me, his sensuous lips on mine ... I finished my drink and slipped off the stool. 'And now I really must get home,' I said. 'Thanks for the drink.'

He straightened from where he had been leaning on the bar. 'But I haven't bought you a drink,' he objected.

I pointed to my empty glass. 'I've had the one I came for,' I said.

Just then a bald head peered through a hatch in the wall behind the bar, where I gathered there must be a tap room. 'Hugh,' said the man. 'Fancy a game of darts? We're a man short in here. Bring your friend, if you like.'

'Thanks,' I said, 'but I'm going.'

Hugh looked from me to the man, clearly torn. 'I ought to see this lady home,' he said.

'You need do no such thing,' I said, repeating what I had said earlier to Olivia and Patrick, showing my torch and Bob's lead. I really didn't mind walking home alone. In truth I thought it would be safer in lots of ways than allowing Hugh to accompany me. I slipped my arms into my coat, zipped it up and seized the door handle.

'You stay and play darts. I'll see you again, I hope. Good night.'

I walked home across the slumbering marsh, the air around me still and peaceful, but bitterly cold. I was happy to see the soft glow of the light I had left on in the cottage, to be greeted by the warmth inside.

Chapter Eighteen

The next day I walked out across the Moss—as I now knew I must call it—with half an idea that I might come across Hugh. Surely I was not alone in feeling there had been unfinished business between us?

There had been a hard frost in the night; the bracken was rimed with crystals, the water in the rills skinned with ice. The Moss lay out like a tapestry, its usual russet and olive tones silvered and bejewelled where the frost was melting, strewn over with a gossamer of cobwebs. It was an enormous expanse and the idea that I might just happen upon one person in its wilderness was ridiculous; that kind of thing happened in novels, not in real life. Flocks of birds swooped overhead in the fathomless blue of the sky. I wished I could identify them. But I was a town girl, after all. What would I have in common with a countryside ranger like Hugh? I clambered up onto the horizontal branch of the trysting tree while Bob pursued his own agenda in the undergrowth. The air was sharp in my nostrils, but it cleared my head, which was somewhat muzzy after all the gin. I began to think straight. I was there to work, to write, not to enter a dalliance with a local, no matter how personable or handsome he was. I needed to get a grip.

It was tricky though. I was assaulted again, as I had been on my first visit to it, by an air of enchantment in that little glade. The air within the trees was stiller, poised, and thick with history; the birds unaccountably quiet. I was *sure* something—perhaps many things—had taken place at this spot that had in some way defined or redirected lives. It is not often that one gets such a decidedly vivid sense. Sometimes in churches or in ancient manor houses, castles and fortresses, you can almost hear the history oozing from the stones: the hue and cry of battle, the bell tolling crisis, the whimpers of hidden priests and walled-up women. I suppose, in those cases, a knowledge of the facts of history informs our sixth sense—we hear those echoes because we have thumbed through the guidebook or read the information plaques. But, in this case I had no absolute knowledge of what had taken place at the trysting tree. I just *felt* something had.

I scrambled down and marched purposefully back towards the cottage. I had to write. I felt the need with an urgency that I guess addicts feel for their narcotics.

Jamie was in his hen house. I called a greeting as I passed, adding, 'Great fireworks, by the way.' It did not occur to me until I got inside that he might misconstrue my remark; the last he had seen of me I had been arm-in-arm with Hugh and heading for the pub. Not that I cared what Jamie thought, but I regretted adding another stone to the uncomfortable shoe of our relationship.

I took my coffee upstairs and opened my laptop, eager to begin. Before I could, though, an email notification reminded me I had not spoken to Mrs Harrop about the roof, the vacuum or my groceries, but I recalled Mrs Snooty-Knickers up at the manor house ordered *her* provisions via email. Why should I not do the same? It didn't take me long to find the shop's website and I fired off a hasty email. A reply fell into my inbox fairly promptly. It was signed by Olivia. Ah yes! Saturday was her day for helping out at the shop.

> *Mrs Harrop says Mr Harrop will come over this afternoon and bring your groceries. I'll box them up for you now.*
>
> *Love from Olivia x*

It occurred to me that I had not spent much time with Olivia the previous day. I was making a pretty poor show of being "a real friend." I sent her a message to say how much I had enjoyed the bonfire and that I hoped we could get together soon for a girly natter.

Walter Harrop was more or less as I had pictured him—diminutive of stature, narrow-faced, wirily built. I tried to imagine him and Mrs Harrop in close juxtaposition and failed utterly; they were both too bony and angular to provide any comfortable version of marital concourse. He arrived in a newish-looking pickup truck, ladders strapped to its cargo bed along with an assortment of timber, and lost no time in leaning the ladders against the gable end of the house and shimmying up. Jamie appeared from nowhere to assist, joining Walter on the roof where I could hear the low murmur of their voices interposed with the teeth-sucking and chin-stroking that usually punctuates men in contemplation of DIY. I remained in the front bedroom, tapping at my laptop, only half aware of the scrape of slates above me, the rasp of a saw. After a while there was a knock at the door, and I found them both on the doorstep armed with tools. The difference in their heights made me smile, veritably the Little and Large of the roofing world.

'We need to access the loft from the inside,' said Jamie, addressing the door jamb. He had a sheet of foam insulation under his arm. I stood to one side to let them in. They scraped their boots assiduously on the mat before ascending the stairs. Jamie removed the loft hatch without having to climb on anything to do so, lifted his foot to the banister rail and hoisted himself into the attic. Walter made for the cupboard under the stairs and produced a key.

'Keep the step-ladder here,' he announced. '*I* can't get in like him. Won't be a mo.'

He disappeared *inside* the cupboard. Curiously, I put my head inside too. It was not a cupboard at all, but stairs down to a cellar.

'There's a cellar?' I cried. The news put a whole new spin on the creakings I had heard a few days before; they had not necessarily emanated from Jamie's end of the building at all, but from right below where I had been sitting.

'Oh, aye,' came Walter's disembodied voice. 'Goes right through. This was all one house, at one time. Moss Farm, for a long time; and then, when Todd Forrester bought it, Winter Farm.'

'Oh, yes?' I prompted. But I had clearly received all Walter Harrop's conversation, for he added nothing more.

I descended the stairs cautiously. They were steep, made of stone, cold beneath my stockinged feet. The ceiling was very low—even Walter had to duck his head as he probed amongst the assorted lumber stacked around its walls—and lit only by a single, meagre light bulb. To one side of the stairs was a small space that related to the sitting room above. To the other it went on and on, into impenetrable gloom, beneath the dining room of my cottage and the whole of the other two cottages in the row. A cold, stale breeze seemed to come out of the murk. For some reason I was seized with a frisson of panic. A cellar! Did the other houses have access to it? Could Jamie, for example—if he wanted to—get into the cellar from his house and bring himself directly underneath mine? I couldn't think why he would want to do such a thing, other than to scare me witless. He would have to crouch in two to do it. Heaven knew there would be nothing to *hear,* nothing to *see* … I looked upwards. *Was* it possible to see through the floorboards of the hall and dining room? No. I could see no chink of light.

My musings were interrupted by Walter, who had found the small set of folding steps and was advancing with them up the cellar stairs.

'Wanted the hoover, did you?' he asked, motioning with his head to where one stood at the bottom of the cellar steps. I grabbed it and pulled it up into the light of the hall. It was a much better model than the one I had battled with. I manoeuvred it into the kitchen and stashed it in a corner before closing the cellar door and turning the key, which I slipped into my pocket.

My sense of the cottage's security, its self-containedness, had undergone a radical shift. Instead of an independent dwelling it felt to me now like an addendum to some larger whole in which I had no independent stake. I did not like to feel that, from below, I was vulnerable to Jamie's prying. And, if from below, why not also from above?

Walter made his way up the stairs, lugging the stepladder. 'Thirsty work, roofing,' he threw over his shoulder.

I carried their cups up the stairs and then mounted the ladder to put my head through the hatch. Walter and Jamie were squashed awkwardly into the eaves, Jamie lying on his back and holding the insulation in place while Walter, precariously balanced on narrow wooden trusses, hammered in tacks to secure it. The space was lit by a powerful torch that I supposed one of them had brought with them. The attic was empty of the usual detritus people store, except for a large plastic box marked 'Xmas Decs' that spanned two beams. I put the cups down on the ledge of the access and swivelled my head with a kind of fatalism. Sure enough, like the cellar, the attic stretched away through the ribcage of the roof across the whole building. I was snatched back to my first night in the cottage, the sense of movement above me, the soft thud of the loft hatch being put back in place, the curious deposit of dust on the landing carpet. *Had* Jamie been up there that night? Had he slipped down through the hatch and looked down on me as I slept? I stared, horrified, into the long, narrow throat of the attic, my eyes fixed on its far end. I could not actually see that far, but my imagination conjured for me an access point just like the one I was standing in, the ladder of spars bringing him closer and closer, the fumble with the hatch lid, the soft fall of his stockinged feet onto the carpet ...

Suddenly I was aware of silence behind me; the percussion of the hammer had ceased. I swung round again, almost losing my footing on the narrow rung of the ladder and, as though hooked and reeled in, my eyes met Jamie's. He crouched awkwardly, supported by one elbow and one knee on the rough wood of the joists, his head bowed but twisted, almost tortured, to enable him to meet my eye. His cringing attitude was at total odds with the predatory behaviour I had just been imagining, but there *was* something remorseful about it. The look in his eyes was shrinking, as though he hardly dared look at me but could not look away. Did he know I had rumbled him? Was he worried I would call him out? Walter rummaged in his tool belt, oblivious to the tether of acute attention that connected Jamie and me across the roof space. For my part I poured all my angst into it: hurt, affront, anger, disgust. Then I wrenched my gaze from his, went down the ladder and shut myself in my study.

Much coming and going later, much sawing and hammering, climbing and descending, I sensed—rather than heard—that the work was done. My front door closed softly. Walter's truck started up and pulled away. Jamie melted into the twilight, which was then descending on the

159

cottages, the shadow cast by the hill behind enveloping us in its pall. Across the Moss the sky was aflame, the topmost branches of the trees irradiated by the sun's dying rays, a striation of purple cloud feathering the sky and I was galvanised by the need to escape this shroud of gloom and get out, into the light.

Bob made his customary query and got up from the futon. I saved my work and stretched. On the landing there was no sign of the stepladder, no dusty footprints, no sawdust. The loft hatch was firmly lowered into position. Downstairs I found the little stepladder leaning against the cellar door and my groceries left on the kitchen table, but no other sign. What had I expected? I don't know.

Chapter Nineteen

I shrugged on my coat, laced my boots and stepped out into the chilly air, turning resolutely left out of the gate and taking the path through the willows. The sunlight had gone, leaving a violet half-light that melded into darker heliotrope shadows beneath the trees. The air was still. Somewhere in the depths of the copse I heard the crack of a snapping stick. Bob, a little way ahead of me, cocked his ear, one paw raised off the ground in a classic listening-dog stance. But after a moment he relaxed, and, with an effort, I followed his cue. We walked on beneath the overhead structure of branches, my feet rustling through the leaves, my head in the ethereal realm of my story.

The pathway terminated at another five barred gate. Beyond it, the dune landscape—a medley of grey and greyer shadows, humps, bumps and indeterminate contours—stretched off in every direction. The pale rim to the west, where the final vestiges of light still brightened the horizon, was the only clue as to the compass. I had been sheltered in the willow wood but here I felt the gentle touch of a sea breeze on my face, heard the hoarse hushing of grasses. I had arrived at the dunes Hugh had spoken of. Curiosity drove me on and, again, the half-formed but wholly ill-advised idea that he might be here, somewhere. I opened the gate and ushered Bob through, closing it carefully behind me. In the dimness I could see the faint line of the sandy pathway as it slalomed left and right between cushions of grasses, the rhythmic rise and fall of it over the undulating topography, as enticing and irresistible as a yellow brick road. I cocked my ear—as Bob had earlier—to see if I could filter, through the noise of shushing grasses and whispering wind, the ebb and flow of the sea.

I walked cautiously through the crazy lattice of pathways that criss-crossed the dunes, soft sand beneath my feet, the brush of the marram grasses against my trouser legs. Every so often I paused to look behind me, to fix in my mind the point where the gate gave access back into the wood, but the further I got from it the more difficult it was to pinpoint. I ought to have gone back. Night had fully fallen, but the disc of the moon threw a pearly light over the scene, turning everything to shades of cloud and spectre, and as my eyes adjusted it did not seem I was walking in the night, but in an eerie, half-real world of dusk and dreams. The wind was benign, a soft caress of angel-wings; the noise of air amongst the grasses a sort of ghostly music.

I came at last to the edge of the dune, where it dropped sharply down to the pebble of the beach, about five feet below. The tide was well out, a smear of ink in the distance. Across the firth I could see the wink and shimmer of lights that laced the coast on the opposite side. It seemed to me more than ever like a faerie realm, a far country of myth and legend. I felt that if I really honed my ears, I would be able to hear the strains of elfin merry making as they danced across the smooth sands of their shore.

Bob leapt down onto the beach and began to quarter the shingle, his nose to the ground, his tail a constantly waving banner of pleasure. I continued along the cliff top, enjoying the exercise after my day sitting at a desk, and the sense that, here at least, I was free of Jamie's skulking gaze. My night vision discerned nuance in the shades of grey that made up the landscape, picking out the charcoal sketch of denuded shrubs against the lighter, ashy shading of the grasslands, the metallic medley of the pebbles: steel, lead, silver, some shot through with a startling streak of quartz. Here and there a strew of anthracite must have been a collection of seaweed, or perhaps the stump of a tide-carried tree.

I must have walked for about ten or fifteen minutes, keeping to a straight path that skirted the edge of the dune, but that gradually fell to the level of the beach where time and tide had eroded the sandy bluff that separated the two. Bob had ventured further out across the dun grey of the beach. From time to time I saw a flash of white as he bounded here and there. A little way ahead, and about twenty or so yards into the grass and scrub of the dune, a dark outcrop of some kind caught my eye. It stood at about chest height, proud of the surrounding vegetation, much darker and more substantial than the silvered grass fronds and coal-black skeletons of gorse and wild rose. I altered my course so I could look at it more closely, leaving the beach and following a faint and much-less-frequented by-way that was half-overgrown and difficult to navigate.

What I found was a structure that at first defied comprehension. It baffled me. It was clearly man-made, but for what purpose I could not fathom. I groped my way around it, fighting through the tangle of marram and the clutch of some thorny bush, running my hands over its odd joints and protuberances, willing my eyes to differentiate solid material from shadow, fact from fiction. I estimated it was about the size of an average garden shed, but roughly circular in shape, with a narrow opening on the landward side that made it more into the shape of a C or a horseshoe. From what I could gather in the uncertain gloaming of moonlight, it was made of flotsam and jetsam, mainly sun-bleached branches and skeletal sticks that I presumed had been scavenged from the beach, and also ragged skeins of netting, old oil drums, planks and pallets. These had been woven together in the way that a bird might construct a nest, forming a substantial wall that was so thick it exceeded the length of my arm when I reached across it. It was clear to me this was not a new construction. Grasses grew up through the spars, knitting them together, amalgamating the disparate parts into a whole that was solid and curious, a relic of the past. If it had not been made from wood, I would have likened it most closely to an ancient round house; it lacked only the thatched roof to make it complete.

I walked around it again, coming to the curious, narrow entrance on its leeward side. Within the curtilage of cleverly wattled bone-like sticks all was dim and dark. I couldn't tell what—if anything—might be there. I hesitated to step inside, not just because, whatever this was, it belonged to someone, had been painstakingly constructed over years at no small expenditure of effort and ingenuity, but also for fear of what might lurk inside. With the size of the structure and the thickness of the walls, I estimated an internal space easily large enough to conceal a sleeping person. The homeless man was still on my mind, and I had to admit that, for a place to escape the worst of the wind and weather, this would certainly be better than a hedge or a ditch. Other no less alarming or unsavoury ideas sprang to mind. There could be broken glass, fishing tackle barbed with hooks, jagged timbers spiked with rusty nails. Stupidly, in my hurry to come out, I had forgotten my torch, but I was not sure even if I'd had it to hand, I would have been so brazenly intrusive as to have turned its beam on the interior of that odd little igloo.

I felt a shift in the wind and gave an involuntary shiver. Somehow, the half-light that had seemed so magical now felt more like half-dark—sinister and bleak. I looked up and found the moon veiled by cloud. More towering galleons of cloud bore down across the tent of the sky, masking the stars. When I looked back down it was to see, not two feet away, the dark silhouette of a figure. I had neither heard nor seen its approach, and I did not think it could have emerged from the nest in front of me. I supposed it had been lying hidden in the grass all the time I had made my examination of the edifice because it was not possible it had simply materialised out of thin air. At first, I thought it was Hugh. It was like him to play such a joke, I thought. The height and broadness of the shape was right, but then not quite right—the outline strangely hazy, the actuality less substantial than the illusion. I made out—but dimly—a darkish, indeterminate overcoat, a woollen hat pulled low over the forehead; not the professional park-ranger rig I would expect of Hugh. And then, the figure did not speak, as I was sure Hugh would have done, but only stood in the shroud of night, stock-still, knee-deep in the vegetation of the dune. He—if it was a he— seemed, if anything, more startled and disorientated than I was. I held my breath and I sensed that he held his too. I peered through the gloom but of his face I could make out very little—a paleness between the collar of his coat and the welt of his hat, his eyes and mouth no more than pooled shadows.

Far out across the beach I heard Bob bark and the affronted squawk of some bird he had no doubt roused from its roost on one of the groynes. At this the man did turn his head, stiffly, as though unused to the motion, and seemed to look about him, assimilating his own whereabouts—on the dunes, by the sea, next to the … whatever this construction was. I could almost see his realisation dawn. The smudged outline of his body seemed to become more substantial. Then he looked at me.

'Mary?' he said, in a voice not much more than a croak. He swivelled slowly left then right before adding, 'Where are the others?'

'I'm afraid there's only me,' I said. 'I'm Dee.'

The droop in his shoulders told me he was disappointed.

'What *is* this thing?' I asked him. I wanted to know, of course, but I wanted more to dispel the weirdly charged atmosphere that cloyed around us and to anchor him to something that I felt would ease his patent disorientation.

He regarded the thing beside us. 'Den,' he said at last. 'We *had* to build it because …' he trailed off, the effort of speaking—or the memory—too difficult.

'Ah yes,' I said. 'Of course. It's a splendid den.' I was aware of a slightly patronising note in my reply, that I was humouring him, even though he had only given a straightforward answer to my question. 'You built it when you were a boy?' I said, hoping to rebalance things.

He nodded. 'Yes. We built it when we were boys. Look. Is Mary coming?' he asked, and I sensed a slight impatience.

'Did you agree to meet her here?' I enquired.

He contemplated my question. 'No,' he said at last. 'But I *hoped* … she's been gone so long.'

'I see,' I said, although I didn't see at all. I had heard the name Mary at some time but I couldn't place it just then and, in any case, there could be dozens of Marys. 'I've been out here … oh … about an hour now. I haven't seen anyone else. Except you, of course. Have you been waiting long?'

He shrugged. 'I don't know.'

A few moments passed. Eventually I said, 'I think I ought to be going home. How about you? Do you have far to go?'

That he was considering this I gathered only from a slight alteration in the angle of his head. I wished I could read his face but the cloud that covered the moon seemed to suck all the light from the air; the hues of grey, from pearl to pewter, that I had been able to make out before were just layers of murk and gloom now and he was at the centre of them, scarcely a shadow on the backdrop of the night. Sometimes I couldn't see him at all; he seemed to altogether meld with the air, but then the slightest possible movement in the ether told me that he remained.

Out of this barely-there element I heard the words, 'No, I think I'll wait.'

I shuffled my feet. 'All right,' I said. 'Well, good night then.'

It felt wrong leaving him there, his confusion all too palpable, but what could I do? I turned and walked away, taking the longer route around the outside of the den to avoid having to pass him too closely because something in me sensed his oddness was more than just intellectual bewilderment. I found the half-hidden track back towards the beach and whistled for Bob. When I looked over my shoulder, I could just make out the dark silhouette of the den, but of the strange man I could see nothing at all.

Chapter Twenty

The clouds that chased me home that night brought rain, and lots of it. The rest of the week was lost in a continuous deluge of mist and mizzle. On the occasions that Bob's needs forced us outdoors it was like being draped around by a water-logged gauze of moisture. The rain did not so much fall as saturate the atmosphere. When it was caught up by the wind it flapped like ragged bolts of tulle across the expanse of the Moss, smearing all its colour and texture into one amorphous smudge. The trees behind the cottage and in the willow wood dripped, the crisp carpet of leaves underfoot turning to mush.

I'd be lying if I did not admit I hoped Hugh would call. So much easier for him—who knew exactly where I could be found—to make contact, than for me to wander aimlessly around the Moss and the dunes in the hopes of coming across him. My sense of a powerful mutual attraction remained. I had certainly not misread it. But then it dawned on me that we had exchanged no personal information at all during our brief conversation at the bar. I knew he was a sort of countryside custodian, but that was all. I didn't know whereabouts in the village he lived, how long he had been associated with the village, even if he was single. Day followed day and he did not make an appearance. In fact, I saw no one at all, until one day, as I scurried along one of the water-logged pathways of the Moss, his High-and-Mighty Lordship's helicopter swooped low overhead, whipping up the wetness that drenched the vegetation and sending it showering over me, causing my coat to flap and lashing dripping tendrils of hair over my face. I made a rude sign with one finger, and he banked steeply away.

In the absence of any contact from Hugh and in view of the awful weather, I hunkered down, glad of the provisions Mr Harrop had brought with him, thankful for the stock of firewood in the yard behind the cottage and for the warmth of the range that dried coats and boots and the old towels I had found in the cellar and used to dry Bob after our twice-daily forays into the rain.

Venturing into the cellar had taken some courage. I had been acutely conscious of the yawning chasm that stretched off beneath the middle cottage to Jamie's. The beam of my torch hadn't been strong enough to see much and nothing on earth would have made me creep through that chill, damp, spidery darkness. I had made a quick assimilation of the cellar's contents, taken what I needed and retreated back upstairs, locking the door firmly behind me.

My most important item of booty was a roll of duct tape. I carried the folding step ladder up to the landing and taped around the edges of the loft hatch until I was sure it could not be lifted from above. Realistically, I thought it unlikely Jamie would make any further attempt. The abject shame in his eye had told me he regretted his action. I was wise to him now.

I worked, experimenting with ways I might knit the story of the pele tower into the Forresters', but without much success. My instinct said there *had* to be a connection; my story would require it. I had posited a squire and—randomly, as much as a counterpoint to Todd Forrester as for any other reason—a young daughter, so I had made a start. I shouldn't have needed any absolute fact; my imagination should have been sufficient but, in some way I couldn't explain, I was reluctant to proceed. It was almost as though I was waiting for something, but I didn't know what. While it worked itself out, I read the book about pele towers that had been delivered to me and made notes about aspects of their annals I thought might be incorporated into my narrative.

I received regular messages from Olivia, one of which concerned a meeting of the book club, scheduled for the following week. Would I like to go along? I thought that, on balance, I would, but only if the rain stopped. We both bewailed the weather, but agreed that getting together wouldn't be possible until the rain let up.

All week, at the back of my mind, lurked the stranger I had met on the dune. Who could he have been? And why had everything about him seemed so ... peculiar? The odd quality of the night had made his physical presence seem almost insubstantial—a shade, an illusion? And yet his bafflement, his sense of disorientation, had been absolutely palpable, *more* palpable in fact than his bodily manifestation. Clearly, he was confused. Heaven knows, my own mind had been clouded enough, taken with fancies, carried away with the romance of the night air, the splendid desolation of the dune. It is always hard, after a period of writing—of being lost in the realm of your narrative—to lift your head and refocus on the real world. That day I had not eaten much, adding to my distraction. No, I could not say *I* had been in full grasp of my faculties, but it had seemed to me at the time—and seemed even more to me afterwards—*he* had been seriously befuddled. Could he be suffering from dementia? One thing I could be sure of in the whole, perplexing and dreamlike encounter: he might have been strange, but he was not a *stranger*. He knew the dune; he knew the den. I only hoped some rope of memory had served him that surreal evening, that some beacon of recollection had lit up, and guided him home.

The cottage continued to regale me with its own peculiar concerto. The drone of rain on the windows, the pelt of it on the roof and the gurgle of it down the gutters overlayered the occasional percussion from further along the row. The wind, gusting through the trees on the hill at the back of the house and buffeting the roof added itself to the sonorous choral accompaniment from next door that I had noted previously. That went on and on hardly without ceasing, day and night, like a radio left on at low volume.

The weekend came. I did my laundry and restocked the log baskets. I ran the vacuum over the house and cleaned the bathroom. The wheelie bin in the back yard was getting full and I wondered what I was supposed to do with it. It irked me, but I knew I would have to ask Jamie. I found him—as I knew I would—cleaning the hen house in a brief respite between showers. Bob, wholly unaware of the troubled subtext that existed between Jamie and me, bounded up to him for an ear fondle. Jamie put down his wheelbarrow to oblige.

'Good morning,' I said, in as determinedly bright and self-possessed a tone as I could muster. 'I wonder if you could tell me what I should do with the wheelie bin. It's getting full and ...'

I had been trying to show I had got past our embarrassing connection in the attic the previous week. He had been outed, I knew his nasty little game and his nefarious prowlings would have to cease. I didn't expect him to be past it though; some vestige of lingering shame would surely remain. But no. 'The lorry comes as far as the gate,' he said levelly, as though that excruciating exchange had never taken place. 'The bins have to be taken up. Friday is their day, so you've missed it. There's post in the box for you, but it's been too wet to bring it down.'

'Thanks,' I said. I looked up the rough, pitted slope that must be negotiated with the cumbersome bin. I didn't relish the prospect at all but I was damned if I was going to ask *him* for any help. Jamie followed my gaze. 'Hmmm,' he said, with what I decoded as barely suppressed glee for the onerous task ahead of me. 'Walter takes it on his truck, *normally*. But you're not a *normal* holidaymaker, are you? So, I don't know if he'll think of it.' He folded his arms and looked at me mulishly, and it dawned on me he was waiting for the little battle between my pride and my helplessness to resolve itself.

I drew myself up. 'If I see him, I'll mention it,' I said, 'but if not, I'll take it up next Thursday. Thank you for letting me know about the post.' I whistled Bob and turned on my heel.

Later, I walked up and collected my post, locating the box beneath a sort of lean-to that protected it from the worst of the weather. Even so, I noted my bundle of mail had been wrapped in cellophane to further insulate it from the damp. It might have been the postman, but, somehow, I doubted it. This, like the lighted log burner, like the rescue on the boardwalk, like the eggs, like the dozen other proofs of kindness I had received from him, smacked of Jamie. A different Jamie to the moody outsider on the periphery of the bonfire, to the skulker in attics, to the hot-tempered, sneering neighbour. He was a conundrum I could not make out at all.

It was the following Monday before I made it into the village, driven by a need for milk and bread and—frankly—human company. A week with no flesh-and-blood interaction had left me feeling strangely light-headed and odd, more like one of my characters than a real person.

I wanted to check a couple of things in the graveyard; the time had come to introduce Rose into my narrative, the girl who would become Todd's wife. It was easy to imagine Rose as a poor waif likely to be crushed and dominated by the Todd Forrester I had created, but I thought a feistier woman would make a more interesting story. Either way, I wanted to check the dates on her grave. Also, niggling at the back of my mind, was the Mary the mysterious man on the dune had mentioned. Where had I heard her name, and in what context? It must have been in the village and so that seemed the best place for the memory to return. The book club meeting was to be held at the vicarage at eight, and I had it in mind to buy myself an early supper at the pub before going along.

I set off from the cottage at just before half past three. It wouldn't be long before the evening fell, a bluish twilight sinking down onto the Moss as though burdened by all the cares of the day, but I thought I would have enough time and light to return to the graveyard in search of the dates I needed.

Jamie's cottage seemed deserted as I walked by, the curtains open just a fraction, but no light glimmered from within and I saw no smoke rising from the chimney. The chickens pecked disconsolately in their coop. I walked along the boardwalk. It was slick with leaves from its fringe of trees. I checked the hide but it was empty. The Moss seemed weighted down by its cargo of water, the bracken darkened to beaver-brown, the grasses bent over, dripping tears. The drainage rills were full to the brim with brown, peat-tea. The boggy field that bordered the Moss was a pool, tufts of milk weed drowning waist-high in the black, silty liquid. A lone donkey stood hock-deep in one corner, where a lop-sided lean-to provided some shelter from the weather.

The graveyard was tenanted. I do not mean by the quiet souls at rest beneath the sod, but by a living visitor. The squeak of the gate from the boardwalk alerted a mourner in a practical but unflattering blue anorak. She stood near an ostentatious memorial stone close to one of the back corners of the church, a wreath of greenery and berries in her hands. It took me a moment to recognise Mrs Harrop, out of her usual pinafore and her usual habitat of home-baked hams. She saw me but returned to her contemplation of the obelisk, her head bowed. I loitered at a good distance, touring the Forrester graves to see if I could find any more characters to add to my narrative. John Forrester's flowers had been cleared away; no doubt they had been battered and ruined by the rain. The little solar light lay on its side, the glass of its lantern besmeared with soil. I picked it up and set it straight, but gently, as though I might wake the slumbering occupant of the grave. The mound of earth looked bare and brutal without its floral covering; however we might seek to sweeten it, death is a cold, raw end.

Rose's inscription on the stone she shared with Todd was brief: *Rose Forrester, 1923 – 1976*. Not much, I thought, to sum up a life. I felt a momentary indignation on her behalf, that her whole life had been distilled to such a meagre memorial. There were other gravestones in the vicinity, but their engravings were too worn away to make out; like the people they memorialised, the tributes were gradually fading, crumbling, and sinking back to earth. I wished that the power of my prose could resurrect them, restore their decaying flesh and reignite their souls. But characters in books are only figments of their creators' minds—briefly real enough to ensnare a reader in the threads of their stories before being sealed up between the covers and left on a shelf to gather dust.

When I looked up from my reverie Mrs Harrop was making her approach. She was erect and business-like again, the cloud of her recollections and mourning thrown off.

'Roof all sorted, is it?' she asked, making no preamble of greeting.

'It seems so,' I said. 'No more funny bumps in the night, anyway. *Was* there a bird's nest?'

'Walter didn't say so. A slipped slate, he said. Anyway, I'm glad it's fixed. I wouldn't want a repeat of last year's drama. That leak last year was such a nuisance.'

'Yes,' I agreed. 'I'm sure it was. I didn't know that the whole row had originally been one house. It gave me the willies to find out the cupboard under the stairs was actually the access to a cellar!'

'Did it?' She raised a wiry eyebrow, and I feared that she might not—as I hoped—provide me with chapter and verse on the place. But then she said, 'It was Moss Farm, at one time. Never much of a place. Just a small holding really. Peat-digging was allowed in those days, and they let a few cows graze the Moss. But they were always getting stuck in the dykes and the place went to pot. No one knew why Todd bought it, except to rile *us*.'

My story siren began to sing in my head, throwing out enticing notes. 'Todd *Forrester?*' I enquired in a squeak, and then, 'Us?'

'Oh yes,' Mrs Harrop said. She cast a withering eye over all the Forrester graves; it was not just Todd, then, that she detested. 'No matter what the Forresters like to think, by rights the village belonged to *my* family. It pleased Todd to take it off them, bit by bit.' She brought a tissue out of her coat pocket and wiped her nose and—surreptitiously—her eyes. 'Come and look,' she barked out.

She marched me over the grass to the ostentatious tombstone where she had been standing before. 'The Winters,' she spat out, pointing an arthritic finger at the inscription, 'owned everything hereabouts, gifted it by James I, we were; the pele tower, the land all around it as far as the eye could see, not to mention the fishing rights, the baronetcy … but that was a red rag to a bull, to the Forresters.' The legend on the monument was written out in letters I thought might be lead; *they* would not fade. *Sacred to the memory of Rowan Winter, 1906 - 1962, cruelly killed by fire, by hand or hands unknown. "Be sure your sins will find you out."*

I was struck almost dumb by the coincidence of it. Normally, a snippet of fact will propel a writer forward into fiction but here things seemed to have been reversed. My fiction had uncannily become fact. I had posited a Miss Winter and here, indeed, she was; born, just as I had said, in 1906. What had I just been thinking about the power of prose to resurrect the dead? I hadn't even noticed this monument on my first visit to the church, my attention having been distracted by the strange old man. It amazed me, but it pleased me too, that my instinct had been right on the money. I had thought I was ready for Rose, quite done with my Miss Winter, but here was proof that Miss Winter was not done with *me*.

I hadn't named my character. Rowan. It felt eerily familiar, as though I had known it all along but had simply forgotten it. I reminded myself that although *this* guess had proved right, I still had no proof that the Winters' story overlapped the Forresters'. Having said that, Mrs Harrop's patent antipathy toward the Forresters was unlikely to be based on nothing. It was a waving tentacle of possibility I was determined to catch.

'She was my grandmother.' Mrs Harrop went on, her usually abrasive voice made scratchier still by emotion. 'She was bringing me up, but then she was burned to death in that tower on the hill yonder. I was three at the time, only just pulled out alive.'

'Oh my God,' I breathed. 'That's terrible. What a dreadful tragedy.' I laid a hand on Mrs Harrop's sleeve, hesitantly, because I was not sure she was the tactile type. 'How were you rescued?'

'A young lad pulled me out,' she said, 'but nothing could save her. You know about pele towers, I suppose? The ground floor was used to protect livestock, in the days when the Scots and the Reivers were raiding the coast. Stairs went up to the living quarters above.' I nodded. This accorded with my research. 'Well,' Mrs Harrop went on, 'she was a keen horsewoman, my grandmother, and kept horses in the under croft, and all the bedding and hay for the feed. It all went up like that bonfire the other night.' She gave an involuntary shudder. '*I* never go to *that*. You were there though, I hear.'

'I was,' I said, feeling as though I ought to apologise. 'I'm sorry; it must bring back painful memories for you.'

'I don't really remember the fire in the tower,' she said. 'But the idea of it ...'

'Of course,' I said.

The wreath Mrs Harrop had placed on her grandmother's memorial stone was made of laurel leaves, sprigs of spruce and yew, and interlaced with what I now recognised as rowan berries. 'What a beautiful wreath, and a lovely tribute,' I said. 'Rowan. Is it ... is it the anniversary of her death today?'

She nodded. 'Everyone else was here last week, for the Armistice. And the vicar did a nice remembrance service on Sunday.' She half turned her head and I saw the poppy wreaths laid against the church wall, below the war memorial. 'But I always wait with mine, and bring it on the fifteenth.' She looked around her, at rain-blackened gravestones and the soggy, dispirited turf. 'It had been wet then, I'm told. Rain, rain, rain, for days on end. Then, the first dry day, there was the fire. You'd have thought everything was too wet to burn ...' She trailed off, lost in her thoughts.

Presently I ventured, 'And ... the remaining members of the Winter family?'

'There's only me now.' The utter desolation in her voice struck a deep, resonating chord in me.

I wanted to press her. It wasn't just so that I could garner in the threads of the Winter story to be knitted into the fabric of my novel where they belonged. I felt—on Mrs Harrop's behalf, and with a genuine stab—the tragedy of it. No wonder she was such a bitter, difficult woman; she'd had a bitter, difficult life. Mrs Harrop threw a caustic look across the graveyard to where the Forresters were buried, and I knew in my bones that there, somehow, lay another casualty of this story.

Sure enough, she said, 'My great-aunt Rose ought to have been laid here, with my grandmother. But he wouldn't allow it.'

He, I knew, could only be Todd Forrester.

Rose Forrester had been a Winter! There it was! Not just a coincidence but a fact—the link I had felt certain *must* exist between the two story threads. I do not know how I stopped myself punching the air in triumph. I schooled myself to remember that *my* Todd Forrester was a figment, a fabricated man, not necessarily anything like the original. I must not let the contents of my word document escape, to bias me against history. On the other hand, his pull on me was strong. I knew I was treading a fine line, a precipice between reality and fiction, between the truth, and the fantasy that lured me. I knew Mrs Harrop had more to offer me, if only I could tease it out of her. I spoke low, level, as I imagined one would to a skittish horse. I didn't want to spook her. 'Rose Forrester ... she was your ... I think you said she was your great-aunt? She was also a Winter? And she married Todd Forrester?'

'Aye. Twice her age, he was.' She shook her head in bewilderment. 'What a life she had,' she said sadly. 'But I'll give her this: she made her bed, and she lay in it.'

Fact and fiction met in my mind, like a shaft of illumination that comes from the heavens and lights up a dull acre into the colours of the rainbow. It's a trick of the light and yet, for that moment, unarguable. I had already connected the Miss Winter of my narrative with Todd, preparing the ground for some future intercourse between the two families. That, I knew—I thought I knew—was fiction. But here was fact and the two met each other, as a flowing estuary meets the incoming tide of the sea. Their waters mingled and who could say what had originally been fresh and what salt? I pursued its current. What if, rejected by Rowan, Todd had transferred his attentions to Rose? Both girls would— should—have been beyond his reach. He would meet them secretly ... of course! At the trysting tree. First one, and then the other ...

My hand still lay where I had placed it on Mrs Harrop's arm. I dragged myself back to earth and squeezed gratefully. I wanted to thank her for the door she had opened that would lead my story in the direction I knew it needed to go, but of course I couldn't do that; and in fact I felt bad that this had been my first instinct. 'Thank you,' I said, 'for sharing this with me. It means a great deal.'

I walked, in company with Mrs Harrop, out of the church yard and down the street towards her shop. She spoke, but of generalities now; the temperatures were due to plummet. Had I enough fuel for the fires? I'd want to stock up on provisions, she expected. She had made another batch of lasagne ... Bob trotted at my heels although I had neglected to attach his lead.

'Good dog, that,' Mrs Harrop remarked, and I realised that, from her, who must come across any number of farm dogs and holidaymakers' pets, this must be praise indeed.

'He is,' I told her. 'In fact, I haven't had him that long. He's a sort of rescue, saved on the way to be euthanised.' Even as I spoke, I doubted Ivaan's impossibly theatrical version of Bob's salvation. That, no doubt, had been an embellishment added to appeal to my good nature. Well, in this instance, I did not mind Ivaan's mendacity. Bob had turned out to be the best thing Ivaan had ever done.

I selected more groceries from Mrs Harrop's shelves and she promised Walter would deliver them the following day and take away my rubbish at the same time.

'I fear I'm turning into a bit of a nuisance,' I said. 'I *could* drag the bin up myself, I suppose.'

As a sort of answer, Mrs Harrop held her card machine out. Somehow, my bill had exceeded the contactless limit although I did not know how. I hadn't bought *that* much.

'That's all right,' she said briskly. 'You're less trouble than *some*, believe me. And I'm getting an idea of the kind of things you like now. From now on, I'll just send down a box every week, shall I? If there's anything different, or extra, that you need, you can always email.'

I had a distinct sense of having been caught in the mesh of Mrs Harrop's mercantile net, but agreed to her suggestion. It would be one less thing to worry about.

It turned out the pub did not open until six. It was hardly quarter past four when I stepped out of the shop, so I had a good long time to kill. I wished there was a library in the village, but of course there wasn't. I wished I had had the foresight to buy a hot drink from Mrs Harrop. But I hadn't, so I wandered down the street looking at the cottages and houses. Some—dark and vacant—were clearly second homes. Others had lights spilling from uncurtained windows. The air was acrid with the smoke of a dozen open fires. I superimposed, in my mind's eye, the village a hundred years ago, as I had sketched it in my novel, over what I could see now. I swapped the tarmacked road for a dirt track, removed the satellite dishes and television aerials and placed rows of vegetables, hen coops and a goat into the small front gardens. Further down the village, where the glowering grey fishermen's and ship-breakers' cottages huddled together in clannish proximity, I scrubbed out goats and vegetables and replaced them with lobster pots, saws and axes.

But then the school bus roared past, depositing a dozen or so children at the bus stop and dragging me back to the twenty-first century. The children shouldered their bulging bags and trooped off towards Mrs Harrop's shop, and I remembered she baked cakes to entice them in. Briefly, I likened her to the witch in *Hansel and Gretel*. Hadn't she lured *me* in with her promise of a regular grocery delivery? But the insight she had given me into her family history quickly obscured that impression. I found I rather admired her; from being orphaned at three, she had risen to prominence—even dominance—in the village, married an honest, hard-working man and established a thriving business. As the great granddaughter of an extant baronet her fate would have been somewhat different, though not as different as it would have been a hundred years before. But, given her situation, I thought she had done remarkably well.

I walked to the far end of the village, to Low Farm, hoping the reality of it would not dispel my imagined version. The yard was brightly illuminated, a beacon in the fast-encroaching night. I could see cows in a barn, hear the bleat of goats. An engine—a generator perhaps, or some other piece of farm machinery—rumbled in a low key. From what I knew of them the John Forresters were a tight-knit family, working together in their family business. Olivia had told me John could be frightening. The floral tributes around his grave had given me the impression he had engendered real affection from his children, but now I gathered no one had been back to visit in some days—no one else, anyway, had set that lantern to rights. There was as yet no headstone, so I did not know how old he had been, and I had no idea what he had died from. I imagined him dying at home, surrounded by his children, but the likelihood was he had died in a hospital in a cold, narrow bed, surrounded by strangers, as *my* dad had.

I wandered on. Past Low Farm the pavement petered out so I walked along the road as far as the tree where the witches had been hanging on the day of my arrival. There were no streetlights there; the road disappeared into a throat of gloom. The hanging tree was spectral, leafless. From somewhere high in its canopy, branches ground together, making a creaking noise that chilled my blood. I shivered, and followed a tramped down path towards the sea, unclipping Bob's lead as I did so.

The tide was coming in, relentless barrages of churned water crashing onto the shingle, the foamy wave-tops miasmic in the dim. I hadn't been conscious of the breeze as I had walked along the village street, but here it was lively, teasing my hair and making the hood of my coat flap. I pulled it over my head and fastened it tightly as a way to stop both these annoyances, thrusting my hands deeply into my pockets as I trudged through the shifting stones of the beach and mulled over what I had learned from Mrs Harrop in the manner of someone who has a diamond hidden in their shoe. I felt its value, its potential, but it was uncomfortable. I knew I ought to be making my own story rather than simply unearthing one, but what was I to do when corpses kept rising from their graves before my feet? Potentially, I was trespassing, exhuming skeletons long-since laid to rest. Chance, my writerly instinct, uncanny hindsight—I didn't know how to define it—had made me lucky so far, but I could go on to make links that were wildly wide of the mark; they could be offensive or even libellous. At the very least I could be accused of exploiting my new neighbours who did not even know that what they told me could end up in a novel. What, I asked myself, really was the relationship between history and fiction? That history is considered a legitimate subject for fiction goes without saying; look at the many thousands of books based upon it. Novels about the past transport us right back there, so that we can understand the whats and the whys as well as how the present has been affected. Armed with such insight, hopefully we will not make the same mistakes. Those books were rooted in history that is a matter of public record, I reminded myself, and it could be argued that their subjects were of legitimate public interest. Not so *this* story, which was private and probably of interest to no one but those involved.

I sighed. Those involved, and *me*. The untold story of the Winters and the Forresters intrigued and excited me to the extent that its voice drowned out the whisper of my reservations.

The pele tower, thus far only a potential sub-plot in my story, suddenly clamoured for its share of attention. I considered it; the ancient seat of a proud family, a bastion against marauders, a fortress and look-out point. It perched on the very edge of the land, clung there, as though by its fingernails, against the elements: wind, rain, sea. I squinted along the beach towards its far end, where the headland rose up, a dark mass against the dusky sky. Fifty years ago, to the day, that bluff would have been illuminated by flames—lurid, an inferno, sparks shooting up into the wind-tossed sky. I imagined the maddened horses straining at their halters, lunging and kicking, the flames reflected in their crazed eyes. I fancied the screams of the trapped woman, caught up and tossed on the wind. The image sickened me but excited me too—in a way I am not proud of—because of its dramatic potential. The tower, which had stood for centuries, was just a shell now, burned out and crumbling, a remnant on the edge of the map. The family, once exalted, was extinct too. There, I thought, were tragedy, pathos, drama. There was social comment too— the transience of life, of worldly honours. What a story it would make!

But the Forrester plot—embodied by my tyrannical iteration of old Todd Forrester—was resilient; it was not to be relegated, indeed the more I knew of the Forrester family the more it seemed to be cast in the role of villain. In much of what Mrs Harrop had told me of the Winters, the Forresters were implicated. Some of her indictments against them were clear: Todd had bought Moss Farm, a place with no particular value except to the Winters, just to spite them. Todd had had the temerity to marry into their family, wooing—probably—first one and then the other, finally marrying a woman who was much younger—too much younger?—and above him in every way. How had Todd prevailed against all the opposition he must undoubtedly have encountered? The sheer determination of the man—his power, his persuasiveness, his potency—must have been extraordinary. Then there was something … had Mrs Harrop implied it? Or was I adding a twist that did not exist? She blamed the Forresters for a great deal, but did she add to that tally the death of her grandmother?

And then, last of all, a niggling but exciting possibility I hardly dared consider, especially since Mrs Harrop had been so kind. It would be an indictment, a slur, it might be a hundred miles wide of the truth. But Mrs Harrop had made no mention of her mother—Rowan's child.

What if …? What if …?

The Trysting Tree
1924

Rowan Winter's favourite place was the big silver birch tree that stood on the Moss. Todd Forrester took her there when they were children, in the days, during her evacuation from the London blitz, when he was tasked with her care. In those days the Moss was not a safe place to play and it was unlikely, without Todd, that she would ever have found the tree on her own. The peat workings were sheer and deep, and often filled with water. After rain, the whole ground could be a quagmire of sink holes and bog. Brakes of thorn and gorse were liable to shred a young lady's petticoats, not to mention her skin, and an unwary ankle could easily be turned by the clinging tufts of heather and myrtle. The tenants of Moss Farm kept cattle on the Moss that were mostly wild and could be unpredictable, especially when they had calved. If consulted, Sir Hector would probably have opined that it was an area to which Todd should avoid taking his charge. But he was not consulted, and Rowan did not enlighten him as to the exact parameters of their playground.

In spite—perhaps *because* of—its dangers, Rowan liked the tree on the Moss better than the beach and the dunes and often begged to be taken there. She liked to sit on one particular bough that grew horizontally out of the main trunk about three feet from the ground and was easily wide and strong enough to accommodate them both. From this vantage point she would regale Todd with her prattle. She knew it bored and irritated him, but he did not box her ears like her governess did, or plead important business as an excuse to leave her, as her papa did. She told him of her life in London—that was over now because the Germans had bombed their house—of walks in the park and horse-riding lessons, of ballet classes and deportment tuition. Some of what she told him was true, or *had* been true—the various tutors had all been dismissed for some time, on the grounds of their expense—but some was pure fantasy. She had never, for example, danced before His Majesty. Nor had a runaway horse borne her all the way across Hyde Park until a passing Grenadier Guard managed to bring it to a halt. She told him of the animals in the zoo. Again, some were perfectly real, others—the woolly mammoth and the dappled unicorn—were projections of her imagination. She watched him carefully to see which of her lies he would swallow and which he would question, a smile of amusement on her lips when he allowed that she had played with Prince John in the gardens of Buckingham Palace. She liked Todd. Despite his rusticity and lack of information on many topics he was much better company than her governess. He had no idea what was due to a young lady of her class and so he enabled her to try things that, otherwise, she would never have been able to enjoy. She got filthy dirty, wet and scratched on their days together, but she did not mind. To her, they were glorious adventures. She found Todd to be taciturn, but rather appealing, with his white-blond hair and beautiful blue eyes. He was smaller than she, but strong and brave.

Todd disliked the necessity of taking Rowan around with him but then, when she was taken away in the wintertime or for her terms at school, he found he missed her. The time spent with her sometimes dragged, but the food served up from the kitchen of Winter Hall at the end of each day he spent with her—and the increase to his mother's income—were significant compensations. The girl confused him in ways he did not understand. She made him irritated and cross, then hot and drenched with sweat. He found himself blushing, crippled with self-consciousness one minute, urged to acts of reckless bravado the next.

On one day in the hot spell of July 1917, when both children were twelve years of age, they were sitting high in the canopy of the tree on the Moss, looking out over the intense green coverlet of bracken and enjoying the breeze on their faces. Then voices below brought Rowan's narrative to a stop.

The two children looked at each other, both aware that probably they were too high up in the tree for safety and that a reprimand might therefore be in the offing. Also—and almost as awkwardly—that unless they did something to signal their presence, they could not help but be unwilling eavesdroppers on the passers-by.

'Perhaps they will just go on their way,' Rowan said in a hushed tone.

Todd could not be so sure. The Moss, in summertime, was not readily accessible other than by people who had a pressing reason. People intent on travelling up the firth would use the beach. There were peat-cutters, but the cuttings were on the far side of the Moss. No, anyone who had come this way had come—as *they* had—on purpose, in search of privacy or solitude, or the kind of amusement—Todd was old enough to have a vague understanding—that could not be had in public.

Rowan peered down through the thick interlacing of leaves and branches. 'I can't see,' she hissed.

Todd did not need to see. He had already recognised his mother's voice—low, diffident, with a tinkling musicality it never had when his father had been at home. She was supposed to be at Winter Hall helping the housekeeper in the sewing of some new, thick curtains that would block out the draughts come winter. What was she doing *here*?

The other voice was male. It was not a village voice. It had the round vowel sounds of a southerner. The curate? Todd knew he ought not to be straining to hear. He ought to make a sound, call out, begin his descent. He did not suspect his mother and the curate—if it *was* the curate—was a trustworthy man. But any two people out alone in such a remote location would open themselves to gossip, however unfounded, and he would protect his mother from *that,* if he could. He was sure the curate would understand.

He moved his hand from where it supported his weight on an upper limb of the tree, and made as though to slide from his perch, but Rowan grabbed his arm. 'It's Papa!' she breathed into his ear. 'I can smell his cigar.'

Todd sniffed the air. Yes. He recognised it too. Now both their parents were compromised, and while Todd was sure the curate would have quite understood the necessity of intruding on their *tête-à-tête*, somehow Todd was not certain the squire would see his interference in the same light. So much had been better since Sir Hector had taken an interest in them. His mother had been happier, the farm ran more smoothly. Todd's own life—Rowan notwithstanding—was immeasurably improved. And Todd did not know for certain that Rowan had identified Ellen Forrester as Sir Hector's companion. He decided that on this count alone, much more harm might accrue by disturbing the pair—and exposing his mam—than by letting whatever was in train follow its course.

'He won't like to find us here,' Rowan whispered. 'We mustn't make a sound.'

Todd nodded, though miserably enough.

In truth they could see virtually nothing. The two adults' heads were far beneath them, and the leaves and twigs of the tree made an effective screen in both directions. That the two grownups loitered beneath the tree was evident by the fact that the fumes of the squire's cigar rose in a constant plume, and that the muted conversation—inaudible as to words—did not fade into the distance but stayed at an unvarying pitch from below where the children hid. Perhaps the squire and Ellen rested on the horizontal bough of the tree, enjoying the shade. Perhaps they sat a while on the dry leaf litter and soft moss below the tree. Gradually, as the minutes passed, their conversation tapered away, reducing itself to sighs and murmurs. At one point Todd's mother gave a little cry, and Todd wondered if she had hurt herself on a sharp thorn. The squire seemed to soothe her with crooned condolences and then he, too, barked out a sudden exclamation. Then there was the sound of rustling skirts, the pat-pat-pat of clothing being dusted down, the crack of a snapping branch—and the trysting couple passed back through the screen of the copse.

Todd looked at Rowan; confusion, doubt, the dawning kernel of shameful realisation all writ large on his features. He expected to see something similar mirrored in her face, although he hoped she would not have understood all of what had passed below them. He was not sure he understood its entirety—especially in-so-far as the involvement of his mother and the squire was concerned—but he was a country lad and he was not ignorant of country ways.

Her face, though, was not at all the same as Todd's. She was lit up, as if by a beacon—her cheeks aflame, her eyes almost wild and burning with a light Todd had never seen in them before. She passed her tongue over her dry lips. For once—for *once*—she spoke no words.

They stared at each other for a few moments. Then, in a flurry of arms and legs, she lunged at him and fixed her mouth to his. He stiffened, so startled as to be poleaxed, barely able to keep his seat on the narrow branch beneath his thighs. Her lips continued to press themselves to his. They were moist from where she had licked them; they nudged his own lips apart and then he felt her tongue—hot, soft and tasting sweetly of the apples they had shared earlier. Something moved fiercely in his groin. He gasped and pushed her away, lost his balance and fell out of the tree.

Bruises and a sprain were all the injuries that Todd sustained from his fall, but when they were faded and healed some residue of the children's awkward encounter remained between them. He found he could not quite look Rowan in the face. The sight of her brought a hectic pounding to his pulse and flushed flutterings to his torso. He began to see her not as a child to be occupied and mollified in return for a good dinner, but as a young woman who had a curiously powerful impact upon him. A dangerous impact; for whatever liberties the squire might allow himself with Todd's mother, he would certainly not look upon similar meddlings with his daughter with any kind of pleasure.

Rowan was quite aware of the effect she had on Todd. It increased her pleasure in teasing him; she liked the power she wielded over him. Often, as that hot summer wore on, would she hoik her skirts and petticoats up to above her knees to wade in the surf, or wet herself completely so that her blouse turned transparent and clung to her budding breasts. She tore the fixings from her dark, wavy hair and let it roil around her face in the ever-present sea breezes, and curl in tendrils on her bare neck. The impact on Todd of these ploys was exquisite. He would blush to the roots of his white-blond hair and turn away in an agony of confusion.

~

The summer of 1918 saw the Winters return to the pele tower, and Rowan's assault on Todd's pubescent manhood began again. She, by this time, was more woman than child, having crossed that mysterious Rubicon some few months before. An awkward explanation from her governess, augmented by more lurid details from the girls at school, meant she was fully cognisant now to what her flirtations portended. Danger, disgrace and utter degradation would attend any loss of virtue, as would deliciousness and delight beyond imagining. Rowan's attraction to anything new, the appeal of the untried and the natural recklessness of her spirit—plus the increasingly powerful urgings of her own body— drowned out the governess's dire imprecations. And who, she reasoned, in fashionable London or at Miss Marcheson's Boarding Academy, would ever hear of her experimental fumbles with a Cumberland yokel? She continued to tease and provoke poor Todd who, although her equal in age, was far behind her in maturity.

That summer the squire had provided two ponies, and so the young people's adventuring could extend far beyond the precincts of the village and the dunes. Rowan was an accomplished horsewoman. She rode astride and did not stint Todd flashes of her petticoats and underdrawers as she mounted. Todd, of course, was familiar with horses although he had no formal training in riding one. He did the best he could with his mount, hindered by the basket of foods provided for their midday meal that he must carry, plus the additional burden of parasol and blanket insisted upon by the housekeeper for Miss Winter's comfort, and the importunate erection that was, it seemed, his constant companion while Rowan was in view.

They rode up the firth and picnicked in the dunes. Rowan took her sketchbook in hand and pretended absorption in her drawing while allowing the shoulder of her blouse to slip down over one provocatively naked shoulder. They went down the coast to the fishing harbour where they viewed the boats and fed the screaming seagulls with their crusts, and Rowan licked a smear of jam from Todd's cheek with a long, lingering tongue. They rode inland, across the scrubby farmland and through plantations, up to where a tarn lay like a polished mirror in a dimple of the fell. Here, Rowan dismounted and removed her clothes to swim. Todd, appalled and transfixed, busied himself with the blanket and the food. He tried not to look at the pinkness of Rowan's body as it glided through the mercury waters, the down at the vee of her legs, the dark and puckered circles of her nipples. He ignored her calls that he should join her—ignored them in an agony of desire, crouched near the blanket, his hands across his bulging groin. The next moment he was on his feet, tearing at his shirt and trousers, kicking off his boots and running down the slope to where she skulled a little way offshore laughing at him. He waded towards her, feeling the mud between his toes, the cold grip of the waters on his skin, led on by the unanswerable primal impulse. Her hair was wet, plastered to her skull, her breasts as soft and tender as puppies, her skin cool to the touch except there, where she directed his hand. There, it was hot and slippery. She kissed him once, her mouth open, pressing her breasts against his boyish chest, and then she lay back on the surface of the tarn and opened her legs while his fingers, under her guidance, pressed and probed. Soon, she stiffened and made a whimpering noise and pushed herself beyond his reach, floating on a membrane of pleasure. He was left standing, chest-deep in the water, puckered with gooseflesh. He stroked himself until he, too, convulsed with release.

And so it went the whole summer long. What agonies of conscience each suffered after their clumsy encounters, what sense of wrongdoing and perilous consequences assailed them, still they were helpless to resist the draw of sexual imperative that found them, in glades and byways, behind haystacks and folded in the dunes, panting and enraptured in each other's arms.

~

The return of Caleb Forrester from war, and the permanent departure of the Winters back to London, was a kind of relief to Todd, removing as it did the source of his troubling addiction. Todd and Rowan moved out of each other's orbit for seven years.

By the time Todd Forrester turned nineteen, he had changed exponentially. He was as tall as he would ever be, but he was well-proportioned and he had inherited his mother's beauty of face and colouring. He was wirily strong, fleet of foot and indefatigable in energy. He did not talk much, but what he did say was generally thought worth listening to. Everyone knew he had an incendiary temper and could fight—*would* fight—at the least provocation. He was not precisely liked, but he was respected. There was a certain sympathy for him. It was well-known he had been the butt of his father's brutality—often beaten, forced to sleep in the barn, sometimes deprived of food, worked like a dog.

His mother's recent death and his father's incapacity meant that by 1924 Todd was effectively sole master of Low Farm, a considerable position for so young a man. He had stopped consulting his father as to crop rotation and a regime for drainage many years before. He worked all hours in all weathers to bring forth what he could from the unpromising land; took what he grew to market and sold it cannily. The flock of hens was larger and housed, now, in a purpose-built shed at the side of the farmhouse and Todd had a contract to supply the local branch of the co-operative. As a second benefit, he was able to sell chicken manure to farmers who were unable to source their usual fertilizers. The cultivation of willow had been reinstated, to the benefit of the land itself and to the farm's bank balance. Despite his youth and the burden of his father, Todd was making a success of his life, within the admittedly small sphere of opportunity afforded by his locale.

Between himself and his father there existed a state of tired enmity. They rarely spoke to each other, hardly acknowledged each other's existence. In the past they had fought—and that violently—the father at first inflicting horrible injury on the son, but then Todd gradually gaining the ascendant as the other grew feeble through drink, inactivity and morose introspection. The old man—he seemed old although he was not much more than fifty years of age—was incapable, now, of mounting the steep stairs to his bed and Todd had brought the cot in from the barn and placed it in the kitchen, although he was tempted to relegate his father to the barn as he, himself, had been relegated so many years before. Todd comforted himself by taking up occupation of the large bed in the marital bedchamber. Caleb spent his days and nights by the range, staring broodingly into the flames, one hand on the old Bible, the other holding a glass of spirits. Occasionally he would rouse himself and attempt to harangue Todd, brandishing now the Bible and now the liquor, as though each were weapons with which he would browbeat his son. But his toothless state, and Todd's imperviousness to his father's moods, made the exercise fruitless. Todd could not—*would* not—be moved by his father's tirades, but waited for them to burn themselves out before wearily clearing the debris of broken crockery and spilled food. He provided his father with adequate meals and clean clothes, and tended to his needs with neither tenderness nor cruelty but rather with the same disinterested efficiency with which he cleaned out the goat shed or fed the hens.

His hatred for his father was a simmering cauldron of icy ire. He despised and reviled the old man for the unhappiness and early death he had caused his mother and for the brutality he had meted out onto Todd himself. He blamed his own limited prospects on Caleb's failure to contribute to the farm. Why had he not, by charm and diligence, improved their situation? The two of them, working side-by-side, could have achieved so much! Was it Todd's lot to be forever confined to the lowly, unproductive parcel of Low Farm and lumbered with this burden? Occasionally, in the evenings, he would pause from the perusal of his accounts to throw looks of venom towards his silent, sullen father. Todd's ambition and resentment made a potent brew that scoured his innards when he thought about his lot in life. He looked around him and saw opportunity everywhere, if only he could have amassed some capital to exploit it.

There were, at that time, three farms in the village—all owned by Squire Winter, of course, but worked by tenants. Low Farm, despite Todd's improvements, was the poorest, apart from Moss Farm which was a hovel indeed, crouched on the edge of the marsh, subject to clouds of mosquitoes and gnats in the summer and isolated from the village by water for many of the winter months. Its acres were worse even than the boggy paddocks of Todd's place. Its few cattle were thin from lack of proper grazing and often injured by falling in the dikes. A small flock of fly-blown sheep fared little better; they suffered from dreadful foot-rot and frequently aborted their lambs.

The third farm was Roadend farm, which had recently incorporated the acreages of two smallholdings whose tenants had abandoned the thankless task of farming them. Roadend Farm occupied a central and slightly elevated position in the village that gave it a decided air of superiority over its lower-lying neighbours. It had a good quantity of comparatively fertile fields stretching up the slight slope behind the farmhouse and to the left and right, behind the cottages of the herring fishermen and the ship-breakers to one side, and the church and schoolhouse to the other. They were better drained than any other fields and both crops and livestock did well. There were plantations of softwood which had been planted at the end of the previous century and would soon be ready to harvest. The farmhouse was excellent—stone-built in the Georgian style—and the ancillary sheds, barns and milking parlour were all in good repair. It was Todd's ambition to take over the tenancy of Roadend farm, although he did not know how he would do it since farmer Axby had been in possession for as long as anyone could remember, was a good manager and prompt in his payment of rent. But Axby had no sons; his boys had been killed on the Somme. He had a daughter, and a marriageable one, but she was a tall, angular girl, ill-favoured, and Todd did not think he could bring himself to woo her even if it might allow him, in time, to replace Mr Axby as the leaseholder of the farm.

Todd husbanded his resources as efficiently as possible, and although his work was as much as he could manage—often more—he made time to assist Mr Axby when he could as a means of learning the lay of the land. He did so without any absolute plan in view, but with the idea that, at some time in the future, it would be useful to claim knowledge of the farm.

In the summer of 1924, the squire and Rowan returned to Roadend. That they were due was no surprise—the previous week their housekeeper and a retinue of servants, plus a string of horses had arrived. Room had been secured at the inn for a gentleman who was to be Sir Hector's guest—accommodations at the tower being insufficient to house the entire party—and indeed the quantity of servants was so numerous that the most unfortunate amongst them had been billeted at Moss Farm. Village women had been employed to clean out the dusty and neglected rooms of Winter Hall, provisions had been purchased from growers, groundsmen tasked with taming the bare and rugged grass of Winter Hill to something approaching a garden. Much, it was apprehended, was expected of the squire's visit to his demesne and the appetite to partake of his bounty—after such a long absence—was considerable. Todd himself was eager to make a favourable impression on his landlord, particularly because Farmer Axby had lately been unwell and Todd could see the chink of an opportunity of which he might avail himself.

The squire was a little greyer, his sideburns shaved away to be replaced by a luxuriant moustache, but still, in his early forties, a good looking fellow. Despite appearances to the contrary, his financial circumstances were not much improved and he had been forced to take up employment in a governmental department as an advisor. However, he had a plan in view—schemes afoot—in pursuance of which he had made meticulous preparations for his trip to the country. Everything must go well. An impression must be made. He sent ahead a large and impressive entourage with exhaustive instructions. The party that he was to bring to the pele tower included his daughter, now nineteen years of age and, lately, a successful entrant into the maelstrom of London Society, and a pair of relatively new acquaintances, Captain Frederick Broughton-Moore and the captain's sister Evangeline. These latter two, it may be surmised, constituted the receptacle in which the squire's hopes rested.

The party travelled up in Captain Broughton-Moore's Velox Tourer and arrived in the village one sunny afternoon in July.

Todd, in shirtsleeves and braces, mucking out the goats, watched them pass his farm gate with astonishment—motorcars were rarely seen so far away from Carlisle. He recognised the sartorial form of the squire immediately, but he had to look and look again before he recognised the fashionable young lady at his side as Rowan. She had lost all her youthful plumpness and now had the boyish thinness of figure *à la mode* for girls of her era. Her face had lost its girlishness. It had an elfin quality, with a small chin and a pert nose, but her mouth was wide and her eyes bright and alight with the same mischievous fire. Her hair—cut short, into the style of the day—was as unruly as ever, refusing to sit in the sleek, glossy cap required of it. It blew around her hatless head as the car negotiated the pitted surface of the lane. He could hear her laughter even above the stuttering percussions of the engine. At the last possible moment, she turned her head in his direction. He felt her frank appraisal although he could not tell what, for her part, she made of his well-sculpted form and sun-burned, dirt-streaked face. Her expression was proud, detached, even haughty, but her eyes could not quite meet his, and he thought he saw the bloom of a blush creep up her skin from the low neckline of her dress.

Then they were past, and Todd was left with the fumes of the car's engine and the dust of the road as it blew into his eyes. For the rest of the day, he attended to his work, collecting and sorting eggs for transportation to the markets in nearby towns, weighing the piglets to see which were ready for slaughter, and tending the vegetable garden. In the later afternoon he walked along the lane to Roadend farm to aid farmer Axby with the milking, then drive the cows back to their grazing in the top field when the job was done.

He walked back along the shingle. The tide was in and the sea, for once, was blue and inviting with barely a ripple of wave. The sun was still high in the summer sky. On an impulse he stripped down to his under garments and dived in at a place where the beach shelved steeply, swimming out with strong strokes until the herring women were indistinct figures as they cleared away their tackle for the day. He lay on his back for a while, sculling with his hands, watching high clouds as they crossed the wedge of blue between the Cumberland coast and the Scottish peninsular across the firth. Then he struck out back towards the shore. He lay on the warm stones of the beach while he dried, and allowed his eyes to travel to Winter Hill and the pele tower. He could see the motorcar parked on the turf in front of the tower, the sun glaring off its bonnet and windscreen. An awning had been erected to the seaward side of the tower. He could see movement beneath its canopy but he was too far away to make out individuals. He imagined the squire and Rowan and their friends taking tea from china cups, and eating dainty sandwiches. The thought of it made his mouth water. He had not eaten since breakfast; he was hungry. He drew his breeches back over his legs, but gathered up his soiled shirt in his hands and walked back to Low Farm.

The sun would not set until almost ten o'clock so far west and north. From nine, the air began to cool, and often the wind changed, bringing cooling breezes from off the sea. Todd sluiced himself beneath the pump and put on a clean shirt before assisting his father into his cot. He checked that the hen houses and the barn were locked, and then set off.

His route took him along the village street, past the inn and the church and up the hill towards the pele tower. As he climbed, the view of the sunset sky opened up before him—purple striations of cloud like bolts of exotic silks laid out for sale. The copper penny sun hung over the land on the far side of the firth, as though poised to drop into a slot cut into the summit of Criffle. The pele tower threw an elongated shadow over the grassy top of the knoll, and strains of music came to him from a gramophone machine. He turned to the right, crossed through an area of longer grass and vaulted over a gate, taking the track down towards Moss Farm.

The grass of the Moss was like tinder. Dehydrated sphagnum crackled beneath his boots. He pushed through the bracken, his arms over his head to avoid ticks attaching themselves to his skin.

The tree was in shadow, the sunset blocked out by the hill that rose up between the Moss and the coast. Its silver branches had a strange luminance of their own, though, and he had no difficulty navigating his way through the encircling screen of willow and elder to the still heart of the glade. The evening was windless—a rarity—and a deeper level of quietude shimmered amongst the saplings so Todd almost felt as though he was under a spell. He perched on the horizontal branch of the tree–smiling to himself, because once he had had to scramble and hoist himself on to it—and set himself to wait.

An early owl flew low over the marsh, calling to its mate, and in the east a silver moon rose into the pearly sky.

He felt her before he saw her—the slight flex of the bough beneath his thighs, the shiver of leaves above his head in spite of the utter calm of the night. He remained still for a few moments, as though he had felt nothing, as though he still waited. He could feel her impatience mounting, a pulsing vein through the fibre of the tree. He knew she was stifling laughter. If he honed his ears he could hear her breath, muffled by a hand clapped over her mouth. Leisurely, he removed a packet of cigarettes from his pocket and took his time about lighting one, lifting his head to blow the smoke up through the canopy of the tree, but keeping his eyes down. It would madden her, he knew, that her trick had backfired. Now *she* was the one who was kept waiting.

At last he said, 'Are you going to come down?'

The tree above him shook, and her hoot of amused frustration erupted. 'Oh!' she cried out, 'I thought you'd never cotton on.'

Then he looked up into the branches of the tree, squinting past their tracery, the glow of their bark in the moonlight making a miasma that dazzled his night vision. He heard the scrape of her shoe on the bark, and a little rending noise that might have been the fabric of her clothes catching on a twig. The tree trembled and she emerged from it, like a dryad, dropping lightly onto her feet on the bough beside him.

'I knew you'd come,' she said, lowering herself until she was sitting beside him.

He did not turn his head to look at her but inspected the tip of his cigarette with casual interest. 'I knew *you* would,' he returned levelly—much more levelly than he felt. His hands were sweating. A pulse throbbed in his throat, and he felt the old ache of his desire for her in the pit of his stomach. He was suddenly very conscious of his flat vowels, the narrowness of his world. Her accent was like a shard of glass in comparison and he could not even begin to imagine the life she led in London. He inhaled, and she smelled of roses and something astringent he could not name.

'It wasn't easy to get away,' she said. 'The others are having dinner. I excused myself on the pretext of a headache.'

'Dinner? It's late for dinner.'

She gave him a nudge. 'What you call dinner, we call luncheon,' she said, but not unkindly.

He shrugged. 'It's been a long time,' he said.

'Seven years,' she agreed. 'A lot has happened.'

'Not here,' he said. 'My mam died, that's all.'

'Oh,' she said. Her hand travelled from where it had lain in her lap and took his. He winced, that she would feel its dampness; *her* hand was cool and dry. But he didn't refuse her gesture. Still, they did not look at each other. 'I'm sorry.'

He didn't reply, because his throat was suddenly thick with grief and he knew that if he spoke his words would come out as a sob. He swallowed, choking down his sadness.

She said, 'Have you got a spare cigarette?'

He had to let go of her hand to fumble one from the packet for her, and when he struck the match his hand shook. He could not help but turn to her then, to hold the flame to the end of her cigarette. They looked at each other through the flickering tongue of light, their faces inches from each other. Her eyes were dark wells made fathomless by an application of smoky makeup and thickly blackened eyelashes. He realised her whole face was painted—powder, rouge and a gash of red lipstick. The match went out but he continued to look at her, seeing both the impossible image of the fashionable debutante that had burned itself onto his retinas and also, in his mind's eye, the softly delicious girl he had known before, his old playmate, the brave, impish, teasing vixen. He loved her. He had always loved her. The hectic exasperation he had felt about her as a child had been love, but he had been too young and stupid to recognise it.

Slowly he raised his hand to her face and, with his thumb, smeared away the greasy coating from her mouth. Then he leaned towards her and kissed her.

She didn't respond at first, and he could almost hear the debate in her head as she balanced her duty with her desire. Then she sighed and melted into him.

It had not been quite true of Todd to say that nothing had changed for him in the seven years that had passed since their last encounter. It is not to be supposed that a boy's raw and fumbling inexperience with sex will stay with him into manhood, and Todd had learned enough to acquit himself with considerable expertise. At the end of half an hour Rowan was limp and trembling, a satiated soup of requited desire, and Todd's back was raw with the raking of her nails.

He sat with his back against the trunk of the tree, cradling her in his arms as she recovered. 'Tomorrow,' he said, 'I'll come up to the hall and speak to the squire.'

She shifted fractionally. 'What about?'

He laughed. 'About us, of course. We must be married.'

It was her turn to laugh. 'We cannot be married, Todd,' she said languidly.

He frowned and pulled her round so he could look into her face. 'Why not?'

'Because ...' she shook her head in bewilderment, as though he had suggested something impossible—almost ludicrous. But his serious expression sobered her. She lifted her hand to his cheek. 'We just can't,' she said.

He pushed her away from him and got to his feet, reaching for his cigarettes. 'Don't you love me?' he said.

'Oh Todd, if it were only about love ...' She began to smooth her hair, picking leaves out of her curls.

'What else?'

She heaved a sigh. 'So many things. You wouldn't understand.'

'I'm not stupid,' he barked out. 'Tell me why we can't get married?'

'Well,' she began, 'where would we live?'

'At Roadend Farm,' he said promptly. 'Axby's on his last legs. I'm going to ask your father to transfer the tenancy to me. It's a fine house, Rowan, with two parlours ...'

Rowan looked down at her delicate, white hands. 'I don't think I'd be a very good farmer's wife,' she said.

'In London, then,' Todd threw back. 'I can set my hand to most things ...'

'What about your father?'

'Well ...' this gave Todd pause. He ground his cigarette under his foot. 'It couldn't be straight away, I suppose,' he admitted. 'But, all the more time for me to ...' he bit back the words *better myself,* '... to get things settled. I could look after you, Rowan. I know I could. And I love you.'

He went back to where she still sat beneath the silver birch tree, and knelt beside her. 'I've always loved you. And I know that you love me. Nothing else matters, lass. Didn't we just *prove* ...' He gestured towards the soft, dry, leafy ground, where only a few moments before their bodies had been joined. 'You can't deny *that.'*

He took her face between his hands. The moonlight showed him the pooling of tears on her lashes. One of them spilled over and ran down her cheek, ploughing a furrow through the powder and rouge that was already ravaged from their lovemaking.

'You don't understand,' she gasped out.

'Then *tell* me.'

She pressed her lips together, as though to seal in the explanation. He kissed them gently open again.

'*Tell* me,' he said again.

'I'm engaged to someone else,' she said in a rush. 'To Captain Broughton-Moore. We're to be married next spring. And Papa is to marry Evangeline. She's ten years older than Frederick, but still young enough to produce a son, and Papa *so* wishes for an heir.'

He sat back on his heels, astonished. 'What?'

She nodded mutely.

'But ...' he gestured again to the ground, '... how could you?'

'Oh Todd,' she sobbed. 'I don't love him. He's nice enough, and quite funny. I mean, he isn't *awful* ... but he's rich, Todd, and Papa's broke.'

'Broke?' Todd gazed around him, not at what he could see with his eyes but at what he could see with his mind—the Moss, Moss Farm and all the rest of the squire's property—the mill, the farms and cottages—the trees and fields, the fishing rights—*all* of them generating rents and profits to pour into the squire's coffers. 'He can't be,' he said. 'It just isn't possible.'

'It *is*. You just don't understand,' Rowan said. 'He's been forced to work. He's been advising on some bill or other; the transfer of freeholds by payment of a fee simple.[2] So terribly plebian, for a man like Papa. Can you imagine? Too, too trying.'

Todd only half understood her. Whatever it was, it didn't sound much like "work" to him. He had no sympathy for the squire. 'Let the squire marry then, if he likes it,' he said. '*You* don't have to.'

Rowan got to her feet and began to repair her clothing. 'I *do*, for the money. Evangeline hasn't much, and if I break things off with Frederick, Evangeline will back out of marrying Papa.'

The chimes of the church clock came to them through the thin night air, tolling the half hour.

'It can't be half past eleven! Oh dear. I'm in the soup. I must dash. Look, Todd, I *can't* explain it properly. You wouldn't understand.'

She was on the point of slipping away, but he caught her arm. 'Stop telling me I don't understand,' he said fiercely.

'Ow! You're hurting me,' cried Rowan, trying to free herself.

Todd tightened his grip. 'I'll be up at the hall tomorrow, to speak to the squire,' he said through gritted teeth.

He could see her stricken expression in the moonlight, 'No,' she croaked. 'Don't do that. Let's … let's meet again tomorrow … no, not tomorrow, we're going to Lord Flimby's tomorrow … the next night. Yes. Let's meet here the day after tomorrow and we can talk it over again.'

---

[2] Law of Property Act, 1925

Todd narrowed one eye, but he released his grip enough for her to be able to slip free. 'You'll think about it, then?'

'Yes, yes,' she said, too quickly. 'I'll have a think and see what can be done. But I *must* go now, Todd. Let me get away and past the farm, before you leave. Kells is staying at Moss Farm. He's Papa's valet. If he sees me, he'll tell ...'

Todd saw the look of panic in her eyes, and his heart sank. 'All right,' he said mulishly, turning away. 'I'll keep your secret, for now.'

Rowan did not keep her appointment with Todd. Every evening for a week he went to the tree on the Moss and waited, his anger rising higher, his resentment burning hotter with every hour that she did not appear. He saw her during the day, riding along the lane with her fiancé, driving in the motorcar, and once on the beach with the other young lady, bathing in figure-hugging swimsuits while the gentlemen lounged on deck chairs beneath parasols. Todd stood at a distance and glowered, willing her to look up and see him, but she kept her glance resolutely away from his surly, scowling figure. She seemed happy—he had to admit that—laughing uproariously at some quip of the squire's, smiling up at the captain, linking the arm of the woman who would be her step-mama. She was always dressed beautifully. They all were; the captain often in uniform—an unnecessary affectation—and Todd could not help but compare his own rough working clothes and shabby boots with their linen and leather. The men were close-shaven and pomaded, cool even on the hottest day, while he was grimed with filth and smelled—no doubt—of goat and pig and human sweat. Far from establishing in his mind the utter impossibility of a union between them, the discrepancy in their lives made Todd's desire for it even more fervent. His resentment—that class and education should stand between them—was caustic in his belly. His poverty and disadvantage ate him alive, and his spite invented schemes whereby he could get what he wanted.

One day he saw her alone, waiting outside the inn while the captain had gone inside to fetch something. She sat on the low wall, her hat in her hands, allowing the breeze to disarrange her hair. Todd was on his way to Roadend Farm, where the pastures required topping.

He addressed her angrily, all his disappointment apparent on his features, careless of who might see or hear. 'I've been at the tree every night,' he spat out. 'Where have you been?'

She glanced anxiously around. 'Good afternoon, Mr Forrester,' she shrilled in a high, artificial voice. 'How are you today?'

'I'm steaming mad,' re-joined Todd, not troubling to lower his voice. 'I'm being made a fool of, and I don't take kindly to it, *Miss Winter.*'

'*Stop it,*' Rowan hissed out. 'Someone will hear.'

'I don't care. You said you'd come. You said you'd work things out. I've waited, but my patience is waning.'

'*Please,*' Rowan begged, mashing her bonnet in her hands. 'I *will* come, tonight. I *promise,* only *please* leave me alone now. Frederick will be back any moment.'

He could see tears were near, and his anger melted a little. He took a step back and made a show of tipping his hat. 'Tonight? You promise? If not Rowan, I'll have to take matters into my own hands. You do see that, don't you? For both our sakes.' He did not say it with much idea of making a threat, only of making clear to her that if she could not mend their situation, he would do so. That she took his words as a threat, though, was evident from the light of panic in her eyes.

'What do you mean?' she croaked out, her mouth a maw of horror. 'What do you *mean,* Todd?'

He leaned a little closer. 'I mean that I promised I'd look after you, and I will. That's all.' He extended a finger and pushed aside the lace of her blouse, so that the faint bruise of the love bite he had given her on the top of her breast could be seen. 'How did you explain *that?*' he asked, roguishly.

She slapped his hand away. He saw movement at the door of the inn, and Captain Broughton-Moore emerged into the sunshine, fixing his hat to his head. Todd raised his finger to his hat again. 'Good day, Miss,' he said, and went on his way.

She did not come to the tree that night. Todd waited in an agony of hope and gall, pacing around the tree and scuffing at the leaf litter with the toe of his boot. At last he abandoned his vigil, and marched up to Winter Hall. He did not care who saw him. He almost hoped a member of staff would step out of the night to challenge him. He would relish the opportunity to blacken an eye or thicken the lip of any limp-wristed footman who might decide to stand in his way. Better, he would like to reduce the captain's face to pulp. He clenched his fists as he walked, stoking his ire. But he arrived at Winter Hall unchallenged.

There was no moon that night—a slew of stars across the inky firmament provided the only natural light—but torches burned around the awning beside the pele tower making a scene as bright as a circus ring. Todd stood in the shadows, outside the halo of light, and watched the squire and his guests as they enjoyed the cool evening air. Something, at the last minute, held him back. The gentlemen wore dinner suits. The ladies shimmered in fringed evening dresses, their jewels glinting like ice at their throats. There were numerous bottles and a cocktail shaker on a table, and crystal glasses containing drinks of various lurid hues. A gramophone played dance music. Presently the captain put his hand out to Rowan and they began to dance. Todd shuddered as she placed herself in the captain's arms. Her dress was almost backless and Todd watched, appalled, as the captain allowed his hand to slip further down the skin of Rowan's naked back until it rested on the slight curve of her buttocks. He saw the middle finger curl, surreptitiously stroking that sensitive place just below the base of her spine.

Todd could stand it no longer. He marched into the light, knocking the needle from the gramophone record so that it made a screech like an injured dog. The sudden silence was shocking. The two dancers sprang apart. Rowan's hand flew to her mouth, her eyes wide with terror. Todd squared up, his hands in fists, his breathing quick and ragged. The squire half rose from his seat. The other lady clutched her diamonds.

'What's this?' the squire enquired, looking angrily at Todd. 'Forrester, isn't it? What's amiss?'

Todd didn't reply but remained beneath the awning. He felt his clownish state amongst all the paraphernalia of gentrified entertainment, but kept his eyes fixed on the captain.

'Forrester!' the squire barked out again.

It shocked Todd from the pinnacle of his spleen. He turned, slowly, to face Sir Hector. 'Excuse me, sir,' he said, suddenly seized with alarm at his own impulsiveness and yet very determined to make good on it. He threw a covert look at Rowan, waiting, giving her the opportunity. Would she speak? Would she step forward and stand by him, and confront her father with the facts? No. She took a step backwards, taking herself out of the light. From this obscurity she shook her head slowly and mouthed the word *No*.

Todd sighed and turned back to the squire. 'Excuse me, sir,' he said again, moderating his accent as much as he could but hating himself for it. 'Excuse the intrusion, squire. I wanted to ask you, sir ...' he hesitated. Behind him he heard the smallest possible sound, a stifled whimper of dismay. He took a breath. He would make her this one, last concession. '... If you could spare me a few moments tomorrow to discuss some ... business. At your convenience, sir. It may be,' he went on with heavy significance directed, not at the squire, but at Rowan, 'that by the time we see each other, you will have been informed ... but if not, sir, I will apprise,' he dragged the word from some repository of his memory, 'you fully.'

'The squire gave an irritated smile. 'Of course. I will call on you tomorrow morning. But really, Forrester, *this* was neither the time nor the ...'

'I know that sir,' said Todd. 'I know that. I was forced to it. Goodnight, sir.' He turned to the others. 'Good night, ladies and gentlemen.'

~

Todd did not sleep much that night. The air was stiflingly hot, and increasingly charged with electricity. A storm was brewing. In the morning he fed and watered the stock early, and did his best to tidy the kitchen, hurrying his father through his ablutions and into his clothes, spooning porridge down him at pace.

'The squire is coming, Father,' he explained as he settled the old man in a chair in the yard. 'You're to stay here, and leave things to me. Do you hear me?'

Caleb swivelled a wrathful eye at him, but made no objection. Todd placed his Bible and a glass of ale on a rickety old table and walked away. He needed to decide what he would do—what he would say—to Sir Hector. Much depended on whether Rowan had taken the opportunity he had made for her, and taken her father into their confidence. If she had been brave enough to do that, he would meet her courage ounce for ounce. If she had not …

By the time the squire arrived the sky was purple with impending rain, and a warm wind winnowed straw and dust from the yard and swirled it into little dust-devils. The old man slumped in his chair, half asleep, and did not acknowledge the squire's greeting as he passed. Sir Hector stepped into the kitchen and if he recalled his first visit there, and the lady who had amused him for a few weeks during those last summers of the war, he made no mention of it now.

He laid his hat on the kitchen table. 'You wished to speak to me, Forrester?'

Todd watched him carefully for signs of discomposure, for any clue that he had been informed already of the nature of Todd's request. But the squire's gaze was frank and level, empty of sub-text except perhaps a slight annoyance for the interruption of the evening before.

'Yes sir. You have no idea of why I have asked to speak to you?'

'None at all. I am at a loss. I must say your manner last night has not inclined me to be indulgent, though.'

'I see.' Todd wetted his lips. He knew what he must do.

'My request is about Roadend Farm. I wish to take over the tenancy. Axby is failing. I already do more than half the work. If I did not, I do not think he could manage the place. Without me, he would fall behind with his rent, and the land would suffer.'

'I see.' Sir Hector stroked his moustache. 'You already do half the work, you say? Why does not Farmer Axby simply pay you for your labour? Then you would not be out of pocket.'

'You mistake my intention, squire. I help Axby in kindness, as a neighbour. But I am ambitious, sir. I wish to improve myself. I am more than equal to running Roadend. Soon, you will need a new tenant. I wish that tenant to be me.'

Sir Hector appeared to consider. 'I do not think so, Forrester,' he said at length. 'Roadend is a valuable property, by far the best farm I own. I'd need an experienced tenant in there. A man with a wife and sons, to help him run the place. You're a single man. I've no doubt you're capable …'

'I'm *more* than capable, sir,' Todd interrupted him. 'And, as to a wife, I have a lady in view.'

'Do you? Capital. I wish you joy. I myself am to remarry. You may have heard? But as to Roadend … no. I do not think I can accommodate you.' Sir Hector looked around the kitchen—mean enough—and by extension the whole waterlogged and unpromising farm. 'You've done pretty well here, Forrester, but Low Farm is a challenging prospect. I would not find another tenant who is willing to put in the labour that you do. Perhaps we might make a small accommodation on the rent, if that would assist you. But, as to Roadend …'

'You mistake me again sir, with respect. I do not wish to relinquish Low Farm. I shall run *both* farms.'

'I doubt that,' said the squire. 'You have your father to care for, and, as I say …'

'You underestimate me. I assure you I am quite capable, more than capable.'

The squire shook his head and picked up his hat from where he had placed it on the table. He had decided the interview was over. 'I admire your pluck, Forrester, I really do. But I cannot assign the tenancy to you. Where would Axby live, for a start? I cannot absolutely put him out.'

'Here. We will swap farmsteads. He will be as comfortable—more comfortable—here than he is at present. He and his daughter in that great house. It is wasted on them. I shall soon have a wife …'

'No, Forrester,' said Sir Hector firmly. 'My answer is no. I wish you good day.'

He placed his hat back on his head and turned his heel, but Todd said, 'In that case sir, you leave me no choice. I *will* have Roadend farm.'

The squire half-laughed. 'You *will* have it? What affrontery! I don't think so.'

'You will change your mind when you hear what I have to say.' Todd fixed the squire with a steely gaze and called to mind the liberties the man had taken with his mother, the risks he had caused her to take. He summoned all the iron of his determination, the dreams that had made the years of drudgery bearable and, most of all, the bitter, bitter disappointment of his love for Rowan.

The squire raised an enquiring eyebrow. 'How so?'

'My belief is that much rests on your forthcoming marriage to the young lady who is just now your guest. But much *more* depends on the marriage of your daughter to Captain Broughton-Moore.'

The squire stiffened. 'What do you know about that?'

'More than you may think. It is true, though, isn't it?'

Sir Hector's silence affirmed it.

Todd took hold of a chairback and gripped it tightly. What he was about to say would end for ever any chance of happiness with Rowan. It would be a terrible betrayal, but hadn't *she* betrayed *him* already?

He opened his mouth. 'I wonder,' he said, addressing a ceiling beam, 'whether the captain knows—as *I* do—that Miss Winter has a mole on her left breast. It is the shape of a sickle moon and the colour of a rabbit's ear.'

The squire blanched. 'What do you know of that?' he rasped out.

'Oh, I know it very well sir. I *have* done since we were thirteen years of age.'

'What?' the squire roared out suddenly, seizing his riding crop and advancing towards Todd with it raised high in the air.

Todd stood his ground. 'You can beat me, sir. I have been regularly beaten since I was a child and I can bear it. I shall not retaliate. But I will make sure the captain knows that his betrothed has been trounced countless times by a rustic with calloused hands and dirt beneath his nails. I think then he will be less inclined for the match, don't you?'

The squire towered over Todd, his arm trembling where it held the crop, his face suffused with blood. 'You blackguard,' he cried. 'You filthy, worthless …'

'I am all these things,' said Todd, with icy calm, 'although Miss Winter was by no means an unwilling participant. If I tell the truth, she was the instigator of our romps.'

'Stop it,' the squire cried out. His anger had evaporated. He slumped down onto a nearby chair and put his head in his hands. 'I'm ruined,' he said, brokenly.

Todd looked on with a coldly calculating eye. Any guilt he felt at Rowan's ruination was eclipsed by his sense of icy triumph. Here, he had the squire beneath his heel. He could have eased the squire's distress by mentioning Rowan's willingness to sacrifice herself to the captain for his—the squire's—sake, that there might be an heir for the Winters. He could have informed Sir Hector of the sacrifice he—Todd—was making; the marital hopes that were now at an end. But he was not minded to mitigate to any degree the squire's misery, or to loosen the hold he now had on his landlord's throat. Indeed, the scope of his ambition enlarged. Suddenly the mere tenancy was not sufficient. He wanted more. He was *owed* more.

'No,' he said softly, bending to speak into the squire's ear. 'Not at all, sir. When I am the freeholder of Roadend Farm *and* of Low Farm, no one will ever hear a whisper of it from me.'

Sir Hector raised his head. 'The freeholder?'

Todd nodded. 'I believe that is to be possible, by the payment of a fee simple. There's a new bill to be passed …'

'Do not speak to *me* of the new bill,' Sir Hector spat out. 'It has been my bedfellow these many months. Boredom beyond describing, I do assure you.'

Todd gave the knife a little twist. 'My mother was not a boring bedfellow, was she?'

Neither of them had seen, at the door, the stooped figure of Caleb Forrester, who had brought himself in out of the rain that had begun to fall, like needles from the sky. Some filament of understanding penetrated his mind as his son spoke and he launched himself from the door frame and veered across the kitchen towards the squire.

The squire cowered in his seat, covering his head with his arms.

Todd gave a snort of derision and intercepted his father's trajectory with easy practice. 'Sit down, old man,' he said, pressing his father into his usual chair by the fireplace. 'I have had our revenge upon him. What does the Good Book say? "An eye for an eye"? Well, I have blinded him, and no mistake.'

Caleb mumbled some riposte while Todd busied himself with the kettle and the teapot. Sir Hector remained a broken man, lost in his misery.

Presently, Todd placed an old, chipped mug of tea before the squire. 'Have you considered?' he asked.

Sir Hector nodded miserably. 'It cannot be until spring,' he groaned out. 'The bill will not be enacted until then.'

'That will suit nicely,' said Todd. 'So long as it is *before* the nuptial day, your secrets will be safe. Can that be arranged?'

The squire nodded.

The fine weather came to an end in a summer storm that tore the awning at the tower from its restraints and sent it flapping across the firth. The squire's picnicking was done, and before many days were over the whole party decamped from Winter Hall and drove away.

Before three months were over it became imperative to Rowan that her marriage to Captain Broughton-Moore should be brought forward, and they were wed in a quiet, private ceremony in the chapel of his Sussex estate. The squire and Evangeline Broughton-Moore waited until May of 1925 for their own, much more ostentatious ceremony, by which time Todd Forrester had paid his fee simple, and was the owner of both Roadend and Low farms. By this time also, Mrs Broughton-Moore had given birth to a blonde-haired, blue-eyed daughter. She did so rather earlier than might have been calculated upon, but since the event occurred on a steamship bound for Calcutta where her husband was to serve in his professional military capacity, its untimeliness was overlooked.

Lady Winter also produced a daughter, Rose, in the early months of 1926. Mother and daughter were both feared for, the labour having been protracted and rather complex. In the mother's case, the fears proved founded: she died before the first daffodil bloomed. The child, however, after initial difficulties, thrived.

The squire despaired. There would be no heir for the Winters.

Chapter Twenty-One

By the time I had walked the length of the beach, I had the whole narrative of Todd and Rowan mapped out in my mind. I had lost myself in the contemplation of it and had little recollection of my walk along the dark grey shingle. When I came back to myself, I realised I was freezing, chilled to the bone. I hurried the last few yards to the pub.

The pub's lights had only just flickered on when I pushed at the door and found it mercifully unlocked. Bill was busy in the bar, poking life into the fire and drawing the curtains.

'Oh! You're an early bird,' he said as I peeled off my coat and hung it on the peg.

I rubbed my hands. 'I'm ashamed to say I've been walking for over an hour, waiting for you to open up,' I said. 'I don't know why, but I just assumed you'd open at five.'

'Hardly worth opening at all, some nights, at this time of year,' he replied, shovelling ice into an ice bucket. 'G & T, is it?'

I shook my head. 'I need something more warming. Could you make me a hot toddy?'

His face betrayed the briefest possible expression of annoyance—at the wasted ice, I suppose—before *mine host* stepped back into role. 'Sure,' he said. 'Coming right up. Will you be wanting a meal?'

'Yes, please.'

I settled myself in a seat by the fire, Bob at my feet. The lights were dim; only half of the several branched fittings had been switched on. I didn't mind. After the onslaught of the wind and tide on the beach, and my fevered thoughts, it was soothing to sit in the half-dark and soak up the warmth.

211

Bill brought my drink over together with a menu. 'I'll be with you in a few minutes,' he said.

I heard the soft close of a door somewhere behind the bar, then the tread of feet across the floorboards of the room above. There was a muted conference. I couldn't hear the words but the cadence of the voices was quite enough for me to be able to gather their sense.

'There's a customer wants a meal.'

'Oh no! Really? On a Monday? I've just put my feet up.'

'It can't be helped. We should be grateful.'

'Can't you do it?'

'No. I have to mind the bar. Come on. You need to get the fryer on. She's sure to want chips.'

'Oh, all right then. But really, Bill, what a pain …'

I scanned the menu. He was right, I *did* want chips. In fact, I was ravenous. I chose a starter and a main course and ran my eye over the puddings too. The hot toddy warmed my cockles and my feet began to thaw, so that when Bill came to take my order and later Julie appeared— hastily coiffed and with a brisk smear of lipstick to mitigate her sour expression—I was able to smile benignly.

I ate my deep-fried camembert wedges while Bill stocked up the fridge with bottled beers and soft drinks. From time to time, I looked over at the spot at the bar where I had stood with Hugh, conjuring in my mind the image of his broad shoulders in their cream Aran jersey, the reddish highlights in his softly curling hair. He had been so tall he had to duck to avoid hitting his head on the beams. I remembered the humorous light in his eyes. What colour had *they* been? I couldn't recall.

I walked across to the exact same spot to touch his ghost and order myself another drink, but the place held no vestige of him. I went back to my seat wondering if I had imagined the whole encounter.

Presently the door opened and the old chap I had been introduced to at the bonfire came in. Arnold, I recalled. He unwound a long scarf from around his neck, removed his tweed cap and shrugged off a thick coat. Underneath he was nattily dressed in twill trousers and a shirt and tie, topped with a hand-knitted cardigan; the work, no doubt, of his late wife. Bill reached down a tankard, one of a dozen or so hanging on a row of hooks above the bar, filled it with beer and placed it on the bar without Arnold having to speak a word. Only when he had pushed the exact change across the bar and drunk the foaming top did Arnold say, 'Evening, Landlord. Cold front coming in,' before shuffling across to the seat on the opposite side of the fire from me.

'Hello Arnold,' I said. 'I'm Dee. We met at the bonfire.'

'Aye,' said Arnold. 'Nice to see you again.' He drew a folded newspaper out from underneath his cardigan, opened it and began to read, indicating further conversation would not be required.

I wished I had brought a book. Ordinarily I might have scanned my phone, but of course I didn't have one. I cast about me and found a stack of what turned out to be old parish newsletters on the window ledge behind me. I shuffled through them, reading accounts of fund-raising bazaars, meetings of the parochial parish council, a plan to replace the church hassocks that seemed to have raised a storm of protest. There were rotas for flower arranging, for tea making, for visiting the elderly and sick. The newsletters seemed to be issued quarterly, and this collection went back three or so years. I wondered if anyone—the parish clerk, perhaps—kept a file of back copies, and how *far* back they might go. As far as 1962, the year of the fire? Further?

When Julie came to remove my plate, I said as casually as I could, 'Has Hugh been in recently?'

'Oh no,' she said with a sigh, opening the log burner to throw another log inside. 'He's gone away. His father isn't well. Didn't you hear?'

Well, that explained things, I thought. 'No,' I told her. 'I don't hear much, out on the Moss.'

'I suppose not,' she said. And then, in a sudden burst of frankness, 'I don't know how you stand it, out there all on your own. I think I'd go mad. You could say that some *have* done, couldn't you?' She gave me an incisive glare, a sort of challenge, I thought, but I did not understand it.

'Could you?' I faltered.

'Well,' she straightened up and shifted my plate from one hand to the other, 'yes. What else would you call it?'

Arnold, across the fireplace, gave an odd harumphing noise and shook the pages of the newspaper.

Bill, from behind the bar, said, 'Julie, love. Something's pinging in the kitchen. You'd better go and check on it.'

Julie rolled her eyes and turned on her heel.

I could only think that Julie was referring to the confused old man I had met on the dunes. It seemed cruel to call his affliction madness. Dementia was a disease. It was not caused by loneliness. And he was not directly connected to the Moss or the cottages, so far as I knew.

My chicken and leek pie was delicious. I ate every scrap, as well as the chips. I was thoroughly convinced it was homemade but not, I thought, by Julie. It would not have surprised me to find that this was another of Mrs Harrop's lines.

When I had finished and my plate had been cleared, Arnold surprised me by laying down his newspaper and saying, 'You don't get any trouble, do you, out at the cottage?' And I felt sure his remark was prompted by Julie's earlier allusion.

I hesitated, remembering Marjorie's caution; for all I knew Arnold might be related to Jamie, or to the Harrops. 'No,' I said slowly, 'not really.'

Arnold raised a wiry eyebrow, a question mark.

I proceeded cautiously. 'There have been one or two ... strange things. Bumps and creakings ... odd rumblings ... but Jamie has been really helpful and, all in all, I feel quite settled.'

'Hmm,' said Arnold, sitting back. 'Old houses, you know, they move about. Moss Farm was old when Noah was a lad. It won't have any foundations to speak of and the land thereabouts ... well, it's a bog.'

Arnold's explanation accorded with my own, that if the odd shifts and strange groanings at the cottage were not caused by Jamie's renovations they could only be the natural noises of the building. But it didn't explain Julie's remark. 'You might remember when Todd Forrester bought it,' I mused. 'Who did he buy it from?' I wondered if dune-man was a disgruntled descendant of the original Moss Farm family, whether the loss of his birth right had turned his wits. Could *that* have been Julie's implication?

Arnold gave a chortle. 'Before my time, love,' he said. 'I'm not *that* old.'

I smiled. 'Sorry.'

'I'm the same age as his boys, give or take. We were never pals, though. They had each other, those boys. They didn't seem to need any other mates.'

'I've been told they were at each other's throats,' I cried.

'You heard right,' said Arnold, with a wry smile. 'They regularly beat seven bells out of each other. But if anyone *else* tried it, they'd close up tighter than a ...' he cut off abruptly, clearly having been about to say something not suitable for a lady's ears.

I drained my drink, thinking I oughtn't to have another, but knowing I would. I nodded at Arnold's tankard. 'Can I refill that for you?'

'I normally just have the one,' he said, and I knew it was his habit to make it last all night to put off going home to an empty house.

'But you'll keep me company tonight, won't you?' I cajoled.

The bar was unmanned when I approached it, but I could hear Bill in the taproom, having an altercation with an obstreperous customer.

'No, Joe, I'm sorry mate,' Bill kept saying. 'It's more than my licence is worth. You've had enough, mate, haven't you? Best be on your way.'

Joe—whoever he was—remonstrated angrily, but incoherently, obviously very drunk. I could make out the repeated phrases, 'Give a man a drink,' and, 'Man and boy. *Man and boy!*' I peered through the hatch but could make out nothing of the room beyond.

Bill continued to placate, offering, 'I know. It stinks, but there it is. I couldn't live with myself if you were to take a tumble on your way home.'

This seemed to incense his would-be customer even more. 'Not a stick or stone,' I heard, and again, 'Man and boy.' Then, the scrape of chair legs across the flagstone floor, the shunt of a table, indicated that intoxicated Joe was at last ricocheting his way to the door. It must have been wrenched open; a gust of cold air whistled through the hatch.

'Look. Shall I call …?' Bill offered, and I thought he was going to relent. But this concession, whatever it was, provoked an even more heated tirade, punctuated with slurred expletives and impotent threats. At last I heard the shuffle of feet along the passageway and the slam of the outer door.

Bill reappeared wearing an embarrassed expression. 'Sorry about that,' he said, rinsing his hands and drying them on a bar towel. 'Doesn't happen often. Another round, is it? And what about a pudding?'

I leaned conspiratorially over the bar, 'Does Arnold cook for himself, now he's on his own?' I asked. 'Do you think … would he be offended if …?'

'Loves a plate of cheese and biscuits,' Bill murmured.

'Great. I'll have that then, please. Enough for two.'

'You got it.'

I carried the drinks back and this time I sat next to Arnold. He folded his newspaper away. He, too, seemed affected by the confrontation that had occurred in the tap room. He shook his head sadly, 'A pity,' he muttered and, 'a sad thing to see. He had everything on a plate. Threw it away, plate and all.'

I thought of my character, Caleb Forrester. 'There's many a thing drives a man to drink,' I said.

'You can drive a horse to water, but it doesn't *have* to drink,' Arnold said, cryptically adding, 'That man has no one to blame but himself.'

Our cheese and biscuits arrived just then, and we spoke of other things. Arnold's memory was a mine of anecdotes. He spoke of his childhood, of the Roadend street party that had celebrated the Coronation, the village street end-to-end with bunting and tables laid out for tea. He told me of village fayres, of the year a circus came, of a sports day when the Forrester boys had outrun the whole village in a race across the sands. He spoke of his life on the road as a lorry driver, and of meeting his wife, a newcomer to the village, the sister of a schoolteacher who had briefly taught at the local school before it—and he—had become defunct.

I asked him if he knew anyone called Mary.

He nodded sagely. 'Lots of Marys,' he said, and reeled off half a dozen names. Only the last meant anything to me. Mary Forrester. Then it came back to me: Mary with the hand for baking—much better than Mrs John Forrester—who had done all the cooking when Todd was alive.

'Does Mary still live in the village?' I asked.

Arnold shook his head and, I thought, looked a bit shifty. He didn't meet my eye when he said in a low voice, 'No. She went away.'

I swallowed my disappointment in the consolation that I had secured the next link in my narrative chain. A surviving Forrester daughter! Those two babies remembered on Rose's headstone were not the only girls she had been given ... but I held myself back. I had a lot of writing to do before I got to that episode in the story.

By the time we had finished, and Arnold had taken his leave, it was well past eight o'clock and I remembered with alarm that I had been expected at the book club. Well, it was too late now. I would have to message Olivia when I got home. I paid my bill and put my coat on, rousing Bob from his slumber in front of the fire. I felt sorry for Bill as I left him alone in the bar. I doubted any more customers would come in. He would stand, alone, at the end of the bar, nursing his Scotch, until it was time to turn out the lights.

The air outside had turned arctic, a hard frost forming on the ground. The sky was clear, a high, silken tent embroidered with a million stars. A gibbous moon hung as though from a chain, casting an ivory light over everything. I had no need of my torch. The curtains of Marjorie's front room were tightly closed, and I imagined the heated discussion within. Their text had been *My Cousin Rachel*. So nuanced was the writing that it was always a hotly debated matter as to whether Rachel had been a scheming charmer or an innocent victim. Oh! That I should write something so clever!

I made my way to the church and went in at the lych gate. The tombstones and Rowan Winter's obelisk stood starkly still, like slabs of iron, the grass round about them bright with frost, the wreaths against the memorial wall seemed like fine, filigree lace made of silver wire. I stood for a while by Rowan's memorial. I felt I knew her now—the mischievous, rather forward little girl, the promiscuous woman who had sacrificed herself ... well, *had* she sacrificed herself? Perhaps she had never considered marriage with Todd; he had only ever been her guilty pleasure. Poor Todd. But I couldn't quite believe that. She *had* had feelings for him, but sacrificed them for the sake of Society, for her father, and for the chance of an heir. The idea of her child—hers and Todd's—made me smile. Mrs Harrop detested the Forresters. What would she think if she knew that their blood ran in her veins? But then I had to shake myself. Some of what I had written had turned out to be true, but the rest, I sternly reminded myself, was fiction. I couldn't assume anything I had written about Rowan was true, and the idea that Mrs Harrop had Forrester blood in her veins was especially farfetched. And yet.

The boardwalk shone with diamonds as I walked along it, my feet crunching the crystals. The standing water on the boggy field was a mirror, reflecting the arc of sky above. My breath plumed in clouds before my face. The silence was immense, something almost palpable, a hovering spirit. Far across the marsh an owl screeched and soon afterwards I heard the thin, quailing cry of some poor creature snatched from life.

I walked on, past the hide and alongside the skirt of trees that would bring me to the track, and home.

Unusually, at Jamie's house, every light blazed. Upstairs and down, yellow light poured through streaked and dusty windows. The door was open, and more light flowed from it, down the step and onto the curious jumble of things in the garden. There was music—Shirley Bassey, if I was not mistaken—blaring tinnily into the bitter night air.

What the ... was Jamie having a *party*?

I walked curiously, closer and closer, keeping Bob to my heel and, without really thinking about it, keeping both of us to the thin line of shadow afforded by the line of shrubs on the far side of the track. There were no cars, so any guests must have been on foot. I expected that any minute someone would come out of the house, holding a beer bottle, lighting a cigarette. I sniffed to see if I could smell food of any kind. But no. I could smell only the thin, vegetable air of the marsh and the slight whiff of woodsmoke. I looked up. A tower of smoke rose from Jamie's chimney *and* the one further along that belonged to the middle, unoccupied house.

What the hell was going on?

I tuned my ears to catch the hubbub of conversation, the occasional spurt of laugher, the clink of glasses that emanates from any party, but there was only Shirley—*Diamonds are forever, forever, forever ...*

Abruptly—mid-chorus—Shirley stopped, almost immediately to be replaced by a male singer I did not recognise, crooning a song about love and loss. I was right opposite Jamie's house now. It was so odd. I could see no cram of bodies in what I imagined to be the front room, hear no voices. I felt as though I had happened upon a gala of ghosts—the maudlin warbling of the record, the unnaturally jaundiced light spilling forth, the unaccustomed *openness* of a house habitually in shade and shadow. Looking along the row I thought I could see lines of light seeping from beneath the boards that had been nailed over the door and windows of the middle property. Perhaps, then, it wasn't derelict, not empty after all.

Suddenly, from the open door of Jamie's house, there came a sort of roar. It was scarcely human. There might have been words in there, but if

219

so, I could not make them out. What I could discern was anger, inarticulate fury, laced with a kind of woundedness for which there were no words. Glass—a tray of drinks?—smashed musically. Something else—crockery?—hit a wall with jangling ferocity. A third item—more solid, wooden perhaps—bounced off the inside of one of the hardboard window covers with a hollow thud. I found myself through Jamie's gate and halfway up his path. My foot rested on the step. Bob, behind me, gave a whine. He did not like it. Neither did I, but someone had to intervene.

I raised my hand and knocked on the open door. The hall, beyond it, was without furniture of any kind. The floor was bare boards, sanded down, and reasonably clean. The walls were plain, painted white. Stairs rose up in front of me, sanded also, with turned spindles and a smooth, polished banister. Down the hall I could see what I supposed would be the kitchen. Lights blazed there too but the door was half closed and I couldn't see into the room.

The furore going on in a far room of the house continued, the destruction added to now by apostrophic grunts and incoherent shouts. A fight. I could hear furniture being knocked about, the clatter of fireirons, the sickening smack of a fist on flesh.

I lifted my foot and stepped into the hall. 'Jamie!' I called out, and Bob gave a little bark.

Immediately, the cacophony ceased. There was a taut, listening silence, as though a thief had been caught in the act. I could imagine the two—or more—combatants poised, mid-grapple. The crooning man droned on and on.

'Jamie, it's me. Dee,' I called, my voice ridiculously high, tight with the effort of being light. 'Is everything all right?'

I heard the scuffle of someone getting to their feet, a muttered directive that might have been 'stay where you are,' or 'keep quiet,' then Jamie stumbled through a door that, in my cottage, would have equated to the sitting room, except it was further along the hallway.

Jamie looked terrible. His hair was awry, the beard that had been nascent now grown long and scruffy, the colour of a dirty mouse. There were fresh welts on his face, overlaying the faded bruising of their predecessors. His clothing was filthy. He looked at me through eyes that shot out sparks of resentment.

'What do you want?' he roared. 'Can't you see you're not wanted here?'

He advanced down the hallway, blocking it with his bulk, and I could not tell if he was bearing down on me, or trying to protect me from whatever fracas was in train within. Self-preservation gripped me and I instinctively took a pace back, out onto the step, almost treading on Bob as I did so. Bob gave a low grumble in his throat and not, I thought, because I had almost stepped on him.

'I'm sorry,' I stammered. 'I thought I heard a fight. I was worried.'

'So?' he bellowed. 'What's it to you?'

He loomed over me as I stood on his step, his hand on the door, ready to slam it in my face.

'It isn't any of my business,' I said, feeling my face flush, even in the slap of the cold night air. 'Except that, if something's wrong ...'

'You thought *you* could help?' He finished my sentence for me with a sneer.

From the nether room came a sort of groan.

Jamie flinched, and so did I. Our eyes met, ever so briefly, but what I read in them was too complicated to decode. Obviously, there was someone else in the house. Jamie might not be the person who needed help at all! Who had Jamie been beating up? Perhaps he had someone in there against their will?

I summoned courage to call past Jamie, down the hall and into the room I imagined had been the arena of their combat. 'Hello! Hello in there! Are you OK? Do you need help?'

My appeal was met with silence.

Jamie snorted. His inflated stance suddenly collapsed as though punctured and his shoulders began to shake. He was laughing. 'Oh, that's funny,' he gasped out. 'You think ...' He gestured vaguely behind him, at the door down the hall. 'You think that *he* ...' Jamie gripped the door, helpless with amusement. 'Oh,' he roared out, 'I've heard everything now.'

I looked at him blankly; angry, but also feeling like a fool.

Jamie's mirth seemed to expiate his wrath. At last he controlled himself sufficiently to say, with none of his earlier outrage, 'Thank you, but everything's fine. As fine as it ever is, anyway. Goodnight, Dee.'

He closed the door, shaking his head in amused bewilderment as he did so, and I heard his footsteps as he walked slowly down the uncarpeted hall.

I retreated down the path, but not so far that I did not hear the needle being knocked from the record, strangling as with a garrot its sappy strains. Then, what I guessed to be the record player was launched against a wall; metal, wood, electronics, a smorgasbord of ricochets and twanging destruction.

In the silence that ensured I could hear Jamie and another man laughing.

Chapter Twenty-Two

The next morning the world was crusted with riches. The grasses of the Moss were silver spears, the bracken diamond-dipped, each furl and curl a petrified skeleton of glistening hoar. The waterways were polished ribbons of gilt, and slabs of argent lay in the hollows where water had pooled over the previous few days. Bob and I walked along the crisp, crackling byways of the Moss beneath a cloudless, opal sky. At a distance I saw three or four deer take a brake of low-growing shrubs at a single leap, but other than these I neither saw nor heard a living creature. The Moss, and the row of cottages, seemed unnaturally quiet, exhausted, literally and temporally frozen. The door of Jamie's cottage was closed but the lights blazed on through the smutty windows—a dull, jaundiced light in comparison to the brilliance of the sun and the dazzling white landscape. Unusually, the hens had not been let out. I could hear them clucking in their house. Had things been different I might have released them, checked their water and grain. But I didn't feel I could take such a liberty. Jamie's opinion of me had been made abundantly clear: I was not wanted. I assumed Jamie was sleeping off the dissipations of the night and would not welcome the sound of someone creeping around outside his property, even though it would be a taste of his own medicine.

The previous night I had been kept awake by the noises from the next-door cottage; the sounds that had become familiar to me, augmented by others, and all much clearer than they had been previously, as though the dial of some ghostly radio had been nudged. What had been static now clarified to the rumble of an endless argument that someone—Jamie's guest—had carried on with himself: muttering, grumbling, a catalogue of complaints. Interspersed with these had been the noise of shifting furniture, the rattle of fireirons in a grate that must have been on the other side of the wall that divided my study from the neighbouring property.

No scenario I could come up with could account for the unaccustomed disturbance at that end of the row, let alone the fighting and violence.

Who had Jamie had in there with him? I continued to remind myself it was none of my business. But the idea that the middle, boarded-up house was *not,* as I had thought, deserted—that Jamie and his mysterious guest had access to it—unsettled me. The buffer I had believed separated me from Jamie had shrunk to a thin skin of brick. Add this to the yawning cavern beneath the house and the ladder of crossbeams above and I was left with a sense of being encroached upon. I'd checked the seal around the loft hatch and, for good measure, wedged the little stepladder under the handle of the cellar door.

Even so I had lay in bed with every sense tuned to the peculiar echoes that vibrated through the building, feeling like a sane person mistakenly incarcerated in an asylum, listening in horror to the deranged jibberings of the person in the next cell. This analogy—once it had suggested itself—led me to a worrying possibility. What if Jamie was schizophrenic? It would explain his veering mood-swings and the peculiar, one-sided conversations. What if he was speaking to his voices? Had *they* told him to creep into the loft? Is that what Julie had meant when she had referred to madness? Once this notion had lodged itself in my mind, I found it troubled me a great deal. A moody neighbour was one thing; one with a serious mental illness was quite another.

A hot shower, a good breakfast and a brisk walk through a winter wonderland will put most things into perspective though, and I returned from my morning walk feeling more phlegmatic. I made coffee and steeled myself to climb the stairs with it, going into the study determined *not* to think of what might lurk on the other side of the wall. I had Rowan's thread to weave into my narrative and a strong connection with the pele tower family to incorporate at last.

In the afternoon I was surprised by a visitor: Olivia, well wrapped up against the cold and holding onto Patty's lead with *Hello Kitty* mittened hands.

'Oh, Olivia,' I said, clamping my hand to my mouth because, in all the furore of the previous evening, I had forgotten to send her a message. 'I'm so sorry about last night. I got held up and then, when I got home … but do come inside, and I'll tell you all about it.'

Olivia's face, usually pale, was flushed, her lips pressed into a thin line, her eyes held unnaturally wide and prone to blinking. She stepped indoors but did not remove her coat.

'Oh! I've upset you,' I said, mortified.

'You've upset Mummy,' she admitted, and I realised that, with Marjorie and Olivia, it amounted to the same thing. 'She'd gone to a lot of trouble to get a good crowd at the book club. People who never usually come had agreed to, because *you* were going to be there.'

'Did she?' I asked, creasing my face into a smiling frown I hoped would express both my gratitude and bewilderment that Marjorie should go to such lengths.

'Yes. So that you could meet people and make new friends,' said Olivia, 'and also because ... because ...' I could see her battle with herself— something she knew, but must not reveal to me. Her self-possession won the struggle and she concluded, 'Mummy was disappointed. And so was I.'

'I'm so very sorry,' I said. 'I'll call Marjorie later and apologise. It was thoughtless of me.' I hoped I looked as contrite as I felt. Marjorie had been nothing but kind and helpful to me, and I had failed her. I knew I had let Olivia down badly too. 'I'm mortified,' I said. 'Please come in and have a cup of tea with me,' adding, in a winsome tone, 'I have chocolate biscuits.'

Olivia added fuel to the log burner while I made the tea and tried to explain why I had not attended the book group meeting. Even in my own ears, cheese and biscuits with an elderly man in a deserted pub did not sound like a particularly appealing alternative to a room full of book enthusiasts and potential friends, but it seemed to provide acceptable mitigation to Olivia who said, 'Oh, well if you were keeping Arnold company, I think Mummy will forgive you. You could have brought him, of course.'

I trod more carefully with the next stage in my narrative, not wishing to tarnish Olivia's idealised vision of my neighbour. I spoke vaguely of a sense of something being not quite right at Jamie's house, of overhearing an altercation, and that this had made me forget to message Olivia. To my surprise, Olivia's reaction was neither shock, curiosity nor bewilderment. She simply nodded and sipped her tea. 'Yes,' she said. 'I see. Yes. Poor thing.' I was deluged again with the sense that other people in this village knew things I did not, and—churlishly—that there was a conspiracy to exclude me.

'It seemed very out of character,' I pressed, nibbling a Hobnob with specious naivety. 'Jamie is usually so quiet. He seems hardly to be home, most of the time. He's never had a friend over before, that I know of.'

'It wasn't a friend,' Olivia mumbled into her tea, and I knew—we both knew—we had approached one of those invisible borders, an inviolable divide, across which her mother would not venture because it was "other people's business." If she were here, I knew Marjorie would issue an admonishing, 'We mustn't gossip.' Olivia hovered at the barrier for a few moments before attempting a limbo move that would get her under it undetected. 'It's his dad,' she whispered.

'His *dad?*' I breathed.

Olivia nodded, looking at me owlishly through her spectacles. 'He lives in the middle house.'

Her voice was so breathy I had to virtually lip-read. 'He *lives* in the …' I repeated stupidly. 'What, *permanently?*'

Olivia nodded again and filled her mouth with a biscuit so she did not have to say more. I stared into the flames of the fire, evaluating this information. So, the middle cottage was *not* empty—neglected and boarded up though it might be. Who would tolerate such living conditions? Why had this not been mentioned? How come I had not seen this neighbour? The only possible explanation was that there was something unmentionable, something unsociable, something introverted about him. He was … what? An embarrassment? A disgrace? A danger? Ah! I thought I'd grasped it. He was a *recluse*. He was …

I reached down to stroke Patty, who had snuggled on the sofa between us. 'He's …' I groped for the right word, '… unwell, isn't he, Jamie's dad?' I threw it out not quite as a question because I didn't want to entice Olivia further onto forbidden territory, but not quite as a statement of fact either. I invited her to confirm it and she did, removing her spectacles and polishing them assiduously, but giving the smallest possible nod.

Ah! Now I had it. The man on the dunes was Jamie's father and I had been right—he had dementia. Perhaps also, I speculated, a kind of agoraphobia that permitted him abroad only at night. He obviously had a volatile temper too.

The furniture in my house of assumptions underwent a seismic shift. Foremost of my re-evaluations was my opinion of Jamie, which lifted on a trajectory so steep it was practically vertical. My relief that he was not, as I had half-suspected, a schizophrenic, was immense. Now that I knew that a confused old gentleman was resident in the middle cottage—a man prone to wandering at night, a man lost in his childhood memories, a man who shied away from the light—it seemed unlikely to say the least that *Jamie* had been the late-night stalker, the creeper in the shadows, the attic-crawling interloper I had accused him of being. No. Much more likely that the agent of my niggling anxieties had been his father. But Jamie *knew!* No wonder he had looked at me with such speaking shame in the attic. And no wonder he had laughed at me the previous evening when I had suggested the *other occupant* of the house might be in danger! All along, Jamie had been protecting *me* from his wayward, unpredictable, unstable parent. I was sure there was a term for sudden episodes of explosive rage. Whatever it was, it explained the occasional bouts of violence I heard coming from the cottage. It also explained Jamie's bruises. For all I knew, they might have been the result of his efforts to restrain his father from imposing himself upon me. Marjorie had told me Jamie had been given "a difficult hand in life." Well, she had *that* right. Being left with an elderly, confused parent was certainly no picnic. A violent one was a tribulation I wouldn't wish on anyone.

But it was nothing to be ashamed of, either. I found Jamie's secrecy rather curious.

Oddly, having an all too likely—much *more* likely—suspect in the frame for the strange things that had happened did not unnerve me. If anything, I felt reassured. This was the second outcome of Olivia's revelation. The vague churn of anxiety that had dogged me since my arrival at Winter Cottage had evaporated. The man on the dunes had not seemed at all dangerous to me. He had puzzled me, but he had not scared me. I had felt sorry for him, and I still did. If anything, I would have said *he* was more vulnerable—more a victim of his own dementia— than I would ever be. I had nothing to be afraid of; the more so because Jamie stood—like a colossus—between us. No harm had come to me from his father's erratic behaviour so far and, I was sure, so long as Jamie was around, none ever would.

This train shunted its way around my head while Olivia and I chatted of other things. We both knew we had trespassed on what Marjorie would consider hallowed ground and I did not wish to lead my visitor into further transgressions. She did not stay long and when I waved her off it was with our friendship restored. I had promised to make things up to them both at a dinner that I would host at Winter Cottage on the first evening that Marjorie's busy schedule would allow. Before I shut my front door, I looked along the row of cottages to the far end. The sun was dropping behind the hill, throwing elongated shadows across the track, skewing the size and shape of things, as I had skewed them—or, at least, as my ignorance had. No wonder Jamie was so short-tempered; didn't he have his hands full without looking after me? Heaven knew living on the Moss wasn't easy; but it was a safer, and perhaps an easier location to keep tabs on an errant old man than a village would be. It explained why Jamie had remained at Roadend rather than pursuing the many careers that would undoubtedly be open to him—intelligent, capable and well-read man that he was. I wondered if I would have sacrificed my career for my dad, and knew in a heartbeat that I would have done. But my dad had been quick-witted to the end, dependable. *He* had not been lost in a labyrinth of memory, given to odd impulses or violent temper. He would not have crept through a loft to spy on a woman or have peeped at her through closed curtains. Even at the end he was the man he had always been. Had he been different, irascible, fickle …? well, I did not know.

I was desperate to do something that would repair my relationship with Jamie. That it had broken down before it had even begun wasn't really my fault; I had misread the signs, but I defied anyone else to have come to a different conclusion given the information I had been presented with. Who could have guessed that within the dilapidated shell of the middle cottage, behind those boarded up windows, someone actually lived?

It was too late, after Olivia's visit, to return to my work, but too early for Bob's walk. I decided to make a cake. I assembled the ingredients and began to stir them together, catching up with *The Archers* as I did so. By the time the cake was cooling on the rack the sun had disappeared from the Moss leaving a strange miasma of mist in its wake. I stood on the doorstep, my coat on and boots laced, but hesitant now to venture out. The mist seemed to exude from the ground itself, like steam—a weird emanation of curling vapour and morphing shapes lit from within, much brighter than the surrounding twilight. It boiled up, spilling over the informal hedge that separated the track from the Moss, reminding me of dry ice in nightclubs I had frequented many *many* years before. It snaked in ghostly tendrils towards me. Bob, who had gone off to pursue his own agenda when I opened the door, had disappeared. In the thick, diaphanous mist I couldn't see him at all. I whistled, but the sound of it was deadened, swallowed, and soaked by the damp, writhing air. Up the track, the trees were wreathed in fog, hardly visible through the pall. The lights in Jamie's house—still burning—cast an unhealthy, sallow glow, barely sufficient to keep the billowing haze at bay.

I called again, 'Bob! Bob! Come! Come on, boy!' but there was no answering bark, no disturbance in the wall of roiling vapour that had now filled the track, absorbed the trees and was coiling itself through the gate and into my little garden, around my feet, and beginning to press against my face like a thick veil. I felt suffocated, but I couldn't go back inside and leave Bob out in these conditions. I stepped down into the whorling brume.

Beyond the gate I paused. Which way would he go? I did not think he could jump the five barred gate that led into the willow wood, so I turned right, following the row of cottages by keeping close to the low stone wall. When the wall petered out, I stepped out into a white oblivion, my feet feeling—rather than my eyes seeing—the faint rut of a tyre track. I was blinded by the mist swirling around me. I pictured the hen coop at the side of Jamie's house, the scrubby area beyond that, the bramble hedge that would take me to the turn in the track at the beginning of the copse where the boardwalk branched off. Just before that, a dozen yards or so, was the wide planked bridge across the drainage rill that we often used, then the maze of animal tracks beyond. That was Bob's favourite walk. I told myself the waterways would still be frozen; he would not get stuck in one. I thought of his keen sense of smell; *that* would guide him as unfailingly as his eyesight. I knew it would be madness to cross that wonky and slippery bridge and to venture out across the Moss in search of Bob. I called him again, sharply urgent. I tried to whistle but my lips were too dry. I edged forward along the track, taking small, hesitant steps, my arms stretched out in front of me.

By instinct and the kind of body memory dancers use to learn their moves, I found myself on the bridge. It was thick with hoar frost; I felt the crunch of it beneath my boots. The water beneath the bridge was a floe of cloud that boiled up and up, swamping everything. I turned back to see if I could make out the glow of light from the cottages, but everything behind me was obscured in a cliff of fog. I turned again and took a step. I mustn't have turned a full one eighty degrees—I don't know what saved me from stepping over the edge of the bridge—my boot found only insubstantial murk. Thankfully I hadn't committed my full weight to it and I leaned back, helicoptering my arms to keep my balance, almost fell, stumbling back onto the planks and disorientating myself still further. Now I didn't know which way was which, where home lay, where the Moss, where were the edges of the bridge.

I heard a noise behind me and swung round. 'Bob?' I called into the fog.

'No,' came a low voice I did not recognise. It startled me with its proximity; so close, and yet I could not see a thing. The mist shifted, exuded a hand, an arm, the tenuous shape of a man hardly more substantial than the fog that surrounded it. He could not have been more than two arms' lengths in front of me but the mist was so thick I couldn't make out more than just the nebulous outline of head, shoulder, torso. They melded into one another, barely defined at all.

'Take my hand,' he said.

I hesitated. The hand he held out to me seemed benign, though extraordinarily pale. Palm upwards, it was impossible to discern its age or anything about its owner. It was not calloused, not nicotine-stained, not dirty. It wore no ring. Its lifelines were blurred, smudged, the faint tracery of vein in its wrist was no more than a fine shadow on its pallid skin, disappearing into a colourless cuff.

'Bob ...' I began, looking back over my shoulder.

I sensed—rather than saw—a shake of the head. 'He's all right. Waiting for you, by the gate. Can't you hear him whining to be let in?'

I put my head to one side, straining to hear through the deafening, deadening murk.

'No,' I said. 'No, I can't ...'

'He *is*,' said the voice. The fingers of the hand before me curled its fingers once, twice, beckoning me.

I reached out and put my hand in his. It was so cold that I almost flinched and snatched my own hand back, but his fingers gripped mine and drew me forward across the rough, crusted planks of the bridge and back onto solid ground. I felt the brush of bracken against my trousers, the stony surface of the track beneath my feet. No matter how many steps I took, the man who led me remained obscure, moving as I did, maintaining his distance, keeping himself shrouded in the thick pall of fog. At some point he moved to my side, retaining my hand in his, but still too distant for me to see anything other than an indistinct outline. I reached my other hand out to touch him, to garner *something* from the

231

texture of his clothes, the heft of his figure. My hand disappeared through the mist as through a curtain, with only empty air beyond.

We shuffled on along the track. Then the shoulder of cottages loomed out of the cloud, the meagre light from Jamie's windows painting a sulphur hue onto the impenetrable white smog.

Bob burst out of the mist, materialising as though out of the vapour itself. I let go of the man's hand and bent to greet the dog. His fur was saturated, his ears dripping moisture, his nose wet but his tongue hot.

'You bad boy,' I chastised, but fondly caressed his head.

I turned and said, into the gloom, 'You were right. Thank you so much,' but the elusive figure in the fog had disappeared and I received no reply.

Chapter Twenty-Three

The next day the mist had cleared, leaving a day as pure and bright as a mountain stream, and as cold. I added extra layers to my clothing and lit the log burner before icing the cake I'd made the day before.

Now that I had Jamie's dad to thank—as well as wanting to make a peace offering to Jamie—I wished I had made two cakes. I wondered what their domestic arrangements were. Did they live separately, or were the two cottages connected? Did Jamie cook for his dad, or vice versa? I had no way of knowing. The middle cottage had no usable front door, but I supposed if I ventured along the back alley I might find a rear entrance there. In the end I put the cake in a Tupperware box and left it on Jamie's doorstep with a note saying, *"A thank you and a peace-offering."* I had made the first move. Now the ball was in their court.

That morning the lights were off in Jamie's house, but the curtains had been pulled all the way back and an upper window was open. The hens were out as usual, pecking around their enclosure. I noticed also that the wild birdfeeder had been topped up, and a shallow bowl of water provided.

I walked that morning in a kind of wonderment, looking around me at the quiet country, the bright innocence of the colours, the benign flow of gelid water in the drainage rills. How could the nightmare of last night have given way to such glory?

When I got home I found Jamie loitering in front of the cottage. He looked better—rested—his hair washed and brushed back off his face, his beard trimmed back to a shadow, his clothes clean. His bruises had faded so I could hardly see them. The grazes I had glimpsed on the night of the furore were already scabbed and healing. From the set of his shoulders and the way he held his head I could tell that, like me, he had decided to put the past behind us and begin again. I raised my hand as I approached. Bob rushed forward, his back-end wiggling in pleasure. My eyes met Jamie's and we both smiled. He had a lovely smile—wide, showing white, even teeth. The corners of his eyes crinkled.

'Nice walk?' he opened with.

'Good morning,' I returned. 'Yes, thank you.' I took a deep breath and gestured vaguely at the Moss, the perfect blue sky. 'What a beautiful day.'

'Thank you for the cake,' he said. 'I can't remember the last time we had homemade cake.' But then a shadow crossed his face, as though he *had* remembered, and the memory was painful. He lifted his hand and swatted the recollection away.

'I'm not much of a baker,' I said, 'but I can throw a Victoria sponge together.'

'You certainly can,' Jamie agreed.

We stood for a moment in front of Winter Cottage. I wondered if we would grasp the nettle and speak of the other night; if he might begin to explain about his father and the problems caused by the dementia. I thought about expressing my thanks for the old man's assistance the night before as a way of showing Jamie that, since I now understood the situation, I could cope with any idiosyncrasies it might cause. The silence stretched out between us while we both mulled over the prickly issues that had snagged and wounded our relationship thus far—and how we might broach them. Our smiles became a bit fixed. Jamie ran his hand through his hair. I groped in my pocket for a tissue and made a fuss about blowing my nose. Bob sat between us, looking up, from one to the other, his tongue lolling out of his mouth and his tail sweeping the ground. Jamie put his hand out so as to lean on my gate, but I hadn't latched it properly and so it swung open and he more or less stumbled through. He laughed awkwardly and held the gate open so I could follow.

Before I knew it, I was saying, 'I usually have a cup of coffee when I get back from our walk. Would you like one?'

'Sure,' he said, a bit too quickly. I retrieved my key and led the way into the house.

Of course, he'd been in the cottage before—on the night of the storm, and probably many times before that. In all likelihood he knew it better than I did. But he stood diffidently in the hall wiping his shoes on the mat while I took off my coat and hung it up, and unlaced my boots. It wasn't until I indicated with a gesture that he should follow me down to the kitchen that he moved from the mat. I looked askance at the little step ladder I had wedged beneath the handle of the cellar door, and wondered if Jamie would see it and, if he did, what he would think. But he passed it without a word.

The bulk of him in the narrow, low-ceilinged hallway made me feel a bit breathless. I made straight for the coffee machine while he pulled out a chair and sat at the kitchen table.

He eyed the machine. 'Fancy!' he observed. 'I've smelled the coffee most mornings. I knew it wasn't instant.'

I gave a theatrical shudder. 'I'm a coffee snob,' I said. 'This machine was pricey but it makes good coffee, if you can get the right beans.'

'And can you?'

I hesitated, wondering whether to confess about my black-market delivery from Waitrose. It might implicate Marjorie and Olivia—but I thought, on balance, the secret would be safe with Jamie since Mrs Harrop was certainly no friend of his. 'I had these smuggled in,' I admitted sheepishly. 'You can torture me, but I won't reveal my source.'

He laughed. 'No torture necessary,' he said. 'I think I can guess.'

The machine began its grinding, whirring, steaming routine, rendering conversation impossible for a few moments. At last, I had two perfect flat whites. I carried them to the table then took the seat opposite to Jamie.

'So,' I said, with no idea of how I would continue my remark.

'So,' he returned. He sipped his coffee, rolling his eyes in pleasure. 'That's good,' he sighed, wiping froth from his lips. 'Oh my, that's *very* good. Does everyone have machines like this, out in the real world?'

I looked at him sharply, but there was a light in his eye—grey, flecked with gold—that told me he was teasing. 'No,' I said, 'only the lucky few. I bought this one when ...' I had been going to say, 'when I was flush, after the film came out,' but I clamped my mouth shut on that conclusion and instead said, 'when I lived in Hackney. When I left my ex, I brought it with me. I'd bought it, after all and, to tell the truth, he was a bit of a coffee-slapper.'

Jamie raised a querying eyebrow.

'He was happy to go with any old joe,' I explained, and then, to clarify, 'Joe is ...'

'I know,' he said. 'Slang for coffee. But he had good taste in women.'

I realised he had paid me a compliment. I found myself blushing. 'That's a nice thing to say,' I stammered, 'in the circumstances.'

'In the circumstances,' he replied, 'I have been a jerk.'

'So have I,' I offered. We looked at each other across the table. He smiled and I smiled back.

And that was it. The air was cleared. Nothing more needed to be said.

'So,' I said, leaning back in my chair, 'you're a reader.'

He nodded. 'Always have been. My mum encouraged it. She read to me at nights, all the classics: The *Narnia* books, *Stig of the Dump, The Borrowers* ...'

'Oh, I *loved* those,' I put in. I wondered about suggesting there were Borrowers at Winter Cottage, an oblique reference to the goings on in the cellar and the attic, but I decided against it. No point now, with peace so lately declared, in re-opening old wounds. 'I think *The Borrowers Afloat* was my favourite.'

Jamie nodded. 'I liked books about families, especially brothers.' He gave a sad little shrug. 'I'm an only child. You?'

'I have a brother, but we don't get on.'

'How come?'

I sighed. 'We were OK as kids, but Daniel married a girl who wasn't right for him. When my dad died, she turned into Cruella De Vil …' I shook my head. I didn't want to talk about it. 'Books about brothers,' I mused. 'You've already mentioned the *Narnia* books. What else? *Swallows and Amazons? The Railway Children?*

He nodded. 'Yes. It's odd how books work, isn't it? They tempt us in with the offer of escapism but then, once we're in, they help us see the real world more clearly. I read books looking for a brother, but they taught me that a brother isn't always a blessing.' Jamie had finished his coffee but he continued to toy with the empty cup. 'Your parents are both dead?' he asked.

I nodded. 'Mum died when I was twelve. Daniel was only seven. That's what made it harder. I more or less stepped into Mum's shoes. I wouldn't say I brought him up; Dad did that, but we were very close until …'

'Cruella came along.'

Our talk of parents had brought us close to the tender topic of the old man next door. I approached it obliquely. 'Your mum?'

Jamie pressed his lips together and stared at the table for a while. 'She went away,' he said at last in a low voice. 'I was at Uni—studying literature, you won't be surprised to learn—and I got a call to say … well, I had to come back. Dad couldn't … he needed me.'

I didn't reply. What was there to say? I wanted to reach across the table and put my hand on his arm, but something restrained me. 'That's … tough,' I said at last. In fact, I thought it a great waste. He must feel the same way, I supposed. And to make it worse his dad was ill, but not in a straightforward way—not in need of nursing or regular medication, or of being pushed in a wheelchair—but mentally ill in ways that made him unpredictable and violent. That the subject was a delicate one for Jamie was obvious—if not, he wouldn't have made such a secret of it—so I hesitated to nudge him on it. On the other hand, since we had restarted our relationship at ground zero, I didn't see why we should pussyfoot around it.

'He's unwell,' I said gently.

'Well,' he said in a hard, dry voice, 'that's a nice way of putting it.' A line etched its way between his eyebrows.

'You find him hard to cope with, at times,' I suggested. 'But on the occasions I've met him he—'

'You've *met* him?' Jamie looked horror-struck.

I nodded. 'Just a couple of times.' I almost clarified with, 'Just last night,' but Jamie's panicked expression made me hold my tongue.

'I wish he wouldn't take it into his head to go walkabout,' Jamie said under his breath. Then he looked at me in an appeal that had a note of angry desperation about it. 'I can't watch him *all* the time!'

'Of course not.'

'I mean, I do have to earn a living, or how are we to keep body and soul together?'

'I know. I know,' I murmured. 'From what I could tell, though, he seemed at home in his surroundings. I don't think he'll come to any harm. I know that isn't much comfort.'

Suddenly Jamie was on his feet, the chair legs making an ugly scrawping noise on the tiles of the floor. 'It isn't *his* safety I'm worried about,' he threw out, looking at me with eyes that burned.

I rose to my feet. 'Do you think he's dangerous?' I asked, through thin lips.

Something in my expression must have touched him. He softened immediately. '*You* needn't worry,' he said, with an attempt at a reassuring smile. 'I'd …' he faltered before continuing, '…I'd never let him hurt you.' He blushed then, furiously, and I found I couldn't meet his eyes. I carried our cups to the dishwasher and made a fuss about putting them in.

When I turned around, he was standing at the kitchen door. His head brushed the top architrave and his shoulders touched the frame at both sides. My dad would have said he made a better door than a window and

I was on the point of offering this remark when he said, with a palpable effort at lightness, 'Thanks for the coffee. I'd better let you get on with …' he flicked his eyes at the ceiling, '… whatever it is you're doing up there.'

It was my turn to blush. 'Do I disturb you?' I asked.

'Tap, tap, tap. Tap-tap-tappitty-tap-tap,' he said, deadpan.

I scanned his face but couldn't tell if he was joking or serious. 'I could work in another room,' I said in a small voice.

'Don't be silly,' he burst out, smiling widely. 'I'm teasing you. Tap away! Only make sure I get a signed first edition.'

'Ok.' I narrowed one eye. Was he *still* joking? Or was he probing? I couldn't tell. I decided to play him at his own game. 'I will,' I said, giving him a straight look.

I watched him walk down the track to his own cottage. I couldn't tell if his gait spoke of relief, of a weight off his mind, or of just one less burden on shoulders that were so over-loaded he would hardly notice the remission. He stopped on his threshold, his hand raised, ready to push open his door. He looked back at me and our eyes met across the sorry cottage that divided us. We both smiled and then I went indoors. I leaned against the door for a while, wondering whether our *tête-à-tête* had really cleared the air between us, or simply thrown up more turbulence— the *frisson* of attraction was unmistakable.

Reluctantly—because I liked the little upper room where I had set up my study, especially the view it afforded over the marsh—I brought my laptop downstairs to work in the kitchen. I told myself it was because it was warmer, that, having lit the stove, it would be wasteful not to use it. But, in the back of my mind was the idea that, through the thin party wall, I could be heard. And, as one heartbeat will follow another, it seemed to me inevitable that, having been heard—writing, writing, writing—I would be rumbled, or at least questioned: *what* was I writing? Hadn't Jamie already as good as asked already, with his quizzical, querying, "whatever it is you're doing up there." The question marks suspended from that remark had been legion.

I wasn't doing anything *wrong*—writing is not a crime—but I wasn't ready to be quite open about my project, not the least because it was so intensely *local* and because I wasn't quite comfortable with that. My previous stories had not come to me this way. As I have said, they came from nothing, an idea, a spark that kindled. This one was falling to earth like manna. It seemed I only needed to step outside to gather more. The storylines did not trouble me. Feuds between brothers are commonplace, in fact and in fiction—look at Cain and Abel. Unfortunately, fires are also frequent, and people die in them. But *this* feud and *this* fire were Roadend's and sometimes I felt like a vulture, picking over the corpses. At the same time—like any hunter with its prey—I felt an intense greed over it. It was *mine*. I was nurturing it, privately, in the crucible of my imagination, and my jealousy of it was extreme. No first trimester mother could have been more possessive of their emergent progeny than me, and the idea of it being torn apart by the ravening resentment of Roadend was intolerable. It was a barely budded flower, an embryo, too tender and too filled with potential to be exposed.

Chapter Twenty-Four

The next week or so passed quietly, but productively. I remained in the kitchen where the range and the log burner compensated for the intense cold snap that petrified the Moss in frost. Even though the sun shone in a clear blue sky throughout the ever-shortening days, the temperature never rose above zero. Ice crystals encapsulated bracken fronds and grasses. Pooled water remained as ice. Bob and I went out early in the mornings, in the blue gloaming light that saturated the air above the frozen marsh before the sun rose above the massif in the east. There was something dreamlike about it, the silence so thick it could be sliced, the cold air searing my nostrils like ether. It was impossible to move quickly, bundled as I was into layers of clothing and coat, but also because the instinct to creep—to steal and slither—amongst the ossified plants in the breath-held dawn twilight was so strong. We moved like wraiths along the by-ways of the Moss, Bob and I, sometimes catching sight of other dawn-walkers like us: deer, timid in the thickets; a fox, stealthy, perfectly camouflaged by the russet ferns; a barn owl swooping on silent wings, white against the glacial air.

By the time we went out again the short day had passed and the Moss was in shadow again. Quite often we walked beneath the skeletal branches of the willow trees, our feet treading the frost-crisped leaves of the track until we reached the dune, where a final vestige of fiery light might rim the horizon. The sunset display was spectacular if I could get there in time, the few high clouds ablaze with borrowed light, the sky a rainbow of pink and purple, orange and blue, the sea beneath a still mirror reflecting the firmament above. Often I was tempted to go on, through the gate, and to cross the dunes to the strange structure I had found there before, but the encroaching darkness that seemed to exude from the earth and the sky and even from the water as soon as the sun's last light had died, stayed me.

Between these daily perambulations I remained indoors and hard at work, the log burner glowing and the crocheted blanket over my knees to provide extra warmth. Distantly I might hear the roar of Jamie's motorbike as he came and went. Frequently I heard movement in the next-door cottage; the faint closing of a door, the rattle of fireirons, a deep catarrhal cough. But in truth my mind was distracted, my imagination busy trying to envisage the Moss not, as then, trapped in frost and ice, but as it would be in summer. The sketch I had made in my mind of Todd and Rowan's story had decanted effortlessly onto my screen, arriving fully formed as I had conceived it. I felt the tragedy of it, for both of them. It pleased me that Todd was not quite the monster he was generally thought to be—based on his manipulative treatment of his sons, and also on Mrs Harrop's ironically disparaging account of him. He had feelings. He could be gentle. His treatment of his father in his old age in particular touched me. As much as I might try to blacken his soul, I found I could not quite do so.

My writing absorbed me and, to be truthful, I lost track of the days. They passed quickly. It seemed to be hardly any time at all since I had opened the curtains but it was time to draw them again. I kept the log burner on constantly, banking it up at night so it could be poked back into life in the mornings. I ate the food that Walter Harrop delivered, but distractedly, on the hoof: a sandwich here, a tin of soup there, lashings of tea, and more biscuits than were probably good for me.

I saw Jamie from time to time as he came and went. He left me eggs and returned the Tupperware cake container. When Thursday came around, he hauled my bin from the yard and lifted it into a trailer he had hitched to the back of his vehicle, which turned out to be a quadbike, not a motorbike. When he brought my bin back the following afternoon, I invited him in for coffee again, and again we sat at the kitchen table and chatted amicably for an hour. I did not mention the sounds I had heard coming from the cottage next door; and in truth, now I knew they were human in origin, they did not bother me. Its occupant receded back into the obscurity he presumably preferred, and which Jamie favoured for him. Jamie made no remark about my laptop, which sat open on the table, its screensaver shielding my work—but I found I was acutely conscious of it, of its symbolism of a secret that stood between us.

Our discussion, as previously, came round to books. I asked, 'Do you think fiction is just an arty word for a lie?'

Jamie didn't seem nonplussed by my question. He gave it some consideration before replying, 'At its most elemental, I suppose fiction is untrue, and an untruth is a lie. So yes, I guess you could say that. But that doesn't make it immoral in any way.'

'Oh no,' I agreed. 'So much good can come from it. Books change people, don't they?'

'At its best, fiction gives us something to aspire towards,' said Jamie. 'Right now, I ought to be emulating fiction's perfect iteration of heroic manhood. Who would that be, I wonder? Mr Darcy? Heathcliff? Or has the world moved on to Christian Grey?'

'It depends on who you ask,' I said, feeling that the conversation had veered dangerously off course. 'Most men would say that Jack Reacher epitomises male perfection.'

'What would *you* say, Dee?' He fired the question at me and I floundered.

'Not Mr Darcy,' I said quickly. 'He's too introverted for my liking. And Heathcliff is a psychopath, so no thanks. I haven't read the Fifty Shades books, but from what I hear, Christian Grey isn't for me either.' I thought for a few moments. 'Perhaps Gilbert Markham,' I said at last. 'Do you know *The Tenant of Wildfell Hall*?'

He shook his head. 'Not yet,' he said. 'But going back to your original question, I think books, though untrue in fact, present us with truths. Some we can aspire to and some—the uncomfortable ones—we can choose to confront and change. That was Dickens' idea, wasn't it? He presented us with images of the education system, the law, addiction ... aspects of the world *as he saw it* that were *wrong* and held up a mirror to them so that his readers could see how dreadful things were. There's a difference, I think between *the truth* and what's *true*.'

'I agree with you there,' I said. 'And what about novels that are based on real people?'

'Such as?'

I thought about it. 'Christopher Robin,' I said. 'He grew up to hate the Winnie the Pooh books, didn't he? So, I'm wondering, was he a morally legitimate subject for a story?'

'Well, that's a clever example,' said Jamie. 'I was thinking about the hundreds of books about Anne Boleyn who, of course, was dead when they were written so probably didn't much care.'

'Do you think that's the acid test,' I asked, 'that novels should not trespass on lives that are extant?'

'I think, in this litigious world, they are better avoided by writers,' said Jamie carefully. 'Having said that, if there was a novel about Aung San Suu Kyi, I'd probably read it. Why do you ask?'

'Oh, no reason,' I lied. 'It's just interesting to speculate, isn't it?'

His answer offered me some reassurance. Todd, Rowan and Rose were all dead. Mary Forrester and Mrs Harrop were alive. Were they ever likely to read my book?

I offered to loan Jamie books from my Oxford Pocket World Classics collection and we climbed the stairs so he could choose some. I hoped he would not see the duct tape that still sealed the attic closed. Now that I knew about his father, I felt awkward about my extreme and neurotic response to his nocturnal perambulations.

To my surprise, Jamie chose *Kidnapped* and *The Tenant of Wildfell Hall.* The small volumes looked lost in his large hands. He held them reverently, though, and I was glad; I had few personal possessions but these were amongst the most precious to me. His choice of the second title troubled me a little

On an impulse, I invited him to join Marjorie, Olivia and Patrick when they came for dinner, which was planned to take place the following week.

'And, if you think …' I went on, waving my hand vaguely at the party wall that divided my house from the one next door, '… I mean, if your dad would like to …'

'God, no,' Jamie interrupted, shaking his head vehemently. A stricken expression passed across his handsome features before they resumed the genial mien that was habitual to him now. 'But *I'd* like to, very much,' he finished.

He offered—*sotto voce*—to pick up any groceries I might need from the supermarket the next time he went into town. The idea of a town—not to mention a supermarket—within reach of his quadbike rather unnerved me, threatening to tear down the veil of mystery I was determined to keep draped over Roadend. I agreed, however, and jotted a few things down on a list in the same spirit I might have written a letter to Santa and handed it to an elf. Jamie's raised eyebrow and ironical smile told me he knew *exactly* what was going on.

He glanced over the list before folding it and putting it in his pocket. 'No ambrosia?' he quipped. 'No manna?'

'Just forbidden fruit,' I replied dryly.

He stood on the path preparatory to his departure, shifting the two little books awkwardly from hand to hand before blurting out, 'You ought to think about running the engine of the MG for a while. Those old cars don't thrive on neglect.' He patted his pocket where my list lay. 'You could even get these yourself, you know. I could take you and show you around. It isn't much but …'

I threw a guilty glance at the garage, where the car had been housed since my arrival. I knew he was right, about the car and about my wilful blindness to the world that lay beyond Roadend, but I baulked at breaking the spell. A book called *Le Grand Meaulnes* came to mind, about a boy who, having found a mysterious manor—*le domain perdu*—and fallen in love, had later been unable to find it again. The hopeless romanticism of this notion, its power over me and the appalling frailty of the curtain between *here* and *out there* deluged me with confusion so I missed the remainder of Jamie's halting sentence.

At last, I dragged my eyes back to where he stood, uncertainly, on the path. The sun had gone down behind the cottage by this time, and a ghostly greyness enveloped him, but even in that poor light I could see the furious blush on his face.

'Just a pizza, or something,' he mumbled, and I realised he had asked me out on a date.

'Oh, Jamie, I …' My discomfort was equal to his own.

'Or there's the pub,' he forged on, to head off my refusal, 'if you really can't bear to cross the Rubicon. Julie's cooking—'

'Is excellent,' I cut in. 'Yes, let's have a bite to eat one night. That would be nice.'

He nodded, almost—but not quite—satisfied, and shambled off into the twilight.

Once I had closed the door I stood in the hall and tried to marshal my thoughts. It wasn't a date with Jamie that I found so hard to contemplate, although there was Olivia to consider. Now that things had been smoothed out between us, I found him pleasant enough company. I found his shy manner curiously attractive—not to mention his well-honed physique and handsome features. I knew him to be kind, loyal and caring. I thought him honest. All these things considered, it seemed a miracle that some local girl had not snapped him up years ago. But I had not come to Roadend in search of romance, and it seemed to me Jamie was more than usually vulnerable to having his heart broken. He could not leave Roadend and I could not stay, so what would be the point? That, though, had not prompted my almost visceral reaction to his proposal. No, it was the prospect of leaving the village—even for an evening, or for a trip to a supermarket—that I found untenable. I knew it was ludicrous. Roadend was not a lost domain, it was an ordinary—if remote—Cumbrian village. The road out of it would just as surely bring me back. My story would not evaporate, never to be recaptured, if I crossed the parish boundary. And yet, the idea of doing so filled me with a kind of panic.

I looked down the hallway to where my laptop sat. It had put itself into hibernation now, but the least touch on its keyboard, the slightest nudge of the mouse would reanimate it, it would reanimate *me,* pulling me inexorably back into my story. I felt the draw of it—of my narrative and of this sequestered, detached, slightly unreal existence that I had discovered for myself—with a magnetism that was instinctual. An animal was not called more powerfully to its winter sleep than I was to Roadend, to Winter Moss, to Winter Cottage and to the world-within-a-world that I was crafting.

Rose. Rose was calling to me.

I answered her call, sitting down and diving back into the narrative where I had left off earlier. By rights, it was time for Bob's walk. Night had almost fallen and I knew that by then, Jamie's hens would be tucked up in their coop. But the hour I had lost entertaining him—pleasant though it had been—clamoured to be satisfied. Something else—the indistinct but unsettling threat of the real world Jamie had conjured simply by mentioning it—made the need urgent. I began to write, drenching myself in the world of my story, hiding within its pages. Vaguely I heard the pulse and throb of the helicopter as it passed overhead and noted, in a half-conscious corner of my mind, it was a sound I had not heard for some time. Bob shifted in his bed, and indicated by a polite little grumble that it was time for exercise, or food, or both, but my absorption in my story was absolute, and I wrote on. The last log crumbled in the burner with a sigh. Still I wrote on.

The Trysting Tree

1942

Eighteen years had passed since Todd Forrester abandoned the brief, bright star that had been his hope of marrying Rowan Winter. What became of her, he did not know; it was rumoured she had taken up residence in India.

The pele tower remained empty, but for a murder of crows that had gained access via a broken casement and established themselves in what had been the solar—the topmost storey—of the tower. The building was embattled by weather: winds that scoured the coastline, rain that pelted the old stones like missiles, or exuded from penetrating shrouds of mist, or came at it horizontally in flights of aqueous arrows. The mortar between the stones loosened and then fell away. Dampness seeped up from the ground encouraging a slick green coating of moss and algae. The relentless sea scoured the base of the bluff year after year, eroding the sub-strata of clay and rock until whole sections of it fell away.

It was known the squire had died with hardly a penny to his name. The brief resurgence of his fortunes gained via his marriage had been lost in the crash of '29; there being no male heir, his title and what little remained of his estates had been returned to the crown.

Todd Forrester had taken advantage of this situation to add Moss Farm to his holdings, buying it for next to nothing, and renaming it Winter Farm out of pure spite—apart from the crumbling tower it was the only, sorry reminder of the Winters at Roadend. He had drainage rills dug in the Moss in a grid pattern with a view to it being turned over to productive pasture. He sold peat by the wagonload to horticultural growers. Both of these practices, had he but known it, decimated the priceless habitat and ecology of the wetland environment; but even if he *had* known it, it is doubtful he would have altered his course.

In all these works, however, by his express directive, the silver birch tree at the centre of the Moss remained undisturbed.

It was his only sentimentality. Excepting this one thing, he was known to be a difficult, uncompromising man. He farmed intensively, with a fervid single-mindedness, focused on maximising profits and his personal aggrandisement. He employed a considerable work force, expecting long hours of productive toil from each man and girl be they milkmaid or mechanic, stockman or shepherdess. He drove hard bargains at the auction mart and market. He was respected, but not much liked. He seemed indifferent to the opinion of others. Todd Forrester was his own man. Generally unsmiling, his youthful beauty had been coarsened by the rigours of long hours and relentless work. His hair was still white blond but had thinned on his scalp. His blue eyes were hooded in crêpe skin, weather-beaten, but also guarded and suspicious. What satisfaction and pleasure he knew was enjoyed privately, in the inscrutable alembic of his soul: satisfaction in his extensive acres and large profits; pleasure in observing the steep improvement to Forrester fortunes; gratification, perhaps, in the commensurately downward trajectory of the Winters. What loneliness and regret he harboured in that impenetrable fortress must also be a question of conjecture. He had never married. After his father died, he occupied the elegantly proportioned, two-parloured Roadend farmhouse alone.

War depleted Todd's workforce, as men enlisted and girls departed for munitions factories in the towns, but the advent of the Women's Land Army saved Todd's farms from ruination. It saved Todd in a number of ways, not least because it brought him Rose Winter.

Rose was not like Rowan. She had not her sister's feisty nature or propensity for waywardness. She had not enjoyed the benefit of even a lone father's upbringing, and being a baronet's daughter to *her* brought no expectation of preferment, wealth or advantageous marriage. Essentially alone in the world, she had been adequately educated and quietly brought up in a succession of mediocre schools, spending the holidays with friends when fellow pupils had taken pity on her, or accompanying school mistresses to their summer retreats in Broadstairs or Bridlington when they had not.

A man of law administered the frugal remains of Sir Hector's holdings, paid the school fees and doled out a tiny annual allowance. Rose was a somewhat introverted child and schooled herself to become a self-sufficient young woman—ready, when her education was complete, to earn her crust as a clerk, a secretary or some similar respectable occupation that might be available to women when she should turn sixteen, in 1941.

She left school to find the world at war and many occupational opportunities open to girls in factories, as nurses, as drivers and mechanics. She was too young to be conscripted but she did a variety of clerical jobs in a weaving mill that wove the fabric for uniforms until she signed up for the Women's Land Army in 1943.

So it was, in the summer of that year, fate brought Rose Winter to Roadend.

She came with a group of ten women from a variety of backgrounds. Rose was at home in the company of women, having attended all-girls' schools, and from her work amongst the women at the mill. She made no special effort to establish friendships, as the women journeyed first by train and then by bus through the dramatic countryside of the Lake District, but neither did she reject amiable gestures. When a plump girl with red hair asked if she could sit beside Rose in the bus, Rose agreed readily. The girl introduced herself as Mabel. She had already lost two brothers and an uncle in the war, she said, and had a sweetheart who was a submariner. She opened her bag and brought out a packet of sandwiches—rather squashed—and two apples, one of which she offered to Rose.

She gave Rose a potted history of her life. She had been brought up in Blackpool; her parents ran a guest house. She'd enrolled as a nurse at first but found she couldn't stand the sight of blood. *Her* Roland—he was always referred to in this way—had been an ice cream man before the war; they had fallen in love over his knickerbocker glory. 'He put an extra cherry on mine,' she confided. 'That's how I knew he liked me. Now, what about you?'

Rose couldn't offer much to equal Mabel's story but gave as honest and fair an account of herself as she could. Both her parents had died. She had a half-sister and niece who lived in India but had never met them. Since leaving school she had boarded at the house of a woman who was a martyr to her varicose veins, allowed her paying guests only one bath per fortnight and who unfailingly burnt the toast.

'Oh Lord,' hooted Mabel. 'Mum's guests wouldn't have put up with that! She does a lovely breakfast, does my mum. Eggs, bacon, black pudding … of course, all that is rationed now. Oh! Don't you miss proper food?' Mabel licked her lips and stroked her tummy. Rose thought Mabel didn't look especially malnourished but she forbore to say so.

They looked out of the window at the high fells that sat like sleeping dragons in the misty distance. 'Do you know where we're going?' asked Mabel presently.

Rose shook her head. 'A place I haven't heard of. I looked it up at the library but couldn't find it. A small, out-of-the-way place, I'd say. But I don't mind that, do you?'

'Oh no,' agreed Mabel. 'As far away from the bombing as possible, that's all I care about. I don't know how I'm going to get on. We never even had a garden at home. I've never grown anything. Have you? And as for milking cows and such …'

'They're going to show us,' said Rose. 'Hands-on training, they said. I hope so, anyway. I'm as clueless as you are.'

Mabel sniffed, and Rose wondered if she had given offense. They travelled in silence for a few moments, then Mabel delved into her bag again. Rose waited to see what further foodstuffs might be forthcoming, but instead she brought a skein of wool and a crochet hook. 'I'm a terrible fidget, I'm afraid,' said Mabel. 'Mum says I can't sit still to save my life. You don't mind, do you?'

Rose shook her head and turned her attention to the view.

The bus took them along a road that seemed to go on forever, winding between high hedgerows. At last they came to a town with seagulls wheeling and screeching in the sky above a small stone harbour. Fishing vessels bobbed on the murky water within the sanctuary of the harbour walls. Rows of stone-built houses lined the main street. Then they were out of the town and travelling along a road that ran parallel to the sea. 'Oh,' said Mabel with a nostalgic smile, 'well *that'll* be nice. I'm used to being by the sea.'

The lane continued, fields to one side and the tufted grasses of scruffy dunes to the other. For several miles they passed no house or other dwelling. 'We're in the back of beyond, here,' said Mabel. The thing she was making had grown from nothing to an intricate, lacey circle and then into a square.

'What are you making?' asked Rose.

'It's a granny-blanket,' said Mabel. When it's finished you can have it, if you like, to put on your bed. I've brought an old sweater of my brother's to unravel. Mum says we can't let good wool go to waste. Even with that, it won't be big enough, unless I can get more yarn from somewhere.' She looked morosely out of the bus window. The day was almost over. A spectacular sunset spread itself across the sky above the water. 'It doesn't look as though there will be much to do,' she said. 'I like a bit of life, me. Don't you? I'd hoped for a cinema or a dance hall. *Something* ...'

'I suppose we'll be too tired to have much energy for fun,' said Rose. 'I've heard we're expected to work very hard.'

'All work and no play, though,' said Mabel.

The bus trundled on between the land and the sea. The sun sank down and then disappeared in a blaze of orange and pink. 'Glorious,' murmured Rose.

'Oh,' said Mabel with a shrug. 'We see that kind of thing all the time in Blackpool.'

The light became too poor to crochet and Mabel put her work away. She squinted at her wristwatch. 'I hope there'll be something to eat when we get there,' she said.

Finally they came to Roadend, the bus slowing to a snail's pace and swerving abruptly from one side to another to avoid the potholes.

'Blimey!' moaned Mabel as they were thrown from side to side. 'I hope we're nearly there. I shall be sick if we carry on like this.'

Rose tried to see through the window, but made out only a few huddled cottages. Their windows were dark, thickly covered with blackout curtains, she supposed.

At last the bus came to a halt. The door swung open and a fresh-faced, freckled girl stepped aboard. She scanned the women, doing a head count 'Oh,' she said, half to herself, 'that's going to be awkward.' Then she gave herself a mental shake. 'Hello everyone,' she called. 'Here you are at last. This village is Roadend and, trust me, it is aptly named. My name is Vivien. I came with the last cohort and it's my job to show you new girls the ropes. But for now, you must be exhausted and hungry. Refreshments have been provided for you courtesy of Mr Forrester, your employer. They have been laid out in the inn.' She lowered her voice to add, 'Don't expect this kind of hospitality after tonight.'

Rose and the other girls got up from their seats and made their way off the bus. The driver was already unloading their cases. In the dark, one looked just like another and it took the women a while to locate their own belongings. Then they trooped up a gravel driveway to the inn.

There was soup—hearty enough—followed by indeterminate stew.

'You'd have thought,' said Mabel, who had stuck close to Rose in the melee of queuing for the lavatory and then finding dinner seats, 'that in the country, on a *farm,* they could get proper meat, at least.'

Rose made no reply. She thought the stew was all right, although the potatoes were burnt.

While the girls ate, Vivien and two other land girls huddled next to the bar, engaged in hushed discussion. They seemed to agree something and the two others hurried away, leaving Vivien behind.

When the girls had eaten, she said, 'Now I'll show you your billets.' She paused, as though summoning courage. 'There's no way to sweeten this,' she said. 'The truth is we were only expecting four of you. We've made room in the barn—where the rest of us are accommodated—for four. Even that was a stretch. There simply isn't room for more. The rest of you will have to stay at Winter Farm, at least in the short term. Winter Farm is a short walk away from here and … it's rather basic. Now we know it's going to be needed, a group of us will get it ship shape. That is, as shipshape as possible … for tonight, though … so, we've decided the fairest way to do this is to take the first four girls alphabetically into the barn.' She consulted her list. 'So that will be … Nancy Burke, Gloria Evans, Amy Kitteridge and Deborah Miles. You girls should find your luggage and follow Victoria, who is waiting outside for you.'

The four girls she had named shuffled out of the inn. The others looked glumly at one another.

'When you say "rather basic",' said Mabel to Vivien, 'what do you mean?'

Vivien sighed and came to perch on the edge of the girls' table. 'I gather no one has lived there for years, apart from a group of squaddies doing basic training right back at the beginning of the war. I'm afraid they left things in a mess and nothing's been done since. But Hannah and Beatrice have just taken some clean mattresses and bedding up there for you, and a few candles, some billycans of water, plus some other basic supplies to tide you over. I'm really sorry. It's the best we can do, for now. If you're ready, I'll take you along. Oh! You might want to use the lav again, before we go.'

The women got to their feet. Several of them did go back to the toilet.

'This doesn't sound good,' said Mabel. 'I didn't sign up for sleeping in barns, did you?'

'It isn't a barn, it's a farm, or it *was,*' said Rose. 'Anyway, I think it's quite funny.'

'It doesn't sound very funny to me,' said Mabel mulishly.

'I'm Rose Winter, so Winter Farm will be rather apt, for *me.*'

They took up their suitcases and followed Vivien past a church and up a steep track, then down another path that went through a thicket of trees to a long, low building that they could barely make out in the moonless night. The going was tough, the track stony and uneven. One girl turned her ankle. The others kept stumbling and bumping into each other, burdened down by their cases that had not seemed so heavy at the beginning of the day. The walk took them more than twenty minutes and, in the pitch dark, none of the girls felt confident of finding their way back again.

Their guide said, 'Just follow the path. You'll be right. But make allowances. You're expected at the farm at six. Hopefully at least one of you brought an alarm clock.'

'Six!' squeaked Mabel.

'It's harvest time,' said Vivien. 'We work from dawn to dusk at the moment.' She pushed open the door of the farmhouse and they all trooped in.

'It smells damp,' said one girl, wrinkling her nose.

'It smells of mice,' said another.

'It will all be thoroughly cleaned and aired tomorrow,' said Vivien briskly, lighting one of the candles.

There was a chorus of dismay as they surveyed the cheerless, dusty room. It had a stone flagged floor—very dirty—on which sat a wonky table and several mismatched chairs. In one corner there was a green-slimed sink and a few cobwebbed shelves. A door at the back of the room was discovered to lead to "a disgustingly filthy khazi," with a wash basin. When tested, the tap yielded a thin trickle of cold, brown water.

Vivien walked about in a business-like way making mental notes of what would be required. The other girls stood around looking tired and disheartened. One of them—the one who had turned her ankle—began to cry.

'Let's find the bedrooms,' whispered Mabel to Rose, seizing a candle, 'and get the best of what's to be had.'

They found the stairs and mounted them, dragging their suitcases behind them. There were four rooms, two on one side of the landing and two on the other, each of the pairs joined to each other by an interconnecting door. Each room offered three woebegone bedsteads. There was a stack of doubtful mattresses leaning against one wall, topped by a bale of clean-looking sheets and some pillows that Rose assumed had been brought up earlier. She selected some from the pile.

'Shall we share?' asked Mabel, and then, without waiting for an answer, 'Let's go in one of the far rooms, then we won't be disturbed by people passing through.' They manoeuvred two of the better-looking mattresses through to the room at the far end of the farmhouse and threw them onto the bedsteads, ignoring the plume of dust that rose into the air when they did so. Mabel closed the door of the room firmly behind them, hauled her case onto the nearest bed and sat down with a proprietorial air.

Rose took the bed next to the window and set about making it, running her hand over the rough cotton of the bedding. 'It feels clean enough,' she said, 'and not damp.'

'I'm so tired I could sleep on a washing line,' said Mabel through a wide yawn. 'I'm going to go straight to bed. I'm glad I used the lav at the pub.'

Rose wanted to clean her teeth, but didn't think that would be possible until the water was fixed, and the idea of going back downstairs with only a candle for light, dealing with the billycans … it was too much to face.

She undressed, turning her back in respect to Mabel, although the room was dark. Rose could hear the other girls, who had now come upstairs and were scoping out the sleeping arrangements. Mabel got her wish; no one else came in. Soon the house was quiet.

Rose looked through the uncurtained window. A pale moon had risen in the sky, lighting up a vast expanse of rough, uncultivated land in translucent, milky shades. She saw a white-winged bird swooping low over the vegetation and the shadow of a fox as it skulked along the track. She had a sense of peacefulness that was quite alien to her. She traced it back to the name of the farm: Winter Farm. Absurdly, she felt as though she had come home.

~

The next few days were a whirlwind of work and orientation as the new girls were paired off with more experienced Land Girls and shown the ropes. A cleaning party was assigned to Winter Farm, and Rose found herself on her knees, scrubbing ancient, crusted slime from the floor, ravelling cobwebs and clearing the desiccated remains of generations of bluebottles from the windows. She worked alongside a capable, mechanically minded older woman called Victoria and another of the new recruits, Judith, who turned out to be the daughter of a bishop. Like Rose, she had led a cloistered life, and the two got on pretty well.

Gradually, Winter Farm lost its sad, neglected air and became almost a pleasant place for the women to return to at the end of their hard day's work. Victoria bullied the lavatory into flushing and scoured it with a noxious brew of chemicals that ate the strata of limescale and other noisome stains as well as the glaze, but which at least left the toilet clean. An ancient kerosene geyser had been coaxed into life and they had hot water in the kitchen. Victoria managed to rig up a hose and a rudimentary shower bath with a screen around it in the yard at the back of the kitchen. 'It will be fine while the weather holds,' she said. 'What we'll do come autumn, I don't know.' A lady in the village offered to make blackout curtains for them and Rose helped to hang them at the windows. At the end of a week Winter Farm was, if not a cheerful abode, at least a clean and serviceable one.

Mabel had baulked at such menial work and had instead been co-opted onto the team in the fields, harvesting wheat. She complained about this too: the sun was too hot for her fair skin and she was sure she was allergic to the chaff; her boots rubbed her heels. Rose learned to tune out Mabel's endless litany of complaints each evening as they prepared themselves for bed, in the same way that she distanced herself from Mabel's tears as she unravelled her brother's sweater and crocheted the yarn into Rose's blanket. What *was* there to say? To tell the truth she rather rued her friendship with Mabel. Judith, she thought, would have been a better—certainly an easier—roommate. But it was too late to suggest a change now.

The weather held and the harvest was gathered in, the women working hard in the heat of late summer. They had the farmer, Mr Forrester, and one lame, indefatigable but monosyllabic male farm worker to guide and advise them. Mr Forrester kept a distant but watchful eye on all aspects of the farm's running; he was known to be surly and the girls tended to avoid communication with him if they could. The farm worker—Harry—was more approachable but would rather tackle any difficulty himself than take the trouble to explain its solution. Thankfully Vivien had been brought up on a farm and knew how to do most jobs. She took upon herself the role of leader, and she was the one who dealt with Mr Forrester, if necessary.

Rose knew him by sight; his white-blond hair was unmistakable. It seemed to her that wherever she was working—in the dairy, in the henhouse, in the packing shed or in the fields—he would be there, watching. When she noticed him, he would look away, narrowing his eyes to survey the fields or inspect the silos. He would bend down suddenly and lift a handful of grain to his nose, smell it, then crumble it between his fingers and let it fall back to the ground.

The girls worked—nominally—for five and half days a week. On their day off two or three of them took the bus to town, to buy provisions and toiletries for the rest, to buy a cup of tea and a bun in a tea shop, and to wander along the harbour as they waited for the bus back to the village. On one such occasion Rose got separated from the rest of the girls and she chose a bench on the quayside to wait for them. A shadow fell across her and she looked up to see Todd Forrester standing beside her.

'You're Rose Winter,' he said abruptly.

Rose stood up and smoothed her skirt. 'Yes. And you're Mr Forrester.' She held out a tentative hand. 'How do you do?'

Close up she could see he was not an ill-looking man for someone who, she guessed—rightly—must be past thirty-five. His skin was tanned, and perhaps prematurely lined around the eyes, but those eyes were bright, intelligent, and a beautiful periwinkle blue. Now, he gave her a half-smile—she could not tell if it was scornful or shy—revealing good, even teeth. He was no taller than she was and she looked at him levelly, eye-to-eye.

Rose's scrutiny of him had been met by his own minute examination of her face. She felt as though he had been looking *into* her, to some inner version of herself. She found it quite unsettling.

Finally, he took her outstretched hand. His palm was rough but warm. He gripped her hand hard before letting go.

'Humph,' he said, as though he had confirmed something to himself. 'You're Rowan Winter's sister, all right.'

'I am,' she cried, surprised. 'Do you know her?'

'Used to,' he said. 'A long time ago. Is she still alive?'

Rose shrugged. 'I can't tell you. I had letters from time to time, before the war. But since then, nothing. She was in Singapore.' Rose dropped her head. 'I think things have been very bad, there,' she mumbled.

Todd nodded. 'If I know Rowan, she will have got out.'

259

Rose sank back onto her bench but sat askew, because it seemed rude to turn her shoulder to him. 'I hope so. She has a daughter about a year older than me.'

'And her husband?'

'Oh yes. But he will have been deployed somewhere. But tell me, how do you know Rowan, Mr Forrester?'

He lowered himself down onto the bench beside her, sitting at an angle to mirror hers so they remained face to face. 'You don't know?'

Rose shook her head. 'I have no idea. It seems a coincidence.'

'Your father owned everything hereabouts, at one time, and his father before him going back generations. He brought Rowan here in the first war, while London was being bombed. I met her then. The old tower on the hill … you will have seen it? That still belongs to your family, as far as I know. But it's the only thing that does. I own everything else now.' He sat back and folded his arms across his chest.

'So, Winter Farm…?'

'That's mine,' he said quickly. 'Used to be Moss Farm, but I renamed it.'

'Ah,' she nodded. 'My family never …?'

'Oh no, they never lived *there*. Dreadful run-down place it was. Damp in the winter. No pasture to speak of.'

'I hate to break it to you,' Rose said with a laugh, 'but it isn't *much* improved. You haven't been there recently?'

Todd gave a little shake of his head. 'I don't trouble myself with it. I just wanted to *have* it. I don't care if it sinks into the Moss.'

Rose felt a stab of disappointment—in *him*, if she was honest—and at the likely fate of Winter Farm. 'That's a pity,' she said wistfully. 'I have felt an uncanny sense of being *home* since I've been there. I've never had a home, you see. I went straight from school to a mill, where I worked as a clerk and then learned bookkeeping, and then I came here. I'm a bit of a lost soul, to tell the truth. A stray dog. I haven't found the place where I belong, yet, so *Winter* Farm struck a kind of chord.'

'You're young,' said Todd and, for all his reputation for being gruff, his voice was not unkind. 'How old are you?'

'I turned eighteen in April.'

Todd seemed to consider. 'So, you were born in …?'

'1926.'

'And you say Rowan has a daughter a year older than you?'

Rose nodded. 'She was born at sea in about May of 1925, I think. Her name is Sylvia …'

Todd's eyebrows shot up to his hairline. 'You don't say! May …' His fingers counted absent-mindedly on his knee. Then he smothered a smile with his hand. 'Silver?'

'Close; Syl*via*. I'm sorry that I've never met her. A *sort of* sibling would have been lovely.'

'Oh yes,' said Todd. 'I'd have liked one of those as well.'

They sat in silence for a while, watching the fishing boats in the harbour. Presently Todd got up. 'I'm driving back to the farm. Do you want a lift?'

'Oh no, thank you, Mr Forrester,' she said. 'I'd better wait for the other girls and get the bus. It's been nice speaking to you though.'

Two days after this encounter Vivien sought Rose out in the packing shed, where she was sorting eggs into boxes. 'Mr Forrester has a new role for you, Rose.'

'Oh?' Rose wiped her arm across her damp, dusty brow.

'He says you have bookkeeping experience.' Vivien gave her a narrow, penetrating look. 'Is that true? And how does *he* know?'

'I met him by the harbour the other day. I … I might have mentioned it in passing,' Rose stammered.

'Hmm. *Did* you now.' Vivien seemed seriously displeased. 'Well, I can't say I'm happy about it. You're one of our best workers. And I shall be contacting HQ because I'm not absolutely convinced it's within our remit. But he says you're to report for duties in the farm office from now on. He wants you to see to the accounts and so on. You are up to it, I suppose?'

'Oh yes,' said Rose. 'I can do the books and I've a fair typing speed.'

'I think *filing* is going to be the name of the game to begin with,' said Vivien. 'From what I've seen of it, the farm office is a mess. You might have imagined you were getting a cushy number for yourself ...'

'No, I didn't ...' Rose protested. 'Really, Vivien, you mustn't think that I—'

'Well,' said Vivien, cutting Rose off. 'Whatever you *thought,* you've made your bed now, and you'll have to lie in it.'

Chapter Twenty-Five

The freeze continued for another few days, the Moss all a-sparkle with thick hoar frost, the ice pools cracking with cold. It was a surprise to me, at times, to look up from my work—where summer sweltered the land and the Land Army girls laboured in its heat—and find the Moss in its winter clothing.

Writing Rose, Todd and Rowan was unlike anything I had ever done before. Normally characters extrude from the writer in shining filaments, like silk from a spider. The briefest sense at first, hard to capture, it has to be shaped and honed and structured layer by layer. Gradually, caught in the mesh, the author sees facets that provide nuance and vagary, the qualities that make characters real. Often it is necessary to go back, because an aspect emerges later—a quick temper, a phobia of frogs—that something earlier in the narrative will contradict. But Rose, Todd and Rowan came to me whole, like an apparition I only needed to capture in words and stick to the page. In Rose's case she met with quite a battle, because I had envisioned her as a much more vibrant character than the one she turned out to be. I had expected her to be gregarious and witty, popular with the other girls. But the more I forced Rose into my conception, the more I tried to bring her out into the light, the more she fought back; in the end, I let her have her own way. Part of me bridled—I had wanted so much more for her—but if there was one thing I had learned as a writer it was this: when characters begin to do things you hadn't expected, you're on the right track.

Once I had conceded to Rose, I felt her presence quite strongly. In my imagination she had lived right where I was, sheltered by the walls and roof of Winter Cottage. I liked the convergence of my narrative with my life, and thinking of Rose—of her echo—assuaged my loneliness. The crocheted blanket—hers, I was convinced—seemed to ooze her comfort.

I wrote furiously, but felt more like a conduit than a creator, a portal through which the ghosts of these people channelled themselves. I felt that I wrote at their behest, that they *wanted* me to tell their story, that they *needed* me to give them voice. My writing, in some strange way, seemed to project itself onto the past, rebuilding something that—like the pele tower—had crumbled and fallen away. It felt like fraud; stealing bare names and naked circumstances I knew were historical, rather than summoning them myself from my own imagination. Was I being lazy? But then I would be gripped by an uncanny sensation that they craved the flesh I had put on their importunate bones, that they clamoured for the clothes with which I had covered their shivering nakedness. They were substantial to me; I felt and saw and heard them, a telepathy I could neither explain nor deny. One evening I stood at my bedroom window and felt Rose right beside me. We *both* looked out at the moon-spilled moss, we *both* saw the owl and the fox—I because I was there, and she because I had conjured her.

November ended and December began, my second month at Winter Cottage.

The day of my dinner party was drawing near. Reluctantly, a couple of days before, I put away my laptop and began my preparations. I cleaned the house, made up the spare beds in the back bedroom with clean linen and found a spare duvet and pillow for the futon in case the evening should go on too late—or alcohol consumption be too excessive—for my guests to contemplate going home. I did not plan an elaborate menu, as I am not a particularly skilled or ambitious cook. I thought a lovely homemade lasagne with a fresh salad and garlic bread would hit the spot, with a dessert from one of Nigella's books that I had successfully prepared before and for which I could google the recipe.

Jamie delivered my groceries on the morning of the day before the party, declining coffee when I offered it, pleading—with a mischievous look in his eye—lots of things to do. I set about making the meat sauce for the lasagne, playing *The Archers* on catch-up, and then an adaptation of a Trollope novel. At some point during the afternoon I must have missed the flap of the letter box, because when I started getting ready for Bob's afternoon walk I found a folded scrap of paper on the mat with the message *follow the lights*.

Intrigued, I put on my coat and boots, adding a hat, scarf and gloves, and wrestled Bob into a fleece coat that he hated, but which I felt sure, in the freezing conditions, he needed. By the time I had made sure the log burner was safe and my meat sauce safely covered while it cooled, the short day had ended, throwing a shroud of purple gloaming over the Moss.

I opened the door and stepped out. Across the Moss, a line of brightly glowing solar lanterns strung out into the dusk, beginning at the wide planked bridge and ending at the copse where the trysting tree stood. Their light shimmered in the vaporous air, throwing out halos that dazzled my eyes, turning the dusk into every shade of violet.

I smiled. My imagination and a deep—but rarely touched—quixotic gland was wholly entranced by the romance of the illuminated pathway in front of me. Who would have thought shy, inscrutable Jamie capable of such a gesture! I followed the beacons through the meandering pathways of the Moss.

Bob bounded ahead, his nose to the ground, his tail an ever-waving ensign of enthusiasm. I followed more slowly, wondering how I would handle this unexpected gesture. Undoubtedly it was romantic, its intention to impress, to excite, perhaps even to seduce, very clear. But hadn't I already warned myself about the dangers of a relationship with Jamie? How would I manage to show appropriate appreciation for all the trouble he had gone to, without succumbing to the heady romanticism of it? At the same time, I wished I had cleaned my teeth and put on a slick of lipstick before setting out.

As I drew nearer to the copse, strains of music drifted out to meet me—the mellow tones of a saxophone playing a soulful jazz number, not at all what I would have expected of Jamie. Also drifting in the air was the enticing smell of food—some meaty stew—and the unmistakable scent of charring potato skins. The collision of fact and fiction assailed me again, bringing me to an abrupt stop on the path. These would have been the smells that had greeted Rose as she entered the inn, and I stood in wonderment for a moment, thinking of the miasmic catalyst of fiction that seemed able to emanate from my laptop, wreathe through the vaporous air of the Moss and coalesce again as fact—here, in the present. If it could travel spatially, was it too much of a leap to infer that it could also travel temporally?

A fantastical notion gripped my soul. Did Rose, *all those years ago*, eat stew and burned potatoes *because* I had written it so *now*?

The idea sent an arrow of elation through me, adding to the erotic charge that already trembled in my stomach. I walked on, my footsteps on the crisp, desiccated bracken feeling in some way portentous.

The lantern chain petered out at the entrance to the copse. I began to push my way through the entwined branches that shielded the trysting tree from prying eyes. I knew *he* knew I was close. Bob's arrival ahead of me would have seen to that. The trees stood immobile; no breath of breeze disturbed their leafless branches; no sigh of wind came across the Moss. It seemed as though the whole earth was waiting. I could sense Jamie, within the bower, holding his breath. His anticipation—like mine—intense, poised to see what new flower might bloom from the frosty night, the spectral trees, the frost-bound earth, under the dome of the star-studded sky.

I pushed forward again, the snap of twigs behind me and the shiver of branches as I passed through them giving me away. Through the last interwoven screen, I could see into the heart of the arbour. A canvas awning had been lashed up between the trees, sloping down steeply to the ground to make an open-fronted tent. Within it I could see a scattering of cushions and fleece blankets on a groundsheet. In front of the tent a circle of stones had been collected, holding a brazier that burned brightly, the only source of light in the clearing. Its smoke rose thinly through the branches of the trysting tree and up into the sky. An iron pot was suspended above the brazier—no doubt the source of the delicious smell—and over this stood a man I took to be Jamie by his height and the broadness of his shoulders except his hair was shorter and his clothes were like none I had ever seen Jamie wear. A thick, woollen Fair Isle sweater over the kind of trousers worn by professional mountaineers and adventurers—thick, warm, waterproof, many-pocketed and very *very* expensive.

This was *not* Jamie.

I must have taken a sharp intake of breath. The man turned from his cooking to peer into the darkness of the grove.

'Hugh!' I pushed through the screen and into the lurid light of the clearing.

'Ah, good,' he said, putting down a wooden spoon and taking a step or two towards me. 'You're here.'

'I got your note,' I said faintly. 'I didn't … you were the last person I expected to see.' I was genuinely flabbergasted. I hadn't given Hugh a second thought for weeks.

He looked slightly nonplussed by my remark. He held out his hands, palms upwards. 'Surprise!' he said uncertainly. Then he regained his composure. 'A glass of wine,' he announced, reaching down to where a bottle nestled between the stones of his fireplace. He lifted a glass from a wicker picnic hamper I had not noticed before and poured wine into it. Then he advanced across the clearing towards me.

'I'm sorry I disappeared so abruptly, before,' he said, handing me the wine. I found I needed it rather badly and took a long draught. 'I meant to call on you in the next day or so after the bonfire, but … events overtook me.'

'Your father was ill,' I supplied.

He turned to pour himself a glass of wine so I couldn't see his face when he replied. 'Yes. That's right.'

'And how is he?' I asked.

Hugh shook his head. 'Stable for now, but … I'm afraid the prognosis isn't good.'

'I'm sorry,' I said. 'So, you're not back for long?'

He shrugged. 'Who can say? The doctors tell us it could be days, or weeks. Knowing Dad, it will be soon. Once he's made his mind up to a thing, he generally gets on with it. Won't you come and sit down?' He began to wrestle with a folding chair, clearing away impediments so it would sit on its spindly metal legs without wobbling. 'Here. I think that's pretty stable. It isn't too close to the fire, is it? I have blankets for later. That's the only thing about a campfire; you get too hot on one side and too cold on the other. The trick is to keep turning round.'

I sat gingerly on the chair and allowed him to drape the blanket over my shoulders although in fact, with the fire and in my warm coat, I wasn't cold.

Hugh continued to adjust things in the clearing, turning the music down a notch or two, rotating the wine bottle by forty-five degrees, stirring the contents of the pot over the fire. At last he took a seat across the fire from me and sipped his wine.

'How have you been?' he asked.

'Busy,' I replied.

'On your work project? Yes. How's that going?'

'Quite well,' I said, trying to remember if I had told him anything—however vague—about my self-imposed task. 'How about you? Have you got lots to catch up on, after being away?'

He smiled. 'The land is always here,' he replied. 'It doesn't wait for anyone, but, thankfully, it moves slowly.'

'What *is* your remit?' I asked. 'Conservation?'

He nodded. 'Yes, and restoration.' He waved his wine glass to indicate the marsh around us. 'This is a peat bog. It's holding untold quantities of carbon safely underground. Collectively the world's peat bogs store more carbon than the world's forests. Did you know that? But originally it was a wetland. These drainage channels might have seemed like a good idea at the time, to dry the Moss out sufficiently for it to be productive.'

Ah yes, I couldn't help thinking to myself, and because Todd Forrester wanted his pound of flesh. I looked up through the winter canopy of the trysting tree, following the whorls of smoke as they rose from the fire. He saved *this* though.

Hugh was still speaking. I dragged myself back to the present. 'But *now* ...' he was saying.

'Now that peat cutting is banned?' I extemporised, 'and, clearly, this can never be productive pasture, can it?'

'Well ... What I really meant was, now we realise the value of this environment. There really is no reason for the Moss to be drained. Apart from anything else, when it rains heavily or for prolonged periods, the water from the Moss joins the field run-off in the beck behind the village and the resulting storm-surge is so powerful it's beginning to erode the coast. There used to be a path, you know, along the beach below the pele tower, but it's been washed away. One day the tower itself will fall into the sea.'

'That will be a tragedy,' I remarked. 'And that building has already seen enough of that.'

In the firelight it was hard to read his expression clearly. His colouring was artificially heightened by the glow of the flames. Something I could not interpret passed across his good-looking face but almost immediately he was on his feet again, fussing with the food.

'Yes,' he said, quietly.

'So, you want to stop them up? The drainage rills, I mean?'

'Ideally. The water is leaching carbon from the peat all the time and releasing it back into the environment. That has to be stopped.'

I allowed my mind to drift over the beautiful hues of the Moss, the heathery tussocks and waving grasses, and imagined it all covered by water. I thought, too, of all the history that had been enacted here—of Sir Hector and Ellen Forrester, of Todd and Rowan and, in a future I had not yet mapped, of Todd and Rose. It would be a shame to swamp all of that. 'Such a pity,' I sighed.

'How so?'

'Oh.' I gave myself a shake. 'All the plants would die,' I said.

'Others would come and thrive. Not to mention wildlife. This could be a waterfowl sanctuary. You've seen the geese pass overhead? They'd come here to breed. Imagine that!'

Another thought struck me, another casualty in Hugh's scheme to restore the wetlands. 'What would happen to the cottages?'

'Ah.' He threw me an apologetic look. 'Yes. I'm afraid they'd flood.'

I felt a pang for Jamie and his father. They had so little, barely clinging on to a subsistence, unable to afford the renovations of the middle cottage. When the old man died, what would there be to keep Jamie at Roadend? Now I thought about it, apart from John Forrester's offspring and the saggy-trousered lad who had been helping with the bonfire, I hadn't seen many young people in the village at all. No doubt they—as Jamie surely would—had exodused to brighter lights and better prospects. But then I told myself not to be ridiculous. Hugh's scheme was hardly likely to come off. I knew little of the landowner beyond the fact he had a shrewish and unfriendly wife, but it seemed unlikely to me he would care enough, let alone have the altruism, to invest time and energy into the kind of rewilding Hugh had in mind.

'So, you're compiling some kind of report for the Environment Agency? Or the landowner?' I probed.

'Amongst other things,' he replied. 'This is ready. Are you hungry? Let's eat.'

The stew was delicious although the potatoes were charred black on the outside and raw in the middle. I teased Hugh about it and he laughed good-naturedly. The wine was particularly good, though, and the atmosphere in the clearing—beneath the arms of the trysting tree and in the midst of the magical, glistening moss—couldn't help but be romantic. My initial attraction to Hugh resurrected itself precipitously like a phoenix from the stasis that his disappearance and my absorption in my work had imposed upon it. He was suave, worldly, well-travelled, speaking of plays he had seen in London and on Broadway, of treks in the rainforests of South America, of sailing amongst the Cyclades and skiing in Whistler. I got the clear impression that whatever his remuneration from the Environment Agency, it was by no means his only source of income. What had brought him here, to Roadend, I could not imagine unless it was simply his conviction that his work was important. I rather admired that. Hadn't I followed a similar lodestar? Our conversation ranged from Michelin starred restaurants we had both frequented to celebrities with whom it turned out we had both brushed shoulders. The anachronism of these topics here, in the hinterland, didn't seem to strike either of us particularly. We talked on as the moon travelled through the sky above us and the fire crumbled to molten ash.

Presently I threw a look behind me at the tent Hugh had erected. *Tent* was too prosaic a word for it, with its improvised lashings and lavishly strewn soft furnishings. In my mellow, suggestible, slightly inebriated state, I thought of it more as a *yurt* or a Bedouin bower. It's sturdy fixings high in the trysting tree's canopy made it all of a piece with the romantic connections I had woven around the place—my particular associations with the whole sequestered nook.

'How did you get all this past me?' I asked. 'Did you just *magic* it all into being?'

Hugh smiled. Somehow, without my noticing, he had moved his chair round the fire and now sat close beside me. 'I won't pretend it wasn't something of a logistical nightmare,' he said. 'I felt sure you'd see, and spoil the surprise.'

'It certainly was a surprise,' I said with a laugh, but stopped myself from telling Hugh that the biggest shock of all had been seeing him, and not Jamie. 'But I've been working in the kitchen this past week or so. If I'd been in my study, which is at the front of the cottage, I'd have seen everything.'

271

'That was my good luck, then.' Hugh upended the last of the wine into my glass. 'Oh dear, this is gone.'

'I have more, at the cottage,' I said, unwisely.

'I'm sure you do,' he said in a low voice. Suddenly, his arm was around my shoulders. I could feel the heat of his breath on my cheek. I was deluged with desire, with an overwhelming sense of *déjà vu*. This had happened before. Sir Hector and Todd's mother. Todd and Rowan. And, I decided there and then, I would give Rose this, too. It was so tempting to step into their shoes, their bodies, to really experience what, so far, had only been words on a page. My creative gland yearned to be engulfed in the narrative. It was not enough to *write* about them. I wanted to *be* them.

My rational voice protested weakly. What had I told myself, again and again, about beginning a relationship *now* ... *here?*

I made a grab for the empty bottle and made a pretence of examining the label. 'It won't be as good as this, though,' I said, getting up abruptly.

'Well,' said Hugh, getting up also and coming to stand beside me, 'any port in a storm.'

His proximity was more intoxicating than the wine. I could feel the heat emanating from his body and it seemed to conjure forth an answering intensity from my own. He towered over me, the fair highlights in his hair burnished into filaments by the fire, the golden flecks in his grey eyes glowing like sparks. His face—so handsome, so uncharted and yet, oddly familiar—wore an unequivocal expression. Well, what had I expected? Hadn't the whole production—the enigmatic note, the lights across the Moss, the fire, the wine, the seductively inviting arbour beneath the awning—been leading exactly to this point? Not to mention the entangling threads of my own imagination. He took a step closer and I found the horizontal bough of the tree at my back. It surprised me to find that when he pressed me into it, it gave slightly, flexed, like an outsized limb, oddly human and wholly erotic.

My feeble attempt at resistance crumbled to insubstantial dust. Metaphorically, I stepped through the mysterious veil that divides reality and fiction. Suddenly I was not me at all. I was Rose Winter—an absolute inhabitant of her flesh—lured to the trysting tree by Todd Forrester, drawn by the very recklessness of the deed and helpless to resist the overpowering sexual charisma of the man before me. The sigh that came from my lips carried the breath of Rose Winter as we both yielded to his kiss.

Chapter Twenty-Six

On the whole my dinner party was a roaring success—with just one slightly wobbly moment. Really, I hadn't gone to much trouble, but I got the impression such entertainments were so rare in Roadend that even the most meagre effort would have been a triumph.

My guests from the vicarage arrived in good time, flushed and breathless from their walk. Marjorie carried a capacious shopping bag from which she produced a bottle of wine and another of gin, and some soft drinks. Patrick carried a bouquet of flowers, somewhat woebegone from their trek and the cold evening air. He, on the other hand, looked much improved from when I had last seen him. I could see that his stay with Marjorie and Olivia was doing him good. Olivia had brought her rabbit-ear slippers for herself and a charming card made from pressed flowers for me, thanking me in advance for a delightful evening. I put the card on the mantelpiece for the time being but promised I would put it with my collection of very precious things.

'I'd like to see your collection sometime,' Olivia said. 'I have one too. Mine is just pebbles and sea glass from the beach, and some leaf skeletons, and … a few other things.'

'I'd love to see it,' I said, dropping ice into tall glasses. 'Mine isn't so varied. I have some books I'm particularly fond of, and a ring my mother left me. I did have some earrings from her as well, but someone stole them. But now I have your card too.'

Patrick offered to pour the gin but I took hold of the bottle myself, having the idea he would be parsimonious with it. My dad had taught me that nothing got a party going better than a stiff first drink and over the years this maxim had helped me pull off some rather enjoyable gatherings. Patrick stepped back good-naturedly but I immediately felt guilty. Perhaps he felt more comfortable in social situations when he had something to occupy him. I pointed out some dishes of nuts, crisps and crudités I had prepared earlier. 'Could you offer those around for me instead?' I asked.

He nodded and got to work.

I called out, 'Olivia, will you have a G & T?'

'Oh, no,' Marjorie began, but Olivia, quite forcefully, contradicted her.

'I *will*, Mummy, thank you.' Then she turned to me. 'But just a tiny one if you want me to stay awake until dessert.'

This little altercation surprised me. Clearly, Olivia was beginning to find her mother's treatment of her somewhat chafing.

I caught Patrick's eye and he raised an eyebrow, his thoughts evidently coinciding with mine. He said, 'Just beer for me, if you have any.'

I realised with a falling heart that beer was something I hadn't provided.

I was disturbed in my hosting anxiety attack by Jamie's arrival. I mustn't have told the vicarage party I had included him in the invitation, so a startled hush fell on everyone as he made his diffident entrance into the room. Patty began to yap around his ankles, causing Bob to pause in his more-than-usually euphoric greeting of our neighbour to let out a few antiphonic barks. I stopped mid-pour, my hand and the gin bottle in it suspended over one of the glasses. Jamie, blushing, hurriedly stowed a six pack of beers, more flowers and a box of chocolates on the dresser as though to disassociate himself from them before nodding to the other guests and shaking Patrick's proffered hand as if he was handling delicate porcelain.

'Oh, Jamie,' I called out. 'Once again, you're the saviour of the hour. Patrick's a beer drinker and I haven't bought any. Are you happy to share?'

'Of course,' Jamie replied, wrestling open the pack. He handed a bottle to Patrick and opened one for himself before retreating to a far corner of the kitchen.

Olivia scooped Patty up onto her knee as a way of silencing the noise and of covering her own furious blushes. Marjorie—the guest every host prays for—immediately engaged Jamie in conversation, leaving Patrick to continue handing round the nibbles.

'Cheers, everyone,' I cried.

My toast was echoed and everyone took a long drink.

'My goodness,' Marjorie spluttered, looking askance at her glass. 'I thought *I* made a strong gin and tonic …'

'*Upon my word, we shall be absolutely dissipated,*' said Jamie quietly, throwing me a querying look across the kitchen.

'Mrs Elton,' I mouthed, smiling broadly.

Patrick said, 'Jane Austen's *Emma?* Gosh, she had a poor opinion of the clergy, didn't she?'

And so, the evening took off, as we discussed curates and vicars as depicted in literature, everyone able to offer an opinion or an insight. Olivia hadn't actually read the nineteenth century classics but she was an avid watcher of the various films and television adaptations. I only just stopped myself from making reference to the role Ivaan had played in *The House of Shame.* Marjorie, despite being a member of the clergy herself, told us anecdotes of dotty old archdeacons and vile vicars she had come across over the years. Patrick mounted quite a spirited defence of his prospective brothers and sisters in cassocks but the whole discussion was jolly and genial and when we sat down to dinner it was in high spirits that lasted, with one exception, for the rest of the evening.

Marjorie and I moved from gin to wine. It became apparent quite soon that although Marjorie might think her capacity for drink quite large, it was in fact comparatively modest. Her increasingly risqué stories and her decreasing ability to enunciate made that crystal clear. But I liked to see my friend relaxed, she who did so much for the parish and for others. I wanted to indulge her and so I did not stint in topping up her glass. Jamie took a glass or two of wine but then reverted to beer. Patrick stuck with beer and Olivia, after her gin, drank one of the soft drinks Marjorie had bought, but insisted on having it in one of the rather lovely crystal wine glasses I had found in the sideboard, declaring, at her mother's objection, 'I won't break it. I'm not five, you know.' She soon got over her fluster at being so close to Jamie, and indeed after a while I thought she paid more attention to Patrick than she did to my neighbour. I noted again how improved Patrick looked from when I had last seen him. He had put on weight. His arms and shoulders had filled out and his face had lost its cadaverous look. His teeth no longer seemed too large and his blue eyes sat more comfortably in their sockets. He was almost handsome, I thought to myself. The mumbling and under-confident young man who had arrived had disappeared. Whatever troubles had brought him to Roadend, it was working its magic on him, as it was on me.

I nursed my secret pleasurably in my breast, from time to time finding my attention straying from my guests to my hectic recollections of the trysting tree the night before. The cosy insulation of the bivouac, the feeling of the hard ground under my back and the soft heft of Hugh above me, then later, the gentle rocking of the tree's bough beneath us both as we snuggled, swathed in blankets, against its trunk. Afterwards, I had tried to take a step back, to place myself at a distance to note—dispassionately—the juxtaposition of limbs, the way the plumes of our breath had melded with the fire's smoke, the increasing volume of our ardour. But at the time I had been incapable of dissevering myself from Rose. Hugh, of course, was nothing like Todd physically, but his sexual charisma had been a new revelation. *Todd's* charisma, that is. The two were mish-mashed in my mind.

I'm sure my guests noticed my distraction. I caught Jamie's eye upon me more than once, quizzical in the candlelight, as he looked over the rim of his wine glass towards where I sat at the other end of the table. He must have seen the lights, I mused. Perhaps he had even ventured across the Moss to investigate, but he could not have come near enough to see anything because Bob would have alerted me. What would I care, anyway? I had done nothing to be ashamed of except, maybe, in my own eyes: I had crossed a boundary I had erected for myself, not through ignorance—I could not claim that—but certainly through weakness and my own deliberate fault. That's how Rose would have viewed it, I was sure.

I had not invited Hugh to join us, not because I did not want him there—I *did*. I found I wanted him everywhere—but just because, for now, I wanted to enjoy the secret thrill of it. I wanted to feel as Rose had felt—as she *would* feel—when I had written it: wanton, reckless, clandestine.

For the occasion of the dinner party, I had opened up the dining room of the cottage, polished the dusty table and chairs and lit the fire in the grate to air the mustiness away. As I worked, I had thought about my neighbour—not Jamie, but his reclusive father. What did he do all day in that dark and desolate cottage? I knew there could be little or no natural light in it. I envisaged its comforts would be meagre indeed, imagining ladders, piles of rubble, tins of paint, the materials of the slow renovation I felt sure Jamie had in hand. No wonder, I had thought, the old man periodically got fed up and overcame his agoraphobia to venture as far as the dunes and the peculiar "den" where I had first encountered him.

Now, as my guests finished the last few spoonsful of their dessert, I wondered if Jamie was as acutely aware of his father as I was. Did he wonder if the old man was, even now, crouched with his ear to the chimney breast, trying to garner a vestige of company from the murmured echoes of our conversation? Would our gales of laughter disturb his reverie? Or did the muted reverberations of our talk only meld into the half-remembered snippets of memory and the ghosts of his past?

I looked up to find, once more, Jamie's eyes on me. I held his gaze until my eyes began to water with the intensity, the dazzle of the candles, and the muzz of the alcohol in my brain. I could not fathom whatever communiqué Jamie intended with his forceful and penetrating stare. He sat at his ease, his elbow resting on the arm of his chair, the chair itself angled slightly away from the table. His hair, pushed back off his face and wet from the shower when he had arrived, had fallen forward again. It was thick and lustrous, with reddish tones brought out by the flickering candles and the glowing coals of the fire. I don't know what made me do it—a sudden impulse, I suppose, and too much wine. I got up from my seat and walked round the table so I was behind his chair. I gathered his hair into my fist and pulled it back into a ponytail. I felt him stiffen.

'Are you working on a man-bun?' I asked, playfully. 'I think it would suit you.'

'Do you?' His voice was carked. He heard it himself and coughed the impediment away.

The conversation around the table faltered to a halt. They must all have felt—as I did—the electricity that all of a sudden crackled and fizzed in the room. Every eye turned to Jamie and whatever they saw galvanised them. Standing behind him as I was, I could not see the look on his face, but was critically aware of the radical change in his air, from tranquil to tense in a heartbeat.

Patrick got to his feet, pushing his chair back abruptly. 'I'll clear these plates, Dee,' he said, and began to gather them towards him.

'I must visit the little girls' room,' slurred Marjorie, groping beneath her seat for her handbag. 'Is it upstairs? Oh dear. Olivia, darling, I think you'll have to help me. Mummy's had too much wine again.'

Olivia gave a heavy sigh and a distracted little shake of her head before getting up and going round to help her mother, but without taking her eyes from Jamie as he remained, pinioned by my hand in his hair.

I remained rooted to the spot as the two women manoeuvred themselves past me. As they did so Marjorie murmured, 'Are you going to shear Samson's locks, Delilah?' I stared after her, amazed—confused as to what could have altered the atmosphere so precipitously and startled at her use of my penname.

I let go of Jamie's hair and at last he too rose, turning slowly to look down at me where I stood, awkward now and mortified, in the shadow cast by the half-open door.

'Was it …' I faltered, swallowing tears that gathered in my throat, '… was it your bruises? Hadn't they noticed them before? I'm terribly sorry.'

'I don't know,' he murmured, and I could see by his expression he was as curious about their reaction as I was. The room was suddenly stiflingly hot, an inferno, the fire and the candles too intense. 'Perhaps,' Jamie ventured, but distractedly, as though it was not the main thing on his mind at all, 'perhaps I look terrible with a man-bun.' He gave me a half smile and took a small step towards me. I felt his hand on my arm. It was reassuring, gentle, and yet through it ran the coursing voltage that had fizzed around the room a few moments before. He must have felt the power of it. He removed his hand as though from a burning coal. 'Don't worry,' he said, and I almost wondered if he was reassuring himself. 'Don't worry. Everything's fine.'

I spent a long time extinguishing the candles and tidying up the glasses from the table. When I went back into the kitchen Patrick was elbow-deep in a sink full of suds while Olivia and Jamie dried up. Marjorie lay slumped on the settee, snoring quietly.

'I've put the kettle on,' Patrick threw over his shoulder, 'I hope that's OK.'

'Of course,' I gushed.

'Although Dee does have that fancy coffee machine,' offered Jamie. 'I wonder if it does decaf.'

'Yes, it does,' I cried, throwing myself towards the machine.

'Patrick doesn't drink coffee, remember,' Olivia said. 'Can it do hot chocolate? We can open the chocolates Jamie brought.'

The rest of the evening passed off pleasantly. Whatever hiatus had occurred in the dining room was soon forgotten. We played a hilarious game with cards and spoons around the kitchen table whilst Marjorie slept off her excess of wine. It was gone one in the morning by the time the party from the vicarage gathered their coats and outdoor shoes and stumbled off in the direction of the boardwalk, in spite of my repeated declarations that they could stay, that I had plenty of room, that the beds were all ready.

'Always sleep better in my own bed,' Marjorie slurred. 'Olivia, take my arm, dear. I don't want you to trip on the lane.'

'All right, Mummy,' sighed Olivia. 'Although you're more likely to fall than I am.'

Jamie remained long enough to help me put the plates and glasses away. We spoke little in the low light, moving around the kitchen in a way that seemed choreographed to ensure we were never within an arm's length of each other. At last, he too took his leave, thanking me for a lovely evening. I showed him to the door and he stepped out into the cold, frosty night.

'This will all thaw tomorrow,' he said, indicating with a vague gesture the ice-clad moss. 'The glass is falling. We will have rain by Sunday.'

'A pity,' I returned, thinking of the copse around the trysting tree, its magic dispelled, its ground mushed.

Jamie remained on the doorstep and I had, again, the sense that he wanted to say something but didn't know how, or what.

'Good night, Jamie,' I said. 'Thank you for the flowers and the chocolates.'

'You're welcome,' he said. Then he lunged at me, his hands on my shoulders. I couldn't help but shrink from the suddenness of it, but his kiss was chaste, on the cheek, and then he was gone.

Chapter Twenty-Seven

Jamie had been quite right about the weather. I woke late on the Saturday morning to find the radiant, crystalline aura of the Moss had disappeared, leaving it drab and sagging. A low cloud coated the sky. Skeins of geese arrowed listlessly across the Moss, squawking tetchily to one another as they looked for feeding grounds. I thought about Hugh's vision of the Moss, a lagoon of shallow waters alive with fowl, but the secret by-ways of the bracken all submerged, the trysting tree in all probability felled or drowned, the jacquard of colours which, even now in its subdued state, had a kind of beauty, all reduced to one reflective plate of sky. These very cottages would be mouldering remains, if they were not demolished. All their history—as Moss Farm in the Winters' time, and Winter Farm as cynically renamed by Todd Forrester—would be gone. But then, if it were not, and if the destructive force of the run-off was not stopped, the pele tower would fall. I wondered why life often offered such impossible alternatives, and found the truism incredibly depressing.

It was 5th December, my dad's birthday. Another cause for dejected spirits.

I showered and dressed and took Bob out for his walk. Jamie had already cleaned out the hen coop. There was no sign of him or his quadbike. I stood for a moment in front of his house and felt unaccountably lost; I could have used a friendly face and someone to talk to.

The curtains of Jamie's house were drawn back but the middle cottage, of course, was shuttered and silent. I was reminded of Boo Radley, the recluse in *To Kill a Mockingbird* who lived vicariously through the children in the neighbouring house. Would Jamie's father respond if I were to rap at one of the boarded-up windows? What if I slid a note through the gap I could see between one of the peeling boards and the rough masonry of the house? Hadn't he already proved to me, on the night of the fog, that he would come out and save me, as Boo saved the Finch children? But then I was struck with the idea that the Boo of my neighbours' household might in fact be Jamie. He, after all, was the one who had been virtually imprisoned, if not quite by his father then at least by his father's neurosis. I knew that, from time to time, Jamie took a beating, as Boo had from Arthur Radley. Their relationship—like many families', I supposed—was complex and, without being able to discuss it with anyone, I couldn't comprehend it.

My walk took me along the boardwalk and into the village, where I saw to my surprise that some houses were already decorated for Christmas. Seeing the brightly twinkling lights and the Christmas trees added to my stab of longing for my dad and my brother. All the bonhomie from the previous evening, the sense of having made friends and a little social circle for myself, went up in smoke.

Dad had always made a big thing of Christmas. Daniel and I were deluged with gifts, taken out for treats, provided with every festive foodstuff that man or machine could generate. One year after Dad died, I had spent Christmas with Daniel and Bianca. It had been a total disaster. Their artificial tree should have warned me of what was to come. I arrived weighed down with extravagant gifts from Harrods and a hamper from Fortnum and Mason, hard on the heels of the case of fine wines I had sent to them from Berry Bros & Rudd. My contributions completely overshadowed their meagre provisioning, paltry presents and lack-lustre décor. Bianca resisted any attempt I made to help her in the kitchen and whatever became of the fayre I had provided I do not know—certainly, none of it made it onto the table. Bianca seemed delighted with her gifts—a cashmere sweater and some luxury toiletries—but I could see that I had embarrassed Daniel with my munificence. The expression on his face as I opened the voucher for a high street store was excruciating. My suggestions for filling the long, awkward days of the holiday—that we go out for walks, try the all-weather skating rink that had been put up in their town centre, get tickets for the pantomime—were all met with refusal. They were only interested in the *Radio Times*, keen not to miss the Christmas episodes of their favourite soap operas or the annual re-run of *The Sound of Music*. Although I had been due to spend New Year with them, I made my excuses on the 29th and left. That, I realised now, as I walked past the light-framed windows of the little cottages and the well-staked tree in the children's play park, was the last time I had seen Daniel.

I called into Mrs Harrop's shop and paid my grocery bill, and at her prompting agreed to the delivery of a free-range chicken, a small boiled ham and a box of seasonal vegetables for Christmas. It seemed early to me, to be thinking of such things, but she insisted I needed to place my order so as not to be disappointed.

While I was there, I asked her where the crocheted blanket had come from.

'Oh,' she said, 'I can't recall now. Why? Have you damaged it?'

'Not at all,' I said. 'I like it, that's all.'

She narrowed an eye. 'There's a full inventory of contents,' she said. 'We don't expect things to go missing.'

'Nothing *will* go missing,' I assured her.

I stamped out of the shop, thinking her suspicious and small-minded but now doubting my conviction that the blanket I had become so attached to had been Rose's.

On the march home I allowed myself to wonder if Hugh might come and spend Christmas with me. The idea of us cosied up in the cottage, the open fire blazing, a small but beautifully decorated tree on one side of the hearth and an expensive bottle of wine on the other was rather pleasing. Failing that, I wondered if Marjorie might invite me to join her and Olivia and whatever other strays and lame ducks the village might leave unprovided for on Christmas Day. If push came to shove, I thought I would spend it alone, working, just as though it was any other day. Of course there was another possibility—Jamie—but I did not dare to think about *that*. I liked him but my relationship—if I could call it that—with Hugh predated and mired its waters into more turbulence than I suspected either Jamie or I could cope with. Then there was his father. I had a vision of the three of us around the Christmas dinner table, a facsimile of a mad-hatter's meal too bizarre to contemplate.

It being Saturday, Olivia was working in the shop, but had little time to speak to me other than to agree that, yes, we had had a lovely evening the night before and yes, Mummy was feeling "very tired" today.

I walked slowly home along the damp and slippery boardwalk, thinking partly of Daniel and partly of Hugh—my mind therefore both in the past and in the future, poised in that uncomfortable realm between regret and foreboding. There were some things in my own behaviour I regretted in regard to Daniel. Why, for example, had I gone so overboard that Christmas? Who had I been trying to impress? What had I been trying to prove? In general, though, I simply regretted the rift that had opened up between us. My relationship with my brother was a good thing that, in part I had allowed to go bad. Looking forward, I had a degree of apprehension about Hugh, well-mixed with a quivering and sexually charged anticipation. We had made no arrangements to see each other again after our tryst on the Moss and I knew that his father's illness might take him away without notice at any time. We hardly knew each other. I knew very well that sexual attraction alone was no basis for a grown-up relationship, nice though it might be. And then I had such a powerful sense that the woman Hugh had made love to had been a stranger to us both, an incarnation of a woman long dead but, for that night, resurrected. Writers are encouraged to *know* and *see* their characters but they are not, so far as I know, supposed to *be* them. In this regard I had not dealt honestly with Hugh. If we had been role-playing it should have been with the agreement of both parties. Notwithstanding these things, I did look forward to seeing him again and, through Hugh, of reinhabiting the body and brain of Rose. Being Rose had been exhilarating—a fully immersive experience of creativeness I had never encountered before, the ultimate melding of fact and fiction that I suppose only actors ever get to know. It might be disingenuous of me, but I knew I would not step back from a relationship which was probably a bad thing to begin with and which had little prospect of coming good.

With hindsight, I can see that in respect of all these men—Daniel, Hugh and Jamie—I was lonely—cripplingly, abjectly lonely—but I did not have the perspective to see that at the time.

When I got home, in the absence of any sign or note that Hugh had called, I opened my laptop with the idea of writing a long email to Daniel. It should have surprised me—but somehow, didn't—to find one from him in my in-box, sent from his work email address rather than the danielandbianca one they shared for friends and family communications.

Dear Dee, I hope you're OK. Where are you? No one seems to know or, if they know, no one will tell me. I've had countless messages from that bloke of yours. Ivor? He says you've split up, but that you have a dog that he needs to return to its owner. Is that right? He thinks you may have got the impression that the dog was yours to keep, but in fact it was just a temporary arrangement, while the owner went away. I gather money changed hands and now the dog's owner wants the money or the dog back.

Anyway, that's your business and I wash my hands of it. I'll let Ivor know that I've passed the message on as best I am able.

I've been promoted at work—longer hours but better pay—and so Bianca has handed in her notice. You know she's always hated working in that soulless council office. She'll look for something else in the new year, or maybe she will re-train. In the meantime, she has joined a gym and a wild swimming club and is learning to play golf and bridge. She is at the golf club this morning, so I thought I'd take the opportunity to drop you a line and get that bloke out of my hair.

I drove past the old house last week. The new owners have added an orangery to the back and had the drive block paved. Dad's veg patch has been put back to grass. I thought that was a shame. The apple tree where we had our treehouse has been felled. I sat outside for quite a long time and thought back to those days.

Let me know where you are and that you're OK, sis. But don't drag me into the situation with Ivor and the dog.

Daniel

This communiqué gave me much food for thought, not least the surprising information that Ivaan—the swine—had taken money in return for "caring" for Bob. What a joke! And he had been prepared to allow me to bond with Bob before announcing he was not ours to keep. I looked down at where Bob lay, half in and half out of his bed, spilling onto the hearth rug as was his wont. I wouldn't part with him now for all the tea in China. Let Ivaan find the money from his earnings in Acapulco.

I was sceptical about Bianca's declared intention to find another job in the new year or at any other time. She would enjoy Daniel's increased earnings by becoming a lady-who-lunched. As a child, Daniel had been a quixotic, imaginative, impulsive boy. Our tree house, I recalled, had been his idea. Dad had followed Daniel's vision in affixing the boards for the floor, the lookout turret and the winding stair. I had provided endless "feasts" for consumption and been the Indian to his cowboy, the squire to his knight, the Robin to his Batman—whatever flunkey, foe, hostage or sidekick his imagination had required. Bianca had extinguished all the light from Daniel, diverting him from his ambition to teach Maths in a deprived inner-city school to the grey and stilted world of Accountancy. She had objected to his predilection for amateur dramatics and his season ticket for the local football team to the point that both had been given up. With her he had become a dull, middle-aged, middle-class nonentity. He had been absorbed into her narrow, hidebound concept of bourgeois respectability, squashed, suffocated and effectively extinguished. In all our battles over our father's Will he had taken Bianca's side and, that last Christmas, I had accepted that he—the Daniel I had nursed and played with and loved and admired—was lost to me. But now I thought it strangely significant that he should write to me *privately,* from an email address that she could not monitor, and at a time when she could not pry. And on Dad's birthday, too. Perhaps, I mused, there was something of the old Daniel left after all.

I wrote back to him, assuring him I was fine, working hard on a new book, living in a remote corner of northern England and—yes—had a dog that I would under no circumstances be returning to its previous owner. Let Ivaan pay back the money. Since he had taken Mum's earrings and an expensive designer handbag without my permission, it was the least he owed me. I told him I remembered the treehouse vividly, and all the fun we had in it over the years. I said I was thinking of Dad today especially, as I was sure he was too. I made no reference to Bianca. As far as Daniel and I were concerned there *was* no Bianca. I signed it "with love" and added a kiss. I pressed "send" and felt at least a little of my burden of loneliness lift from my heart.

A little more of it disappeared later, well after dark, when a soft tap on my window made Bob utter a warning woof and broke my chain of concentration on the novel I was reading. I was in the sitting room, the coals glowing in the grate, a cup of tea balanced on the arm of the sofa. I opened the door a crack to find Hugh on my doorstep in an expensive waxed jacket, his hair damp from the drizzle I had not realised had begun to fall. I glanced into the lane beyond my garden wall. No vehicle. There was no moon that night; or if there was one, it was hidden behind the curtain of cloud that had draped itself across the landscape.

He smiled—that warm, charming smile I found so hard to resist. 'Fancy some company?' he said. Of course, he could not have said anything more calculated to weaken any small vestige of resolve I might have had against him.

I opened the door and he stepped inside.

Throughout the next weeks of December our affair carried on in this manner. The sky rarely seemed to get light at all on some days, the sun forever blocked behind thick grey cloud, the day made night by drizzle, while the days grew so short they were over before they had begun. The palette of the Moss was all dun and drear: soggy green, dirt-brown, mud-rut grey. It was in this half-lit, half-awake world we found each other, the murk throwing itself over our relationship like a shadow, rendering it in secret tones. Hugh would arrive under cover of darkness, stay until the small hours and then disappear before the lazy light of dawn struggled over the massif in the distance. Or we would meet by some unplanned serendipity, near the trysting tree on the path beneath the willows, Hugh weighed down by detailed maps in sealed wallets, or once, a GPS locator he carried in a backpack. I would sense—rather than see—the bulk of him in the seasonal dimness that seemed to both press down upon the marsh and exude from it; a shifting in the gloom, the dull green of his coat emerging from the dull gauze of rain, and then the solid warmth of his embrace. His appearance conjured Rose Winter as a medium conjures a spirit, and I stepped into her as I stepped into his arms, leaving the wraith of myself behind.

I avoided telling him anything about myself. How could I? I was *not* myself. And I asked no questions of him. I did not ask where he lived, much less to be taken there. I did not want to know because if I could think of him as covert and ambiguous, I did not feel so bad about my own deception. With Hugh I was not me at all. I was Rose—coyly bashful, but also reckless and lustful. My relationship with Hugh was a dream, a fantasy, a thing of fog and phantoms, the manifestation of the scenes that were pouring out from me and onto the screen. Outside of that manufactured environment I convinced myself it wasn't happening at all.

In the meantime, Jamie was a frequent visitor. I did not mention Hugh. Why should I refer to something that, in my own mind, was imaginary? I could not tell, by Jamie's demeanour, if he knew about my secret assignations or not. It seemed inconceivable to me that he had not seen the lanterns on the Moss. He must know *something* had occurred. But he made no mention of it. He did not, however, repeat his gesture on the night of the dinner party. We said goodbye in a friendly manner, but not with a kiss. He delivered my mail from the box at the top of the lane, brought logs and coal, and one day he scaled the roof to clear a blocked gutter that annoyed me at night with its drip, drip, drip. We sat in the bright light of the kitchen drinking coffee and discussing books. *Kidnapped* and *The Tenant of Wildfell Hall* were returned, and *Lorna Doone* and *Treasure Island* taken in their stead. I waited, in a little trepidation, for Jamie to make some allusion to Gilbert Markham. Was he, in his mind, the young gentleman farmer intrigued and attracted by the mysterious new lady tenant of Wildfell? Was I the Helen Graham of his fantasies? But he made no allusion to it, and I was relieved.

One Saturday morning we had a hilarious episode trying to recapture a hen that had escaped from the coop, chasing it up and down the lane, our arms spread-eagled as we tried to corral it into a corner while it squawked and flapped and at last laid an emergency egg on the verge. The rain had stayed away that morning. There was a freshness to the air that we had not enjoyed for some time. On the spur of the moment, I asked Jamie if he'd like to drive out with me in the MG, and he took me a circuitous route through by-lanes and greenways that hardly warranted being called roads to a gravel car park further up the firth where, miraculously, a lone coffee van waited to provide hot chocolate and brownie.

'It's as though he's waiting here just for us,' I remarked, as I sipped my drink. 'There can't be many customers at this time of year. I'm amazed he even bothers setting up.'

Jamie gave me a half smile but said nothing. Not long afterwards the coffee van trundled away, its driver giving Jamie a sly wink as he went by. I suppressed a cynical remark, and we sat together looking out over the roiling, brown, foam-topped waves towards the far country which, from this vantage point, seemed to be not so very far at all.

When we got back to the village, I realised Jamie had managed to take me out of Roadend without breaking its spell. I had crossed no checkpoint, seen no town or even so much as a bus stop that would break my self-imposed illusion that I was in some way cast adrift. My Oz, my Narnia, my looking-glass world had not been breached.

We put the car back in the lockup and Jamie said his goodbyes. It was hardly past three o'clock in the afternoon but the brief light of the day was dimming, the dark ground rising up to meet the darkening sky. Jamie's bulk shambled into the twilight as though into a daydream, and by the time I had put my key in the door, night had come.

The Trysting Tree
1943 – 1944

Todd Forrester did not feel the bitter sting of his loneliness until Rose came to remind him of Rowan. She was not *like* Rowan—he soon discovered that—but she looked as Rowan had looked as a girl. She was the grown-up iteration of the child, the woman Rowan should have become had not promiscuity and upper-class pretentions skewed her soul. Rose had the same thick, brown, waving hair, the same smooth, peach-coloured skin. Her smile had all the same gusto, but her eyes were free of guile. Her courage was not physical—Rose would not, Todd thought, climb trees or risk being swept away by the tide—but she had a resilient core. She was self-sufficient and capable and had come to terms with being alone. In many ways, Rose reminded Todd of himself.

And, of course, she was a Winter, and as such she held a special fascination for him. Even though she had inherited none of the Winter lands and, in her self-effacing demeanour, by no means represented the patrician legacy of lordship, yet—in his mind—it was in her blood, lurking there, like an undiagnosed disease. She symbolised, however unwittingly or unfairly, everything he had set his face against. Like the squire, like Rowan, like the land itself, everything related to the Winters must be brought to heel. The chip on the Forrester shoulder must be assuaged.

He had seen her name on the list that the Land Army Commission had sent through to him and had made it his business to watch her. Unbeknownst to her he had even been in the shadows of the inn as she

291

had trudged thither with her suitcase that first evening. He had expected her to visit the pele tower, even to throw her name around the village in the expectation of some vestige of forelock-tugging subservience, but she had done none of these things. She had worked, diligently and hard alongside the other girls, and sought no preferential treatment. In the end it had been Todd himself who conferred that preferment, taking her out of the draughty dairy and the monotony of the egg-packing plant and into the warmth and comparative comfort of the farm office. There she had gradually, without fuss, brought efficiency. Her draw on him was powerful. He found himself returning to the farmhouse for lunch and a cup of tea in the afternoon—surprising the village woman who cooked and cleaned for him; this had never been his habit before. In the evenings, when Rose had gone back to her billet, he would sit in her chair in the farm office—the weight of the empty house pressing down and around him, and lay his hands on the keys of the typewriter.

In the autumn of 1943 half of the Land Army girls departed Roadend. Some were absorbed into factories for the manufacture of aircraft. Others—like Victoria and Vivien—became Lumber Jills in the forests of Scotland. Mabel's Roland was invalided and sent home. Mabel—who had not enjoyed her brief sojourn in the country—resigned from the corps and returned to Blackpool to marry him. There was just as much work to do on the farm, if not more, as the autumn ploughing got underway, ewes were put to the tups, drainage ditches cleared and hedges trimmed. Harry was busy cleaning and servicing the farm machinery and Todd had to shoulder more of the work, leading and teaching the remaining cohort of girls by his example. This did not come easily to him. He was taciturn, not given to the lengthy explanations the women seemed to need. He had not the patience to coax or encourage them. He certainly had no time for their girlish spats and gossip. Returning to the sanctuary of the office with Rose was a respite he found he looked forward to more and more. *She* did not require conversation beyond a brief greeting, would not trouble him with her woes, and allowed him to fulminate his angst away over the accounts and correspondence that she had laid ready for his inspection. Apparently, though, she heard from the girls. They told her Mr Forrester's manner was gruff and unfriendly and that they were sometimes afraid to ask about things they had not understood. Some had been reduced to tears. Rose broached the subject with him cautiously one afternoon, when atrocious rain had sent everyone indoors. Her solution—made with shy diffidence—was to offer her assistance back out on the farm again, but he shook his head at this; she was to pay the bills, do the wages, and deal with the endless correspondence from the Ministry of Agriculture. As for the Land Girls ... well, he supposed he would try to be more tolerant with them.

The winter of 1943 was the hardest many could remember. Snow fell and stayed, coating the land in a crystalline blanket that was beautiful, but treacherous. Two pregnant ewes drowned in ditches. Harry slipped in the yard and injured his back.

Winter Farm was uninhabitable. Any heat from the log-burner in the kitchen was instantly lost through the draughty windows and sucked into the sandstone walls. Water froze in the pipes which, one day, burst. Gelid water flowed over the stone slabs of the floor and then turned to ice. By then only Rose and Judith remained at Winter Farm, the others having left or taken up the spare bunks in the comparatively cosy barn.

Rose mentioned the matter to Todd Forrester one afternoon after several hours spent over some bewilderingly complicated forms sent by the Ministry.

'I don't know what can be done,' she said. 'Probably nothing. But I think, if this cold weather continues, Judith and I will have to transfer elsewhere.'

Todd put his cup of tea down. 'Transfer?'

'Oh yes,' said Rose, shuffling some documents together. 'People are needed in all kinds of places. We'll be snapped up.'

The idea of Rose leaving filled Todd with a strange alarm. 'Why don't you move into the barn?'

'There isn't room, and, frankly, since Betty ...' Betty, one of the newer recruits, had unexpectedly delivered a baby a few days before. 'I'm told no one is getting much sleep in there.'

'She's to be sent home, as soon as she's well enough to travel.'

'Yes, I know. But that only makes one vacancy. There are two of us.'

Todd looked around the farm office, now neat, the slew of invoices, lists and inventories having been tamed into organised files and put away in properly indexed drawers. The drawers themselves, and the old desk that Todd had inherited with the house, had been polished; he had never noticed before what a fine grain the wood had. The desk was empty apart from Rose's typewriter and a pot plant she had brought from somewhere, and which thrived under her care. Through the—clean—window he could see the girls coming back from their work. Their faces were pinched and blue and he had a sudden stab of conscience about their welfare. They lived in a barn, while he ... In his mind's eye he travelled through the elegant but neglected rooms of his farmhouse. In most of them the furniture was shrouded and the shutters kept closed. Only his bedroom and a small room that might at one time have been a study but which he now used as his parlour were in use. The rest were empty, wasted, their fireplaces cold. Perhaps he should have invited Betty to bring the baby into the house? But here was a much better idea.

'You must move in here,' he threw out, turning to leaf through a catalogue so she would not see his blush. 'Plenty of unused bedrooms here. Take your pick.'

'Oh,' Rose cried out. 'Oh no. I couldn't. I mean ... it wouldn't be proper.'

Never had her difference from Rowan been more evident. Todd smothered a smile. Rose's probity touched him. It also challenged him. 'Why not?'

'Because, at night ...' she stumbled to a halt.

He let her squirm for a while before he said, 'We wouldn't be chaperoned?' He raised a rakish eyebrow. 'Surely you don't think *I* could pose much of a threat to your maidenhead?'

Now it was Rose's turn to blush. 'You aren't *that* old,' she mumbled.

'Well, thank you.' Todd felt absurdly pleased. So, she didn't think of him as an old man! Well, he *wasn't* old. Not *too* old, by any means. He was only the age that the squire had been the summer when he had seduced Todd's mother. 'If it will make you feel better, have that other girl in here too.'

'Judith?'

'Whichever one you like. I don't mind.' He put his catalogue down and came to stand beside her chair. He was glad she had remained seated. It meant he could lean over her. It made him feel dominant. 'Haven't you said it yourself? You feel at home here. You *belong* here. You're a Winter, aren't you? Where else do you belong, if not here?'

She gave a sort of shrug, and he could see that being a Winter meant virtually nothing to her. It was a name, just a name. It pleased him to see the Winter pride so wholly eradicated. On the other hand, if he wished Rose to stay, he would have to employ other arguments. He lowered his voice to say, 'I don't want you to leave Roadend. You're too important.' He waved his arm, gesturing at the room, at all the order she had wrought. Unconsciously, his other hand rested on his heart. 'How would I manage all these forms, and the quotas and everything, without you?'

She turned her head slowly and met the sapphire penetration of his gaze. 'You managed before,' she returned, her voice oddly husky. She swallowed. He watched the slight spasm of her throat and it took all his will not to reach out and stroke the soft, vulnerable skin.

'Don't go, Rose,' he said.

Life in the farmhouse was a vast improvement for Rose. Now with a fire in her room, she was warm, her bedding remained dry, her belongings were not shredded by mice. She and Judith gave their ration books to Todd's housekeeper and were provided with proper meals—far better than the bread and dripping and cold, tinned meat they had been forced to subsist on at Winter Farm. It was unspeakable luxury to take a bath now and again, and this delight was not limited to Judith and herself. Rose persuaded Todd to permit the other girls to avail themselves of the bathroom once per week.

The water at Winter Farm was shut off once more, and the place left to the mice, the damp and the ghosts.

At Rose's behest, Todd opened up the large parlour, and had a piano tuner come out to coax the instrument—that had at one time been played by Farm Axby's daughter—back to melodiousness. He grumbled, feigning reluctance, but privately he found a heady pleasure in pleasing her. Crates of beer and other treats that could be bought on the black market, and sheet music and records for the gramophone appeared in the parlour as though by magic. If Todd's right hand had a role in it, his left did not know it. He could not readily admit even to himself the delight he felt in having her beneath his roof, in the smile that came so readily to her lips at his little acts of kindness. In the evenings Rose and Judith invited the other girls in, and there was singing and laughter. Todd, from his private retreat, found his attention to the newspaper in his hand distracted, his ears tuned to the sound of their merrymaking through the wall that divided the parlour from his private sitting room. He liked to separate out the strands of the different voices so that he could isolate Rose's low, clear tones. Once or twice he was invited—politely, without much conviction—to join the fun, but he refused. In part, it suited him to keep his distance, to maintain the curmudgeonly exterior that ensured discipline and deference. But in the main he feared he would reveal the feelings he was less and less able to deny.

It was increasingly clear to him that he had to have Rose Winter. She was a Winter. If it meant nothing to *her* it was still important to *him*. Like everything else pertaining to the Winters, she must be obtained. He must add her to his collection—thus the bitter and resentful part of his mind reasoned. He mulled over ways in which she might be subdued. She was a courageous girl but she was not physically strong and he could easily take her by main force. He considered it; it would be easy, he thought, to take her by surprise, to go into her bedroom at night, and clamp his hand across her mouth, throw the sheets asunder, and force himself between her legs. But he knew such an act would only make him repellent to her. She would pack her suitcase and leave, and *having* had her, just once, and in such a way, would not do. He must think of another way. He did not think she would be bought; he could lavish her with gifts but she was as likely to give them away as to enjoy them herself. And he did not wish her to think of him as some doting, elderly sugar-daddy. He was much older than she—twice her age, in fact—but he did not think age, on its own, would be an impediment to her … he struggled to name it … to her *loving* him. That, he realised, was what he most desired.

His desire for Rose was deep-seated: an extension of his early deprivation; his disappointment over Rowan; his *need,* since that time, to put the Winters beneath his feet. He must have her. Yes, yes. And then he would have possessed the last of the Winters, and his demon, perhaps, would be assuaged. But there was more—*much* more—to it. The girl plucked a hidden string in his heart. At night, when the farmhouse was quiet once more, the soft shift and sigh of the cows in the shed the only sound, her presence on the other side of his bedroom wall was palpable to him. He lay and tuned himself to her, listening to the faint susurration of the sheets as she shifted in her bed, the occasional sigh or cough in the night. He must *win* her.

Spring came, and then summer. Vast numbers of ships launched from the south coast and landed troops in Normandy, the final offensive. Land Girls came and went but Rose remained, and Todd Forrester launched his own attack: gradual, thoughtful, tender, as a groom will approach a skittish horse. By slow degrees he chipped away the carapace—his own aura of grumpy reserve—and allowed her to see the man beneath. He smiled at her, creasing his face into the unaccustomed expression, but was otherwise aloof, pretending disinterest. He would go to lengths to manoeuvre himself into her company, meeting her on her evening stroll along the beach as though by accident, walking a little way with her but then making an abrupt excuse to go in a different direction, leaving her confused and a little bereft, wanting more.

Rose was surprised to discover she *did* want more. Judith had left to marry a curate with whom she had long had "an understanding." None of the original cohort of Land Army girls remained at Roadend. Although the current lot were friendly, they were mainly city girls, coarse and worldly; there were none with whom Rose felt she might strike up a friendship. One of them—a sly, spiteful girl called Gaynor who had caused trouble amongst the others—had been permitted to move into the farmhouse to replace Judith, but Rose had little to do with her. Rose was not invited to join the rest for their summer evenings on the beach, where they drank gin and discussed their various sexual encounters. In the evenings she would do her laundry, or read the novels and occasional magazines that got passed around the women. Sometimes she played the piano, but it was out of tune once more and she did not wish to ask Todd to send for the piano tuner again. She liked the farmhouse. It was spartan in its furnishings, but the wood panelling in the hallway, the elegant shutters, the Adam fireplaces and ornate ceiling corbels were delightful. She would miss it, she thought, when she had to leave. She toured the rooms and felt their emptiness was a manifestation of her own loneliness. Sometimes Todd would come and sit with her, and they would discuss farm business, but then he would make an excuse, and she would be alone again. Once or twice she saw him in town, where she had gone alone. She longed for him to invite her to have a cup of tea in the tea shop, or to offer her a lift home, but he never did either, walking away and leaving her on the pavement by herself.

She saw past his crankiness. He was lonely, she realised. Just as she was. She decided he was also shy—a bachelor, unaccustomed to the company of women. His reticence added to his attractiveness; she would not have liked a "fast" man, a modern, unthinking, young man.

One warm Sunday afternoon Todd said to her, 'Come with me. I want to show you something.'

She lay her book down on the seat she had been occupying, beneath the shade of a horse chestnut tree, and rose immediately at his summons. They passed between the farm gates and turned right, towards the church. The church was closed now, the morning service having concluded, but the verger and one or two others were mowing the grass around the gravestones.

'My parents are buried in there,' Todd remarked as they passed by. 'I shall be too, bye and bye. Do you know I have never been further than Carlisle?'

'Have your people always lived at Roadend?' Rose asked, because—unusually—he seemed disposed to speak of his past.

He shook his head. 'I don't know where we came from. At first, we were cold-shouldered. We were "incomers," and my parents were Methodists. There was a chapel, way out over the dunes. I never go there these days.'

'You have unhappy memories of it?'

'My father was a difficult man. The war addled his wits and turned him to drink.'

'I'm sorry. That must have been difficult.'

Todd threw off her sympathy. 'I have made up for it since. No one can say *now* that I don't belong at Roadend. I *am* Roadend. There's barely a stick or stone that I don't own. Of course, it all used to be your father's.'

Their way took them up the slope of the bluff, and Rose wondered if they were going to Winter Farm, to see what might be done about making it habitable again, for more Land Girls would be coming for harvest and there was no room for them in the barn. But they passed the track that went down that way and continued to climb steeply, towards the pele tower. The sight of it—embattled, weather-beaten and desolate—seemed like an adequate illustration of Todd's last remark. The Winters and everything relating to them was ruined.

'I have no memories of my father,' she said. 'I was an infant when he died. Perhaps that is kinder than unhappy ones.'

'I remember him,' said Todd, thinking of their final interview, in the kitchen of Low Farm. He—Todd—had felt triumphant then, having reduced the squire to cinders, but his victory had tasted of gall, because he had been forced to give Rowan up to achieve it. 'You have heard nothing from your sister?' he asked suddenly.

'Nothing,' said Rose with a sigh. 'I fear she is dead, and Sylvia too. I would have liked to have met them, just once.'

They had reached the top of the rise. A few sheep scattered at their approach. The pele tower stood silent in the sun, bleak against the intense green of the turf and the blue of the sky and sea.

'This is your birth-right,' said Todd, perhaps a little cruelly. 'I suppose, technically, it is yours. You could move in, if you wished.'

The double doors yielded at his push, and they entered the cool of the lower floor. Straw still lay about the cobbles and an old hay net swayed in the breeze.

Todd began to mount the stone steps, pausing at the top with his hand on the heavy oak door. 'May I, my lady?' he asked with affected gallantry, to offset the meanness of his last words.

'By all means,' said Rose, frowning, because she did not understand his mood or his purpose.

The main chamber of the tower had been relatively untouched by the years. A large, probably very ancient table sat before an enormous fireplace. In one corner, shielded by screens, was a cooking range, a much more utilitarian table and a few shelves containing basic kitchenalia. It surprised Todd to see how rudimentary it all was; somehow, he had expected more grandeur. As a boy, when he had come there with his mother, it had *seemed* magnificent.

In the corner of the room more stone stairs led up to the bedrooms, just two of them—no wonder Captain Broughton-Moore had to be accommodated in the inn. The bedrooms were empty of furniture; whatever had been left behind by Sir Hector had long since been looted. The casement of one room—the seaward room—was broken and swung from its hinges. The floorboards below it sagged with rot, and Todd put out his arm to prevent Rose from going to look at the view. 'It's not safe,' he said, pulling her close to him for a brief, delicious moment. He had a momentary impression of her body—soft, warm, smelling astringently of the cider vinegar he knew she used to rinse her hair— before he released her. 'I can send Harry up, if you like, to board that window up,' he said. 'But the floorboards will be a bigger task.'

'What's the point?' said Rose, 'unless you want me out of the farmhouse?' It was the only explanation she could think of. She looked at a further flight of stairs, wooden this time. 'What's up there?'

'They called it the solar,' said Todd. 'Sir Hector used to conduct his business up there. His tenants said he liked to wear them out by the stairs. We can go up, if you like. I'll make sure you're safe.'

From above them a sudden gust of wind through some aperture made a hollow moaning sound. A crow, in startling proximity, cawed shrilly.

Rose turned away. The thought of being sent here depressed her. She thought she would rather go back to Winter Farm if Todd no longer wanted her at the farm. 'I think I'd like to go back outside if you don't mind,' she said. 'This place means nothing to me. It makes me feel rather sad.'

Back out in the light and warmth she tried to rally her spirits. Todd opened a bag he had been carrying and laid a blanket on the turf on the seaward side of the tower exactly where, twenty years before, Sir Hector had erected his awning.

'I had the woman put us up a picnic,' said Todd, laying out slices of pie, cheese and apples. 'And this,' he said as he produced a bottle of wine and two glasses. 'This is French wine. Chablis. You have to know the right people to be able to get this stuff.'

Rose looked askance at Todd, at a loss to understand him. 'Is something wrong?' she asked at last, accepting the wine from his hand. It was warm, and, when she sipped it, rather sour, but she swallowed it without comment.

'Wrong? What could be wrong?'

'Well,' Rose said, with a half-laugh. 'You've never brought me out for a picnic before. I wondered if perhaps you're softening me up for ...' But she could not finish her sentence.

'You're soft enough,' said Todd, looking out at the sea. Then, 'No. I just thought you should see the tower. I don't think you've been up here, have you?'

'No. I *meant* to, after you told me about it. But there never seemed time. And, to be honest, the Winters ... they feel alien to me.'

'You've been alone in the world,' said Todd, 'as *I* have. But you have *this,*' he indicated the tower beside them, which, from their position on the grass, rose up to a seemingly impossible height into the azure sky, like the tower of Babel, 'which is more than *I* had, to begin with.'

Rose picked up an apple and bit into it. 'What use is it, though? I couldn't live in it. And it's too far from anywhere I could earn a living.'

'You're thinking of the future?'

'Isn't that what *you're* thinking of? But, until the war ends, it's hard to contemplate, isn't it? I suppose, at some point, we'll all have to think about what we'll do afterwards, what life will be like. Of course, *you'll* stay here and farm. But for me ...' She trailed off, unable to go on. She looked out, over the sea to where the Scottish peninsula basked in the sun. She could make out the white obelisk of a lighthouse on the far shore.

Todd gulped his wine. Now, if any, was his moment. 'Rose,' he began.

'Have you ever been over there?' Rose suddenly got to her feet and walked across the grass. The bluff narrowed, sticking out like a tongue into the sea. She made a visor with her hand to shield her eyes. 'Don't you wonder what *here* looks like from over *there?*'

Todd swallowed down his frustration. 'I told you,' he replied gruffly, 'I've never been beyond Carlisle.' He had to raise his voice; she was too far away from him to be able to hear properly. She spoke again, her words snatched away, and he scrambled to his feet to go and stand beside her. 'What was that you said?'

'I was asking,' Rose went on, oblivious to his annoyance, 'whether you didn't think it would give you some perspective? To go over there, I mean, and look back. Roadend is a small place, off the map, in many ways, and it can get a bit suffocating after a while ...'

'Do you feel suffocated?' The wind tugged and riffled the skirt of her frock and he felt the brush of it against his leg. He wanted to put his arm around her waist—she was too close to the edge—but he thrust his hand into his pocket instead.

'No,' she replied slowly. 'In fact, since I've come here, I've felt ...' she groped for the word, '... cocooned. I've felt insulated from the outside world, the war, the need to make my way ...'

'So why would you need "perspective"?'

'Oh,' she turned to him, 'you know.'

He shook his head, confused.

She took a deep breath, 'Just to prove to yourself that it's real, and that it really is as lovely as it feels.'

He frowned. 'Lovely? So, not "suffocating"?'

'I used the wrong word. Sometimes Roadend, and my life here ... it feels *unreal.* I feel no connection to my ancestors; but to this place ... I don't know. *Here,* I have felt ... at home.'

He took his hand from his pocket and caught hold of hers. She looked down at where their palms met and their fingers entwined, looked down in surprise but in dawning understanding.

'You *are* at home,' said Todd.

He had wanted to kiss her by the tower, perhaps even seduce her. It would have pleased him to have stamped his ownership on the Winters' youngest scion beneath its baronial crest. Suddenly now none of that seemed important to him. He had enjoyed showing her the ruined tower.

He had hoped the contrast between it and the elegantly proportioned and comfortable farmhouse would have struck her. He wished—callously, perhaps—to have emphasised the contrast between her peripatetic future with his rooted security at Roadend. Now, with her hand in his, all his scheming ambition evaporated and was lost in the smallness and tender vulnerability of that hand.

'People will say I'm too old for you,' he mumbled, still looking down at their knitted fingers.

'Who?' she breathed. 'I have no one to object.' She thought, briefly, of Mr Chisholm, the lawyer who doled out her allowance. She didn't think he had any remit that would create an obstacle.

'Your sister ...' Todd suggested.

'Rowan? I don't suppose she'll care, even if she's alive.'

Todd pressed his lips together, unsure as to how much he should say. But Rose was right. Rowan had probably been a casualty of the Japanese occupation of Singapore, and her daughter—*their* daughter—with her. 'And there really is no one else? No one you feel you ought to consult?'

Rose shook her head. 'But,' she said, stooping a little so she could look into his eyes, 'are you really asking what I think you're asking?'

He raised his face to hers. 'I want you to marry me, Rose,' he said. 'I can offer you a good life here. And I think we suit each other. We've a lot in common, don't you think?'

'Well, yes,' said Rose wrinkling an eyebrow. She was waiting. She wanted more.

He forged on. 'In a way there's a sort of ... poetry in it. Your family used to rule here, and now I do.'

'Oh yes,' laughed Rose, 'in ye olden days it would have been thought quite suitable for the old squire's daughter to marry the up-and-coming knight! And now you're going to tell me what a good team we'll make, you running the farm and me doing the books!'

Todd narrowed an eye. Was she laughing at him? It was exactly what he had been about to say. He knew what she *wanted* him to say, but it was hard, getting his mouth to form those words, however true they might be. 'I love you, Rose,' he got out at last. 'I'm not a man who's good with words ...'

But his speech was smothered in her kiss. He thought, fleetingly, of Rowan—the moistness of her lips, the bold exploration of her tongue. Rose's kiss was hard, but chaste. Her lips tasted of apples. *That* much, at least, was the same.

~

There was no reason why their engagement should be kept secret and yet, without discussing it, Rose and Todd kept the news to themselves. For Rose's part, she had no one, really, to tell. She thought she ought to write to Mr Chisholm, the lawyer, at some point, but the point did not come. She had kept in touch with Mabel and Judith, but the idea of telling them she was engaged to marry the man that they would think of as curmudgeonly old Mr Forrester gave her pause. *She* knew him better now, and she did not think of him as old, but she had the notion they would think she had mercenary motives so she failed to mention the matter in her letters.

Todd was well-known in the locality. He had business connections, tenants, customers and suppliers. But he had no friends. No one who would stand him a drink and slap him on the back and tell him he was a lucky old dog. His neighbours were nosey. Gossip abounded in the village and not just because most of the menfolk were away. There would be *interest,* he supposed, but not much congratulation. Rose was a Winter, so he did not think she would be considered as an in-comer. But the Winters, in local ethos, were still looked up to. They would think he aspired too high.

The real motivation of keeping their romance to themselves, though, was the *frisson* it added. Todd had never had the opportunity to tire of Rowan; she had been taken from him at the very height of his prowess and his passion. He felt sure, however, that even the most fervent liaisons cooled in time, and he did not want his burning desire for Rose to consume itself too quickly. He had a notion that she was a sleeping princess who would need awakening—slowly, by small increments of passion.

At night they were alone in the farmhouse. The housekeeper slept beneath her own roof and Gaynor, by this time, had struck up a romance with one of the ship-breaker's sons, recently invalided home. She rarely came back to her room before midnight and sometimes did not come back at all. If the weather was inclement, Todd and Rose sat together in the large parlour, she purporting to sew, he feigning interest in a feed catalogue, but their eyes again and again meeting across the empty fireplace between them. When the longcase clock struck ten, they would rise, and douse the lights, and he would walk with her up the fine, curving stairs and along the landing to her room. There he would kiss her, lingeringly, but she would enter her room alone.

If it was fine in the evenings they went abroad, walking together in the twilight. He took her up the hill and into the plantation behind the farmhouse, where they kissed beneath the overhanging branches of the trees. He unleashed more ardour, pressing her to him and allowing his hands to roam over her body until she broke away from him, breathless and feverish with desire. One evening they went to Winter Farm, stumbling together in the gloaming, the light of their candles throwing grotesque shadows onto the peeling walls. Distractedly, they discussed the improvements that would be needed before the new girls arrived, Rose jotting notes on a pad of paper she had brought with her. From time-to-time Todd would lift his hand and stroke her cheek, or snake his arm around her waist, and she would forget what she was going to write. When their list was made—the next day she struggled to make anything of the scrawls and hieroglyphics—Todd asked her to show him the bed she had slept in. She took his hand and led him up the stairs. Her bedstead and mattress remained, bathed in moonlight, the blackout curtains having long since been removed and deployed elsewhere. They lay down together on the narrow bed and Todd kissed her, his tongue gentle but erotic in her mouth. She sighed and reached for his hand, needing something but not knowing quite what. She placed his hand on the bodice of her dress and he undid the buttons one by one. He slipped his hand beneath the cotton and caressed her breast, feeling her nipple harden beneath his thumb. She arched her back, her need for him suddenly urgent, and he moved over her and pressed himself against her groin, her dress rucked up round her hips but himself still fully clothed, until her breath came short and panting. Her little moans and cries grew louder—pleasure and astonishment. Her hands gripped his shoulders so hard he thought they would be bruised. At last, she rose up beneath him, shuddering. Afterwards she clung to him, sobbing against his neck, and he soothed her and told her he loved her, and that when they were married he would make her feel that way every day.

They walked home together across the Moss, which was tinder-dry and crackled beneath their feet. They walked languidly, hand in hand. The moon lit up the silver birch tree in stripes of luminous light. Its sighing branches and whispering leaves were the only sound in the hollow of the night. But Todd's steps did not slow as he took Rose past the secret copse.

The episode awoke something in Rose, just as Todd had hoped. Her dormant sexuality was aroused and became a ravening, insatiable beast, filling her with urgency at the most inconvenient times. She, now, was the one who looked for opportunities to be with Todd, feeling wanton and reckless; she spent hours imagining clandestine trysts. At night, she left her door ajar, but Todd never crossed the threshold.

The new contingent of girls arrived at Roadend Farm just as harvesttime came on. They were, if possible, a less salubrious bunch than the existing cohort—mainly munitions girls who had tired of the heat and noise of factories. Most of them had never seen a farm, let alone worked on one, and Todd was kept at full tilt stopping them from letting all the stock loose, mangling their arms and legs in the machinery and setting the barn on fire with their cigarettes. In view of their extreme inexperience, they brought a supervisor—a senior organising committee member who had expressed herself interested as to the work "on the ground" undertaken by the Land Army recruits. Mrs Bellis was a formidable woman: a widow, mother of four grown girls, and by no means to be hoodwinked by any ploys or dissimulations young women might make. She was eagle-eyed, particularly tasked with overseeing that decent standards were upheld, both by the farmers in their provision of accommodation, and by the girls themselves. In pursuance of this Mrs Bellis insisted on wholesale improvements to the accommodations at Winter Farm: indoor bathing facilities and an additional lavatory, reliable hot water and a refrigerator. Todd grumbled but complied.

Mrs Bellis of course had to be accommodated in the farmhouse. Gaynor was caught sneaking into her room in the small hours and dismissed on the spot. Mrs Bellis eyed Rose's situation sceptically at first. She was suspicious that Rose did no physical farm work, did not fraternise with the other girls and seemed to have been particularly marked out by Mr Forrester for privilege and preferment. Seeing the efficiency of the farm office mollified her slightly, and once she understood the low calibre of the Land Girls, she rather praised Rose's decision to keep herself at a distance. She swept Rose under her wing, realising immediately that her situation—so often cloistered *alone* with Mr Forrester in the farm office—could give rise to remark.

Again, it would have been easy for Todd and Rose to have explained their relationship but, again, they chose not to. It became a game with them to evade Mrs Bellis' detection, snatching kisses behind the henhouses, sneaking onto the Moss while Mrs Bellis was occupied with her endless committee minutes or yelling down the poor telephone connection to Committee HQ. Though both were fully occupied during the day, they found ways to "accidentally" encounter each other. Todd might return to the farm office on some pretext when he knew Mrs Bellis—bonneted against the sun but still puce and pouring sweat—was supervising the girls' midday repast. Rose found that she needed urgent—and utterly spurious—stock lists of feed, fertiliser, hoof treatments and udder salves which would excuse her being in the store alone for long periods of time. She even convinced Mrs Bellis that an up-to-date count of hay bales was essential, which allowed the couple to rendezvous at a far-flung haybarn for a long afternoon of pleasure.

For Rose's part, the pleasure was immense and astonishing. She had never imagined such delight between a man and a woman. Todd had coaxed her gradually, touching her at first through her clothing and then, as he gained her trust, beneath her flimsy summer layers. He had not attempted intercourse, nor had he shown her what she could do to please him. She admired his restraint and selflessness. It elevated him in her mind's eye. Here was a man—the first, the *only* man she had ever encountered—who would take care of her. He answered needs she had not even known that she had.

The harvest was brought home, and in the nick of time. The weather broke in late August and the stubble fields pooled with water. Mrs Bellis declared her intention of leaving Roadend and invited Rose to accompany her.

'We have paid roles within the committee,' she said. 'We need a secretary, and from what I've seen of your efficiency, I think you're more than competent enough. I can put in a word here and there …'

But Rose said, 'Oh, no, Mrs Bellis. Thank you, but I want to remain here.'

'Here?' Mrs Bellis allowed her eye to travel over the farm office, and then through the window at the empty fields and the dun swell of the sea. 'There's nothing for you here, dear. If you're worried about what will happen when the war is over, let me tell you that women who have singled themselves out in the various voluntary corps will be ripe for work in the Ministry, and not just on an administrative level.'

Rose held back from explaining her reasoning, and Mrs Bellis took her silence as agreement. 'I shall assist you with your application and I, myself, will provide a reference. Once we're home, I can really put the wheels in motion for you. I recall from your file that you have no family living. You can stay with me until you're in post, and then we can make some more permanent arrangements.'

Rose nodded. She wished Todd was about the farm, so they could stop Mrs Bellis' interference, but he was away at the auction mart that day and not expected home until late.

'It's my intention to leave tomorrow,' said Mrs Bellis. 'The bus leaves at ten. Make sure you are packed and ready.'

'Tomorrow?' Rose gasped. 'Oh, but that's too soon, Mrs Bellis.'

'Nonsense,' said the other woman, dusting her hands together as though she had performed some arduous task of work. 'There's no reason to delay, and if I don't get your name forward by the end of the week Mrs Aikton will have her own candidate installed before you can say Jack Robinson.'

Rose waited up for Todd to return home. It was late when he came in; the trailer had had a puncture on the road and it took a long time to fix. Then he had the new stock to unload and bed down. When he came into the kitchen, where Rose waited, he looked tired and out of sorts, but he brightened at the sight of her.

'You needn't have waited up, lass,' he said, going to the sink and washing his hands.

'I wanted to,' said Rose, lifting the plate of dinner that the housekeeper had left in the oven onto the table for him.

She sat down and watched him eat. Suddenly, she was filled with misgiving. She had given herself to Todd in every way but one. She had trusted him implicitly, but now that the moment had come, she doubted. Had she been only a distraction to him? Had his talk of marriage been only a ploy to undo her? Their romance had come upon her unexpectedly. It had been so *exciting* … but now here was real life knocking at the door. If she was not to go with Mrs Bellis on the morning bus, Todd would have to make his intentions clear.

'Mrs Bellis wants me to go away with her tomorrow,' she blurted out as Todd swallowed his final potato.

'The devil she does,' he said, wiping his mouth. 'How so?'

'She says she has a job lined up for me with the committee.'

'Damn her committee.' Todd got up from the table abruptly and went to the barrel of ale that sat in the corner. He drew himself a glass.

'But ...' Rose began, willing him to say the words she wanted to hear.

'But?' repeated Todd. He turned to look at her. A single lamp burned on a sideboard and Rose's face was in shadow. 'You don't *want* to go with her, do you Rose?'

'It would be a good opportunity,' she replied, 'if ... if things *here* aren't ...'

'But they *are!*' Suddenly he was beside her, kneeling by her chair. He gathered her hands in his. 'We're to be married, Rose. Look.' He let go with one hand and fumbled in his shirt pocket for a piece of paper. 'I got the licence today, look. We're to be married next week, at the Registry Office. I didn't think you'd want a church wedding—and, in any case, they take too long. I can't wait any longer, Rose.'

She flung her arms around his neck. 'Oh no,' she sobbed. 'Neither can I.'

The following week Todd Forrester and Rose Winter were married. He was forty—twice her age—his beginning as low as hers had been high. They had no guests, and the witnesses were two people who happened to be passing by at the time.

The poor weather had abated, and sun shone on the new Mrs Forrester as she stepped from the unremarkable council building. They had tea in a café and then Todd drove her home to Roadend.

She spent the rest of the day moving her things into Todd's room. It did not take long; her possessions were few. They made up the bed together with fresh sheets and Rose topped it with the crocheted blanket that Mabel had made for her.

The farm was unusually quiet; the girls had gone to the beach to take advantage of the sun. The animals shifted in their stalls. Somewhere, Harry tinkered with a gear box.

'Come,' said Todd.

He took her out, across the Moss, to the silver birch tree. Clouds of insects rose from the bracken as they passed, and a late blooming of wildflowers made an iridescent haze over the ochre grasses. Within the bower of the copse it was cool and dry. The silver birch tree spread its limbs in welcome.

'I haven't been here before,' said Rose, her voice lowered as though she was in a church.

'I haven't been for a long time,' said Todd. He looked around. Some saplings had rooted and struggled through the brush for light and air, but otherwise the place looked the same to him, as if caught in time.

He lay a blanket on the ground and opened a bottle of wine, handing Rose her glass as she dropped to the ground beside him.

'It's special, though,' he said. 'I have lots of memories all entwined with the branches. I came here as a boy many times, with your sister.'

'Did you?'

He nodded. 'She liked it. She'd climb right up.' He tilted his head and peered through the foliage, as though Rowan might, even now, be hiding in the canopy, her hand clasped to her mouth to prevent her laughter from bursting forth. 'She was braver than I was, in lots of ways.'

Rose sipped her wine. It was cold this time, and sweet. She felt it in her belly and in her head, a *frisson* of delight. 'Tell me about her,' she said.

Todd considered. 'She was not like you,' he concluded.

'That doesn't tell me much!'

He leaned towards her. 'It's all that matters,' he said, and kissed her.

As he made love to her, though, Todd knew, in some distracted ventricle of his consciousness, that Rose *was* like Rowan in some ways—in how, she abandoned herself to the moment, now it had come, holding nothing back. He had unearthed—quickly in one case, slowly in the other—an innate wantonness of sexuality that would delight any man. He was glad he had waited, glad he had been patient. Such depths of ardour would not have sprung from Rose on the spur of the moment. If he had been precipitate, she would have shrunk from him. No, it had needed coaxing, but it was there as strongly as it had been in Rowan. In this mysterious fundamental, the sisters were the same. But in other ways they were different. Rose had not Rowan's inconstancy, nor her selfishness.

Todd buried himself in his wife, exorcising in her flesh the ghosts of his past. *She* would not disappoint or desert him. Rose was all softness. It was Rowan who had borne the thorns.

Chapter Twenty-Eight

I saw Hugh three or four times a week, always at night or in some gloaming realm that aided my fiction that our affair was not happening at all. I enacted Todd and Rose's story. When Hugh kissed me, I imagined I was Rose—inexperienced, overwhelmed by his attentions—and he rose to this fiction with manly gallantry. Like Todd, Hugh was a man who inspired confidence; clearly, he was well set up in life, mature for his years. In my rational mind I despised the idea that a twenty-first-century woman *needed* the care and protection of a man, but I was hardly in my rational mind and Rose was not a twenty-first-century woman. I saw what Rose saw: that she was alone in the world and could do much worse than marry a well-to-do landowner.

In between my times with Hugh I walked Bob, kept house and entertained Jamie in what was becoming our own, very specialised and exclusive book club. And I wrote. For many a day I was more in my book than I was in my cottage, my laptop always on the kitchen table, meals taken sporadically around and over it. The morning saw me pad downstairs in dressing gown and slippers to make tea and stoke the fire back to life. I would sit, "just for a few minutes" to re-read what I had written the day before, only to find that hours had passed, the tea was cold and the fire had crumbled back to barely-glowing ash. Then I would be galvanised to eat breakfast, get dressed, walk Bob, before submerging myself once more into the depths. The day would pass and night would fall and I would work on, sometimes looking up to find the room in darkness, the fire out, and Bob sitting hopefully by his food bowl.

On such a day as this I lifted my head from my work to find the cottage being battered by wind. I could hear it in the chimney and skimming the slates above my head. At dawn the day had begun oddly with a weird, portentous light struggling from behind a cloud that smothered the massif in the east. Not long afterwards the sky was blocked out by cloud, as though a blind had been drawn across the dome, and the day plunged into preternatural darkness. I had felt sure snow would come but none materialised.

Now, I stretched my arms over my head and cricked my back. Bob came to rest his head on my knee.

'Poor old lad,' I murmured, fondling his ears. I knew I had neglected him recently.

Even though the evening was upon us, I decided we could both do with some fresh air. I bundled up warmly in my thick coat and boots, added a hat, and affixed Bob's flashing collar and fluorescent jacket. We stepped out into the storm. The wind hit me immediately, far more strongly than I had expected, but I bent into it and we made our way to the willow walk.

I half expected to encounter Hugh—it had happened before. I thought it would be exciting to make love in the midst of a storm—exciting and dissociative, feeding into my obsession with Rose and Todd. We were their avatars, inhabiting the shades of their history. There is something about extremes of weather that I find extraordinarily erotic and I thought of the trysting tree, flexing and bucking in this wind, the sigh and sough of it like abandoned cries … but we got to the end of the path without meeting anyone, and I opened the gate onto the dunes.

We must have been protected from the full force of the wind within the tunnel of the willows. It hit me now like a steam train. The waves crashed onto the shore in a furore of sound. Bob didn't seem to care. He dashed off along the narrow path that I could only just make out between the darker mounds of grass on either side and was soon lost to view. I wasn't worried. I didn't think he would venture into the surf and the wind—although buffeting and strong—could not harm him. He would run and run along the dunes and down onto the shingle, and all his patience over the past few weeks would be paid off as he answered the call of *his* wild, archetypal nature. I followed, bent forward, each step a struggle against the gale, but the power and noise of it energised my blood. The grasses on either side of me shivered and rippled, making a panicked, hissing clamour that added itself to the fizz of the sand beneath my boots—strangely liquid, yielding and slippery. When I got to the bluff where the dunes met the beach the wind redoubled its intensity. It felt like two hands on my chest, pushing me backwards, ejecting me from that untamed and primeval place. I struggled to stay on my feet. It was dark and yet, in some weird way, light. Cloud-like galleons crowded the sky but occasionally the moon—full—broke through. The sea emitted a peculiar luminosity of its own and my eyes adapted to shadow and contour sufficiently to allow me to make slow progress along the top of dunes.

I had never seen the tide so high; its waves broke just a few feet of the bottom of the dunes. A thick line of flotsam had built up along the lip of the sea. In the distance I could see the flash of Bob's collar and the glow of his jacket as he ran deliriously along the tideline, nose to the ground, tail high.

Presently the bluff descended to the beach. I scurried down it, the sand giving way to wet shingle that glistened in the eerie light, my feet finding contorted branches and tangled seaweed and other detritus that caused me to trip and stumble. The sea pounded onto the beach; I could feel the vibration of it through the soles of my feet, and the spray of it on my face. I tasted salt. It stung my eyes and they began to water. The noise was all but deafening, the wind relentless. I tried to focus on it—the multisensory experience of it in my ears and eyes and on my skin, even in my mouth. But all the time I found my mind drawn to the undulating dunes to my right, to the den that I knew to be nestled amongst the taller grasses and spikey shrubs a few yards further inland. It called me with a ghostly urgency, its voice drowning out the note of reason that told me both that it had been a figment of a feverish imagination and that I would not find it again, *and* that I would, but it would be just an ordinary shamble of sticks and wood.

There it was: indeed, a tangle of sticks and sun-bleached branches, old pallets, fishing net and hemp rope, but woven together into the stuff of boys' imaginations, as my dad had woven Daniel's fantasies into the tree house at home. A momentary shift in the clouds allowed the full illumination of the moon to light it up, a beacon, bright where all around was a wind-tossed, tousled blur. My feet turned from the beach and followed the winding way towards the den almost of their own volition.

By the time I reached the place the moon was shrouded once more, and I felt my way around the den by some species of second sight until I stood close to the opening on the landward side. The interior was impenetrably dark, a hollow of mystery. The wind moaned through its sticks and spars, the grasses that had grown up through its structure struggling to be free from their restraints. Then a voice that was at one with the wind's groan—thin and reedy—issued from inside the den.

'Why don't you come in and shelter? The wind is less, in here.'

From the dark throat of the den came a hand—the same hand that had been extended to me in the fog a few weeks before—unnaturally pale and, when I took it, as cold as ice.

I resisted its pull. 'If there's only room for one,' I said, 'you ought to stay where you are. This isn't a night for old men to be abroad.'

'Or for young women, either,' came the reply.

I was pulled into the hollow of the den and guided towards a low chair— canvas and metal, slightly tacky to the touch. The respite from the gale was immediate, as though I had stepped out of a tempest into a womb of calm. I felt the eddy of air between us as we exchanged places. A whiff of damp wool, of chill earth and salty sea, the darkness parting like a veil as he moved through it. I could hardly see the outline of his torso as he stood at the den's entrance, dim on dim, scarcely more substantial than the night at his back. His voice, when he spoke, came to me on the breath of the wind, filtered through the wattle of the den.

'Have you seen … the others?'

'Not tonight,' I extemporised. 'You?'

Perhaps he shook his head. He didn't reply, but I gathered a negative.

'You're still looking for Mary?' I ventured.

He sighed. 'Always.'

'I was told she'd gone away.'

'She'll come back. All of us will come back, in the end.'

'All of you?'

The air above me shifted slightly. I inferred a nod.

'Do you talk to Jamie about it?' I asked gently.

A beat, quizzical. 'Why should I do that?'

I paused. Could he have forgotten? 'He's your son.'

A dry bark. Of laughter? Of chagrin? It was hard to tell. 'Someone else will answer for that. I won't have it laid at *my* door.'

'Oh,' I said, nonplussed. 'OK.'

The conversation faltered. I listened to the storm as it howled around the den; the sea as it heaved and pounded onto the shingle beach; the thick, muffled silence of my dark little tomb.

It started to oppress me and I burst out, 'I heard from my brother, recently. We've been … estranged.'

The silhouette at the entrance to the den stirred. I had struck a chord.

'His wife …' I babbled on, 'she's come between us.'

'Ah, yes,' he said heavily, as though he understood. 'That happens.'

'I've resented her,' I admitted, surprising myself with the admission, here, now, to this strange confidant. 'The relationship between siblings … it's …' I groped for what I wanted to say, '… it should be unbreakable, shouldn't it? After all, you never know anyone in your life for as long as you know your brother or sister, do you?'

Waves of understanding emanated from the outline in the doorway. He understood *that*, at least. But then he said, 'I didn't resent Mary. Oh no. Mary was … we *all* loved Mary.'

'I see,' I said, although I didn't see at all. There were connections that I couldn't make; his fractured mind and my own ignorance causing the misalignment of things that ought to join up. Mary Forrester, the daughter of Todd and Rose, how did she relate to Jamie's father? Had there been—I speculated—in their youth, some romantic entanglement? Had it caused her to leave Roadend? It was a conundrum I needed to explore.

I opened my mouth to ask a question, but suddenly the den was full of hot breath, wet tongue and saturated fur. Bob launched himself onto me, delirious with joy.

I crawled out of the den, back into the teeth of the gale. I scanned the dunes, but they were empty of all but the tossing maelstrom of the night, the thunder of waves and the whisper of grass.

When I made it back to the cottage, a dark shadow separated itself from the lee of the wall where it had been crouching, perhaps for some time.

'There you are,' said Hugh, enveloping me in his arms. 'I thought you'd like some company. Tonight's the longest night. Did you know?'

'The longest night?' I repeated, groping in an inner pocket for my key.

'Yes. December 21st. And this year, a full moon too. Portentous, don't you think?'

'I don't know,' I mumbled. After the wild battering I had received on the beach, and the oddness of my encounter in the den, some human company, some warmth and affection, were just what I needed. But there was so much I wanted to think about; and I was surprised to find that, for the first time, I wasn't pleased by Hugh suddenly turning up.

Nevertheless, I opened some wine and began to pull things out of the fridge for us to eat while Hugh lit the fire in the sitting room.

'You haven't got a tree,' he remarked. 'Don't you "do" Christmas?'

I shrugged. 'There didn't seem much point, just for myself,' I said. Christmas felt like Passover or the Hajj, a celebration that had nothing at all to do with me. The usual London parties had taken place without me. I had bought some token gifts for the vicarage crew—to hold in reserve in case they should invite me to join them at the last minute—and sent a Christmas card to my brother. I had found it in Mrs Harrop's shop, showcasing a view of the Moss under snow, taken by a local photographer. I had dithered over whether to buy anything for Hugh. Ours was a peculiar relationship, carried on in the shadows for no reason other than that was just how it had worked out. In the end I had bought him an e-reader with the idea of loading it with the classic novels he insisted he had not read just because there was no room for books in his rucksack. His itinerant lifestyle was just one more little fiction it pleased us to maintain. I pretended he lived in his tent, yomping from one location to another, bathing in streams and eating foraged food, with only those possessions he could carry on his back and he abetted me in this illusion. I knew it was a fantasy; of course, he lived *somewhere*—I just chose not to know where.

'And *will* you be alone for Christmas?' Hugh asked, taking a couple of slices off the loaf and buttering them.

'I expect so. What about you?' It was a dangerous question and we both knew it. He took a huge bite of bread so he could think about what answer he would give.

'I'm making no plans,' he said at last. 'I may have to leave at any minute, because of Dad, so it wouldn't be fair.'

I nodded. 'That's what I thought,' I said.

Later, I said, 'There *is* a Christmas tree though, and decorations and so on, in the loft. I don't normally approve of artificial trees, but then again, I don't like to think of real ones being cut down for such a frivolous purpose either.'

'I know what you mean,' Hugh agreed. 'They say an artificial one has to be used for ten years to offset its carbon footprint.'

'I have no idea how old the one upstairs is,' I said. 'I suppose Mrs Harrop keeps it for when she has Christmas guests here.'

'Do you want to get it down? I don't mind helping,' said Hugh.

I shook my head. 'No. I can't be bothered,' I said.

The storm raged round the house all night long. I snuggled into Hugh's arms and listened while it battered the house and thrashed the trees on the hill behind us, and thought about the old man next door, and what might have been portended by his remark, 'We *all* loved Mary.'

Mary Forrester intrigued me. So far as I knew she was alive—the only living person who would have the inside track on the Roadend of my book, who had known the flesh-and-blood iterations of the characters I was channelling. Naturally, she would have first-hand information about the Forresters—about her parents Todd and Rose, and about her feuding brothers, who, although detesting each other, I included in the "all" who loved her. She might remember her aunt Rowan. She might also, I speculated, have information about the fire at the pele tower. I knew, in my logical mind, that my job was to create fiction; I wasn't a detective or a historian. I certainly wasn't a clairvoyant. But somehow the world I was creating shouted down logic. The real and the fictional were becoming ever more confused in my mind, the real exuding from the fiction, like a snake regurgitating its own tail, the story becoming truer and more vital to me than the hints and happenstances it was built upon. This was a complete reversal of the usual process, when fiction was extrapolated from fact. My Roadend was at least as real to me as the one round the shoulder of Winter Hill. My version of Todd and Rowan and Rose revivified the remains that mouldered beneath the graveyard sod.

When I woke in the morning, Hugh had gone. Only the two wine glasses on the drainer offered proof he had been there at all.

Chapter Twenty-Nine

Naturally, I had searched for Hugh on various social media platforms but had come up empty. When I asked him about it, he had dismissed the whole on-line business as "a frivolous time-bandit." We had not exchanged email addresses and I still had no phone, so unless we saw each other in the flesh we had no means whatsoever of getting in touch. It was no surprise therefore when, a few days later—on Christmas Eve, in fact—I discovered from a completely different source that his father had taken a turn for the worse and that Hugh had gone.

I had walked into the village late in the afternoon to get a few bits and pieces from the shop and to call in at the vicarage to offer my friends there the season's greetings. In truth, I had been feeling rather sorry for myself. My idea of ignoring Christmas, of blithely working through it regardless, felt less and less appealing as the day drew nearer. I watched little television but whenever I did switch it on, I found carol singers, lavishly decorated trees, cherubic children enacting the nativity and corpulent, middle-aged men pretending to be Santa. Rather than finding all this irritating I found it depressing. I knew my being at Roadend was entirely my own choice. I could have done much more to integrate myself into the windswept little community. I *still*, for example, had not sought out Mrs Ford to see what she made in her studio, and another book club meeting had passed by without my attendance. Lastly, the clandestine nature of my relationship with Hugh had suited me, so I could not complain that I had been excluded from the kinds of things that acknowledged couples did at Christmas. My loneliness was my own fault and yet I resented it bitterly. Those other companions of mine—Todd and Rose Forrester—had retreated from the limelight of late, and no replacements had so far hoved into view, leaving me feeling adrift.

The December weather did not help. After the excitement of the storm, we had been plunged in drizzle, low cloud, dreich and smir. The Moss oozed and dripped. The sea, when I had walked to it, was a turgid soup of silt—a perfect metaphor for my own morose mood.

A young woman I did not know served me in the shop and there was no answer to my knock at the vicarage door other than the distant sound of Patty's bark. More out of loneliness and frustration than because I really wanted a drink, I made my way to the pub. Its door was open and the lights were on. I could see paper chains strung across the ceiling through the tinsel-framed windows. I pushed open the bar door to find quite a crowd inside, both Bill and Julie working the bar and Jamie amongst the tables, clearing plates. Marjorie, Patrick and Olivia sat at one of the larger tables, surrounded by a dozen or so elderly people in paper hats and various stages of inebriation. Arnold was amongst them. At another, smaller table, sat Mr and Mrs Harrop with two other extremely aged people I did not recognise. Three other groups of senior citizens took up the other tables; one of those had pushed the detritus of their meal to one side to deal a hand of cards. It was clear I had intruded upon some Roadend Christmas get-together and I hesitated on the threshold, doubtful as to whether I should proceed.

But Bill shouted, 'Ah! Come in, dear! Merry Christmas!' and even Julie managed to smile.

I approached the bar. 'Is this a private function?' I asked.

'Old folks' Christmas lunch,' said Bill, placing a gin and tonic on the bar even though I had not asked for one. 'Pretty much over now, bar the shouting,' he added. 'They'll all be at home and asleep in their chairs before the clock chimes the hour, I shouldn't wonder.'

'Let's hope so, anyway,' muttered Julie. 'My feet are killing me.'

'You go up and take it easy,' said Bill. 'Jamie and I can clear up.'

She needed no coaxing and I found myself marooned at the bar drinking a large gin and tonic I had not really wanted while Bill served more drinks and Jamie carried dirty plates back through to the kitchen. He gave me a nod and a smile on his way past, but we exchanged no words, and after a while he stayed in the kitchen from where the gush of a tap and the rattle of crockery gave me to understand he had got to work on the washing up.

I scanned the wrinkled faces, myopic eyes and impossibly perfect dentures for someone I might recognise as Jamie's father. I thought he might have been persuaded from his stronghold for such an occasion as this. But none of the grizzled old-timers seemed to fit the bill and it came to me with a jolt I had only encountered him in mist and darkness and shrouded in dark clothing that had obscured any identifying feature. Even if he was here, I probably would not recognise him.

Presently the partiers began to disperse, wobbling their way to the toilets, stopping for disjointed and slurred conversations and then genially searching through the enormous collection of coats on hooks, their coloured hats still perched askew on their grey, white or bald pates. Marjorie and Olivia helped one extremely arthritic lady who had sat between them, so they had no opportunity to do more than say hello, and wish me a Happy Christmas. I replied with festive enthusiasm, suppressing my dismay that they clearly intended leaving me to my own Christmas devices, with a bright and entirely specious smile. It wasn't until Patrick—sent back to the bar to retrieve someone's lost walking stick—took a moment to tell Bill how much everyone had enjoyed themselves and what a treat it had been for Marjorie—who was "at this moment" heading to open up the church for the Christingle and, later, the midnight mass, and who would be working *all* the next day—that I made the belated connection between Christmas and Marjorie's role. Of course! With her religious and pastoral duties, she would have no time to eat, let alone cook a Christmas meal. I scolded myself for being pathetic and needy, and gulped down my gin.

Mrs Harrop wobbled past me, her habitually rigid frame softened for once. She looked down at my bag of groceries. 'Been to the shop?' she asked, her words somewhat slurred.

I nodded. 'Just needed a few bits and pieces. Happy Christmas. I expect Christmas at Roadend Farm is really lovely.'

'It was ... eventful, usually, in the old days,' she said. 'You know by now what the Forresters are like. There's just me and Walter these days.'

'In the old days?' I prompted.

Mrs Harrop made a fuss about placing her handbag at her feet and leaning against the bar, settling in for a chat. 'I lived there with Rose and Todd and the family, after the fire,' she said. Her eyes were glazed—whether from alcohol or memory, I could not tell.

'*Did* you? They took you in?'

'I had nobody else,' she sighed lugubriously. 'I was an orphan. Alone in the world.'

'Like Rose had been,' I put in, forgetting that whatever situation I had invented for *my* Rose Forrester, was not necessarily true in fact. '*She* would have understood.'

Mrs Harrop gave me a quizzical look I interpreted as, "How do *you* know?" But she did not contradict me. 'She was nice enough to me,' she allowed.

'And Todd?'

'Todd was Todd,' she said cryptically. 'Liked to lord it over everyone.'

'Not Rose though,' I said, trespassing again into my fiction. 'Sometimes I feel Todd gets a bad press. But he loved Rose, didn't he?'

Mrs Harrop stared into the distance. 'He could be a bastard,' she spat out at last, taking me aback with her invective. 'The older he got, the worse he became. After Rose died ... and those boys ... but I suppose, if he had a redeeming feature, it was his love for Rose. Yes. I can see that now. For all his faults, he did love her.' Mrs Harrop's eyes turned glassy, and she groped in her cardigan pocket for a tissue.

I felt surprised—but delightfully vindicated—at her change in tune. In the graveyard and before that, in the shop, she hadn't had a single good word for Todd Forrester, but now ... could it be? ... now that I had *re-written* him, softened him, smoothed away his more abrasive edges, she saw him as a rounder, more sympathetic character. What was this alchemy? I had been amazed before at the way my writing seemed to recreate the past, but now I had to ask myself, could it *impose* itself on the facts? I sat in the sort of wonderment a seer must experience when a lucky guess turns out to be right, and hardly acknowledged Mrs Harrop as she took Walter's arm and the two shuffled out of the pub.

When I came to myself the bar was empty. Bill paused in his loading of the glass washer to say, 'Hugh's away again, I hear.'

I pretended only the vaguest interest. 'Oh? His dad again, is it?'

Bill nodded. 'I heard so. Took a sudden turn, apparently. Touch and go if they got there in time.'

They? 'Very sad,' I said, 'especially at this time of year.'

'Never easy, at any time,' Bill observed. 'Another?'

I nodded, and he poured me another double. 'Are you open tomorrow?' I asked.

'No. Well, sometimes we open for an hour or so in the evening. But Julie would have my head on a plate if I suggested opening on Christmas Day.'

'Do you have family coming?' I was goading myself, I realised, with impressions of other people's perfect family Christmas celebrations. The gin had hit some depressive nerve, and I was drinking it on an empty stomach.

But Bill shook his head. 'Our son's abroad. He works in the Gulf. It'll just be Julie and me. You?'

I shook my head.

'Silly, really,' Bill remarked. 'All this fuss for just one day.'

'I agree,' I said.

From the kitchen I heard the clatter of plates and a disembodied 'Bah humbug!'

In spite of my morose mood, I smiled.

On an impulse I lowered my voice and said, 'Jamie's father couldn't be persuaded to come out with the other old folks?'

Bill frowned, as though the idea was not an attractive one. 'No, thankfully,' he said, polishing a glass to a high shine. 'I feel for him but, really ...' He trailed off for a moment. 'He doesn't give you any bother?'

'Arnold asked me the same question,' I said. 'No. Not really. He keeps himself to himself, mainly.'

Bill nodded, and we remained in companionable silence for a while. The Christmas CD trawled its way through melancholic renditions of *White Christmas* and *Edelweiss*. From the kitchen I could hear the clash and clang of saucepans and, very low, a more upbeat selection of festive music.

'Bill,' I said, tentatively, 'what do you know about Mary Forrester?' I had expected him to be surprised at the conversational leap from Jamie's father to this long-gone Roadend resident, but he seemed to take it absolutely in his stride.

'Not much,' he said, levelly. 'Julie and I came here in 03 and Mary left a couple of years later, so we didn't know her well. People here were shocked at her going, but we weren't.'

'Oh?' I could hardly breathe. The anticipation was intense. At last, someone who would talk about Mary.

Bill pressed his lips together. 'He was awful to her. He was awful to everyone. He hadn't a friend left in Roadend. He was so far gone a saint wouldn't have stood for it.'

'Her ... husband?' I ventured.

'Of course. Who else? She did her duty. She saw the lad off to university. Launched him out on the world, safely away from the old man. And then she packed her bags and left. She wasn't to know he'd come back, was she? *I* didn't blame her. Neither did Agnes Harrop, although of course she's no friend to the Forresters, you'll know that by now.'

'Yes,' I murmured.

'But you'd be surprised at how much feeling there was against Mary, notwithstanding. People can be so judgemental, can't they?'

I nodded. I had so many bells clanging in my head, alarms, broken circuits trying to find connections. My glass was empty and although I knew it was a mistake—that the very thing I wanted was probably the thing that was interfering with my cognitive processes—I held my glass out for a refill.

'They just had the one son,' I observed, probing, although I already knew the answer.

Bill placed my glass on the bar and then leaned over to hiss, 'Surprising that, isn't it? When the other lot …'

The kitchen door swung open and Jamie appeared, wiping his hands on a tea towel. 'That's the place shipshape,' he announced. 'Anything else I can do for you, Bill?'

Bill stood up so sharply I felt sure he would put his back out, but he seized a cloth and began polishing the bar. 'I don't think so, Jamie. Thanks for all your help.'

'No problem.' Jamie folded the towel and put it somewhere under the bar. He looked at me. 'Are you walking home? I could give you a ride.'

I held up Bob's lead. 'I am not alone,' I said stupidly. 'I have my faithful companion.'

Jamie grinned. 'No problem,' he said again. 'We can squash him between us. Or I can leave the bike here and walk.'

I looked at my untouched drink, and at Bill, who had retreated to the till and was counting out money. I was desperate to continue my conversation with him, but something in the way he had leaned so conspiratorially towards me to make his last remark, and something else, something shrilling and fluting and piping in my brain like an orchestra tuning up for a big number, told me that, with Jamie present, our conversation would not—could not—continue. 'I've just got this drink,' I said. 'You go ahead. I might catch you up.'

Jamie gave a cynical smile. 'Somehow, I doubt that. Are you sure you're fit?'

'Of course,' I said, but even in my own ears my voice sounded slurred.

Jamie breathed out through his nose. 'Alright then,' he said in a fatalistic tone.

Bill pressed money into his hand and Jamie was gone. I sipped my drink, but without relish. Bill continued to busy himself with the takings.

Presently I said. 'Perhaps I should have gone home with Jamie. I don't think I want this after all. And you must want to have a rest before the evening rush. Can I pay my bill, Bill?' The joke made me smile, foolishly, but Bill must have heard it a million time. He named a sum of money and I brought out my card.

'What was Mary's husband called?' I bought it out in a low voice.

Bill looked up sharply from the machine, a query etched on his forehead. 'Joe. Joe Forrester, of course.'

'So ...' I laboured it out, '...so she wasn't born a Forrester, then? Mary, I mean. She was a Forrester by marriage.'

'Yes.' He spoke patiently, as though I was one of the blotto old folks who had crowded the bar earlier.

I slipped off my stool and fumbled over putting my card back in my bag. 'She was married to ...?'

'Joe Forrester,' he repeated. Again, that tolerant, even tone.

I nodded, as though he was only confirming something I already knew. I bent down and clipped Bob's lead onto his collar. It took me a couple of tries because I had drunk too much gin and Roadend was tilting on its axis. 'John's brother,' I muttered. 'Joe and John. The feuding Forresters.' I walked slowly to the door and pushed it open, then turned to ask my final question. 'What happened to Joe Forrester, Bill?'

Bill laughed, but in a perplexed manner, shaking his head and reaching for the bank of light switches that would plunge the bar into darkness. 'Nothing happened to him, dear,' he said. 'He's your neighbour.'

Chapter Thirty

It was full dark when I left the pub, a moonless night, the village veiled in shadow. A chill, damp breeze blew off the sea. I had no notion of the time but I thought it could not be much later than seven o'clock.

As I passed the church, I could hear the low strains of an organ. Light shone dimly through the small, stained-glass windows. The door, for once, stood open, propped by a heavy metal stop moulded into the shape of a knight.

On impulse, I pushed the inner door open and slipped inside. The place was deserted, illuminated by candles placed in sconces around the walls and by the feeble twinkle of the lights on a small tree just inside the door. The interior was small; a narrow nave with five or six rows of elderly pews on either side facing a rustic pulpit. Beyond, a simple chancel, the altar covered in a white cloth strewn with holly and ivy and incorporating a nativity scene. A low communion rail divided the chancel from the nave, and along its length were the children's Christingles, extinguished now, but explaining the strong aroma of citrus in the church. The whitewashed walls were unadorned apart from behind the pulpit where a faded illustration of some kind suggested an early attempt at embellishment. The floor was made of stone flags, worn smooth. An envelope of brighter light spilled onto the flags from a door in one of the transepts, and I assumed Marjorie and perhaps Olivia also would be sequestered in some inner room, preparing for the next service. The organ continued to play but I could not see its pipes and concluded the music was a recording. The church was surprisingly warm and I unzipped my coat and slipped into a pew. Bob settled at my feet and laid his head on a hassock.

I am not a religious person although I would say that I am quite spiritual; when I write I feel as though I am touching something that is bigger than I am, tapping into a creative force that is wholly outside of me and yet accessible to me. I find something inspiring about buildings built by faith to honour a higher power. They are saturated by prayer, I suppose, their very stones imbued with fervency. I gave myself up to the oddly comforting quietude for a few moments, the gin assisting in a sense of ethereal connection; respite from what, for me, that year, was a drear and cheerless season.

I may even have dozed for a few moments.

A slight movement in the air brought me back to myself. I had never seen Marjorie in her clerical garb before and for a confused moment I thought I had opened my eyes to find an angel before me.

'Hello,' she said, nudging me further into the pew so that she could perch beside me. 'Having a moment, were you?'

I nodded. 'I think I'm a bit drunk,' I said, although in fact my head did feel somewhat clearer.

'God approves of wine, but only in moderation,' she said.

'What is His opinion of gin?'

She made a moue. 'Strictly for prostitutes and publicans,' she said.

I indicated the nativity scene on the altar. 'I expect Mary could have done with a slug or two of something, in that chilly stable,' I said. The name Mary brought back to me all I had learned at the pub: that Mary Forrester was married to Joe; that Joe was my reclusive neighbour; and that Jamie was their son.

'Indeed,' said Marjorie. 'It must have been terrible for women in those days. Not so much as a whiff of gas-and-air.'

'There isn't mention of a midwife, is there?' I remarked. 'She managed the whole thing alone.'

'The shepherds may have assisted, although according to scripture they didn't turn up until afterwards. But we must remember all the gospels were written by men, who may well have been too squeamish, or too ignorant, to have recounted the gory details.'

'Or just too respectful? Descriptions of Mary sweating and grunting and pushing a baby out of her vagina may not have sat well with later iterations of her—the eternal virgin, worshipped almost as much as God.' This, I thought—respect—might well explain the reticence of the people of Roadend to talk about Mary Forrester.

Marjorie nodded sagely, indicating she thought I might have a point.

'Do you think,' I asked, 'that because it was a situation God had sort of foisted upon her, he would have made it easier on Mary?'

'Birth? I doubt it. Jesus was fully human, so he would have arrived with all the trauma and pain of any human baby.'

'Poor Mary,' I breathed, and again my thoughts went back to Mary Forrester, who had suffered, and then had to say goodbye to her son.

'Are you alright, Dee, dear?' said Marjorie, taking my hand and sandwiching it between hers.

I didn't know how to even begin to answer her. I wanted to tell her everything—that I had *stolen* a story that did not belong to me and now I was being punished for it. My lucky guesses were turning out to be unnervingly on the money. Was I psychic? Fiction was becoming fact and I was beginning to doubt my ability to distinguish between them. What the hell was happening? The past had turbo-charged itself and come hurtling into the present and one of my protagonists was alive, if not well, and living next door. I mean, for God's sake! It was just too close to home. Two of my five months in Roadend had gone by and I had effectively nothing at all to show for it. My new "big thing," the follow up to *The House of Shame,* the book that would cement me into the psyche of readers and movie producers, was dead in the water.

I wanted to tell her I had made a mess of things in Hackney and had run away with the idea of making a fresh start—but here too, I had bemired myself in mistakes. I was having an affair with a man I hardly knew, who could, from what Bill had hinted, be married. Bad. Very bad. But if he had been untruthful, so had I.

Then, I could not ignore the fact that Jamie was developing feelings towards me that I thought I might reciprocate a little, but what would be the point? He could no more leave Roadend than I could stay.

My idealised—not to say fanciful—notion of Roadend as a place of fantasy, a storybook realm, was dissipating more by the day, leaving only the harsh light of reality.

Roadend was not the fiction here. I was.

But none of this could I articulate to Marjorie. Instead, I began to cry, and she put her arm around me and let me weep my desolation into the shoulder of her crisp white cassock until the first attendees of the Mass began to make their way into the pews.

Chapter Thirty-One

I do not know whether Marjorie sent Jamie a text after she had seen me off home along the boardwalk or whether my remark, overheard in the pub, had determined him to hijack my Ebeneezer Scrooge impression, but on Christmas Day I was awakened from where I had fallen asleep on the settee by a series of loud bangs on the door.

I groped my way along the hall and found Jamie on my doorstep, freshly showered, his hair slicked back and—yes!—tied in a tiny man-bun behind his head, a box of groceries in his arms.

'Happy Christmas, neighbour,' he said brightly, shouldering his way past me and into the kitchen, deaf to my protestations. 'Rough night, was it?' He filled the kettle and switched it on.

'Drink was taken,' I admitted. 'I'm afraid …' I paused. Could I—*would* I—be honest with him? 'I'm afraid I'm in a slough of despond,' I said lamely. 'Not great company, especially today. I'm sure you have other places to be.'

'And yet I choose to be here,' said Jamie, bringing mugs from the cupboard and dropping teabags into them. While the kettle boiled, he turned and gave me a direct look. 'I presume you are not expecting other company?'

My expression must have given him all the answer he needed.

I sat down heavily on the kitchen sofa and raked my hair back from my face. I probably looked a mess; I certainly *felt* one. Then Jamie was beside me. Gently, he took my hand, as Marjorie had done, and I was reminded of Help, who pulled Christian from the slough in *Pilgrim's Progress*. I knew Jamie had the same thing in mind, though he did not speak the words; his action was a sufficient demonstration. I raised my eyes to his— concerned, kind. The same current flowed between us that had electrified me on the night of the dinner party, but it was a benign flow now, assuaging rather than shocking. We sat for a moment as he poured his care into me, until Bob came and rested his head on our conjoined hands and the kettle began to boil.

'Tea,' he announced, 'and then, for you, a shower, while I get that tree out of the loft and put it up.'

'Oh no, Jamie,' I protested. 'There's no point *now* ...'

He held up a hand and gave me a look. I knew there was no point in arguing.

'Then we'll have a walk. There's a place I want to take you to. After that we'll put whatever scrawny fowl old mother Harrop has pawned off on you into the oven.'

'But surely, you have something organised at home, for your dad and—'

Again, that admonishing hand. 'He has no idea what day it is,' said Jamie. 'If you're in a slough, he's down a rabbit hole. If you don't mind, I'd *much* rather spend the day with you.'

What could I possibly say?

In the end, we had a lovely day. I showered and Jamie pulled the little tree and the box of decorations from the attic. He made no remark about the duct tape that sealed the loft hatch. By the time I was dressed the tree was up and the lights draped round it. I was left to add the baubles and tinsel while Jamie grilled us some bacon and made sandwiches oozing with butter and HP sauce which, it turned out, we both preferred above tomato ketchup on bacon.

We cleared up and then went out. The day was fine—a thin blue sky washed over with shreds of high cloud, a weak sunshine bathing the Moss. On the far fells I could see a dusting of snow.

'Does it ever snow here?' I asked Jamie.

'Yes, sometimes, but it tends not to stay for long. We're too close to the sea. But I have seen snow on the beach. Mainly it's too cold for snow. The shallows are sometimes partly frozen. They look like that slushie drink you can buy, but not the same lurid colour.'

We walked along the willow walk, and I had an inkling of the place Jamie wanted to show me. Sure enough we went through the gate and onto the dunes, and followed the narrow pathway in single file. Bob went ahead of us. The tide was on its way in, but there was still a broad expanse of sand and boulder fields for him to explore. He loped deliriously down the beach, through rock pools and into the surf, disturbing a large flock of seabirds. They rose, squawking angrily, into the sky. We were the only people to be seen as far as the eye could see. The air was cold, fresh, blowing away my cobwebs; the sparkling sea and the far country across the firth, if not quite filling me with hope, at least dispelling my clouds of doom.

'Do you want to tell me about your slough?' Jamie asked in a tentative voice.

'Oh,' I waved my hand. 'Just feeling sorry for myself and … the thing I've been working on … I think I'll have to abandon it and start again.'

'How come?' His enquiry was casual, as though he was only half interested, but I knew it was just his way. Rather than confront a thing, and spook it, he would sidle up to it. And he knew I could be prickly, so I guessed he felt he had reason to be cautious.

'I've been writing a book,' I said heavily, and waited for his reaction: surprise, suspicion, amusement.

'Uh hum,' he said, nodding. 'I thought so.'

'A novel,' I added.

'Uh hum,' he said again.

'It isn't my first,' I said. 'In fact, it's my …' I counted up on my fingers, '…my seventh.'

He did raise his eyebrows at that.

'So, I know what I'm doing, or I thought I did.'

He turned away from me and lead us further along the dunes. 'And it isn't going well?' he threw over his shoulder.

I laughed, a dry, cynical laugh. 'It's going well,' I said. '*Too* well. It was based on a tiny snippet of something I heard that intrigued me; a minuscule, unformed nucleus of story I thought I could develop. Gradually other bits and pieces came to me … it's hard to say *how* exactly, but they seemed to fall into my lap. Whether they *drove* my narrative forward or if they just *confirmed* the direction it was already going in or if …'

'Or if?'

How could I possibly have concluded my sentence? Was I mad enough to believe the narrative I was laying down could impose itself on the past and become history? I had invented a daughter for the squire and she had materialised. I had felt sure that the Winters and the Forresters were connected and so it had turned out to be. I had written a much more nuanced version of Todd Forrester and suddenly Mrs Harrop's opinion of him had softened. How could all of that simply be good guesswork? If I was mad enough to believe it, I certainly was not mad enough to articulate it.

'Novels are supposed to be fiction,' I said, 'based on real life, perhaps; believable, but not *actually* true. I mean, they *have* a truth, a truth of their own, but when they *are* true, well, that isn't fiction, it's history.'

'Or biography,' he put in. 'But I don't understand. Surely when you begin a new book, you *know* how it will end? Don't you plan it all out beforehand? I don't get how its progress can surprise you, even if it will surprise the reader.'

'Some writers do,' I said. 'They have spreadsheets and maps and storyboards that lay the whole thing out from beginning to end. But I don't work that way. I begin with an idea and then I develop it—or, I should say, I allow it to develop itself. Usually, the story gets further and further away from its start point but *this* one seems determined to end up exactly where it began.'

'And that is …?' He had been walking ahead of me. Now, he stopped and swung round to confront me.

I looked at him, and the looking at him was the reply I gave him. *He* was the answer, if the narrative was to pursue its logical—its historical—course. I knew that now. Todd's story ended with Jamie and *that's* what made it impossible. As Jamie himself had warned me, novels about flesh and blood people were dangerous.

We had come to the place where the path descended to the beach. I could still see the line of detritus left behind by the high tide—wood and weed flung onto the dunes, the deep gouge scoured by the waters.

At last I said, 'My book is getting too close to the truth. Having believed all the people in it were long-dead, I *now* find …'

'Ah.' Jamie nodded, understanding at last. He appeared to ponder my dilemma, but we came to the den in the dunes and the whole topic seemed, for the time being, to have slipped his mind.

'This is what I wanted to show you,' he said, taking my hand to help me through the thorny bushes on its seaward side.

'I have stumbled across it,' I admitted, not wanting to spoil his surprise. 'Twice, in fact. But at night.'

'Oh?' He turned to face me. 'What were you doing here at night?'

I shrugged. 'Just walking,' I said. 'Not *late* at night but, you know, it *felt* like night. It was probably only seven o'clock.'

'You could have turned an ankle or something,' he said with a frown.

'In point of fact,' I said, 'I was not alone. Your dad was here both times.'

'Dad? Are you sure?'

I nodded. 'Quite sure. We had … an odd kind of conversation. He was looking for …' but I bit my words off for fear our two threads of conversation would clash too precipitously and painfully together.

Jamie was having none of it. 'Looking for …?'

'Your mum,' I answered in a small voice. 'Mary.'

'That's strange,' said Jamie, looking over my head to the rise of the dune behind me. 'He never speaks of her to me.'

I kept quiet about what Joe had said to me when I had suggested he should do precisely that. *That,* I thought, would be too hurtful a thing for Jamie to hear, even from a man far-gone in dementia.

'Do you have any contact with her?' I asked.

'Oh yes,' he said. 'She's in Canada. We have relatives there. She calls and we email.'

'But you must …' I probed, 'you must feel … that she abandoned you.'

He denied it. 'She waited until I'd left home before she went. She'd given me all I needed, and *him* all she had to give. It was my choice to come back.'

The air blew briskly all around us. Seabirds wheeled and cried overhead. Down on the beach I could hear Bob barking.

Jamie smiled at me. 'I shouldn't be surprised that he comes here,' he said, stooping down and peering into the hollow within the walls. In the bright daylight it wasn't sinister at all. There was nothing creepy about the rickety chair, the loops of fibrous rope and the upturned beer crate, which were all its contents.

'He built it?'

'*They* built it, when they were boys. You can see how much work they put into it, can't you?' Jamie stood back and admired his father's handiwork. 'I wonder why they never finished it.'

'Isn't it finished?'

'It needs a roof.' But then he pointed at something. 'But look. Somebody's been adding to it,' he said.

I looked. Sure enough, a few new spars had been woven vertically into the fabric of the walls, one jagged end of each dug deeply into the sand at its base, the other ends pointing skyward; tide-bleached tree-limbs and what looked like a couple of old fence posts, no doubt garnered from the beach after the high tide. 'Supports for a roof, do you think?' I asked. 'Do you mind?'

339

Jamie thought about it. 'No,' he said at last, 'I don't think so. It always amazes me that it has been allowed to stand all these years. You would expect it to be blown away, or burned down or something, or at least filled with litter. But people seem to respect it.'

'People?' I asked ironically, looking round at the empty beach, the deserted dunes.

'In summertime this path is like the A1,' laughed Jamie. 'Tourists walking the coastal way, campers from the various sites, picnickers, birdwatchers, beachcombers, fishermen …'

I tried to imagine it but couldn't. I indicated the additions to the den. 'So,' I said, 'whoever is making these improvements is *local*.'

'They must be,' he mused. 'I wonder who …'

'Your dad?' It seemed not inconceivable to me that Joe would have spent his time at the den in continuing its construction. Given his mental confusion he may even have believed himself still to be the youth who had begun it.

But Jamie didn't buy it. 'He can't manage a knife and fork, some days,' he said. 'He couldn't have managed *this.*' In proof of his assertion, he stepped forward and waggled one of the new spars. It was solid, well-embedded.

Fleetingly I wondered about Hugh who, in my imagination hovered in some make-believe gloaming but who might, in reality, in pursuance of his peripatetic wanderings, have adopted the den as a refuge. For all I knew he had decided to take its completion into his own hands. Something stopped me from offering this suggestion though.

'I think it's an extraordinary thing,' I said, feeling that, having been brought to the den as a kind of treat, I ought to show due appreciation of it. 'My brother had a tree house when he was a little boy. That place was everything to him: spaceship, pirate ship, fort, castle … he told me recently that it—the entire tree, in fact—had been pulled down.'

We began to walk back, down the dunes and out onto the beach, where the sea crept inexorably over the land. Bob raced across the sand to join us, one ear inside out, a tendril of seaweed attached to his tail. Jamie bent to detach it, taking the opportunity to fuss Bob so his eyes rolled in ecstasy. Then we turned and walked back along the encroaching tideline, towards the end of the beach that terminated in a sheer cliff.

'You heard from your brother?'

I told Jamie about the email, about the change in Daniel's circumstances that I feared would make Bianca take even more advantage of him, that I would like to protect him from her, if I could.

'People have to live out their own stories,' said Jamie. 'Maybe your brother will realise his wife is a taker and leave her, or maybe he won't. Either way, there's nothing you can do.'

'No,' I said miserably. 'I know.'

We came to the base of the cliff, gouged out by the relentless waters. Cascades of fallen stones lay scattered about. The sand there was claggy; the clay eroded from the hill and melded with the sand. There were fresh falls of mud on the beach.

'That lot must have come down on the night of the high tide,' I said. 'Thank goodness no one was standing underneath. I'm told you used to be able to get round here to the village.' I looked along the formidable face of the cliff and up to its towering crag. 'I wouldn't fancy it,' I said with a shudder.

'You *can*, at low tide, but it's dangerous. You can see how fast the water comes in. And there are dips and hollows in the beach that fill up first. You can get cut off. They re-routed the coastal path past Winter Farm ... oh, I don't know ... maybe thirty years ago? After the big fall.'

'The big fall?'

He nodded. 'One winter night years ago. Another high tide. All this lot and more came down.'

'Climate change?'

'I guess so. Word is that one day the whole lot will come down, tower and all.'

341

'I've heard the same.'

Jamie gave me a sidelong glance. 'I would expect so.'

'And … you know the solution that's proposed?'

Jamie nodded. 'Come on,' he said.

It was the closest we had come to acknowledging Hugh. To say I felt conflicted would be an understatement, especially at that moment. Jamie had been so kind. Hugh had not been *unkind*—anything but—yet he had been away such a lot and even when physically present he had, for me, an ambiguity I could not readily explain. Objectively, I would describe him as an important, travelled, sophisticated man. No one could claim that for Jamie. And yet there was, with him, a cerebral quality I had not found in Hugh. Certainly, as far as *books* were concerned, Jamie and I were on the same page. As far as *looks* were concerned, there was nothing to choose between. Both were my type: tall, well-honed, ruggedly good-looking.

We began to walk back on ourselves, skirting the cliff in the direction of the dunes, to the path that would lead us to the gate, and home. Presently we came to the place where cliff and dunes met—the far side of the hill upon which the pele tower sat. I began to look about for the stately pile of Mr and Mrs Aspiring Squirarchy. A pair of gates—much more modest than the ones on the other side of the hill—and a rough, grassy track told me we had come to what was effectively their rear entrance.

'Winter Hall is up there,' I observed. 'Have you been?'

'Haven't you?' He seemed surprised.

I shook my head. 'I met Her Ladyship once. Can't say we hit it off,' I said. 'But then, she did catch me trying to break in.'

Jamie gave me a puzzled smile. 'No, she wouldn't have liked that.'

'What kind of a place is it?' I imagined something tasteless, a MacMansion.

'Oh,' said Jamie, 'I think you'll like it.'

It wasn't until Jamie had summoned Bob with a piercing whistle, and we were back in the willow walk that he said, 'Lots of books are based on fact. Charles Dickens really experienced the blacking factory he described in *David Copperfield*. At the other extreme, Stephen King really stayed at the haunted hotel he recreated in *The Shining*. There's a genre—I think it's called Uchronia—that takes history and gives it a twist. It asks, "What if?" What if Germany had won the war, for example. They are all considered to be legitimate. How is yours different, so long as you make your own truth of it? I think you should just go ahead and write it.'

'Oh,' I exclaimed. I had thought the subject abandoned. 'But I can't. It's too intrusive. I can't just let it have its head, like a rampant bull. It might wreak havoc. And the people concerned—they'll know. I worry that, if—when—they find out, they'll feel I've trampled on them, used them, exposed them. As Christopher Robin did.'

What I *meant*—but could not say—was that I feared *his*—Jamie's—reaction to the revelation that I had wantonly plundered his family skeletons.

Jamie said nothing for a while. We came to the row of cottages. I half expected him to part company with me, his earlier talk of sharing a meal just a way to rouse me from my torpor, but he held open the gate and accompanied me to the door.

'Do you know what?' he asked. 'I sometimes think *everyone* could benefit from seeing their own life through someone else's eyes. We have such tunnel vision sometimes that we can't see beyond our own point of view. To get a glimpse of another life—other lives—we could have lived … lives we could *still* live …'

He threw me a look, fleeting but speaking, and I wondered what kind of life he would choose for himself. Did he picture *me* in it? I pushed the question away.

'I hope everyone will feel as philosophically as you do. In any case,' I concluded with a sigh, 'it might never get published. Not all of mine have made it that far.'

'There you are, then,' said Jamie with a cheerful smile. 'Now let's get the oven on and that poor excuse for a chicken into it. Good lord, Dee. The Cratchetts' fleshless little goose had more meat on it than your chicken does! I hope you've got plenty of spuds.'

Chapter Thirty-Two

The remainder of Christmas passed quietly, but not unpleasantly. Hugh did not return. Physically, I missed him, although now his mystery troubled me a little. I began to worry about all the things I didn't know about him, especially his marital status. The gaps—which had seemed so exciting before, and which had fuelled my transubstantiation—now began to fill me with foreboding.

I walked Bob, ranging more widely than we ever had before, through farmland I presumed belonged to the Harrops since it lay behind their farmhouse, but which I had already depicted in Todd and Rose's story. As I had foretold it, a footpath went along the edge of a ploughed field and into a managed forest of pine trees where I'd had them canoodle out of Mrs Bellis' sight. The plantation rose up the slope of a slight hill, more of a knoll, just as I had imagined it, and when I emerged at the top I walked along a ridge, seeking the tarn where Rowan and Todd had swum.

For New Year's Eve I was invited to the vicarage where Marjorie, Olivia, Patrick, and some half a dozen other waifs and strays were treated to a buffet of cold meats and cheeses, a judicious quantity of wine and games like charades and twenty questions. When midnight came, we raised our glasses and pecked each other on the cheek, or shook hands—all except for Olivia and Patrick, who embraced each other less decorously, and then blushed furiously about it.

The following day I screwed my courage to the sticking point and video-called Daniel on my computer. He answered quickly, and carried his phone through to his study, shutting the door firmly behind us.

'Bianca has friends from the golf club coming over,' he said in a half-whisper. 'She's in a flap over the canapés. Apparently, there isn't half enough smoked salmon and the blinis are stale.'

'Oh dear,' I said, chancing a tongue-in-cheek riposte. 'Questions will be asked in the House.'

'Letters written to *The Times*,' Daniel chimed in, like his old self, but then he straightened his face. 'No, seriously, she's in a real stew about it, poor thing. She went out to get extra, earlier, but of course all the shops are shut.'

'I'm sure it will be fine,' I soothed. 'People are coming to see her … that is, *you*, not to assess the quality of your catering.'

'I don't know,' said Daniel, chewing the inside of his cheek. 'We went to the captain's house on Christmas eve. You never saw such a spread. I thought they'd had outside caterers, but Bianca said definitely not. Suffice it to say, the bar was set pretty high.'

'How was the rest of Christmas?' I asked, feeling the subject of members' provender had probably been exhausted. 'Fun?'

'Quiet. I spent quite a bit of it by myself. Bianca had rounds of golf booked, and there's a new tennis coach at the club who was offering lessons at half price, so she had a few of those.'

'You didn't want to go with her?'

He shook his head. 'To be honest, I'll be glad to get back to work.'

'Has Bianca found anything she wants to apply for?'

Daniel's eyes slid away from the screen, which was all the answer I got. 'Tell me about you,' he said.

I filled him in with sketchy details.

'When I come back,' I said, warily, 'I'd like us to see more of each other.'

Daniel's expression was hard to read—the desirability and impossibility of such a thing.

'I can settle anywhere, so long as it's a reasonable commute to London,' I said. 'Your neck of the woods is as good as any other. I'm fed up with the itinerant life. I want to buy a place. It'll have to have a small garden and access to a park or the countryside. Apart from that I have no preference, really. What do you think?'

Before he could answer I heard a shriek and the crash of smashing crockery. 'Oh God,' he said. 'I'll have to go. Sorry Dee. Happy New Year.'

January was a dismal month—damp without being particularly wet, chill but not freezing. We rarely saw the sun and all the Moss's colours were muted.

I wrote to my agent with an outline of the book. It wasn't finished but I had got to the point where I could posit the ending—the ending I had in view, even if the story itself had other ideas. She asked me for a synopsis—always the hardest thing to write—and I laboured over that for about a week, honing my summary of the plot down to its sharpest teeth and thinnest bones.

I had come to a hiatus. Todd's story was done and I needed to introduce the next generation of Forresters: the two feuding boys, Joe and John, and Mary who, I instinctively knew, held the key to the whole history.

But I couldn't. To begin it felt like an act of vandalism, an insult to my neighbour, a cruelty I could not inflict. I could not trespass on the living.

I sat and stared at my screen for hours. Not a word was written. I distracted myself by checking reviews and sales, trawling Facebook, playing solitaire. The story called me in a voice so plangent it kept me awake at night; or perhaps it would be truer to say that my visceral need for the story kept me awake. Either way, I was stuck. The words would not come. There is no doubt that writing gives me a kind of high, a sense of being in the right place and of being the person I am meant to be. Now that my story had stalled I experienced a kind of withdrawal. I drank far too much coffee. On a more prosaic level, perhaps I should blame the coffee for my insomnia.

So it was that one morning, about six, I rose after a sleepless night, got dressed and went out. Bob seemed reluctant. If it is possible for a dog to frown then he did just that as I fussed with his halter and lead. The Moss was unrelievedly dark. There was no moon, so no glint of light on the slowly flowing water in the rill. I could not even make out the silhouette of the trees in the copse where the trysting tree stood. It would have been madness to walk that way. Madness too, to climb the track to the pele tower, where the crumbling cliff edge would be invisible. I thought about following the boardwalk to the village, where I guessed the light in Mrs Harrop's shop might already be shining out, where I could get a hot coffee—albeit only instant—and where the everyday comings and goings of the flesh-and-blood residents of the village might chase away the importuning ghosts of my characters.

Instead, I turned towards the willow walk, my torch clasped tightly in my hand. The fastening of the gate made a blood-curdling screech as I pulled it back; enough, I thought, to wake the dead. Across the Moss a fox barked, and another answered from the direction of the village. I paused to see if the lights in Jamie's cottage would come on, spilling their comfort over the track. Maybe that's what I'd really wanted. But no bright knife sliced the darkness, and I turned and went on my way.

The trees on either side were spectral, eerie. No breath of wind moved their branches. Ahead of me the beam of my torch caught a movement, a flash of white, and three roe deer bounded away. Bob stiffened, but did not attempt to follow them. I heard them distantly as they crashed through the trees, and then silence like outer space descended again.

I turned off the torch. It's light only showed me the thickness of the dark, as the full beam of a car's headlights will only illuminate the utter depth of fog.

I almost bumped into the gate at the end of the track, its steely greyness melded so absolutely with the surrounding dim. The dunes beyond were absolutely immobile, as though caught in a picture. The grasses did not so much as quiver, the sky above and the air within its dome were opaque, inert, a canvas I felt I could reach out and touch. I passed through the gate, treading almost reverently as though on holy ground. I bent and unclipped Bob's lead, the snap of its clasp like a thunderclap in the petrified air. Unusually, he did not disappear along the path. He looked up at me with the kind of wonder I felt myself at the unaccustomed otherworldliness of the scene, and contented himself with walking at my heel as we trod the narrow pathway towards the shore.

The tide must have been far out; I could not see the water and, although I honed my ears I could hear no lap or splash of wave-on-shore. The beach, as far as I could see it, was a moonscape of pits and craters, strewn with odd-shaped boulders and tortured tree stumps. The whole panorama was a study in purple, the air like a bruise, the land an extension of it, with only the merest possible contour and shadow to differentiate one from another. I walked, dreamlike, along the edge of the dunes and then dropped onto the shingle. Even the stones beneath my feet were mute, their habitual crunch and grate and rattle not much more than a sigh. I walked straight out towards where I assumed the sea must be, the felt of the night parting in front of me and closing behind, and I lost sight of the dunes after only a few steps. The darkness was an entity, nebulous; I could feel its eddy against my face, at one with the quiet that pressed down from the air and oozed up from the ground.

We walked on. I found myself ankle deep in a rock pool, but splashed on through it. At one point the sand was soft and yielding and it was hard to make progress. At another I found a field of stones, slick and treacherous. Then I was amongst some ancient timber piles, supports for a long-since-rotted pier. At last I found the sea. It lapped with barely a ripple at the shore, viscous with silt and emitting no glimmer of light.

I turned to look back. An ocean of indigo lay behind me but far, very far away, over the dunes, slashed across the impenetrable slab of sky, I could see the faintest possible streak of violet outlining the massif.

Dawn.

I turned and walked in the direction of the village. I had no idea of circumnavigating the bluff and coming round as far as the village—it never occurred to me the tide could have been as far out as *that*—I expected to follow the route Jamie and I had taken on Christmas Day. I thought if I followed the tide line—as we had then—it would push me unerringly up the beach and leave me at the bottom of the cliff from where I would be able to re-join the dunes and head home. I walked slowly, keeping the water to my right, watching it carefully as it crept over the sands in little baby rushes, each foray gaining more ground. I reasoned that if I did not allow my boots to get wet, I would be alright.

I don't know how long I walked. I kept my eyes on the gradually-encroaching water and also on the far eastern horizon, which was lightening from violet to lilac, the rim of the high fells differentiating itself from the arc of the sky. The indigo bowl of the beach and the dune dissipated into amethyst and I could make out the line of the dunes against the shingle, the silhouette of the bluff rearing up. It was much further away than I had expected. I stopped, a clutch of panic in my throat, Jamie's admonitions about the treacherous nature of the beach and the tide echoing in my ears. Between me and the hill, the featureless terrain that should have been solid sand had an oddly molten quality; the tide was creeping in behind and around me. A cold swill of water covered my boots. I looked down to find myself two inches deep in water.

Bob whined and made a dash forward. He was hock- then knee-deep in the sea. I followed him quickly, walking towards the shore but seeming somehow to be sinking deeper and deeper into water. The faster I walked the more quickly the tide seemed to chase me, coming at me from all sides now, closing in. The water was icy cold. It filled my boots and soaked the bottoms of my trousers.

All the while the sky lightened from lilac to pink. The outline of the fells was on fire, streaking the dawn half-light with gold and orange—beautiful, but throwing my own circumstances into dreadful relief. I was surrounded by water. The innocent-seeming baby-waves were now malevolent toddlers, slapping up my legs as I forged through the surf. No matter how strongly I strode forward it felt like the tide was before me. Bob was almost swimming now, the water halfway up his body. He turned in circles—making progress but then doubling back to urge me onward, losing all the ground he had gained. I was thigh deep. My foot met a stone beneath the water and I stumbled—almost fell—but managed to remain upright.

The sepia tideline seemed far away and ever-receding, as though enchanted. I was hundreds of yards from safety. At that point I felt more foolish than endangered, wondering if I could get home without being seen, without my stupidity being found out. I looked around to ensure my idiotic situation had no witnesses and was appalled to find my nemesis, Her Bloody Ladyship, standing at the rear entrance to the grounds of Winter Hall gesticulating wildly in the grey dawn. Her voice came to me, disembodied and shrill, but I could make no sense of her cries. I raised an arm to indicate that, yes, I was an idiot but, yes, I was ok, and would make my way towards her to receive the withering remonstrance I was sure she had prepared for me.

I took a few more steps forward. Her cries became more voluble. Her frantic gestures redoubled in their energy. I shook my head and cupped my ear with one hand to indicate that I couldn't hear her. With another step forward I was chest-deep in ice-cold water. Bob, swimming now, paddled around me whining piteously, his eyes wide with panic. He took hold of my hood in his teeth and tried to pull me along. I was saturated. My legs were trembling and could barely hold me up. The water surged around me. I looked across to where Her Ladyship had been standing, but she was gone.

I took hold of Bob and clasped him to me, both of us swaying in the ebb and flow of the sea, water lapping over my shoulders. The undertow pushed me about this way and that, my coat yanked and dragged as if by vandal hands. The sea had morphed from naughty child to spiteful teenager.

My teeth chattered. Tears spilled down my face. 'Swim to shore Bob and I'll follow. Good boy. You're a good boy. You've been a very good boy.' I squeezed him tightly, kissed his wet head, then pushed him violently away from me on the crest of a wave. 'Swim Bob,' I urged him. The wave carried him away from me and I lost sight of him in the rolling surf. I swallowed a sob and tried to swim, but my arms were leaden and my feet seemed anchored. No amount of thrashing brought me nearer to safety. I was moving backwards rather than forwards.

It was almost light now. The sea was its usual brackish colour; the beach—far away—a striation of dull greys and muddy brown; the dunes an ordinary wilderness of grass and sand. What an unremarkable place to die.

I had almost given myself up to that prospect—ceasing to struggle, feeling tired and extremely cold—when the air above me was rent by the throb of a helicopter. Ridiculously, my heart—not, at that moment, very buoyant—sank even further. Oh no. The chinless wonder to the rescue. How humiliating.

The helicopter rose precipitously from beyond a copse of trees that clung to the side of the hill. It made a wide circuit and came to hover about thirty or forty feet above me. I looked up with dreadful resignation, wondering if the prospect of drowning wasn't preferable to the potential of being rescued by the interloping, ogling Lord of the Manor. I regretted pushing Bob away. If rescue was to come, I wanted it for him too.

The door of the helicopter slid back and a figure wearing a red drysuit and a large crash helmet began to descend on a rope. The blades of the aircraft beat mercilessly, bludgeoning my ears and whipping the water around me so that it filled my mouth. Gasping for breath and flailing my arms about, I panicked. Then I was pulled beneath the surface of the water. When I opened my eyes all was murk and cloud. But beside me in the water was a figure in red. With a strong grip on the shoulder of my coat I was hoisted back above the surface where I took an enormous gulp of air, coughed, retched and was sick. The harness was slipped over my head, my arms unceremoniously thrust through its loop. The two of us were pressed together in an awkward embrace as we rose, dripping, from the sea.

I was pushed gracelessly into the helicopter, sprawling across its metal floor. The noise was extraordinary—a percussion of metal and the vibrating thrum of air. I was crying for Bob, pointing back at the water, but my voice was lost in the cacophony. My rescuer leapt back into the cockpit with enviable aplomb. The door closed. The aircraft swooped away. I covered my face with my hands and wept miserably. I hardly noticed the blanket that was draped around my shoulders, or the soft shudder as the runners touched back to earth.

I heard the grate of the door as it slid open again, a whistle, and then Bob was in my arms, smothering me in water and slobbery kisses, leaving a trail of silt and water all over the cabin. I looked across at the winchman to thank him, but his face was obscured by the visor of his helmet. He moved between the two seats in the cockpit and sat down beside the pilot. The aircraft was off again on the short flight back to the helipad at Winter Hall.

Chapter Thirty-Three

My memory of the next half hour or so is dim. I recall feeling like the still point at the centre of a maelstrom of activity, and then like the target of a bombardment of information and revelation.

The sound of the helicopter's blades gradually diminished as they slowed. I was given a mug of hot, too-sweet tea. The pilot and the winchman barked irritably at one another from inside their thickly-visored helmets. I got the impression my rescue would cause ructions for someone, at some point.

A lady in light blue chinos and a lambswool sweater appeared. Perhaps she had given me the tea? I couldn't remember. She swathed Bob in an old candlewick bedspread and rubbed him down. Then she threw another one around me. She was trim, with neatly styled grey hair and kind eyes, perhaps in her early sixties. She rubbed my arms and shoulders with the same sympathetic vigour she had used on Bob.

I cast a few glances around me. I had an impression of a close-cropped lawn, some shrubs, a gravel pathway, but no stately home, no pseudo-Palladian façade or mock-Tudor mansion. My teeth were chattering and I slopped the tea I had been given onto my coverings.

'You're in shock,' the grey-haired lady said. 'Come inside. Let's get those wet things off you.'

I saw the winchman remove his helmet, shaking free a head of dyed, permed hair. She—for it was Her Ladyship—threw me a withering look, grasped Bob's collar and then disappeared with him through a screen of shrubs. The pilot remained, hurriedly filling in a form on a clipboard. As he began to remove his helmet I braced myself to thank the man it had suited me to revile and ridicule for no logical reason at all.

Hugh.

Before either of us could say anything, the grey-haired lady steered me away from the helipad and I found myself inside, although I had seen no building. I was taken through a cool, stone-flagged hallway into a cosy room with a brightly burning log fire.

'No one will disturb you here, dear,' she said, helping me out of my wet coat and kneeling to fiddle with the sodden laces of my boots. 'There now,' she said, when she had removed them, stripped off my socks and put both to dry on the hearth. 'I'll leave you to do the rest. Wrap yourself in that dry blanket there, and I'll be back with more tea in a few moments.'

I looked around anxiously.

'Oh! There are no windows,' she said, 'only in the roof, look.' She pointed up, to where three portholes were set into the ceiling, throwing streams of light into the room. 'Odd, isn't it? I thought so too. It's an eco-house, apparently. Very environmentally friendly. Well! What else would you expect of Hugh? It reminds *me* of a hobbit house. But I mustn't stay here nattering. You need to get those wet things off. I'll leave you to it.'

She made for the door, but turned when I said, 'Where's Bob?'

'Don't you worry. Warm by the Aga with a tummy full of porridge, I shouldn't wonder.' She smiled. Such a reassuring, kindly smile. A mother's smile. It made me want to cry. I *did* cry a little bit, while I took off my wet things and swathed the large, fleece blanket around me. Then I fell into one of the comfortable fireside chairs.

The shock of my ordeal, added to the revelation about Hugh—my friendly neighbourhood countryside ranger and the wannabe Lord of the Manor—put me into a kind of swoon. I tried, in a dim, disconnected part of my consciousness, to fit my knowledge of one into the caricature of lascivious aristobrat I had drawn for the other, but failed. Nothing about the Hugh I knew could square that circle. He was not arrogant. He was not a snob. He was anything but aloof. Certainly, he was not Todd Forrester, and I did not know how I had ever managed to convince myself of that ridiculous mutation.

Perhaps this was Hugh in his true light—a model landowner, an environmental champion, a thoroughly good bloke. His father must have died. That was the only explanation for his returning to Roadend. Like any good son, he had brought his widowed mother—the grey-haired lady—with him.

And, of course, he was married. Any Lord must have his Lady and Hugh's was the domineering harridan I had made an instant enemy of on my first day at Roadend. The impact this revelation had on my confusion was less than the sense of my own utter stupidity for not realising it. What other reason was there for the secrecy of our assignations, his clandestine comings and goings, his reticence about where he lived? I didn't blame *him*—I had been a fool. He had not been honest with me, but this was no time either for recriminations or for histrionics, and I was by no means blameless.

When I roused myself from my doze, Hugh was in the room with me, sitting in the opposite chair, mashing his hands. The moment I opened my eyes he was up, sweeping me into a fierce embrace, murmuring cross endearments and concerned reprimands. 'What were you doing? What were you *thinking?* Oh, Dee. Thank God Caroline saw you.'

The mention of Caroline made me stiffen, and I disentangled himself from his arms. 'Someone will come in,' I said.

He gave a puzzled smile. 'Why would that matter?'

I took my seat and hoisted the blanket back up around my naked shoulders; they felt gritty with sand and salt. 'Our game is up, Hugh. Surely you must see that? It was one thing, while I didn't *know* … although, frankly, I do think you should have told me. But now I *do* know, I couldn't possibly carry on.'

He frowned. 'Know what?'

I sighed. Would I have to spell it out? 'About Caroline.'

Still, that quizzical, confused expression. To mask it he went over to a table and poured out two stiff whiskies. He placed one down beside me. 'What difference does she make?'

I raked my hair. It was matted and stiff with salt. 'Well, you know,' I said cynically, 'she's not going to like it, is she?'

Some light seemed to come on for Hugh. 'Oh!' he said, relief flooding his face. 'Well, you didn't make a *great* first impression, I'll admit. But she'll get over that. It was an honest mistake.'

I wrinkled an eyebrow. 'I don't think that forcing your gates will be her *primary* objection to me, do you?'

Hugh threw his drink back in one swallow. 'I don't understand. What else have you done to upset her?'

I hesitated, casting around the room for some clue that I wasn't having a bizarre dream, that *I* wasn't the one here to have lost their grip on reality. It was an odd-shaped room, roughly circular, with low beams, but not so low that Hugh—or Caroline, who was almost as tall as he was—would bang their heads on them. It was comfortably and tastefully furnished. I might have said it was *expensively* furnished also, but for me the expense was secondary to the taste and comfort. On a low table was a silver-framed photograph of Hugh and Caroline and an older man I took to be Hugh's father. This brought me back to firmer ground.

'I'm so sorry about your dad,' I said. 'I presume he passed away?'

Hugh nodded. 'Yes. We've brought him home. He wanted to be buried here. The service will be in a few days.'

Home? The Lord of the Manor was Canadian, wasn't he? An odd note chimed in my head.

I silenced it. 'How was it … in the end?'

'Peaceful,' said Hugh. 'We were all there with him. He just … slipped away.'

I could see the recollection moved him. In other circumstances I would have gone across and knelt beside him, offered him the comfort of my arms; but that, of course, was impossible now.

Instead, I said, 'Hugh, I had no idea you were ... the person who lived here, *with Caroline*. That you were *in effect* the Lord of the Manor. That's your title *in fact* now, isn't it? Are you Sir Hugh?'

'God, no,' he said. 'I'm nobody. But Dad thought it would be funny to buy the title. He was born and brought up here, although most people here haven't made that connection.'

There it was again, a knell. I picked up the heavy cut glass tumbler and brought it to my lips. My hand was shaking. '*Was* he?'

'Oh yes. His family owned virtually everything hereabouts, at one time.'

'He was a Winter?'

Hugh shook his head. 'No. He was a Forrester. My grandfather bought all the Winter lands.'

My head was clanging, and not from the whisky, which I had barely tasted. 'Yes,' I said faintly. 'I know about Todd and Rose. They were your *grandparents?*'

So Hugh was a Forrester. How had I not known? But then it came to me—we had never told each other our full names and I had never heard him referred to as anything other than Hugh.

He nodded. 'That's right. But I never met them. Dad left Roadend and went to Canada, where he married a rich Canadian woman. He made a pile himself. Hence, when he heard how things stood here—with his brother, I mean—he stepped in. He meant it kindly but Joe—'

'Joe is his brother,' I murmured.

'Yes, one of them. There were ...'

'Three brothers,' I breathed. '*Three* Forrester brothers. Joe, John and—'

'Jack. Dad wanted to buy Joe out of his financial troubles, save the farm. He wanted to *help*.'

'But wait. He did it anonymously? No one knew he was Jack Forrester?'

'There was a mix up on his immigration papers. When he got to Canada he was listed as Forster. He stuck with it. So that muddied the waters.

But yes, he thought it would be less hurtful to Joe's pride to sell the farm to a stranger.'

'But Joe didn't see it that way?'

'Joe didn't see it *any* way. He was already on a slippery slope.'

Hugh sat down heavily across from me. I tried to shuffle a third Forrester brother into my lexicon.

'This is going to come as a shock to people, you know. They think your dad is a stranger, a foreigner.'

'Oh, I know. I've had the devil's job to gain acceptance here. Thankfully I had one person on my side.'

'Jamie?' I was doubtful.

Hugh sighed, and I saw disappointment in him. 'Jamie *knows* but ... I guess it's hard for him. *His* dad ...'

Yes, I thought, the two brothers had been dealt such different hands in life.

'Mrs Harrop knows the truth,' Hugh told me, 'and as you know, where Mrs Harrop leads Roadend will follow.'

This puzzled me. 'Mrs Harrop is no friend to the Forresters though,' I mused aloud, holding aloft, metaphorically, another handbell that added its noise to the din.

'Not to the others. But she has a soft spot for my dad.'

This set more bells ringing, so loudly that it was like oranges and lemons and the bells of St Clements in my head. I summoned all my strength to dampen them, because I was not ready, then, to hear the tale they were telling. They were taking me too far, too fast.

'Was your dad, Jack ...' I ventured. 'Was he ... like the others?' Argumentative, I meant, feisty, irascible.

'No,' said a voice by the door. I turned my head to find the lady who had been so kind earlier. She carried a tray with a plate of sandwiches and two fresh cups of tea. 'No,' she repeated, advancing into the room. 'He was nothing like the others.'

Hugh stood up and took the tray from her. 'Thank you, Mary,' he said.

Chapter Thirty-Four

I sat and looked at Mary Forrester. I could see Jamie in her, especially in the eyes. Jamie had told me his mother had gone to stay with a relative in Canada and now I knew this to have been her brother-in-law, Jack Forrester. I remembered being told the new Lord of the Manor had come from there, but had not made the connection. Caroline's accent, which had eluded me on the two occasions I had heard her speak, was Canadian. It all added up.

Mary was still beautiful. It didn't surprise me that everyone had loved her. Given Joe's treatment of her—"awful" Bill had said—I was surprised anyone would blame her for leaving. But they did, and I thought her rather brave to come back, even for a funeral—*especially* for the funeral of a man Roadend had obliterated from its memory.

'Have you seen Jamie?' I asked, as she fussed with sandwich plates and napkins.

'He knows I'm here. We only arrived last night. *Such* a long journey. Our body clocks are all at sixes and sevens. That's why Caroline was out so early.'

'I'm ... very grateful,' I mumbled. 'I haven't seen her properly to ...'

Mary waved her hand. 'I shouldn't worry. Caroline's a bit of a porcupine; prickly on the outside but soft in the middle. She can come across as ungracious, can't she, Hugh?' It struck me as a surprising thing to say to a man about his wife.

'Scares me witless,' said Hugh, munching a sandwich.

'She'll think I was reckless and stupid,' I said. 'I've caused trouble, I know.'

'Well ...' said Hugh, swallowing his mouthful. 'There is a little caveat in the insurance. We're not supposed to do search and rescue.'

'I won't sue,' I said.

'I've written it up in the log as a test flight,' said Hugh. 'I don't suppose there were any witnesses, so we should be OK.'

I ate a sandwich, and then another. I found I was famished. I managed to get the second cup of tea down without spilling it but after that I was engulfed by tiredness. The heat of the fire and the hum of conversation between Mary and Hugh as they discussed the details of the funeral—pallbearers, the eulogy, hymns and so on—lulled me into a torpor that was as hard to fight free of as the sea had been earlier. I gathered a memorial service had already taken place in Canada; the burial, here, would be a low-key affair … I gave up the struggle and let my eyes close.

I woke up hours later in a room I did not recognise—smallish but neat, with the same round portholes in the ceiling. They rattled with the sound of falling rain. My clothes—all washed and dried—lay in a pile on a chair. I struggled up. The blanket I had been wrapped in was full of sand. My body and hair felt stale and crusted. Off the bedroom was a small shower room. A clean towel lay folded on a stool, so I took advantage of it.

When I emerged into the hallway there was no sign of Hugh or Caroline and I felt relieved. Better to slip away, I thought, and let sleeping dogs lie. Jamie and Mary stood on the threshold, engaged in an affectionate hug. Bob, who lay nearby, lifted his head when he saw me, his tail beating a tattoo on the floor.

'Ah, here she is,' said Mary. 'Feeling better dear?'

'Much better. I slept like the dead.'

'By rights, you should *be* dead,' said Jamie tersely. 'I *told* you about the tide.'

I held up my hand. 'I know. I was a fool. I don't know what I was thinking of.'

'I do,' he muttered. 'You were lost in your book, I suppose.'

Mary patted his hand, which she still held between hers. 'Don't scold, Jamie. She's had a terrible ordeal.'

He looked down at her, his love for her written in letters a mile high. 'Alright Mum.'

He looked at me. 'I'm just heading home. Do you want a ride?'

I nodded. 'Yes. I must get out of these kind people's way.' I turned to Mary. 'Do thank Hugh and Caroline for me, won't you? I owe them my life and—'

It was her turn to offer an admonishing hand. 'It's what anyone would have done. All in a day's work for them, at one time. They were in the Canadian Air Force, you see.'

Here was another fact about himself that Hugh had kept from me—and no wonder, if he had met his wife whilst enrolled.

'They've pulled people out of glaciers and avalanches …' but she tailed off, seeing, as I did, the peculiar expression on Jamie's face. Not envy, but perhaps a shade of resentfulness. He—through no fault of his own—could not boast such exploits, and it did not surprise me that it upset him to hear his mother sing the praises of his so-much-more-successful cousin.

Mary pressed his hand again. She said, 'Hugh would be your friend Jamie, if you'd let him.'

Jamie shrugged. 'We have nothing in common,' he replied. 'My other cousins kept their distance. He has no reason to do any different.'

'He *does*.' Mary was emphatic.

Jamie shifted from foot to foot. 'I should get back,' he said. 'It's time the hens were locked up, and I need to check on Dad.'

'Of course.' Mary relinquished his hand, as though, at the mention of Joe she suddenly felt she had no right to hold it. 'But you'll come again?'

Jamie nodded. Then he turned to me. 'Mum will be able to help you with your research,' he said. 'She remembers lots of stuff about Roadend, from when she was a girl, and … afterwards.'

'Research?' Mary's enquiry was polite.

'Yes. Dee's a writer. She's working on a novel based loosely on the area. Local history, you know.'

And although it felt like having my clothes ripped off in a public place—being exposed, *finally,* for who and what I was—I was glad. Mary was not a person I could have pumped covertly for information as I had pumped Olivia and Mrs Harrop and Bill and even poor old harmless Arnold. No, Mary was too close to the nub of my story for me to be sly. If she told me her story, she would know, first, why I was interested. But if things ran true to course, one sentence from her would be all my rampaging bull of a story would need to throw itself into the china shop of the Forrester family.

Mary said, 'Oh! I'd be delighted to help. A writer? How thrilling. Will I have heard of you?'

I was gripped by self-consciousness. This is always a tricky question for a once-nearly-briefly-famous writer to answer, because if I said "yes", and then she hadn't heard of me, we would both feel awkward and I would come across as egotistical. So I said, 'I shouldn't think so,' and looked at the floor.

'You might be surprised,' Mary urged. 'I'm a voracious reader, aren't I, Jamie?'

'What is your penname, Dee?' asked Jamie in a low voice.

I mumbled it.

'Gosh!' cried Mary. 'Really?' She clasped her hands together. 'What a thrill!'

'But I'm here *incognito,*' I warned. 'Nobody knows. To be honest, even if they knew, it wouldn't mean anything to them. But I've chosen to live very much under the radar.'

Jamie laughed, but not unkindly. 'Let's be honest, Dee. You haven't been here at all, really, have you? You've been … I don't know … in Earthsea? Somewhere along platform nine-and-three-quarters?'

I lowered my eyes. 'Until this morning, yes. But I had a wake-up call.'

'You can rely on me,' said Mary. 'I'm *very* good at keeping secrets.'

Jamie drove us home on his quadbike, with Bob squashed between us. The day was all but over, the blanket of night hauling itself across the Moss.

'You liked Bag End?' he threw over his shoulder above the din of the machine.

I giggled. 'It wasn't at all what I expected,' I said. From what little I had been able to see, Winter Hall was built almost entirely inside the hill. Its roof was turfed, apart from those port holes. From the air it would be impossible to tell there was a dwelling there at all. The ruined pele tower would remain the dominant feature of the landscape for as long as it remained clinging to the bluff. I thought this fitting, and admired Hugh for his decorum even though my admiration would now have to go unexpressed.

'You're a dark horse,' I shouted. 'You never said you were related to the folks at the big house.'

'*You* can talk,' he threw back. Then I felt him shrug. 'We don't have much to do with each other.'

'It's a pity,' I said, half to myself. 'You could have some great adventures together.'

'I don't have time for adventures,' came the pithy reply. 'I have a living to earn and a father to care for.'

'That's a bit cruel,' I hit back. 'Hugh's just lost his dad. However challenging yours is, at least you still have him.'

Jamie's shoulders dropped, and I knew my reprimand had hit home.

We whizzed down the slope to the cottages and Jamie killed the engine. I climbed off, stiffly, and handed back my crash helmet. I didn't want to leave things on that slightly sour note, but the only topic I could think of was tricky to broach. I grasped the nettle anyway. 'Jamie,' I said, 'I didn't know ... about Hugh.'

Jamie pushed his hair back off his face. 'Didn't know what about him?'

I sighed. He was going to make me suffer. 'Anything.' I gave Jamie a direct look. 'I knew nothing of his ... situation at all. I thought he was a ranger, or something. Itinerant, working for the Environment Agency. I had no idea he lived ...' I gestured, '... with her, up there.'

Jamie did not hold my eye. He turned his helmet over and over in his hands, regarding it intently, as though he had never seen such a thing before. 'Hum,' he said at last. 'And now you *do* know ... I suppose ... well, it will change things.'

Still he did not meet my eye. Little light still remained but, through his lowered lashes, I saw the glint of a tear.

'Yes,' I said. 'Of course.'

He heaved a huge sigh. 'You'll be making plans to leave,' he said, with specious lightness.

'At some point.'

'Sooner than you'd planned?' He squeezed the query out, and my heart gave a little contraction.

I thought about my unfinished book, about what Mary might be able to tell me that would put me back on track again, and set this against the awkwardness of the situation with Hugh. Jamie was right. To go away— as I had come—without fanfare or planning, to pass through the veil and leave Roadend to its obscure, timeless existence on the edge of the map would be the best course. And yet ...

'I don't know,' I said. I was suddenly tired—dog tired—and wanted nothing more than my bed. 'I can't decide now,' I said, the misery and exhaustion plain in my voice.

He nodded. 'We'll see you in a few days? Mum and me?' He said it almost as if he did not expect me to stay even that long.

'Yes.' Mary had arranged to come down to my cottage one day later that week. Of course, I had invited Jamie to join us. I knew he could not spend too much time with his mother and I had an idea that, whatever

Mary might tell of her early life in the village, it might help Jamie come to terms—if he needed to—with her leaving.

I woke up the next day more energised than I had felt in ages, Mary's story already complete in my head. It was as though I had dreamed it, and the dream had stayed with me, vividly detailed in technicolour, a long, intricate tapestry. I could scarcely believe it had happened again. I had needed Mary and she had arrived, as though summoned, releasing the floodgates that had been holding my narrative back. I knew nothing about her at all other than that she was kind and lovely. On the other hand, in my imagination I felt that I knew *everything* about her; her whole story was mapped out in my mind. It couldn't possibly be the truth—how *could* it be? I might have got the gist, the generality of it, but the specifics of it would only—*could* only—come from her. And yet … I wrestled with the weird sense of inspired hindsight, of bringing forth a tale *not* from my imagination but from history.

And I dabbled again with that incredible idea that, more than simply *discerning* history, I was actually *making* it.

I hesitated at the blank screen that had tormented me for so long, my fingers poised over the keys. Was it possible, I wondered, that whatever I wrote today could not only foreshadow but actually dictate whatever Mary might tell me in a few days' time?

The Trysting Tree
1960 – 1978

Todd and Rose had their first son in 1950. They christened him Joseph, but he was always referred to as Joe. He was a sturdy child, lusty and forever hungry. He also had an appetite for mischief and adventure from the moment he could crawl across the stone flags of the kitchen floor. In spite of being active during the day, he was a poor sleeper, and many was the night hour Rose spent pacing up and down the landing of the farmhouse with him on her shoulder. In truth, he wore her out; she grew thin and harried, torn between watching him and running the farm.

Farming during the fifties was hard; several years of drought hit the UK, adversely affecting yields. Many farmers sold up, and large tracts of land were amalgamated to form enormous commercial enterprises. Whereas Todd's holdings had been considered large, now they were small in comparison to others, and he struggled to compete. Mechanisation had made life for farmers easier, but machines cost money and, for Todd, money was hard to find. Too proud to admit to his struggles, he made an effort to continue in the role of influential, affluent farmer in the eyes of his peers, sometimes spending more than he could afford on breeding stock and the upkeep of his buildings. More than once he was approached with decent offers to take the whole parcel of Forrester land off his hands, but the bearers of these propositions were sent packing.

Rose did her best to encourage and support her husband, but it was no surprise when the stress caused her two stillborn babies—both girls—in '51 and '53 respectively. Their tiny bodies were laid to rest beside Todd's mother, Ellen, in Roadend cemetery—a place visible to Rose from her bedroom window.

There was consternation amongst farmers about what would happen in 1953, when rationing was due to end, but in fact the government committed to continue subsidising food production, and this security eased the burden on the Forresters' farm. Todd swallowed his pride and negotiated a substantial loan to fund investment in machinery and infrastructure. The Forresters took a holiday for the first time in their married life, and a second son, John, was born the following year.

Like his brother, John was a strong and vigorous child. Although four years separated them, it seemed like John was always on his brother's heels. Whatever Joe could do, John could do too. Sunny days saw six-year-old Joe marching off to the shore with his fishing rod, or up to the tarn to swim, with two-year-old John toddling resolutely behind him. Joe enjoyed his brother's admiration but disliked the responsibility of looking after him. He resented, also, the fact that John seemed to achieve by brains what he himself accomplished by brawn. John was quicker-witted and more imaginative than Joe, overcoming obstacles with apparent ease that had taken Joe many attempts to master. Joe invented challenges he hoped his brother would fail at: shinnying up smooth-trunked trees, scrumping apples from an orchard where a notoriously bad-tempered boar was housed, whittling sticks with knives that were murderously sharp, swimming a brimming drainage channel from end-to-end without a breath. Joe would always go first, having had days or even weeks to practice or at least to plan his offensive. John would watch—in awe and admiration—but then, on the spot, come up with a cleverer scheme. It was a wonder, with all these exploits, that John survived his childhood, but he did.

Joe could be cruel, but no amount of meanness seemed to dint John's affection and veneration for his older brother until the boys were twelve and eight-years-old respectively. Then, a seismic shift took place between them. Their household was augmented by Agnes, the orphan granddaughter of Rose's sister Rowan who had died in a tragic fire. The child was sulky and difficult and this perhaps decreased Rose's time or her ability to mediate between the boys. Puberty no doubt impacted Joe's temper; it certainly did increase from that time. Whatever the cause, John's esteem for his brother soured and an outright and bitter rivalry commenced between them.

Both lads were big for their age, the Forrester gene that had skipped over Todd manifesting itself with extra pugnacity in them. Both took up Cumberland wrestling, Joe prevailing by sheer strength and John by skill and clever sleights as well as more muscle than would be expected of a boy his age. The wrestling gave them an outlet for their excess of physicality; they were often found tussling in the street or the yard, but their adherence to the rules went by the wayside as personal hostility swamped any sportsmanlike instinct either of them may have possessed. Biting and hair-tearing and attacks below the belt were the norm. They vied for ascendancy in a noisy, bloody campaign of black eyes and split lips that drove Rose to distraction. Both boys grew up to be characteristically angry and obstreperous; they could pick an argument with one another in an empty room. They were over-large, over-loud and over-handy with their fists. As they grew to be young men, Joe and John could out-drink, out-shout, out-swear and out-fight any of their contemporaries—but were only interested in out-doing each other. Let any outsider malign the Forrester name, though, and the two boys acted as one. On these all-too-rare occasions, they were a formidable team.

Their size and their combative characters brought out the worst in Todd. Never a man to play second fiddle to anyone, he was certainly not going to allow his sons to dominate him. Both were taller than him by their mid-teens and either could have crushed him with a blow. Todd's pride in them metamorphosed into beleaguered defensiveness as he felt his own supremacy come under threat. He would wade into the fray, taking indiscriminate sides with one lad or the other, often changing allegiance mid-argument in order to prove he was a match for them both.

Those years were acrimonious ones in the Forrester household. Poor Rose was hassled by running the farm and feeding her family's voracious appetites, and being utterly unable to keep the peace. It distressed her to see her boys at each other's throats, and she disliked seeing her husband behaving as badly as they did—equal to them in his spleen and violence. In private she feared she was unwell, dogged by constant tiredness but unable to sleep at night. Her appetite was poor. She dug deep into the self-sufficiency she had propagated as a child, and spoke to no one of her worries.

Her only consolation was her youngest boy, Jack. He was two years younger than John. Their closeness in age should have made them more natural playmates—if it had not been for John's obsession with his older brother—but Jack was more self-sufficient than either of his siblings and, as a child, was happy to play on his own. He was of a quiet, contemplative bent, an easy child and one for whom Rose thanked God. Though quite the physical equal of his brothers, and in time taking on his share of the work, he never involved himself in their on-going rivalry, and looked on with mild disgust as they rolled in the dirt over some imagined slight, or punched each other black and blue. Once their cousin, Agnes, was added to the Forrester household it was more likely to be her, than one of his brothers, with whom Jack spent his time. He took the little girl under his wing, and she adored him. Jack's care of Agnes relieved Rose of that burden. His air of peacefulness in the eye of the Forrester storm was a blessing to her. When battles raged on over the dinner table it would be Jack who would calmly pour his mother a cup of tea before clearing the table of anything that could be used as a weapon or a missile. One afternoon he led Rose up the attic stairs to where his room was located and showed her an old armchair he had hauled up there to sit in an envelope of sunshine that came through the rooflight. He had accumulated a collection of dog-eared books, an old kettle and a chipped cup and saucer.

'You can come up here whenever you like,' he said. 'I doubt anyone will think to look for you up here, and I won't tell them where you are.'

He had simply seen his mother needed a refuge and provided one. No further explanation was necessary and Jack offered none.

By 1970 Joe and John were both working full time on the farm, Although Jack would have to remain at school until 1972 there was no question of him pursuing another career or leaving Roadend when that time came. Todd insisted his boys would inherit and carry on his dynasty at Roadend; there was land enough and there were houses enough to accommodate them all, and his dream was that they would continue what he had started when he was laid to rest in the ground. Accordingly, he demolished the farmhouse at Low Farm and built a square, brick, utilitarian farmhouse in its stead. It was no thing of beauty, but it had piped heating and a modern kitchen and bathroom. As Rose toured it, admiring its sleek and easy-to-clean kitchen surfaces and its labour-saving gas fires, she tentatively suggested she and Todd take up residence there; the older boys, by that time, were capable of looking after themselves and frankly, she would have been glad to escape their constant quarrels. But Todd wouldn't hear of the move. The Forresters were the premier family in the village and Roadend farm was the premier house. One of his sons might, in time, occupy Low Farm, but he, the head of the household, would remain where he was.

In order to pay for the new farmhouse at Low, Todd sold the row of old ship-breakers' cottages he had acquired some years before. Ship-breaking as an industry had ceased at Roadend and the cottages were hardly fit for human habitation as they stood. It came hard to Todd to sell his land, but as he could not afford to demolish and rebuild the cottages himself—and being in sore need of some ready money—he grasped the nettle. A builder bought all the plots and constructed half a dozen modern bungalows. They were ugly to look upon, and wholly out of keeping with the rest of the village architecture, but bought up by retired couples and the odd family keen to begin a country life.

One of the new residents was a widowed professor, who brought his daughter to Roadend to take up residence in one of those new dwellings in the early spring of 1974. The professor had taught history and classics at a number of universities until the death of his wife, which coincided with the publication of a historical novel he had been working on in his leisure hours for about ten years. The novel's immediate popularity opened up a new career for Professor Leon; one that did not tie him to a campus or a schedule of lectures and seminars. The death of his wife made him feel that a new start, away from the places where he had been so used to seeing her, would be a good thing.

His daughter Mary had been sorely afflicted by her mother's death. Her studies had suffered and it seemed unlikely she would get the grades she needed for university, even if she could be persuaded to take the examinations. She was seventeen years old when she came to Roadend, depressed and grieving, her life so utterly shattered she doubted she would ever regain the joy she had once known. Listlessly, she arranged her father's books on the shelves of his study and put the rest of their belongings away in the custom-fitted wardrobes and cupboards thinking—morosely—that this god-forsaken, dead-end place and their soulless bungalow would be a perfect metaphor for her life from then on. Roadend seemed to her an intellectual wilderness—the nearest library was a five-mile bus trip away. There were no museums or galleries. No lectures or societies. She could not imagine meeting a single soul with whom she might have anything in common.

Her bedroom was at the back of the house. Its window looked up the narrow strip of garden to a field beyond that sloped up to a fir plantation. She knew there was a public footpath running up the far edge of the field to the trees, and she wondered if she would have the courage—or the energy—to walk up there one day. She opened her window to hear the sough of the wind in the swaying treetops in the hope it might motivate her to escape her stultifying torpor of grief. It was a bright, breezy day, with high clouds skimming a perfect, eye-blue sky. The juxtaposition of her bleak mood with the light, airy panorama struck Mary with particular poignancy. She longed to shake off her depression and step out into whatever possibility this new locale could provide, but somehow she felt rooted, anchored as though by a hawser, in a mire of thick grief. Even if she could summon the will to take herself outdoors, she doubted her legs would carry her.

A tractor was making ever decreasing circuits of the field below the plantation, turning over the previous year's stubble, revealing the deep, black soil beneath. Mary wondered idly what the next crop would be. She knew nothing of farming but assumed some seed or other would be sown once the field had been ploughed. She hoped it would not be used for cows because these scared her. If there were cows in the open field, she would certainly not risk the footpath. The tractor was filthy, so bespattered with mud it was impossible to tell what colour it might once have been. No glint of chrome or gleam of glass reflected from the dun vehicle despite the brightness of the sun. Within the cab though, she could see a bright corona—the white-blond hair of the driver, a beacon amidst the smirch and smear.

The furrows behind the tractor were neat, mesmerising in their slow exuding from the blade of the plough. The soil was rich, starkly dark against the bright light of the early spring day. Overhead, dozens of seagulls carked and swooped to pick up whatever food the turned soil offered, the sun glinting off their feathers, making another vivid contrast to the scene. It seemed to her that the tractor spooled out both the endless furrows and the flights of birds as a conjurer produces reams of handkerchiefs from his sleeves. The gay connotations of this image against her own melancholy increased the vague urge that she should go out, *do* something, but she remained, fixed and almost transfixed at the open window.

As she watched, a second tractor came through the narrow gate of the field and trundled directly towards where the first one laboured up the incline of the field. The second drove across the perfect spiral of troughs, squashing and spoiling them, and sent the seagulls flapping in disarray from their feeding grounds. The first tractor stopped and its driver got down from the cab, his hair lifting in the breeze like the birds' feathers. He was not an old man by any means, but he was a man as opposed to a boy. He was broad in the shoulder, tall. The second driver also descended. He was of the same mould—well-built, substantial—his hair—wildly curly—was also fair but not as blond as the other man's. A heated argument ensued. Mary, her interest piqued, opened her window more widely, but she couldn't hear any of the words that were now being bandied with great energy between the two men. There was arm-waving and pointing. The blond man took a wild swing, which the curly-haired one dodged with ease. He placed his hands on his hips and threw his head back in an exaggerated mime of derision. While he was thus occupied the first man lunged in earnest, and then the two were on the ground, rolling backward and forward but caught in a deep furrow so they were effectively unable to escape one another. Showers of earth flew here and there as they kicked it around. Their arms and fists were a blur as they took punches at one another. Mary did not know whether to be alarmed or amused but stood at her window riveted by the violent encounter.

Then a third man—younger, lankier, but definitely a scion of the same tree—come walking up the periphery of the field to where the fight was taking place. The two combatants didn't see him until the new arrival bent and grasped the collar of the uppermost wrestler and hauled him off the other. The second fighter staggered to his feet and it seemed for a while that both would set upon the third—they advanced upon him menacingly. The peacemaker took a few steps backwards and held up his hands in a gesture of surrender. Then he pointed at his watch, before turning to look over his shoulder to where a battered Land Rover was making its slow way along the narrow track that dissected the ploughed field from the one next to it.

The sight of the vehicle, or perhaps being reminded of the time, galvanised both the tractor drivers immediately. They leapt into their respective cabs and resumed their work, driving in perfect tandem, side by side.

The lad thrust his hands in his pockets and walked swiftly up the field towards a stile at its top. By the time the Land Rover appeared at the farm gate, he had climbed the stile and disappeared into the plantation.

~

Summer came, and gradually Mary's depression abated enough for her to venture into Roadend. She walked up the field—a shimmering, shivering fabric of green now, as the spring wheat thrived in the fertile soil. From the top of the hill, she looked back down at the village, laid out like a child's model, with prick-neat houses, the undulating common, the wide ribbon of beach against the tawny, foaming sea. She went to the butcher's, baker's and green-grocer's vans that parked up on the green near the little bridge, and got on nodding acquaintance with the other women who came to buy. She made friends with a local girl named Nancy. Like Mary's, Nancy's plans for the future had been scuppered; she had intended to train as a hairdresser but a long bout of glandular fever had caused her to miss the beginning of her course. This was about the only thing the two girls had in common. Nancy had little intellectual capacity and less ambition. She had never heard of Dickens, Tolstoy or Steinbeck and had no curiosity about them once she discovered they were not in the hit parade. She was interested in clothes and makeup and the kind of pop music that gave Mary a headache. Nancy consumed magazines voraciously, cutting out pictures to put in a scrapbook or stick on her bedroom wall. The girls met on the beach where both were whiling away the interminable days, their friendship forged from their mutual loneliness.

Nancy and Mary met Joe and John Forrester on the night of a disco to be held in the nearby harbour town. A disco was not Mary's idea of fun but Nancy was keen so she had agreed to go along. The girls were waiting at the bus stop when a rusty, rattling Cortina drew up at the kerb and John wound down the window.

'Want a lift, girls?'

Mary held back, having had it inculcated into her from an early age that accepting lifts from strangers was dangerous, although she recognised the two young men in the car as the combatants in the field and so she supposed they were not, *strictly speaking*, strangers. Nancy yanked open the rear door of the car without hesitation and Mary could do nothing but slide in beside her. Nancy's giggling demeanour, as the car followed the lane out of the village and along the line of the coast, suggested powerfully the offer of a lift had not only been anticipated but also planned. The car had hardly come to a standstill before John and Nancy leapt out of it and disappeared together up a narrow side street.

Joe, who had been driving, watched them go with a baleful eye. Then he turned to Mary. 'You don't want to go to the disco, do you?'

Mary blushed. She hadn't wanted to go, but whatever alternative this enormous, swaggering lad was going to suggest would surely be worse.

'Isn't that where you're going?' she asked, and, looking up the street in the direction Nancy and John had taken, 'Isn't that where *they've* gone?'

Joe shook his head, his white-blond hair, worn long in the style of the day, falling like fine silk across his broad brow. 'I doubt it. Off to the pub, I should think.'

'Nancy isn't old enough,' said Mary, knowing she sounded prim.

Her companion gave a scornful smile. 'So what? Anyway, you don't have to have a proper drink. Come on, I'll buy you a lemonade, if that's what you really want.'

He took off after his brother. Mary tripped after him, regretting her platform soles.

'I don't know your name,' she said breathlessly, after a few minutes.

Joe turned incredulous eyes upon her. They were the intense blue of iris flowers. 'You're joking!'

'No,' said Mary. 'I have no idea who you are.'

Joe seemed to consider this remote possibility. 'You're new,' he said, excusing her ignorance. 'I'm Joe Forrester.' He held out his hand awkwardly and she placed her small palm against his huge one.

'I'm Mary,' she said.

'I know,' Joe replied.

The pub was busy, with a press of bodies up against the bar. It was thick with cigarette smoke and the smell of beer and aftershave. Loud music blared from a juke box. It met Mary's every pessimistic expectation. Where were the groups of students in earnest debate? Where the solitary scholars crouched over their books? Across the crowd, hemmed in at the bar, Mary saw Nancy and John. She waved, but they were too absorbed in each other to notice her. Mary felt she had been taken for a fool, dragged to the disco as an excuse for Nancy to meet up with John and possibly set up with Joe as a kind of double date. She felt manipulated and used, and looked up at Joe to see if she could make out what part— if any—he had in the arrangements. Perhaps he would take the first opportunity to abandon her.

But he seemed to have no objection to the situation that had fallen out. He scanned the pub and soon spied an unoccupied table by the empty fireplace. He took Mary's hand and shouldered through the fray, dragging her behind in his wake. The crowd parted, one or two preparing to offer objection to being so unceremoniously jostled out of the way until they took in Joe's heft and height. Then they stood aside meekly enough. Joe pressed Mary into a chair and forged his way to the bar. Mary surveyed the scene with alarm. She had never been in a pub before and she was not sure her father would approve of her being in one now. The male clientele was all older than she, holding pint pots. The girls were heavily made up; she doubted half of them were old enough to drink but they all held wine glasses. The raucous, sexually charged atmosphere made her feel uncomfortable. One or two blokes without female companions threw curious glances her way. One sidled up and asked if she would like a cigarette, proffering his packet. He wore a paisley shirt unbuttoned to his navel and the wide-legged trousers that were all the rage. Mary hardly had time to stammer out a refusal when the chap was elbowed rudely aside as Joe returned with a foaming pint for himself and a Coca-Cola for Mary.

'Back off, mate, this one's spoken for,' he growled.

Mary opened her mouth to protest—she certainly was *not* spoken for and did not wish Joe to assume so—but closed it again abruptly when she thought about the alternative. She was alone in an unfamiliar town. She was not sure when the next bus would run to Roadend and it would mortify her to telephone her father to ask him to collect her. So long as she could keep Joe at arm's length, she thought she would be safer in his company than not. She would sit tight and drink her Coke and hope she could reunite with Nancy bye and bye.

Joe returned to the bar twice more, bringing drinks and packets of crisps, refusing the money Mary offered. Three Cokes was enough for her bladder and she finally had to excuse herself to find the Ladies'. She pressed herself through the crowd towards the door Joe had indicated. On her way back she saw Nancy, half on and half off a bar stool, her hair mussed and her lipstick smudged.

'Nancy,' Mary said, 'are we going to the disco or not?'

'I thought you weren't keen on it,' said Nancy, focussing a bleary, mascara-blackened eye on Mary. 'This is much more fun, isn't it?' She gestured vaguely at the pub. 'I'm having such a lovely time with John. He's *so* dreamy, isn't he?'

Mary looked over at where John was in conference with another man. John's hair—she could see now that it was permed—hovered in a static halo round his head. That aside, Mary thought perhaps John was slightly better looking than Joe although both, with their broad shoulders and impressive height, were physically arresting specimens.

'You've been drinking,' said Mary, turning back to Nancy. 'Are you OK?'

'I'm fine,' slurred Nancy, turning to the bar where her glass stood on a bar mat. 'In fact, I'm ready for another. I'm drinking sweet martini and lemonade. John! John!'

John half turned, frowning. Then he saw Mary. Immediately, his face cleared, the scowl replaced by a broad smile. He turned back to his companion for long enough to mutter something under his breath. His friend turned and surveyed the two girls, then he gave John a ribald leer and walked away.

John returned his attention to the girls. 'Hello, Mary,' he said, all charm. 'Let me buy you a drink. What'll you have?' He raised his arm to attract the barman's attention.

'No, thank you,' said Mary. 'I think I ought to go. I think we *all* should, or we'll miss the disco altogether.' She glanced at her watch. It was half past eight and, to her knowledge, the disco ended at ten.

Nancy slipped her arms round John's neck. 'Perhaps we should, Johnny,' she crooned. 'We can dance the slow numbers. Wouldn't you like a smooch?'

John pried Nancy's arms from his neck. 'You're pissed,' he said witheringly. He turned to Mary. 'I'll dance with *you,* if you like.' Mary felt his arm snake its way around her waist. John's eyes were not like Joe's— they had a sly glint to them, their blue more of ice than of iris. She did not trust him.

Nancy's face, at John's remark, had crumpled. It looked like she was going to cry.

Mary looked helplessly from one to the other, and also over her shoulder, to where she had left Joe sitting by the fireplace. Joe had bought her three drinks and so perhaps she ought to consider herself honour-bound to remain with him for the rest of the evening, if he desired it. Also, Joe had the car keys—although he had consumed three pints of beer. As though reading her thoughts John brought his mouth close to her ear and whispered, 'I can get Joe to take Nancy home. You and I can go to the dance, if you want.' His hand gave her waist a little squeeze. 'Or, how about a little stroll around the harbour? I know a few shadowy nooks and crannies where no one will see us. If I'd known you were the blind date Nancy suggested for Joe, I'd never have agreed to it. You're much prettier than she is and I can't have my brother stealing *that* march on me.'

Mary stepped away, pushing his arm from her as though it was a snake. 'But you *did* agree to it,' she said firmly, above the din of the music. 'You asked her to the dance, and you've plied her with drink. I think you ought to look after her.'

'I can look after *both* of you,' said John, waggling a suggestive eyebrow. He did not seem at all put off by Mary's manner.

Suddenly the crowd parted and Joe appeared. He took in the situation—Nancy's inebriation, John's lascivious suggestion and Mary's distress—at a glance. He pulled Mary into the protection of his arm. She fitted beneath his shoulder comfortably and she found surprising reassurance within its circle. She cowered under his wing while Joe leaned forward and delivered a few choice epithets into his brother's ear. The record came to an end and there was a sudden, deafening silence. John squared up to his brother, his expression bullish. Mary heard someone say, 'The Forresters are going to kick off.' The throng shrunk back as one, some downing their drinks and leaving the pub in a fluid retreat, others holding back to see the fight they felt sure would ensue. The Forrester boys' spats were a source of local entertainment. It was not infrequent for bets to be placed, and here was one in the offing right now. The barman said, 'Take it outside, if you please gents,' while Joe and John eyed each other, neither yielding an inch of ground.

Mary quailed at the idea of a fight—she had seen the violence of the brothers' antagonism before in the ploughed field—and was stupefied at the idea she might be the cause of it.

John said, 'I have as much right to Mary as you have, Joe.'

Mary bridled. She was not a chattel and no one had "rights" over her. Joe must have felt her anger. He stroked her bare arm with his thumb—a tiny, hardly perceptible motion, but one that spoke to her. 'I know, I know,' it seemed to say. 'Don't worry. *I* don't think that way.'

'Oh John,' wailed Nancy who had been forgotten in the standoff. 'I thought I was your girlfriend.'

John gave an irritated shake of his head and fixed his eyes on Mary. 'You'll come to the dance with me, won't you Mary?' he said with a confidence Mary was sure was pure bluster.

'I … I thought we were *all* going,' said Mary, desperate to diffuse things.

'Take *me* to the dance, John,' Nancy whined. 'You promised you would.'

Mary cringed. The public bar was deathly still and silent, every eye and ear tuned to the little theatre of altercation around the four of them. She certainly had no intention of going anywhere with John, but she felt if she accepted the invitation implicit in Joe's encircling arm, she might aggravate an already volatile situation. What she really wanted was to get Nancy home, away from the malign influence of both the Forrester boys.

Without taking his eyes from John, Joe bent his head to plant the briefest of kisses on Mary's head. His arm tightened around her. She could not tell if it was intended as a reassurance or as proof of possession. Whichever it was, a bolt of electricity shot through her brain, fizzed through her solar plexus and curled itself into her groin. She felt suddenly breathless and panicked, the encirclement of Joe's arm now more of an entrapment than a shield, but one she was not minded to escape.

Help came in the shape of the gangling younger brother—Jack—who had come into the bar unobserved by anyone. 'Joe, John,' he said, his quiet voice somehow more startling in the taut silence than a blood-curdling yell would have been. Every eye turned to him, including his brothers'. 'That heifer has started to calve. It's breech. You're to go home. Dad needs you.'

John and Joe were released as though from a spell. Their enmity simply evaporated, and they dashed together through the door.

Nancy crumpled from her bar stool and Mary only just managed to stop her from falling.

'Come on, girls,' said Jack, taking Nancy's other arm. 'I'll run you home.'

The night of the dance had been a Saturday. On the following Tuesday, Joe arrived at Professor Leon's front door with a bunch of wildflowers, a freshly baked pie and an invitation to take Mary for a stroll up to the pele tower. The request was delivered to Mary's father rather than to Mary herself. She hovered in the gloom of the hallway while Joe—his hair slicked down, his shirt obviously freshly pressed—exuded respectful but not demeaning deference. He introduced himself, and waved to the gates of the farmhouse, some fifty or so yards along the lane. The pie, he explained, was for the professor from his mother, as a welcome to Roadend. The flowers—he held them out, the blue of his eyes as innocent as the cornflowers wilting in his grasp—were for Mary. He explained he had met Mary at the dance on Saturday, and finding she was new to the area would be happy to show her the local sights, if the professor did not object. Professor Leon allowed Joe's charm-offensive to wash over him, neither impressed nor alarmed by Joe's appearance, just rather annoyed to have been disturbed from his work.

'By all means, if Mary wants to,' he said, once he had understood the somewhat old-fashioned nature of Joe's application.

Mary and Joe set off along the lane. It was evening. Joe's long shadow threw Mary into the shade. She fought the rising tremor of her nerves to say, 'The pie was a nice touch. Did your mother really bake it for us?'

'Of course,' said Joe. 'She's sorry not to have been down to say hello. She knows what it's like to be a stranger in town. But she's so busy and then, in the evenings, so tired.'

Since Saturday night Mary had thought of little else besides Joe Forrester—how handsome he was, how big and strong. But then also, how much older he was than she; a man, who would expect more than she—a seventeen-year-old virgin—was ready to offer. As she walked beside him she noticed the thick mat of golden hairs on his forearms and the nick in his chin from his razor and felt herself to be young and impossibly unworldly. She groped for some topic of conversation. 'You must all work hard on the farm,' she said, lamely in her own opinion. 'I've seen you, ploughing and so on.'

Joe seemed to think her remark a perfectly reasonable one. 'It's dawn to dusk, pretty much,' he said. 'But I never wanted to do anything else.'

It was Joe's turn to ask a question, but he made no attempt at it and they passed the church and began the climb up the track to the pele tower in awkward silence. 'What's this place, then?' Mary blurted out.

Joe stopped. 'We don't have to go up there, if you don't want to,' he said, suddenly disarming in his palpable uncertainty. 'I just said it because I thought your dad would approve.' He squinted up the hill to where the burnt-out remnant of the tower stood, a jagged silhouette against the setting sun. His air of manliness had drained away, leaving him coy and awkward. He mumbled, 'If I'm honest, the place gives me the creeps,' and thrust his hands into his pockets.

'I don't mind,' said Mary, confused by the sudden alteration in his mien.

He looked at her feet. She wore canvas lace-ups. 'What about going on to the beach?' he suggested. 'At least you're wearing sensible shoes. Not like on Saturday.'

'Those platform shoes made my feet ache,' Mary admitted.

They turned from the track and walked across the scrubby turf of the green, then onto the shingle. The bluff rose up to the right of them, its layers of rock, soil and cobble exposed by the winds and tides. Presently they found an old sea-bleached log, worn smooth by endless pounding of wind and weather, and sat down upon it. Joe had not spoken and Mary felt a surge of panic. She guessed him to be at least five years her senior. What would she do if he made a move on her? She could not outrun him, she didn't think, and she certainly had no chance of fighting him off. On the other hand, his initial confidence seemed to have vanished; he was as tongue-tied as she was.

Joe reached into his pocket and brought out a packet of chewing gum. He offered her a stick and Mary accepted it even though she considered gum-chewing a slovenly habit. They chewed companionably for a while, Mary somewhat reassured; she did not think it was possible to kiss—or rape—someone with a mouth full of gum. Also, it was an excuse to delay conversation.

Nevertheless, she said, 'What is it, between your brother and you?' surprising herself because she had not known she was going to pose the question.

Joe shrugged. 'John's always been jealous of me.'

Mary stopped herself from correcting him—*envious,* not *jealous*—and nodded, encouraging him to continue because she felt here, at last, she would get a glimpse of the real Joe Forrester.

'Everything I have, he wants,' Joe went on. 'I'm the oldest, so I'll get the farm when Dad dies. It's up to me to carry on the Forrester name. John doesn't like that he has to take second place.'

'Won't John get anything?'

'He'll get something. But I'll have Roadend Farm. It's the best house and has the best land. It's only right: I'm the oldest.'

Eldest, Mary wanted to say, but didn't. Instead, she remarked, 'Things may have changed, by then.'

Joe turned to her. 'What do you mean?'

Mary considered. 'Your dad isn't likely to die *soon,* is he? Years may go by. You may decide to do something other than farming. Or John might. And what about your other brother?' Discreetly, she removed her gum and wrapped it in a tissue from her pocket.

'Jack? I doubt he'll care, one way or the other. He talks about university, travel … I can't see him sticking around here.'

The idea of anyone in that backwater having such admirable ambitions cheered Mary. She picked up a smooth, white pebble and turned it in her fingers. She supposed it was only fair that she told him something about the real Mary Leon; that she too had plans beyond Roadend. 'I was supposed to be going to university, in September,' she said. 'But I didn't take my "A" levels.'

'It's a waste of time,' declared Joe, taking the pebble from her hand and hurling it down the beach. It bounced once, and then split into a dozen shards.

'I don't think so,' replied Mary hotly, thinking of her father. 'Study, research …'

'Achieves absolutely nothing,' Joe finished. He held out his hands—large, meaty, calloused. 'Good, honest toil is the only thing that gets you anywhere,' he said. 'What were you going to study, anyway?'

'English literature.'

Joe let out a burst of laughter. 'There you are,' he said. He spat his gum out and reached across and took her hand in his. The impossibility of any kind of friendship between them had never been more apparent to Mary than at that moment but then, with her hand in his, and the proximity of his hard, muscled body, it was hard to focus rationally on anything.

In front of them the last sliver of sun stretched out elongated fingers, grappling on to what remained of the day, bruising the striations of cloud in hues of pink, orange, magenta and violet. The blue of the sky dimmed to heliotrope. The turgid sea became mercury, the beach a lava of glinting mica and winking quartz. Suddenly the wind picked up, puckering the flesh of Mary's bare arms; she gave an involuntary shiver. Joe wrapped his arm around her shoulders and pulled her close. 'I like you, Mary,' he said, turning so he could look her square in the eye, blocking her view of the sunset, the silken sky and the bejewelled beach. His face was shadowed and she could not make out his expression. She wrinkled an eyebrow, not knowing if she could trust him. She felt very young and hopelessly disorientated by his alacritous changes—one moment shy and uncommunicative, the next brash.

'Have you ever been kissed?' he asked.

She shook her head. Her heart was beating wildly. She didn't know whether she wanted to be kissed by him. She hardly knew him. She wasn't sure if he was just toying with her. At the same time, roiling in her belly was a snake of desire that almost made her squirm with pleasure.

He smiled—she could see the white of his teeth in the dark, indistinct smudge of his face. 'I didn't think so,' he said. His mouth was close to hers. She could smell the minty flavour of the gum on his breath. His hair was lit up into rose gold filaments by the dying throes of the sun; she could see the halo of it round his head. He licked his lips. Then, with a suddenness that was astonishing, the radiance faded and the bright iridescence sank away leaving the beach dull and grey.

Joe heaved a sigh and released her. 'It's getting dark,' he said, pulling her to her feet. 'Time I got you home or your dad won't let me see you again.'

Mary trudged back up the shingle behind him, feeling both relieved and strangely cheated.

At her door he did lean down and kiss her, but too briefly, a mere brush of his lips against hers. Then he strode off into the twilight.

When he had gone it occurred to Mary that he had not asked her if she wished to see him again. He had taken that as read.

John's offensive on Mary was markedly different to Joe's. He came by night, a stealthy knock on her bedroom window. She found him crouching on the path, stifling his glee.

'What are you doing?' she hissed at him.

He stood and leaned his arms on her window frame. 'Aren't you going to invite me in?' He pushed her curtain back and peered into the room.

'Certainly not,' she said, appalled at the idea. 'It must be past midnight.'

'It is,' he agreed. 'I thought your old man would never go to bed.'

'He often works late,' she said, thinking how ridiculous it was to be having this conversation in these circumstances.

'I've been waiting an hour at least,' he said, 'waiting for his light to go out. And I have to be up again at five.'

'You should have called at a proper time, and in the proper way,' said Mary stiffly, thinking of the formality of Joe's visit. 'At the front door, for example?'

John gave her a grin. 'Boring,' he said. 'This is much more exciting. Move over. Let me in.'

'No!' Mary protested, but John had hoisted himself up and was in her bedroom before she could do anything to stop him.

'Well, this is nice,' he said, strolling around the room, examining her bookshelves, desk and the large beanbag where she liked to sit and read.

Now that he was inside she could smell the beer on his breath. 'You've been drinking.'

He shrugged. 'I had to pass the time somehow. I told you, I've been waiting over an hour.'

'Waiting in the pub,' she sneered. 'What do you want, anyway?'

He waggled his eyebrows. 'Isn't that obvious? I want you.'

Mary backed away, clutching her dressing gown to her. 'What about Nancy?' she said. She knew Nancy had seen John since the night of the disco. Indeed, it seemed to please Nancy to give Mary lurid chapter and verse on their liaison while they drank coffee and played records at Nancy's house or at Mary's. From what Mary had gathered Nancy had—so far—resisted John's pressure to go "all the way" but she had allowed him to get what she called "fresh." In spite of how mean he had been to her, Nancy considered herself to be John's girlfriend.

'Nancy's a nice girl,' said John, 'but she's got nothing on you.'

'I think she'd be very hurt if she knew you were here,' said Mary. She had backed herself into a corner between her bed and her wardrobe. The tumbled bed had an intimacy and an implied invitation that horrified her. She saw John's gaze flick across the rumpled sheets. She said, 'Nancy's your girlfriend, isn't she?'

'Nancy's a nice girl,' said John again.

Suddenly he seemed to notice how uncomfortable Mary was with the situation. His assertive demeanour relaxed and he said, 'Don't look so much like a cornered rabbit. I only want to talk. Is that OK?' He sank down onto the bean bag. 'What are all these books for?'

Mary emerged from her corner and perched on the bed. How on earth was she to answer such a question? 'For reading, obviously,' she said.

'And you've read all of these?'

Mary considered. 'I've read most of all of them, and all of most of them,' she said. 'What do you want to talk about?'

John seemed at a loss—all his bluster dispersed into the shadowy corners of the room. 'I don't know,' he mumbled.

'Tell me about your brother,' said Mary impulsively. 'Tell me about Joe. What *is* it between you two?'

John's brow darkened. 'Joe has this idea that he's *better* because he's older. It annoys me. There's nothing that he can do on the farm—or *anywhere*—that I can't do just as well, or better.'

'If that's true, he'll have to accept it,' suggested Mary.

'It *is* true, but he'll never accept it,' said John bleakly. 'His answer to everything is that he's the oldest.'

'Your dad must …'

'Dad *likes* the fact we compete all the time,' said John, kneading his large hands together. 'If anything, he encourages it.'

'I wonder why.'

John pondered. 'It makes him feel big,' he said at last.

Presently, John stood up to leave. He perched on the window ledge, fighting the curtain that billowed in the breeze. 'I *do* like you, Mary. I want to you to go out with me—properly, I mean. I want you to be my girlfriend. Will you?'

'What about Nancy?' said Mary. 'She's my friend. I wouldn't want to see her hurt.'

'I'll let her down gently,' said John. 'She'll be starting college in September. She'll meet lots of new lads there and she'll soon forget me.'

'I'll be going back to school,' said Mary. 'I'm going to retake the last year of "A" levels, then I'll be off to university.'

'What a waste of time,' said John—exactly, Mary recalled, as Joe had done. 'But that's ages away. Will you go out with me?' In the pinkish light of her bedside lamp John's face was flushed, eager, hopeful.

Mary shook her head. 'I don't think so, John. If you can treat Nancy this way, how could I ever trust you?'

The earnest, winning expression on his face metamorphosed to one of cunning. 'I could just tell everyone I've been in your bedroom at night,' he said. He surveyed the room. 'I can describe your bed, your books, the poster of Blackpool Tower you have on your wall.'

'That's the Eiffel Tower,' said Mary in a small voice. 'You wouldn't do that, would you John?'

His shoulders slumped. 'Probably not,' he said.

He lifted his leg over the sill and was gone.

The summer passed quickly. Long days of bright but breezy weather saw Joe and Mary walking along the shore when his work on the farm permitted. In the evenings he drove her along twilit lanes to flat areas of the dunes where they could park up and watch the stars appear in the velvet sky. He would kiss her, his mouth roving over hers, his tongue a tentative explorer, his arms a crushing cave around her. When they talked it was of the farm, of Todd's iron grip upon it, of Joe's drive to win his father's approval. 'He won't trust me,' Joe complained. 'He won't let any little bit of it go, so I can prove myself. I do the work of three men some days, but it's never enough.'

'Have you tried talking to him about it?' Mary ventured.

Joe threw her an exasperated look. 'He wouldn't listen.'

John's nocturnal visits continued. Like Joe, John was in Todd Forrester's thrall, afraid of him. But John also nursed a sour hatred of his father, a resentment that burned like gall. He was made to feel his second-son status as a branding that would never fade.

In some ways Mary enjoyed John's company more than Joe's. Joe had gallantry but John had charm. There was a rigid formality about Joe's courtship that Mary—and Professor Leon—appreciated. He respected her, but he lacked imagination. John was more unconventional, and more fun. One night he brought her a chick, just hatched, that hid beneath her bed and cheeped plaintively for the duration of the visit. They would squash together on Mary's beanbag and flick through magazines, talking in low voices. It would be a while before Mary realised John's arm had slipped around her waist. Once or twice he managed to kiss her. His kisses were harder than Joe's, his tongue intrusive and his hands wayward. It was a struggle to keep him in check. He pleaded with her to ditch Joe and be his—John's—girl. At times he was importunate, wild-eyed with longing. One night he knelt at Mary's feet and kissed them. She could feel the drip of his tears as he implored her to love him. Mary stepped away, appalled. His act had been convincing, but she suspected the only reason John desired her was that Joe had laid first claim. She knew John was still seeing Nancy and, what's more, that things between the two of them had progressed "all the way." Mary distrusted John, but when he rapped on her window, her resolution to deny him admittance always wavered.

Naturally, Mary did not mention John's visits to Joe. She knew he would be angry and she was not sure whether John or she herself would be the object of his ire.

On one occasion she was invited to the farmhouse to meet Rose and Todd. It felt significant—an official introduction to Joe's parents—although Mary did not know what exactly it portended. Rose greeted Mary kindly, with a swift hug. Todd eyed her narrowly. Agnes, Rose's great-niece, then aged fifteen, looked witheringly at Mary's neatly buttoned cardigan and sensible, polished shoes; she wore a pair of work-stained dungarees and had straw in her hair. John threw Mary lascivious looks whenever he thought Joe wasn't looking. Jack busied himself with assisting his mother, carrying dishes and fetching condiments.

Dinner was served in the kitchen, a matter that Rose apologised for several times, lamenting she had not had time to do the dusting in the dining room. Todd occupied a carver chair at the head of the table. Mary noticed its seat was bolstered by several cushions so he could meet his sons eye-to-eye. He held forth at length about his rise to prominence from nothing, his discourse occupying the main course and the dessert. No one else spoke. They kept their eyes fixed on their plates and allowed the old man's diatribe to wash over them. Rose wore a fixed smile, pulling back thin lips from teeth that seemed too large in her emaciated face, her eyes bright points of anxiety. Occasionally, passing back and forth between the table and the sink, she grasped Mary's shoulder with a hand that was surprisingly strong. Agnes' scorn shrank under the weight of crippling embarrassment and under cover of the tablecloth she briefly took Mary's hand and squeezed it, her eyes pouring apologies. Joe, on Mary's other side, pulled his chair close, and when he filled her water glass she could see his hand was shaking. John glowered while the meal was served, wolfed down his portion and excused himself before the others were even half finished.

At last Todd's monologue came to an end. He leaned back in his chair and said, 'You could do much worse than Joe, young lady. You've no farming experience, but then, neither had Rose.'

Mary blanched and Joe blushed. Both of them opened their mouths to deny the old man's imputation but Rose gave a minute shake of her head and Jack, speaking for the first time, said, 'When will the delivery of chick crumb come, Dad? There's hardly any left in the feed store.'

Afterwards, Joe said, 'I'm sorry about my dad. He spoke out of turn.'

'That's all right,' replied Mary in a small voice. Todd's implication had startled her. She wasn't ready to think about getting married; she had her exams to take, and then university to attend.

But Joe said, 'Since he mentioned it though, I want you to know I do want to marry you, Mary.'

Although Joe had never broached this topic before, he had made it plain he liked Mary, so his declaration wasn't a complete surprise. Being admired by a man like Joe was very flattering, but Mary tried not to let it go to her head; what would be the point? Who knew what would happen once she was absorbed back into academia? She *had* feelings for Joe, although they confused her. Sometimes she felt intimidated by him; he could be stroppy and insistent and there was no doubt he was a chauvinist. His greater maturity awed her and she almost envied his clear-eyed vision for his future on the farm; *she,* in contrast, had no certainty about what her future would hold. At other times she found herself moved and sympathetic and perhaps even a little sorry for him. When he opened himself just a chink—to allow a glimpse of the vulnerable person beneath the apparently unassailable exterior—she saw his desperate need to stay one step ahead of John, for example, and his abject need for his father's approval. Then there was her own treacherous body—the writhing serpents in the pit of her stomach, her roving hands that slipped inside his shirt to feel the cladding of hard muscle on his chest and belly. She and Joe had nothing whatsoever in common, and she knew in her heart he wasn't right for her. Yet, in those hot, quick-breathing moments in his car, that didn't seem the least bit important.

'I know,' she said, looking down at her hands. 'But Joe …'

'Don't say anything else,' Joe breathed, kissing her.

August came and both boys were busy with harvest. The weather was forecast to turn foul. Rain hovered but never fell. A grey, lowering cloud blanketed the sky. The wind was warm, taut with latent thunder and biblical rain that would decimate the crop. Todd, driven into a frenzy by the threat to their livelihood, kept his sons working day and night, bringing in the wheat and barley and the final silage cut of the year. Mary lay in her bed listening to the throb of the machinery as it toiled up and down the fields. When she rose and pushed aside her curtain, she could see the yellow eyes of the tractors' headlights illuminating tiny arcs in a field of dim and shadow. She wondered which Forrester boy was driving which vehicle, and why it was that at times like this both boys felt as far from her as were the last men to have stood on the moon a couple of years earlier.

In September, Mary returned to school. That Joe was disappointed was evident; he had never in so many words told her he did not wish her to pursue her studies, but that he considered it a waste of time was abundantly clear. He made it his business to take and collect her from school as often as possible. Having a boyfriend who was an Adonis—with a car—marked Mary out. Girls were envious of her and shut her out of their covens. Boys' interests were piqued, but the sight of Joe at the gates, his arms folded over his wide chest and an intimidating expression on his face prevented any from daring to approach her. Consequently, Mary was lonely at school—isolated as perhaps Joe had intended. He allowed Mary what he considered reasonable amounts of time for her studies, but then insisted she accompany him in his car to out-of-the-way places, where his kisses melted her marrow and she dissolved to liquescent neurons beneath his touch. Afterwards he would cajole her—wouldn't she like to lay in his arms all night long and allow him to make proper love to her? Study, reading, a degree, all that could come *afterwards,* if she was still fixed on it, he said, but didn't she feel—like him—that she would explode if they could not be man and wife?

Mary would sigh and straighten her clothing and remind him *again* that she had always been adamant about her university studies. It was what she had always wanted. Indeed, having been brought up in the rarefied atmosphere of a university town, it was the life she knew best. To give it up was impossible. Afterwards, perhaps—she would offer as a concession—once she had her degree, she might consider becoming Joe's wife if he could overlook her lack of experience and her utter unpreparedness for the farming life. In the privacy of her mind she added another caveat: if *she* could overlook Joe's intellectual shortcomings and his tendency to be a bully.

On these occasions Joe would climb out of the car and walk crossly up and down for a while, waiting for his ardour to cool. Mary wondered why he did not just take what he so badly wanted. She did not think she would refuse him, although she would not, herself, initiate it. She wondered if *that* would satisfy him, *pro tem*. Then again, if she went away and met someone else, her lost virginity might prove a stumbling block. In her heart, she thought that if she was to have intercourse with Joe, she would consider herself irrevocably committed. For a girl of the 70s, Mary's was an old-fashioned attitude, but there it was.

~

Nancy began her college course in September too, but she was never to complete it. She discovered she was pregnant with John's baby at Christmas and the two were married in haste in January. Mary stood as bridesmaid. She was secretly appalled at the shoddiness of the wedding, at Nancy's bump—which no amount of white nylon could conceal—at the lacklustre buffet laid on at the pub, at the swift deterioration of the guests into drunkenness. Joe, the best man, fulminated for the whole day, furious to have been relegated to second fiddle. His speech was grudging, brief, and by nine o'clock he was blotto, stumbling about the makeshift dance floor, ready to pick a fight with anyone who looked at him askance. At one point Mary found herself grabbed on her way to the Ladies' by the groom. He manhandled her down the narrow passageway and into a dark cloakroom.

'I wanted you,' John almost sobbed into the crimplene ruffle on the neck of her dress. 'And now look what I'm stuck with.'

'You're drunk, John,' she said, pushing him away.

'How else can I get through this?' he wailed.

'I don't know,' said Mary stiffly. 'But you *must* do, somehow.'

John and Nancy's first son, Johnny, was born in April of 1975. John's marriage and the arrival of a baby rankled Joe more than he could express. It went against every grain that John, the second son, should have reached this milestone first. Knowing how it provoked, Todd wasted no opportunity to brag about John's fecundity, rubbing Joe's nose in his brother's success. Joe redoubled his efforts to persuade Mary to give up her plans for university. They spent the year locked in battle over the question, neither prepared to compromise. At times it looked like they would part ways over the issue. They argued; Joe's inability to articulate made up for by a loud voice that drowned out Mary's reasoned opinions. His sexual frustration reached a peak and one day he pushed his way inside her. Afterwards, Mary did not know if she had been raped. She had not fought him off, not remonstrated or uttered the word "no." They had been petting for months—this outcome should have come as no surprise—and only a naive fool would have expected anything else. On the other hand, she had been taken by surprise, had not been ready, and the act had been painful and unpleasant. The location—the back of Joe's car—was not one she would have chosen. She was not sure what—if any—precautions Joe had taken. When it was done, Joe said, 'There, now you're mine. Even if I have to wait three years, I'll have you in the end. No one else will want you now.' That was Mary's own opinion. She stared up at the vinyl ceiling of his car with bleak acceptance. Later, when he tried to arouse her as he used to, she found she could not rise to it.

The sex seemed to assuage some of Joe's exasperation and the matter of Mary's studies was put in abeyance. She worked hard at her course and attended interviews at various universities. Joe even drove her to one or two of them, touring the libraries with disinterest and looking sneeringly at the students gathered in earnest groups in the quads.

In late September of 1975 Mary packed her bags and left Roadend to begin her university course. She suggested to Joe they break things off; it seemed only fair to him and, frankly, her own appetite for a continuance had been blunted. But Joe clutched her to him and swore he would never giver her up. 'Three years,' he hissed fiercely. 'Three years, and not one day more.'

~

Joe visited Mary at university any weekend when he could be spared from the farm, but that was not often. Rose was ill—less and less able to manage the farm accounts, run the household and provide the constant running buffet of food required to keep Todd and the boys fed. Nancy had moved into the farmhouse but she was useless in the kitchen and anyway, had Johnny to look after. Agnes, still only sixteen, was more of a help, taking on her shoulders increasing numbers of Rose's responsibilities while Nancy sat in a chair by the kitchen range and nursed the child and called plaintively for tea.

Rose's illness—her gradual diminution as cancer occupied her body—allowed Todd's inflexible and sour nature to re-emerge. She had kept things in balance, her steady kindness keeping his surly nature at bay; but now the equilibrium was lost. He was angry and afraid, furious that Rose would be taken from him; but his fear manifested itself in a resurgence of the tyranny that had characterised him before she had come to the farm. She could only look on helplessly from her bed—weak, pallid, little more than a spectre beneath the sheets—as Todd drove his sons before him. They worked punishing hours in all weathers.

Relations between John and Joe deteriorated still further as Todd indiscriminately disparaged one and praised the other. What little leisure time they had was spent hurling insults and any loose object that came to hand, and often ended in a fight. Rose moaned as she felt the reverberation of doors slamming and crockery smashed in the room below her. Jack—her most patient nurse—quietly closed the bedroom door and increased the volume of the little radio that comforted Rose's wakeful nights.

By the end of the year, it was plain Rose had only days to live. Mary, home for the Christmas vacation, looked around the farmhouse kitchen in horror. The sink was piled high with dirty dishes, the floor had not been swept in weeks, little Johnny occupied himself in the cats' food bowl. There was no sign of any supper being prepared. The whole family was upstairs, consulting with the doctor, debating loudly as to whether Rose should remain at home or be taken to a hospice.

Mary rolled up her sleeves and got to work.

Rose lingered until the new year, and then slipped away from Roadend. There was a funeral in the frozen churchyard, her sons lined up beside her grave thick-lipped and swollen-eyed from a massive fight that had broken out the night before. Todd stood head and shoulders shorter than his sons, rigid with the effort of holding back his grief. Afterwards, Mary went home, reluctant to join them for the funeral meats that had been laid out in the pub.

Two hours later Joe pushed past a startled Professor Leon to burst into Mary's room. His tie was askew, his eyes bleared with drink. 'You *must* stay now,' he shouted, half-stumbling over a stack of books that sat by the door. He kicked them roughly away, Mary's careful page-markers and interleaved notes fluttering everywhere.

'You know I can't,' Mary said quietly, getting up from her beanbag. 'You have Agnes and Nancy ...'

'Agnes is a child,' Joe spluttered. 'And Nancy is pregnant *again* ...' His fury at this seemed to eclipse his grief at the loss of his mother as well as his imperative for Mary.

Mary regarded him, at a loss to know whether to comfort him or to stand up to him. He bent such a look upon her—impotent rage, abject loss, crippling envy—it permeated his body making his breathing ragged while sweat oozed from his forehead. His hands clenched at his sides. She did not know if he would hit her, or whether his agony would be visited on himself. She almost wished he had drunk *more,* to reach the level of inebriation that brought incoherent oblivion. She had seen him like this before. Sometimes sex would assuage him, sometimes only violence but—so far—that violence had never been directed at her.

There had been times—when he had visited her at university—when he had rampaged through the halls of residence, over-turning tables and kicking chairs. Once he had picked on a porter and been arrested, though released the following day without charge. He sneered at her friends but could not answer their cutting ripostes; their clever erudition infuriated him. Drink and violence were his only outlets. She had been ashamed of him. Then, on Sundays, when he set off—bleary eyed and hung over—to drive back to Cumbria, he wept and said he was sorry. He told her he missed her and, yes, that he resented her being there, studying, learning things that would be no earthly use to her back on the farm. In between visits he wrote her letters—blotched with mud, scrumpled and smelling of silage—which were tender and contrite although poorly spelled. She would relent and agree to another visit, and the snake would swallow its tail again.

She thought of these things as Joe simmered like a volcano in the dimness of her bedroom, despairing of a relationship she felt was doomed and yet from which she could see no escape. The trajectory of Joe's emotions went on unabated—the thoughts and feelings he could not express. They filled the room and swamped her with their potency. Then he lifted his arm and swept it across his face. He was crying. Astonishment and compassion overcame her, shrivelling her doubts. She went to him and put her arms around his neck. He sagged within her embrace and lay his head on her shoulder. They made love, Mary stiff and terrified that her father would disturb them. Joe unwontedly gentle, tears all the while pouring from his eyes and soaking her hair.

Mary gained her degree in July of 1978 and married Joe Forrester two months later. By that time, to John's crowing satisfaction, two more children had joined Johnny, another boy and a girl. John was in the ascendant with his father, Joe relegated to drudgery, but his marriage restored some balance, especially as Mary soon took on the task of running the farm office and the provision of victuals. Agnes had persuaded Todd to allow her to convert a little-used dairy into a shop, where she sold groceries and farm produce. The grocer's and baker's vans had ceased their deliveries in the village when a supermarket had opened in the nearby town, but many older people did not drive or were disinclined to go so far afield for their shopping. The shop did well and

Todd was happy to rake in the profits, but it occupied Agnes' hours and by the time Mary entered the house it was in a poor state of cleanliness—neglected, bashed and smashed about by three rampaging children and the brothers' on-going war.

Professor Leon's success in the literary world had made staying in Cumbria untenable. He was needed for book signings and readings, literary festivals and interviews. He had sold the bungalow in the Spring of that year and moved back to the metropolis.

Mary returned to Roadend alone, and entered the Forrester fray.

Chapter Thirty-Five

The day of Jack Forrester's funeral was dreary. The empurpled sky threatened rain which did not fall but hung in the air, unpleasant, a damp cloth of moisture.

I had brought out one of my London suits for the occasion, pulled on stockings and forced my feet into court shoes. Bob looked at me as though I was a stranger. My hair—uncut for months now—was long enough to put up and I wrapped it into a sort of chignon, but the moist air plastered it to my head within minutes of leaving the cottage, and by the time I had walked to the church along the boardwalk the backs of my stockings were smattered with mud. I must have looked a sorry excuse for a mourner, but I slipped into a back pew and hoped no one would notice me. I felt like an interloper but, for Mary's sake as well as for Hugh's, I felt it right to put in an appearance.

I felt I knew Mary now; not from our afternoon of tea and chat, but from my writing. I understood the bleak sense of obligation that had taken her into a marriage with Joe; her old-fashioned upbringing; her ability to see—beneath his armoured exterior—glimpses of a man hungry for affection. She must have hoped she could change him, by loving him. But her departure a quarter century later proved her hopes had been doomed.

Roadend had taken the news that their Johnny-come-lately Lord of the Manor had in fact been the youngest Forrester boy with its customary phlegmatic acceptance. I heard more than one person refer to Jack Forrester as "the best of the bunch," but not in the hearing of any of the John Forresters. There was more surprise that Mary Forrester had returned; she had passed so completely from the Roadend consciousness that she had been in effect deceased. Now she was back, in company with the Jack Forresters, of all people. Speculation as to how this might be was rife but, for once, Mrs Harrop kept her counsel. It must have been tempting for her to crow that she had known all along, both about the new squire and about Mary, but she didn't. Mary had kept a low profile since returning to the village. Suffice it to say that the church environs were crowded with people purportedly desirous of paying their respects to Jack Forrester but actually avid to get a glimpse of Mary. I was lucky to get a seat inside at all. Olivia slipped in beside me.

'A good turn out,' I mouthed.

'Free food,' she mouthed back.

At my suggestion, the wake was not to be held up at Winter Hall, but in the pub. 'Bill and Julie will be glad of the custom,' I had observed. 'They struggle, you know, especially at this time of year.'

This nugget of information has seemed like news to Mary, who duly sent Hugh to make the arrangements.

Now I was glad for Bill—the bar tab was likely to be large—but sorry for Jack, that his mourners should be more interested in the sandwiches and *vol au vents* than in him. I had no qualms on Hugh's behalf. The expense would be nothing to him. By all accounts he could afford to buy the pub lock, stock and barrel and I almost wondered about suggesting it to him, if he really didn't know that Bill and Julie were ready to retire. But my days of influence over Hugh—if I had ever had any—were done. I had avoided seeing him, and when he arrived on my doorstep under cover of darkness, as was our previous wont, I had simply not answered the door. It was not appropriate, now I knew the truth. And in any case, I felt ashamed.

An elderly lady at the front of the church played a series of random, dolorous chords on the piano. A couple of be-hatted women stood either side of the door clutching collection bags, which they jingled hopefully as the funeral-goers filed into the church. Marjorie, wearing a flowing black cassock, moved up and down the aisle greeting people. The church was filled with flowers; blue iris and maple leaves for Canada, a selection of sea campions and wild orchids to symbolise Jack's native county. I thought it beautiful, and saw Mary's hand at work in all the small details. I knew she had supervised the decoration of the church herself even if she had not been seen in the shop or the pub. She was unwilling to scratch off old scabs, and especially keen not to upset Joe, who had taken her return to Roadend very hard, Jamie said.

Indeed, I had not needed Jamie to tell me. The usual echoes of groan and complaint from next door had escalated and every day, recently, there had been a major ruckus of some kind, accompanied by a tirade of yelling and the sound of smashing crockery.

I watched Mary scuttle into the church and take a place at one of the front pews, but hard against the wall in the shadow of a buttress. She wore a neat, grey woollen coat and a tasteful little hat, and kept her eyes resolutely on her small, gloved hands. Caroline pressed in next to her, almost shielding her from view which, with her bulky frame, she was well qualified to do.

Hugh would follow. It had been arranged, after much tricky negotiation, that he and Jamie would carry the coffin, assisted by John Forrester's two oldest boys and two men belonging to the funeral director. Jamie's involvement had been Mary's particular wish, although I was not clear why she should hold more than ordinary sway over matters. I supposed she was grateful for the shelter Jack had given her on her exodus from Roadend, and had been fond of him. Since she could not carry the coffin herself, of course it was natural she would wish Jamie to do so in her stead.

The front row on the other side of the church was occupied by the John Forresters. It was my first actual sighting of Nancy, who had "no hand for pastry" and who "was always ill and left all the work in the dairy to the girls" but she was exactly as I had imagined her—a painfully thin, hatchet-faced woman, wearing a shabby anorak and an expression I judged would probably sour the milk in the dairy. She was opposite to Mary in every way. I felt sure I was right in my idea that John Forrester would have given Nancy up in an instant in preference for Mary. Nancy was accompanied by her two daughters and the two sons not tasked with carrying the casket. The pew could barely hold them all. They wriggled and shuffled in an unseemly way. Across from them, Mary and Caroline sat like carved marble statues.

Suddenly the lady at the piano struck a particularly resonant chord, and the funeral procession commenced. Marjorie walked at the front, reciting words from the Bible. The coffin followed. It was large, to accommodate the characteristic Forrester breadth and height, and made from environmentally friendly willow. It rested without apparent effort on the shoulders of the men as they supported their burden. I could only see the backs of Jamie and Hugh, who walked at the front. Both men wore grey suits—I gathered that Hugh had bought or at least hired Jamie's as I was certain he did not possess one. Jamie had his hair tied back. Hugh's fell as usual in soft fair waves to just above his collar. If it had not been for Jamie's hair, I should not have been able to tell them apart. There was something about the way their arms were entwined—braced beneath the casket—that I found rather moving. Jamie had always lamented being an only child, I remembered. I glanced at Mary, who had turned to watch the short procession. Her eyes were running with tears. The two undertakers carried the middle section of the coffin. Johnny and Adam Forrester brought up the rear. Adam's suit still had the vent sewn shut. I imagined it had been new for his father's funeral and not worn since. Johnny's shoes were scuffed and muddy on the heel. I hoped Mary would not see.

The coffin was lowered onto two trestles and the pallbearers took their seats. Hugh and Jamie slid in next to Mary and Caroline. Hugh turned his head, scanning the congregation. When he spotted me, he gave me a wan smile, and I returned it. Johnny and Adam, for whom there was no room in the other front pew, were forced to sit behind. I could see that this annoyed them.

Marjorie spoke a few words of welcome and the lady pianist pounded the introduction to "Abide with Me." We rose and began to sing.

Afterwards, we assembled in the churchyard. Some effort had been made to tidy the grass around the other Forrester graves. The bare soil around John's had been covered with a mat of artificial grass. There were more flowers, but the lowering sky and the general air of dankness gave the scene a dismal atmosphere. The trampled pathways soon oozed with moisture and turned to mud. I felt the heels of my shoes sinking into the ground. We could still hear the indefatigable pianist working on a refrain of the final hymn, "Jerusalem."

The pallbearers brought Jack Forrester's coffin out of the church to the opened grave, but at this point the family members handed over the delicate task of lowering it into its final resting place to the professionals. Hugh stood between Mary and Caroline. Jamie made as though to lose himself in the crowd but Mary took his hand and pulled him to her side. The John Forresters lined up on the other side of the grave, as though in opposition. I allowed myself a small smile because, although I had not yet written the burial scene of Todd Forrester, I'd had in my mind exactly this disposition of the characters; the brothers glowering at each other over their father's remains.

Marjorie had just begun the committal when a disturbance at the wicket gate began to make itself heard—a roaring, inarticulate diatribe, bitter and angry. I had placed myself at a little distance from the main group, close to the war memorial, where the gravel was easier on my heels than the grass, and because I had no business being any closer. I turned my head, as did a good many others. The man I knew as the tramp came into view. He was hatless, his white hair wild and dishevelled, his sallow cheeks unshaven. He wore a suit—albeit a very old and disreputable one— several sizes too big, frayed at the cuffs and badly stained in several places. A bottle of spirits peeked from the jacket pocket.

'You bastards,' he yelled, waving an arm to encompass us all in his epithet. He stumbled against a gravestone, swerved round a group of mourners and tottered towards the main funeral party, his body uncoordinated, his knees buckling. It seemed incredible to me that he was able to remain upright.

'Drunk, as usual,' a lady muttered.

There was general tutting and eye-rolling amongst the villagers.

Marjorie tried manfully to continue with the committal but I could see from a kind of concerted shrinking of heads into shoulders and a hasty exchange of horrified looks that everyone knew what was about to occur and eventually she paused in the service, bringing forth a large handkerchief and making a great show of blowing her nose and clearing her throat until the disturbance should be over.

The tramp butted the people at the back of the gathering out of the way with a strength I would not have believed him capable of, barking, 'Move, will you? Shove over. Get out of my bloody way if you don't want your face kicked in.' People shrank aside, one after another, no-one offering the least resistance as he pushed and shouldered his way to the front. He forced himself into a space that didn't exist between Jamie and Mary, swaying so alarmingly that if Jamie had not taken a firm hold on him he would certainly have followed Jack Forrester into the grave. The only thanks Jamie received for this aid was a violent blow, sending him cannoning backwards a few paces. I, and several around me, cried out in protest. Hugh made as though to lunge forward. Mary gave a little cry and pressed her hand to her mouth, shrinking closer to Caroline, but Jamie did not respond at all other than to hold up a hand to stall Hugh. I couldn't understand why Jamie would allow himself to be treated so badly by the revolting old hobo, other than in an effort not to make a bad situation worse. He recovered himself, however, and took up his position once more.

'I'm here now,' panted the tramp, nodding vigorously a few times. He swept his hands through his unruly haystack of hair in a vain attempt to tame it and looked with an unfocussed but pugnacious eye on the gathered company. I thought, rather than showing any inkling of shame, he looked rather pleased with himself. Then he looked at Mary. The expression on his face was hard to read, both wounded and wounding. Mary's ashen countenance, on the contrary, was easy to interpret—she was horrified and afraid.

The vagrant allowed his eyes to linger for a long time, taking in Mary's face, hair and clothes and travelling down even as far as her shoes. Her eyes remained averted as she bore his inspection.

At last, he dragged his eyes from Mary and addressed himself to Marjorie. 'Carry on, Vicar,' he said.

The ceremony continued. The coffin was lowered into the earth. Marjorie intoned the liturgy. Hugh, then Caroline, Mary and—at her prompting—Jamie each threw a handful of earth onto the coffin lid. Not to be outdone, the John Forresters followed suit. For a terrible moment I wondered if the tramp would spit into the grave, as I had seen him spit onto John Forrester's. He contented himself, however, by standing amongst them wearing an expression of superlative satisfaction, his arms folded across his chest, his bleary eye triumphant, a contemptuous smile affixed to his face.

Marjorie said, with particular emphasis and a look that would have pierced the tramp's soul if he had been even a quarter sober, "*Those who walk uprightly* enter into peace; *they* find rest as they lie in death."[3]

The service was over. Hugh and Caroline linked their arms through Mary's and led her from the grave. Others began to melt away in the direction of the pub. The vagrant remained by the graveside, as though asserting his entitlement; although, so long as he remained, so did Marjorie. Jamie stayed also, his face ashen with remorse, blinking back the tears his pride would not allow him to weep. I stayed too, half-concealed behind the war memorial. I couldn't understand why this dreadful man had been allowed to disrupt proceedings, or why Jamie had allowed himself to be so abused.

Suddenly the old man cried out, 'I'm the last! The last man standing, see?' A few folks who had not yet exited the churchyard looked over their shoulders at his outburst. Jamie flinched. The tramp was oblivious. He thumped himself on the chest but his fist was ineffectual now, his whole demeanour one of drooping exhaustion. He was weak, old, spent—but not in his own eyes. He looked witheringly down at the open grave where Jack Forrester's coffin lay, and then allowed his groggy gaze to travel to the fake-grass mound of John Forrester. 'You two,' he blurted out, spittle spraying onto his grizzled chin, 'you two ...' He attempted a laugh—harsh, cold. 'Ha! Look at me,' he barked out, stabbing his gnarled old finger into his chest. 'The first. The best. The last. Still standing!'

---

[3] Isaiah 57:2

Then he wasn't standing. His legs buckled and he sank like an empty sack so he half-lay, half-knelt on the turf between the two men's graves. 'Still standing,' he cried out in anguished defiance, oblivious to the irony of his words. His voice was breaking and his face collapsed into a contortion of misery. He bowed forward until his forehead touched the ground, a facsimile of contrition, his shoulders shaking as he brought forth hard and bitter sobs. 'Still standing,' he gasped out one last time, his face buried in the mud.

Marjorie must have felt the climax had passed. She bent her head in a brief prayer before walking briskly from the site. The churchyard was deserted now, the piano within silent. The wind sighed across the graves.

I looked at Jamie, who had stood stoically by while this scene played itself out, his face a complexity of shame, compassion and endurance. He raised his eyes and met mine. I could think of no word or gesture that could comfort or encourage him. My confusion was complete.

Perhaps Jamie saw it. He stepped forward, bent down and gently hauled the old man to his feet, fishing a handkerchief from his pocket to mop the muddy, tear-stained face.

'Come on, Dad,' he said. 'Time to go home.'

The tramp made no objection and but allowed himself to be led away from the grave, through the little gate and onto the boardwalk.

I remained alone in the churchyard, the memorial stone the only solid thing in the whirling maelstrom of my understanding. It began to rain. Not a hard, pebbling rain, but the mizzle that saturates the air without falling, a vapour that nonetheless penetrates every layer. I felt it—slicking my skin, wetting my hair, soaking into the shoulders of my suit—but still I remained, anchored to the monument like a lost mariner tied to the mast.

Presently two men arrived with shovels. They hovered uncertainly for a few moments until I indicated that they should proceed with their task, whereupon they began to fill the grave.

The truth lodged like a stone in my gullet. The old vagrant was Jamie's father, my reclusive neighbour, the querulous man I sometimes heard through the walls. His illness was alcoholism, not dementia. Julie, I was reminded, had implied madness, which, even in the circumstances, I had thought unfair at the time. Alcoholism *was* an illness, but there was more to Joe's mania than that. When I had referred to his father as "unwell" Jamie had said, 'That's a nice way of putting it.' That had struck me as odd at the time. Now, I knew why.

This much I could fathom: faulty connections, misconstrued inferences, the fact that—though ever a brooding presence—the real Joe Forrester had remained hidden behind the boarded-up windows of the middle cottage, kept in check by the vigilance of his son. I had never made the link between the recluse next door and the wild-haired hobo I had briefly glimpsed the day of my arrival at Roadend, and then again the night of the bonfire. Instead, I had related my querulous neighbour with the man on the dunes. Who could blame me? What other conclusion could I have jumped to? But now I knew better. It was almost—in that violently-altered perspective I now struggled to get into some kind of focus—the *only* thing I *did* know. The two were definitively, beyond doubt, *not* the same.

The question that haunted me as I walked home along the boardwalk in the rain, was this: whose then, had been the pale, bland hand I had grasped in the mist? And who was the bewildered old man I had met on the dunes? Because I was certain it had not been *this* poor derelict. *That* man's form, his voice, his manner, his hand, *everything* about him had been other than this. And yet his essence, his preoccupation, his experience had been the same. I knew, in some bizarre and baffling way I could not begin to elucidate even to myself, that they were two parts of a whole. They were conjoined.

Chapter Thirty-Six

The rain that had begun to fall on that dour January day kept up for the rest of the week. The sky was an ever-bloated bladder of water that seeped and dripped and sometimes hammered down on the village without let up.

I had moved my laptop back upstairs; although the weather was unremittingly wet, it was reasonably mild, and I did not need to keep the log burner alight during the daytime. Plus, I had other motives for the move. I wanted to be on the lookout for Hugh, in case he should attempt another interview. And I wanted to be closer to the party wall, to hear for myself the cantankerous drone of my neighbour's perpetual soliloquy. Rationally, I knew the author of this meandering rhetoric was the white-haired old man I had thought of as a tramp, and *not* the perplexed, cold-handed man from the dunes, but I was desperate to superimpose my vision of the one onto the other, no matter how awkward the fit, because any alternative was just too outlandish to contemplate.

If dune-man was *not* Joe Forrester, who, *who,* could he be?

I could hear him—Joe—from time to time, in the scrape of a chair leg across an uncarpeted floor, the thunk of the poker amongst the coals, incoherent muttering. And I sometimes heard the deeper timbre of Jamie's voice urging, soothing, cajoling. But these interactions were never more than the tune of a song whose words were indistinct. I thought about unlocking the cellar door and creeping beneath the middle cottage to see if I could make any sense of the drone. I wanted to pick out something—anything—that would connect one broken old soul to the other. But I held back; outright spying was for others.

The view over the Moss was drear: soggy, boggy, its colours darkened to dingy brown and olive drab. The drainage rills were full to capacity and in some places had spilled over onto the Moss, creating pools that pocked and dimpled with rainfall. The massif in the distance was blotted out by the pall of the weather. Yet I stared at the prospect beyond the window for hour upon hour, trying to make sense of things.

I worked hard on the chapters of my book—honing, polishing, agonising over commas and semicolons. Consigning Rose to the grave had been hard but I knew we had to release each other if my story was to move on. As a little act of symbolism—and because I no longer needed its warmth—I folded the blanket and laid it back on the settee. My narrative had brought me to 1978. For now, I had by-passed the fire, which occurred in 1962, but I knew it was an episode in Roadend's history that must be dealt with, somehow. All the while, my ear was tuned to the cottage next door, my attention divided between the fiction I was spinning and the fact that lurked, unsettled and brooding, next door—trying to comprehend the connection between the two.

In a brief email Daniel informed me Ivaan had continued to make a nuisance of himself. He was back from the US and had the cheek to turn up at Daniel's house in search of me. Daniel had not been home—as, probably, Ivaan had calculated—and Bianca had been gushing in her welcome, giving him tea and scones and taking plenty of selfies to share with her golf and bridge buddies. She had swallowed his sob-story about Bob hook, line and sinker, and eventually rummaged out the Christmas card I had sent to reassure Ivaan that Bob was in a place perfectly suited to the happy existence of a dog. This worried me, because the card—a picture of the Moss in wintertime—would give Ivaan exactly the information he had been seeking: my whereabouts.

I was glad of the respite that a visit from Olivia brought. She arrived one afternoon, splashing through the puddles of the track, carrying Patty under one arm and a Recorded Delivery package under the other.

'This came,' she said, handing it over. My agent's name and address were boldly printed on the back. It was impossible that anyone who had handled the envelope would have missed the name and profession of its sender. What was more, she had used my penname as the addressee. 'Mrs Harrop signed for it,' said Olivia, removing her glasses to wipe them dry.

'She asked me to deliver it. She says, "Can you make sure this doesn't become a habit?".'

'Yes,' I said, placing the package unopened on the hall whatnot, and resolving to email my agent to give her a piece of my mind. 'Isn't Patrick with you?'

'I left him in the hide with his binoculars and a notebook,' she said. 'He'll be happy there for hours.'

As Olivia removed her coat I went into the kitchen to put the kettle on. 'What's the news?' I threw out.

'*You* are the news,' said Olivia, coming in behind me. 'To Mrs Harrop, anyway. Mummy's known for ages.'

'So, it's all over the village?'

Olivia pulled out a chair. 'Of course it is, *now.*'

'Oh dear,' I said, biting my lip. 'I didn't want to make a big thing of it.'

'People are beginning to wonder what you're up to,' said Olivia. 'But you know Mummy. She says it's no one's business but yours. *Are* you writing a new book?'

I nodded, avoiding the need to see her face by busying myself with the tea.

'Am I in it?'

I thought she sounded rather hopeful.

'I don't know,' I said. 'Tell me about your big romance, and I'll think about it.'

Olivia blushed, and smiled so widely I thought her cheeks would crack. 'Oh,' she said, beautifully coy. 'Well, yes.'

She spent an hour regaling me with the details: lingering glances, little brushes of the hand, small acts of thoughtfulness and then, at last, a kiss. 'It was the first time I'd kissed anyone,' said Olivia, squirming with pleasure at the remembrance of it. 'Patrick had kissed a girl he knew at university, so he knew what to do. He did it just right. He does everything just right.'

'How wonderful,' I sighed, sharing her joy. 'What does Marjorie think about it all?'

A shadow passed over Olivia's features. 'She thinks I'm too young. But, in her eyes, I'll *always* be too young, won't I?'

'I expect every mother feels the same about her daughter,' I prevaricated. 'She'll come round to the idea, I expect.'

'I hope so,' said Olivia, staring abstractedly into the fire.

'Patrick seems so much better,' I observed. 'I gather … of course your mum never divulges people's secrets … but I gather he'd been rather unwell.'

'He tried to kill himself,' Olivia said matter-of-factly. 'He was in care all the time he was a child, lots of foster homes. Some of them weren't nice. And children's homes. I think they were worse. And then, when he was eighteen, he was just left to himself. He didn't cope very well.'

'Poor thing,' I said, placing Olivia's second mug of tea into her hands. 'But he went to university?'

She nodded. 'But he was always lonely, he says.' She sipped her tea. 'I know how *that* feels.'

I reached out and gave her arm a little squeeze. 'I'm glad Patrick has been able to talk to you about it all,' I said. 'It's so important—to not have secrets.'

Olivia roused herself. 'Is that why Hugh's cross with you? Because you hadn't told him who you really were?'

I kinked an eyebrow. '*Is* Hugh cross with me?' I tried to keep my tone light, but inside I was almost screaming, 'What? Hugh is cross with *me?*'

Olivia blew on the surface of her tea. 'He was cross that you didn't come to the pub after the funeral. People say all kinds of things in front of me. They think I don't understand, but I do. Mostly, anyway. He kept craning

413

his head to the door, to see if you were coming in, and asking people, 'Where's Dee? Have you seen Dee? Is Dee coming later, or what?' Caroline told him you were an inverted snob, and now that you knew he was rich you would give him a wide berth just to spite him. Are you an inverted snob? What *is* an inverted snob, anyway?'

I threw my hands up, 'No! *That* isn't the reason I've broken things off. How can he not realise?'

'Oh,' she narrowed her eyes. 'So there *was* something between you?'

I clamped my lips shut.

'Well, obviously there *was*,' said Olivia. 'Is Hugh a good kisser?'

I laughed, in spite of my annoyance. 'Yes,' I said. 'He *is* a good kisser. But when I was kissing him, I did not know he was married.'

Olivia almost choked on her tea. 'Hugh's *married?*' she spluttered.

I stared at her, open-mouthed. 'Of course Hugh is married,' I cried. 'He is married to Caroline!'

Olivia dabbed the spilt tea from her pink mohair jumper with a tissue. 'No, he *isn't*,' she scoffed. 'For a famous writer, you're not very bright, are you? Caroline is his sister.'

I gawked, aghast. 'His *sister?*' I mouthed.

Olivia gave a smug smile. 'His half-sister. Hugh's mum already had Caroline, from her first marriage, when she married Jack Forrester.'

I put my head in my hands. I could hardly believe it. And yet, everything told me it was true. I wanted to cry. How many mistakes was I destined to make? What else would I misinterpret? When would I realise that things were rarely—almost never—what they seem?

Olivia said, 'Dee, have you got any make up? And will you show me how to put it on?'

I looked at her. 'I've got some bits and pieces,' I said. 'I haven't worn so much as a slick of lipstick since I got here. Why do you want to start wearing make up? Has Patrick said anything?'

'No. It isn't to do with him. I just want to try.'

'All right,' I said, getting to my feet. 'I'll see what I can find.'

We spent the next hour experimenting with mascara and eye shadow. I impressed upon Olivia that less was definitely more, and that even more important than the application of makeup was its removal. She should buy some cleansing milk and so on if she did not want to come out in a rash of spots. 'And you have eczema,' I reminded her. 'You ought to look for brands suitable for sensitive skin.'

The afternoon was almost gone when Olivia took her leave. The rain had ceased, the clouds spent. A full moon—the wolf moon, since it was the first one in January—rose in a nacreous sky.

My time with Olivia had been pleasant, but once she had left the ghosts of my errors came crowding back to taunt me. They clamoured indictments at me—'How could I have misunderstood *this*? What kind of idiot would get *that* wrong? Call myself a people-watcher? An observer of life! What a joke!' There I had been, flattering myself I had a sort of sixth sense— No, more than that—I had half-believed my narrative had imposed itself on the past; that affairs had turned out in Roadend *because* I had written them so! And all the time the truth—the *facts*—had been staring me in the face. Oh! How blind I had been; how entangled in the mechanics of story, poking about in other people's business but utterly unable to see the utterly, blindingly obvious.

I stood with my back against the door for a heartbeat or two, appalled and humiliated at all my wrongheadedness. Then I could bear it no longer. I threw on my boots and coat and stamped off into the twilight, slamming the door behind me. Bob, at my heels, lay his ears against his head and looked up at me with wide, anxious eyes.

The willow walk dripped scorn on me as I passed beneath its bare branches. The undergrowth rustled its derision. I sloughed through the puddles that had gathered on the path—quite deep in places—my hands thrust down into my pockets.

415

At the gate I took a different route through the dunes, avoiding the beach and the tide—which I could tell just by the sound of rolling surf was already quite high. And avoiding also the rear entrance to Winter Hall and Hugh, to whom I supposed I owed, if not an apology, certainly an explanation. The marram grasses scoffed as I walked. Skeletal shrubs shook with laughter in the stiff breeze. A chevron of geese passed overhead, and over the scrubland a murmuration of starlings swooped and darted in a cohesive swarm. The opalescent sky paled to silver. Over the massif, the first stars blinked into life. I trudged on through a landscape that was leached of colour, a monochrome iteration of itself.

It seemed, though, all tracks led to the den. I came upon it suddenly, bathed in ethereal moonlight, its colours all sepia and dew. More work had been done on it since I had last been there on Christmas Day with Jamie. The new spars had been used to anchor roof trusses to support it in a conical peak. The wood was driftwood, gnarled and ancient, brought in by some storm and then left to bake on the sand. In the moonlight it looked as white as bones. I admired the enterprise of whoever had struggled to carry these not insubstantial branches up and across the tricky terrain of the dunes, through thorny shrubs and tough, thigh-high grasses. I looked to see if I could trace the route—trodden-down plants, a site where timbers had been sawn—but the area around the den looked undisturbed.

Well, it had been more than a month since my last visit—plenty of time for the wind to scour away any disturbance of the sand, and these grasses were by their nature extremely resilient.

I bent to peer inside the den. The rickety chair was still in place, and I ducked down and sat myself upon it. Bob, sensing my distraction, lay down on the soft sand of the den's floor.

The respite from the chill wind and the noise of unfurling waves was immediate. The den was a cocoon, quite well-insulated by its interwoven sticks and pieces of mesh and by the action of the weather itself, which had filled up the gaps with insulating sand.

Unfortunately, it offered no respite at all from my thoughts, which continued to goad and accuse me. Thinking back over the conversation I'd had with Hugh in the odd-shaped sitting room of his hobbit house, I did not know how I could possibly have misinterpreted his remarks about Caroline. He had considered her no reason for us not to embrace, and said so. I had read his remarks as crass and insensitive to us both, seeing subtext where there was none, reading between lines that were utterly *un*ambiguous. Then I remembered the strained conversation I had with Jamie. He had suggested my relationship with Hugh would change. At the time, I had assumed it was because Hugh was married. Yes! Naturally, in the light of *that,* it would change. But now it crashed upon me that Jamie had meant our affair was *more* likely to develop into something serious because ... well, because there was even more incentive for me to ally myself with such a man. And therefore—I burrowed deeper into what Jamie might have meant—therefore I was so much *less* likely to ally myself to a man like *him*. Like Jamie. Now I understood the glassiness of his eye, the teardrop that had trembled on his lashes, and it made me sick at heart.

I had been so blind! I had maligned Hugh to a woeful degree. His pride would be wounded and I did not suppose he would ever forgive me for misjudging him so badly. He was a good man, an honourable man I had used in pursuance of my own fantasy. Now that illusion had been swept away, I could appreciate I had lot in common with Hugh. I could envision a life with him, in the real world outside of this charmed enclave. But that was wasted now. And I had hurt Jamie, whose heart I had always known was vulnerable. I had ignored those sparks of attraction that had zipped between us from the first and channelled them into a meeting of minds that was, perhaps, even more powerful than the largely physical magnetism I had with Hugh. But I could not imagine Jamie *outside* the realm of Roadend and—it came to me in a deluge—for all that I had relished its storybook enchantments I could not imagine myself permanently *within* it.

The turmoil of my thoughts was interrupted by the sound of children's voices. They were distant at first, carried on the little wind that managed to winnow itself through the interwoven spars of my refuge. I thought it odd that children should be abroad at that hour—although in reality it was not much later than six o'clock—when night had fully fallen. I waited to hear an adult's voice—someone who was in charge—but only two fluting voices came to me, as light and airy as the sigh of breath over a bottleneck. I sat rigidly still in the den in the hopes they would pass by. I certainly did not wish to be encumbered with responsibility for two children, out too late and far from home. And neither did I want to alarm them, as I was convinced my sudden emergence from the den would surely do.

'*We're* collecting wood, and *he's* to get the matches,' said one, who I guessed was perhaps eight or nine years old.

'So, there *will* be a bonfire?' chirruped the other, younger, not more than five or six.

'Yes. Like a beacon, on the top of Winter Hill. In olden days, they would light beacons along the coast to tell people things.'

'What kinds of things?'

'That marauders were coming.'

'What are marauders?'

'Baddies. Vikings. Scots, coming to rape and pillage.'

'What's rape and pillage?'

'I'm not sure.'

'And what will *our* beacon say?'

'It will say that no one stops *us* from doing what we like. Come on, Jack. Keep up.'

The children—boys, I speculated, by their talk—had passed the den now. Their high voices were snatched away by the rolling waves and pining wind. Their conversation put me in mind of Daniel as a child, a parroter of information he had picked up but did not quite understand. Much like myself, I thought glumly.

Then, from much closer, a man's voice—breathy as breeze—said, 'Can't we stop them?'

I tensed in my seat, turning my head left and right. Bob remained curled at my feet, not even so much as lifting his head. The fabric of the den shivered as a stronger gust of wind hit it.

I had opened my mouth to reply, to offer after all to go after the lads and see them home, when the voice of another man came to me in a rattle of dry gorse. 'They can't hear us.'

I gripped the arms of the chair. That was dune-man, *my* dune-man. I raised a cautious head up to peer over the parapet of the interwoven walls of the den. The moon continued to throw a milky light over the dunes, rendering the grasses unnaturally pale and casting convoluted shadows. No figure showed itself. I wondered if they had hunkered down in the lee of the den, below my eyeline. If I wanted to *see* them, I would have to get up and go out. But something—some unthinkable but inescapable possibility—kept me in my seat.

The wattle of the den creaked, as though weighed down 'So, we have to watch ourselves make the same mistake, over and over again?'

The air around me eddied and I inferred a shrug. It was uncanny, the way their voices emanated both from without and within the little burrow, even from the very lathes of it. The den was an echo chamber, steeped in memory—Could it be … the memory of the boys who had built it? And those boys, the ones who had just passed by, could *they* be …? The aberration clogged up the channels of my mind with its absurdity. I tried, *again,* to connect disparate threads, but my facility for the task had proven so unreliable I baulked at the conclusions that suggested themselves.

A moment or two passed. Waves threw themselves onto the shore. The shingle rattled and chattered. 'Is it always this cold?'

'It's winter.' A reverberation from the stoical boulders.

The wind shifted a little, whiffling a piece of netting that had been stretched across the slats, worrying at it with a restless flux. 'What's happening? What are we doing here? What's all this about?'

And then, from far out across the dunes, a strange, disembodied cry of just one word—'Joe.'

The spars above my head sawed against each other, rasping out, 'It was all Joe's fault!'

'*What* was Joe's fault?' I burst out. My voice was shockingly loud, even in my own ears. Bob lifted his head then, a querying look in his eye.

Outside the den there was a scurrying movement, like an animal darting in the undergrowth; abrupt and startled. Slowly, slowly, I rose from my seat and stepped through the little aperture and out into the wide acres of the dune. I stepped round to the side of the den.

Nobody was there.

I turned three-hundred-and-sixty degrees, scanning the oddly colourless dune, the opaque nickel sheet of the sea, the vast dome of space that was punctuated now by a strew of stars. The impassive wolf moon illuminated everything in its bland, unambiguous light.

My question remained, pressing and importunate: *what* was Joe's fault? *What* was eating at that shattered, tortured occupant of the derelict cottage and *what*—really—was the source of the caustic acrimony that had embittered the Forrester brothers? I didn't believe it was *just* rivalry over Mary. I also couldn't see that it was caused by Todd's vindictive division of his holdings. There was something else. And there was only one way to find out.

Chapter Thirty-Seven

When I got back to Winter Farm all was quiet. I put Bob in the kitchen and went back out to make my way along to where Jamie's quadbike was usually parked. The place was empty, and no lights shone from his windows. I knocked at his door anyway, loud and imperative. I *had* to speak to the old man inside. I listened carefully for the least sound—the usual low chunnering of his endless complaint, the sound of a chair pushed back—but heard nothing.

The gate to the middle cottage was stiff with disuse. Weeds had entwined themselves around its wrought iron bars and I had to force it open. The garden was strewn with wire and rubble, old pallets and oil drums. I clambered through and over the obstacles until I arrived at the boarded-up window. Previously I had seen a slice of light peeking from the edge of it but on this night the shadow was unbroken.

I looked up, to where the upper window—also boarded—gazed blindly out. Ah! There, at one corner, I could make out a weak glimmer.

I called up, 'Joe! Mr Forrester! It's me, Dee, from next door. Will you let me in?'

I could not say I *heard* a response, but I sensed, in the air, a tense, listening stillness. I was *sure* he was there.

I shouted again. 'I just want to talk, Joe. About Mary, and about when you were a boy. Wouldn't you like some company?'

Again, that palpable pause. The whole Moss seemed poised, alert.

Then I heard it, the creak of a floorboard, a voice so low it was more of a vibration than a sound.

'Joe?' I tried to make my voice light, friendly.

There was a rasping, tearing noise behind the upper window, the fumble and judder of an ancient mechanism and I gathered the occupant was struggling with the sash window.

Then, a clenched-tooth grouse. 'Who's there, damn you? Bothering a man ... Jamie? Is that you, lad?'

'It's Dee, the woman from next door,' I reiterated. 'Can I come in?'

It took a few moments for my words—and the sense of them—to penetrate the fog of his brain. Then, 'Can't,' he barked out, and I detected a tinge of regret. 'Locked in.'

'But ...' I called, desperate not to lose the tenuous connection I had made, '... if I could get in, would that be all right?'

Again, with the slow churning of his mind as he digested the idea I caught, 'Locked the bloody door ...' and, 'Can't stop her ...' and, 'Poor old soul some peace ...'

'If I can get in,' I called up again, 'will that be all right?'

'Easy to get in,' came the reply, a quicksilver shaft of light in an otherwise dark sky. 'Harder to get out.'

I let myself back into Winter Cottage. Bob lifted his head from his bed and blinked at me blearily. I unlocked the cellar door.

Even with my torch, the darkness in the cellar was a wall of thick black felt. The beam seemed to bounce and refract in odd ways, pulling ordinary things into grotesque facsimiles of themselves, throwing elongated shadows and tortured reflections that teased my peripheral vision. I shuffled along the rough surface of the floor, feeling for impediments with my feet, one hand extended in front of me to sweep away the cobwebs.

My cellar was reasonably tidy, but as I pressed beneath the brick archway that separated it from the one next door I encountered immediate obstacles: packing cases, stacks of timber, something soft and dusty that disintegrated when I touched it. Amorphous shapes loomed into the halo of my torch like spectres. A row of garrotted children turned out to be a line of old coats hung from nails. My head hit a pendant light fitting and then I found myself at the foot of a steep timber staircase. I climbed it on hands and knees, getting splinters in the heel of my palm and knocking one shin painfully on the sharp edge of one of the treads. The door at the top of it would not yield to my push.

I retreated backwards and continued to grope my way through the cellar, beneath what must have been Jamie's part of the building. Things there were more orderly; boxes of books neatly labelled, tinned goods arranged on a shelf, plastic containers of assorted nails and screws, a variety of power tools. Lined up along one wall was a vast collection of empty scotch bottles, evidence of the old man's addiction. I could not decide if they were a sad metaphor for each other—empty vessels, kept in the dark—or whether some deeper alchemy was at play. Had the spirit's fire and brimstone poured into the old man's soul in a perpetual fermentation of angst and regret that would not let him rest?

The stair up to Jamie's cottage was built of stone, like mine. I mounted it with trepidation, my heart in my mouth, the beam of the torch quivering on the back of his cellar door. I turned the handle and found myself in his hallway. As before, the hall was clean, empty of furniture. Moonlight spilled in through the glass of his front door and threw a milky envelope of specious innocence onto the broad planks of the floor. After the oppression of the cellar, it was unspeakable relief to breathe air that was fresh, to feel liberated from the nebulous phantoms below. At the same time the peace and respite of Jamie's house indicted me—I should not have been there without his knowledge or permission. I knew I ought to have waited. But the bizarre episode on the dunes, the snatched conversation I had overheard and my strong impression I was within touching distance of the heart of the mystery of Winter Moss justified, in my own mind, my course of action.

I stepped through a door and found myself in the sitting room. It was spartanly furnished with a settee and a mismatched easy chair, on the arm of which sat one of the books I had lately loaned to Jamie from my collection. A low table and a modest television made up the rest of the furnishings. The walls were whitewashed and unadorned and lit by the moon. The whole room was little more than a monastic cell—orderly, clean, restrained. A door in the corner of the room would lead me through to the middle cottage. It was bolted top and bottom. Joe had been right: he *was* locked in. I slid back the bolts, questioning the morality of *literally* locking someone in their own home, even if it was for their own safety. Mrs Rochester came to mind. My hand hovered on the top bolt, the idea that I could be unleashing a fiend suddenly quelling my determination. I felt like Pandora—who knew *what* lurked beyond the door? But the sense that the crux of my story was waiting to be uncovered was too compelling. It called me as enticingly as any siren, the force of it too strong to resist. Was I being summoned to right some past wrong? *Could* history send echoes to the present? Did the narrative have its own volition? No matter, the call was not to be denied. I slid back the bolts.

The room beyond the door was as unlike Jamie's sitting room as it was possible to imagine, even though in shape and size it was the mirror image of it. Where *there* had been light and order, moderation and calm, *here* was darkness and chaos, intemperance and abandon. Everything was in disarray, broken, upended, tottering and ravaged. The window was boarded over on the inside with cardboard as it was covered on the outside with ply. A curtain rail hung askew with thin dusty curtains drooping from one end. Two chairs tilted on three legs. Another lay in smithereens—I could see the place in the plaster where it had hit the wall. A tabletop was smashed in two as though sundered with an axe. A fractured mirror reflected my appalled, torchlit face. I saw cracked crockery, tattered clothing, thick dust and skeins of furry cobwebs. The air was stale, slightly damp and chill. The wind sighed in the chimney.

Above my head I heard movement, the creak of a chair as weight was shifted.

I found the stairs—a dark well of shadow—and began to climb.

'Joe!' I sang out, trying to make my voice light and unthreatening. 'I made it! I'm here. Can I come up? We can have a talk about things.'

I sensed Joe was trying to remember who I was, to connect the woman here now with the voice from a quarter of an hour ago.

His grumbled soliloquy paused and he said, 'Talk? Talk? I do nothing but talk. Trouble is, nobody listens.'

'I'll listen,' I said, climbing further. My torch beam picked out the narrow landing with three doors leading off it. I made for the room that would be the front bedroom and knocked lightly on the door. 'May I come in?'

The room surprised me. It was ramshackle, as below, with furniture such as comes from bric-a-brac shops—mismatched, old-fashioned. But it was not dirty. No one could say the old man was kept in squalor. His bed was made up with sheets that appeared clean, although they were extremely rumpled. There were thermos flasks—presumably containing hot drinks—a carafe of water and a large plate of sandwiches sealed in clingfilm on a gateleg table. As downstairs, the window was covered over, apart from in one corner where the cardboard had been peeled back. A cold draught whistled through the gap Joe had made when he tried to open the sash. A lamp glowed dully from behind a pinkish shade. A coal fire burned in the grate, protected by a substantial fireguard. Before it sat Joe Forrester. In his hand was a tumbler of whisky.

From the other side of the party wall, I had become used to the sonorous narrative my neighbour kept up—the rise and fall of his spleen, the endless repetition of his woes, the occasional outburst of anger that had sometimes been accompanied by the sounds of smashing glass and splintering wood. For a long time I had misconstrued the cause of it, believing it to be the house itself, or the sound of Jamie's renovations, or even a forgotten radio left murmuring into the night. Even after I had been made to understand the noises came from a person, they had been more song than soliloquy, the words indistinct. I had hoped that, here in the room with him, the static fuzz of his verbiage might at last be comprehensible as words and sentences. But no. I could make nothing of his mumbling rant. Its cadences were empty.

It broke off abruptly as my foot caused a floorboard to squeak. He turned his head and regarded me through drink-mazed eyes. 'Jamie? Mary?'

I ventured further into the room. 'I'm Dee, from next door,' I said, speaking low, as though to a skittish animal. 'I wanted to talk about when you were boys.'

It took a moment or two for my remark to penetrate the wool of his brain. He squinted at me, as though I might be an apparition. Then, he stiffened. 'Boys? What about when we were boys?'

I shrugged, as though I had no particular agenda. 'I found a den on the dunes,' I said. 'Splendid, it is. Made of driftwood and stuff. Do you know who built it?'

'Oh aye,' he said, turning back to stare into the orange heart of the coals. '*We* built that.'

'You?' I took another step into the room, bringing me to the bed.

'John and Jack and me. But … but we never finished it.' From my position I could see his face in profile. His expression was stricken. 'We *should* have finished it,' he croaked out vehemently, a little fleck of spittle on his dry lip. His hands gripped the arms of his chair. 'We *should* have,' he said again, 'we *needed* to. But we couldn't get away from the farm …' his recollection stalled and his murmured homily began anew.

I lowered myself gingerly onto the bed. 'Your father wouldn't let you?' I spoke sharply, to rouse him from his reverie.

'We had our chores,' Joe broke off to bark, with such fervour that I half-rose in alarm, 'and then, before we knew it, we were men, and the farm had to come first.'

'Of course,' I soothed, eager to assuage the palpable nature of his regret. I dared to lower myself back onto the bed. 'Everybody understands that. It was a big farm.'

His white hair was lit into ruddy filaments by the reddish glow of the fire and the pink filter of the lampshade. His skin was flushed, mapped with broken veins, the cheeks sunken and bristled with stubble. His eyes were dull, the whites yellowed. His mouth moved ceaselessly.

'The biggest,' he blustered. 'Everybody knew the Forresters. In the end there wasn't a square foot of land that wasn't ours.' He lifted his glass and took a drink, wiping his lips with the back of his hand afterwards.

'You bought the Winters out,' I put in.

'We did!' he cackled.

'The old tower …'

'Burned 'em out,' he boasted, nodding vigorously at the recollection, but then with less energy. A guilty shadow passed over his features. He drank again. His hand shook so much that the liquid slopped up the sides of the glass.

I took a deep breath and reached out a tentative hand to part the thin veil between the past and the present. 'The other boys collected firewood off the beach,' I suggested. 'You brought the matches.'

His brow furrowed. 'Did I?'

'It was to be a beacon,' I said, 'like in the olden days.'

I felt as though I had dropped my words down a well that had no bottom. It seemed an age before they plummeted the fathomless depths of his addled comprehension. At last–at long last—he nodded.

'It had rained for weeks,' he murmured. 'The village bonfire had been cancelled.'

There it was. I had brought him to the threshold of the memory, to where the blinking cursor on my screen had stopped and could go no further.

Mrs Harrop's words came back to me. I repeated them, "Rain, rain, rain, for days on end. Then, the first dry day, there was the fire. You'd have thought everything was too wet to burn …"

'It *was*,' said Joe, the memory suddenly illuminated. 'That's why we needed the straw.'

I held my breath. Joe's head swivelled on his neck. 'Did you bring anything to drink?'

I suppressed my irritation. 'I'm sorry,' I said. 'I didn't.' I nodded at the carafe of water. 'Shall I pour you some—'

'Pah!' he spat out. He reached down to the floor where his whisky bottle stood against the chair leg. The process was tortuous. He manoeuvred the glass between his knees, hoisted the bottle from the floor, fumbled with the cap and then, with a hand that trembled, poured the whisky. He squinted at the amount of spirit that remained in the bottle. It was almost empty. 'Jamie will bring more,' he said to himself. At last, the glass was replenished, the bottle back on the floor. He drank, smacking his lips.

'The straw?' I nudged.

'What straw?' he slurred. His eyelids flickered, his head drooped. I was losing him.

I got up from the bed and knelt at the side of his chair. I put my hand on his arm. For all his bluster, his violent tendencies, his pent-up vitriol, his arm was fleshless. 'The straw you needed, to get the fire going,' I urged, giving it a little shake.

He looked at me groggily. 'The fire?' he rasped out.

'The beacon,' I pleaded. 'The other boys brought the wood. You brought the matches. But everything was too wet, and so you needed the straw from the stables beneath the tower, didn't you?'

His eyes widened, just for a moment, and I saw in them such a well of trauma and remorse, a Kraken that roiled and coiled and tortured its host without ceasing. And at its core beat three hearts.

Now, it roared. Joe catapulted himself from his chair fuelled by an energy I would not have believed him capable of. He launched himself across the room at some vision I could not see, his eyes on fire, his wiry arms flailing. I was knocked off balance and sent sprawling, hitting my head on the bed frame. The bottle of whisky and the glass both smashed—one dropped from a floundering hand, the other knocked by the chair, which was sent backwards by the velocity of the old man's precipitate motion. I could see a trickle of fluid seeping across the hearthrug and towards the grate. I scrambled to my feet and, grasping the jug of water, threw its contents onto the Scotch. Joe hurled himself across the room, ricocheting off a chest of drawers. He stumbled over the broken glass. It must have cut his feet—he wore only socks—but he seemed not to feel it. His movements were so uncoordinated, made unstable both by his inebriation and his fit, that I feared he would fall into the fire. I placed myself before it but he began instead to claw at the cardboard that covered the window, ripping it off, admitting an arctic blast of cold air that blew the glowing coals behind me into sudden, crackling life. He wrestled with the old sash window as though frantic for escape from whatever demon had besieged him in the room. The sash was restricted in such a way as to open only a few inches. Joe wrenched at it in vain. Then he laid hold of his head, tearing at it until I thought he would do himself a real injury in the effort to release the devil that tortured his soul. All the while he ranted, his voice hoarse but agitated, his words incoherent but their sense perfectly plain. There was white-hot anger and irredeemable loss, caustic resentment and aching regret. I heard—I fathomed, I inferred, I intuited—the whole history of the man and the boy.

Then his eye lit upon me. 'Mary,' he roared, launching himself towards me. I found myself in his grasp. Although emaciated he was taller than I was and surprisingly strong. I feared violence but in fact his hold on me was more of an embrace. 'You've come back,' he crooned. 'I knew you would. Oh Mary, my Mary,' he mumbled into my hair. I shuddered at the reek of spirits on his breath.

'I'm not …' I began, trying to disentangle his arms from around me.

'Shhh,' he hissed, shuffling his feet so that we moved like two exhausted participants at a dance marathon. I felt the edge of the bed behind me, Joe's weight and height making me bend over backwards until at last I had no option but to collapse onto the rumpled sheets. Joe fell on top of me. I felt his hands move from behind me. Then they were on my neck.

'I'll teach you to leave *me.*'

'I didn't …' I croaked out, but his grasp on my neck was too tight for me to say more. I began to struggle, to writhe beneath him. His eyes were crazed, on fire with inner torment.

Then Jamie was in the room. 'Dad!' He seized his father, yanking him off me and pinioning the old man in his strong arms. Joe writhed and struggled, kicking ineffectually with his stockinged feet, punching wildly at Jamie's torso until his reserve of strength was spent. I scrambled off the bed and retreated to a corner of the room, gasping for breath, my hands at my throat where my skin was red and sore. Jamie threw me a look so layered with nuances of emotion—betrayal, concern, shame, outrage—that I could hardly decode it. Slowly, Jamie relaxed the cage of his arms, supporting his father's drooping weight, and at last led him, unresisting, to the bed. He drew the covers over him with a tenderness that moved me, then perched himself on the mattress, the old man's hand held gently in his own.

I stayed where I was, rooted knowing I ought to go—or at least to offer some explanation—but Jamie asked no questions.

Ten minutes might have passed. A coal fell in the grate sending a spark onto the hearth. I crossed the room to sweep the spark to safety with the fire brush, my feet crunching on the broken glass that littered the carpet. When I straightened it was to find Jamie on his feet and standing in the centre of the room. I waited, expecting the accusations and outrage I more than deserved for trespassing in his house, disturbing the peace of his father and putting myself at such risk. Jamie's gaze was level, his eyes inscrutable in the half-light. Then he strode the two paces that separated us and took me in his arms. His kiss was passionate beyond anything I have ever experienced, laden with desire, with longing, with emotion that had been pent up but now poured out in untrammelled floods. His caress was protective, nurturing, giving everything and asking for nothing at all, and I surrendered myself to it.

When we broke apart, each of us breathless, Jamie said, 'There.' Then he turned and left the room.

Chapter Thirty-Eight

I had hardly got back into my cottage, hardly pulled off my coat and kicked off my boots, hardly got halfway up the stairs to where my empty screen begged importunately for the dramatic climax of my narrative, when a series of sharp raps on the door brought my impetus to a halt.

I supposed it was Jamie. We certainly had unfinished business, not least my explanation for having effectively broken into his house—but also the matter of the kiss, and what it might portend. The problem was I didn't know. My mistake about Hugh needed to be unravelled before I could even begin to think about Jamie. It was a mess I wasn't ready to sort out. I glanced longingly up the stairs, to the room where my laptop waited. My desire to sit at it and disappear into the world I had created *there* was as strong as any narcotic, not lessened by my desire to escape from the consequences of all my errors *here*. The boys, the tower, the wood, the straw, I could see it all in my mind's eye. Surely the ghost of Rowan Winter deserved justice?

My visitor knocked again and I heard someone calling my name. Bob woofed and padded through to the hall where he stood with his head cocked, his tail wagging uncertainly from side to side.

I sighed. It would have to be faced. I went back down the stairs and opened the door.

Ivaan stood on the doorstep, carrying a small but stylish portmanteau, and wearing his most boyish and winning smile.

My expression must have shown my utter dismay.

'Surprise!?' he cried, his tone a perfect iteration of the interrobang.

Bob's tail began to wag with more energy and he moved forward to greet our visitor. Ivaan dropped his bag and squatted down to fondle Bob's ears. 'There you are, old boy,' he crooned. 'I've been looking everywhere for you.'

'You can't have him back,' I said, taking hold of Bob's collar and hauling him away from Ivaan.

Ivaan stood up again. 'Hello, you,' he said, ignoring my remark. 'I've been looking everywhere for *you*, too.'

'You went to my brother's,' I said coldly. 'Hardly an exhaustive search.'

He shrugged. 'I was lucky,' he said. 'My first point of investigation paid off. Are you going to invite me in? I sent my car away, and it doesn't look to me as though this place has many hotels.'

'There aren't *any*,' I confirmed. 'You should have thought about that before you set off. Certainly, as regards sending your car away, it would have been better to see what kind of a welcome you were going to get before you did *that.*'

I stood in my doorway and folded my arms. The night was dark now—the moon must have set—but in the shaft of light that fell on Ivaan from my hallway I could see he was inadequately dressed for a stay in Roadend. He wore a light jacket over an open-necked shirt; no sweater, fleece, coat, hat or scarf—the garments that to me, now, were as intrinsic as my skin. I thought his face looked thinner than when I had last seen him. His hair—ink black and usually rather lustrous—was greasy and dull.

He bore my scrutiny for a few moments and then he said, 'Dee ...' in that wheedling way he had.

'What?'

He gave a half-laugh. 'Well, if we must have this conversation on the doorstep ...'

'We must, until I hear what you have to say.'

He cleared his throat, and I had the powerful sense he was commencing a prepared speech, an audition piece. 'We parted badly,' he began. ' I behaved very poorly; I know that—'

'Which part of your behaviour did you think particularly poor?' I enquired archly. 'Stealing my belongings? Or leaving Bob to die of neglect? Oh! Or lying about Bob in the first place?'

'All of it,' he said promptly. 'I make no excuses. But, to be absolutely accurate, I ought to say that in fact I didn't *steal* your things, I pawned them.' He fumbled in his jacket pocket. 'They can be redeemed. I have the tickets here—'

'You didn't think your apology might carry more weight if you'd actually redeemed them *first?*' I spat out. 'What good are pawnbrokers' tickets to me here?'

'No,' he said, dropping his head. 'I didn't think that through, did I?'

'That's your problem right there,' I said. 'You don't think *anything* through Ivaan. And I can't have a man like that in my life.' I put my hand on the door and made to close it.

'Oh Dee! Please don't ... I mean ...' he looked over his shoulder into the impenetrable blackness of the night. '... where can I go?'

I rolled my eyes. I could see I had no alternative but to ask him in. He might even have to stay the night if his car could not be recalled.

I stepped to one side. 'You can come in,' I said, 'but make no assumptions about staying. I presume you can call your driver?'

Ivaan picked up his bag and took a tentative step into the hallway. 'The signal seems quite patchy,' he murmured. 'I can try, but ...' He cast a glance around himself with what I took to be an air of ill-founded complacency. 'Nice place,' he remarked.

I realised I was hungry. I had no idea what time it was. I had not eaten or drunk since Olivia's visit and that seemed a lifetime ago. 'Don't make yourself comfortable,' I warned, 'but I'll make us something to eat. You can tell me more about how wrong you got things, back in September.'

He followed me through to the kitchen and I set about making us omelettes while he tried to explain what he described as "the misunderstanding" about Bob. Apparently, Bob was a valuable stud dog that Ivaan had agreed to care for while his owner was in hospital. Yes, he admitted, bringing his famous dimple into play, he had been paid a "small fee" to look after the dog. There had never been any question of euthanasia, though; that had been my "overly dramatic imagination." As far as not coming home in time to look after Bob, that was a comedy of missed trains, lost tickets and a cab-drivers' strike. Ivaan's story was entertaining but wholly unconvincing. It lasted for the duration of our omelettes and the pot of tea I made afterwards. At some point Ivaan excused himself to use the bathroom and appeared downstairs again in his stockinged feet. His bag had disappeared—I later found it on my bed. He had clearly treated himself to a tour of the cottage because he remarked how spacious and well-appointed it was, as though he were a prospective tenant. He offered no help with either the cooking or the clearing up and eventually settled himself on the settee with every air of having decided to stay for a long time.

'Your story has more holes than a string vest,' I said, when his rendition came to an end. 'A valuable stud dog would not be palmed off on a stranger for a paltry sum. I simply don't believe you. You *did* tell me he was on his way to the vet, so don't tell me I imagined it. As for your story about the trains and so on—absolute bollocks. I checked the trains. There were no delays. And remember, I have the email you sent me from Acapulco, in which you say you went straight to Heathrow from Wales. By your own admission you made absolutely no attempt to get back to the flat. For all you knew Bob could have been there for days. You're a liar, Ivaan.'

He had the grace to look ashamed of himself. 'I just want you back,' he cried out at last, throwing his arms wide in appeal. 'I've come all this way. Don't you find that romantic? Darling. things will be different. I've got this film in the bag and the producer wants me for the sequel. Others will follow, I *know* they will. Chrissie says ...'

'Oh!' I broke in, 'yes, do tell me. What *does* Chrissie say? Did she throw you out on your ear?'

'There was never anything between Chrissie and me.' But Ivaan's eyes would not meet mine, and I knew—again—that he was lying.

'I don't care,' I said. I was tired of it. I glanced at the clock. It was after eleven. 'You can stay tonight, in the spare room, but you must leave tomorrow. If necessary, I'll take you to the station myself. Bob will stay here with me.'

'Please, *please* Dee …' Ivaan's face crumpled, and I thought he was going to cry.

He stood and I looked at him without a flicker of emotion. He cut a pathetic figure and I could not see what had ever attracted me. I waited for his performance to end, for his face to clear as actors' faces do when the director shouts "cut" or when the lights go out on the stage. The show is over, the take is in the can. The role is cast off and reality emerges from the artificial.

I waited. He was milking it. What did he want? A round of applause? A standing ovation?

Tableau. Then someone knocked on the door.

I stamped along the corridor and threw the door open to find Hugh on my doorstep.

'Ah,' he said, his face illuminated by a wide smile, '*there* you are.' He looked benign, not at all angry, not the least bit resentful—as I would have been—to have been deserted in his hour of bereavement. I realised he was infinitely better than the adulterer I had lately imagined him, and that I had degraded him by relegating him to a role-player in my castle-in-the-sky. I owed him an explanation and I realised I could not in all conscience put it off any longer.

'Hugh,' I said, stepping to one side. 'I'm so glad you're here. I need to explain things to you. I'm afraid I've been an utter fool.'

'Oh,' he said, ducking his head to get beneath the lintel, 'I doubt that. I'm just so glad to *see* you.'

I caught movement in the kitchen. Ivaan—no doubt—was hovering just out of sight, listening.

'Please come into the sitting room,' I said, leading Hugh into that room, switching on the lamp and quickly closing the curtains. 'I'm sorry there's no fire.'

'I can light one,' Hugh offered, removing his coat and hanging it on a hook on the back of the door.

'If you like,' I said distractedly. 'The thing is, I have a visitor, someone from London. He turned up unexpectedly and sent his car away and so I've had no choice other than to ask him to stay the night. In the spare room, of course.'

'Of course,' echoed Hugh. He held out his arms in an invitation for an embrace and I found I really *really* wanted what he offered. After the day I had had … and now Ivaan … but there was also Jamie. I could still taste him on my lips. I really didn't want to compound an already fraught situation with more layers of trouble.

'Give me five minutes,' I said, backing away. 'Let me get my visitor settled and then I'll be back. There are things to say, but I need to …' I gestured at the door.

'You take all the time you need,' said Hugh equably. He turned and began to assemble the makings of the fire.

In the kitchen I surprised Ivaan in the act of going through my handbag. 'You bastard,' I hissed, snatching it off him.

'Just looking for a tissue,' he said, springing away.

'Get yourself upstairs,' I said in a stage whisper. 'Your room is at the back, the one with twin beds. Go into it and shut the door. I don't want to see you again until the morning, preferably the back of your head as you disappear out of my life for good.'

'Oh Dee,' he remonstrated, assuming the expression of a chastised puppy.

'No.' I held up my hands. 'I mean it, Ivaan. It's *that*, or you can leave right now, on foot. I don't care if you fall in a ditch or drown in the sea. Take it or leave it.'

'All right,' he said, and slunk from the room.

By the time I returned to the sitting room Hugh had a bright fire burning in the grate. I had taken in my bottle of Spanish brandy—the best thing I had in the house to offer him, and the least he deserved—and two glasses. At length, I stammered out my confession, at least so far as my mistake about Caroline. I baulked at further revelation. Hugh took it with good humour, although I could tell he had been both angry and disappointed with me, confused by my suddenly distancing myself from him.

He sat on the edge of the sofa with his elbows resting on his knees and watched me intently as I poured out my story from where I knelt on the hearthrug.

At last, he said, 'I can't see how you leapt to such a conclusion. Caroline? Surely you can tell she's gay from a mile away? But anyway, I accept that, for whatever reason, you made a genuine mistake. But while you have been labouring under that misapprehension, I can't help wondering … in fact, it's the thing that's plagued me, these past weeks … I wondered if your affections have been engaged elsewhere.'

I almost laughed. Had he been reading *Sense and Sensibility*? It was a phrase I would have expected of Jamie, not Hugh. 'Engaged elsewhere?' I prevaricated.

Hugh nodded. 'Mary tells me you see a good deal of Jamie these days.'

What could I say? 'Yes,' I admitted. 'I do. We started off badly but then we cleared the air and now I'd say we're pretty good friends.'

'Friends.' It was not a question. Hugh was weighing my words. 'And where does that leave us?' He looked across at me, his grey eyes very direct.

I could not meet them. 'I don't know,' I muttered. 'I'm sorry. I *really* don't know. I've made so many mistakes lately, Hugh. I've misunderstood things that ought to have been obvious. And then, I've begun to believe things that really are incredible. Ridiculous things, but things that ... well, I can't see any other explanation for them. I'm writing and ...'

'Ah yes, you're writing.' I looked up from the rug, where my eyes had been fixed, to find Hugh's eyebrows raised in mock surprise.

'Yes,' I said, rolling my eyes, 'I'm writing. I'm a writer. My secret is out.'

'Oh, it surely is,' said Hugh, suddenly relaxing and leaning back on the sofa. He took a sip of his brandy.

'And, when you find out *what* I'm writing,' I began, but just then the door of the sitting room swung open and Ivaan appeared. He wore silk pyjama bottoms and the expression of a pantomime Lothario.

'Dee,' he began, 'aren't you coming to bed?' Then he pretended to see Hugh. 'Oh, do excuse me,' he said, acting surprise, 'I didn't know you had a visitor.'

Hugh stood up, his instinct as a perfect gentleman vying with a sharp surge of jealousy.

I struggled to my feet. 'This is the friend I told you about, Hugh,' I said. 'His name is ...'

'Ivor Kash,' said Ivaan, extending a hand and advancing into the room, 'although I'm sure I need no introduction.'

Hugh took his hand and shook it briefly. He towered over Ivaan, who had to bend his head back in order to meet Hugh's eye.

'I'm sorry,' Hugh frowned, looking down at Ivaan in every way, 'who are you?'

'He is a person who is going to get dressed and leave immediately,' I said through clenched teeth. 'Ivaan, I told you to go upstairs and *stay* upstairs. That was the deal. Now you've ballsed it up and you can leave.'

'Like this?' Ivaan looked down at his pigeon chest and ridiculous paisley silk pyjamas. 'You wouldn't be so cruel.'

'I would,' I said. I marched from the room, intent on fetching down his case. As I passed the door someone knocked on it and I turned the handle with grim resignation. The evening—the entire day—was turning into a black comedy, a farce, a nightmare. Meeting all my expectations, Jamie stood on the threshold.

'Perfect,' I said, flinging the door wide. 'Do come in. The more the merrier.'

I don't know what kind of welcome Jamie had expected but it was not this one. He hung back, unsure.

'Is everything all right?'

'Not really,' I threw off. 'My lying, cheating, stealing ex-boyfriend has turned up out of the blue. Hugh is here too. The jury is out on whether he is ready to accept my grovelling apology. Now you're here ... Oh! *So* much unfinished business! You'd better go in and pour yourself a brandy. I think we'll all need one before the night is out.'

With that I mounted the stairs to find Ivaan's suitcase on my bed, its contents flung everywhere, and every evidence that he had been making himself at home between my sheets.

When I got back to the sitting room with Ivaan's hastily repacked case, I found my ex-boyfriend sandwiched uncomfortably between the twin colossuses of Hugh and Jamie. It was laughable, really—or perhaps I was verging on hysterics. Whichever, I let out a peal of laughter. Ivaan clearly found the situation far from amusing. He looked anxiously from one man to the other, at their broad and well-muscled shoulders, their large, meaty hands, their towering stature in the low-beamed room. Their expressions were a mirror-image of each other. They looked at Ivaan as though he was something unpleasant brought in on the bottom of a shoe.

'It looks like you're more inclined to leave now, Ivaan,' I said, putting his portmanteau down in front of him. 'You'd better get dressed.'

Ivaan grabbed his bag and scurried from the room. Hugh and Jamie both guffawed at his cowardly demeanour. I wondered why I had never noticed what a poor excuse for a man Ivaan was. Perhaps it had taken the comparison with *these* two men. I realised it was the first time, apart from at the funeral, I had seen Jamie and Hugh beside one another. Their Forrester likeness was striking and—just for that moment, while they shared the joke about Ivaan—I sensed a tenuous but promising connection between them. I really understood Mary's desire that they should be friends.

Presently we heard Ivaan speaking on his mobile phone. Then he reappeared, dressed, and wearing the jacket he had arrived in.

'I'll have those pawn tickets, before you go,' I said.

He held them out. 'Here you are,' he said.

Then he backed out of the room and we heard the front door close softly behind him.

'What an unpleasant man,' said Hugh, taking his seat again. 'Who did you say he was?'

'He's Ivor Kash,' said Jamie. 'He's an actor, isn't he Dee? Quite famous, I believe.'

'Infamous, some would say,' I replied. 'I had the misfortune to fall for him. I'm wise to him now though.'

'An actor,' said Hugh thoughtfully, swirling what remained of his brandy round his glass. 'A *famous* actor. And you know him?'

'He was in Dee's film,' supplied Jamie. 'He played a curate, I think. Rather apt. A mixture of servility and self-importance, wouldn't you say?'

I smiled—but bleakly—at Jamie's reference to *Pride and Prejudice*. I wondered if he was trying to make a connection with me that would exclude Hugh. If so, he succeeded. The Jane Austen quote went right over Hugh's head. He only turned surprised eyes on me to say, 'A film?'

'One of my books was made into a film,' I explained. 'I was a success, briefly shining in the firmament. But since then …'

Tears suddenly pressed behind my eyes because it seemed to me I would never regain that brief but oh-so-glorious pinnacle. My current book could never be published; it preyed too cruelly on a family's tragic history; its truth was too uncomfortable. Can a book be too true? Up to that point, I would have said not.

The room was full of a strange atmosphere; the presence, *together*, of Hugh and Jamie brought a potent dimension to it. They sat at opposite ends of the sofa, as alike as bookends and yet their paths in life so different. One had enjoyed privilege and plenty; the other had suffered a life of toil and burden. It didn't seem fair when both were scions of the same tree and should, all things being equal, have followed similar paths. They must have felt it. I know Jamie did. I tasted some of Jamie's gall in my mouth. Through Joe, he should have inherited the best of what Todd had to leave, but Hugh, via Jack, had wrested it from him. Wrested it with every kind intention, but still …

I looked around the room again. It was charged with the awkwardness of our trio—the ridiculous idea that these two men might be rivals for my affections and the unfinished business I had with both of them. Also, projecting itself with particular emphasis was the business between Hugh and Jamie that had not even begun. They shared so much, these two, in terms of family history and connective strands of DNA. They could share so much more, had not the disgruntlement of Joe stood between them. While he lived, I did not think Hugh and Jamie could ever be friends.

All this swirled like relational soup in the little room, yet in spite of it I felt a vacuity. Something was missing. I looked at the hearth rug, the empty place beside me.

'Bob,' I cried, scrambling to my feet. 'Ivaan has stolen Bob.'

My words galvanised Hugh and Jamie. They both leapt from the sofa and there was a comedic moment as they both tried to exit the narrow doorway together. I wore stockinged feet but thankfully neither of them had removed their boots and they ran together out into the night and up the lane, where the red glow of taillights showed a vehicle making its tortuous departure over the pot-holed road.

I returned to the house to push my feet into my boots, but by the time I got past Jamie's cottage a flash of white streaked towards me and Bob was in my arms. He slobbered over me, his tail a frenzied metronome. Hugh and Jamie appeared side by side, their strides matching, both grim-faced but oddly gratified. Hugh rubbed the knuckles of his right hand with his left.

I gabbled my thanks and we walked slowly back towards my cottage.

'He won't look very pretty for a day or so,' remarked Jamie. 'I hope he isn't due on set.'

'I hope he *is,*' said Hugh. 'We know how to deal with reivers[4] round here, don't we Jamie?'

'Some of us do,' said Jamie. He looked at his watch. 'It's late.'

We stood in a little huddle on the dark lane, and I realised neither man wanted to yield the field to the other. Jamie and Hugh threw covert glances at each other, and both of them looked at me—waiting, perhaps, for me to invite one of them to come back inside with me. I bent and stroked Bob, meeting neither of their eyes, feeling awkward and suddenly, overwhelmingly tired. Then, simultaneously, both men took a breath and stepped away. I stole a glance at Hugh. His expression was hard to read, but I gathered he had concluded—as I had—that although our misunderstanding had been cleared up, things would not go back to how they were. At least, they would not go back *yet*.

Jamie's face was much easier to interpret. He had hoped that, with our kiss, we had crossed the divide that had stood between us since my arrival at Roadend. He could not conceal a look of longing in his eyes. But he, too, saw that now was not the time.

'I've had quite a day,' I said, more lightly than I felt. 'I'm bushed, chaps. I hope you'll excuse me if I call it a night.'

'Of course,' they said, in unison.

---

[4] Border reivers were raiders who terrorised the border region stealing livestock and practicing arson, kidnap and extortion from the late 13th to the early 17th century.

I turned back to the cottage. Its door stood open, light pouring onto the path.

'Goodnight, Dee,' said Jamie, turning towards his own, dark cottage. He added, 'Goodnight, Hugh.'

I walked up the path to my door. From behind me I heard Hugh say, 'Goodnight.' I turned to see Hugh still hesitating at the spot where we had stood. I had half expected him to be staring after me—hoping, perhaps, for a reprieve, for a last-minute invitation to accompany me indoors. It was not me, however, that Hugh was looking at but Jamie, his slowly retreating back. It occurred to me he was being discreet, waiting until Jamie had gone inside his own house before following me into mine. But I was wrong about that too. Suddenly Hugh called out, 'Jamie!' and set off at a lope in pursuit of his cousin. He caught up with Jamie just at his gate. Jamie half-turned. Hugh held out his hand and then, when Jamie took it, wrapped an arm around Jamie's shoulder. They exchanged some words I could not hear, then Hugh disappeared up the lane and Jamie went inside.

The Trysting Tree
1962

The year 1962 was appalling weatherwise, with snow in late February and early March delaying the sowing of spring crops. Heavy rain in the late spring caused standing water on the fields, preventing germination. The crops that did emerge were spindly and feeble. A dry summer caused further issues. The autumn was wet and windy, heralding the historically awful winter to come.

At Roadend, the doughty villagers struggled through heavy rain to build their Guy Fawkes Night bonfire, the children turning out in oilskins and wellington boots to drag windfallen branches, hedge trimmings and gash timber onto the pyre that was to stand in its traditional place on the beach. Joe, then aged twelve, had done the work of two boys his age, wrestling boughs into position alongside the men, while John and Jack—eight and six respectively—had built their Guy Fawkes effigy in the dry of the barn. Their idea was to trundle the completed Guy along the village street and to wait with it outside the doors of the pub in order to collect pennies with which to buy fireworks. This had been their tradition since any of them could remember. They expected no assistance from their parents and they got none. Todd and Rose were preoccupied.

Earlier that year Rose's long-lost sister Rowan had returned to Roadend. They had received no warning of her coming. A Land Rover towing a horsebox had made its appearance in the village, not stopping at the pub or the church but travelling directly up the rough and snaking path to the pele tower. It was only afterwards, when an unnaturally brown and very wizened woman had presented herself at the door of Roadend farm that Rose had understood the visitor to be Rowan Broughton-Moore.

Rose surveyed her sister, appalled. This sallow, wrinkled and ugly woman was not the sister she had been imagining all her life. On the other hand, she was smartly dressed in Bond Street clothing and her hair declared its styling by Vidal Sassoon. Rose, in comparison, wore farm slacks and a stained apron. Her hair was carelessly tied in a loose bun. Her hands were calloused, her nails torn. She felt ashamed.

Rowan brought with her a toddler, a girl perhaps three years-of-age, who was also swarthy and who spoke in an accent so impenetrably thick that the Forresters doubted she was even speaking English.

The meeting of the sisters was by no means an emotional or even a particularly friendly affair. Rowan was disgruntled, complaining about the state of the pele tower, which she declared was scarcely suitable even for pigs. She smoked voraciously—a habit disapproved of by Rose—sending clouds of acrid smoke up to the ceiling of the kitchen, contaminating the strings of onions and bunches of herbs that dangled from the rafters. Rowan seemed offended to have been shown into the kitchen, as opposed to the parlour.

'Oh, we never use those rooms,' said Rose, kneading her hands. 'We tend to live here, in the kitchen mostly.' As a compensation, Rose had brought out the best china tea service from its glazed cupboard in the dining room, despairing to find the milk jug was chipped. On the stained kitchen tablecloth, though, it looked pretentious and out of place.

'How very rusticated of you,' sneered Rowan, handling her teacup with pinched fingertips, as though it might be dirty. She looked witheringly at Rose's three large, sturdy and handsome boys as they slurped their tea and gobbled wholesale amounts of cake. 'Goodness,' she said, half to herself, 'who would have thought Todd could have produced these great hulking things?'

'Todd will be … surprised to see you,' said Rose, sitting on the edge of her chair and trying to imply by frowns and shakes of her head that the boys should display better table manners. 'To be honest, Rowan, we all thought you had perished years ago.'

'I don't know why,' said Rowan, lighting another cigarette although the butt of the previous one still burned in her saucer. 'I kept the lawyer informed. What's his name?'

'Chisholm,' supplied Rose. 'But he's been dead and buried for years, and his practice sold.'

'Oh,' said Rowan. Her mouth was slicked in bright red lipstick that had crept into the etching of wrinkles around it. 'I wondered why he didn't write back.'

'So,' said Rose, with forced brightness, 'you've been in Australia?'

'Lately, yes.' Rowan tapped a worm of ash from her cigarette and shook her head at the plate of cake Rose proffered. 'But now I'm home, and something will have to be done about the tower. It's untenable, as it stands. I'll need a carpenter, a roofer and a chimney sweep, I suppose. A plumber ...'

'You can't mean to *live* there,' cried Rose. She got up and fetched a dishcloth to wipe the boys' jam-smeared faces. In her distraction she also wiped the face of the little girl, although she had eaten not a morsel of cake. 'You can go and play, boys,' she said, 'if you've done your chores. Joe, go and find your father and tell him we have a visitor. I think he's in the three-acre field. John and Jack, you can take your cousin to see the calves.' She turned to Rowan. 'What's this child's name?'

'Agnes,' said Rowan. 'She's my granddaughter.'

The boys trooped out of the kitchen, Jack taking Agnes' hand although she was reluctant to let him do so.

When the boys had gone Rose said, 'She's Sylvia's child? Has Sylvia come with you?'

Rowan shook her head. 'She's dead,' she said baldly, without a glimmer of emotion. 'She married late and died giving birth to Agnes in the bush.

She was only thirty-five. Agnes goes as Winter, though. Her father was Indian.'

'Not as Broughton-Moore?'

Rowan gave Rose a narrow look. 'No. That would hardly be appropriate, would it, since Sylvia wasn't a Broughton-Moore.'

'Sylvia wasn't ...?' Rose repeated. 'But you had her almost straight away.'

'I had her three months too soon,' said Rowan, pushing her cup forwards for more tea. 'She wasn't Frederick's. He knew it, of course, but by then, what could he do? He made a good job of pretending. We *both* did, for *years.*'

'How sad,' said Rose, pouring more tea. She added milk straight from the bottle, wishing she knew how her milk jug had been damaged; one of the boys, she'd be bound.

'Better *that,* than a lie,' said Rowan cryptically. 'You'll have to put me up here, *pro tem,* Rose. The tower really isn't fit for a beast.'

'You should go back to London,' said Rose. 'I haven't room for you here and,' she looked her sister up and down—nylon stockings, polished nails, high-heeled shoes, hoity-toity attitude—'I don't think you're cut out for country life.'

'Nonsense,' said Rowan, lighting yet another cigarette. 'I was virtually born and brought up here. I spent the summers here anyway. I know this area like the back of my hand. I bet I know some places Todd has never taken *you* to. We were childhood playmates you know, and then, not-so childish ones ...'

'I know he was made to look after you,' said Rose in a small voice.

'Made?' Rowan let out a carking laugh. 'Well, I don't know about that. But look, the thing is, we're here now and frankly, we've nowhere else. The house in London was sold years ago. What fortune my husband had was lost in death-duties and squandered at the gaming tables. The tower is all that remains to the Winters and so to the tower I must go. I've brought my horses. Do you ride?'

Rose shook her head.

'No, I didn't suppose so,' said Rowan.

'I haven't room for you here,' said Rose again, with steely directness. 'If you're determined to stay, you will have to put up at the inn.'

Todd had been prepared for their visitor by Joe—although had he not been told beforehand that Rowan Winter sat in his kitchen, he would certainly not have recognised her. He spent a little time in the scullery washing his hands and splashing water over his face and hair before coming into the kitchen. He told himself his racing heart was due to having walked too quickly from the three-acre field.

He took a breath and pushed open the kitchen door. 'Rowan,' he said, 'you're here.'

'I am, darling Todd,' said Rowan, rising immediately and crossing the worn slabs of the kitchen, her heels clicking, to stand before him. She put her exquisitely manicured and heavily jewelled hand on Todd's cheek and locked her eyes on to his. 'Hello, you,' she said quietly. Then she kissed him, lingeringly, on the lips.

Todd felt the old stirrings, although he was fifty-eight now and not the virile man he had once been. This feeling confused him, for neither was Rowan the girl she had been. She was dried up and bony. The taste of tobacco and the grease of her lipstick on his lips made him feel nauseous and he wiped it away with the back of his hand.

At their kiss, Rose had given a little cry, shot up from the table and busied herself about clearing cups and plates and washing them in the sink. Now Todd looked at her back, bent over the Belfast as she scrubbed furiously at something. Her hair had fallen out of its bun. It was threaded with grey, perhaps a little lank. It stuck to the sweat of her neck. He felt a surge of tenderness for her—his Rose—and crossed the kitchen to put his hand briefly on the small of her back, at the place where he knew it ached. Then he sat down and poured himself a cup of tea although he would usually have expected Rose to do it for him.

'What do you want, Rowan?' he asked.

'Why, I've come home,' said Rowan, taking the chair next to his. She steepled her hands and rested her chin on them in the manner that, forty years before, might have been winsome. 'I'm going to need a bit of help, darling. The tower is in an awful state. More really should have been done to maintain it.' She let her implied criticism float in the air. 'It's all the Winters have left.' She gave a false tinkle of laughter. 'You seem to have acquired everything else that used to be ours,' she said, throwing a significant glance at Rose. 'If I'd known about that scheme in time you can be sure I would have stepped in to prevent it.'

'It was none of your business,' said Rose with a flash of savagery quite unusual to her. She turned from the sink. Her eyes were red from suppressed tears, but also full of angry fire. 'You couldn't have prevented anything.'

Rowan raised a finely plucked eyebrow and reached for her packet of cigarettes. Rose dried her hands hastily on the tea towel. She sawed a slab of cake for Todd and slapped it onto a plate before sweeping the cake off the table and carrying it into the scullery, slamming the door behind her.

Todd made no remark but drank his tea and ate the cake with studied attention.

Rowan needed another line of attack. She leaned back in her chair and swept an invisible thread from her skirt. She kept an eye on the scullery door in case Rose should return but the sound of smothered sniffles suggested Rose would be ensconced in there for a while. 'Of course,' she said, lowering her voice, 'I did take away something that was yours. You do know that?'

A flicker in Todd's cheek was her answer.

'Does Rose know?'

Todd turned his cold blue eyes upon her. 'What do you need at the tower?' he asked.

~

In spite of all the work there was to do on the farm, Todd supervised the renovations at the tower. Rowan stayed at the inn and did not trouble Rose with her company much. Rowan spent her days at the tower, camping out amongst the builders and carpenters, making tea on a little camping stove and smoking interminable cigarettes. She rode her horses daily, out along the dunes and back through the shallow surf. She left Agnes more or less to her own devices, and on most days the child found her way to the farm, particularly after school, when she would find Jack or one of the other boys about their appointed tasks.

Rose found she did not resent the little girl, who put her in mind of the two daughters she had lost. It was easy to lay an additional place at the table for lunch and to coax the child into eating something. Gradually she was able to decipher the infant's speech. It became apparent that Agnes was confused and disappointed by what she had found at Roadend; she had been led to believe that Winter Tower would be a castle fit for a princess, with bright fluttering pennants atop the turrets and a posse of gaily dressed courtiers ready to do her bidding. 'Because I am the last of the Winters,' she explained haltingly, 'and my great-grandfather was a Knight-of-Old.'

Tentatively, Agnes began to respond to Rose's affection. Rose could not believe the girl had received much in the way of *that* from Rowan although clearly, from someone, she had been fed a great deal of romantic nonsense and persuaded to think much too highly of her Winter connection.

Agnes was the only bright light in the black storm of Rowan's return to Roadend. Todd and Rose did not discuss what her advent meant, and they avoided like the plague any discourse on the relationship Todd and Rowan had had previously. Rose, of course, had assimilated all of Rowan's darkly suggestive hints; obviously, there was *something* she didn't know, but which was easy to guess. She was hurt and angry Todd had been less than truthful with her although she could not honestly say that knowing would have made any difference. Nevertheless, she felt excluded, on the outside of a circle of historical intimacy that bound Todd and Rowan together. Rose became silent and withdrawn. Her boys saw it. Life with Todd had never been easy—he was volatile and domineering—but Rose had always been able to shield them from the worst of his humours. Rose had provided the lightness and laughter in their lives, smoothing off Todd's sharp edges with her kindness and indefatigable good humour. Now, since Rowan's arrival, she seemed less inclined to occupy this role. Meals—hastily prepared and flung anyhow onto the plates—were taken in silence. The little touches with which she had shown her care—neatly mended shirts, freshly baked biscuits, the thoughtful gifts she sometimes left beneath their pillows—ceased.

The boys disliked their aunt Rowan; she was scathing of what she described as their hobbledehoy natures and rough, agrarian manners.

'Not a single one of you enrolled at Sedbergh school[5],' she said one day, looking down upon them from the saddle of her horse. 'What does your father hope you will ever make of yourselves?'

'We'll be farmers, like he is,' said Joe, bullishly.

'Or better,' put in John.

Rowan sighed and kicked her horse onwards. 'I rest my case.'

Rowan was installed in the tower by October. The renovations were necessarily not extensive, but the tower was water-tight, the windows and roof repaired, rotten floorboards replaced and some rudimentary plumbing installed. As in days of yore, the ground floor was given over to the stabling of her horses. The upper floor was a vast living area with a solid fuel cooking range installed into the fireplace. Rowan and Agnes occupied the two bedrooms above, but the old solar on the top level had been left unfurnished and was unused.

---

[5] The north of England's premier public school, situated on the border between Cumbria and Yorkshire.

Regardless of her straitened circumstances, Rowan lost no time in establishing connections with the few remaining land-owning families in the area. These people had retained their country residences even though many of those were now open to public, had caravan sites sequestered amongst their ancient woodland acres and sold tea and scones at exorbitant prices. She disappeared for weekends of what Rose called hobnobbing—shooting and bridge, charity dinners and exhibitions of questionable art—leaving Agnes at Roadend farm. Rose didn't object to looking after the girl, but she found she resented—unreasonably, because she had never sought it—the hand of friendship that had so readily been extended to Rowan, but denied to Rose herself.

In her more clear-eyed moments, Rose acknowledged that her *real* resentment was against Rowan, and not the lingering remnants of squirearchy. Since her coming, Todd had spent many hours—surely *too* many—at the pele tower, liable, at the drop of a hat—just whenever Rowan had the whim—to disappear off to revisit what Rowan referred to as their "old haunts." Rowan and Todd rode up to the tarn on one rare, sunny afternoon, leaving Rose to supervise the milking and the lorry that came to collect the eggs. Rose had never seen Todd on horseback, and here was *another* reminder of something that he shared with Rowan, but not with her. They were gone such an unconscionably long time that Rose had contemplated sending Joe to see if an accident had occurred. But then, as twilight fell, the steady clip-clop of the horses' hooves had been heard in the yard.

On another occasion Rose was horrified to find Todd and Rowan at the silver birch tree on the Moss. Rose thought of it as *their* tree—Rose's and Todd's—because it was the place he had taken her on their wedding day; the place where, *at last,* they had succumbed to their mutual passion. They still liked to go there on their anniversary, and it was on this occasion that Rose had made her way towards the tree with a picnic. She had waited for Todd to appear in their time-honoured fashion, to lead her out on to the Moss and the trysting tree. But the hours had gone by and it had become plain that, this year, there would be no romantic rendezvous. So, she had set out alone, her heart heavy, the shadow of the pele tower falling across her metaphorically if not in fact as she climbed the hill and then took the track down towards Winter Farm. The bracken on the Moss was turning from green to orange, subsiding with infinite elegance to reveal a labyrinth of mysterious tracks through its foliage. Rose remembered being taken through them, feeling as though she was the first to tread these faerie by-ways, the first to find the magnificent accommodating tree at the heart of the copse. As she approached the coppice she paused, hearing voices. She laid down her basket and crept forward, peering through the thickly interweaving branches of the surrounding saplings. The voices were low and confidential, the figures shrouded from view, but she recognised the smell of Rowan's cigarettes and then heard Todd's voice in the soft, intimate iteration she had believed had been reserved only for her—indistinct, but unmistakable.

Rose turned and walked away, her picnic basket forgotten.

The atmosphere at Roadend farm soured still further. Mealtimes in particular were curdled by a bladder of unspoken angst. On one occasion Rose lost her temper and deliberately dropped Todd's plate on the floor, sending stew and dumplings in a splatter over the slabs. Another day she caught the early bus to town and did not return until night had fallen and the boys, despairing of any dinner, had assuaged their hunger with what they could purloin from the larder, and enormous pieces of cake. It had seemed fun at first—as well as rebellious, as they were not really allowed to help themselves to cake—but as the boys munched at their hacked off slices of bread and barely chewable wedges of cheese they regarded each other with round, alarmed eyes. Jack began to cry. Joe got up and wiped his brother's eyes and running nose with the edge of the tablecloth. John left the table, abandoning his supper, and went into the unused parlour to wait for his mother's return. Their father was nowhere to be found.

It rained for most of October and the whole of the first week of November. On the 5th, the rain came with a blustering gale that made the Guy Fawkes' celebrations impossible. The boys were distraught. Their fireworks were bought and stored in old biscuit tins in the scullery. Rose had made treacle toffee and parkin[6]—both traditional bonfire night treats—and their Guy was in the barn, stuffed with straw and ready to hoist onto the top of the bonfire. The Guy, wearing a tweed skirt and with a gash of red material coarsely stitched in place as a mouth with a thin roll of paper in one hand resembling a cigarette, was easy to recognise. But the rain fell relentlessly and word arrived the bonfire would be postponed until the weather was better.

Day followed day and another whole week went by, the sky a perpetual sieve, pouring water without reprieve. The bonfire was saturated beyond saving, its spars blackened and soaked, the dry kindling that had been pushed to its heart no more than mush. The boys and the rest of the village children went to look at it on their way home from school, their anoraks dripping water from the hems, their school shoes oozing. The consensus was there would be no bonfire that year. They shook their heads and made their way home.

Only the Forrester boys remained. '*They* might have given up, but *we* haven't,' declared Joe.

'No,' agreed John, although he had no idea how the situation could be rescued.

'This bonfire is no good,' wailed Jack, snivelling.

'This one isn't,' said Joe, 'but we'll build another. A better one.'

John looked at his brother. 'Not on the farm,' he warned. He knew fire on a farm was a calamitous thing.

'Oh no, not *there*,' said Joe. 'Somewhere better. Somewhere everyone will be able to see. The Forresters don't give up. We can do what we like.'

---

[6] A moist ginger cake

Jack had stopped blubbering. He wiped his nose with his sleeve. 'Can we, Joe?'

Joe put his arm around his brother's shoulders. 'Of course we can. But don't tell anyone, or they'll all want to join in. This will be just for us.'

The boys turned away from the bonfire and trudged back up the beach. The day was drawing in. Already it was almost dark, but the pall of night was hardly distinguishable from the gloom that had overwhelmed the day. On the bluff, the pele tower was an umbra silhouette against the surrounding shadow of sky, and in one of its narrow windows, a dim light shone out.

On the 14th the rain finally abated to a drizzle, but a brisk wind began to herd the clouds away to the west and, in the evening of that day, the glimmer of rain-washed stars and a thin sliver of moon shone from a cloudless sky. Undimpled puddles reflected the meagre streetlights along the lane and the boys went to bed unaccountably troubled by the sudden absence of rain pebbling their windows or drumming on the roof above their heads.

The following day—a Thursday—Joe pretended a stomach-ache and was sent home from school. The secretary's call to his home went unanswered—as he had known it would—but he assured her his parents would be at home, out and about on the farm. He did not go home, however, but set about gathering driftwood from the beach beyond the bluff where he would not be seen, dragging it doggedly up the slope, through the trees and depositing it just over the brow of the hill, concealed by some low scruffy shrubs. It was hard work and he lacked gauntlets or stout boots because he had not risked returning home to get changed. He knew that, ordinarily, his mother would be angry with him—about the uniform, and about having lied about being ill—but these days she was distracted. He could waylay any letter that came from school and claim a lunchtime football game had got his uniform in a mess, and she would probably believe him.

All afternoon, as he worked, he pondered the logistics of his scheme. The driftwood was damp and would not light without assistance. He would need kindling of some kind, and also possibly an accelerant—paraffin or petrol—as well as matches. He knew where the matches were to be found—on a high shelf in the scullery—and he knew his father kept paraffin which had been used to heat the hen houses before he'd had electricity laid in. Getting either of these things from the farm without being seen would be a challenge, but one he felt confident he could overcome.

By three o'clock he was scratched and muddy but he had a not-inconsiderable cache of wood, and made his circuitous way back to the village. At half past three he met the school bus and collected his bag from where he had stashed it in the bin beside the bus shelter. He walked home with John, apprising him of the progress he had made during the afternoon.

'We'll light the bonfire tonight,' he said. 'Straight after tea, you take Jack out onto the dunes and bring as much wood as you can carry. I'll get the matches and meet you there.'

'Where?' John's eyes were round with admiration, but his mind calculated on ways he might be able to improve on what his brother had begun. The toffee and the parkin had all been eaten up, but their fireworks remained, sealed into their tin boxes. 'How will we launch the rockets? Dad sinks a kind of tube into the—'

'We won't be able to have the fireworks,' said Joe. 'We'll need to manage the fire. I promised a fire, not fireworks. It will be like a beacon. They used to light them all along the coast to warn of marauders. Vikings, Scots, coming to rape and pillage …'

'Oh,' said John, impressed in spite of himself, although unclear as to what rape and pillage might be. 'Where will the bon … the beacon be?'

Joe leaned in to whisper, 'On the hill, by the tower. That's where it *would* have been, in olden days.'

The clocks had gone back at the end of October and so by the time the boys had eaten their tea it was fully dark, although only a quarter past five. They had got changed into rough gear and told their mother they were going out to play. She waved them away with a vague instruction that they should be back by six thirty. Todd had not made an appearance for the meal. It was market day and generally he liked to spend a few hours in the pub with his farming cronies once the auction mart had concluded. She assumed that's where he would be, although these days she was never sure.

Once they were free of the farm, Joe sent John and Jack to scavenge more wood from the beach beyond the bluff, telling them to meet him at the top of the hill in half an hour. When they were gone, he doubled back, creeping into the farm store and pulling the paraffin can from where he had stashed it beneath some old tarpaulins. Next, he went into the kitchen. The light was off, the pots all cleaned and put away, the tea towel draped over the rail of the range. His mother would be somewhere in the house, sewing perhaps, or in the farm office. Joe stole across the kitchen and into the scullery, groping on the shelf for the matches. There were not many in the box. He must not waste them.

The two younger boys ran helter-skelter up the hill, their eyes soon becoming accustomed to the dark, past the tower and down through the woods on the other side. The night was chill, but dry. A winnowing wind riffled the marram grasses as they hurried along, picking up what sticks of bleached, balsa-like driftwood they could find until their arms were full. Then they turned to make their way back to the hill.

Jack complained. 'These are heavy,' he said, although in truth John carried far more than he did. 'Why didn't Joe come with us?'

'We're collecting wood,' John said, 'and he's to get the matches.'

Understanding dawned in Jack's mind. 'So, there *will* be a bonfire?'

'Yes,' said John, parroting the details Joe had given him earlier. 'Like a beacon, on the top of Winter Hill. In olden days, they would light beacons along the coast to tell people things.'

'What kinds of things?'

'That marauders were coming.'

'What are marauders?'

'Baddies. Vikings. Scots, coming to rape and pillage.'

'What's rape and pillage?'

'I'm not sure.'

'And what will *our* beacon say?'

'It will say that no one stops *us* from doing what we like. Come on, Jack. Keep up.'

By the time the boys had laboured up the slope and through the trees of Winter Hill, Joe was already there. He had hauled his own stash of wood onto a patch of bare grass twenty yards or so from the base of the tower on its seaward side, and erected it in a conical structure, emulating the fire that had been built on the beach. John and Jack approached with caution, throwing anxious looks at the tower.

'What if she's in there?' Jack stammered.

Joe assured them there was no one home. 'We have Winter Hill to ourselves, just as we should have,' he crowed. 'It's the only bit of Roadend we *don't* own. When I have the farm, it will be mine.'

'Or mine,' said John. 'You won't get the whole farm, you know, Joe.'

'I *will*,' said Joe with great vehemence, adding the wood his brothers had brought to the fire. 'I'm the oldest. But don't worry, John, I'll look after you.' He stood back to admire his handiwork. 'There,' he said, walking round the pyre with an air of great satisfaction. 'What do you think?'

John said, 'We'll need something dry to start it off with.'

Joe lifted his hand in a "Just wait and see," gesture and went to retrieve the effigy of Guy Fawkes from where he had left it, some yards beyond the fire towards the edge of the spit. In the darkness the doll was surprisingly life-like and Joe felt a peculiar reluctance to pick it up. Something gnawed at him, an inkling, a presentiment. He felt queerly as though he was balanced on the edge of something, but the edge of the bluff was nowhere near where he stood. He paused, looking down at the gruesome image of his aunt. What if this was all a really bad plan? But he shook it off. The Guy had been a last-minute idea, but one he was particularly proud of. 'I brought this. It's as dry as tinder. I know it should go on the top, but that can't be helped.'

Jack looked up at the tower, still unconvinced it was untenanted. 'Are you *sure* there's no one in there?' he said.

'The horses, that's all. Look. Her Land Rover isn't there. She must be out with her posh friends.'

'Where's Agnes then?'

This gave Joe pause, but he said, 'She must have gone too,' with such confidence that neither of his brothers was minded to question it. The truth was that Joe was so fixated on the bonfire, on the splendour and kudos of having planned, built and lit it himself, that the occupants of the tower had not for a moment featured in his calculations. He produced the can of paraffin and began to pour it liberally over the stuffed figure. It soaked up the fuel like a sponge. Then he pushed the dummy into the space he had made at the heart of the fire.

'Ready?' he said, pulling the box of matches from his pocket.

His brothers nodded, their faces pale in the moonless night, both a little awed at their undertaking and, if truth were known, suddenly doubtful of it. Instinctively, they both took a step backwards. The breeze on the top of Winter Hill was much stronger than it had been on the dunes. It lifted the feathers of Joe's hair as he knelt to strike the match.

The first few were instantly blown out. 'Come round this side, John, and shield the wind,' said Joe, crouching lower and reaching in between the spars of the fire so the flame might instantly catch the reeking Guy. 'There aren't many matches left.'

John moved round as instructed and placed his body between the breeze and the match. This time it flared and Joe laid the match against the paraffin-soaked straw. It ignited with a woosh that threw Joe and John backwards, bright blue flames reaching up through the lats as the effigy caught fire and disappeared in a bright corona of flame. The noise—a reverberating buzz, like a million bees—seemed deafening in the wind tossed night, and the flare of light was spectacular. The boys looked on in amazement as their fire seemed to take hold, the on-shore wind pushing the flames and smoke toward the tower.

'It's too close to the tower,' said a worried Jack, but his voice was lost in the crackle of the flames.

The Guy disintegrated and the paraffin was consumed, and soon the dampness of the wood began to tell on the fire. The flames—initially high—began to sink, the branches failing to catch.

'It's going to go out,' said John, not quite knowing if he was pleased or disappointed. He glanced down the hill, sure that lights and a hurrying crowd of angry grown-ups would soon be on the scene.

Joe could see John was right. The Guy had not generated sufficient heat to ignite the green wood and the wind on the hilltop was more of an enemy than a friend. He cast about him for dry tinder. A nicker from within the tower gave him an idea. He rushed to the tower and pushed open the door, which yielded easily. It was dark inside, and he struck a match to get a quick glance around. Two horses were tethered in stalls with hay nets suspended from hooks, and plentiful straw to make soft and comfortable bedding. To one corner, a flight of stone stairs led to the upper floor. A tower of six or seven bales of dry straw stood just inside the door. That was all Joe needed. The match in his hand curled, the flame perilously close to his fingers. He dropped it on the floor, reaching by memory for the straw bales and hauling one through the door. Straw bales are heavy and cumbersome, but Joe had been handling them for years and he carried it quickly to the fire and thrust it into the gap where the stuffed doll had been. It caught, and the fire renewed itself instantly, the flames curling round the base of the bundle and reaching out into the more substantial wood. Soon snaps and crackles denoted that the timber was well alight. The breeze snatched embers from it and tossed them away. By the light of the fire the tower looked stolid and imposing, just as it must have done centuries before when occupied by Winter ancestors. The boys, dazed by their feat and awed by the trouble that was sure to come of it, looked as one down at the village, half expecting to see it as it would have been in Jacobean days—a collection of hovels lit only by tallow, the church new built, the graveyard empty, themselves only a glimmer of a premonition.

'It's a beacon,' said Joe, summoning more confidence than he felt because the fire was an enormous entity now, raging with heat, a white ball of incandescence with bright shards detaching themselves and rising up, and a plume of black, acrid smoke that seemed to follow him wherever he stood on the fire's periphery. He surveyed the coast to north and south, and the place across the firth—invisible except in his mind's eye—where the Scottish coast mirrored their own. Of course, no answering fire showed. In truth, he had not expected that. What he *had* expected was a surge of delighted villagers swarming up the hill and clamouring to be part of the Forresters' triumph. Where *they* had given up, *he* had prevailed. He had expected their congratulations; that somehow mothers would produce cake and sweets, and that fathers would begin to set off fireworks; that he would be lauded and—most of all—that his father would be proud. But the village was quiet and dark. It looked like his victory would go unremarked.

Then, from the stable behind them, a high, dreadful, scream rang out. The boys rushed to the stable door and flung it wide. All of the straw on the floor was alight, a choppy sea of flickering flame. The horses lifted their feet to avoid the fire in a terrible dressage, their eyes rolling. They skipped from side to side, cannoning against the flimsy partitions of their stalls, kicking out with their hindlegs but only adding shards of wood to the fire. The hay nets burned like braziers, too close to the animals' noses to be avoided. The screams of the horses went on and on. The boys stood rooted, aghast.

The door at the top of the stone stairs opened and Agnes appeared in her nightdress, her eyes terrified, as first one horse and then the other was consumed in flame. The whole of the stable was on fire—the floor, the partition and the racks where tack was stored, the purlins that supported the floor above—a cube of blue and purple and caustic orange. The stack of bales near the door was also alight but burning more slowly because it had less air to feed it. The heat was overpowering and the smoke so thick that they lost sight of the child.

Joe and John backed away. Their instinct was to run, to go home via the dunes and Winter Farm, and deny all knowledge of—all connection with—the fire. They could say they had … their frantic minds thought of scenarios, things they could legitimately be doing *away* from the hill that could have occupied them and made them forget the time, for by now it must be well past their six-thirty curfew. Both boys took to their heels, running past the tower on the side opposite to the fire and heading for the woods on the far side of the hill. They were a good way through the trees before they realised Jack was not with them. They looked at each other in horror, half driven to run on, half persuaded they ought to go back and find Jack—a mire of doubt and indecision that effectively prevented them from doing anything at all.

Then, through the trees, they saw him—little Jack, six years old, dragging behind him what at first they thought—impossibly—was the stuffed effigy, but which they then made out was their cousin Agnes. She was limp and singed, as was Jack, his clothes charred and his hair a frizz of scorched ends. His face was illuminated as Moses' must have been having glimpsed the glory of God, but smeared with soot and snot and a spigot of tears that would not stop. He hacked and coughed and eventually made himself sick, but after that he was surprisingly calm— perhaps in shock. Agnes was insensible, drooping from Jack's arms like an outsized doll.

Behind them, the flames engulfed the pele tower, a beacon indeed. The glass of the windows shattered in the heat, the ancient beams creaked and disintegrated into iridescent ash. In the far distance, they heard the wail of fire engines that must have been summoned from the harbour town.

Joe said, 'No one will notice we're gone for a while. We must think. We have to come up with a plan.'

John, still traumatised by the burning horses, said, 'You'll have to own up.' His voice was high and thin. He was thirsty—oh, so thirsty—and licked his lips with an arid tongue.

'*I'll* have to?' queried Joe, turning on his brother. 'We're *all* in on this.'

'*You* built the fire. *You* lit it. It was all *your* idea. And you … you were the only one who went in there, so you must have set the place on fire,' John retorted. Then he burst out, 'Oh God, those horses. They burned up like … they burned up. It smelled like meat.' He turned and retched onto the ground, a spume of bile to add to Jack's.

'It was a spark, that's all,' said Joe, plucking lies from the air. In the darkness, he rubbed his finger and thumb together. He could feel the ghost of the matchstick between them, the sting of the fire as it had reached his fingers just before he had dropped it. His face felt hot and tight, shrunken by heat and panic and shame. 'It must have blown through the door …'

'That *you* left open,' concluded John bitterly, wiping his mouth with the back of his hand.

'Agnes is hurt,' said Jack. 'I think she breathed in smoke.'

Joe said, 'Why did you have to bring her, Jack? How are we going to explain *that?*'

'It was all burning,' said Jack confusedly. 'She would have died.' He looked down at the child as she lay on the leaf litter of the woodland floor.

They all looked at the little body curled up by their feet.

'We could just leave her here,' said John. 'Someone will find her.'

'No,' said Jack, surprisingly firm. 'She needs a hospital.'

Joe squatted down so he could look Jack in the eye. 'Look, Jack,' he said with forced patience, 'we're going to be in trouble. *A lot* of trouble, if they find out we lit the fire. The bonfire, I mean. The fire in the tower was an accident. Nobody's fault.' He threw a glance over his shoulder at where John loitered in the shadow, waiting for a contradiction, but none came. John was sullenly silent. 'So, what we need to do is think of something that will mean no one will suspect us … I mean, no one will think it was us. And …' he took hold of Jack's shoulders and gripped them tightly, '… when we've thought of something we must stick to it no matter what. Do you understand? We can *never* tell the truth. Otherwise, they'll put us in prison. Do you understand, Jack?'

Jack wiped his streaming eyes with his sleeve. His lower lip began to tremble but he nodded solemnly. 'Yes.'

'So,' Joe stood up again and began to pace around the little clearing. 'Let's think. We were …' he cast about, trying to grasp ideas, but ideas had never been his forte.

It was John who came up with it. 'We were on the dunes, building a den. How about that? And we lost track of the time.'

Jack nodded, but uncertainly. 'And Agnes was helping us?'

'No,' snapped Joe, but adopted John's suggestion immediately. 'No, because she's *obviously* been in the fire and so have you, so … let's think. We were on our way home from our den and we saw her running away from the fire …'

'But that wouldn't explain why Jack's clothes are burned,' said John mulishly.

'No, all right.' Joe pondered again. 'We were on our way home and we *saw* the fire, and Jack went in and saved Agnes. That's the truth, more or less, isn't it? And the important thing is that we didn't see anyone else. Right?'

Agnes began to stir. Jack said, 'But what if she remembers?'

Joe gathered her up. 'Let's hope she doesn't,' he said.

When they were halfway down the hill John said, 'We'll have to build the den, or they won't believe us.'

'Oh, all right,' said Joe.

~

The cause of the fire at the pele tower was quickly established—a spark from the fire on the grass nearby had ignited the straw of the stable. *Who* was responsible was never proven. The lady in residence, the tragic victim of the fire, was thought by some to have been the author of her own demise, having begun a fire that had got out of hand. It is wrong to speak ill of the dead but folks *did* criticise her for her carelessness. A post-mortem, however, established that the victim had been asleep in her bedroom at the time of her death not—as would be expected— struggling frantically to save herself and her granddaughter, not to mention the poor horses. Evidence was provided that Mrs Broughton-Moore had spent the day with friends—her granddaughter also— assisting with the Christmas decorations at a stately home that would be open to the public for the festive season. Afterwards there had been cocktails, which the victim had imbibed liberally. Her car was found on the road, its petrol tank empty, and it was concluded that she and the child had walked the four or so miles back to the pele tower where, exhausted—and in Mrs Broughton-Moore's case, intoxicated—they had fallen asleep.

The child was of no use to the enquiry. She could be persuaded to say very little indeed, but what was coaxed from her confirmed at least this much: yes, she had been with her grandmother and yes, they had to walk home and yes, they had been very tired.

The Forrester boys' story was never questioned. It was not questioned by their mother, who could not ignore the reek of smoke that permeated all the boys' clothing nor the almost empty box of matches that she found in Joe's pocket. It was not questioned by their father, who found his old paraffin can amongst the rubble of the pele tower.

Chapter Thirty-Nine

The weather remained wet, every day bringing rain in some form—either steady downpour or drenching drizzle. Sometimes wind added itself to the mix, driving the rain horizontal so it spattered onto the windows like a turbo-charged shower. The track in front of the cottages was a constant pool those days, and I had abandoned my stout walking boots for neoprene wellingtons.

The night of Ivaan's visit had been a sort of watershed in my relationship with Hugh *and* with Jamie. We all knew things between us hung in a fine balance. Hugh had forgiven me for my wrong-headedness but we had not agreed to pick up where we had left off. He must have guessed that, in the interim, my friendship with Jamie had changed. It *had* changed—although Hugh could not know it—that very same evening. Jamie's kiss had been the natural and inevitable outcome of all that had gone before, including our scratchy beginning, our instinctive affiliation over books, his little acts of kindness and our mutual attraction. That, too, hung in the balance. Since that night I hadn't seen much of Jamie. Perhaps he was waiting for me to make a sign, waiting to see if things with Hugh would recommence.

I remained caught on the horn of the dilemma that had plagued me from the first moment I had recognised my feelings for Jamie. In so many ways Hugh was my ideal partner. He existed outside of Roadend. He moved in my milieu. He was sophisticated and well-travelled. He was immersed in his own career that would allow me plenty of scope and space to pursue my own. All of these things were true and yet I felt that, in many ways, I did not know Hugh at all. Our relationship had been a thing of make-believe, on my part. I had subsumed myself into Rowan and Rose and enjoyed Todd, vicariously through Hugh. In that respect he had not been much more than a vehicle into whom I had integrated my iteration of Todd.

Jamie, in contrast, had hardly had a chance to live his life. He was unworldly, untravelled. He must have so much that he wanted to do once he was released from the shackles of his father, but how long might that be? When it did finally come about, in all probability a steady relationship would not be high on his agenda. He would want to play the field, and who could blame him? On the other hand, he might be fixed here in Roadend for the rest of his life, as his father and grandfather had been before him. Yes, we both liked books, and that was a strong connection, but—and it pains me to say it—books are not life.

All these things my reason repeated, a rational exegesis of the situation before me. My heart spoke also, irrationally, in lurid flushes and yearning dreams. Also vociferous was a voice that told me I had made enough false starts with unsuitable men already. My past failures indicted me: I was not cut out for monogamous relationships and had better give them up.

Last of all, it seemed that evening had marked a turning point between Jamie and Hugh. Their joint effort to rescue Bob—they had acted uncannily as one—and then that parting embrace I had witnessed spoke to a nascent, budding friendship that could mean so much to both of them. There would be a poetic justice if Hugh and Jamie could heal the rift that had swallowed their fathers whole; and it might, in time, extend to John Forrester's children.

It seemed as though we had all seen the sense in leaving things in abeyance for a while. I saw Hugh infrequently, out on the Moss or flying overhead in his helicopter. Mary, who became quite a frequent visitor to my house, told me the legalities of tying up his father's estate required Hugh to travel to London, and further afield. She said he was committed to the on-going management of the estate and would probably remain at Winter Hall for the majority of the time. He had offered her a home there, if she wished it. Caroline, she thought, would return to Canada. The summer months, when others of her set were in the country, drawling and guffawing and doing whatever the tweedy set do—my words, not hers—had been enjoyable to her, but she had found the winter rather lonely. Mary threw me a glance when she recounted this fact, and I felt bad. Caroline and I might have forged an alliance, had I not begun things in such a stupid way. For herself, Mary did not know how long she would remain at Roadend. It was clear to everyone that her presence had unsettled Joe to a severe degree; almost every day now I heard a rumpus coming from the cottage next door. I gathered Joe's alcohol consumption had increased. More than once he managed to slip out behind Jamie's back and I was called upon to help in the search. He was found on these occasions to be attempting to scale the wall of the pele tower or—as I had—forcing the gates to Winter Hall. As much as Mary loved being close to Jamie, she had to admit her being there made life difficult for him. When Jamie joined us for a cup of tea or a bite of supper, I think we were all conscious of the party wall that divided my cottage from the one that Joe occupied. The bruises on my neck had faded but the memory of Joe's assault on me remained raw and I had reapplied the duct tape to the loft hatch and kept the little step ladder wedged under the handle of the cellar door.

I spent the rest of January and the beginning of February writing diligently—the story of the fire at the pele tower. There was no doubt in my mind that I had hit on the truth of it. However the boyish voices across the dunes had come—echoing from the past, or simply a distortion of shifting shingle and whiffling grasses—Joe's own words were incontrovertible. I wrote the narrative with a heavy heart, dredging it up as one exhumes a corpse. My overall impression was one of tragedy and sadness—for Rowan, of course, and for Mrs Harrop—but also for the boys themselves, who were at least equal victims of that terrible accident. The confluence of truth and fiction still confounded me. The boundary between my story and history remained nebulous in my mind, the chicken-and-egg of it confusing me. I just abandoned myself to it, allowing the story to spew forth onto the screen, which it did spontaneously. I was powerless against its vital integrity. It was sacred to me; it had its own truth, now.

All in all, I felt my story was virtually complete. The dramatic climax—the tragic death of Rowan—provided an all-too-sufficient reason for the Forrester boys to be ever afterwards embattled. Their guilt over their deed—however accidental, however young they had been—would skew their relations with each other to an extent that Jack would eventually leave Roadend altogether. Todd's deliberately divisive will would be the death knell between the remaining brothers, who were already at loggerheads. I had previously described the impact Mary's coming had upon the brothers' relationship. All I needed to do was to cover the period between that and Todd's demise, the reading of his fatally divisive will and its fallout. It would make for an unhappy ending, which is rarely well-received by readers and does little to guarantee a book's commercial success. But there it was. I could see no other endpoint—no uchronia—to the Forresters' story.

The package from my agent had been a dossier of offers from various publishers, all of whom were keen to secure the rights to the finished book, some of whom added film rights and foreign translations to sweeten the deal. For all that I had got wrong during my winter at the cottage—my blindness and blunders, my reckless liaison with Hugh—the book, at least, looked likely to be a success. The taste of this in my mouth was like nectar. What a shame that it could never be published. I would finish it though. I felt I owed that to Roadend, to the Forresters and to myself. In any case, the story was such a distinct entity now, with its own life and energy, I knew nothing would silence it except the words "The end."

In the beginning of February, I duly paid Mrs Harrop the two months' rent that would bring my tenancy at the cottage to an end. I was due to leave at the end of March. The book might be unpublishable but there was much work to do on it before I could lay it to rest, and the peace and quiet of Roadend would be the perfect place for the gruelling weeks of rewrites and edits that I had in front of me.

My "outing" changed Mrs Harrop's attitude towards me; nothing, now, was too much trouble but, at the same time, she was sneeringly derisive of what she called "London ways." Subtly, my grocery bill increased and my weekly grocery box began to include all kinds of provender she clearly believed were staples for residents of the metropolis but which I had absolutely no use for. I found tins of caviar, copious quantities of quinoa, tofu, kefir and, once, the most over-ripe and sorry-looking avocado I have ever seen.

Mrs Ford—whose studio I had *still* not visited—came to see me, proffering a copy of *The House of Shame*, and a pen, so that I might sign her book. 'If only we had known,' she said. 'I've seen the film ever so many times. That poor girl, buried away in that lonely old house … where *did* you get the idea for it?'

I invited her in and we sat at the table discussing my characters as though they were real people, my heroine's dilemma as terrible to Mrs Ford as it had been to me while I had conjured it, our horror of the villain so vivid we both shrieked at the idea of him. When she left, I felt as though I had spent the afternoon with a group of much-loved friends.

One thing I chalked up as a win. I felt my relationship with my brother was getting back on track. I heard from him in early February, again using his work email address. He implied—but was not so disloyal as to state outright—that Bianca had pushed him away so far that he was seriously considering whether their marriage should continue. The question of children was raised. Their childless state had been Bianca's choice that now Daniel regretted. In regard to the suggestion I had made at New Year, Daniel indicated yes, he thought it would be a good thing for me to relocate myself in the vicinity of Oxford, where he himself lived. He said he would look out for properties if I would give him an idea as to my budget. From that time, we exchanged frequent messages, generally related to my prospective house purchase but occasionally touching on more personal topics as we tested the change in the ground that had kept us apart. It felt good to have him back in my life, but I was determined that our rediscovered connection should not be limited to emails.

Chapter Forty

In the last week of February, we had a storm. Heavy rain was forecast, on top of all we had already endured. The drainage channels in the Moss were already at capacity, the wide plank bridge submerged and the boardwalk under threat. The stream in the village that ran under the little humpbacked bridge and past the play area was choked with silt and tangled debris from further upstream. For safety reasons the play area had been locked. When the tide was high the water backed up the stream in the village, threatening some of the cottages with flooding. Sandbags appeared along the main street. The water from the stream splurged onto the beach in a torrent that had scoured a channel, both deep and wide, into the shingle, perilously close to the base of the bluff. Every day, Jamie told me, there were further falls of mud and debris. He and a party of workers erected barriers, sealing off that end of the beach. Hugh was amongst them, and I detected, between them, a kind of truce, a developing comradeship I thought would do them both good. I liked the way Hugh allowed Jamie to take charge of the project, directing the men and deciding where and how the barriers should be secured. This did nothing to aid my conundrum, however. Hugh's tact spoke as many volumes as Jamie's unassuming authority and instinctive understanding of the job. I was proud of both of them. Fond of both of them. But I was not in love with both of them.

The storm was predicted to hit by Friday evening. Olivia messaged me to ask if I would like to relocate to their house for the duration, as power was likely to be cut and it was not inconceivable that all of the Winter cottages would flood.

I considered her kind offer, while I watched black clouds boil up across the sky and heard the wind strengthen.

When I heard Jamie's quadbike come stuttering down the hill, I went out to consult with him. Rain hit my waxed coat like pellets so I had to shout to make myself heard. Already, the sky was preternaturally dark although it was not much later than three o'clock.

'Do you think the cottages will flood?' I yelled. 'Olivia wants me to go over to their place.'

'If you're going to go, you should do it now,' he shouted back. 'The boardwalk will be under water in an hour, I'd say. I won't be chancing it again on the bike. The water is already almost up to the boards.' He looked at the lake that now constituted our lane. 'You won't get the MG through this, I shouldn't think. Of course, I'll take you if you want.' He indicated the bike. 'This will get us through, and up the track.'

We stood and looked at each other, blinking away the rain that stung our eyes. Unlike me, he wore no coat, just a thick guernsey that seemed impervious to the rain. His hair was almost always tied back these days, but a tendril had come loose and I had to stop myself reaching up and pushing it behind his ear.

'*You* won't …' I began.

He shook his head. 'I'll have to stay, for Dad's sake. God knows what he will take it into his head to do if I'm not here to stop him.' He lifted a bag from the back of his bike. It chinked, suggestively. Jamie gave me a shamefaced smile. 'His panacea for all ills,' he said. 'I feel terrible, but dosing him up to the eyeballs is the best way to keep him where I can see him.'

I made a sympathetic moue.

Suddenly Jamie said, 'What about the Hall? Mum would be happy to have you and, from there, you could check back here from time to time. I suppose …' his eyes slid away and he stared at a spot in the middle distance, ' … I suppose it's time you made up with Hugh, if you're going to.'

'Made up with him?'

'Well,' his forehead furrowed, 'he hasn't been around for a while, has he? *I* thought, once you found out he was … you know …'

'Rich?' I supplied.

He nodded. 'Yes. I thought that would cause things to move forward.'

I tilted my head to one side. 'You thought I was that shallow?' We held each other's eyes for a moment, then I shook my head, dislodging rain from my hood. 'Things moved backwards, instead. You see, I thought he was married. To Caroline. I think he's forgiven me but …'

'Is it … is it over, between you?' He looked at me then, with a light of such hopefulness in his eye that it penetrated the rain, the brooding cloud, the premature night.

I made my decision. 'I'm going to stay,' I said. 'Sit out the storm here. I'll move as much upstairs as I can. There are candles in the cellar, I think, and I have the log burner, so if the power goes out for a few hours I'll be OK.'

'I'll come over, as soon as Dad's settled, shall I?' Suddenly the storm, the prospect of a power cut and even of a flood, seemed irrelevant to Jamie.

'All right,' I said. 'Yes.'

I splashed back to my gate. The water was halfway up the garden step. I pushed my hood down to eliminate the exaggerated sound of the rain on its waterproof surface. Still the sound of water was everywhere, puckering the puddles, surging through the rills, splattering on the roof and gurgling down the downspouts. I looked out across the Moss. It wallowed in water, its grasses saturated, bent and beaded. The little canals were full to the brim, the tannin-coloured water carrying blobs of foam, sticks and scum along. Wind scoured the Moss and boomed over the roof of the house, making the overhead electricity and telephone cables sing a shrill, discordant note.

I messaged Olivia, thanking her for her offer but declining it, then spent an hour or so emptying the lower kitchen cupboards of their contents and stacking everything along the worktops. I carried the sofa cushions upstairs and lifted the carcasses onto some crates I found in the yard. I tied the curtains and stuffed them onto the window ledges so they were away from the floor. The dining room chairs were piled on top of the table along with the contents of the sideboard but there was nothing I could do about the table or the sideboard themselves, or the carpets. Everything electrical was carried upstairs, including the television.

Then I remembered the candles. I opened the cellar door and ventured down the stairs. When I got to the bottom my foot disappeared into six inches of oily water. Things were floating around on its surface—the white wings of an instruction manual, a bottle of carpet shampoo, some sponge scourers that had escaped from their packet—and a whole flotilla of empty whisky bottles that must have floated down from Jamie's end of the cellar. From up there, through the throat of darkness, I heard splashing and saw the dim gleam of a torch beam.

'Jamie,' I called. 'Is that you?'

'Yes,' he replied. 'The electricity consumer units are down here. When the water reaches them, they'll trip, but before that there'll be sparks. We need to remove anything combustible, like turpentine or gas canisters. Can you see anything like that? And then anything flammable, like paper or cardboard the water won't have soaked already.'

I looked around me. There was some decorating paraphernalia on one of the shelves including a bottle of white spirit, and, further back, a bottle of butane for a gas barbecue.

'Yes,' I said. 'There's a gas bottle. I'm not sure I can lift it.'

'That's OK.' I could hear the swish of water as he came through the cellar towards me; even through my anxiety, I was conscious of a little thrill of pleasure at his approach.

Then, there he was, bent half double, as I had seen him that first day in the hen coop. He carried a powerful torch in his hand. The water lapped round the shins of his wellingtons, the bobbing bottles nudging at him like importunate ducklings. I pointed out the things I thought ought to be removed and he began to gather them up.

'I just came down for the candles,' I said, looking ruefully at my stockinged feet and my jeans, which were soaked to the knee. 'Do you think we'll flood?'

He shrugged. 'Who can say? This,' he indicated the water at his feet, 'is not uncommon. It happens every few years. I told Walter, when he installed the new electricity supply, that it ought to be put in much higher up, but he wouldn't have it.'

'I'm surprised,' I said. 'They must have quite a bit invested in this place, and I guess it brings in a reasonable income.'

'The Harrops don't own it,' said Jamie, seizing the gas bottle. 'It's all Hugh's now.'

'Hugh's?'

'That's right. Mrs Harrop manages it for him, but we're all here by His Lordship's grace and favour.'

I stepped to one side as Jamie passed me on the stairs. 'Even your place?'

'Yep. Lucky, weren't we, to be allowed to stay on?' He pressed his lips together into a hard line. For all that he might be forging a hesitant friendship with Hugh, I could see Jack's philanthropy towards Joe—however well meant—still rankled.

I grabbed the candles off the shelf and followed Jamie up the stairs. He carried the cannister and the other things through to the yard and then returned to rinse his hands at the sink.

'It's a lake out there in the yard,' he said. 'Have you seen? The water comes down the hill. That's how it gets in the cellar. Sorry about the wellies.' He looked down at the little pool of water around his feet. 'I think, in a few hours, a few wet footprints will be the least of your worries.'

I waved his apology aside, pointing at the water dripping from my jeans. I knew I ought to go and get changed. 'You do know,' I said cautiously, 'that Jack bought your father out as an act of kindness, so the farm would all remain in Forrester hands? Isn't it what any brother would do?'

Jamie dried his hands. 'How would I know?' he retorted, but then he mastered his resentment. 'Yes, of course,' he said. 'But Dad didn't see it that way. He saw it as a failure. Just another failure to add to the list.'

Privately, I wondered if Jack had intended the gesture as an act of forgiveness—for the fire, for the falling out, or even as an apology for having walked away. I said, 'Whatever Jack's motivation was, Hugh is as much a …' I did not want to say "victim" because it would feed into Jamie's sense of being hard done by. '…is as much caught up in it as you are,' I amended. 'Whatever happened between your fathers, you two don't have to continue it.'

'No, I know.' Jamie regarded me. 'He's actually a nice bloke, isn't he?'

'Very nice,' I said, adding—rashly—'like you.'

Then, with a pop, the lights went out. Only the glow of the log burner lit the kitchen. Jamie launched himself towards the cellar but came back soon afterwards to report there must be a general power cut as the water was nowhere near the consumer units.

I brought some cold cuts, fruit, cheese and salad from the fridge and cobbled together a meal while Jamie waded back to his place to check on his father. We ate by candlelight in the kitchen, polishing off half a bottle of Pinot I had also found lurking at the back of the fridge.

'How's your book coming?' asked Jamie, helping himself to grapes.

I hardly knew how to reply. 'I have offers for it,' I said slowly, 'but I don't think I can publish it.'

'Why not?'

I chewed, choosing my words. 'Truthfully,' I said at last, 'I'm rather afraid of it—of the power of fiction. The wonderful thing about being a writer is that *you* are in control. *You* create, *you* describe, *you* dictate … but with this, I have hardly felt in control of it at all.'

Jamie sipped his wine. In the candlelight, I could see red and gold filaments in his hair, and the golden flecks in his eyes were like embers. He knew there was more, and he waited patiently until I got it out.

'And then there are all the reasons I explained to you on Christmas Day,' I said at last. 'It's too close to the truth, too close to home. And really, I feel I've cheated. It isn't *my* story, it's other people's and … I don't think they'll like it.'

Jamie put his knife and fork down. 'And do you remember what I told *you* on Christmas Day? I told you that a little perspective can't harm people. The problem is, we're all stuck in our own shoes, looking at the world through the window of our own eyes. Isn't that why we read books, you and I? To get a chance at a fresh point of view? To experience vicariously the things we may never encounter in real life, like war and love and flying on a dragon?'

'I haven't given up on love,' I mumbled.

'And I truly hope to ride a dragon. But can you see what I mean? Things get ingrained in us: resentments, entitlements, patterns of failure and the expectation of success. Chips on our shoulders and silver spoons in our mouths—they're passed on down the generations and nobody knows their origins and the idea of breaking free of them never occurs. We just imbibe them with our mothers' milk. Forresters are farmers. That's the mantra I was brought up on. Mrs Harrop has never let go of the idea that, as a Winter, she's *better* than everyone else. History repeats. But what if there's a different way? What if there's an exit to that maze but we've never spotted it? Being able to see ourselves at that one step remove— through a writer's eyes, for instance—might just be the catalyst we need. *Any* alternative version is worth seeing, don't you think? Even just one tiny twist of the kaleidoscope can be enough to change our view of the whole picture. Sure, it might be wrong—way off the mark—but so what? If it is, we can dismiss it and move on to the next book. But what if it's *right?* Just imagine what a *gift* that could be! When Dee, *when* can too much perspective, too much insight, too much empathy be a *bad* thing?'

'You just want to read the book,' I said with a laugh.

'I've been promised a signed first edition,' he replied.

It was on the tip of my tongue to tell him the truth, that the story was *his* story, the tale of his family, but my courage failed me.

Chapter Forty-One

I cleared away the plates and Jamie went out to check on the water levels. The gust of wind as he opened the door blew out the candles. I tuned my ear to the weather; stronger wind, I thought. In answer, something in the yard behind the house shifted and the gate that divided my yard from the one next door began to flap and bang. I guessed its catch had broken loose. I found my Neoprene boots and put them on, struggled into my coat and went out into the dark box of the yard. Immediately, the hood of my coat filled with wind and billowed out behind me like a sail. The wind caught my hair and writhed it into snakes around my head. It whipped across my eyes and got caught in my lips. The narrow passageway behind the houses was like a wind tunnel. The gate flailed like a mad thing, slamming itself again and again against the wall and then against its frame. I caught it, but another volley yanked it away from me, giving me a glimpse down the row of cottages. There was no light at all and yet I felt sure I saw a stooped figure, pressed close to the wall, moving away from me. I called Jamie's name, but my voice was snatched away.

I secured the gate using the bolts top and bottom, and then let myself out of the yard on the other side. I battled my way around the house. The growl of the wind was thunderous, the rain like sharp stones. Whoever had made his way behind the cottages should have emerged by now. I should have been able to see him on the lane, but the track in front of the cottages was empty of everything but water. Jamie had taken a torch with him but I couldn't see its beam.

I made my way back inside.

'There you are,' said Jamie. He must have come in by the front way as I had gone out by the back. He had removed his boots and coat and had opened another bottle of wine.

'Jamie, did you check on your dad?' I asked, wiping the water from my face. 'Only, I think I just saw someone at the back. Could he have got out?'

Jamie reached for his coat. 'The old bugger's capable of anything, you know that,' he said, fumbling with the zip. 'He can crawl through roof spaces if he has to. I'll go and check. You sit tight.'

'If he's gone, come and get me. He can't have got far.'

It didn't take long for Jamie to return. 'You were right,' he said grimly. 'The old coot's gone walkabout. Come on.'

Quickly, I led Bob upstairs and shut him in my bedroom, lest the water come in whilst we were out looking. Then I secured my hood as well as I was able and Jamie and I stepped out into the teeth of the storm.

I was struck immediately with the danger inherent in the situation for Joe. The Moss was saturated, more lagoon than land, with submerged trip hazards and areas of gloopy bog, not to mention the steep-sided peat-workings at the far side which, by now, would be full of water. The only saving grace was the plank bridge was under water, so I did not think Joe would have gone that way. The boardwalk was impassable with any degree of safety and anyone who mis-stepped would end up neck deep in the drainage channel. Surely, he would not risk it? But the strongest probability was that he was making his way, again, up to Winter Hall. Jamie must have drawn the same conclusion. He fired up his quad bike, I climbed on behind him and we rocketed through the water of the lane, up the slope and into the trees. At the top I got off and opened the gate.

The wind on the top of the bluff was stronger still, a pulling, pushing, grasping, shoving bully of a thing that would scarcely allow me to stand straight. It howled like a banshee around the ruined tower. The trees of the coppice creaked and thrashed behind us, the wind in their branches a high-pitched scream. Over the brow of the bluff, I could hear the sea. The tide must be right in, hurling itself at the base of the cliff, dislodging mud and scree, hollowing out the earth beneath the lip of the bluff. Rain billowed in thick curtains across the hill, falling slantwise. I narrowed my eyes against it, trying to make out the figure of the old man, somewhere on this blasted heath, as mad and broken as any Lear. The ground was lumpy, tufted with grasses, cratered here and there where perhaps boulders had been excavated for incorporation into the tower. An old man prone on this terrain, soaked to the skin, would be hard to see and would not survive long before hypothermia took him.

Behind me, Jamie had cut the engine, but in truth the onslaught of the storm was so cacophonous I hardly registered it. I felt him beside me, reached for his hand and squeezed it.

'I can't see him,' I shouted, cupping my free hand round my mouth to channel my voice.

Jamie looked wildly left and right, water pouring over his face. Then he reached into an inner coat pocket and brought out his phone. He crouched over it to protect it from the rain while he scrolled through his contacts, then pressed the device to his ear.

I heard him shout, 'It's me. He's out. Have you seen him? He may be … yes. Ok.'

He put the phone away. 'Hugh and Caroline are coming,' he yelled. 'They'll check the grounds on the way. Then, together, we can do a sweep of the tower.' He took my hand again. 'You stay close to me, do you hear?' he shouted. 'And, whatever you do, don't go anywhere near the edge. It isn't safe.'

I nodded to show I understood. While we waited, I looked down at the village. It was hard to make anything out through the scouring rain, but I was surprised me to see there was power down there. The streetlights lit the scene in a lurid, sodium glow. I made out that the playground was under water, a greyish spume bubbling round the swings and the slide. The stream must have broken its banks. I looked again. Yes, the carpark had become a lake and the street was a turgid river from the far side of the church, where the Moss's outlet was, to where the beck would have been. Now, the water burst like a geyser from the watercourse and surged over the road on both sides of the humpbacked bridge, which had been closed off with a makeshift barricade, dividing the village in two. From there it boiled down to the beach where it met the smash and crash of the sea. I could see villagers in hi-vis out in force, a man on the back of a trailer distributing sandbags. Cars—axel-deep in floodwater—

blinked orange eyes and emitted the mournful blare of alarms, their electrics soaked. The lights in the church were on and I knew Marjorie and Olivia would be making endless cups of tea for the bedraggled, beleaguered residents. On the other side of the bridge the pub would have opened its doors to anyone who had been flooded. I scanned the track towards the church to see if I could see Joe—perhaps confused by the new topography of the village—but it was a rain- and wind-lashed wasteland.

Jamie put his arms around me and drew me to him. I could feel the heat radiating from him. The rain flung volleys at us. It was like standing on the deck of a ship in a hurricane. The very ground seemed to shift and plummet beneath our feet. We clung on, each the other's only anchor in an ocean of storm.

Then, from the gates of Winter Hall I saw torch beams, and three figures came into view.

'Mum's come,' he murmured, releasing me. We crossed the sodden turf to meet them.

'No sign of him so far,' said Hugh, looking fixedly at Jamie. I wondered if he had seen our embrace. 'Do you think he would have gone to the village?'

'Not by the boardwalk, I hope,' I said. 'Certainly not this way. We'd have seen him.'

Caroline looked broad and capable, her face a stoic mask against the weather's attack. She wore the same capacious coat I had seen her in on our first encounter. Mine was identical. She gave it an appraising glance and me a sly, narrow look. Mary wore a long, padded coat that must have soaked up more water than it repelled. The shoulders were dark with water but the hood was pulled up and tightly fastened. She looked small and burdened within it, but threw me a brave smile.

'If he was down in the village, someone would have called me,' said Jamie. He surveyed the bleak camber of the hilltop and the rain-soaked

481

monolith of the tower. 'He's here somewhere. He's drawn to the place. I don't know why.'

I knew why, but of course could not say.

'Let's spread out,' suggested Hugh, 'but only two or three meters between us. Keep each other in view. We'll approach the tower but cautiously. We don't want to spook him.'

We all nodded and spread out as Hugh had suggested. The two men took the outer positions in our cordon, Caroline was in the middle and I ended up between her and Hugh. We set out across the heath, up the slope towards its summit, raking the ground with our torches, investigating every hump and shadow for Joe. The higher we got, the more exposed we were to the blitz. Rain like hypodermic needles pierced my skin and stung my eyes. I wanted to turn away, to put my back to it, but there was no escape; the deluge came from everywhere and I had to do my part in the search. All around us the wind was a wild animal, howling and making us stagger, but it was nothing to the thunder of the sea against the cliff. It boomed and bellowed in fury. I was sure the ground shuddered from the impact. I looked up at the tower, a jagged, black buttress against the maelstrom but crumbling, weak and unreliable. I was gripped with a sense of panic. What were we doing out here, where the ruin could collapse upon us at any moment, or a stray blast of wind pick us up and hurl us into the sea? I looked along the line. Caroline strode with purpose and little apparent effort but Mary was bent, hardly able to stagger through the tumult. Beyond her I could see Jamie, gale-lashed, his hands cupped around his mouth. He must have been shouting his father's name. Nobody met my eye until I glanced at Hugh. His smile reassured me, and I soldiered on.

We walked doggedly forward. My trajectory took me to the only corner of the tower that remained and, to an extent I was within its lee. It was blessed relief, just for those few moments, to escape the incursion. I wiped my face with a sodden handkerchief I had found in my pocket and then blew my nose, which was streaming. I cast about in the long grass and brambles at the ruin's base while Hugh, to my right, proceeded along the back wall, his strong torch beam raking the grass and the implacable—surely unscalable—wall of the tower. Caroline, to my left, disappeared around the shorter wall that would have taken her, with Mary and Jamie, to what remained of the tower's precinct and what would then be an unimpeded view of the remainder of the bluff—the grassy sward at the side of the tower and then the gentle slope that terminated abruptly at its perilous edge.

I heard a cry. Mary, I thought. I followed the sound and rounded the wall, feeling again the full force of the tempest. The rain seemed redoubled, added to by the sea spray that rose from below and hurled itself into the fray.

I scanned the ground, the brambles and long grass, the base of the wall, the odd, tumbled block of stone, but could see nothing. I looked at my comrades and then, following their horrified stares, I saw Joe. He was right on the edge of the bluff, about twenty yards from the tower, looking down at the ground in concentration. His coat—a loose, flapping, wholly unsuitable affair—billowed around him. His white hair was plastered to his head. I couldn't see what he wore on his feet but certainly not boots or wellingtons or anything remotely apt. He seemed oblivious to everything, his gaze fixed on a single point on the ground.

It came to me in a sickening revelation that he was in the place where the boys' fire had been. Perhaps, in his crazed, drunken distraction he had imagined himself back there, still a boy, with all his life in front of him until a simple error, a moment of childish distraction altered everything. Almost in confirmation, Joe bent and seemed to lift something and then place it, something we could not see but which, to his eyes, was real.

The fire, I thought. He's building the fire.

But no, I told myself. I made that up! It wasn't real, only a random detail. The fire must have been somewhere close to the tower and I had thoughtlessly identified a spot, but its truth was only lines of type on a page. This ... this must be something else. But *what* else could it possibly be? I was poleaxed by dread and terror, tortured by the appalling certainty that my rendition of that night, the arbitrary placing of the fire just there, had brought Joe to this. Why had I not had them erect it on the other side of the tower? Why, I asked myself miserably, had I allowed them to light the fire at all? I could have cited Rowan, burning the builders' off-cuts and sweepings or … I don't know … the spontaneous combustion of the muck heap? Where there are horses there is *always* a muck heap—Even Rose, I thought wildly, might have decided to force Rowan from Roadend by burning the tower. Any one of those alternatives would have saved us this! I wanted to turn and run, back across the brow of the bluff and down the path to the cottage. I wanted to open my document and erase it all, delete it and consign it to the wastebin. Would *that* be enough to avert this awful aftermath?

I was roused from my panic by movement. Jamie, at the end of our now ragged and appalled chain, waved his hand to indicate we should all remain where we were. Then he took a few, casual paces towards his father.

'Oh Jamie, no!' Mary shouted. I think I, too, cried out. Caroline moved closer to Mary, shielding her as much as possible from the weather but also, I thought, from what might, in the next few moments, occur. Hugh moved slowly to his right, perhaps with the idea that when Joe noticed Jamie he would turn and be distracted sufficiently to allow Hugh to grab him from behind and pull him away from the edge. I moved closer to Mary and Caroline. There was nothing we could do now but watch. My mind was frantic, unknitting the whole fabric of the fire I had created and cobbling together something—anything—different, but the fates were set. The fiction had too powerful a hold on reality and now it would not let go. All the while, Joe remained busy with what must have looked like a senseless, phantom activity but which, to me, was horrifyingly plain. He was lifting wood and stacking it into a conical pyre, every so often stepping back to admire his handiwork.

Jamie and Hugh continued their cautious approach. Jamie's disembodied voice calling, 'Dad! Dad! What are you doing?' came back to us, carried on the wind.

At last Joe saw the boys, Jamie and Hugh. He smiled, as though he had been expecting them, which of course, he had—these two representing, in his addled mind, John and Jack. The thought made me sick to my stomach. Joe smiled and stepped to one side, showing them the fire which, of course, Hugh and Jamie could not see. Still, he was dangerously close to the soft and unsubstantial cliff edge. Still, the squall shrieked and plucked at his coverings. Still, the downpour continued, unrelenting, on his head.

There seemed to be some words exchanged. Jamie gestured at the tower, urging his father towards it, but I knew only too well what Joe would have heard: Jack's anxious enquiry, *'What if she's in there?'*

I knew exactly what Joe's reply would be—a cold, dreadful voice in my head recited it even as I saw the movement of his lips. *'We have Winter Hill to ourselves, just as we should have. It's the only bit of Roadend we don't own. When I have the farm, it will be mine.'*

I could see Hugh and Jamie exchange frowning glances, trying to make sense of this odd—and, to them, irrelevant—assertion. Hugh made a self-deprecating gesture and some reply that in Joe's mind would have stood in for John's retort, *'You won't get the whole farm, you know, Joe.'*

Joe—this Joe, the real Joe, shouted, 'I *will*,' startling Hugh and Jamie into taking a step or two backwards, losing what little ground they had gained. Jamie held up his hands in a placatory gesture. Joe, confused, looked from one to the other, perhaps unsure as to how boyhood John and Jack had metamorphosed into these two grown men, or trying to tell one from the other. I couldn't blame him. Silhouetted as they were against the torrent, soaked to the skin, their hair plastered to their heads and any distinguishing feature in their clothing utterly lost, I would have been hard-pressed myself to say which man was Hugh and which was Jamie. Their size and shape, their bone structure and colouring, their bearing, even some of their facial expressions ... a germ of an idea coalesced in my mind but I thrust it aside.

Joe likewise shook his head, dismissing whatever question had momentarily perplexed him. He puffed out his chest and pointed to it. In my head and perhaps also caught up on the wind and tossed towards me, I heard the words, *'I'm the oldest. But don't worry, John, I'll look after you.'* The storm continued to whir around us, gusting in fierce erratic eddies. It

485

howled like a harridan across the top stones of the tower. Below us, against the clay of the cliff, the sea boomed in reply.

I racked my brain to recall the next move in this chillingly pre-ordained script. Joe looked with great satisfaction at the imaginary fire before him.

He's going to walk round it, I thought. From where I stood it was impossible to tell how close to the precipice Joe was. It seemed likely to me that even if the ground remained solid beneath his feet, the force of the wind might well snatch him away. With a stone in my heart, I watched him circumnavigate the patch of ground. Jamie let out a cry and lunged forward even though, from that distance, he could not possibly have reached his father. Hugh, to my surprise, threw himself not at Joe but at Jamie, seizing his arm in a steely grip. We all looked on in breath-held panic but Joe completed the circuit and came back to his starting position.

'*Well? What do you think?*'

Again, Hugh and Jamie searched each other for some clue. Again, they edged nearer, pretending to examine whatever it was that Joe thought he had built.

Jamie stammered out some words—I couldn't hear what—and took two or three more studied, casual paces towards his father, Hugh alongside him.

Joe would have heard, '*We'll need something dry to start it off with.*'

I think I started forward. I'm sure I shouted out a warning because, oh God! Oh *God!* I *knew,* with a terrible presentiment, what would happen next. I had foretold it.

Joe lifted a hand in a "Just wait and see," gesture. Then he turned and walked off the edge of the bluff.

Jamie yelled and hurled himself forward but Hugh still held his arm. The two grappled for a moment, Jamie struggling to be free of Hugh's restraint, his eyes wide and staring in shock at the empty space on the cliff edge where Joe had stood only a second before. Hugh grappled

Jamie to him, cradling him in a gesture that I found surprisingly affectionate, fraternal, enfolding him in both his capacious arms.

Beside us, Mary gave a strange little mew at the moment of Joe's disappearance and clapped her hands over her mouth, but I thought I read, mingled with her natural horror, some other emotions. Her face, as she observed Hugh and Jamie, was soft, gratified, glad.

Caroline led her quickly away towards the gates of Winter Hall.

Presently Jamie stopped struggling and abandoned himself to his grief. Hugh, his arm anchored to Jamie's shoulder, guided him over the turf to the far side of the pele tower and, I presumed, back to the Hall where tea and heat and dry clothes—and the comfort of family—would be waiting for them.

Perhaps they expected me to follow. I don't know. I remained where I stood, alone, in the accusing storm.

Chapter Forty-Two

I walked home alone, hardly conscious of the excoriating storm as it battered my body. The water in the basin of the lane was almost to the top of my wellingtons and, as I went through my little garden gate, the water had got there before me. It swilled around the bedraggled plants of the garden but it had not got as far as the step into the house.

The house was dark of course, as there was no power, and also chilly because the boiler had stopped working and the log burner had long-since gone out. It was dry, though, which was an unspeakable relief. I stripped off my wet clothes and carried them into the kitchen where I wrapped the crocheted blanket around me and stuffed my sodden gear into the washing machine. I lit just two or three candles and lifted one of the Aga's hotplate covers, praying there would be enough residual heat to boil the kettle. I stood, shivering, while it heated up. I knew I probably ought to go into the cellar and check the water level, but I couldn't face the idea of putting my wellingtons on again and I had a notion that to step into the water might be dangerous.

I blew out the candles and felt my way up the stairs. The storm continued all around but the house next door emanated an eery silence. I had got used to the spooky hubbub through the party wall and without it the atmosphere was, oddly, *more* ghostly, not less. I went into my bedroom where Bob greeted me with his usual rapture. I climbed into bed, and, for the first time ever, invited Bob to come up and lie beside me.

I drank my tea, curled myself around him and fell instantly asleep.

I woke to silence. At least, the weather was silent—an unnerving, exhausted calm. I could hear neither wind nor rain. The absence of weather was like being under water—a hollow, muffled quiet that pressed on my eardrums. The birds, however, were cacophonous, clamouring under the eaves and chittering in the willow trees. At a distance I could hear the squawk of geese as they crossed the Moss.

I got up and opened my curtains. The Moss was a lake, silver-mirrored, reflecting the pale-washed blue of the sky. A watery sun shone down, turning the moisture that beaded the grasses into multi-faceted diamonds. The brightness was so intense it made me squint. As I stood before the window, I realised the radiator was warm. The power was back on!

I had a hot shower and got dressed, and then went out to release Jamie's hens from their house while Bob explored the watery world that our little enclave had become. I felt sure Jamie would have stayed the night at the Hall with his mother. The last thing on his mind would be the hens. They chucked and cooed at me, happy to be out, although their run was more puddle than paddock. I found grain in a bin that I scattered around for them, and in the boxes, three beautiful fresh eggs I decided to use for an omelette. I stood for a while in front of Joe's house, the warm eggs nestled in my palm, looking up at the boarded windows, feeling an immense weight of sorrow for the poor man who had lived within that self-imposed prison, choked with gall for what I could not see in any light other than my own part in his death. Of course, I knew Jamie would carry the burden of guilt, not me. He would be plagued by what-ifs: what if he hadn't come over to my place? What if he had checked on his dad that last time, instead of just the water levels? What if instead of waiting for Hugh and Caroline we had gone straight away to the tower, where we would have seen Joe just that few moments sooner? If I attempted to explain my part, I knew I would not be believed. A coincidence, they would say, an unlucky guess. I hoped—oh, sweet God I *really* hoped—they were right.

I wondered if the police or an ambulance had been called, or if there would be any search for Joe's body. He could not possibly have survived the fall from the bluff. And even if he had, the frenzy of the tide would have snatched his body and broken it. In all likelihood it might never be found.

With a sigh, I went indoors and set about undoing all my flood preparations. As I did so I wondered if it would be a kindness or an intrusion to let myself into Jamie's house and perform some similar tasks for him. With all he would have to do in clearing out Joe's rooms, it might be nice to have his own place set to rights. But I decided against it. That was a job for family, and I was not family.

I made my omelette and ate it at the kitchen table, pondering the previous night, especially the meaning of that odd impression—so fleetingly glimpsed—of Mary's expression as Hugh and Jamie embraced.

I received a text from Olivia, asking if I was OK in the aftermath of the storm, and after witnessing Joe's fall. She said her mum was up at the Hall already and would come and see me if I wanted her to, if I felt I needed someone to talk to. I replied briefly, declining Marjorie's offer, but asking Olivia to forward the information that Jamie need not worry about his hens, I had them covered. As kind as Marjorie was, I knew she would feel obliged to bring religion with her, which would be no comfort to me at all. I wanted to be by myself and, happily, I saw no one at all for the whole of that day as I tried to process events. I felt strangely eviscerated—stunned by the storm and by what I had witnessed, and what I still felt—despite it being utterly irrational—had been my part in the tragedy.

I walked Bob along the willow walk, which was squelchy with decomposed leaves but not too muddy. There was a scattering of broken branches and some of the trees did seem to lean at a more acute angle but other than that they seemed undamaged. The day was beautiful— fresh, vibrant, blithely unaffected by the dark turmoil of the night before. There was a hint of spring. I found a patch of snowdrops in the scrubby undergrowth beneath the willows and saw a bluetit with a beak full of nesting material. The resilience of nature astonished me. Winter was all but over. When spring came I would be gone.

As I returned to the cottage, the thrum of Hugh's helicopter began to reverberate in the air. I stood in the waters of the lane—already receding—and watched it swoop over the wooded hill behind the cottages and over my head and then away, across the Moss towards the smudge of the far distant hills. I wondered if Jamie was with him in the cockpit or if he remained up at the Hall, cosseted by his mother, putting off the time when he must come back and face his father's empty room.

It put me in mind of the day Daniel and I had gone back to Dad's house to begin sorting through things. Even though we thought of it as home, we had both been reluctant to trespass on Dad's privacy. I remembered standing on the threshold with my brother, staring at the envelope of sunshine on the hall parquet, seeing a tumble of motes in a shaft of light that refracted off the mirror, and having to stop myself from calling out Dad's name. Daniel's face had been white, as I suppose mine was, his lips clamped firmly shut but his eyes glassy. Rather than allowing us that few moments to cross the barrier of our grief, Bianca had shouldered past us and marched into the house, trampling any last vestige of our father that might have remained in the dim echoes and flurry of dust.

After my walk I made tea and lit the fire in the sitting room, watching through the window as the lowering sun threw the Moss and the trees into the bright facsimile of flame. Bob, perhaps emboldened by the previous night's privilege, scrambled onto the sofa and put his head on my knee. I stroked it absent-mindedly and thought about what Jamie had said to me the previous evening about fiction, and how it could open a new perspective on an old thing. The alteration might be infinitesimal— the difference between looking through one eye and then through the other—but the inclusion of one extra peripheral thing could change the whole view. I thought about my book. Fiction? History? Biography? Augury? I had no clue. Had I just made good guesses? Put correct flesh on the random bones I had been thrown? Or had I been guided? My man on the dunes, then the boys' voices, then *two* men ... what *was* all of that? My over-active imagination, perhaps? Or something else, something weird and inexplicable by any law I knew of. I might call it psychic hindsight. How else could I explain the sickening scene that had played itself out the previous night on the edge of the bluff? What I did know was the book I had produced had its own vitality, its own truth. Who was I to suppress it? I was reminded of George Orwell's assertion that history is written to suit the needs of the present. There, perhaps, lay the crux of it. In some way that I couldn't possibly explain, something or someone, here and now, needed my story—my version of their story—to be told. If that was the case then I ought to set it free, but the only way I could do *that* was to allow the people most closely enmeshed in it to read it first. And to do *that,* I must finish it.

The Trysting Tree
1978 – 1993

Everything in Mary Forrester's kitchen was exactly as it had been when her mother-in-law had cooked in it, except that Mary had managed to persuade Todd to buy an electric cooker to replace the solid fuel range. Mary cherished that cooker; there wasn't a sprink on the enamel stove-top and the chrome of the hot-plates was as bright as the day it had been delivered. At the same time, she resented it. A cooker was such a prosaic, ordinary thing, a sad icon of her life. How had she been reduced to such drear domestic considerations? But it was the only thing in the whole farm apart from her clothes that she could really claim sole ownership to. The very bed she and Joe slept in had been his parents' beforehand, and the antique bedroom suite likewise.

Sometimes at night, lying awake and staring at the elaborate cornices—so awkward to get at to dust—she felt as though she was her mother-in-law's living ghost, treading the careworn grooves in the cold floors from sink to washing line to ironing board, from cooker to table to sink, an interminable grindstone. But where Rose had managed to spread sufficient cheer to counterbalance Todd's ire, Mary felt she herself had failed. It seemed to her that Rose's mortal remains were not the only thing that had been buried in the churchyard. Any humanity Todd had ever possessed had been interred there too, with Rose. What was left to their children was a scratchy, desiccated and caustic old man who soaked up all the colour and brightness into the dryness of his pumice heart.

Todd allowed his sons to do most of the work, but according to him it was still *his* farm, and he permitted them almost no say in its overall management. It pleased him to countermand their orders and to overrule their suggestions. It appeared to Mary, on occasion, that Todd would choose a course tangential to the one urged by his sons just to make the point that he could. He retained control of the bank account, doling out the boys' wages every Friday with a parsimonious hand.

Upon Joe's marriage Todd had permitted his own things to be moved into the parlour, a room that had never been much used by the family. John and Nancy occupied the second-best bedroom and their increasing brood of children took up all the other first floor rooms apart from the one that was used by Agnes. Jack remained in the attic, where there was another room that could have done for Todd, but *he* was not going to be relegated *there*. As the years went by, and as Todd grew more infirm, Mary rued the decision to set him up in the parlour, where he could rap on the dividing wall with his stick to get her attention; she was *always* at his beck and call. She wished he had been found a room at the back of the house. From *there* his notorious temper, with its lurid and blasphemous connotations, would not have been able to carry over the paddock, across the green and through the thick stone walls of the church to appal and embarrass the handful of worshippers there.

But then, Mary had much to rue and regret. What dreams she might have had when she arrived at Roadend Farm as a bride had quickly been smothered by the weight of work both inside and out. Under the tutelage of Agnes, she had learnt to "cater"—it was an operation on too large a scale to be called "cooking"—for the vast and numerous Forrester appetites. She had to feed not just her husband but both his brothers, Nancy and their three children and Agnes. They all had voracious appetites that needed satisfying on the dot of eight, twelve and five. Supplementary sustenance, in the form of home-made cakes and biscuits, was expected to accompany beverages between meals. Nancy—perpetually pregnant or nursing—was excused domestic duties, and spent her days on the only comfortable chair in the kitchen while her children scattered their toys around the floor and got under Mary's feet. Once

Agnes had inducted Mary in her responsibilities, she had taken a step back from the domestic scene to concentrate on her shop. Six months a bride and Mary found herself producing three square meals a day plus auxiliary pastries, laundering the family clothes and bedding and keeping the house clean, as well as having to answer frequent calls to help on the farm in all weathers, calving, maintaining the kitchen garden and assisting the Veterinarian with vaccinations and castrations.

What other disappointments Mary had to bear can only be surmised. The older he got the more like his father Joe became, inheriting all Todd's cantankerous character. Joe's voice could be heard as far as Low Farm on a still day and his vocabulary was not choice. Those glimmers of a softer, vulnerable Joe Forrester—the Joe who needed Mary—ceased to show themselves once they were wed. He gave no credence to the fact that she knew nothing about farming; he left her to sink or swim. His feud with John showed no sign of being resolved; they harangued each other across fields and argued over the dinner table so that any other conversation was impossible and usually one or all of John and Nancy's children ended up in tears. Todd would weigh in, naturally, stirring the hornets' nest with a kind of sadistic pleasure, and Agnes was not beyond adding her two-penn'orth. Mary was powerless to make herself heard between them.

One evening, after a particularly vitriolic fracas, Nancy and Mary had regarded each other over the decimated meal table. Nancy said, 'You don't marry *a* Forrester, you marry *the* Forresters. You throw yourself, your genes and your dreams into the Forrester soup. And then you drown.'

Mary wondered if Nancy knew how true her words were. Although John was careful, he did not let Mary forget his feelings for her. These seemed to be prompted as much by ingrained sibling covetousness as by Nancy's shortcomings, which were many. Nancy had let herself go. Her hair was often unwashed, she never wore a slick of lipstick and she made no effort with her attire. More than that, she was shrewish, with rarely a kind word for anyone and certainly not for her husband. Each successive child seemed to sap more of her personal entity so that, after three babies, she was little more than an exhausted strew of stained clothing in the chair. She was nothing like the girl John had married, and Mary could see why John felt he had chosen unwisely. As for his being attracted to Mary herself, she was convinced it was part and parcel of everything that characterised the two eldest Forresters. Whatever one did or had, the other must either spoil or steal. Mary would catch John watching her as she hung the laundry on the line, her brown, abundant hair blowing in the breeze, the curve of her breast exposed by her raised arms, and she did not like the look in his eye. She was sure that if Joe were to notice it, he would not like it either. It would add to the various bones of contention that Joe and John felt impelled to return to day after day, year after year. It made her quail, to think of herself caught between those two sets of jaws.

Joe had never been violent towards her, although he could be cruel. His large physical presence, which Mary had once found to be a comfort, had revealed itself only as a form of self-assertion; it was how he dominated and got his own way. On the farm, at the auction, with his father, even with his brother, Mary could see why Joe needed to assert himself—but why with her? If a gentler iteration of Joe could have revealed itself in the bedroom, that might have mitigated some of Mary's unhappiness, but it did not. Joe's efforts in the marital bed were a means to an end; he liked sex and took pleasure in having a wife, but essentially he wanted children, lots of children, like John, but preferably more. And here was the core of the acrimony between Joe and John. It grew more abrasive with every passing month that Mary did not conceive. Five years passed, and John and Nancy added a third son, a fourth child, to their brood, but Joe and Mary remained childless. Gradually, Joe turned his disappointment upon Mary herself.

Her only ally in the house was Jack. Like Mary, he shied away from any involvement in the family acrimony, letting it flow over and around him, or simply leaving the field of engagement altogether. He became an instinctive if covert friend to Mary as she strove to come to terms with the rancorous atmosphere of the household, the burden of work she was expected to undertake and—not least—the surprising speed with which

Joe reverted to Forrester type. Quietly withdrawing from the fray as the brothers berated each other over the table or hurled insults from different rooms, Mary would frequently find Jack already ensconced in her chosen refuge—the hayloft or the byre. Once she came across him seated on a convenient bough of a silver birch tree that stood on the Moss. He would acknowledge her with a nod, shift over to make room, and the two of them would sit in peace while the booming antagonism of the warring brothers, the acerbic interjections of their father and even Agnes' occasional incisive parries raged on.

Without saying a word Jack somehow made Mary's life amongst the rampaging Forresters almost bearable. He would catch her eye as the brothers railed and Todd flailed and Agnes harangued them all, and pass her the peas.

On one occasion he came across her as she stood at the window of the farm office and watched, aghast, as the two brothers tussled in the mud of the yard in the pouring rain, and he simply drew the curtains and placed her in a chair.

'What are they arguing about?' Mary asked, despairingly.

'The den,' said Jack. 'We never finished it. It all goes back to that.'

Mary turned an exasperated eye on him. 'A *den*? Really?'

Jack offered a sad, inscrutable smile. 'Let me bring you a cup of tea,' he said, 'and your book.'

Mary had little time for reading but she nevertheless kept a book handy for those few moments of respite that the day might provide. More often than not she would find the book under the kitchen table, or used as a drip mat, or scribbled on by Johnny or Adam.

Jack brought the tea and placed her book in her hands. 'This is a good one,' he said, 'but I prefer the Barchester books to the Pallisers.'

'You like reading?' Mary said, trying to keep the incredulity from her voice.

He nodded. 'I don't get much time for it though.'

'Neither do I,' said Mary with a sigh, 'more's the pity.'

On arrival at Roadend Farm Mary had placed her books on some shelves in the bedroom, but they had been elbowed out by feed catalogues and machinery manuals and now they lived in a store cupboard under the stairs. She said, 'If you wanted to borrow any of mine, you'd be welcome.'

'Thanks,' said Jack, 'and likewise. Mine are upstairs in my room.' He paused, as though considering. 'It's quiet up there,' he said slowly, 'and people don't think to look there. Mum used to sit in my room sometimes. There's a chair and … the light is nice, through the rooflight. I wouldn't mind at all if you wanted to spend time up there during the day, and you could see if there are any of my books you haven't read. I like American literature, mainly—Faulkner, Steinbeck, Whitman.' Then he left the room.

Mary looked at the place where he had stood, as though she had seen a ghost. Or an angel.

In 1984 Nancy lost a baby, her first miscarriage. Nancy was a distant, detached kind of mother who allowed her children to crawl over her and amuse themselves as they wished without much in the way of correction or even oversight. In truth Mary did more practical caring for the children than Nancy did, but the loss of her fifth child affected Nancy deeply. She took to her bed where she remained all day, eating with disinterest the food Mary prepared and often dissolving into tears.

Todd was seventy-eight, slowing down physically even while maintaining an iron grip on the farm's finances and management. He rose late and liked to have his breakfast brought to him on a tray before taking a dithering constitutional down the village street. His return journey was via the pub, where he drank pints of beer until the landlord called Mary to come and help the swaying old man home and put him to bed for an hour. Then, the sharp percussion of his stick on the wall declared he was ready for his supper.

With two invalids to care for, plus all the John Forrester children to manage, Mary's workload was redoubled and sometimes it was all she could do to wash one lot of dishes before another meal had to be begun. Her legs ached from running up and down stairs to Nancy. Todd's complaints and barked out instructions made her head pound. She was concerned that Joe's recourse to alcohol had increased. These days he went to the pub almost every night after supper, the beer occasionally mellowing his mood but more often bringing him home fired up and spoiling for a fight.

Drink-fuelled altercations between Joe and John were even worse than their sober ones. They sensed their father's deterioration and vied for the day when one or other of them would take over the farm. Neither was above ingratiating themselves with the old man, taking opportunities for confidential confabs during which they inflated their own standing and denigrated their brother's. Joe's approach was to take a bottle of whisky into Todd's room. They would drink to the small hours, "setting the world to rights," sometimes keeping the whole household awake with Shirley Bassey and Frank Sinatra records played unsociably loud. Joe would stagger to bed, drunk and reeking, to prise Mary's legs apart and fumble his way inside her, crooning, 'Make me a baby, Mary. Make me a baby, damn you.'

Nancy recovered sufficiently to wash and dress herself each day and transport herself to the chair in the kitchen, which at least saved Mary the stairs, but buoying Nancy's mood was just as much effort. It wasn't that Mary wasn't sympathetic—she was. She understood only too well what the absence of a baby felt like.

Rarely did Mary manage to sequester herself in Jack's room, to sink into the accommodating chair and let the warmth of the sun filtering through the rooflight ease her fatigue. Now and again though, she occupied that refuge, and was glad of it.

One evening in 1985 the usual animosity between John and Joe over the supper table got out of hand. There was a scuffle. The gravy jug got knocked over pouring scalding gravy onto Harry, aged two.

Mary's temper snapped.

'This has got to stop,' she yelled, leaping up and fetching a cold cloth to put on Harry's burns. 'You two men are dangerous. What kind of example do you think you are setting for these children? John, how will you like it if these boys behave like *this* when they're older? Or, never mind that, only yesterday I caught them at it, Johnny and Adam, throwing their toys at each other. It's already started!'

Joe and John were so surprised by Mary's outburst they floundered, finding no reply. Harry yelled lustily, his mouth an open maw of distress. Nancy dabbed ineffectually at the pool of congealing gravy on the table. Todd tottered in from the parlour, eager to see what had transpired, his eyes bright with vindictive pleasure.

Mary turned her spleen on him. 'You have *encouraged* this, Todd. You set your boys against each other like two dogs. Now look what's happened.' She lifted the cloth to show the angry weal on Harry's arm. 'The fact is, this house is too small for John and Joe, let alone the rest of us poor hapless occupants.'

She sank down on her chair, exhausted by her outburst, and swept her hair off her face. Jack lifted Harry from his highchair saying, 'A dunk in the trough for you, young man,' and carried the bawling child away. The silence in the room was stunning. For a few moments, while Joe and John recovered themselves and the children stared in amazement at Aunty Mary—and even Todd, lost for a riposte, leaned on his stick in the doorway—only the sound of the slowly dripping tap could be heard, a maddening erosion of the peace.

Then Agnes said, 'Mary's right. There are too many people in this house and Mary can barely cope. Let's face it, John and Joe are *never* going to get on. The more distance put between them the better. There's Low Farm standing empty, and Winter Farm could be put right. Walter Harrop's asked me to marry him. If you give us Winter Farm, which by rights should be mine anyway, he'll do the place up. I'll still run the shop, of course.'

The momentary respite came to a cataclysmic end as Joe and John both argued *they* would not go to Low Farm. Todd took a chair and allowed himself to be importuned, first by one and then by the other.

The obvious solution was for Joe and Mary to move down to Low Farm, a small satellite holding at the other end of the village which had a functional if unattractive house and some decent ancillary farm buildings. The grazing was poor, rather waterlogged, but Todd had made good there and believed either of his sons could do the same. The entire poultry enterprise could be moved there, if necessary. Joe could certainly manage it if Jack went with him. It made sense for John and Nancy to stay at Roadend; the house was much bigger; the larger farm would support the bigger clan. It would not be too long before Johnny and Adam could start helping out. Nancy would have to start pulling her weight. Agnes' suggestion that she and Walter Harrop set up at Winter Farm was a good one. Walter was a stockman who worked on a number of different farms in the area. It would not matter that it had no land.

Joe was outraged at the idea *he* should decamp from Roadend. He was the oldest and ought to inherit the family farm. Roadend was his birth right. Already—he said—suppliers and customers were beginning to look to *him* in matters of business. It was galling that the bank account was *still* withheld from him. The egg business had always fallen to John's lot. It— and John—should be transferred to Low Farm. Egg production was all it was good for.

These arguments, couched in different terms, sawed on for weeks, each son taking every opportunity to apprise their father of their opinion. Todd sat back, appearing to ruminate, but enjoying very much the proof that whatever might occur in the future, here and now, *he* was in charge and nothing could be done without his say-so.

Mary hesitantly intimated to Joe that she would like the move to Low Farm; she liked the idea of choosing her own furniture. The house was modern and would be so much easier to maintain. Appealing to what she knew was Joe's greatest vulnerability she suggested that, if she didn't have to run round after the whole family, there was a chance she might be able to make a start on their own. She had no objection to Jack coming with them, she concluded. He was no trouble.

There followed a period of entrenched and vicious warfare. The brothers refused to co-operate on the farm so that jobs which needed two pairs of hands went undone unless Jack stepped in. The atmosphere in the farmhouse was corrosive. Periods of stony silence were split asunder by sudden outbursts of vitriolic invective. Two of John's children started to wet the bed. Nancy's depression returned. The feud ground interminably on, night and day. Attempts at reasoned argument soon descended into pointed accusation and knee-jerk rejoinder and ended in smashed crockery and broken furniture. One evening the entire evening meal— the product of Mary's labour—ended up on the floor.

It was October. The bracken of the Moss was subsiding again, revealing its secret pathways and opening up the trail to the silver birch tree. Mary found herself, coatless, halfway to that refuge without quite knowing how she had got there. The sun had all but set—just a few stray filaments of iridescence stroked the pale sky in the west as the indigo of night crept to meet it from the east. The air was chill. A frost was not unlikely and she thought distractedly of the last few courgettes that remained to be harvested in her kitchen garden. She ought to go back, gather in that last harvest or at least cover the plants with sacking as some protection. She dithered momentarily, her dismay at the spoiled dinner evaporating into the thin twilight air. But distantly, she could still hear the Forresters braying at each other. The fight was still in train. She could imagine the kitchen. No one else would clear up the spilled food, and in all probability the whole family was trampling heedlessly through it, spreading the mess through the whole house. Her heart failed her. She could not go back.

In the clearing, perched on the extended bough of the tree, she found Jack, almost as though he had been waiting for her. He lifted the book he was holding. 'Too dark to read now,' he said.

Mary hoisted herself up onto the branch beside him. 'What are you reading?'

'Thoreau.' He peered at the page, "*I had three chairs in my house,*" he quoted. "*One for solitude, two for friendship and three for society.*"

'Ah!' breathed Mary. 'What bliss! Where did you get your love of books, Jack?'

'Your father,' he replied promptly. 'After you'd gone to university, he invited me in and offered to loan me some books. All I possess, more or less, he gave to me.'

The news gave Mary pause. Her father, nowadays, was a sought-after celebrity, appearing on panel discussions about the arts on Radio 4 and producing a succession of best-selling historical novels. He had recently remarried to an American lady who had been nominated for the Pulitzer Prize. They had bought a villa in Spain. Mary heard infrequently from him, although she had a standing invitation to visit. 'I'm glad,' she said.

They sat in companionable silence, watching the day fade and the night come on. Mary shivered and Jack put his arm round her shoulders. He was as big as Joe but leaner; recently, Joe's muscle had been running to fat—a result, she was sure, of excessive alcohol consumption.

Presently Jack said, 'I'm sorry about the supper, Mary.'

She shrugged. 'It provides an excellent metaphor for pretty much everything I do,' she said. 'Wasted, disregarded ...'

'I don't disregard you,' said Jack in a low voice. 'I see everything you do, Mary. And, what's more, I see everything you are.' She heard him inhale, a deep draught of courage. Then he said, 'Why did you marry Joe? He was never good enough for you, you know, and neither was John.'

She turned her head to look at him. In the gloaming light she could not make out his expression. 'You know about John?'

He lifted his eyebrows. 'I see a lot of things. I *know* a lot of things. But I don't speak of them.'

'John and me,' began Mary falteringly, 'we never ... we didn't ...'

'I know,' replied Jack. Mary had not turned from him and now he laid his forehead against hers. 'You should leave,' he whispered. 'You don't belong here. You should leave whilst you still can.'

The idea that she could just pack her bag and leave had never occurred to Mary. 'I couldn't do that,' she said, leaning back to look at Jack with a better perspective.

'Why not?'

'Because I'm married, and ...'

'It isn't working though, is it? You're a drudge, and all Joe wants is babies. Any local girl could provide those for him. There are farmers' daughters up and down this coast who would kill to be in Joe's bed. Mary, you're made for so much more. Just leave. *I'm* going to.'

Mary gasped. 'You're going to leave Roadend? When? Where will you go?'

He considered. 'I've thought about Europe. I could stay with your dad for a while. But on the whole, I think probably America or Canada. There are opportunities there and,' he flapped the book that he still held loosely in his hand, 'I know the culture.'

'But what will Todd say?' Mary was incredulous.

Jack made a moue. 'I don't care, really. I don't owe him anything and I don't see that he owes me anything either. Joe and John squabble over the farm but really Dad's right, it *is* his farm. He built it up. Why don't *they* do something of *their own?* I know they've worked hard on the farm all these years; we all have. But that doesn't give us any rights over it, I don't think. Other men don't look to their fathers to provide a home and an occupation. They go out and they forge their own. That's what I'm going to do. Soon.'

'Oh Jack.' Mary took his hand. *Walden* fell to the ground. 'I'll miss you.'

'You can still use my room,' said Jack softly, tightening his arm around her shoulders. 'You can move all your books up there and have it as your own refuge.'

Mary found herself crying. Jack lifted his hand to her face and wiped away her tears. 'Don't cry, Mary,' he said, his voice hardly more than a susurration on the little breeze that whiffled the few remaining leaves on the tree. 'Oh, please don't cry.' He began to kiss her tears away, his mouth on her eyes and her cheeks. She tilted her head just a little and his lips met her own, soft and tender. There was a moment when they both paused, poised on the edge of an abyss; the least movement by either would have drawn them back. But neither of them made the move. Mary sighed and opened her mouth. His tongue was beautifully erotic, stirring a creature she had believed long dead in her core. She pressed herself closer to him and he lifted her onto his lap. She sat astride, facing him, pressing her body to his, the gentle flex of the bough beneath them—the tree's vital force—quivering up through him and into her.

~

Todd took the opportunity of Christmas Day—a brief, artificial ceasefire—to announce that he had decided John and Nancy must move to Low Farm. The truce disintegrated; all hell broke loose and another meal was ruined.

John was incensed, importunate, broken, but could not change his father's mind. Early in January the John Forresters moved down the village, taking the entirety of the egg production enterprise with them. Joe watched their departure, triumphant; but without a view of John's disappointed face, his victory was a pyrrhic one. Mary lamented her new furniture, her modern kitchen, the respite from caring for Todd. She had no idea how Nancy would cope, but that was not her concern. From that day on Joe and John never exchanged a civil word. Mary became estranged from her sister-in-law and the clutch of nephews and nieces she had helped to nurture. Jack neither stayed at Roadend Farm nor went with John to Low; he left without a word. Mary missed his companionship, his quiet peacefulness in the hayloft or on the bough of the silver birch tree. She sat and thought of him and stroked her swelling stomach.

Jamie was born in the summer of 1986. Joe was delirious with joy at the arrival of his son, returning from the hospital to batter at the door of the pub, although it was barely ten in the morning. He drank toast after toast to his son while the day wore on, the cows neglected and the farm work undone.

Mary held the child to her breast and delighted in his rosy mouth on her nipple. She had an address for Jack; he was settled in Vancouver and working as a forester for a landowner with vast tracts of both agricultural and wooded land. She would write to him, and to her father of course, with the news.

When she returned to the farmhouse, she found Agnes had been deputising for her but this was not a situation that could continue indefinitely. Agnes and Walter were due to marry in August and all of their spare time was needed to make Winter Farm habitable. Todd had not given it to them, as she had wished, but he had allowed them to live in it rent-free, which was something—the same arrangement, in fact, that John and Nancy had at Low Farm. Jamie was barely a fortnight old before Agnes took off the apron and handed it back to Mary. Of course, without the John Forresters and Jack there were fewer mouths to feed, but Todd, now eighty, needed more and more of her time and care. She did not mind. Jamie was her delight and joy, an easy child who fed and slept and smiled. It was a pity he would not be able to play with his cousins—John and Nancy's children were debarred from their old home.

Agnes and Walter were married in the church, with a wedding breakfast held afterwards at the pub. Judiciously, Agnes seated the John Forresters at a far remove from Joe and Mary, separated by phalanxes of Walter's family. Both brothers worried at their collars and unaccustomed ties, loosening both once the speeches were done. Todd had given Agnes away but he made no speech. Agnes, on-trend with the women's lib movement that had just permeated to the remoter shores of the country, spoke for herself, making much of her Winter ancestry. Once the meal was done both Forrester brothers made straight for the bar, matching each other pint for pint and then scotch for scotch but speaking not one word. Mary did not tarry to see the outcome of this machismo. She took Jamie home.

The following year, 1987, Todd had a stroke, leaving him incapacitated and his speech impaired. His anger at this state of affairs was incendiary. He railed and flung his good arm about in his bed, dribble running down his chin, glaring out of his good eye as Mary washed and dressed him and set him in his chair. She left the newspaper and his spectacles to hand, and a carafe of drinking water, but Todd would have no truck with it. He craned to see out of the window and into the farmyard, to see the cows brought in or taken back out again, the feed lorries coming and going—to maintain his tenuous grasp on the farm. Joe was, at last, given access to the accounts, the bank manager coming in person to deliver the forms and to witness Todd's reluctantly scrawled agreement that Joe should be a signatory.

John did not come to visit his father but only sent a message via Agnes to say that Nancy was expecting again and had been prescribed bed rest in order to prevent another miscarriage. Agnes told Mary that John had lost weight, was hollow-eyed and drawn, and tetchier than ever. 'I don't think he's enjoying having to manage the children as well as the farm,' she said.

Mary suggested to Joe that she should go and visit Nancy, to see what she could do to help.

'You will not,' said Joe, bouncing Jamie on his knee. 'If John wants help, he can ask for it.'

'He's proud,' objected Mary. 'You know he won't come cap-in-hand.'

'More fool him,' said Joe. 'You're not to go.'

Ben, John's fifth child, was born later that year—a difficult labour, but not Nancy's last. Joe began to lobby for another child of his own and was diligent in trying to get Mary pregnant. Mary endured it, sharing his disappointment each month, although she knew by now that Joe could not sire children. Jamie would be an only child.

Agnes and Walter's attempts to produce a family also failed. Agnes' disappointment manifested itself in a strange animosity towards Jamie, who displayed all the Forrester characteristics of form and person; he was big for his age, strong, and could be stubborn. As the only grandchild now accessible to him, Todd doted on him, which compensated a little for the sense Jamie had that he was not enough, for his father at least; Joe wanted *more* sons and made no secret of it.

'What use are you, on your own?' Joe lamented bitterly one evening, in his cups, which was the norm those days. Jamie turned his bottom lip out, but did not cry.

In early 1988 the family received news from Jack. He was married to the daughter of the landowner for whom he had been working. She already had a little girl, Caroline, and would produce another child—Jack's—before the summer's end. Mary read the letter slowly several times, filtering her envy as best she might. Jack's child would be the brother or sister Jamie would never have. And Jack would be the husband *she* lacked. She knew that. Jack had been right, she didn't belong at Roadend; but now that she had Jamie, she could not contemplate leaving. She tried to be pleased for Jack, and said she was, in the letter she wrote in return. She sat at the kitchen table with her Basildon Bond and her Parker, while Joe snored in the chair. She wrote paragraphs of news about the farm and the village, Todd's health, the books she had read and, interspersed with as light a touch as she could manage, information about Jamie's progress. She knew that Jack would understand.

> *Jamie turned one last July and was walking before Christmas. He likes the farm, of course, as all children do, but you can be sure that he has many books about him as well, and I read to him every night. He looks like his father.*
>
> *You will have read Toni Morrison's latest …*

~

One Thursday in April of 1992, Mary walked home from the bus stop where she had waved Jamie away to school. By the time she got home she supposed Todd—now eighty-six—would be awake, and ready for his breakfast, which would have to be fed to him. Many other jobs would occupy her but, for that brief moment, she put them off, enjoying the day. Driving showers in the night had given way to pale sunshine, but a thin wind still bent the stalks of myriad daffodils around the green, their heads continually kow-towed like a group of Far Eastern tourists in Easter bonnets. Sparse stalks of winter wheat shivered across the dun soil. Lambs leapt and sprinted over the tufted pasture.

Thursday was the day in all the week that Mary looked forward to the most. It was market day, and Joe had set off early with a trailer full of yearling calves. He would spend the whole day jawing with the other farmers over bacon and eggs in the auction mart's café and then, later, over pints of beer in the Old Grey Goose in town; he would not be home until late. The man and the lad who helped out on the farm would come and collect their lunch at twelve—a packet of sandwiches each, a flask of tea and some of Mary's famous home baking: rock buns today. She would feed Todd his lunch and give him one of his tablets and that would be him off to the land of nod. Then she would have a few hours to herself, a few precious hours of utter solitude and peace.

Mary entered the farmhouse by the scullery door. The scullery was a mess—its habitual state—the scullery was *farm* as opposed to *house* and did not therefore come under Mary's jurisdiction. It was cluttered with wellington boots and galvanised buckets, coiled up lengths of rope, pairs of wire-cutters and a collection of walking sticks. A row of hooks dangled with the leads of dogs long dead and Joe's overalls and bad weather gear. It smelled overpoweringly of farm—animal and vegetable.

Mary took her coat off and reached for her apron. Without either covering she felt giddy and undressed and she donned the apron quickly and went into the parlour where Todd was awake, his good eye rolling in his head. She dealt with Todd's toilet with the deftness of long habit, but it was not easy. A shrunken relict of his old self, he was still wily and awkward, surprisingly resilient, a coil of prehensile wire contained in a

509

tough, leathery sack. He was uncooperative, likely to impede progress with the sudden jutting of a stubborn, sinewy leg or to capture her clothing in the clamp of a claw-like hand. She lifted him from the bed and folded him into his chair while she stripped the bed, then she peeled the pyjamas from his frame and washed him with brisk, no-nonsense flannels. Mary scraped Todd's chin with a razor, then checked his bedsores and dabbed them with ointment. She hoisted him onto the commode and left him perched there for a few minutes while she fetched clean pyjamas and remade the bed with clean sheets.

All the while he raged at her in a diatribe of verbiage—querulous, carping, incomprehensible—a tirade of remonstrance which remained non-specific and therefore inconsequential while his teeth stayed in the glass on the shelf. Once he was settled back into bed she went to fetch his breakfast—usually scrambled eggs but today porridge. She knew this would raise objection and she was not wrong. Todd clamped his mouth shut and turned his face from her, lashing out with one hand that knocked the porridge bowl from her grasp and onto the carpet.

'Suit yourself,' said Mary. 'There'll be nothing else until lunch. Joe won't buy eggs off John and that's all Agnes has, in the shop. I used the last of ours in a batch of rock buns last night. If you're good, you can have one of those later.' She placed the newspaper to hand and switched the television on. A children's cartoon blared at full volume and drowned out the old man's complaints.

Mary went about her chores, registering the flap of the letter box but too caught up in getting things done to investigate. It was about twelve-thirty before she had a moment to pick up the strew of letters and sort through them. Bills, a catalogue or two, and an airmail envelope from Canada that she clutched, momentarily, to her breast before tucking it into her apron pocket. She was glad Jack still used old-fashioned mail for his communications. The farm had a computer now, of course. Joe treated it with suspicion, firing questions at the man from the shop who had come to install it and give instructions on its use. Mary had stood in the background, trying to assimilate as much as she could without allowing Joe to think that she would be able to operate the thing better than he could; after all, she did most of the accounts and correspondence. They had email and Jack's Christmas card a few years back had supplied an email address. He could simply email them his news but he continued to write, and Mary was glad of it. She treasured his letters.

She placed the farm correspondence on the hall table and went into to the kitchen, where she made a cup of coffee. Peeking round Todd's door, she saw with satisfaction that he was asleep, his head lolling and a silver trickle of dribble on his chin. She took her coffee and the letter up to the attic, settled herself in the chair and opened the tissue-thin envelope.

Jack's wife was dead! A brain tumour, diagnosed late and inoperable, had carried her away in a matter of weeks. The children, Caroline aged seven and Hugh aged four, were naturally devastated, but his late wife's inheritance from her father would provide the best of care for them, and Jack's own business concerns were now such that he could easily take a step back and offer fulltime parenting. He did not ask or expect any of his family to make the journey to Canada for his wife's funeral, but … and here a blot on the page suggested Jack's pen had rested for some time before continuing with the next words … if any of them wished to visit, for a short or a long time, his house was *always* open to them and he would be delighted to welcome them.

Mary laid the letter on her lap and stared up through the skylight at the billow of clouds that scurried across the square of blue. Jack was a widower, with small children—one of whom was Jamie's sibling—who needed care. She could not misinterpret Jack's invitation in the last lines. She thought of her day, a brief respite of calm before Joe came thundering home, hours late for supper, reeking of beer. He would clump through the kitchen in his muddy boots, not even bothering to shower or remove his stinking overalls before seating himself at the kitchen table and shovelling the food she had kept warm for him into his mouth. He would not ask her about her day. He would not notice the bale of washed and ironed laundry. He would not observe that she'd had her hair cut or wore the cardigan she had been knitting for weeks and had finally finished. He would not enquire about the book that lay on the arm of the easy chair—what was it about? Was she enjoying it? Neither would he enquire about Jamie—had the boy had a good day at school? What had the teacher thought of his homework project? No. He would be oblivious to all of that. He would clear his plate and get up from the table, not bothering so much as to carry his dishes to the sink, not pushing his chair back under the table, not saying thank you. He might speak a word or two to his father. He might go out and do a tour of the farm buildings. Then he would go to the pub for last orders. And tomorrow would be the same, more or less, and the day after that, and the day after that. And perhaps, one day, if there was no dinner in the warming oven, and no clean laundry, it might occur to him to wonder … where is … what was her name? The woman that usually … oh yes. Where is Mary?

Todd Forrester died peacefully in November of 1993. The manner of his exit from the world would probably have annoyed him. He would have preferred to have been at the epicentre of a drama, with blue flashing lights and clamouring sirens, a hoard of weeping relatives clustered around his bed. Instead, all attention had been directed to a violent storm that had battered the village and taken out the power, meeting the onslaught of an extraordinarily high tide that had surged into the village, flooding homes and peeling the surface from the tarmacked road. The tongue of the bluff—already fatally undermined—had disintegrated into the sea, depositing hundreds of tonnes of clay and rubble onto the beach—an event that would ever afterwards be referred to locally as "the big fall."

With farm buildings to be secured and stock to check, no one had made their customary bedtime visit to Todd. Mary discovered him as she opened his curtains the next morning—a slight, stiff mound beneath the tidy covers. There had been no fight, no struggle, no thrashing limbs or vain attempt to summon help. The little death of sleep had simply extended itself to eternal slumber.

Mary, for once, was permitted to walk down the village and to knock on the door of Low Farm. She was used to seeing Nancy only at a distance, at the school bus stop or sometimes entering or leaving Agnes' shop. Joe did not allow Mary to speak to her in-laws or to send the children gifts at birthdays or Christmas. But what Joe did not know could not harm him, and the two women had in fact got into the routine of arriving early at the bus stop most days to exchange a few words while they waited for the school bus to trundle into the village. Nancy had had a baby girl, Lucy, the year before, a cherubic little thing who laughed and gurgled at her aunt Mary and held out her arms to be picked up—but of course Mary did not dare to oblige, in case Joe saw.

'Don't you sometimes think back,' Nancy said to her one day, as they waited in the drizzle for the bus, 'to that day we stood here waiting for the bus to take us to that disco?'

Mary looked at her, astonished. She had not thought of that day for many years. 'No,' she said, 'not really.'

'I do,' admitted Nancy. 'I was mad for John Forrester. I'd have done anything to get him.' She shook her head. 'It's funny,' she said wistfully. 'I can't remember that feeling now. I sort of rue the day I ever saw him.'

'Do you?'

Nancy thought about it. 'No, I suppose not. Not really. There are the children. But I can't say I've been happy. Can you?'

Mary stared glassily across the road, to where a brown soup of sea boiled onto the shingle. 'No,' she said, through thin lips.

Nancy picked at a hangnail. 'Mary,' she began, 'if you ever got the chance to leave ... you know, if you met someone else, and you thought they could offer you everything you've been missing ... would you?'

'Nancy?' said Mary, frowning. 'What's going on?'

'Oh, nothing,' said Nancy, too quickly.

'Nancy!'

'Oh, all right,' said Nancy, suddenly wreathed in smiles. 'There's this man. He's a rep for an egg wholesaler ...'

'Stop,' said Mary. 'I don't want to know.'

'I know, it's silly,' said Nancy. 'But ... I don't know, he makes me feel ... special. He notices me. John never does.'

'It'll come to nothing,' said Mary. 'And what about the children?'

'Johnny's eighteen. He works on the farm fulltime. And Adam will join him next year. He won't stay on once his GCSEs are done.'

'What about the little ones?' Mary looked down at baby Lucy, contentedly asleep in her pushchair. 'Anna's fifteen. That's a difficult age. Harry starts at secondary school in September and Ben's only six.'

'I'd take them with me,' said Nancy.

'Here's the bus,' said Mary.

Now, as she walked down the village street towards Low Farm, stepping over tree branches that had come down in the storm, Mary wondered whether Nancy's affair had progressed any. Would she really leave John and her two oldest boys?

Low Farm was compact, with every available square yard of space given over to machine sheds and poultry housing. Mary went round to the back door and knocked. Eventually Nancy answered. She wore an old tracksuit and a towel around her shoulders. Her hair was piled onto her head, larded with orange dye.

'Todd is dead,' said Mary quickly. 'Joe sent me to tell you. Is John at home?'

Nancy waved vaguely at one of the farm buildings. 'He's here somewhere. You'd better come in.'

Mary stepped into the kitchen, trying not to see the pile of dirty dishes in the sink, the laundry spilling out of the washing machine or the tumbleweeds of dog hair that lodged in the corners. Baby Lucy sat in the dog's bed sucking something that looked suspiciously like a bone.

Nancy grabbed the telephone. 'This is an internal line through to the packing shed,' she said. 'If John's there, he'll pick up.'

Mary crossed the kitchen and picked Lucy up, removed the bone from her mouth and replaced it with a toy that had been abandoned on the tray of the highchair.

Presently John arrived. He was thinner, Mary thought, and his hair had receded, but he smiled at her. 'Hello stranger,' he said, coming to kiss her on the cheek. 'Escaped from Alcatraz, have you?'

'I'm the bearer of bad news, I'm afraid,' she said, shifting Lucy from one hip to the other. 'Your dad has passed away.'

'Has he,' said John, musingly. 'The old bugger. I thought he was indestructible.'

'Apparently not,' said Nancy, slapping a cup of coffee down in front of John and pushing another towards Mary. 'Was it painful, the old man's passing?' She almost looked as though she hoped it might have been.

'Peaceful,' said Mary. 'He slipped away in his sleep. We don't know quite when. We were distracted by the storm. Were you all right down here?'

'I hope he suffers seven kinds of hell,' muttered John, slurping his coffee and ignoring Mary's enquiry. 'So at last, we can get things sorted. I suppose there's a will. I hope it's legal, and that Joe had nothing to do with it. I won't be cheated out of a penny.'

'John!' said Mary, putting the baby down. 'There will be time for all of that once we've discussed the funeral. For goodness' sake, can't you lay this interminable feud to rest? Are you going to let that old man ruin your whole life? You and Joe ...'

'Me and Joe have nothing to say to each other,' said John. 'Not since the day he threw my wife and family out of their home.' He slammed the cup down on the table and made for the door. 'Let me know the

515

arrangements and we'll be there,' he said from the threshold. 'And the name of Dad's solicitor. I want to talk to him.'

Then he was gone. Nancy said, 'I'm sorry you had all the care of Todd, Mary. It can't have been easy. But now you're free of him. Life will be easier. One less thing to tie you to the farm, I suppose.' Suddenly, her eyes flew to the clock on the wall. 'Christ!' she shouted. 'My colour's been on ten minutes too long. My *apricot glow* will be tangerine! Let yourself out Mary, will you? Sorry, I must …' and she was gone, leaving Mary and Lucy, astonished, in the kitchen.

Mary took off her coat, rolled up her sleeves, and began to tackle the washing up.

~

Jack arrived the night before the funeral, calling at Roadend—as well as at Low—with his stepdaughter Caroline, aged eight, and little Hugh, then five years of age.

Caroline was sulky, stony-faced and not to be distracted with toys or books, programmes on the television or even by Jamie's PlayStation. She stayed beside Jack with her hand in his for the entirety of his visit and during the funeral the following day. Hugh was different altogether, befriending Jamie immediately, eager to be shown everything on the farm and to look at all Jamie's toys. The similarity between the two boys was so striking that Mary was amazed Joe did not remark it. But Joe was already half drunk by then, stumbling round the farm to show Jack the improvements he had made and not once reciprocating by asking Jack about his business, his home or his life.

Mary thought Jack was extremely handsome; the eight years of his absence sat well upon him. He was bronzed, his physique athletic. He was smartly—expensively—dressed, his hair neat, with a tidily trimmed little beard. He had hugged Mary tightly on his arrival and whispered, 'Oh, Mary,' into her ear, and she had felt the brush of his lips against hers as they had separated. She had busied herself with something to avoid meeting his eyes. Jack had declined to stay at either farmhouse. He said he had reserved rooms at a hotel, naming the new, swanky and eye-wateringly expensive one that had been opened in a converted stately home. He didn't stay long, citing the children's exhaustion after their long journey. Mary gave him the details for the next day's ceremony and of the long-awaited and sure to be contested opening of Todd's will, which was to take place at the solicitor's office beforehand.

Jack waved that information away. 'Never mind about that,' he said, leaning conspiratorially towards her. 'Will we be able to talk? Just for a few moments? There's so much I want to say to you.'

'I expect so,' said Mary, trying to still the trembling of her knees.

The appointment with the solicitor was at nine o'clock, with the funeral scheduled for eleven. John and Nancy, Agnes, Joe, Mary and Jack presented themselves in their funeral attire. It was so long since Joe had worn his black suit, he had struggled to get the trousers buttoned, and Mary had been forced to do some last-minute sewing to move the button. Even so, the jacket stretched tightly across his shoulders and would not fasten at all at the front. Mary felt ashamed of him, especially when Jack appeared in an immaculately tailored and clearly made-to-measure suit. Joe stood in the waiting room, red-faced and bleary-eyed, ignoring John, and surreptitiously drinking from a hipflask. Jack took one of the chairs. Mary sat down next to him and tried to read one of the magazines that were laid out on a coffee table, conscious of the press of Jack's leg against hers. Caroline and Hugh were to be left in the care of the solicitor's secretary for the duration of the meeting, a matter that Caroline was very unhappy with.

She kept whining, 'I want to stay with you, Daddy. I want to stay with you,' her Canadian accent strange to all her British relatives' ears.

Jack said, 'I know. I know. It will only be a little while. I'll be just through that door there.'

Mary pulled a children's story book from her bag. 'Have you read this, Caroline?' she asked, handing it along. 'I'm reading it to Jamie and I bought this copy for Hugh. It might be too babyish, but you might like to look through it.'

Jack threw her a grateful look and Caroline, reluctantly, took the book in her hands.

The solicitor's office was cramped, full of files, and it took a while to assemble sufficient chairs for the family. Even then, there was some jockeying for position as John and Joe avoided sitting near one another. People had only just settled when John said, 'I'm sorry. Could we have the window open? There's a terrible smell of stale scotch in here.'

At last, the solicitor shuffled his papers and began. Todd's will was really no surprise to Mary, although it shocked and disappointed his two elder sons. It seemed to her he had pre-empted it, more or less, in his division of the property at the end of 1985. John and Nancy were to have Low Farm, all the title deeds that pertained to it and the business interests associated. Joe was to have Roadend under the same terms and Jack was left with Winter Farm. Agnes was bequeathed the few remaining properties in the village that Todd had still owned, although these were not many, and a sum of money to make up the difference. Todd's personal savings were to be divided equally between the four of them.

'Four?' blustered John, turning to stare at Agnes. 'Why should *you* get an equal share? You're only his niece.'

Agnes shrugged. 'I don't know,' she said. 'It's more than I expected. All I'd hoped for was Winter Farm. Jack, it looks like you'll benefit from all Walter's hard work.'

'You can keep the farm,' said Jack. 'I don't care about it.' He addressed the solicitor. 'Can I just give it to them?'

'Why would you give it to *them?*' thundered Joe. 'It belongs with Roadend.'

'Look,' said John, thumping his fist onto the solicitor's desk. 'This just isn't fair. Roadend is worth two Lows, even just in terms of the property, not to mention the income. I shall contest this.'

'The fairest thing would be to sell the whole lot and divide the money equally,' said Nancy, 'between the three boys.'

'*Very* sensible,' sniped Agnes, 'depriving us all of our homes *and* our livelihoods. Handy, though, for anyone thinking of suing for divorce. They could just walk away with half the loot.'

'Who's thinking of suing for divorce?' said John, glaring around the room.

'Oh, *I* don't know,' said Agnes, examining a fingernail. 'Why don't you ask your egg rep?'

'You'll sell Roadend over my dead body,' roared Joe, leaping to his feet, over-balancing and landing on top of Nancy.

John lunged. 'Don't you *dare* touch my wife.'

'Why not,' carped Nancy, pushing Joe off her. 'You've wanted to touch *his* often enough.'

Jack said, 'Come on, Mary. Why don't we leave them to it? I'll drive you back to Roadend.'

Jack had a hire car. It was sleek, new, smelled of leather and money. Mary felt cocooned in the plush seat. Caroline and Hugh climbed into the back.

'Read more of the story, Caroline,' said Hugh in a sleepy voice.

'Do you mind if we pick Jamie up on the way?' asked Mary. Excused school on account of the funeral, he had spent the morning with a lady in the village.

'Not at all,' said Jack.

They picked Jamie up—smart, in his school uniform, solemnly aware of the importance of the day—and Jack drove them down the track towards Winter Farm.

'Where are we going?' asked Jamie. 'I thought we were going to the church.'

'There's a little time,' said Mary, swivelling round in her seat. The picture of the three children lined up along the back seat—the life she could have had—made her eyes fill.

Walter and Agnes had divided Winter Farm into three distinct cottages, and had made their home in the end one, which looked cheerful enough. The rest remained drear and neglected.

As they drove up, Walter emerged with a bucket and trowel. 'All over, bar the shouting?' he called out.

'I'm afraid the shouting is still in full swing,' replied Mary. She looked at her watch. 'Oughtn't you to be getting changed?'

Walter blanched. 'What time does the shindig start?'

'Eleven. You've barely an hour.'

'Oh,' said Walter. 'Won't take me ten minutes to get into my suit. I've time for another batch.' He began to mix sand and cement.

Jack smiled. 'Come and look at this tree, children,' he said. 'It's very special to me.'

They made their way across the Moss towards where the silver birch tree stood, amid its copse of trees. The children—even Caroline—ran like hares along the byways of the bracken maze. The day was bright, the sun shedding a little warmth although the wind was chill. Mary, in a linen suit and a thin blouse, shivered. Jack, behind her, laid his hand on her shoulder, and then followed the line of her arm until he reached her hand. He clasped it tightly for a second, and then let it go. They walked slowly. Mary wished time would stand still.

Jack spoke in a low voice. 'Funny,' he said, 'I've imagined this moment so many times, and thought of all I want to say to you. But now it's here I can't get the words out.'

'Oh?' Mary murmured, watching Jamie and Hugh as they zoomed about, their arms whirling.

'That's Hugh being a helicopter,' said Jack. 'It's what he wants to do, when he's older.'

'Be a helicopter? I think he might be disappointed,' quipped Mary.

'A pilot,' Jack clarified. Suddenly, he grasped her arm and turned her to face him. 'Mary,' he began, 'are you happy?'

She could not meet his eye. 'I get by,' she said.

'But that's not good enough,' urged Jack. 'You should be happy. You should be reading … I don't know, maybe teaching. Even writing. You're wasted here.'

Mary knew it was true, but a flare of loyalty made her say, 'I play my part on the farm. I do the accounts, and …'

'…and Joe hardly notices,' Jack concluded for her. 'He's a drunk, Mary. How can you bear it?'

'I don't know,' said Mary. She had put a handkerchief in her pocket for the funeral—not that she expected to cry, but you never knew how these affairs might take you. She got it out now and wiped her nose. When she looked up at Jack her eyes were still wet, but her expression was fiery. 'I just *do,*' she said vehemently, 'because I *have* to. It's the life I chose. I've made my bed and I must lie in it.'

'No,' he took hold of her arms and gave her a gentle shake. 'No, Mary, you don't. Not when there's a much better one just waiting for you.'

She disengaged herself. 'You've been widowed,' she said. 'Naturally, you're lonely. And you've two children. Of course, you're looking for someone to—not replace, I know that no one ever could—but love them *like* a mother.'

'All of that is true,' said Jack, looking across the marsh to where the children played. They had found the tree. He could just see, through the surrounding saplings, the boys clambering up into the branches. Their funeral clothes would be grubby, he thought, but it didn't matter.

His eyes focused back onto Mary. 'But I've wanted *you* from the beginning. Do you remember, when we sat on the bough? I wanted you *then.* I asked you to come with me *then.* I'm not looking for a stand-in, a substitute, Mary. That's what Helen was, God rest her. I'm looking for the original. Come back with me, Mary. I've a good life, a big house—'

'I can't, Mary sobbed, cutting him off. 'You know I can't. It would be wrong. Nancy … she … and I …' She stammered into silence. Words failed her. What she wanted to say was that what was wrong for Nancy would be wrong, also, for her. But then, Jack was not a random sales rep. Perhaps the two situations were not the same at all.

Jack would not press her. He took her in his arms and held her while she cried.

Presently, Mary mumbled, 'We ought to get back.'

'Yes,' he said, releasing her. 'But Mary, if not now, please don't say never. One day … I don't know, it may be years from now, but *one* day, when you're ready, come to me, and I'll be waiting.'

She gave a sad smile, dabbing at her cheeks with her sodden handkerchief. 'I'll be too old,' she said, 'too wrinkled and grey and saggy.'

'No, you won't,' he replied, lifting his hand to stroke her cheek. 'Never, *never* in my eyes will you be less beautiful to me than you are now.'

Chapter Forty-Three

'Yes,' said Mary, dabbing her eyes with a tissue. 'That's more or less exactly how it was. It didn't happen on the Moss or on the day of the funeral, but, in essentials, you've got it all right.'

I had given her my raw manuscript a few days previously—on a flash drive, which she had transferred to her tablet—making her promise that, when she got to the chapter covering 1978 to 1993, she would stop and come to Winter Cottage, and read the rest where I could watch her. Really, what I wanted was for her to be able to vent her indignation onto me straight away. I did not want her to rail *about* me to Hugh or Jamie and especially not to Caroline, who, I thought, might be capable of roughing me up if she thought I had upset or maligned Mary.

Whilst Mary had read her copy of the novel up to that point, I had read it aloud to myself. The cadences of the prose can only really be heard when it is read aloud. When you speak it, you can hear if the dialogue sounds natural, and sentences that go on too long make themselves plainly heard. It is a valuable editing tool, but even as I narrated, I knew I must sound as mad to Jamie, through the party wall, as he cleared away Joe's belongings, as the old man had sounded to me. I tried to read the book as Mary would read it, as—in time, perhaps—Jamie and Hugh and Caroline and Agnes Harrop would read it. My agent was champing at the bit for the finished manuscript and only Mary stood between its publication or its permanent erasure. With or without that, I would leave Roadend at the end of March.

That month was already halfway through. Daffodils were beginning to show in the woodland areas and the willow walk was full of catkins. The air had a softer, more benign iteration, as though the storm had expiated all winter's ire. I was packing, getting ready to leave. It was amazing to me how much stuff I had accumulated in the five months of my tenure at Winter Cottage—stuff that, probably, I would not need in one of the Cotswold cottages I was considering purchasing. Daniel sent me links almost daily to properties that might suit; pretty places built of honey-coloured stone, with roses growing around the doors and nicely enclosed gardens where Bob would be safe from traffic. The Cotswolds are not Cumbria, and I thought probably most of my extreme winter gear could go to a charity shop. Then again, looking over the thermal vests and layers of woollies, I did not like to think I would *never* return to Roadend.

Mary closed her tablet and picked up her mug of tea. 'Of course,' she said, 'there are parts of this that were before my time. But, in terms of Todd—yes, he was bitter and cruel after Rose died, and he *did* stir up disagreements between the boys. About the fire, well, I couldn't say. I know Agnes has always suspected the boys had a hand in it, but she never had any proof.'

'I can't offer any proof,' I said. 'No one can, now.'

'Do you really think Agnes might be Todd's granddaughter?'

'Pure speculation on my part,' I admitted. 'I'm sure she'll be horrified at the suggestion.'

'She didn't like what he did to Rose,' said Mary. 'Rose was a truly lovely woman. I'm sorry I didn't know her better. Agnes thinks—and I agree with her—that she was another young woman who might have had a very different life if the Forresters had not intervened. Plus, Agnes is rather wedded to her Winter antecedents, isn't she? Delusions of grandeur, and all that? That plays a big role in her resentment, too.'

'And what is her grudge against Jamie?' I wanted to know. 'She seems determined to denigrate him.'

Mary thought about it. 'Partly, I think she's envious. For a long time, it looked like I wouldn't have a child and then, at last, along came Jamie. Agnes and Walter weren't so lucky. Year followed year and *her* miracle never happened. Plus, she was always especially close to Jack but once I moved into the farmhouse, I'm afraid Jack distanced himself from her. But mainly I think it's just his name. He's a Forrester, and in Agnes' eyes the whole clan is tainted.'

I ruminated on what she'd said. Mary sipped her tea and, without looking at me, said, 'How did you know about John? I never told a soul about that.'

I paused. What could I say? That the marram grasses had told me? That explanation was at least as incredible as the truth. 'A hunch,' I said. 'If two brothers, why not all three?'

'Hum,' she said. 'But he certainly never climbed in through my bedroom window. Nancy was … difficult. That's true. I suppose he thought the grass might have been greener. Don't *all* men, though?'

'And some women,' I said. 'What about Joe?'

'Oh! *All* true, in the essentials. He started drinking quite early on. Not to excess, then, but it crept up. And yes, he was desperate for more children, a bevy of boys to hand the farm on to.'

'And,' I probed gently, 'I'm right about Jamie, aren't I?'

She nodded. 'Joe was injured during a wrestling bout. I think it resulted in him being infertile, but he refused to see a doctor about it. He always said our difficulty conceiving was *my* fault.'

'Of course he did. But then, when you got pregnant with Jamie?'

'He never suspected Jamie was not his.' Mary ran her finger round the rim of her mug. 'It was just that one time with Jack, you know, before Canada. I wouldn't like you to get the impression that we were sneaking about.'

'It never occurred to me,' I said. 'Why didn't you go away with Jack when he asked you?'

'Oh,' Mary burst out, tears again welling in her eyes. 'I wish I had. My life was so miserable. I felt like a flower that had been trampled on again and again. It got more and more difficult to lift up my head. But I was scared to admit how bad things were. I thought, once I'd faced it, I'd never be able to get it back into its box. And Jamie—how could I uproot him from everything he'd known? His friends? His school? His home?'

'So you decided to wait until he left home?'

She tilted her head to one side. 'No. We didn't *plan* it, but something happened the day Joe and I drove Jamie to the campus. I was so proud of Jamie. But Joe had taken umbrage. He didn't see the point of university. Why couldn't Jamie just work on the farm? Joe blamed me for Jamie's love of books. He blamed me for Jamie wanting to study. It had been a source of acrimony for months, while Jamie did his "A" levels. Anyway, we dropped Jamie off and started home, but on the way, Joe wanted to stop for a drink. We went to a pub and we rowed, and Joe drove off without me. He took my bag and my coat. I had nothing! I had to hitch-hike home. I never told Jamie about that.'

'Oh Mary,' I said, 'that's terrible.'

'Arnold picked me up. You've met Arnold?'

I nodded.

'Thank goodness he saw me from the cab of his lorry and stopped. Otherwise, I don't know what I would have done. I was *miles* from home. Well. After that, things happened pretty quickly. Really, it was the last straw and so yes, after that, we did make plans.'

'You were in touch with Jack?'

'Yes. Jack and I had been communicating by email for a couple of years. I got a private email address and it was such a comfort, to be able to speak to him—almost, anyway—to pour out my troubles and to have him send me pictures, and pieces of music, poems … we read the same books and then discussed them. Sometimes I would sneak out of bed at night and creep down to the farm office, where the computer was. Jack was eight hours behind me, so at three in the morning here it was five in the afternoon there. The children were at school by then and Jack had taken the reins of his business up again. But he'd be home, by then, and we'd chat until it was time for him to put the children to bed. It would be dawn here then, and I'd go back upstairs as the birds were stirring. Joe never even noticed I'd been gone. I felt *dreadful* … so deceitful, but then—apart from Jamie—Jack was the only bright light in my dark, dark world.'

'I understand,' I said.

'So, after that incident I told Jack I was ready and he bought my ticket: first class, if you please! All I had to do was get myself to the airport, get on a plane, and fly away. But I had no passport and applying for that without Joe knowing was so difficult. And then, on the day, I was sick with worry. I knew I ought to tell Joe I was going but by that time he was … so volatile. I didn't dare. There was no telling what he'd do. He might have locked me away. He *had* done, before. I had packed my case the previous Thursday, which was market day, so Joe was out. I'd left it with the woman who did my hair. I told her some lie—All I needed to do was get on the bus. But the bus didn't come that day, it had broken down, and so I called a cab and I was terrified that Agnes would see it from the shop—well, of course, she sees *everything* from the shop—or that Joe would choose just that moment to come back from the fields or out of the shed …'

'Why didn't you leave on a Thursday, while he was at the market?' I put in.

'Because the flight was Thursday. I had to leave on Wednesday. And just as the taxi arrived Joe came into the yard wanting to know where I was going, why I was dressed up, where was his lunch, had I paid those invoices? The taxi beeped its horn and Joe noticed it, parked at the gate, and just at that moment Agnes came flying out of the shop, shouting at the top of her voice, haranguing Joe about something, shoving him in the chest, pointing at something in the barn that she was pretending to object to, all the time motioning to me that I should just *go* … and so I did. I climbed in the taxi and rode away.'

'I think you were very brave,' I said, moving to sit next to her on the sofa. I wondered if—when my moment came—I would be as brave as she had been.

'What was it like, when you got to Canada?' I asked. 'Was Jack waiting for you?'

'Oh!' Mary blushed furiously. 'Yes. Yes, he was. It was … just wonderful.'

527

Later, I said to her, 'So, Mary. Imagine that in the book you've just read, all the names were different, and Roadend was transported to—I don't know—a Scottish island, maybe, like Shetland. How would that be? Would you feel I'd stolen your story? That I'd opened up your private life to the public? Would it be an intrusion, still? Because if it would, this book will never see the light of day.'

She considered. 'In some ways I'd be sorry,' she admitted. 'These are our ghosts and I'd like them laid to rest. That festering feud should be put behind us. For Hugh and Jamie, and John's children, there can be a whole new beginning. On the other hand, if you changed the details, it might be better. I have to think of the whole family,' she concluded. 'Can I be Moira, rather than Mary? I've always hated being Mary.'

'If you like,' I said, laughing.

Mary laughed too, but then she sobered and said, 'But you must promise me this: you won't publish it until we've told Jamie the truth.'

'I promise,' I said

Chapter Forty-Four

Hugh called on me a couple of times—not in the old clandestine manner but in broad day light, respectably, almost formally. If I'd hoped he would let sleeping dogs lie, I was to be disappointed.

'Before,' he said, with a sly smile, 'was lots of fun. But it got us into trouble, didn't it? We didn't properly understand each other. So let me make it crystal clear, Dee. I *like* you, *so* much. I'm not just interested in a quickie now and again. I want to have a relationship with you. I think I'm ready for the real deal. I have a place in Canada I think you'd love. I mean, if you like it *here,* you'll love it there. It's similar but ... so much bigger. You could have your own study, and write to your heart's content. That sounds patronising but what I'm trying to say is, I respect your career and I won't ever stand in the way of it. I know we will both have to travel. I'm really committed to the estate here, to rewilding—but that's too much about me. I should be talking about you. You're an amazing woman, exciting, clever—'

'Stop it,' I said. 'I like you too, Hugh, very much. But—'

'There's Jamie?'

'There's Jamie,' I said with a sigh. I gave Hugh a frank look. 'How much do you know?'

'I know everything,' he said. 'I've known for a long time. But we didn't think it was right to tell Jamie. We *still* don't. It's down to Mary to decide when the time is right. But once I've got probate sorted, there'll be money for him—more than he ever dreamed of, I suspect. Dad was always clear about it. Jamie was his son and would be treated equally. But I don't quite see how that interferes with things between us?'

'Don't you?'

He looked blank. 'No. Not really. Unless—'

'Well, there you are, Hugh,' I said. 'There's an "unless".'

'Oh,' he said, looking glum. 'I see.'

He didn't see—I knew that—but I could not explain to him. I was in the classic dichotomy of head versus heart. My head told me life with Hugh would be amazing, secure and wonderful. Sex with him had been exciting but I had to admit that, in those moments, I had been more Rose than myself. Our liaison had existed in the twilight world of my imagination and I was not sure it could survive out in the midday sun of real life. He did not share my love of literature, and although he *said* he respected my profession I worried that, when push came to shove, it would have to play second fiddle to his environmental work. I thought a relationship with Hugh would be civilised and comfortable, but not much more. A relationship with Jamie, on the other hand, would be full of fireworks. We sometimes rubbed each other up the wrong way and, like Ivaan, he was a man who, through no fault of his own, was young in years. That would annoy me. And yet, with him I felt a compatibility I had never found with anyone else. If we are given soulmates in this life, Jamie was mine. My heart told me he was The One.

All of that, though, was irrelevant, because I could not—I *would* not—intrude myself between those two brothers. Daniel and I had allowed Bianca to come between us and our sibling bond had had years and years to cement. It was only now, as I was repairing it, that I understood exactly how precious he was to me, how much I had missed him, how my grieving for Dad had been made worse by my estrangement from my brother. Jamie and Hugh were both grieving, and sharing that experience would be the fire that annealed their relationship. They needed each other more than either of them needed me. It would give them a basis of brotherliness that would last them a lifetime if they could just have space and time to establish it. If I allowed myself to interfere with it now, just when those all-important foundations were being laid, they would never achieve it. Their every interaction would be complicated by the fact that I stood between them. What would be the point in laying one feud to rest, just to provoke another? No. I could not be the schism that divided them, the kind of stumbling block Mary had been between Joe, John and Jack, that Todd had been between Rowan and Rose. History repeats but—as Jamie had pointed out to me—it did not *have* to. I would not allow it to. I could twist the kaleidoscope and make a different ending by disappearing from these men's lives and giving each of them—as my gift—the brother they had both so longed for.

Jamie returned to his cottage and began the slow process of packing away his father's things. It did not take long; most of the broken furniture went into a skip. If Joe's personal belongings had ever been precious to him, he had ruined most of them in bouts of drunken temper.

In the absence of a body there was to be a memorial service. It saddened me that Joe would not take his place alongside his brothers; then again, I wondered if the three of them could rest easily, side by side in any realm.

In between his labours Jamie came in and drank coffee, and we talked about Joe's death, the trauma of it, his sense of failure, and I did my best to reassure him.

'An accident,' I said. 'A tragic accident. It looked to me as though he was lost in some memory. … His mind had gone.' I was careful not to season my sympathy with what, after all, I only thought I knew, but Jamie knew me too well.

'You know what it was, don't you? What did he think he was doing, Dee?'

'I don't *know* anything,' I protested.

'But you suspect.'

'Playing a game, perhaps,' I extemporised, 'as he had as a child, before the big fall made the bluff so much shorter than it was before.'

'Ah, yes,' mused Jamie.

'He would have known nothing, at the end,' I hurried on, snatching Jamie back from that metaphorical cliff edge. 'It was so quick. A fall, and then … nothing.'

Jamie nodded. 'I hope so,' he said. He raised his eyes to mine and we shared a long and lingering gaze, our unfinished business unwound between us in tangled skeins.

'What are your plans?' I enquired, shattering the moment, 'in the short term, at least?'

'I hardly know,' he said. 'I wondered about finishing my degree. Hugh says he'll pay the fees.'

'That's good of him.'

'He *is* good,' Jamie agreed, with hardly any grudge. 'I don't know why he feels he wants to—'

I bit my lip. 'No?' I croaked out.

'Mum, I suppose,' he offered. 'He can afford it. He's loaded.'

'Jack will have left his children well provided-for,' I said, naughtily. 'I gather the whole probate business is proving complex. Some clash between Canadian and British law. Hugh says the lawyers are having a field day.'

'Hugh's been to see you?' Jamie threw out, as though it was nothing to him, as though he did not care at all.

'Mmm,' I said, topping up his coffee. 'A couple of times, actually.'

'Oh?' He left his enquiry hanging, and I did not pick it up.

I saw a good deal of Marjorie and Olivia during those final days. I suppose it was a way of avoiding awkward situations with Jamie. Olivia and I painted each other's nails and we experimented with ways of plaiting her hair which, she said, she was growing long, like mine. She showed me her collection of precious things, which included—to my surprise—some poems she had written. She showed these to me shyly and I praised them, genuinely impressed. I felt that, on the whole, I had not been as good a friend to Olivia as she deserved. I hoped Patrick would prove a better one.

On a subsequent visit I found Marjorie in the throes of forming a committee to take over the management of the pub. 'A marvellous development,' she cried, shuffling papers around on her desk to make room for her mug. The Lord of the Manor has agreed to buy the place if the community runs it as a not-for-profit enterprise. In time, that will include employing a manager, but for the time being we need a rota of people to man the bar, oversee the accounts … oh! ever so many things.'

'And are people signing up?' I asked, doubtful because, in my small experience of these things, they don't.

'All the usual suspects, of course. You see the same faces on every committee. But Mrs Harrop has taken an active role. Normally, all she wants to do is wear a posh hat and cut the ribbon. But it seems she has a nephew who's a chef so she's wading in on his behalf.'

I stroked Patty, who had struggled on to my knee. 'Where's Olivia today?'

'Out with Patrick somewhere,' she said stiffly. 'I must say that little romance is blossoming. Who would have thought it?'

'You're not happy about it?'

'What mother ever is?' she asked, turning glassy eyes on me. 'It's very hard—to let go—and in Olivia's case, harder still.'

'Olivia was ripe for falling in love,' I said. 'Patrick was in the right place at the right time. I think he'll be good for her, don't you? She has certainly been very good for *him*.'

'I have no objection to him at all, in any capacity except—'

'As Olivia's boyfriend?'

She nodded. 'I really just have to get a grip on myself. He's an excellent young man, and *so* much better now than he was when he came. He's to begin his ordination training.'

'Olivia will make a splendid curate's wife, if things progress that far, ' I said. 'Don't you think so?'

Marjorie considered. 'It is easy to think of people with Down Syndrome as perpetual children. I know I've been guilty of it. They are characterised as having sunny dispositions and child-like simplicity, but they have their struggles. Olivia has struggled with loneliness; and of course, here she lacks company her own age. Olivia has Mosaic Down Syndrome. You've heard of it?'

I shook my head.

'No, not many people have. It means she is more,' she made inverted commas with her fingers, '"highly functioning." She's much more clever than people give her credit for—and I include myself in that. I've mollycoddled her, I know. Patrick treats her as an equal. Which is—Oh!' she cried suddenly, 'just a moment. There's Mrs Ford. Do you mind if I just ...?'

Marjorie leapt up from her seat, barged through her door and flew down the drive, flapping a sheaf of papers in Mrs Ford's face. I knew our conversation about Olivia was over.

I allowed my eyes to travel around the room, to the bookshelves that I had wanted to examine on my first visit. Sure enough, there on the middle shelf, were all of my novels, neatly arranged, my author photo smiling out from the back covers. I lifted Patty off my knee, took the books out one by one, and signed them.

'Marjorie,' I said, when she came back, breathless, but with Mrs Ford's signature appended to one of her documents, 'I think I owe you an apology, and perhaps an explanation.'

'No need in the world, dear,' she said, slurping her tea. 'Bother! This has gone cold. Let me just get a refresher. You?'

I proffered my cup.

'But I think I do,' I said, following her into the kitchen. 'Olivia told me that you knew all along who I was, so you knew I'd been, let's say, less than transparent about it. But you were *so* kind. You gave me the space I needed. I'm not famous. I have no delusions about that, but once people know you're a writer they want to tell you their stories, which is helpful, sometimes, but I wanted one to find me.'

'I understand all of that,' said Marjorie, pouring freshly boiled water into the teapot. 'I *did* try to hijack you, for book club. That was mean of me. I promised everyone a *surprise, exciting* guest, and then you didn't show up. Served me right. So, what are your plans now? Have you written your book?'

I opened the fridge to get the milk. 'The book has sort of written itself,' I said. 'There was a story right here in Roadend, and it offered itself up to me in, oh! such odd ways. In the graveyard, on the dunes, through the weather and, yes, through the people. I feel I have more channelled it, than actually written it. It was a story that was crying out to be told.'

'I can't wait to read it,' said Marjorie. 'Am I in it?'

I laughed. 'Of course not. *"No similarity to any real person or persons is intended or should be inferred."*

'Oh!' said Marjorie, quite crestfallen.

Chapter Forty-Five

I was due to leave Winter Cottage on Friday. Thursday was, cruelly, the most splendid day, the air almost warm with spring sunshine pouring over the Moss. On my last walk across it I could see new bracken buds pushing themselves through the papery skeletons of their winter blankets. Soon the secret pathways would be gone, swallowed up and absorbed back into the undergrowth. Gorse flowers studded the bushes and wild daffodils nodded sage agreement with each other in little enclaves around fallen branches and tree roots. I stood beneath the canopy of the trysting tree and listened to the sigh of the wind in its branches, the voices of the characters I had conjured, soon to be dispersed to the world. An enormous squadron of geese passed overhead, many hundreds, squawking to each other as they began their travels. Before many hours had passed, I would follow them, leaving behind my winter feeding grounds for pastures new.

I spent the day packing up my belongings and squeezing them into the car—all except for the coffee machine, which I had decided I would leave on Jamie's step the following morning. I left the front door open as I trooped in and out. The cottage billowed with fresh air. Bob lay in the sun in the garden and watched me narrowly. Once the car was packed, I set about cleaning. I knew that almost as soon as my car left Roadend, Mrs Harrop would be in the cottage, snooping about to see what damage I might have done, if I had taken anything that was hers. I *had*, of course, but I hoped what I would give her back—closure—would be sufficient recompense.

Evening had fallen by the time I finished, leaving only the clothes I would wear for the journey and my toiletries to pack away into one last bag.

Jamie and I were due to eat together at the pub. I had agreed to the suggestion reluctantly. Goodbyes are hard enough and I thought this would just prolong the agony. However, at seven he arrived and we zoomed together on his quadbike along the boardwalk, Bob squashed between us. I should not have been surprised—but I was—to find all my Roadend friends collected in the bar: Hugh, Caroline and Mary, Marjorie, Olivia and Patrick, even Arnold and Mrs Harrop. Tables had been pushed together and the menu agreed beforehand. All I needed to do was smile and keep the tears at bay. It was a jolly evening, with lots of teasing about what my new book would be called.

At last, I blurted out, 'The Trysting Tree.'

People exchanged puzzled looks. Only Hugh and Mary knew what I meant.

'There's a tree,' I explained, 'on the Moss. A silver birch—'

'Is there? And that's what your book's about? How odd,' they all chorused.

I was careful not to imbibe too much gin, although the temptation was strong. We ate steak and ale pie with chips and lashings of gravy followed by plum crumble and custard. I felt absolutely stuffed at the end, but when it came time to pay Bill waved my card aside. 'All paid for,' he said.

At about nine o'clock people began to take their leave. Arnold bundled himself into his many layers of coat and scarf and shook my hand warmly. 'A pleasure to have known you,' he said.

Mary hugged me fiercely, whispering, 'I know what you're up to. Thank you.' Then she was gone, hustled away by Caroline.

Mrs Harrop said, 'Leave the key in the door tomorrow, please. I'll be along at ten sharp, so be gone by then.'

'I will,' I said. 'Thank you for all your kindness. I especially enjoyed the quinoa.'

I hugged Hugh tightly. 'Goodbye,' I said, my eyes pouring.

'Is it?' he asked, holding me at arm's length. His face was rigid with suppressed emotion. I threw a glance at Jamie. 'I hope not for ever,' I said, 'but for now, it must be.'

Jamie decided to leave his bike at the pub, so we walked back along the boardwalk in the moonlight, beneath a panoply of stars. He held my hand. Bob skipped ahead of us.

'I understand why you have to leave Roadend,' he said at last, his voice thick. 'But I'm not sure I understand why we can't ... why we have to say goodbye. Is it because of Hugh?'

'Partly,' I said.

'You're not over him? He's not over you?'

I nodded. 'Something like that.'

'I don't understand.' He stopped abruptly, bringing me to a halt beside him. 'You *do* feel it too, don't you Dee? What *I* feel?' He looked down at me, his silhouette blocking out the moon's argent light. It bounced off the water meadow behind me and refracted in the embers of his eyes.

'Yes,' I croaked out, my willpower deserting me as though from a tap, pouring between the boards beneath my feet. 'Of course, I do.'

'Then why?' His arms were around me. His warmth, as always, enveloped my body.

'I can't explain,' I stammered out. 'I want to, but I can't.' I lifted my hand and tucked a stray lock of hair behind his ear. 'I can only promise you, one day you'll understand.'

I didn't think he would accept it, but he did. He gave a little shake of his head, dislodging the hair I had just tidied away. 'I suppose I must swallow it,' he said brokenly. 'Can I kiss you anyway?'

I nodded, and he did.

I couldn't sleep that night. I lay in bed and watched the moonlight creep across the floor, stray onto the covers and then point with accusing beams at my holdall. An owl called across the Moss and its mate answered. I listened for the sound of the loft hatch being moved cautiously to one side, the soft thud of feet on the landing carpet, the creak of my bedroom door being slowly pushed open. If Jamie came to me like that, in the night, and we made love, just once ... if we made no promises … if we parted without regret but with something, a hectic memory, to remember each other by … but the loft hatch remained in its place and Jamie did not come.

At two o'clock I got up, showered and dressed. I had decided to leave before dawn, before Jamie's stricken face and my own wavering resolve could change my mind.

I carried the coffee machine along the lane and put it on Jamie's step, wincing at the squeal of his gate. I looked up anxiously, but his bedroom window stayed dark.

I led Bob out along the willow walk. The air was still, sharp with frost, the nude branches of the trees unmoving, a cathedral grove that towered above us. The dune grasses were filigree spikes, reflecting the last light of the setting moon. I moved between them like a wraith, my feet leaving no prints, the sand undisturbed by my passing. Far, far out across the shimmering sand, the sea murmured, a sheet of tempered bronze beneath the dun pewter sky.

I trod the old, accustomed way to the edge of the dunes, where it fell away to the shingle, along the edge to where the den rose, dim on dim, above the scrub. It was finished. The pointed structure of roof lats had been interwoven with brush, willow and whatever else could be scavenged from the beach: fishing net, hemp rope, a piece of ragged tarpaulin. It was a splendid den and I envied the children who would play in it, the walkers who would shelter in it, the lovers who would meet in it. They would never know—as I did—the guilt it assuaged, the penance it represented, the pact between brothers its completion sealed.

All across the undulating topography of the dunes, over the rippling sands and the barely moving sea, from as far as the far country I heard voices. They came to me on the sigh of the wind and in the regular in-out respiration of the sea—the merry echo of three little boys playing, their laughter untroubled, their spirits as free as air.

Epilogue

It took a year for *The Trysting Tree* to make it into print, and another two before it hit the screens because of the disruption caused by the Corona Virus. Needless to say, before giving the go-ahead to my publisher, I had heard from Mary, a brief email informing me that she had explained things to Jamie and that no one had any objection to their story—with names and location altered—being published.

A few months after the final restrictions were lifted, just before the film was due out, Olivia and Patrick were married. I attended the ceremony, which was held not at Roadend, but in the inner-city parish church in the Midlands where Patrick was curate. Olivia naturally looked beautiful, glowing with radiance. Marjorie was resplendent in mother-of-the-bride regalia and wept a bucketful of tears as the couple spoke their vows. I was privileged not to be asked to deliver a reading but also by being seated on the top table at the reception. My *nom de plume* was liberally bandied about so I felt like a celebrity even though most of the guests— parishioners and a handful of Patrick's family members—lost interest in me once they realised I was not a star of a reality television series.

'What news from Roadend?' I asked Marjorie once the speeches were done and the coffee had been served.

'One important development,' she told me. 'Bill and Julie have taken up residence in the Balearics. We have a keen young couple in the pub now—Mrs Harrop's nephew and his partner. They worked marvels during lockdown, delivering food to the old folks and so on. Now, they're open all hours and I cannot help wondering if Mrs Harrop has not rather shot herself in the foot. Her trade in hot drinks and cakes has certainly dwindled to nothing.'

'She won't like that,' I said. 'Isn't it time she thought about retiring?'

'Only death will prise her from her Post Office cubicle,' said Marjorie. '*I* am considering retirement though. Or semi-retirement, at least. A private boarding school for girls is looking for a chaplain. It comes with accommodation, naturally, and will be termtime only. It is not too far from here, so I could continue to support Olivia, if she needs it.'

'It sounds perfect,' I said. 'And … what of Hugh and Mary?'

'They divide their time between Roadend and Canada,' said Marjorie, 'although lately I have thought Mary prefers to remain here. And who can blame her? International travel can be *so* tiring, can't it, even if one does travel first class? She is gradually integrating herself back into village life, which is marvellous. I have got her back on the flower rota for the church and she is a stalwart of the book club. She and Arnold have struck up a rather touching friendship.'

'That's good to hear,' I said. 'I sent her a first edition of the novel. She replied with a lovely note. Perhaps she will suggest it to the book club.'

Marjorie beetled an eyebrow. 'I think *that* might be courting disaster, don't you? Thankfully, Mrs Harrop is no reader. Otherwise, she might sue.'

'Oh dear,' I said. 'What did *you* think of it?'

'Quite the best thing you have ever written, dear. Do you fancy a brandy? I'm paying for this shebang so we might as well get my money's worth.'

When our brandies came, we sipped them appreciatively and watched Olivia and Patrick as they toured the room, speaking to their guests, never for a second letting go of each other's hand.

'Does Hugh have … anyone?' I asked at last.

Marjorie looked shifty. 'Was there something between you two?'

I sighed. 'There was something. But it wasn't …' I nodded at the bride and groom, '…what *they* have.'

'I rather think there might be someone,' Marjorie murmured. 'An old colleague from his Airforce days.'

'That's good,' I said. 'And he and Jamie?'

'Ah yes. They've grown close. They're renovating Winter Farm; the whole row. It's been converted back to one dwelling and it will be used by students of environmental sciences to study the Moss.'

I approved of this idea. It seemed to me it would be the ideal compromise between flooding the Moss and doing nothing at all. I saw the co-operation of Hugh and Jamie in this scheme and was heartened. 'So, Jamie's still at Roadend?'

'Often, but not permanently. In fact,' she threw me a narrow look, 'I'm surprised you're not up to speed. He's in your neck of the woods, isn't he?'

This news surprised me more than I could say. 'Is he?'

'I thought he was at Oxford. Isn't that near you?'

'Very near,' I cried, masking my hurt feelings with astonishment. Mary knew my address and could easily have given it to Jamie if he had asked. Why hadn't he? Come to that, I was easily Googled these days. I had a website with a "contact me" tab. I could only conclude that Jamie had forgotten about me. 'I wonder which college he's in?' I mused dejectedly.

'I couldn't tell you,' Marjorie said.

I had settled in a village about halfway between Oxford and Cheltenham, in a honey-coloured stone cottage with leaded windows set into deep mullions. The village was as close to Jane Austen's Highbury as possible, with its own Miss Bates, a valetudinarian squire who might have modelled himself on Mr Woodhouse, and a suitably unctuous vicar. My house had small but sweet gardens front and rear and plenty of open spaces close by for Bob to enjoy.

Daniel and Bianca had separated in the middle of lockdown. Being in such close proximity for months at a time had been the *coup de grace* to a relationship that was already mortally injured. Not many months after the decree absolute, Bianca married the tennis professional who had supposedly been giving her lessons—in *what*, one can only conjecture—and Daniel moved to a newbuild property on the outskirts of my village, where he set up his own company advising start-ups and mumpreneurs, and now worked from home. We saw plenty of each other without living in each other's pockets, both having joined the local amateur dramatics group. He looked after Bob when I had to be in town or abroad, and at weekends we explored the surrounding countryside together on long rambles. Between us, everything was as it had been before Bianca, before Dad's death. I had just begun to accept that my relationship with my brother might well become the cornerstone on which my life was built; that we might be, in old age, as we had been as children. But then I noticed Daniel referring more and more often to one of his clients— Amy, a single mother with two primary-school-aged children who had started her own company from her kitchen table making decoupage art and greetings cards. Their business meetings seemed rather frequent and I was sure that, before too long, he would have priorities other than me.

I did not mind. I was happy. *The Trysting Tree* had met with commercial as well as critical success—no small achievement. On its back there had been a resurgence of interest in my other books and *The House of Shame* was so popular on various streaming services that I was being offered an impressive advance on a sequel.

Still, after all that time, I was unsure as to the alchemy that had brought *The Trysting Tree* into being. Trying to skirt round it on my appearances via Zoom at literary festivals, and for the various articles and Q & As that always accompany a book launch, had been tricky to say the least of it. I had written another novel since and the process had not been the same. The influence of the ethereal voices on the dunes, the peculiar confluence of fact and fiction, the sense of being a portal through which the narrative flowed—these seemed confined to the Forresters' story; but they were, none-the-less, troubling. I had talked with Daniel about it and he had agreed with me that I had always been prone to flights of fancy, more than usually suggestible, with my head more in the clouds than out of them. That propensity in me might be all the explanation this needed. Nevertheless, some supernatural explanation could not be discounted. Without implying that I was psychic in the usual paranormal sense, he allowed that there was a possibility the tale had manifested itself to me. While Roadend had been keen to close that episode in its history, I had

543

been eagerly open to it—ready, a vessel waiting to be filled. The unquiet spirits may have recognised me as the fissure in the veil and revealed themselves through it. One in particular I thought, had much to gain by my participation. Rose would not wish to see her children tortured into eternity by their childhood errors, or for the consequences of those mistakes to foist themselves on subsequent generations. And had I not felt myself, from time-to-time, inhabited by her shade?

Olivia and Patrick's reception did not go on into the evening, which was a relief. The idea of gyrating on the scuffed floor of the parish rooms to the strains of Justin Timberlake was not appealing. Although I had booked a room at a hotel I left the venue feeling vaguely unsettled, weary and eager to be home. I checked the train timetable and discovered that, if I was quick, I could catch the 19.10 back to Oxford. I cancelled my hotel reservation, called a taxi and we sped towards Birmingham New Street where I arrived on the platform just in time to leap aboard.

The train was almost empty. I supposed that, by Saturday evening, people had got to the places where they wanted to be for the weekend. I made my way towards the buffet car to buy a cup of tea, feeling overdressed in my wedding attire. The steward served me my tea and I asked him where the quiet carriage was. He motioned to the one further along.

The door slid open and there was Jamie, as though summoned by my conversation with Marjorie and from the sequestered repository of my memory where I had fondly consigned him three years before. It was a shock—but a nice one—to see him outside the charmed environment of Roadend, like encountering Mr Tumnus in Tesco. Hadn't I always told myself he would never make that transition? But here was evidence to the contrary. He had been forging a life for himself, *in the real world* as he would have couched it, for three years.

He was alone in the carriage apart from an elderly man down at the other end who was asleep with his head against the window. Jamie was hard at work, referring to the several books he had spread across the table and then typing quickly on a laptop computer. A frown of concentration made a furrow between his eyebrows. He took no notice as the automatic door slid closed behind me and so I was able to take him in. His hair was trimmed short, his beard gone. He wore clothes that, although shrieking student, were top quality for their type. His bulky shoulders and tall frame were too big for the standard class seat; he sat awkwardly, hunched over his computer, one leg and an elbow protruding into the aisle. I noticed his shoes: leather, tooled, very expensive.

The hand that held my paper cup of tea was trembling, a vibration that communicated itself to my whole body—not the thrum of the train over the tracks but the rhythm of my heart and my churning innards. I was close to tears. They welled up behind my eyes and made my throat thick. They hydrated all my old feelings, reanimating the old bones of my attraction and my sense of Jamie and I as kindred.

I dropped into a seat, taking the one next to the window where I would be shielded from Jamie by the row in front. I tried to get a grip on myself, rummaging in my bag for a tissue. He had forgotten all about me *obviously* I told myself—otherwise, he surely would have looked me up. No doubt he had a girlfriend, *many* girlfriends. I calculated it was his final year. He would be occupied with exams and his thesis; and after that, I was certain, had a career mapped out for himself as well as travel—a whole world of plans. I shrank into my seat and stared miserably at the thick glass of the window; the countryside obscured by nightfall. The window was only a mirror displaying back my woebegone face, the stark illumination of the train carriage, the reflection of the seats—and a large figure standing in the aisle beside me.

'Hello Dee,' said Jamie. 'I thought it was you. Didn't you see me?'

I glanced up at him briefly and then looked away. 'Hello Jamie. I wasn't sure,' I said, and then, making myself a liar, 'and you looked so busy.'

'Not too busy to say hello,' he said, lowering himself into the seat beside me. 'You're all dressed up,' he remarked. 'Been somewhere nice?'

'A wedding,' I faltered. 'Olivia's wedding.'

'Ah yes,' he said. 'Mum told me. How have you been?'

He swivelled himself so that he was facing me, his knees crushed up against the seats in front. Counterintuitively, I pressed myself back into the corner.

'Fine,' I said, with specious lightness. 'Busy. You?' I was afraid to look him in the eye, afraid that he would see the brim of emotion I was struggling to suppress. I opened my bag again and began to rake around inside although I had no idea what I was looking for.

'Busy too,' he said. 'I've been up to Roadend to check on a project I've got going up there. Now I'm on my way back to college. I've got my finals coming up.'

'That's wonderful,' I croaked, in a voice I didn't recognise. 'Which college?'

He named it. 'So funny,' I almost shrilled, overcompensating, giving up on the pretence of searching for something in my bag. 'I walk past there every week, on my way to the station. Daniel drops me outside Luigi's Coffee shop and I always get a coffee and a sandwich before I catch the train to London.'

'Luigi does the best coffee,' said Jamie. 'Although I have a fancy machine.'

'It's still working?' I fixed my eyes on the zip of his Schöffel fleece.

He nodded. 'You should come by and see for yourself,' he said.

'Oh,' I demurred, 'I couldn't … I wouldn't … and you'll be so …'

'Never so busy that I couldn't make an old friend a cup of coffee,' he said. He was leaning towards me, over me, his arm on the back of my seat. It was impossible to avoid his regard. At last, I lifted my gaze to his. 'You mentioned Daniel,' he said, as I roasted myself in the embers in his eyes. 'You and your brother are back on terms?'

I nodded weakly. 'Yes,' I said, my voice all breath and whisper. 'And … you?' Now that I was looking at him I couldn't drag my stare away. His face, his body, his expression all pulled me back to that night on the boardwalk, the night we had said goodbye.

He smiled. 'Yes. Hugh is great. We get along *really* well. He's the brother I always wanted. I owe that to you.'

I got out, 'I told you you'd understand one day.'

'Yes, you did.' A little smile played around his lips. 'I liked your book. You promised me a signed copy.'

'I sent Mary one.'

'I'm not her though. I'd like my own copy, please.' He was so close to me I could feel the stir of his breath on my face. His body, beside me, was an inferno and mine an answering blaze. His arm dropped from the seatback to my shoulders. I was as good as in his arms.

'Ok,' I said. My mouth was dry but I made no attempt to drink the tea that was cooling now on the little drop-down table in front of me. I swallowed. 'I didn't know you were at Oxford,' I said. 'It's odd that we never bumped into each other.'

'We *have* bumped into each other,' he said in a low voice, resting his forehead against mine. 'I knew we would.'

I was drowning in him. 'Did you?'

He nodded. 'I never doubted it.' He groped for my trembling hand and took it in his. 'Dee.' His voice was so husky I could barely hear it over the rattle of the train. 'Do you still …?'

'Oh *yes,*' I said, and fixed my lips on his.

YOUR REVIEW MATTERS

Thank you for reading this book. As a self-published author I don't have the support of a marketing department behind me to promote my books. I rely on you, the reader, to spread the word.

A short review provides great feedback and encouragement to the writer, and is a helpful way for others to know if they might enjoy the book. Please write a few words along with your star rating.

Connect with me on social media: @alliescribbler on Twitter and @allienovelist on Instagram. Search Allie Cresswell on Facebook or sign up for updates and blog posts on my website at allie-cresswell.com

ABOUT THE AUTHOR

Allie Cresswell was born in Stockport, UK and began writing fiction as soon as she could hold a pencil.

She did a BA in English Literature at Birmingham University and an MA at Queen Mary College, London.

She has been a print-buyer, a pub landlady, a bookkeeper, run a B & B and a group of boutique holiday cottages. She taught literature to lifelong learners but nowadays she writes full time.

She has two grown-up children, two granddaughters, two grandsons and two cockapoos—but just one husband—Tim. They live in Cumbria, NW England.

The Cottage on Winter Moss is her thirteenth novel.

AFTERWORD
By Deirdre O' Grady HDip

Literature reflects and creates a discourse which can support or subvert the foundation of acceptance within the disabled community. This can influence societal normatives and construct a zeitgeist of acceptance and inclusion or create misconceptions and prejudice.

Conveying accurate portrayals of a character with a disability is imperative to dismantling negative societal stereotypes and allows the reader to comprehensively analyse their own acceptances and prejudices. It is therefore crucial for authors to continue to collaborate with disability advocates in order to adhere to acceptable portrayals of characters which are as accurate and representational as Olivia.

Olivia's character delivers a positive portrayal of inclusivity and immersion within her community and conveys the contributions possible by each individual when diversity is accepted and acknowledged, to allow love and friendships to bloom and flourish.

For more information on Mosaic Down Syndrome and other types of Down Syndrome, visit: https://www.downs-syndrome.org.uk

ACKNOWLEDGEMENTS & AUTHOR'S NOTE

This book had its genesis a few years ago now. Whilst walking on the dunes that fringe the wild and remote Cumbrian coastline my husband and I came across a weird construction nestling in the tall grasses and scrub. Clearly man-made, it incorporated flotsam and jetsam from the beach to form a horseshoe shaped edifice threaded through with grasses, just as I have described it in the novel. It amazed us that it had stood for so long. We wondered at it. Who had built it and why?

I mused upon this for some time, but other writing and real life prevented me from making a start on the story that I felt must be lurking there, somewhere.

In 2020 we moved to a small hamlet very close to the coast, right next to a marsh area—locally known as the Moss—which is an SSSI. Throughout the second Covid lock down and over the winter of 2020-21, when restrictions meant we hardly stirred from home at all, we took our permitted exercise across the Moss every day with our two dogs, marvelling at the landscape, the wildlife, the amazing variations of weather and light. I was writing *The Lady in the Veil* at the time, but the impact of my surroundings and the possibility of a story there really began to call me.

I began the book in the late summer of 2021 but didn't allow Dee to arrive at Roadend until the end of October, so that I could write her story in real time. The vista outside my window as autumn ended and winter came on, the periods of frost, rain and wind that assailed us here were replicated in Dee's world. Accordingly, in March of 2022, the book and Dee's story came to an end as daffodils bloomed and the sparrows and bluetits began to gather nesting material.

The Cottage on Winter Moss is a book about writing. I had not expected that aspect of it to emerge but as Dee wrote her book and as I wrote mine, I found myself increasingly fascinated by the process of writing. Where does a writer get her ideas? What real-life events, people or prompts are legitimate material for a writer? Every novel should have its own truth, but how "true" can that be? How can a writer explain that curious alchemy, when characters who are fiction nevertheless insist on forging their own destinies? Does that autonomy make them, in any sense, "real?"

Dee says, 'Characters in books are only figments of their creators' minds, briefly real enough to ensnare a reader in the threads of their stories before being sealed up between the covers and left on a shelf to gather dust.' Now that I have written this book, and you have read it, will you think of Hugh and Marjorie and Dee out there, somewhere, carrying on their lives? Will you journey to Cumbria to find the curious little den on the dunes in the hope of hearing for yourself the distant laughter of little boys at play? Or will the characters fade back into the ether they came from, so that in a day or so, or when you meet your friends at your book group, you can hardly recall their names?

My thanks to Molly, my granddaughter, now aged 8, who held my hand as we walked up the Moss together. She never failed to ask me about my book, enthusiastically encouraging me to introduce a family of unicorns into the enchanted glen where the trysting tree stands. I'm sorry I didn't manage it, sweetheart. Molly, along with our other grandchildren, Zack, Parker and Ivy, ran through the curious maze of the bracken and scrambled on the horizontal bough of the trysting tree while I mused upon my story, filling the place with happy memories for me.

Thank you to Tim and Becky (B Fleetwood) who were my alpha readers, picking up my many errors and falling obligingly into the traps I had set for them. Thank you to Deirdre O'Grady, my sensitivity reader, who made sure I had got Olivia just right. Thanks to Chris Moss JP, who helped me understand the change in the law that enabled Todd to wrest the freehold from Sir Hector. Thank you to Sallianne Hines, Quinn Editing, for her patient and painstaking work. Thank you to my launch team and the bloggers who so kindly set the book on its way. Thank you to Sarah Reid for her beautiful cover art. Thank you again, and always, to Tim, who supports and encourages me every day. Meet me at the Trysting Tree!

ALSO BY ALLIE CRESSWELL

Game Show

Relative Strangers

Crossings

Tiger in a Cage

The Widows Series comprising:

The Hoarder's Widow

The Widow's Mite

(Coming Soon) The Widow's Weeds

The Talbot Saga comprising:

The House in the Hollow

The Lady in the Veil

Tall Chimneys

*The Highbury Trilogy inspired by Jane Austen's Emma,
comprising*:

Mrs Bates of Highbury

The Other Miss Bates

Dear Jane

Printed in Great Britain
by Amazon

84170436R00317